Praise for the Eagles and Dragons s‹

Historic Novel Society:
   "...Haviaras handles it all wit
century Rome—both the city and its African outposts—is colourfully
vivid here, and Haviaras manages to invest even his secondary and
tertiary characters with believable, three-dimensional humanity."

Amazon Readers:
   "Graphic, uncompromising and honest... A novel of heroic men and
the truth of the uncompromising horror of close combat total war..."

"Raw and unswerving in war and peace... New author to me but ranks
along side Ben Kane and Simon Scarrow. The attention to detail and all
the gory details are inspiring and the author doesn't invite you into the
book he drags you by the nasal hairs into the world of Roman life sweat,
tears, blood, guts and sheer heroism. Well worth a night's reading
because once started it's hard to put down."

"Historical fiction at its best! ... if you like your historical fiction to be
an education as well as a fun read, this is the book for you!"

"Loved this book! I'm an avid fan of Ancient Rome and this story is,
perhaps, one of the best I've ever read."

"An outstanding and compelling novel!"

"I would add this author to some of the great historical writers such as
Conn Iggulden, Simon Scarrow and David Gemmell. The characters
were described in such a way that it was easy to picture them as if they
were real and have lived in the past, the book flowed with an ease that
any reader, novice to advanced can enjoy and become fully immersed..."

"One in a series of tales which would rank them alongside Bernard
Cornwell, Simon Scarrow, Robert Ludlum, James Boschert and others of
their ilk. The story and character development and the pacing of the
exciting military actions frankly are superb and edge of your seat! The
historical environment and settings have been well researched to make

the story lines so very believable!! I can hardly wait for what I hope will be many sequels! If you enjoy Roman historical fiction, you do not want to miss this series!"

Goodreads:

"... a very entertaining read; Haviaras has both a fluid writing style, and a good eye for historical detail, and explores in far more detail the faith of the average Roman than do most authors."

Kobo:

"I can't remember the last time that a book stirred so many emotions! I laughed, cried and cheered my way through this book and can't wait to meet again this wonderful family of characters. Roll on to the next book!"

The Blood Road and the Eagles and Dragons series

Copyright © 2021 by Adam Alexander Haviaras

Eagles and Dragons Publishing, Stratford, Ontario, Canada

All Rights Reserved.

The use of any part of this publication, with the exception of short excerpts for the purposes of book reviews, without the written consent of the author is an infringement of copyright law.

ISBN: 978-1-988309-39-2

First Paperback Edition

Cover designed by LLPix Designs

*Please note: To enhance the reader's experience, there is a glossary of Latin words at the back of this book.

Sign-up for the Eagles and Dragons Publishing Newsletter and get a FREE BOOK today.

Subscribers get first access to new releases, special offers, and much more.

Go to:
www.eaglesanddragonspublishing.com

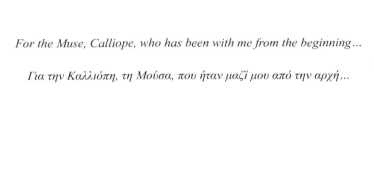

For the Muse, Calliope, who has been with me from the beginning...

Για την Καλλιόπη, τη Μούσα, που ήταν μαζί μου από την αρχή...

THE BLOOD ROAD

A Novel of the Roman Empire

ADAM ALEXANDER HAVIARAS

PROLOGUS

R ome, A.D. 212

It was the month of Februarius in Rome, the cold still clinging to that eternal city of brick and marble. Winter held on with iron fists as it prepared to gust for yet a little longer, before Proserpina crawled her way out of Hades.

Rome pulsed, as always, at every hour, the silence in places broken by music from taverns, or giddy laughter sweeping out of brothels. The darkness of those ancient streets, when the moon crept behind a sliver of cloud, was broken by torches of the urban guard, or the fires in tripods before temples and shrines where they called for the Gods' attentions.

But the light was not everywhere. In the shadows along the swift-flowing Tiber, two wolves slinked along the icy shore, pausing to sniff the air when a noise erupted, and then continuing on with a purpose like wraiths on the hunt.

The countryside was their domain, but with the winter months their survival was threatened, and the city needed to be risked.

There were two of them, one of deepest black with violent, yellow eyes, and the other an undecided shade of grey that leaned more toward white and brown in places. The second wolf's blue eyes followed the first, his eyes darting from side to side as he went, his tongue licking the bits of flesh that yet clung to his muzzle from the gorging they had undertaken in the necropolis outside the city.

Both were still hungry, wishing for more, eager to the point of risking death at the hands of the men of Mars.

The lead wolf paused suddenly and cut away from the cold river water, up an alley that led into the streets toward a hill ahead of them.

A few times did people stumble upon them, but one look at the pair of slavering brethren was enough to send them scurrying behind closed doors.

The wolves walked on, hunting, drawn to that hill, to that high place. Close to walls and in angled shadow they crept, up the hard slopes, until they came to a broad open space and stopped, the start of a growl in the black one's throat as it observed an enormous man upon a horse.

When the horse did not move at their snarls, they crept closer until they were beneath the legs of the horse and the man sitting astride it with his hand outstretched.

Footsteps echoed in nearby porticoes, and a gentle thrumming voice emanated from the open doors of the great temple before them.

Did Jupiter see them standing there before his shrine? Did he think to strike them down before the damage they might do, the havoc they might wreak on Rome?

No.

Divine laws are stringent, and the Gods themselves must uphold those timeless laws, lest they collapse like a vein bled dry, or like the heart of that ancient metropolis itself.

The wolves looked around, hunger still gnawing at their guts.

And then they saw it, heard the cry.

At the base of the steps of the house of Jupiter, a wounded eagle wept upon the marble slabs, one wing outstretched, but the other broken and bent.

The wolves spotted this noble lord of the skies, and felt their hunger keenly in that moment. They crept forward, their heads low and hackles high. They bared their white teeth as they approached.

The eagle's mouth opened and closed, his voice lost, though his head was still high, keen eyes looking at the oncoming enemies.

Just as the wolves were about to pounce, the black one stopped, turned sideways and growled with a ferocity that startled the other. Then it leapt, its jaws clamping down on the neck of its sibling.

The eagle flapped its good wing, and stood, its talons scratching on the marble that was now wet with spattered blood.

The wolves twisted and turned, jaws gnashing and claws scratching. Howls and yelps filled the square until the black wolf found his hold once more and bit out the neck of the other.

Blood dripped from his maw as he turned to the eagle. It was a moment, but the eagle knew.

As the jaws opened before it, the eagle's tallon struck out at the eyes, just as razor teeth tore into it, shook it, sawed at it and crushed it, a memory of mountain clouds and eyries in its wild eyes.

Men were there then, running out of the temple and down the stairs, brandishing weapons at the wolf.

He fled, back to the shadows, and ran away from the hill and the light, and the unfinished meal he had left behind in the blood upon the steps.

The crowds of men and women thickened as he sped downward and came to an open area where fire burned at every turn, and more screams sent him in different directions, desperately searching for darkness.

Voices followed him now, more and more of them. He could smell their anger, hear the clang of their weapons.

Then, a ruffle of feathers ahead drew his eye. His nose flared.

Pigeons in a soft, still mass before him... It was too much to resist. He would grab one and run, sate his hunger one more time.

The wolf ran and lunged, but something bit him and he turned violently, howling.

Another bite, and another...and another.

He lay still now upon the enormous cobbles of that human forum, looking up at the iron teeth of the men who had hunted him.

Then...darkness.

It had been a calm morning on the Palatine hill, the quiet a gift from the Gods that extended throughout the day.

From the high window of her private chambers in the Severan palace complex, Julia Domna had watched the sun rise and soar across the wintry sky until late in the day.

Wrapped in furs, she had lain upon her couch reading over piles of correspondence that had been sent to her sons. She read more slowly now, her eyes tiring easily, even in the light of day.

She sighed, reaching up to touch the tight weave of her hair, wondering as she did so how the sacrificium at the temple of Concord in the Forum Romanum had gone.

The senate had offered to perform the rites to honour her sons, the joint emperors, successors to their father Septimius Severus, whose loss the empress yet felt. However, her grief had hidden in the shadows for long now, for she had been busy trying to bridge the widening divide between Caracalla and Geta.

Rather than working together, pursuing the harmony their father had wished for them, each brother had retreated to a separate wing of the palace under guard at all times, food, water and wine tasted by others before passing imperial lips.

She had to admit that she had had her misgivings, especially with the chaotic jollity of Saturnalia when she had arranged for Geta to be shadowed at all times to ensure his safety.

It was not long before the boys spoke of an empire divided, the East for Geta, and the West for Caracalla.

"I too, together with earth and sea, would be partitioned between you!" she remembered yelling at Caracalla not three days before.

It had been that moment, that loss of composure, that had, she believed, rattled her son and brought him around. For the very next day, Caracalla had sent word to her that he would accept the senate's offer to perform a sacrificium before the sacred altar of Concord, that he was willing to sit, as a family, with his mother and brother to find a harmonious solution.

Julia Domna smiled as she felt hope fill her, and she sipped the wine in a golden cup that sat upon the table beside her couch.

There was hope, and yet…all the blood spilled to get to that point still haunted her. She remembered her cousin, Papinianus. She missed speaking with him of home, of their other cousins, of the warmth of family recollections, and memories of Severus.

Her sister, Julia Maesa, spoke little of all that was happening. In fact, she saw her little, and wondered if she, her husband and daughters, Julia Soaemias and Julia Mamaea, had decided to pull back for fear of their safety. If Papinianus, Euodus, and Castor had not survived, then…

Stop this, Domna! she told herself. *I must think of the present, of peace between my sons… Oh Goddess Concord, bless this day for me…*

She breathed deeply as the saffron curtains of her window blew inward with a gust of wind, and she closed her eyes as the cool wind of winter kissed her face. *Are you there, Septimius…watching?*

She was startled by a sudden knocking on the door, and waited a moment before speaking.

"Enter!" the empress said, turning her head to look at the gilded, double doors at the back of the room.

"Empress," came the gruff voice of Macrinus, the new Prefect of the Praetorian Guard.

"What is it?" Julia Domna answered, not bothering to rise. She did not like Marcus Opellius Macrinus. Not only was he lowborn, but he had also been a legal advisor to her old enemy, Plautianus, before becoming director of the via Flaminia and of her husband's properties. He was boor and upstart, she knew, but she dared not gainsay Caracalla's choice. Not yet, anyway. "What do you want, Macrinus?" she asked again as he walked slowly into the room, admiring the gilded furnishings and armour that had belonged to her husband.

"Empress," he bowed, "the sacrificium at the temple is finished."

"And?"

"The senate seems propitiated."

"And did my sons perform their duties admirably?"

"They would have, I am sure…were they in attendance."

She sat up then. "They were not there?"

"No. They were not." He stood there, hand upon his sword hilt, looking down at her with no regard for her station, for all that she had done for the empire. "I suspect they stayed away because of the ill omens last night."

"Omens?" she asked.

"Two wolves crept into the city. They fought on the Capitoline where one of them died. The other fled, but was cut down in the Forum Romanum."

That gave her pause. She tried to abide by the stars more than anything, but such omens could cause a panic among the people, especially on the eve of an important sacrificium.

"I will speak with them, Macrinus. Are they still planning on attending me soon? We have much to talk about together, as a family."

"Oh yes, Empress. They are coming." Macrinus stroked his long beard as he said so, the hint of a smile behind his whiskers, but the empress did not notice, for she could not bear to look upon him for too long.

"Very well. Please go and bring them to me."

Without a word, he saluted and went out, casting a backward glance at her as he closed the door.

"My lady?" asked one of her serving maids from a quiet corner of the room. "Shall I have food brought for your conversation with the emperors?"

"Yes. Do. They will be hungry, I'm sure. They eat so little now."

The slave went away to make arrangements, and Julia Domna settled back down onto her couch to watch as the first stars began to alight in the sky beyond her balcony.

Her eyes closed briefly, and a smile began to play about her lips. She loved the stars, and she knew she could, that very night, turn the fortunes of her sons around for the better.

It was dark in the marble corridors of the palace, the light from the intermittent braziers casting wavering shadows upon the walls and smooth floors outside the empress' quarters.

Geta approached with one of his men from the east end of the corridor, his eyes searching the dark, but not too much, for he always felt safer near to his mother.

The Gods knew he had done his share of plotting against his brother, but Caracalla, he knew, had done more, and so he hoped this conversation with their mother would be the olive branch they needed to heal the rift, to make sure he would survive to rule from a distance in the East.

It had surprised Geta when Caracalla had sent word that he wanted to talk together with their mother. Such a thing had not happened in a long while.

"There he is, sire," his man said beside him.

Geta stopped before the doors of his mother's chambers and watched Caracalla approach from the western end of the corridor.

There was a sudden gurgling beside him and he turned to see his man with a pugio jutting from his neck, eyes bulging in surprise.

Geta turned to scream, but the heavy fist out of the dark that connected with his check sent him to the floor.

"Help!" Geta tried to yell through the shock. "Help!" He looked up and saw Caracalla bearing down on him, a glinting blade in his right hand, his eyes holding a flame of determined fury in them.

Geta kicked out quickly, sending Caracalla back.

A hand gripped at his cloak, ripping it away, and he lunged for the double doors, crashing into his mother's chambers.

"Mother!" Geta yelled, his voice cracking with fear. "Mother! I'm being murdered! Help me!"

Julia Domna felt her heart explode out of chest as she jumped up from her couch to see her younger son running toward her with outstretched arms.

"What is happening?" she demanded, ready to take Geta into her arms.

Geta stiffened suddenly, and Caracalla's face appeared over his shoulder.

"No! No! NO!!!!" the empress cried, but the sound of the dagger plunging into the body of her son would not stop. She fell backward onto the couch, still holding onto her boy as his head slumped against her chest and his blood spattered all around her.

She looked up and saw the face of her son's murderer, not his brother, nor her son, but that of a cold and bloody fratricide, a distorted theatre mask of hatred.

She began to shake, her face drenched with her boy's blood, her furs, her stola, the couch…the blood was everywhere.

Caracalla stared down at them, grabbed Geta's hair and pulled his head back abruptly to ensure there was no life.

"Leave him alone!" Julia Domna cried, swatting desperately at the murderer's hands, her son's hands!

"We will not divide the empire!" Caracalla roared, before being pulled away by the Praetorian Prefect.

Julia Domna sat there shaking, her mind and soul exploding like a star in its death throes. Her voice came to her then, from deep within, a loud terrible wail that shattered the peace of the Palatine hill, and could be heard across the city.

Part I

PAIN

A.D. 213

I

VITA AMARUM

'The Bitter Taste of Life'

It was a world apart, a place of peace…beautiful and serene, full of life, and of colour…truly, the eye of a great storm that raged without.

Dagon, the lord of his people, a king, sat alone upon the slopes of one of Ynis Wytrin's hills, beneath the limbs of the tree planted by the strange Christian, Joseph. There he found it easy to think, to remember the hurt, the betrayals, the horrors they had all experienced. There, he could grapple with them, stare them in the face and bring them to their knees for another short period of time.

It has been almost two years since those frightful days when the vipers of Rome had destroyed their lives, murdered his brothers, his people. The god of the sacred sword had not come to their aid then. They had fought alone on foreign fields.

He prayed to Epona that wherever his surviving men were, that they were safe from Rome's grasp, from Caracalla's hunters.

Dagon closed his eyes and felt the sun upon his face, its soft, warm light filtered through the misty wall that surrounded the Isle of the Blessed.

Blessed? he thought, shaking his head and feeling his eyes burn. *Not for everyone.*

Even there, the shadows of the world were able to creep in with fingers of guilt, resentment, anger, lack, and hatred. Even there, among the dancing petals of the apple blossoms and the winking leaves of the ancient oak groves…even there, the poison of the outside world leeched into the Goddess' veins, or tightened the thorny crown of the Christus. Even there.

And it was his own happiness that tortured him most of all, for even with his brethren scattered to the wind, and the silent torture of his best friends, he still managed to feel joy.

Why did the Gods choose to bless me in all of the chaos? To be angry and bitter would have been easier than all the guilt that accompanies this joy...and yet...I would not change it.

And the Gods multiplied his guilt at this.

Dagon turned to his left and saw Briana walking slowly up the slope of the hill toward him. He could not help but smile.

Their daughter was walking more steadily now, pulling to get away from Briana at every chance, wishing to explore the world around her.

Briana caught his eye and smiled. She bent over to hold the girl's hand as she wandered in the direction of the steep slope to their left.

"Baba!" the girl said when she spotted her father and toddled toward him with her arms out.

Dagon stood and knelt to receive her. "Antiope!" he said as he wrapped his arms about her and picked her up. "You're getting stronger every day!"

The child blew at the wisps of sandy hair that danced about her face and placed her tiny hands upon his cheeks.

I will never let anything happen to you, he thought.

"Are we disturbing you?" Briana said, coming to his side and kissing him.

"Never." He smiled, but then sighed deeply, one arm holding his child, the other around Briana. The flowering thorn beside them whispered in the wind that blew across the levels from the sea, and the two of them felt the longed-for calm that they always got when they were alone in that spot.

Briana looked up at her husband and felt the weight of his worries again, the great guilt that chained him to the world outside of Ynis Wytrin.

"How are they today?" Dagon asked her.

"Phoebus and Calliope are helping Father Gilmore, Rachel and Aaron with the lambing... It is keeping them busy."

"I'm glad to hear it." Dagon felt his heart tighten. "Those children... they've been through so much. The last months have been a trial for them."

"For everyone," Briana added. She looked at her husband's eyes as they strayed to the slopes of the Tor and the hill of the Chalice beside it.

From where they stood, they could see the roof of the lone round-house where the three of them lived peacefully together beyond the apple orchards, alone, away from the others.

That too was a source of guilt.

Antiope gazed into her father's eyes and her little hand reached up to wipe away the tear that wended its way down the creases of his face and into his beard.

The Gods, it seemed, had turned their backs fully upon the Dragon's family, and now that they all knew the truth, a great distance had opened up in the earth between them, a gulf no horse and rider could leap over.

"Come," Briana said. "Let us show Antiope the children at work."

Together they walked back down the slope of the hill, past the chapel and the orchard, now in full bloom, and made for the animal pens.

Dagon and Briana looked toward the great oak and saw her, Adara Metella, sitting alone as she seemed always to be, gazing out at the dark lake waters, the mist. She had not spoken for so long, and yet now, the truth, the reality of it all, seemed to have sealed her voice and soul up more tightly.

"You go ahead," Briana said. "I will try."

Dagon nodded and took Antiope's hand. "I love you," he said.

Briana smiled, and then turned to walk away as her husband and daughter joined the others. She watched them for a moment, saw Antiope run to Phoebus and Calliope who both knelt to hug her, to welcome her with their open arms, desperate for affection.

She wanted to weep, but knew it would not help things in that moment. Briana turned back toward the oak and the black-cloaked figure of her friend. She would not give up on her. She would be there for her no matter what, no matter the resentment.

Adara Metella felt cold as she sat upon one of the stumps beneath the broad, ancient limbs of the oak, the thick wool of her cloak doing very little to shield her body from the breeze that blew from across the lapping water before her. Every day, she sat there, watching the reeds and rushes sway, and the birds skirting the surface about the silent, wading herons.

There was life all around her and yet, she felt a loneliness she had never felt before, a loneliness of such brutal strength that she could not break free of its grasp. Even with Phoebus and Calliope behind her, the sweet sound of their young voices joining with the other children, trying to move on, she could not withdraw from the dark, choking cloud that surrounded her.

Her hand instinctively reached beneath her cloak to the ugly scar across her abdomen, that talisman of bitter memory and loss.

So much loss...

She could not shake the memory of Death standing before her, reaching out to rip her child from her hands as she lay beaten and bleeding. Her life had burned down all around her, and she had felt helpless to do anything but weep.

And she had wept. During her weeks in the healing houses of Ynis Wytrin, she had wept in her sleep, and while awake. Her sadness had known no end, but there had been a ray of light through the dark that she had clung to.

Phoebus and Calliope had survived the chaos of that night of fire and death, even as so many had perished.

And Lucius... *Lucius...*

His light had fallen and faded before her eyes, plunged into an engulfing darkness.

She could still see it clearly, her love plummeting, hear the crack of his body upon the earth like a god tumbling out of the sky.

He had died before her, for her, and she had not known...none of them had known. Not Dagon or Einion, Briana, Weylyn, Gilmore or even Etain.

Adara Metella had shed her tears for her lost infant when she had come out of her tortured and healing sleep, drawn by the voice of her daughter and son at her side - the three had wept together - but those waterways had run their course over the months since. Now, they had opened up again, but only when the tide of anger and betrayal ebbed away.

It was easier to shutter the soul at that point.

"Adara?"

Briana's voice invaded her thoughts, but she did not turn her gaze from the dark water in the distance, the depths she had considered joining permanently at times.

She felt a hand upon her shoulder and fought the temptation to lean into its possessor beside her.

"Please Adara…look at me," Briana said.

"Please leave me alone," Adara whispered.

"No. I won't, because you are not alone. You are surrounded by friends, people who love you."

Adara was silent.

"You've come so far. I know it doesn't seem like it, but the Gods have watched over you. In the ways of nature, neither of you should have survived, but you did. And you have a purpose - your children."

Adara turned slowly to face the Briton. "Not all my children."

Briana looked down, unable to face that angry gaze. "Please…don't. I have wept with you and for you. It is not my fault, nor anyone else's but the evil man you slew. He is gone."

"Do not speak of him, or of my slain child."

"I won't," Briana said, removing her hand. "But I will speak of the living." Briana turned to kneel in front of Adara and look up at her pale face beneath the cowl of her cloak.

Adara's once-brilliant green eyes were shot and faded now, the strands of her long dark hair streaked with grey. The tightly clenched hands were thin and pale too, the ring of intertwined dragons loose about her finger.

Briana pried the hands open to hold them and held Adara's gaze.

"Phoebus and Calliope need you! They need your love. No one else is their mother. Do you know what they have been through? Have you pondered that? They watched you lingering on the verge of death for weeks. They watched their father die before them as his body sank to the bottom of the red waters of the chalice…"

Even Briana wept at the memory then, of what they had all seen as Aaron and Rachel had reached in to pull the Dragon out.

Adara had not seen it, but she had imagined it over and over again, tried to make sense of it all.

Now, with the truths she had recently learned, it made sense. It made her angry.

"I have failed my children," Adara whispered, her guilt so very heavy upon her hunched shoulders. "I know I have."

"No! You haven't!" Briana snapped. "You survived. You fought so that they could escape fire and death."

"By sacrificing my baby."

Briana could feel her desperate frustration, but she reined it in. "By living, Adara. You are still here for them. No one else can be what you are for them."

Adara could feel the tears stinging her eyes, and her head sank a little lower into her trembling hands.

Briana leaned forward to wrap her arms about her friend, to hold her.

This time, as had happened so many times before that moment, Adara did not push her away in disgust or jealousy. Briana held her quivering body tightly, making her feel that she was not alone.

After a time, Briana stood, pulling Adara to her feet, wanting to take her to her children. But she had to say it. She could not stop herself.

"He...he needs you too."

"He lied to me!" Adara snapped, pulling away. "After all that happened to him in Dumnonia...all that he learned!"

Briana could see the anger flaming up again in Adara's eyes, burning away the tender tears she had wept for her children, to be replaced by the feelings of anger and betrayal she had pinned upon the man she had loved so very deeply.

"The man I knew is gone. Dead."

"But he's not! He lives, Adara!" Briana pointed up to the high slopes of the Tor beyond to the lonely, black silhouette against the sky. "Lucius is there! He is the same man who loved you. He is the father of those two blessed children behind us. And he needs you more than ever." Briana felt her patience waning quickly, and pulled back before she said things she did not mean, things she would regret having uttered. "He hid things to protect us all, truths he could not fathom because the Gods had kept him in the dark. Think of the burden he carried before the flames took him. He fell trying to keep us all safe, to make the world better."

"Out of selfishness," Adara said bitterly, though she knew it was false.

"No, Adara. Out of love and a belief in something greater. And that something has turned to ash all about him. He fell harder than any man has...and he needs you to help him rise again."

Briana walked away, back to her husband and child, to the light of life that pulsed in the Isle of the Blessed, leaving Adara alone again.

For some time, Adara stared up at the Tor to where Lucius stood gazing out at the world, wrestling with his own darkness.

Gods...do not forsake us again, she demanded now. *We have put our faith in you, and lost so much. Do not repay it with silence.*

. . .

I died... This was my choice...my choice...

As he stood beneath the sky at the top of the Tor of Ynis Wytrin, Lucius Metellus Anguis' arm reached out slowly from beneath his long black cloak and the loose sleeve of his tunic. He held it up, and observed the molten hand and arm, and he did not recognize it.

Most men would recognize their hands, every scar, every oddly-shaped knuckle, every path that criss-crossed the palm. But Lucius Metellus Anguis, the one-time 'Dragon of Rome', now felt like a stranger to himself, a misshapen horror who no longer recognized his own hands.

Frustrated and feeling the anger rise again, he lowered his arm and closed his eyes, trying to remember how he had once felt, to feel the kiss of the wind upon his skin, rustling his hair. It was not to be. He felt only the tight pull of his body, his mottled, drum-tight skin, the pain in his muscles, and the spotted vision in his eyes.

"Apollo...Father...why didn't you tell me?" Lucius found himself whispering.

I did, my son. I did. You chose this pain...

The god's response was cut off, as if the memory of that moment on far-off Olympus was too painful, the moment when Lucius had rejected his place among the immortals, opting for unimaginable pain.

And it had been unimaginable...a pain like no other.

Lucius remembered more and more as he emerged from the months and months of horrific semi-consciousness in which he had been harassed by dreams of fire and of death. He had wandered alone through the dark wood of his psyche, lost, angry and shouting. Then, one day a few weeks ago, his eyes had opened wide to see worried and scared faces hovering above him in a dark, candlelit room in the healing house.

Etain, the priestess of Ynis Wytrin was the first person he saw and heard speaking, but she had not been speaking to him. Her voice reached to somewhere farther afield.

Lucius remembered his newly-opened eyes swimming in the fire-lit dark, seeing the druid, Weylyn, mixing something as he looked down at Lucius' body. There had been a tang of vinegar and resin in the air, a scent that followed Lucius around still, in addition to another mixture of wine and myrrh.

"Welcome back to us, Lucius Metellus Anguis," Etain's soft voice said as she had looked down at him, her eyes meeting his. "You are alive and with us, but you cannot move, or go outside. Not yet."

Lucius' eyes had sought the sunlight at the window, but it burned him, adding to the pain that laced his body.

"Drink this, Anguis…" Weylyn had said, putting a cup to Lucius' lips. "It will help with the pain."

In truth, nothing had helped with the pain since the moment Lucius had tumbled from the heights of Olympus and emerged from the blood-red waters of the Well of the Chalice, gasping and screaming in agony, his mind exploding in confusion as he looked up to see the familiar faces of men, women, and weeping children.

He remembered little of the months of standing at Death's gates, little of the bitter and resinous skin salves the priestesses had spread daily over his burned body. He did remember, however, the short visits by Father Gilmore and his two charges, Rachel and Aaron. Lucius had not seen his own family for so long, his wife and children, but the faces of those two dark youths were clear and radiant to him in moments of darkness. Their faces lingered over his as they prayed with words he did not understand, as they laid their soft, healing hands upon his brow, his heart, and his eyes.

Those had been moments of relief, a light to pull him back from the dark depths he felt himself plunging toward.

Those moments still confused him.

The faces he had wanted to see were Adara's, Phoebus and Calliope's. Lucius had not known that Etain and Weylyn insisted it was crucial that the number of people who visited Lucius was limited to prevent infection, and so the days and long months had turned into a sort of waking coma from which he had emerged only a short time ago.

Now that Lucius was awake and finally able to move, he felt his anger more acutely. He knew that his self-pity, and self-loathing was unfair to all those around him, but he could not stop himself. It was easier to lock oneself in the dark, to be alone upon that windswept hill where he wandered painfully every day since he had regained movement in his limbs.

As he lay upon his back staring up at the sky and ravens soaring in the wind, he felt horror at the shocked look upon his children's faces when they had seen him, or Adara's quiet, grief-stricken gaze when she had told him their child was lost.

Daily, Lucius thought on that loss, remembered the faces of the dead - his men scattered to the winds, hunted...Barta...the child he would never know...

He thought bitterly of his own hubris that had brought them all to that place and time, that life of pain.

He thought of Apollo, his true father, and chewed on the resentment of his own godhood which had not allowed him to stop all that had happened. Lucius decided that he deserved all of the pain that was a part of him now, for all that he had done to his friends, and to his wife and children.

So many have been trying to help me... I don't want it, he would tell himself. *I don't deserve it.* "I need to make things right again. I want my life back!"

Only days before, he had sat with Adara beneath the oak, in an effort to comfort her, and it had only caused further pain for them both.

Adara looked at him differently now, and in those once-brilliant and loving eyes, Lucius saw only disappointment and loss, and it was caused by him.

For so long, he had wanted to tell her the truth he had learned in Dumnonia, in the realm of Annwn, but he had not been able to. However, beneath the leaves of Ynis Wytrin's oak, he had finally told his wife, his true love, who he was.

She had stared at him in that moment, and wept. She had accused the Gods of toying with them, Lucius of lying to her. She would not hear his pleas, his explanations, the confession of the painful weight that knowledge had heaped upon his shoulders.

Neither of them had been able to reach each other through the flames of the fire that had burned their lives down.

They had not spoken since.

So, every day, Lucius Metellus Anguis made his way to the top of the Tor, alone, his mind searching for a way to win his life back, to make the pain stop.

From the valley below, Etain, Weylyn, and Father Gilmore watched the Dragon descend the spine of the Tor, alone, a shadow in Elysium.

"He cannot stay here," Father Gilmore said.

"He must stay here," Weylyn countered, rubbing his white beard. "He has much healing to do still."

"You cannot chain a dragon," Etain said, stepping forward to watch Lucius more keenly. She had suspected the truth they now knew for some time, though it had been hidden from her sight. "I feel that he is not yet ready, that something stands in his way."

Weylyn stepped to her side.

"His inner physical healing has been…miraculous," Father Gilmore said, shaking his head. "He seems ready, Etain. Our ministrations have healed him, and kept infection at bay. The Metelli can go home now."

Etain turned on her long-time friend, disappointment in her eyes. "I was not speaking of his physical being," she began to walk toward the apple orchard where white petals were tumbling gently to the grass beneath. "Lucius Metellus Anguis is the son of a god…he is a dragon…" she sighed, "…and both of those carry a weight we cannot imagine."

"I disagree," Gilmore said. "All of us carry a weight." He stopped to look to where Rachel and Aaron played with the Roman children. Ever since they had come here in dire need, the four of them had grown too close for his liking, developing a bond that made him uncomfortable. He knew his charges had played a key role in healing the Dragon and his family - they still did - but that came with repercussions. Rachel and Aaron had to be his priority. They were his duty, and they needed the proper guidance. He felt Etain's hand upon his shoulder.

"Do not let your worries for the children close your heart to kindness, my friend," Etain said. "Did not the Christus have a world of worries upon his shoulders and yet seek to help others, to love?"

Father Gilmore was silent, looking down at the grass like a child who knows they have done wrong.

"You are right, I know. I just feel that this will all come to no good."

"This land needs them, Gilmore," Weylyn reminded him. "Etain has said it for some time. It is our duty to help them, for in helping them, we help this land, we help Ynis Wytrin, and we help Rachel and Aaron."

"They did not shy from the horrors of what they saw when the Metelli arrived here, their bodies, home and lives consumed by fire. God urged them to help, as did our gods. We must trust in that," Etain said to Gilmore.

Weylyn was quiet, watching for Lucius who had disappeared in the darkness of the trees at the foot of the Tor.

Be strong, Dragon...we need you.

When Lucius reached the bottom of the Tor, he found Adara standing in the middle of the shaded path, waiting for him. He pulled his cowl lower over his face so as to hide it.

"Don't do that," Adara said, and she reached up to gently lift back the wool. She tried not to weep as she looked upon him. His hair was thin like a newborn child's, only just recently beginning to grow back. His once-smooth skin was now scale-like and mottled, constantly glistening from the resins and oils the priestesses put on him.

She was afraid to hold Lucius, to squeeze him as tightly as she wanted, for fear of damaging the muscle and bone that had once been as iron beneath his skin, but were now brittle and emaciated.

It was Lucius' eyes, however, that filled Adara with fear, for she could not see the man she loved in those eyes, she could not see him past the bitterness and resentment and angry emotions.

"I wish you had told me, Lucius...everything...before...before all of this."

"I wanted to...I..." He closed his jaundiced eyes and felt the shame coming upon him again, fought the urge to hide away from the world.

"Come," she said, taking his hand in hers.

Together, they walked along the avenue of yew trees until they reached the Well of the Chalice.

The familiar gurgle of the healing pool filled Lucius' ears as they sought the bench beside the pool and sat together.

Lucius gazed at the red waters, the pool from which he had come back into the world, and he grunted at the remembered pain he had felt in that moment.

"He told me this would happen," he said.

"Who did?"

He turned stiffly to look at her. "My father...Apollo..." Lucius looked back at the water, felt Adara's hand leave his. "I was on Olympus, Adara. I was there. They said I could live there, that I could be free of pain and of suffering. I had to chose."

"Why didn't you stay then?"

He stood and stepped to the edge of the pool, gazed into its depths, a part of him wishing he could dive in and return to Olympus, if only to be free of the pain and guilt and torment he felt and was putting others through.

"Because I chose you and our children, my love." Lucius looked at her, at the tears that streamed down her cheeks, the angry expression of utter loneliness she felt. He walked toward her and slowly knelt upon the ground, though it tore the skin of his knees.

"I'm sorry I wasn't there soon enough, that I was not really here for you since the fires." He placed his hand upon her belly where their child had grown. "I...I wanted to make this world better, for all of us. And yet..." he looked her in the eyes, worried she would recoil, but she did not. "I failed you and our children, my love."

There was so much Adara wanted to say, but could not. A part of her wanted to hold him tightly and wish it all away, and another part of her wanted to slap him across the face and tell him he was not the only one who suffered. Her anger at herself and him, merged into one, leaving her numb.

"We've been through so much, Lucius, and yes, I wish you had been there, that you had not left for war, or decided to take the world on your shoulders without speaking to me." Gently, she pulled away from him and stood, unable to look into his eyes any longer.

Lucius pulled his cowl over his head again as he stared at her back.

"We have lost our child, Lucius. I have had over a year to think on that loss by myself. But what torments me now, perhaps even more so... is that I have lost you!" She turned to face him. "I don't even know you. You went into Dumnonia a man, and you came out wounded and full of torment, and you didn't even tell me. Why?"

Lucius shook his head. It seemed like another lifetime, another man. "I...I didn't want to frighten you. My world had turned upside down."

"The son of Apollo?" she asked. "I married a man, a man I loved with all my being."

Lucius felt his heart tighten painfully. "I understand if you don't love me, especially now. How could you love this?" he raised his arm to show the melted, red and angry skin.

"When we were married, we swore to journey through this life together, Lucius. Through all things. But it's time for you to decide who you are. How are you going to make things right again?"

It was the very question Lucius had been asking himself since he awoke.

Suddenly, the shield wall of Adara's emotions broke, and she wept as she fell to her knees beside the red waters of the pool.

Lucius went to her side. "I am your husband still, if you'll have me, and I would continue to suffer this pain if it meant I could stay with you."

Adara looked up. "We are better than this, Lucius."

"I will make it right, somehow…"

"Mama? Baba?"

Lucius and Adara turned to see Phoebus and Calliope standing beneath the arch of ivy at the end of the path, holding hands as they watched their parents. It was as if they were seeing them for the first time in a long while.

Phoebus and Calliope both looked older now, taller and stronger, but more world-weary behind the eyes, as if they had now been fully robbed of their childhood, sent adrift upon a raft, alone with no captain.

Adara wiped her eyes and stared at them, felt such sadness and guilt at her neglect of them. But those feelings were nothing compared to the gratitude she felt that they were alive, and she opened her arms to them as she struggled to her feet.

The children came to her and their arms held her fast, as if taking advantage of the minute crumbling in the hard wall that had been mortared up around her since the destruction of their home and the loss of the baby.

Together they wept and held each other in the calm, green quiet of that healing place.

Lucius, however much he wanted to join that familial embrace, to allow that love to sooth his burned soul, could not bring himself to go near. He pulled his cowl closer about his face and turned away, unable to weep. Instead, he only felt anger at all that he had been robbed of.

His enemies had come to kill his family, and somehow, they had survived, but their family had been wounded beyond recognition, and that attack upon them all would not let him rest, for every painful movement of his body, every terrifying memory, reminded him of the loss and betrayal.

"Baba?" Calliope's soft voice reached out to him, and Lucius felt her fingers upon his.

He pulled away. "Don't look at me, my girl. Please."

"I want to," she insisted, sniffing as she wiped her sodden eyes. "The Gods told me I can help you, and I shall."

"The Gods?" Lucius muttered. "Help us?"

"We are all here," Phoebus added, coming to his sister's side, staring at his father's back. He held his sister's hand tightly beneath the folds of their cloak. "Please look at us, Baba."

Lucius felt desperate to walk away. *But how can I turn my back on them? They fought and lost too.* Finally, slowly, he lowered his cowl to reveal the rough skin of the back of his head, and turned slowly to face them.

Phoebus gripped Calliope's hand tightly but he kept his eyes upon his father's face, forced the tears back as he looked upon the wasteland of Lucius' visage.

Calliope stepped forward and stood before Lucius, taking both his hands in hers and kissing them. She stood to the height of his chest now as she placed the palms of her hands upon his face.

For a moment, Lucius' eyes closed, and his burning skin felt soothed, but it only lasted a moment until he was overcome with the feelings of self-loathing that had become a part of him.

They are beautiful...and I am a monster.

Lucius slowly removed his daughter's hands from his face, and Calliope stepped back, afraid to hug him tightly for fear of hurting him.

They've even robbed me of my children's embrace, he thought bitterly, the faces of his enemies floating at the back of his mind.

"Come," Adara said as she approached the children. "It is getting late, and we should eat. I want you to tell me about the lambing."

They began to walk away, hand in hand, but turned to look back.

"Lucius," Adara said. "Will you come home with us?"

There it is, Lucius thought as he observed the tenderness he so loved, beginning to break free from behind the shades of Adara's eyes.

"You go ahead. I will come later."

Adara nodded sadly, and the three of them left Lucius there, alone beside the pool.

He stared at the red water, that gateway from which he had emerged. It looked soothing, cool, and as he gazed upon it, he let his cloak fall to the ground so that he stood only in his loose tunic and sandals. He slipped off the latter, and stepped slowly into the water.

Lucius sighed as he lowered himself and leaned back so that the water covered his body.

There is no going back, he heard Apollo say.

But Lucius ignored his immortal father, and focused on his pain, and on his anger.

II

IGNIS MEMORIA

'A Memory of Fire'

T he weeks slipped by, and time began to heal for some in the isle, that misty place of peace, hidden from the brutal world without.

The bonds of family and of friendship began to mend, if not quickly, then surely.

Adara spent more time with Briana, Dagon and their child without bitter jealousy invading her heart. She began to be a mother once more to her son and daughter too.

Etain, Weylyn, and Father Gilmore all watched the transformation and smiled gratefully among themselves. However, they worried for Lucius, for he only seemed to grow more distant, nursing a secret anger which they knew could come to no good.

"We need to move him out of the healing house and back with his family," Etain said one day. "We have done all we can for him."

Weylyn nodded, but Gilmore shook his head, still determined that the Metelli should leave Ynis Wytrin.

"I will speak with him," Etain said, looking up at the leaves of the oak under which the three of them sat that morning.

Etain knew where to find Lucius. He lingered often at the gateway to Annwn, as if drawn to it, longing for the forgetfulness of the Otherworld. She began the slow ascent along the sacred path that led to the top of the Tor on an afternoon filled with birdsong and sun.

She enjoyed the walk, moving slowly and reaching out to touch the boughs of oak and yew, rowan and ivy as she went, feeling her connection with them, with the earth at her feet.

It had been a strange night.

In her dreamless sleep, the Gods had asked for her help with the Dragon.

She had gazed into the star-whirling eyes of Apollo and Venus for the first time, and it had left her with a calm purpose, but also a weight.

And the Dragon has felt that gaze the whole of his days…

She felt pity for Lucius as she wended her way up to the top of the Tor where she found him standing alone in the wind, crows diving in the sky above. The sight filled her with a little dread, for in that moment, she thought she spied the Morrigan standing in his place. But she was wrong.

It was the Dragon. Though she and her priestesses had helped him to heal muscle, sinew, and bone, they had not managed to get at the root of the pain he still felt. None but he could do that.

And that was worrisome, for as Etain stared at Lucius where he gazed across the levels to the ruins of the hillfort, she knew he was nursing a darkness that had no place in Ynis Wytrin.

"I feel your thoughts, Lucius Metellus Anguis," she said, her voice reaching out with the kindness she knew he needed. "You are not alone."

Lucius was silent for a moment. "We had thought to make our home there. We did…and it was beautiful…"

Etain walked slowly to Lucius' side, her fingers reaching up to touch the crescent moon that hung about her neck, wisps of her red hair blowing sideways across her brow.

"I can't feel the wind upon my skin," Lucius said to her.

"That will return in time."

"I feel little of anything."

Etain's green eyes looked at him.

"That's wrong," he added. "I do feel… I feel anger and hate…toward those who did this to us…toward Rome…"

"Anger and hate will not serve you now, Lucius Metellus Anguis."

Lucius turned his burned face to her.

She did not flinch, but gazed back with kindness in her brilliant eyes.

"I hate myself too."

She shook her head, but could not answer, for she could indeed see and feel that he meant what he said.

"I did this, lady. Me. I had hubris enough to believe that I could change the world, that I could make it a better place for all of us-"

"And you did!" Etain took Lucius' hands, and even though he tried to pull away, she held them fast. "That home you built on the sacred hill of our ancestors had lain dead and dormant for three generations before you came, before you brought life back to it. The Britons who dwelled about it were practically slaves before you arrived, forgotten by the Gods. But then you built that temple and allowed them to honour all the Gods."

"It was a little thing," Lucius said, pulling his hands away slowly.

"No. It was not. It was a great thing, and so much so that they risked their lives to help you and your family when you were in need. Such sacrifice is not given lightly or for no reason."

"And now the hillfort is destroyed forever."

"No. It only sleeps now, but I have had a vision of it alive again, a place of beauty and inspiration, a home of dragons once more."

"You dream, lady," Lucius said bitterly. "Just as I dreamed, just as I thought I could be emperor and right all the wrongs of this world."

"You are so blessed. You have no idea."

"I was blessed."

"You are!" Etain said, her voice more stern. "You are blessed in that you did not perish in the flames. You are blessed by the Gods-"

"Pfft!"

"You are blessed in the wife and children who have survived along with you and who love you."

Lucius was silent. *I've failed them most of all,* he thought.

Then be there for them! Etain answered, having heard his thoughts.

Lucius stepped away from her in surprise, but she remained with him, close, intent.

"Your wife and children need you more than ever now, and you need them!"

Lucius had no answer, no angry retort. He knew that if there was any goodness left in the world, it was them.

"I don't know how to be there for them," he said sadly, his hand reaching up to touch his burned face.

Etain reached up to take his hand away. "Go to them. It has been well over a year. It is time to leave the healing houses. Live together as the Gods intended."

"The Gods?" Lucius said, the angry edge returning to his voice.

"Yes," Etain answered him. "For they are your family too." She began to go back down the spine of the Tor and leave Lucius with his thoughts. "We are all here for you, Dragon. You are not alone."

With those parting words, Etain turned and began the long walk down, leaving Lucius alone at the top to think on what she had said.

She had tried, and she would continue to try for she knew in her heart that Lucius Metellus Anguis and his family still had an important role to play in the future of Ynis Wytrin and all who dwelled there, though she did not yet know how.

Three days later, Lucius was moved from the sterile world of the healing houses to the large guest house where Adara and the children had been living for over a year.

It felt strange to be a family again, to try and move on after the trauma they had all experienced. Each of them was quiet, wary of happiness.

However, the silent, soft embrace each of them gave to Lucius as he stepped through the threshold of their small dwelling was the first step in a long process of rebuilding, a process Lucius and Adara were not sure was possible.

They each had separate beds in different corners of the long room, for Lucius could not sleep beside his wife yet, his skin still too fragile, though he felt very little himself.

A wooden shelf upon the stone wall now held the phials of oil and pots of resin that Weylyn had prepared, as well as fresh linens to wrap about Lucius' limbs. The old druid had instructed Adara on how to apply them daily so that Lucius' skin could continue to heal.

"He will mend, my dear," Weylyn had said to Adara as they waited for the priestesses to help Lucius down the hill from the healing houses. "It will take time for you all."

"I don't believe he knows how much you have all done for him," Adara said. "Thank you." She gripped Weylyn's hands.

"He was between worlds for a long time. That alone will be difficult for him to fathom. Be patient with each other...and look to your children." Weylyn glanced at Phoebus and Calliope who sat with Aaron and Rachel beneath the oak tree nearby. "They are our greatest teachers."

Adara smiled then, and though there was sadness behind the veil of that smile, it did feel good and true. "Thank you," she said, beginning to weep.

Weylyn reached out and held her to him, let her weep into his robes as they waited for the wounded Dragon.

Slowly, life began to attain some form of rhythm, even if it was broken and harsh at times.

Though he was present with his family in that house near the misty shores of Ynis Wytrin, Lucius Metellus Anguis was often withdrawn and quiet.

Adara tried to be understanding, to set aside her own thoughts of pain so that she could reach out to him, but it was no easy task.

There were moments, however, and she clung to those moments just as she clung to her children who waited for the father they had known to emerge from the physical wreckage that sat in their midst.

Calliope was often content to sit beside Lucius, to wait until that moment when he would reach out and hold her hand in his. No words were spoken, no glances exchanged.

It was more difficult for Phoebus, for the young man was now himself withdrawn in his father's presence. It was as if Phoebus held the fact that his father had not been there when their world went up in flames against him. The son also seemed to fear the father somewhat, for he had heard the truth of who he was, and pondered the implications for all of them.

The nights, however, were the worst.

It was then that Lucius spoke, or cried out in pain. It was then that all of his anger and rage emerged as he tossed and turned in his sleep. He wept and raged alternately as if he were still on fire, as if he relived the burning.

With the children weeping in the darkness, Adara invited them to her own bed where she held them close, as if they were talismans of hope against the pain of the world.

Almost nightly, they would watch Lucius' shadow writhe in the darkness, waiting for him to awaken so that they could care for his wounds anew.

It had felt strange when Lucius left the healing houses of Ynis Wytrin. He was not ready to face the world, to face his family.

The other day at the Well of the Chalice, there had been hope, and so he wondered if maybe, just maybe, that was a good starting point.

However, when he saw Adara and the children waiting for him outside of the guest house as Etain and Olwyn Conn Coran led him there, he began to worry, to feel the guilt begin to chew at his flesh once more, like some horrible beast that followed him everywhere he went.

And now that beast followed him into the home he would share with his wife and children.

They don't deserve this, he thought as they approached, his eyes looking up from the ground occasionally to meet Adara's before she and the children crowded around him and held him as the others looked on.

It was a beginning, but just as the days nurtured that beginning, the nights fed the trauma of the past.

After a week of restless nights in the guest house with his family, Lucius relived that dread night of fire, as if the Gods wanted him to burn all over again.

This time, as Lucius dreamed, Adara and the children listened to it all, as if in the audience of some ancient, grisly tragedy.

Lucius was bound in the dark with the faces of his enemies surrounding him. Praetorian spies laughed at him and prodded him. Serenus Crescens and his hateful son chided him, and beat him. And Marcus Claudius Picus laughed at him as he spoke of his wife and children and what he would do to them.

Lucius cried out in rage but the faces before him only shimmered in the darkness.

The doors of the roundhouse where he had been tied shot open and there, ahead of him, he saw it again.

Barta, his friend and bodyguard, was tied between those two trees as Claudius cut him and tortured him.

"Anguis!!!" Barta cried. "HELP ME!"

And then he was dead, his head flying through the air.

Claudius approached him laughing, sneering, full of hate and jealously.

Then his face changed, contorted until Caracalla stood before Lucius.

The son of the emperor Lucius had served for most of his life laughed at his pain, raged at his plans to supplant him, blamed him for all that had gone wrong.

"I'll kill you!" Lucius yelled in the darkness as he strained at his bonds.

"No. You won't, Metellus!" Caracalla laughed. "You and your family will die!"

And it was then that the house burst into flame and the dragon's jaws engulfed Lucius as the Gods looked on from afar.

"AHHHH!!!!" Lucius shot up in his bed, weeping and raging at once, his fists clenched tightly, his skin bleeding in places. He looked around the dimly-lit room, not knowing where he was, seeking to put out the fires that burned his flesh.

Adara was at his side in a moment, a cool cloth in her hand, pressed gently to his forehead.

Phoebus and Calliope crowded around him too, tears in their eyes at all they had heard.

"Lucius! You're safe, my love!" Adara pleaded. "All is well!"

Lucius swatted at his arms and chest, and pulled at the sweaty tunic he wore as if it burned him. "Get it off of me!"

Adara pulled the blood-stained tunic over his head. "Phoebus, build up the fire in the hearth please."

Phoebus hurried to do that, and soon there was light burning brightly behind Lucius, where he could not see the flames.

Calliope brought down the clean bandages, resin and ointments from the shelf as Adara dabbed at Lucius' skin and whispered to him.

"We're safe, Lucius...all is well..." she said through her tears.

"It was just a bad dream, Baba," Calliope said, her own tears starting anew as she looked closely at the flesh of his torso.

There, upon Lucius' chest, was the sharp outline of the dragon. It was branded onto him, a mirror image of the dragon with outspread wings that had decorated his armour which was all but gone.

Lucius' breathing began to return to normal, but his hands kept going to the beast upon his chest, as if it were the only thing his fingers could recognize.

"I'm sorry..." he mumbled as his wife and daughter cleaned him and spread the resin upon his skin before covering his flesh in fresh linen bandages. "I'm so sorry."

Phoebus observed the branded image upon his father's chest and then went to a table in the far corner where Lucius and Adara's things had been set - their swords, the daggers, and the wrapped bundle. He reached for the latter and placed it in the middle of the table, looking down at it. Slowly, Phoebus folded back the flaps and there, in the middle, glinting brightly as if it were newly wrought and polished, was the image of the dragon. It was all that was left of the ancestral armour that he had thought would one day be his.

He remembered watching through his tears as the priestesses and Weylyn had pried it from his father's flesh when they arrived in Ynis Wytrin, when both of his parents had lingered at the doorway to Elysium.

That dragon image had glowed before his eyes, not with the orange light of fire, but with a starry brilliance that outshone the blood that covered it.

Now, he looked upon it, untouched by the horrors of all that had happened and, compared to his father's flesh, his soul, that dragon seemed at peace with itself.

"Phoebus?" Lucius' voice croaked from his bed as Adara and Calliope tidied up the bloody linens. "What is it?"

Phoebus turned and held up the shining image of the dragon for his father to see, but upon seeing it, Lucius grasped his chest as if he could feel it burning still.

"Put that away!" Lucius growled. "I don't want to see it!" Lucius stood and stumbled to the door.

"Lucius, please! You need to rest. Stay in bed!" Adara said.

"I need to get out," he answered, opening the door and going out into the dim dawn mist of the isle.

Adara walked over to her son. "He is not angry at you, Phoebus."

"Poor Baba," Calliope wept then. "How can we help him?"

Adara shook her head and reached out to take the dragon image from her son. "I don't know that we can, my girl," she said as she wrapped the dragon back up in the linen and set it back upon the table. She turned to Phoebus and put her hands upon his shoulders. "Though much has changed...he is still your father."

Phoebus nodded silently and turned to the table where the gladius he had wielded that fateful night - his father's gladius - lay upon its side. They had not been allowed to practice on Ynis Wytrin since their arrival, but nor had he wanted to. He reached out to force himself to touch it with a shaking hand.

"It's all right, my son. You have fought your battle, and won. It is a time for peace now."

Phoebus withdrew his hand and looked at his mother. "Is it? It doesn't feel like a time of peace."

Adara had no answer as she stood there looking at her two children, her one hand upon her belly.

When the sun was up, and the bell of Father Gilmore's chapel began to ring in the misty morning, Adara walked with the children to the Christian temple for their time with Rachel and Aaron.

It had become their habit to spend time with the twins under Gilmore's protection, for they had a way of making Phoebus and Calliope calm, happy. They liked watching the Christian rites and talking about Gilmore's Christus and the love he had for the world.

It sounded strange that a son of some god should be so open and caring to the world, and yet treated so terribly by his own people, and by Rome.

Adara had, of course, known Christians before, but Rachel and Aaron were different, had a deeper understanding of their beliefs. She saw no harm in her own children spending time with them, hearing about the love and optimism of that Christus in those dark days. They would always honour the Gods, of course, but like Ynis Wytrin itself, the two beliefs could live in harmony within.

"Good morning, Phoebus and Calliope!" Rachel and Aaron ran up to them as they approached the wattle and daub chapel.

"Good morning," Phoebus answered, hugging them in greeting.

"Are you not well?" Rachel asked, concern upon her face.

Phoebus was silent.

"Their father had a difficult night," Adara said.

"And you, lady?" Aaron asked. "How are you feeling?" He reached out and took her hand.

It gave Adara pause, for she felt an immediate lightening of her heart, despite the task she was about to undertake. "I am well enough," Adara answered, "if not very tired."

Nearby, birds twittered in the branches of a tree, and rays of sunlight poured through the mist.

Still holding Adara's hand, Aaron closed his yes and listened to the birdsong, felt the sun upon his face. "All will be well, lady, for no matter how bad the world seems, there is always hope."

"With our Lord to watch over us, hope is eternal," Gilmore said as he came out of the chapel. "Are you all coming in?"

Aaron released Adara's hands gently and turned his dark eyes to Father Gilmore. "We are coming, Father."

Phoebus noted that Aaron did not look at Gilmore when he spoke, but merely touched the priest as he passed.

Together the four children went inside the chapel, Gilmore smiling tenderly at them all as they passed. He then turned to Adara. "Will you join us today, lady Metella?"

"No. But thank you, Father Gilmore. I look forward to hearing more from Phoebus and Calliope." She pulled her cloak about her as she stood there in the wet grass. "You have helped them through this difficult time, and I am grateful to you for it."

"It is not I, but Rachel and Aaron who have done so. Their hearts are as pure as they can possibly be, and the love they have for those around them is the only thing that can help Phoebus and Calliope heal from the trauma they have experienced."

And their father and mother's love, if they can get it, she thought. "They are indeed special children," Adara agreed. "They all are."

Father Gilmore nodded and bowed to her slightly before turning and entering the chapel to join the children and begin his ritual.

Adara turned to walk up toward the slope of Wearyall Hill then, going slowly, in her mind seeking the Gods' guidance, for herself, her children, and for Lucius.

The things he said in his sleep...the fear, sadness...the anger... It was all terrifying, and she did not know how she could help him. *I don't know if I am strong enough to help him.*

When she ascended the spine of the hill, she saw her husband sitting, leaning against the thin trunk of the lone, windswept tree, gazing to the south in stony silence.

"Lucius?" she said as she got closer, unsure if he could hear her, not wanting to surprise him.

"I'm sorry I woke you in such a way," Lucius said. "I…I dreamed of…"

"I know."

He turned to look up at her from the shadow of his cowl. "I can't stop thinking about it."

"I'm so sorry, Lucius."

"You didn't do anything."

"Yes. I did. Had I not left the hillfort to lead Claudius away, our child might have survived, and you…you would not have fallen so far."

Adara felt the tears begin to burn at the rims of her eyes as she sat down in the grass beside Lucius.

He turned to look at her, his jaundiced eyes wide and intense. "Is that what you think? Had you not led him away, he would have hunted you and the children down, and you would all have been slain by him and his men."

"I still see you falling, Lucius…so far…"

His voice was calmer in that moment than it had been in a long time. "And I would do it again and again if it meant that you were safe."

She looked at him, and wrapped her arms about him as gently as she could, but he squeezed back, and the feeling was a wonder to her.

"We will get through this together," Adara said.

But Lucius released his hold on her and looked back out to the South. "Yes, we will. But the road is not yet ended. Those who have done this to us…they are still out there."

In that moment, Adara felt fear grip her heart anew, but she was afraid to ask what he meant by it, to ruin the momentary peace between them. She felt Lucius' body relax again beside her.

"I'm sorry I wasn't there for you these long months," Lucius said. He shook his head. "I can't believe the Gods have robbed me of so much time."

"It was time you needed to heal."

"Yes…heal…" He held out his arm to gaze upon the melted flesh where the dragon tattoos that had once writhed upon his skin were now gone. "But who is Lucius Metellus Anguis now?"

"You're my husband. You're a father. You are a dragon, a leader of men…a friend. You are…a son of Apollo." Adara closed her eyes.

"A son of Apollo…" Lucius said bitterly. "But what does that mean? What does it mean to have been ignorant of the truth for the whole of my life, to only find out as I lay bleeding to death upon the grass of the Otherworld?"

"I don't know, Lucius." Adara looked up at the sky. "But I do know that, despite the pain we've suffered..." She tried to steady her voice. "...we are blessed...*you* are blessed..."

Lucius breathed a deep, ragged breath, but he did not say anything.

Adara had said the words to comfort him, but she knew that he did not believe them. He would have to come to that conclusion on his own. And so would she. For she did not fully believe it either. *Blessed? After all the trials we've endured...can such a life be called 'blessed'?*

In that moment, Adara felt the coolness of a morning breeze upon her neck as she sat there with her eyes closed.

Yes, it can, the voice said in her mind, the voice of the goddess she knew stood behind them both with her hands upon their shoulders, binding them, reminding them.

Venus held firmly to her favoured two, and felt the sadness that burned in each of them. Pity filled her heart then, for she knew she and Apollo had failed them, that they could have helped them more.

Love also felt the anger burning deep inside the dragon before her, the half-mortal man who had been through so much. It pained her to know that he yet had a long road before him, before he could achieve his true self and realize the world he wished for inside.

I am here for you both, she said before disappearing from their midst.

"She says so now," Lucius muttered. "Where was she as I burned?"

The lightness Adara felt in her being departed at his bitter words.

"Where are the children?" Lucius asked, as if he just remembered them.

"They're in the chapel with Father Gilmore, Rachel and Aaron."

"Why?"

"Because it helps them to heal. Those children have been their saviours these many months since we arrived here."

Lucius could not argue with that. He could still see them pulling him out of the red waters. But he knew that Father Gilmore did not want them there, and worried that the priest would try to turn them against him.

"What has Gilmore been telling them?"

"He has been telling them of the Christus and of his love for the world, his wish for peace."

"Then he was a fool," Lucius said. "For there will be no peace until wicked men are made to pay for their crimes."

"Please be calm, Lucius." Adara laid her hand upon his arm, but it was stiff, his mind removed now. "We are here to heal, to be at peace."

"Peace?"

"Lucius, my love." She stood and moved to kneel directly in front of him. "We need to pick up the pieces of our lives before we can move on. Before we can go home."

"Adara, we have no home. All we had is gone."

"Not all of it. We have each other. We have our children! Did you know that Phoebus killed someone in the battle? Did you know that he has been haunted by that ever since that night, in addition to all else that happened to us? All that we have learned about you?"

"I did not know."

"No. You did not. But he is resilient, despite the weight of seven worlds upon his young shoulders. He cannot heal alone, and those children of Gilmore's help him to do so. But he needs you to come back, to speak with him."

"I will."

Adara stood, her arms crossed as the wind began to whip around them on that lonely hilltop. "We need to stay close to each other, Lucius. We need to help each other. Because if we don't, we truly have lost everything." She looked down at her belly, the empty womb beneath her clothing, and as her hands reached for it, they fell limp at her sides as her tears fell. "I don't want to lose anything more in this life."

Adara turned and walked away, gone before Lucius could stand and reach out to her, to hold her.

Gods, what have you done to us? he thought.

It took Lucius some time to make his way back down the slopes of Wearyall Hill, but eventually, he found himself skirting the edge of the marshes to the West of the crops and orchards. As he moved along the shoreline, his eyes searching for the world beyond the water and tall reeds, the priestesses and priests who tended the crops watched him move silently along the water's edge. The Dragon filled them all with awe, but also with fear. They had all seen his wounds, and heard his nightmare screams, crashing upon the walls of the healing houses.

It was also whispered that he was of immortal parentage, and that the Gods themselves visited him often to tend to him, to heal his body.

The Dragon should have been dead. They all knew it. And yet he was not fully alive, it seemed, a shadow of the man he had been, walking among them.

Lucius could feel their eyes upon him, but he ignored it, knew stares were something he would be forced to get used to.

He carried on walking for some time until he heard a series of pained cries echoing along the water's edge. Lucius stopped and listened as best he could through the sound of his own, pumping blood in his ears.

The sound was a loud whinny that broke into a sort of keening each time, full of pain and fear.

Xanthus? Lucius thought, as he heaped more guilt upon himself. In all that had happened since the fires, he had completely forgotten his old friend, the one who had led Dagon and the others to him, who had saved him countless times before, who had been loyal above all else.

Lucius hurried along through the trees until he came to an open grass area where a large pen had been erected and there, in the middle of it, pacing back and forth and calling out to the sky, was the enormous black stallion.

As soon as Lucius came into view, the stallion stopped in the middle of the paddock and stared directly at him through his enormous, dark eyes.

Lucius wanted to weep as he approached, but his eyes were not able to, though his heart cried out at the sight of the animal before him.

Xanthus stood very still as his old rider came to the edge of the fencing, unwilling to immediately approach.

"I'm so sorry, boy…" Lucius said. "Don't be afraid. It is me."

Xanthus tossed his enormous head and stepped backward a few feet.

"Have they been taking care of you?" Lucius tried to climb over the fencing, but his skin pulled painfully as he did so. He stopped, and looked along the rim of the paddock for a gate. When he found it, he made his way there and opened it to go in. Once the gate was closed behind him, he stood still and watched Xanthus from a distance, unsure of how the stallion would react to his presence. "I'm here, Xanthus…"

For some minutes they watched each other until, eventually, the stallion stepped a few feet closer, and Lucius did the same. The grassy space between them lessened slowly, more and more until eventually they were only three feet apart.

Lucius could see Xanthus' eyes observing him, looking him over. He could tell the stallion was feeling what he was feeling, the torment and sadness, the trauma. It broke Lucius' heart to see him like that, and in that moment, he knew that he could never ask the animal before him for anything else but friendship.

"No more battles, my friend. No more blood. I release you from all of it."

Xanthus, as if waiting for confirmation of those very thoughts, then closed the final space between them, and laid his thick neck across Lucius' shoulders.

Lucius' arms reached out to hold him, and in doing so he could feel a great shuddering inside of Xanthus. "It's all right, boy. It's all finished."

He was worried about you, a soft voice said from Xanthus' other side.

Lucius paused and looked down at the grass to Epona's sandalled feet.

"What are you doing here?" Lucius asked, unable to look the goddess in the eyes.

Epona said nothing at first, but stroked Xanthus' neck slowly, calming him. *I have been here the entire time, Lucius.* The goddess walked slowly around the front of Xanthus' head and stood beside Lucius. She reached out to lower his cowl, but he pulled away.

Please...let me help... she said.

"Now you wish to help?"

I have always done so for you and your men...my warriors. Epona reached out and placed her hands upon Lucius' ruined face and, just as the spring blooms green and blossom, or as the crops grow strong at her touch, Lucius' skin ceased its bleeding. The goddess' hands lingered there for several moments.

Lucius felt some of his pain dissipate, but when she removed her hands, it returned.

I am sorry, Lucius... Epona's voice was full of sadness and pain. She wanted to hug him, to hold him close after all he had been through, but she knew that he was too far distant, too full of anger. *I thought I could help.*

"No one can," Lucius answered.

His words saddened her, and she stepped back. *Only you can make things right then, Lucius Metellus Anguis...for yourself.*

Lucius looked her in the eyes then and she felt his pain and anger more than ever, the twisted life of a man with a foot in two worlds, bleeding over the threshold between them.

I never abandoned you, my dragon. And I never will. She reached out to hold his hands. *Do not abandon yourself.*

Lucius felt the truth of her words, but inside, he pushed them away, for his guilt and anger urged him to do just that. "It would have been better for everyone had I remained on Olympus, unable to bring more sadness into people's lives."

Epona shook her head. *It was one of the bravest things I have seen any man do.* She looked down, and then back up at Lucius and Xanthus. *I will go now, but you must speak with him now, for he needs you.*

"Who?"

Your son, Lucius Metellus Anguis...your son...

"Baba?"

Lucius turned to see Phoebus climbing over the fence of the paddock and walking slowly toward him and Xanthus.

The stallion moved away from Lucius and went to Phoebus who carried a bucket of vegetables and oats.

"Phoebus? What are you doing here?" Lucius asked.

"I've been taking care of Xanthus for you while..." Phoebus paused. "Well... I'm the only one who can get near enough to him to brush him and feed him. Sometimes he lets Dagon, but mostly it's just me. But no one can ride him."

Lucius smiled at his son and looked at Xanthus as he ate happily of the vegetables the boy fed him.

"Thank you, Phoebus. You seem to have done well with him." Lucius sighed and stepped closer to his son. "I know too that Xanthus is not the only one that I've neglected... I..." Lucius felt light-headed, and as he stumbled a little, he felt his son's strong arms hold him up and lead him to the fence so that he could lean against it while Xanthus ate out of the two buckets. "I haven't been there for you either."

Phoebus was quiet.

"I have seen things that..."

"I know, Baba. I've heard you speak of them in your sleep...the things that happened to you." Suddenly, Phoebus was hugging his father.

With shaking arms, Lucius held him. "I don't know where the time has gone. I wanted to make this world a better place for you...a safer one."

Phoebus looked up at Lucius then, tears in his young, bright eyes.

"But I only hurt everyone I ever loved in the process. I'm so sorry."

Phoebus shook his head. "It wasn't your fault, Baba. It was the men who attacked our family and tried to kill you."

"In some ways, yes. But I was not there for you when you needed me."

They were silent for a few moments before Lucius decided to bring it up. "Your mother told me what happened during the attack. That you saved your sister from Crescens' son."

Phoebus looked down and Lucius could see his fists clenched as he relived the moment he killed a man for the first time, a moment that every warrior remembers.

Lucius turned his son to face him and looked into his eyes. "Listen to me carefully, Phoebus..."

The boy looked up at his father.

"You did nothing wrong. To kill another is a serious thing, but sometimes, it is needed. He was a wicked man, the son of another wicked man who sought to do harm to all of us."

"He was going to kill Calliope. I had no choice."

"You did have a choice, Phoebus, and you chose well. You saved your sister, and if you remember anything from that night, remember that."

Phoebus nodded and then looked back at Lucius. "They all came, you know. To help us fight."

"Who did?"

"Culhwch, Alma, Paulus and the rest of the villagers. They were there for us. And Briana fought the Praetorians as they attacked...and Mama too and-"

The boy was pouring the memories out now for his father, overcome with the fear that had haunted him for over a year.

"It's all right," Lucius said, holding his sobbing son, forgetting momentarily his own pain and anger. "It's finished."

As Lucius held his son in that green pasture, he imagined Phoebus slaying Crescens' son, the boy who would have been a willing apprentice of Claudius Picus, the boy who had looked Lucius in the eye before the fires had engulfed him. Phoebus had done well to kill him, but there were others who yet lived.

Should I have my poor boy do my killing? Lucius chided himself, the familiar anger returning. *No more…never again…*

In that moment, he thought of their once-beautiful home, and the friends that had surrounded them there, who had come to his family's aid through fire and blood.

What was left of all of it, their friends, their home?

I need to go back, Lucius thought, and the urge to do so was overwhelming.

III

DOMUM REDITIO

'Homecoming'

A s Lucius Metellus Anguis began to move more easily about Ynis Wytrin, accustoming himself to his scarred body and its way of moving, Etain, Weylyn, and Gilmore observed him from a distance. They watched as Lucius slowly allowed his wife and children to get closer to him, an act that allowed the healing in all of them to truly begin, for they were stronger together.

However, even as the physical healing progressed, and Lucius' strength began to return minutely, Etain worried about other aspects of Lucius' return to the world.

"He still spends most of his days alone," she said to Weylyn and Gilmore one morning as they sat beneath the oak tree watching the waterfowl along the loamy shore. "He lingers at Annwn's gates and waits for I know not what."

"We cannot imagine what he is thinking," Weylyn said. "Ever since we discovered the truth of his lineage..." He struggled for the words. "For a man in the mortal world to be faced with such a realization... It has not been easy for him."

"I agree," Etain said. "He told me as much during his time in the healing houses. He had reached a point where he believed he felt he finally knew himself, truly. How many men can say that? He had made a great decision in the North, a decision supported by the legions, and by his friends."

"And it all came to nothing," Gilmore added, "and endangered all those around him."

Etain turned on her friend. "I am constantly surprised by your lack of empathy for a man who tried to protect this blessed place from those who would seek to destroy it. He has suffered for all of us."

"Has he?" Gilmore said, rubbing his temples. "Or was it his own hubris that brought the world crashing down upon him? Even he believes in his own guilt." Gilmore stood and leaned against the trunk of the tree. "You say he is the son of a god, but...I just can't..."

"What is it, my friend?" Etain asked.

"How can it be?"

"You ask this?" Weylyn said. "Your own Christus was the son of your god, born by a mortal woman. You know it is possible."

Etain rose then, her priestess' robes straightening about her as she stood tall, commanding. "We have debated this many a time, Gilmore. All are welcome in Ynis Wytrin, and that includes the Dragon."

"A Roman!" Gilmore hissed.

"A friend," she answered calmly.

"And a warrior whom Etain has seen will protect this place, this land, from the coming trials whenever they may be."

Gilmore stopped himself and stood still, staring at both of them. "I'm afraid...afraid for this sanctuary, for Aaron and Rachel."

"It was they who helped to bring the Dragon back from death," Etain reminded him. "Trust in your charges, for they too possess a spark of the divine, do they not?"

Gilmore lowered his head and stared at the grass about his feet. Then he heard laughter and turned to see his charges and Metellus' children playing in the spring sunlight near the orchard.

"Perhaps the future is a coin with two faces, harmonious and supportive of each other rather than at war?" Etain reached out to touch Gilmore's shoulder. "Do not build up walls when none are needed. Let us all consider this together."

Gilmore grasped her hand and nodded before turning and going back to the chapel.

Weylyn stepped to Etain's side. "Is he right to worry? Lucius is a good...*man*...but there is a growing anger in him the more conscious he becomes. The more he heals physically, the more other wounds open up."

"It is true. There are wounds we cannot help him with. He will need to seek his own remedies sometime soon."

"We cannot lose the Dragon, Etain," Weylyn said, grasping her hand.

Her green eyes turned toward him, intense and full of emotion. "No, we cannot. The future of Ynis Wytrin and our people depend upon it."

. . .

It was a night of spring thunder around Ynis Wytrin, and the crashing symphony of the Gods woke Lucius with a start. He had been dreaming that he lay swallowed in mud, gazing up at the heavens and falling rain. Pain was everywhere as he had raced through the dark to a great fire in the distance, surrounded by the sounds of screaming, death and dying.

Lying in his bed, he felt his chest where the dragon brand spread across his torso. He wondered if he had screamed in his sleep and looked to his wife and children, but they slept soundly still.

I wish I could lie next to her, he thought as he gazed at Adara's sleeping form, but the blood upon his sheets where his back had bled told him it was not yet time. He wondered if they would ever lie together again, and the thought kindled more anger.

He went over to the broad table at the far end of the house, away from his sleeping family, and lit the clay lamp that sat upon its surface. As the flame sprang to life, Lucius looked upon the items that had been laid out there.

He had not touched his sword in a long time, nor his daggers. Adara's sword - the one crafted by the strange smith, Terdra - lay beside his own blade.

With hesitant fingers, Lucius reached out to pull back the linen wrappings and touch the pommel, handle, and dragon-headed hilt. He remembered it in the hands of Claudius Picus as he slashed away at Barta's Herculean body. He paused, fighting back that memory and the urge to scream anew, and grasped the handle tightly in his massacred hand.

Turning away from the table, Lucius held the blade out and felt the full force of its weight straining his muscles. There had been a time when that divine blade had felt like it was a part of his own body, feather-light and reliable, but in that moment, it felt foreign to him, as much so as his relationship to the people and world around him.

Lucius Metellus Anguis felt that no weapon would ever be a part of him again, but he forced himself to grasp it, to feel it, for his muscles to search for the martial memories they once possessed.

He tired, and put the blade down again, trying not to let it drop and wake his family.

He then poured out water from a clay jug into a cup and drank where he sat once more at the table before the array of weapons. He then reached out for another bundle and placed it before him.

Lucius gazed at the linen for a while before peeling back the folds to reveal the image of the dragon glowing in the lamplight before him.

The image seemed to shimmer and glow, its wings waving quietly in an invisible breeze, willing to break free.

What does it mean? he thought as he looked upon the untarnished image. The metal was perfect, though it had been to Hades and back, though it had burned in the same fires that had burned him and all the armour that had protected him.

Can this be all that is left?

A part of him wanted to call out to his divine father, to question him, to demand answers, but he would not. *No,* he told himself. *We were so happy for a time...and now?*

He shuttered up his mind then, for thinking on it only caused more anguish. He wanted to staunch the flow of pain that continued to bleed his soul.

With the dragon on the table before him, Lucius bent over with his head in his hands and wept.

Adara watched Lucius from her dark corner of the room, sitting at the table and weeping to himself.

But she could not bring herself to rise and comfort him, haunted as she was by her own nightmares. She had dreamt of Claudius Picus again, the child he had murdered, and it was all she could do not to weep and wallow in despair. Instead, she focussed on Phoebus and Calliope who slept nearby, and Lucius' form at the far end of the house.

As Adara watched Lucius from the shadowy corner of her part of the room, she felt like they were constantly reaching out to each other in the dark, but unable to touch, the gap between them broadening. She wanted to comfort him, but was unsure how, and that was a new feeling.

Outside in the morning mist of Ynis Wytrin, a rooster called out to herald the new day.

Lucius looked up, wiping his eyes and sniffling, searching for the dim grey light that came in at the window.

Adara watched him shift stiffly upon the chair and decided to go to him.

Lucius did not hear her coming, and flinched at her gentle touch upon his shoulder.

"Sorry, my love," Adara whispered. "I didn't meant to startle you."

He reached up to touch her smooth hand with his rough one, and kissed her fingers. "I didn't mean to wake you."

"You didn't. I was already awake." Adara looked down at the dragon upon the table and felt a chill run along her spine. She had avoided looking at it since she realized it had been the only thing to survive the fires unscathed, nor had she touched the swords whose golden hilts now poked through the open linen wrappings. "What are you doing?"

Lucius sighed. "Remembering. Trying to understand."

Adara felt herself growing nervous. "While you were in the healing houses, I tried understanding and remembering… It causes nothing but pain. We need to move forward and create a new life." Without pause, Adara went to the shelf to get the clay pot of resin.

Lucius pulled back his shirt, and allowed her to start spreading the thick mixture over his bleeding back, arms and chest. He continued his thought, shaking his head.

"I can't forget or move forward until I understand… We had built a new life, a good life-"

"Please stop."

"I need to go back to our home. I need to see it again."

"I can't go back there, Lucius. It is gone. There is nothing there."

"Just one day."

"I can't!" Adara snapped. She stood there, with her eyes closed tightly as memories of fires and screaming invaded her thoughts. "Please, Lucius."

"I'll go by myself then. I need to."

"You're not well enough to travel yet."

"I'll manage. What more could happen to me?" he said stubbornly.

"You could be killed. Caracalla will have hunters looking for you."

"It has been well over a year."

"Lucius, it's not safe-"

"I want to go!" he said loudly, slamming the table and making the sword and dagger blades clang.

"Mama?" Calliope sat up quickly in her bed.

"What's wrong?" Phoebus added, swinging his legs over the edge of his and scanning the room.

Adara turned away from Lucius and went to sit with her children. "It's nothing. Your father and I were just talking." When she turned to look at Lucius again, he was already on his way out the door with his black cloak trailing from his hand.

"Is he all right, Mama?" Calliope asked, still confused from the suddenness of her awakening.

"No, my girl. He is not," Adara said, burying her face in her hands and weeping as her children gathered around her to comfort her.

Lucius walked barefoot through the dewy grass in the direction of the Well of the Chalice and the avenue of yew trees that led from there to the slopes of the Tor.

From beneath his cowl, he could see the forms of the white-robed priestesses moving about the sanctuary, making their morning offerings to the Goddess. Their movements were calm and smooth, like smoke lingering softly in the air, whereas Lucius' own movements felt rough and clumsy as he went, unable to feel the cool earth beneath his feet, or the trunks of the trees he reached out to for support.

He emerged from the avenue and began to climb to the top of the Tor. The effort made him breathe heavily, his stamina not what it had been, nothing as it had been.

When he reached the top, he collapsed upon his back and stared up at the dim, morning sky.

As he lay there, he could think of nothing else except going back to the hillfort. He needed to see what was left, to remember the green slopes of the ancient defences where he had walked the ramparts and watched sunsets with his family. He wanted to see the hall, their home that had echoed with laughter and the gatherings of family and friends about the great, round hearth.

The thoughts angered Lucius and he ridiculed himself for them, pounding his fist upon the hollow hill.

"Gods! What have you done to me?"

A moment later, all sound was sucked out of the world around him and he felt his breathing slow down. He opened his eyes and felt her hand upon his forehead.

We did not do this to you, Venus said, as she looked down upon Lucius, her hand firmly upon his brow. *Be calm...be peaceful...*

After a few moments, Lucius felt his anger dissipate. He sat up and turned to look at Love. Then he shook his head. "I can't do this…"

You are not alone, Love said, her eyes full of sorrow and pity for the man before her. *You have never been alone.*

"Except when I was being tortured and consumed by fire," he answered bitterly.

Venus did not speak. Lucius' own decisions had led to that. As a mortal, he had had to endure certain trials upon his chosen path, that one being amongst the worst.

You do not know how difficult it was for us to watch that…

"All you did was watch," he answered. "You watched me burn."

Tears filled Love's eyes then, and she let them fall.

Lucius looked up at her and could not continue his argument, but nor could he reach out to touch her cheek as he wanted to. He shook his head. "I was a fool to come back here…to live."

No. It is another choice, another path to travel.

Lucius struggled to his feet and stood before the goddess. "And I will travel it alone if I must."

You need not be alone, Lucius.

"No?" he snapped at her, before turning and beginning the descent. Lucius paused to look to the East and there, rising up before the face of the sun was a sliver of smooth smoke. His eyes followed its line downward until he saw the thatch roof of a roundhouse.

Love was at his side again, though she did not reach out this time. *So many people love you, Lucius. Do not turn away from them.*

And with that, she was gone.

Lucius stared at the roundhouse for a few minutes before going back down the long slope of the Tor.

When he arrived at the bottom, he took another path to his left, where the trees hid him from the world and birds flit and chirped among the branches.

Soon, the chorus was joined by other noises - the chopping of wood, soft speech and the sound of laughter.

Lucius paused at the edge of the trees to see the lone roundhouse in the middle of a field fringed with another apple orchard. Sunlight beat down on the roundhouse which was well-kept, and bordered with various vegetable patches. A part of Lucius did not want to intrude.

Briana knelt in the garden, smiling beside Antiope as they pulled carrots from the ground, and Dagon paused in his wood chopping to watch them, smiling as he leaned on the large axe he wielded. It was a scene of utter peace and joy, and Lucius was not sure if he wanted to enter, either for fear of darkening it, or fear of his own jealousy.

Then Dagon turned to see his dark figure standing at the edge of the trees and he raised a hand to him in greeting.

Lucius pulled the cowl lower over his face and stepped out into the light to slowly walk across the grass toward him.

Dagon set the axe down and walked over to meet him.

Lucius noted that he did not look like a king, or even like the great warrior he was. The sword of his uncle, Mar, no longer hung at his side, and his great scale armour was packed away, oiled and linen-covered in a corner of the home they had built themselves. He observed Dagon's plain dress of a brown tunic and bracae, belted with brown leather, and wondered how a king of his people could have ended up here, a farmer, husband and father, and look so absolutely at peace.

"Lucius," Dagon said, his voice soft and full of relief.

Lucius felt his anger dwindle as his friend approached and he reached out to him.

Dagon took his hand and hugged him carefully. He was unsure of what to say, but knew that he was indeed relieved to see Lucius.

"You look well, my friend," Lucius said as he pulled back.

Dagon was silent for a moment, awkward. He turned to look behind him at Briana and Antiope who were wiping their dirty hands upon their aprons as they too approached.

Lucius tried to smile when the child looked up at him, but his features soon contorted as thoughts of his own lost child entered his mind.

Antiope retreated behind Briana's legs, but her mother kept moving forward to take Lucius' hands.

"It's good to see you, Lucius," she said.

Lucius nodded, unable to hold her gaze for very long. He looked around, his hand disappearing inside the folds of his cloak. "You have built a beautiful home here," he said.

Dagon nodded and reached for his daughter's hand. "Thank you. Etain gave us permission to build it. It is small, but enough for the three of us." He looked down at his daughter and hoisted her up in his arms. "Antiope, this is my dearest friend, Lucius."

The little girl, her courage up as she sat in her father's arms, looked directly at Lucius' face. "Are you hurt?"

Lucius observed the wide eyes and wondered what he must look like to the child. He could see the awkwardness upon Briana and Dagon's faces, the unwarranted guilt, and forced a smile.

"I am, yes, Antiope. But I am very...happy to meet you."

She buried her face in Dagon's neck under Lucius' observation, and her father handed her back to Briana.

"Will you take some water with us?" Briana asked.

Dagon looked hopefully at Lucius and the latter nodded. "Thank you."

They made their way to the roundhouse and Lucius ducked under the thatch awning to enter.

Inside it was dark, and the floor was strewn with fresh hay that made the air smell sweetly, mingled with the scent of woodsmoke from the central hearth where a warm fire burned and crackled. Dagon added another log from the pile he had just cut outside, and showed Lucius to a large stump beside the fire.

Lucius, however, hesitated at the sight of it so near the flames.

"I'm sorry," Dagon said quickly. "Over here is better." He went around the fire to the back of the house and a rectangular table with benches.

Lucius looked around at the simplicity of the place, the wooden shelves with clay pots, jugs and plates, the dried herbs hanging from beams. On a small second floor, there appeared to be beds for the family to sleep in.

Dagon sat down and waited for Lucius to follow as Briana took two cups and a jug of water from one of the shelves.

Lucius moved to join Dagon and eased himself onto the bench opposite, his back to the hearth so that he could not see it. His breath was raspy as he sat, but it soon calmed, the water Briana handed him soothing his dry throat.

"You built this yourself?" Lucius asked, looking around the walls.

"Yes, well, with some help from some of the younger apprentices around Ynis Wytrin."

Lucius nodded. "It is beautiful."

Dagon smiled, his eyes meeting Briana's where she sat at the fire with Antiope. He looked down at Lucius' burned hands and remembered how they had first looked. "I'm relieved to see you moving about. Etain, Rachel and Aaron have worked a...what does Gilmore call it? A miracle? Are you feeling better?"

"I don't know how I'm feeling," Lucius said quickly. "I don't know who I am anymore. People stare at me or look away as if they're frightened...even in Ynis Wytrin. My own children and wife hesitate around me and are more my nursemaids than my family. I dream of fire and cry in my sleep, and I can hardly feel the surface of this clay cup I hold in my hands, let alone lift a sword."

Dagon was silent. "I'm so sorry, Lucius."

Lucius looked up to see the tears forming in his old friend's eyes, the anger he too nurtured. "You have no reason to be sorry, Dagon. It was my foolishness, my hubris, that has led us to all of this."

"That is not true," Dagon replied, wiping his eyes. "It was the hatred and jealousy of lesser men, men who would have stopped at nothing to destroy you long before you decided to try for the imperial throne."

"We could all have disappeared, deserted..."

"And then what? Caracalla and Claudius Picus would have burned your home anyway-"

"But I would not look like this!" Lucius slid back his hood to reveal his burned face and thinly-haired head. "And our...our child would still be alive." He slammed his fist on the table, causing his skin to crack, but he did not seem to notice it.

Briana glanced at Dagon over Lucius' shoulder and took Antiope outside to continue their work and allow the two men to speak privately.

"I'm sorry I wasn't at your side when you and Barta were taken. I should have been with you."

Lucius shook his head. "Barta...and so many others." He breathed deeply, his lung aching with the effort. "At least you are happy, my friend. For that I am grateful. Your daughter is beautiful."

"Yes, she is. She and Briana are my anchors in this world." Dagon looked down, and then back up again at Lucius. "But do you think I am happy?" He looked to see that Briana was not near the door. "A part of me is, yes. Absolutely. But there is a part of me - the king - who is constantly at odds with this place. I have abandoned my people, my brothers. They are adrift in the world, hunted and alone."

"You have heard nothing?" Lucius asked.

"I haven't left Ynis Wytrin for over a year...since the day Claudius attacked the hillfort." Dagon leaned against the whitewashed wall behind him. "Yes, a part of me is happy - the husband and father - but there is a part of me who lives in constant guilt and anger. Every night, when I close my eyes, I wonder if the shade of my uncle will emerge from the shadows to chide me for abandoning our people." He sighed deeply. "But it is a choice I have made to live here, to shore up the defences of my life and keep my wife and child safe from the cruelty of the world. It is also my chosen burden."

Lucius was quiet for a long time, and knew that Dagon was beating himself up not only for what had happened to Lucius, but also for every Sarmatian who had died in the wars, or who yet lived in hiding in the wilds of Britannia.

"You have a home and family here that is worth protecting," Lucius said.

"As do you, Lucius." Dagon stared at him. "Adara and the children need you more than ever, and now that you are healing, you should heal with them."

"I know," Lucius said. "I just…I can't forget. I can't forget who is responsible for all of this."

"Claudius Picus is dead, Lucius. You and Adara killed him."

"Not Claudius!" Lucius snapped.

"Then who?"

"Caracalla."

Dagon froze. "You need to forget him. The Gods will make him pay in their own time. You need to move forward, to build a new life."

"I had built a new life, and they took it from me. From all of us."

"And now you live, when you should have been dead by all the laws of nature, men, and gods. Cherish it, and accept things as they are, Lucius. As I have."

"You know what I have learned about myself?" Lucius stared directly at him now.

Dagon looked into his friend's pained eyes and nodded slowly, wondered if it was his friend speaking, or if in the recesses of Lucius' person, there was now a wounded demi-god addressing him. And he found it frightening. "Yes. I know."

"Then you know I cannot sit idly by."

"There is nothing you can do."

Lucius shook his head. "Maybe not, but I want to go back."

"Where?" Dagon asked.

"To the home they took from me. To the hillfort."

Dagon paused. "It's not safe."

"It has been over a year."

"And that is not long enough."

"I want you to come with me. Just once."

Dagon closed his eyes. A part of him dreaded retracing the steps to that place, the images of Lucius and Adara bloody and broken in the barges entered his mind, the silent wailing of their children. *Why does he want to go back? How can he?*

"Please, Dagon. I can't take Adara and the children there."

"But why go? It's all in the past."

Lucius shook his head. "Not for me. I want to see what pieces of my former life I can pick up. Then, perhaps I will be able to move forward."

Dagon was quiet for a few moments, and rose to get more water for them. After pouring, he sat back down.

"Very well. I'll take you."

"Thank you," Lucius said, reaching out to grip his friend's hand.

Dagon could not help but shiver at the sight of the blood Lucius' touch left upon him.

"But why do you have to go?" Briana demanded that evening as they sat around the hearth fire of their home. She had spoken loudly and looked to the upper level to make sure she had not woken Antiope. When there was no sound, she turned back to Dagon. "We are well here, my love. We are safe. Why risk it all by venturing out into world when you are hunted...when *he* is hunted."

Dagon looked at his wife across the fire. She was so beautiful to him and, if it was possible, he had fallen even more in love with her since the birth of their daughter and the life they had begun to build for themselves. He reached up and touched the fall of her blonde hair where it covered her shoulder. He sighed.

"I know it's risky," he said. "I'm no fool. But it has been well over a year since that night, and since Caracalla left for Rome. He has greater concerns in the world than hunting for a man he believes to be dead."

"A man who tried to take the imperial throne for himself!" she said.

"Briana..." Dagon searched for the patience he knew he needed. "We all wanted Lucius to take the throne…me…Barta…Brencis…all of my Sarmatian brothers…the imperial legions themselves… We could all see the potential in the world with Lucius Metellus Anguis upon the imperial throne."

"Could they also see the commanders of the legions executed, your countrymen slain or dispersed? And Vaclar, Badru and Lenya who gave their lives to protect us? Their sacrifice will have been in vain if you and Lucius get yourselves killed now." She paused, and took a breath to hold back the tears that were forming in her eyes. "What about Barta's sacrifice?"

Dagon stared at his wife and then at the fire. "You don't need to remind me of all the friends and brothers I have lost. I think on them everyday."

"Then why even consider going?"

"Because, Briana… I am able to sit here with you and our child, to be peaceful when others cannot."

"Out of guilt then?"

"Can my surviving men sit peacefully by a hearth fire without worrying about a blade in the dark? Can they stay in any one place for long?"

"Perhaps they can?"

"Can Lucius?"

"He is *here* with his wife and children. Yes, he can if he chooses to!"

"And yet, his days are spent in pain and torment. He cannot rest because he carries the weight of all our charred hopes upon his shoulders. He blames himself for everything. He is with his family, yes, but can he lie beside his wife and make love to her? Can his children hug him tightly without tremors of pain wracking his burned body?"

"But how will going back to the hillfort help him to move on, Dagon?"

Dagon stood and walked around the fire, his arms crossed. He turned to look at her. "By seeing that there is nothing left for him there…that it is all gone…perhaps he will be able to accept things as they are and finally move on."

Briana looked doubtful.

"I need to do this for him, not because I owe him anything, but because he is my truest friend, and he is in pain."

She could see there was no changing Dagon's mind. "I need you to

promise me this will be the end of it. No more useless risks. I can't lose
you, and Antiope needs her father."

"I promise. Just this once." Dagon did not smile, but walked around
the fire to take her into his arms as she stood.

"Perhaps some of your men will be lingering around the fort?"

"I can only hope," he said, having thought of that very possibility.

When Briana had gone up to their bed, Dagon remained by the fire a
bit longer, thinking of what they might find at the hillfort. He hoped that
going would give Lucius what he needed to focus on the present, on
healing and family and a life of peace in Ynis Wytrin.

One last deed for the Dragon... he thought.

He rose and went to the back of the house where a trunk covered in
coarse linen sat in the dark. He lit a lamp and set it on the table nearby
before kneeling and removing the covering.

His hands paused over the latches he had not touched in many
months. Then, he flipped the latches slowly and raised the lid. The tang
of metal and oil reached his nose then, and he closed his eyes to its
familiarity, breathed deeply.

Dagon reached in and removed the top layer of dark linen to reveal
his sword and scabbard beneath. Tracing his fingers along the length of
the leather scabbard, he could not help but recall the days...years...of
battle and blood, the victories that he and his men had lived for, victories
given to them by Lucius.

How they had all loved the Dragon.

So many victories...riding beside the Gods themselves!

The Gods... He had not seen Epona since that night of blood and
fire. But he knew that the Gods were everywhere in that place, that now
a part of Lucius was one of them. He was torn between worlds, one half
of him living in pain among mortals, the other half conversing with his
immortal family and struggling with his anger toward them, his sense of
betrayal.

Epona, Dagon prayed, *let us grant him peace at last.*

He reached into the trunk, removed the sword, and stood. Its familiar
weight rested easily in his grip, and as he slid the blade free of the
sheath, the oil upon it glistened in the lamplight. It felt good to hold his
sword again, but then he remembered whose sword it was, and the trust
that his uncle had placed in him as a king of their people.

Dagon's arm lowered, heavy with the guilt that thought brought to his senses…the shame. He sheathed the blade again and set it on the table nearby. He then looked back inside the trunk and pulled aside the second layer of linen to reveal his helmet and the folds of his polished and oiled scale armour upon which he placed his shaking hand.

"No more," he whispered, before placing the linen fold back and closing the trunk's lid.

"I want to go with you and Dagon tomorrow!" Phoebus said to Lucius as he helped him dress. "You will need another sword."

"No, Phoebus," Lucius answered, his patience growing thin at the barrage of begging. "You cannot come with us. It is too much of a risk."

"Then why are you going?"

"To see what I can salvage."

"Then I can help look for things!"

"No!!!" Lucius yelled, his voice choked by phlegm, his head beginning to pound.

Phoebus stopped abruptly. "Dress yourself!" he said before turning away and going out the door.

For a moment, Adara simply stared at Lucius struggling with his tunic from across the room.

"Don't worry, Baba." Calliope appeared at Lucius' shoulder, and her gentle hands helped to arrange his tunic. "Phoebus misses our home, as we all do. He's been talking a lot to Rachel and Aaron about seeing it again lately."

"It's too dangerous."

"If that is so, you should not be going either."

Lucius turned to look at his daughter. Her wisdom had grown as much as she had during his healing. *But there are things she does not understand,* he thought. He reached up to touch her soft cheek, but was unable to feel through the tips of his clumsy fingers.

Calliope gripped his hand and kissed it. "We would rather you did not go, but if you feel you must, then you must." She let his hand down gently and went after her brother.

"And you?" Lucius said, turning upon the stool to look at Adara where she made the children's beds on the other side of the room.

"What of me? My opinion does not matter."

"Of course it does," he answered, though he knew he was dismissing her worries.

"You escape death, only to seek it once more."

"It's a threshold I have always lived in."

"Then may Janus protect you from walking in the wrong direction as you leave that threshold."

Lucius stood and walked across the room to his wife.

As he approached, Adara felt her heart rend at the sight of him. Every day, she remembered the strong, vibrant man he had been, the warrior, the loving husband and father. And then she looked at him, tended his wounds and listened to his bitter vision of life as it was through his eyes, and she realized that the man she loved, whom she had given everything to, was hanging by a thread of sanity over a precipice.

She held him in her arms when he hugged her, but all she could think of was not wanting to see him fall into darkness all over again.

That is exactly what is happening, she thought.

"Go with Dagon tomorrow, Lucius," she said, stepping back and looking him in the eyes. "But I don't want to hear about anything you see. That was another life, and I mean to live in this one."

With those words, Adara took a basket from the table nearby and went outside toward the vegetable garden.

Lucius stood alone in the long room which was filling with morning sunlight that angled in at the small window. He walked over to the table where their swords were lain, and pulled back the cloth covering them. He knew he could not yet wield his sword, and that it would be recognized if anyone saw it.

His hand strayed to a plain pugio to the right and his hand wrapped itself around the wood and bone handle. He pulled it free of the sheath and held the blade up to the sunlight. It was chipped in two places but the blade was sharp and oiled.

He smiled. *Good work, my son,* he thought, realizing that Phoebus had kept the blades in good condition these many months. *But you cannot come with me. Not this time.*

For a moment, he realized that he just might have to use the weapon in his hand, and he took several practice thrusts, slowly at first, and then quicker. His muscles seemed to remember, as if they had been asleep for a while, but he was slower. His arm tired, he slammed the blade back into its sheath and set it back on the table.

I will just have to live in the shadows for now, he thought, *like Death.*

It was still dark when Dagon appeared at Lucius' door the following morning, but Lucius had been ready for a while, unable to sleep the whole of that long night. Adara and Calliope had already helped him with his ointments and fresh bandages applied to his body for the journey, taking extra care to cover his wounds and protect them from dust and dirt.

Lucius was dressed in black bracae and a black tunic belted with a cingulum from which hung the single pugio.

When Dagon entered, Lucius could see that he did not wear his armour but that his great sword hung at his side beneath his cloak.

"I don't know if I'll need it," Dagon said as Lucius looked at the sword, "but I'll be ready." He looked at Adara. "It will be fine, Adara."

"As I told Lucius, I don't want to know what you see."

Dagon nodded. "I understand." He turned to Lucius where Calliope was helping him with his long black cloak. "You sure you want to go through with this?"

"Yes." Lucius nodded, pulling his hood over his bare head.

"I've hitched one of the ponies up to a small wagon that can navigate the path through the marshes. It's poor-looking, so no one will suspect a thing."

"We don't have anything," Lucius said.

"If Caracalla's venatores are out there looking for you, then your life will be of sufficient value to them," Adara said from the middle of the room, her arms crossed as if she were cold, though it was warm in the small domus.

Lucius turned to her. "Even if they are, they would not recognize me. I will be back soon."

She reached out to hold him. "I've been dreading this day for so long, hoping you would not want to go out into the world again."

"I cannot hide forever."

"Just because your father's light touches everything, does not mean you must also." She stood back and looked up at Lucius. "Just come back to us." The words gave her pause, for the last time she had said anything like it, their world had irrevocably changed.

Lucius kissed Calliope on the head and then went to the bed where

Phoebus was pretending to sleep. "I promise, you will leave Ynis Wytrin at some point. Just not today, my son."

Phoebus was silent, unwilling to turn to look upon his father whose shadow receded from his bedside and went out the door with Dagon.

The morning air was cool and damp as Lucius and Dagon walked across the grass of the isle, the light from Dagon's torch casting shadows around them as they went. Finally, they arrived at a clearing at the southern end of the isle to find Weylyn and his servant, Morvran, waiting for them.

"Good moorninga!" Morvran said loudly in his broken manner of speaking. He held the reigns of a white pony that was hitched to the small, two-wheeled cart.

"Quietly, Morvran," Weylyn said to him. "Even the Gods are still asleep."

Morvran shook his head and pointed at Lucius' dark silhouette.

"You are astute," Weylyn said to him, smiling sadly and patting him on the shoulder before stepping forward to greet the two men. "Are you sure you wish to do this?"

"Yes," Lucius answered curtly.

"Very well," Weylyn answered, his voice low and tired. "The pony knows the way through the marshes well. She will not fail you."

"Thank you, Weylyn," Dagon said. "We will try to return by this evening."

Without another word, Lucius climbed slowly up into the cart.

Weylyn approached from the side and looked up at him. "Remember...it is a material world you are returning to. It is fleeting. You have all you need here."

Lucius looked down at him. "It was my world."

The look in Lucius' eyes gave Weylyn pause, for despite all the healing, the help he had received from others for so many months, there were unseen parts of him that still bled with anger and grief.

"Be safe, friends," Weylyn said, stepping back as Dagon seated himself in the wagon beside Lucius.

"We will," Dagon answered, but Lucius stared straight ahead into the darkness of the path that led into the trees and the marshes beyond.

When they were gone, Morvran turned to Weylyn. "D...d...danger?"

Weylyn did not take his eyes from the path ahead. "With dragons? Yes...always, Morvran."

. . .

For some time, either by skill or instinct, the pony navigated the dark, labyrinthine world of reed and water. They travelled deeper and deeper into the mists, the wheels of the cart skirting the edges of the water as Lucius and Dagon held onto the sides, bracing themselves as the vehicle teetered.

After what seemed like almost two hours of slow progress, the pony began to climb a path that led up into a forested slope until at the top, where it levelled off, it stopped to crop at some fern.

"We're out," Dagon said, stepping down off the wagon to stretch his legs. He reached out to help Lucius do the same and together they turned to look out over a vast green land from that forest eyrie. A sliver of orange and pink light was forming on the distant horizon. Slowly, as the Sun's chariot sped upward, the light spread over the land, beginning the process of burning away the mist and dark in hidden places. "Beautiful," Dagon said to himself.

As Lucius watched, however, all he could see was blood pooling over a land that had been his family's home. It was now stained by the work of evil men. In his mind, he still saw the fires burning, of the roundhouse in a field nearby, and of his home in the distance.

"Lucius? Are you all right?" Dagon was beside him, propping him up.

Lucius shook his head and regained his feet. "I'm fine. Sorry…I… Just remembering.

"We don't have to do this. We can go back."

"No. I have to. I want to."

Dagon stepped forward to where the path began to wend its way down the slope to disappear in a field of long grass. "The Gods have guided us this far. Let's continue, then. If you are sure."

"I am." Lucius climbed slowly into the wagon and sat on the bench.

Dagon pat the pony and whispered to it before sitting himself beside Lucius and taking up the reins again. He clicked his tongue and the animal carried on down the path to join the Roman road which they could see on the other side of the sprawling green field. Eventually, they reached the road and turned east.

The pony sped along now at an easy clip upon the flat surface, riding into the morning sunlight. The light burned Lucius' eyes and he lowered his hood and turned back momentarily. Behind them, he saw the road leading in the other direction, toward Lindinis.

How many times had he and his family travelled that road to visit the market in that small settlement full of vipers. He remembered travelling that road on the way to Serenus Crescens' villa that one night for a convivium at which someone had tried to murder him. He also remembered in flashes of pain and dark, his last, furious ride back to his home, in the direction they were now headed, to reach his family before Claudius Picus and his Praetorians did.

Lucius did not notice the merchants' wagons passing them upon the road, nor the strange looks some gave to the strange tattooed warrior driving what appeared to be a leper in a small cart. All Lucius could think of was what he would find when they arrived, and how he would feel at seeing the ruins of his own world before him.

It was not long before the cart pulled off of the main road and cut through the field paths toward the hillfort where it rose up out of the earth like a sleeping dragon.

Dagon reined in and paused to look up at it. "Lucius. We're here," he said, placing his hand upon the latter's shoulder.

Lucius looked up from where he was hiding from the light beneath his cowl, and without knowing it, he cried out audibly as he looked upon the green embankments of those ancient fortifications, the same as the first time his family had set eyes upon their new home.

The roof of the hall he had built was no longer visible. No smoke rose from the round hearth where family and friends had gathered, and no laughter or children's voices rang out from the top. All that remained was grass, trees, and the dark shadows of the crows diving in the wind before the steep slopes.

It was as if the Metelli had never been there.

Lucius felt his throat catch as he stared at the spot upon the western rampart where he had sat with Calliope before he'd left for war in Caledonia, where he had watched the sunset numerous times with her, Phoebus, and Adara.

The man he remembered walking that lofty home was someone else and now, as the cart carried on toward the southwest gate, he felt like an intruder.

Dagon steered the pony around a corner and up until they came to the gatehouse, or the spot where it had been. "It's gone," he muttered, looking at the few fallen timbers, now grass covered and rotting.

Lucius looked up, imagining the great doors that had been there, and the walkway that had stood over the path. Now all he saw was blue sky above, and the dark skeleton of the gate lying upon the ground.

"Keep going, Dagon," he said.

The pony pulled hard to get up the slope and directly ahead, the summit plateau came into view against the burning light of the sunlit morning clouds.

"It's all gone!" Lucius cried as he began to stumble out of the moving cart.

"Lucius, wait!" Dagon said, pulling on the reins and jumping down with his sword in hand. He helped Lucius up and together they looked around the desolation of that place. The dragon's domus was no more.

All that remained of the stables, the barracks, and the hall itself were rotting piles of wood and iron, black and broken tiles. Any cut stone had been carried off, but for a few broken pieces, and the storage pits and gardens where they had grown their food were gone, overgrown, reclaimed by the earth.

Lucius wanted to weep as he walked among the ruins to the top of the summit plateau and stood on the spot where the hearth had been. But the more he looked around, the more he remembered of happier days and that previous life, his more mortal life, the angrier he got. The tears he was about to weep burned away in the fires that now fuelled his rage.

It was all gone - the hall, his children's rooms, their beds, the kitchen where they had made food, the tablinum. *My scrolls!* he thought with pained memories of the valued collection that his old tutor, Diodorus, had left him. *It's all gone!*

Dagon searched the grass and dirt for anything he recognized, anything that was not broken or burned, but there was nothing, and he did weep for the loss. It had been his home too, a place where he had finally begun to feel purpose again among friends and newfound family. He looked at Lucius turning on the spot, surveying the destruction beneath the grass. He could feel his pain, his anger.

Suddenly, Lucius stopped and stared to the southeast corner of the hillfort and the ruins of the temple he had built. "It's still there!" he said, beginning to stumble down the path from the plateau.

"Lucius, wait for me!" Dagon said, clicking for the pony to follow as he went after Lucius.

When they arrived at the ruins of the temple Lucius had dedicated to Apollo, they found more charred beams and broken tiles. The roof had fallen to the side, and the walls were mostly collapsed, but more remained of that structure than anything else.

Dagon and Lucius stopped before the temple to look at the fresh offerings people had continued to leave in that sacred place that had been blessed by Weylyn so long ago. There were bundles of herbs, loaves of bread, and handfuls of nuts. Upon the cracked steps were clay figurines of children, or miniature imagines of loved ones who had died.

Lucius gazed at the faces on those images and wondered if some of them had died while defending his home and family in that very place.

"They continue to honour the Gods here, Lucius," Dagon said, his voice low and full of awe. "They never stopped." Dagon then looked about the spot where he stood and remembered one of the happiest moments of his life taking place right there. "I was bound to Briana here," he said as he stooped down to touch the grass with the flat of his hand, his eyes closed, remembering the wedding and the great feast with his men afterward as they had honoured him and their new queen.

Dagon heard Lucius' panicked breathing then and looked up to see Lucius stumbling over the broken imbrices and tegulae to try and reach the cella of the temple. "Lucius, wait! Let me help you!" Dagon stepped forward to help, but turned quickly as something caught his attention to the left, near the tree-covered embankment of the battlements. He looked, but saw nothing, and continued forward until he reached Lucius. "What are you looking for?"

Lucius rummaged through the debris desperately, pushing rotten roof beams aside with great effort and kicking at broken tiles. "The altar! I need to reach the altar!"

"Careful," Dagon said. "That piece of the roof could fall down!" He pointed to where the one intact part of the roof hung precariously over one side of the altar inside the temple.

Lucius was on his knees now sifting through the rubble for pieces, then he stopped and reached down to pick up a bronze 'A', a remnant of the dedication upon the temple pediment and the name of 'Apollo'. "Father," Lucius said, his voice but a whisper of sadness and despair. "How has it come to this? How have you allowed it to?" He set the bronze letter aside and continued to search, finding pieces of the statues that had been set there - a muscular arm belonging to Apollo, a head of Venus', a leg of Epona's. There was also a piece of Lunaris' statue which Culhwch had made for Lucius after the stallion's death in Dumnonia.

He arrayed the pieces upon the floor before him and stared at them, the pieces of his gods, and his anger began to burn away his sadness once more. He clenched his cut and bleeding hands, his eyes shut tight.

"Lucius?" Dagon spoke softly behind him, placing his hand upon his friend's shoulder. "Perhaps we should not linger too long?"

Lucius opened his eyes to see the pieces of the gods upon the floor spotted with his own blood that had dripped from his hands as he had clenched them. "We're not finished."

Lucius stepped forward to lay his hands upon the intact altar and swept the dust and debris off the top. A moment later, he was pushing against it with all of his might.

"What are you doing?" Dagon said, jumping to his aid.

"Help me push!" Lucius said.

Together they pushed hard, straining at the stone altar until finally it moved an inch, and then another and another until, with a loud grating sound upon the stone floor, the altar swung aside.

"What is this?" Dagon said. "How did you know?"

"I had Cradawg create this as a hiding place," Lucius said. "Before leaving for Caledonia…I hid… It's still there!" Lucius bent over and was reaching into the hole beneath the altar.

"Lucius stop!" Dagon pulled at him. "Your going to injure yourself even more. Let me do it!"

Lucius looked up at his friend and nodded. He knew he could not remove the strong box without too much strain upon his still-healing body. He stood slowly and stepped aside so that Dagon could stand above the stone-lined pit and grab hold of the box.

Dagon heaved with all of his strength until the box moved and he achieved some purchase on the metal strips that covered the sides. He got his hand beneath one side and pulled it up the side of the pit until finally, it reached the lip of the pit.

Lucius leaned over to help him pull until the box was safely out.

"What's in it?" Dagon asked, breathing heavily as he stepped back.

"All that our family has left."

"And what is that?" said another voice suddenly from behind them.

Lucius spun around to see Dagon with his hands out.

Behind him was a man cloaked in deep green wool with the point of a gladius in Dagon's back.

Lucius rose slowly, looking at the man. He wore no uniform, but he appeared strong and capable. "Who are you?" Lucius asked.

"I might ask you the same thing?" the man answered, jabbing his sword a little more into Dagon's back.

Lucius could see Dagon's eyes, could tell he was thinking of spinning to get at his attacker, but he shook his head. He could feel the anger rising quickly, the urge to see the man dead.

"This is my home," Lucius said. "And you're trespassing."

"Your home?" the man said, and his eyes widened "So...you are alive...Praefectus Metellus!"

Lucius felt dread then beneath his anger.

"What have you got there?" the man asked, nodding toward the strongbox.

"You'll be dead before you know," Lucius said.

The man laughed. "I'm not the one who'll be dead. There are a lot of people looking for you, and they're willing to pay close to a talent for your body."

Lucius felt his rage build and build in a matter of seconds, and his hand went to his chest where the dragon brand felt like it was on fire. He wanted to scream, to strike when, suddenly, Dagon's head struck backward into the man's face, and the gladius rose and was about to strike downward.

There was a whistling sound in that moment before the man's arm swung down to strike Dagon, and his body spun to the side and fell into a pile of rubble. He howled, grasping the long-shafted arrow that protruded from his shoulder.

Lucius leapt forward and pounced onto the man, knocking his gladius aside and pressing his pugio to his chin.

"Dagon?" came another voice that Lucius recognized.

"Culhwch?" Dagon said as he stood to see the Briton running toward them with a bow in his hand, and another arrow nocked.

Lucius did not turn to look, but stared into the fallen man's eyes with fury. "Who sent you?"

The man shook his head and spat in Lucius' face.

Lucius pressed harder with the blade of his pugio, his left hand pressing upon the man's neck. "Tell me," Lucius growled, blood dripping from his mouth onto the man's face.

The man shook his head with his eyes closed, Lucius' blood and bile spattering over his eyes.

"Tell me!" Lucius yelled pressing harder so that the blade broke the skin.

"I was hired to watch this place for your return...if you ever returned!"

"By whom?" Lucius yelled.

"Ahhh...by Serenus Crescens!" the man cried.

In that moment, Lucius could hold back no more, and with a cry of rage he plunged the blade upward beneath the chin into the man's head. He withdrew the blade and plunged it in again, and again. "Oh Nemesis! Oh Furiae! I offer you this blood for all our suffering!"

The blade continued to plunge and withdraw, over and over, as Lucius let fall the tears he had held back since they arrived in that place.

He did not feel Dagon and Culhwch's arms pulling at him, their voices begging him to stop.

Finally he collapsed in darkness, his own screams echoing in his mind, as the faces of Nemesis and the Furies hovered in the shadows before him.

The darkness that had engulfed him began to dissipate.

Lucius stirred, afraid to open his eyes, unaware of where he was. He heard muffled voices, and through the cracks of his eyelids, he could see dim golden light. For a moment he wondered if he was dead again, back on the slopes of Olympus, but the pain wracking his body told him otherwise. He groaned and, slowly, he opened his eyes wider.

Before him was a bright-eyed woman with pale blonde hair. She leaned over him, her eyes watery in the faint light. She held a cool cloth to his forehead as she sat beside him, her nose sniffling from weeping.

Lucius looked up at her. "Alma?"

She nodded and tried to smile, and tears flowed down her cheeks. "Yes, my friend... You're alive?" She took a deep breath, and tried to stop her tears. But it was impossible, for the relief she felt was great.

Above her shoulder, Culhwch's own smiling and relieved face

appeared. "The Dragon returns," he said, his own eyes glistening. "We'd hoped the Gods would bring you back to the world."

Lucius struggled to rise, his breathing ragged and pained. "Where am I?"

Alma and Culhwch looked at each other. "You're in our home in the village, Lucius," Culhwch said. "I found you and Dagon at the temple. You were attacked."

"Dagon?"

"I'm over here, Lucius," Dagon said from the table on the other side of the room where he sat with Paulus, Culhwch and Alma's son.

"Paulus," Lucius tried to smile at the boy, but the latter was not able to look directly at him. He tried to rise, and Alma and Culhwch helped him up slowly. He looked around. "Where is my cloak?"

"It's drying by the hearth." Alma pointed. "It was covered in blood."

"Blood?"

"From the man you massacred in the temple," Dagon said, his voice betraying a hint of worry. "Do you not remember?"

Lucius shuffled toward the table and the light there. He nodded. *Serenus Crescens*, he reminded himself. "How could I forget?"

"Here... Sit, Lucius." Culhwch brought up a stool with a back for him while Alma poured water. "What is in that iron chest you risked your life for anyway?"

"Where is it? Is it safe?" Lucius asked quickly.

"Don't worry my friend. It's hidden out back in the cart you came in."

Lucius relaxed a little. "It's all we have left in the world. Some gold and silver, scrolls and..." his voice faded away. "Everything was gone."

"I know, my friend," Culhwch said as he settled on the other side of the table beside Dagon. "We sifted through the rubble after that night, but the fires burned so fiercely that...anyway. But I doubt that all you have left in the world is in that chest. You have much more than that, thank the Gods."

Lucius was staring at his hands which he remembered briefly being covered in blood.

Dagon cleared his throat. "I've been telling them about Adara, Phoebus and Calliope," he said. "That they are alive and well in Ynis Wytrin."

"We had been hoping all these months, of course," Alma added, "but to see you and hear it confirmed-" her voice caught in her throat. "We... we're just so relieved." She placed her hand upon Lucius' rough one. "I'm just sorry that... I wish I could see Adara."

Lucius stared at the table.

"How are you, Lucius?" Culhwch asked. "I can see your injuries, but-"

"I'm a monster, can't you tell?" Lucius snapped.

"I can see you're alive, my friend," Culhwch said calmly. "A gift from the Gods, it is."

Lucius looked across the table where he sat beside Dagon. "A gift? You think so? A curse of my own choosing more like!"

Culhwch looked confused. "What do you mean? You didn't do this to yourself, Lucius. That patrician bastard did it. Rome did it."

"Did Dagon not tell you...that I died?"

The room was suddenly silent.

Lucius nodded. "I died...and upon the slopes of Olympus itself, Apollo - my father - gave me a choice. I could stay there, whole and young and free of the pain caused by this piece of meat I find myself in...or...I could come back to be with my wife and children, and all of you...my friends..." Lucius stopped when he saw the looks upon their faces, and he chuckled darkly. "So much for *The Dragon*...an unknowing demigod burned by fire." He opened the top part of his loose tunic to reveal the brand upon his chest. "I may not have much left, but I will always have this to remind me of what I am." He turned to Dagon. "I felt it burning when I stabbed our attacker."

"It was your blood pumping, Lucius," Dagon said, trying to calm his friend.

"I enjoyed killing him!"

More silence.

"How can you say you don't have much left?" Alma asked him. She pulled her stool closer and leaned in, her hands reaching out to touch his arms gently. "You live because you were able to choose. Your wife survived a terrible attack and the loss of a child...and Phoebus and Calliope are alive!"

Lucius' face softened. "Yes." He looked at Alma and Culhwch. "And I am eternally grateful to you all for coming to our family's aid."

"You have become our family," Culhwch said intently. "No matter who your father is." He winked.

Lucius actually smiled, but then a thought entered his mind. "How many casualties did the village endure?"

Alma and Culhwch were silent, but then the latter spoke. "Quite a few, though not as many as you would have expected. It was dark and we took the Praetorians by surprise."

"Ula and Aina live. It was they who got Phoebus and Calliope to the village," Alma said.

"My uncle is dead!" Paulus said from the end of the table, looking up at Lucius for the first time.

Lucius looked at the boy. He had grown a great deal since, looked more like a young man than a boy now. "I am sorry. Sigwyll was a good man."

"He died fighting on horseback," Alma said. "It could not have been a better end for him. You all helped him rediscover life, Lucius. He was grateful."

"You now have a chance to rediscover life too," Dagon said, staring at Lucius. "Culhwch is right...it is a gift, whether from your divine father, or from yourself. You have a chance to live away from Rome for good now...in peace...to start over."

"In peace?" Lucius asked. "The moment I come back to my home - *my home* - I'm attacked by another spy. How can there ever be peace?"

"In Ynis Wytrin," Dagon said. "I have made a choice to live with Briana and Antiope, even though my men are scattered to the winds and grassy plains of the world."

"They have done so much to all of us. How can they be allowed to carry on without punishment?" Lucius asked Dagon.

"It is the way of the world, Lucius. My people suffered defeat at the hands of Rome a long time ago, and yet we carried on, though the life we led was different in every respect. We all find our peace with Rome, and when we do, a new life presents itself."

Dagon could not hide the regret in his voice, though he did believe what he was saying.

"Have you had no word from any of your men?" Culhwch asked.

"No. We hear nothing in Ynis Wytrin. It is outside of this world, between worlds. When I am there, the pain and regret are less, though they are present. It's bearable."

"Not for me," Lucius added.

"Silvius was down south cutting timber some time ago. He had some business in Isca Dumnoniorum. He told me that he heard a rumour that strange foreigners had been seen crossing the river. I didn't think much of it - a lot of trading vessels come up the river from other parts of the empire - but I do wonder if the foreigners might have been some of your countrymen."

Dagon sat up for a moment, his eyes alight, but then he shook his head. "Likely not. They would not be able to hide from Caracalla's spies. The Praetorians are ruthless, and anyone who supports a would-be emperor is not allowed to live." He rubbed his face and hair. "None of us are safe."

Culhwch looked wistful. "It would have been something though, a new world...if you had succeeded."

Lucius clenched his fists. "It was hubris to think I could do so."

"I don't know what that word means." Culhwch chuckled.

"It means I was arrogant enough to think I could challenge the Gods' plan for me."

"But you are a god!" Culhwch added.

"No!" Lucius snapped, his eyes closed. "And look where it got me. To this!" He raised his sleeves to reveal his red, mottled flesh. "Some god..."

"Lucius," Alma's voice was soft and full of compassion and care, "you are also a man of goodness."

He looked at her.

"None of us can even pretend to comprehend what you must be feeling...the burden you have had to carry with that knowledge...but we do know the mortal man sitting here with us to be a true friend, a good father and husband, a man who always put others, including his men, ahead of himself."

"And look what happened to all of you," Lucius countered. "Look what happened to so many of my men - Dagon's own countrymen - whose bones probably lie open to the sky, unburied and unmourned because of me."

"They made a choice, Lucius," Dagon said.

"As did our village by coming to the aid of the Dragon's family," Culhwch added. "None of us regrets our actions, Lucius. So why do you?"

Lucius could say no more. *They don't understand!* he thought. "It would have been better for all of you if you had not known me."

"Sounds like self-pity to me," Culhwch said, his smile fading fast.

"It's the truth."

"I'll tell you the truth," the Durotrigan said. "The truth is that our people had no champions before you came along. That ancient fortress - the one-time beating heart of our people - had sat still and silent, a place of ghosts for generations until the Dragon and his family brought life back to it, and joy and hope back to our people. Because of you, Lucius Metellus Anguis! Not because of Rome. Because of you...hope and joy... Now those are things that are worth fighting and dying for." Culhwch leaned on the table to catch Lucius' eye. "Don't waste time pitying us. We all made our own choices and were glad to do so. The question is, what choices will you make in this new life the Gods have granted you, that you have granted yourself?"

Lucius thought about the state of his life, about all that he had learned and heard. He thought of his wife and the child she had lost. He thought of the trauma in his children's eyes when they remembered what had happened and when they looked upon their misshapen father. He thought of the charred remains of their once-beautiful home upon the hillfort that sat silent once more in the darkness outside that village, of the spy who had come to kill him that very day.

"I will make things better," Lucius said, staring across at Culhwch.

The Durotrigan nodded. "That's it. Life has changed, but it can still be better. And who knows? You may be able to move your family back to the hillfort again. Emperors never last very long these days. Once Caracalla is out of power, chances are the next emperor won't even care about Lucius Metellus Anguis. The cycle of this life carries on, and they are all leaves in the wind."

"And we will all help you to rebuild, Lucius," Alma said. "Emperors may forget about you, but your friends never will."

"Until then, however," Dagon began. "The Dragon must remain hidden from the world."

Morning came a short time later, its silver and pink light coming in at the window like a note of music on the wind, a warning call that it was time to leave.

"We should return to Ynis Wytrin now," Dagon said. "Briana and Adara will be worried."

Alma and Culhwch stood with Lucius and Dagon.

"We will miss you both," Culhwch said, "but with hope, we will see you soon."

Alma took Lucius' cloak from the hearth and she came to place it upon his shoulders.

He flinched at the heat, but settled.

"I'm sorry, Lucius."

"It's fine," he said, not wanting her to feel badly.

She gripped his hands. "Please give our love to Adara and the children. Tell them we miss them and are always thinking of them."

"I will. They miss you too." Lucius turned to Paulus. "Phoebus and Calliope miss you very much, Paulus. Please know that."

The boy nodded. "I do. I miss them too. Please tell them that...that if they ever need me, I will be there for them."

Lucius smiled sadly.

Culhwch stepped up. "And someday, hopefully soon, we will all be together again."

Lucius turned to him. "Thank you for everything, my friend." He extended his burned hand, but the Durotrigan wrapped his arms about him instead.

"Take care my friend. May the peace of Ynis Wytrin help and guide you in your healing. We will watch over your home until you return."

Lucius nodded and went to wait by the door while Dagon said his own farewells.

"Give our love to Briana, Dagon," Alma said. "I hope we can meet Antiope someday soon."

"That is my hope as well," he said.

"Goodbye my friend," Culhwch said. "If I hear anything about your men, I'll try and send word to you."

"Thank you."

"Oh! I almost forgot!" Alma suddenly said, rushing to the other side of the small domus and taking a leather courier's tube from a shelf. "Perhaps ten months ago, a messenger arrived in the village. He had been up at the hillfort looking for you, Lucius." Alma handed him the tube.

"Was he an imperial messenger?" Lucius was worried now. "If it was, and he knew you accepted this, you will have placed yourselves in danger."

Culhwch shook his head. "No. He said he was privately hired."

"We told him that you were…gone…but that we would hold onto it in case you returned," Alma added.

"He seemed reluctant, but left it anyway," Culhwch said. "I mean, he looked tired, having travelled from Graecia and all."

"From Graecia?" Lucius asked.

"That's what he said."

Lucius looked at the leather tube, his heart pounding. *Please let them be safe,* he thought, his mind immediately exploring the worst scenarios.

"We should go," Dagon said again. "The sun is already risen behind the clouds."

"I'll go bring the wagon around the front," Culhwch said before going out the back door that led to the field behind their home.

Lucius opened the door, gripping the leather tube in his other hand, and stepped out into the street. He found he did not want to leave them, his loyal friends, but he also knew that just by being there, he was placing them in danger. *Nobody is safe with men like Serenus Crescens still around.*

"What is this?" Dagon said as he, Alma and Paulus stepped outside into the misty air of the street behind Lucius.

The street was filled with people, the young, the old, the strong and weak. They stood there like cloaked sentries, all their eyes on Lucius as he stood in their midst.

Lucius recognized many of the faces, people who had drunk with him and his men, who had made offerings at the temple he had built, people his wife and children had talked to and played with. He also noticed many faces missing. He felt his guilt washing over him then, choking him, but he took a deep breath and stepped forward, his cowl hiding his burned head.

"I'm sorry for everything you suffered. I know my words cannot bring back those you have lost, but I will make things right again. I swear to you all. Somehow, I will make-"

He was cut short by someone patting his arm, reaching out to touch him, his cloak, his shoulder, even his foot. More and more hands reached out to him and he heard people whispering in awe…

"The Dragon lives."

Ula and Aina appeared in the crowd, their faces wet with tears as they looked upon Lucius.

"The Gods have blessed us," a hunched old woman said, one Lucius recognized from her daily offerings at the temple. "They have brought you back to us." She held Lucius' hands gently, his massacred skin mirroring her aged and gnarled fingers. "Does the Dragon's family live?" she asked.

He nodded. "Yes...they do..."

"Then it was all worth it," she said.

"None of you must speak of this," Lucius said, but he was unsure any of them heard him.

As the crowd parted for Culhwch who drove through with the cart, the people continued to file past Lucius, reaching out to touch him, their heads bowed, blessings for him and his family soft upon their shuddering lips. It did not matter that he appeared different to them, for they only saw the Dragon who had sought to help and protect them, who had been their friend.

Culhwch jumped down from the wagon and stepped in among the people. He looked over their heads at Alma and Paulus who were both standing before the door of their home, tears in their eyes.

"Tell them not to speak of this," Dagon whispered to Culhwch. "They will all be in danger if they do."

"I will. But...do you see any fear of Rome here?"

Dagon looked around and shook his head. "No." Nor did he notice any sign of hatred, anger, or regret. There were only the good wishes of a kind and brave people. It saddened Dagon to think that the only hatred, anger and regret present among them was burning within Lucius himself, even as people kissed his hands and cloak and wished him well as he climbed into the cart.

Dagon turned once more to hug Alma, slap Culhwch on the back, and then climb into the wagon beside Lucius.

"May the Dragon return to us someday!" one of the villagers called out as the cart began to roll.

Lucius took a last look at all of the faces, his eyes resting upon those of his good friends.

Alma stood there gripping her son close, her hand upon her heart as Culhwch waved one last time to Lucius and Dagon.

"Farewell, friends," Culhwch said.

As the cart joined the road that headed west, Lucius turned to take one last look at the ancient hillfort.

"It is no longer our home, Dagon," he said. "It belongs to all of them."

Dagon smiled. "Spoken like a king who cares for his people."

"I am no king."

No, Dagon thought. *You are so much more than that. If you could only accept it.* "Do you think we will ever return to that grassy mound?"

Lucius continued to stare back at the hillfort. "Culhwch is right. If ever there is another emperor upon the imperial throne, then anything becomes possible."

IV

NEMESIS SUSSURUS

'Nemesis Whispers'

A dara had not slept all of that night. Neither had the children, for it was the first time that they had not seen Lucius, heard him cry out in pain in the dark of the guest house in Ynis Wytrin. Their minds scanned the dark constantly, listening for the anguish that had become normal, but when it was not there, worry set in.

What if he doesn't return? What if Caracalla's men found him?

When morning arrived and Lucius' bed remained empty, their worries intensified. They went out to ask the priests and priestesses if any of them had spotted Lucius and Dagon, or the horse and cart they had taken, but none had.

"They will return," Etain said to Adara who had been sitting beside the Well of the Chalice splashing the cool water upon her face. The priestess smiled at Calliope who had just come up to sit with her mother.

"I was just sitting beneath the great oak, Mama, and a thought came into my mind. We should go and wait in the field where the path leads into the marshes. It will be better that way."

"What do you mean, Calliope?" Adara asked, too tired and worried to read behind the words her daughter uttered.

"We should just go. All is well."

Etain smiled at the girl. During their time in Ynis Wytrin, she had watched Calliope closely and come to believe that she could be one of the greatest priestesses to walk that sacred ground. *But she is perhaps meant for other things, this daughter of the Dragon...* "You should go," Etain said to Adara, helping her up. "The walk will do you a world of good. I believe the southern field is covered in flowers now."

Without a word, Adara reached out to hug Etain. "I'm so worried, lady. I can't bear it."

Etain held her tightly and willed peace to flow from her into the woman she held. "You are one of the strongest women I have ever met, Adara. Whatever the road ahead holds, you will lead your family through the trials."

Adara stood back a little. "What if I don't want to?"

Etain stared at her, understood the words of desperation that Adara uttered, knew that she was far stronger than she believed she could be. "All will be well. For now, follow your daughter." She smiled, and the kindness in that smile, the great sincerity, calmed Adara.

She followed Calliope out of the garden and together they went to find Phoebus at the horse paddock before going to the southern field.

The sun was high by then, the field warm and bright. Bees skimmed the surface of the field from flower to flower, like water bugs upon the surface of the surrounding marshes. A rabbit darted from the long grass toward the edge of the field as Adara and the children approached, and a flock of finches soared and spun from the ground to twitter in the branches of the closest orchard.

Calliope skipped through the sun-soaked grass as if the very place gave her life, and her brother chuckled to watch her.

"It's like she's five years old again!" Phoebus said.

"That was a long time ago," Adara answered, her eyes fixed on the dark path that led into the forest and marshes and out of Ynis Wytrin.

Phoebus gripped his mother's hand. "It's been strange…him not being here."

"It was always strange…empty…when your father went off to war. But this is different. I feel like he is farther away than ever."

Phoebus was silent. He did not want to give power to the worry his mother had just expressed, for he felt it tenfold. And it scared him. He wanted to be strong. He had to be. He looked up from the grass and flowers to see his sister turned, her back to the forest path, a smile upon her face.

"What is she doing?" Adara could not help but smile at her daughter. "What is it?" she called out.

Just then, they heard a whinny from the darkness beyond, and a moment later, the horse and cart carrying Lucius and Dagon emerged.

"They're back!" Phoebus said, running toward them.

Adara stared at her daughter and then began to walk. *She knew they were coming,* she thought, reminded once more of how special her children were.

"Baba!" Calliope and Phoebus crowded around the cart as it came to a halt. "Dagon!"

Adara smiled at Dagon who gave her a nod and smiled but a little. The look confirmed a fear that she had been nursing, that going back had been difficult, had churned up the mire in which Lucius found himself drowning.

"I was worried," she said to Lucius.

"I'm sorry," he said. "But it got dark and we had to stay with Culhwch and Alma."

"You saw Paulus?" Phoebus asked excitedly. "Is is all right? What did he say?"

"They all send greetings and love," Lucius answered, his face betraying how tired he truly was. "They miss us."

"As we miss them," Adara said. "And the villagers? Were they... were they very angry?"

Dagon came around the wagon to stand with them. "No," he said softly. "They too miss the Dragon's family and want you to move back."

"Move back to what?" Adara asked.

"To nothing," Lucius growled. "Our home is gone...all of it...except that." He pointed to the strong box in the back of the wagon.

Adara put her hand to her mouth. "I had forgotten."

"What is it, Baba?" Calliope asked.

"All we have left," Lucius answered. His eyes lingered on Adara for a moment, but then he turned and began to walk in the direction of the Tor.

Adara's eyes followed him, but she stayed rooted to the spot. "Was it very terrible, Dagon?" she asked as they both watched Lucius go.

"Yes," he said. "And the place was being watched."

Adara turned to him quickly.

"Were the emperor's men there?" Phoebus asked.

"No. But one of Crescens' men was."

"What happened?" Phoebus persisted.

"The Dragon's survival remains secret," Dagon said, "but I hope whatever is in that box was worth it." He turned to look at the cart, then back at Adara. "I'll put the box in your domus and then take care of the pony." He put his hand on Adara's shoulder. "The hate is building in him more and more everyday. We need to watch him."

Adara nodded, the bright light of the field dimming in her vision. "On your way to the guest house, stop and let Briana know you're back. She's been worried too."

Dagon smiled and walked on.

"I'll help Dagon with the box," Phoebus said, before running after the Sarmatian.

"Come, Mama." Calliope took her mother's hand and kissed her cheek. "Let's go to the garden to pick some vegetables for the cena. Maybe a nice meal will help Baba."

"You don't really believe that, do you, my girl?" Adara said.

Calliope's smile faded. "No, Mama. But we have to try." She gripped Adara's hand tightly and led her toward the vegetable gardens.

That evening, after a meal prepared for them by Adara and Calliope, the Metelli, along with Dagon, Briana and Antiope, sat before the fire in the guest house talking about their visit to the hillfort.

"What an amazing people they are," Briana said of the villagers after Dagon had told them how they had all come out to wish Lucius and him well.

"They are. And they await the Dragon's return again one day," Dagon said.

"They may be waiting a long time," Lucius said from where he sat farther back from the fire, outside of the others, staring at the box upon the table.

He had not opened it yet, though Dagon had broken the lock that was upon it so that they could get inside.

Adara watched him for a moment, but then turned her attention to Calliope who was bouncing Antiope upon her knees while singing a soft and simple tune. *She would have been a wonderful older sister,* she thought sadly.

Briana saw the look in her friend's eyes and came to sit beside her, lean up against her and grip her hands. No words. Just the comforting closeness of a good friend who was trying desperately to be there for her.

"Was anything left of our home?" Phoebus asked Dagon.

Dagon shook his head. "No, Phoebus. I'm sorry. It is all ruins. But the temple still stands, at least partially." He stopped, remembering Lucius driving his blade into Crescens' man over and over again. "The villagers are still leaving offerings there to the Gods…and to all of you."

Just then, they heard the lid of the strong box make a grating sound as Lucius lifted it to peer inside.

Anger and sadness swept over Lucius as his fingers hovered over the contents of that box. It had been a different life, a different man who had placed those items in there.

He removed several armillae and torcs that he had received for valour throughout his military career and, of course, the pinnacle of those achievements, the corona aurea which he had received for saving the life of his legate, Marcellus, in Numidia. He set all of these on the table where the lamplight glistened on their surfaces.

Adara watched her husband and knew that his mind was, in that moment, walking through memories, days of youthful strength now foreign to him. *What terrible strength lies within him, now that he knows the truth about himself?*

It worried her.

Lucius then pulled out the scrolls he had saved, all that was left of the library Diodorus had left to him all those years ago - copies of Arrian and Caesar, and the gifted scroll of Longus' own *Daphnis and Chloe* which the poet himself had given them and recited at the Metellus domus in Rome during the festival of Venus Verticordia. There were a few other scrolls too, but it was so little compared to all that had been lost.

Why didn't I save more? Lucius rested upon the table on balled fists, his eyes shut for a moment. Once the wave of anger passed, he called to Phoebus.

"Yes, Baba?"

"These scrolls are yours now," Lucius said. "Make sure you care for them."

Phoebus approached the table and stood beside his father. His hands reached down with a reverential touch, his fingers grazing the papyrus rolls. "Thank you. I'll take care of them. What is that one?" he asked, pointing to a couple of final scrolls tied with a string.

"Those are the copies of the deeds to our estate in Etruria, and to the hillfort which your grandfather gave to us on the day we were married," Lucius said.

"And that?" Phoebus pointed to a last scroll.

"My imperial pass to anywhere in the empire."

The room fell silent. What had been a guarantee of safe passage from Emperor Severus with Lucius' own name upon it was now a death sentence.

Lucius picked up the scroll and looked at it. He thought of burning it, but stopped himself. *One day...when Caracalla is no longer emperor...* He placed it upon the table with the other scrolls and reached back into the box.

The jingle of coin filled the room then as Lucius began removing the thirteen heavy leather pouches filled with gold aurea and silver denarii until the box was then empty.

Dagon rose from his seat and came to stand beside Lucius. "Why did you set all that aside, Lucius? It's like you knew something would happen."

"I don't know."

"You don't need all of that here," Dagon said. "Such things are of no use in Ynis Wytrin."

"No. Not in Ynis Wytrin," Lucius answered, putting the pouches back in the box, along with the other items. When it was all packed up, Lucius grasped the handles himself and pulled the box off the edge of the table.

It fell quickly and heavily, and Lucius felt pain shoot through his body.

"I could have helped you with that," Dagon said, angry he had not been quick enough to help.

"I need to build my strength," Lucius said. As he stood straight, he turned to Dagon. "Will you help me train again?"

"It's too soon, Lucius. Allow your body time to heal," Adara said from where she sat by the fire.

Lucius took a deep breath. "I need to train. I can't feel myself anymore. I'm lost beneath this burned exterior. I have strength enough underneath." He thought of killing the attacker the day before at the hill-fort. How it had felt. He had managed, but it had been clumsy. Then he remembered who had sent the man to watch their home, to wait for and kill any of them who approached. "Will you help me?" Lucius said to Dagon again.

Dagon glanced at Adara. "Of course, my friend. Anything."

"We can start tomorrow."

Briana stood with Antiope in her arms. "We should go," she said to Dagon. "She's tired." She kissed Adara's cheek, and went to the door with Dagon following.

"I'll come by to get you tomorrow morning and we can begin," Dagon said to Lucius.

"I'll be ready," Lucius said from where he stood at the table.

Adara closed the door behind their friends, and turned to look at Lucius. "I don't want you to injure yourself. What is the point of training so soon?"

"It's a part of who I am...who I was. Besides...I should always be ready."

"Can I train with you?" Phoebus asked.

Lucius looked at his son. Before, he would have said no, not yet. But he was older now, stronger. He had killed a man. *He is a dragon too,* Lucius thought. "Yes. You may."

"Thank you, Baba," Phoebus said.

"Calliope?" Lucius asked. "Do you want to train too?"

Calliope looked up at her father and shook her head. "I'm to help Etain and the priestesses tomorrow. It doesn't feel right to swing a sword in this place."

Lucius looked at the stone floor then back at his daughter. "Very well. If you change your mind..."

Calliope came to him and touched his arm. "I love you, Baba."

Lucius looked into his daughter's eyes, her face framed by her long hair. He knew she was right about not swinging a sword in Ynis Wytrin, but she did not know of the plans he had begun forming in his mind. None of them did.

With a nod of her head, Calliope indicated that Lucius should sit with Adara by the fire.

Lucius looked to see Adara holding the letter from Graecia in her hands. He had given it to her when they had returned, but she had been unwilling to open it right away, had been silent since it arrived.

Lucius went to sit next to her, and he too felt an inkling of fear as he looked upon the leather dispatch tube.

Phoebus was about to sit beside his parents when Calliope took his arm and shook her head.

"We're going to go outside and see the moon," Calliope said.

Lucius turned to the children and nodded.

They left, and Lucius and Adara were alone with the missive.

"Are you going to open it?" he asked, his hand upon her arm.

"I'm afraid of what it says."

"I know."

Adara turned to look at him, her eyes pleading for help he did not know how to give. "What if…"

"There is only one way to find out. Alma and Culhwch said it came a long time ago."

Adara looked back at the scroll and began to untie the leather straps. When the tube was open at one end, she tipped it and a papyrus scroll slid out into her lap. She unrolled it and angled it toward the firelight so that she could read it.

"It's dated to the time of the emperor's death."

"They would not have known about Severus then, or anything else," Lucius said. "What does it say?"

Adara cleared her throat and began to read…

To Lucius Metellus Anguis, Adara Metella Antonina, and their beloved grandchildren, Phoebus and Calliope,

With love and greetings from Publius Leander Antoninus and Delphina Antonina.

It has been a long time since we have had word from you, and we pray to the Gods that you are all well and safe. This missive may take some time to reach you as we have sent it by private courier instead of imperial postal service. But that is for a reason.

Adara paused, her voice shuddering, and guilt taking hold of her heart. "I should have written them more often," she chided herself.

"Keep reading," Lucius said softly.

Adara nodded and continued reading as the fire crackled in the hearth before them.

. . .

It has been some years since we were all together in Etruria...an age, it seems. We reminisce about those halcyon days when our worries were fewer and there was hope to be found around every corner of life.

How is life in Britannia? When last you wrote, it was of the changes you had made at the hillfort we presented you. Often, we try to imagine what wonders you have worked there, what the hall looks like, and the temple where you said the local Britons have returned to honour the Gods.

We dream of visiting you in your faraway home in that corner of the empire.

Adara's voice cracked and she stopped reading to gather herself. A tear ran down her cheek to blot the papyrus scroll she held in her hands as if it were a wounded songbird. She continued...

Life in Athenae is different also. The great news here is that both Lavena and Hadrea have married and moved away. We do not see them often. Lavena married a wine merchant from Chios and lives upon that distant island. He is a kind man, and hard worker, but his business keeps him away for long periods of time.

Hadrea too has wed a potter from Corinthos. He is very successful and his work is in high demand. Delphina and he have had interesting conversations about painting and perspective. We see them a little more often when he delivers pieces to some of the wealthier citizens of Athenae.

Neither Lavena or Hadrea have had children as of yet, however, and so we dream often of Phoebus and Calliope, and guess at how much they must have grown. We hope to see them someday soon.

Despite hope and sun-filled days that are scented with mountain pine, and evenings that are sweetened by jasmine, there is a fear in the air of this city that we cannot describe. And it is getting worse.

To add to our unease, we should let you know that we have not heard from Antonia and Emrys for quite some time.

.   .   .

Lucius and Adara looked at each other for a panicked moment, and she read on.

Since your departure for Britannia, Delphina and Antonia had been in regular, monthly correspondence, each of them writing long letters about life in Athenae or in Etruria. Antonia seemed ever so happy with Emrys, who is one of the kindest, most reliable men we have met. She never missed sending a letter, but now it has been three months since her last one.

Lucius felt his heart begin to race as a fist of fear and anger gripped it tightly.

We hired a man to go to Etruria with a letter for her and to ascertain whether or not they are well, if anything is wrong, or if they need help.

The man never returned.

I was going to go myself, but then there was some strange activity around our own domus on Hymettos. Strange men have been spotted roaming around the hillside, and it is no one whom the local shepherds recognize. At first, we thought they might be imperial prospectors, but then I would have heard about such activity from the bouleuterion in the city.

We don't want to worry you, but if there is any chance that you have heard from Antonia and Emrys, or even Caecilius or Clarinda, please do let us know.

But on to happier thoughts and the comfort we cling to knowing that you are all safe in Britannia in your home which we are proud to have given to you. Perhaps someday, we will find ourselves there with you, all of us in the same place, a family.

It is a dream we have.

For now, and until that time comes to pass, we ask the Gods to watch over you and bless you.

Please embrace our grandchildren for us, and tell them that they are ever in our hearts, as are you, Adara and Lucius.

All our love,

Publius and Delphina

Adara let her tears fall then as she thought of her family, how she had not seen them in years, and how the world they believed in no longer existed.

"This letter was written so long ago," she said through her tears as Lucius stood, pacing the room. She looked up at him. "Anything could have happened since then, to my parents, to Antonia and Emrys, Caecilius and Clarinda. Surely one of them would have written?"

Lucius shook his head, his mind reeling from the dark thoughts that harassed him, so much so that he forgot the pain his own body caused him. He felt like he was falling through a dark sky, spiralling out of control like a dead leaf upon the winter wind. He looked at his wife as she read the letter again through the blur of her tears. He thought of Phoebus' face, how it had changed with the taking of a life. He thought of how his precious daughter had come to worry about him such that childhood was now passing her quickly by.

He thought of the home that Publius Leander believed they inhabited, what it had looked like beneath the sun, and what he had found only the day before, the charred ruins of a world they had built.

He did not notice Adara leave the room to go outside. His rage and anger were ringing in his ears. He looked at the table where their swords and daggers lay silent beneath the cloth. With the memory of the man he had killed only yesterday in the temple ruins, Lucius reached for the newly-cleaned pugio that lay there.

I don't need to train to do what needs to be done.

He stabbed at the shadows with the pugio gripped tightly in his hands, each thrust spurred on by a worry for his mother, brother and sister, for Publius and Delphina, for the Durotrigan villagers who had sacrificed so much to come to their aid. The list of individuals who had suffered for knowing him was painfully long, They had paid for his own hubris, and for the arrogance and greed of wicked men.

"Wicked men…" Lucius said to himself as his body and mind suddenly grew still.

It was a stillness borne of decision and certainty of action.

Calm again, Lucius lay down upon his lonely bed, his eyes closed. He walked through the ruins of their life again, of their home, and allowed the anger and rage to flow freely through him, to give him strength.

Apollo…Father… if ever I meant something to you, heal me now and give me the strength to do what I must do.

Lucius slept through the night, and when he awoke the next morning, he felt less pain than he had in some time. As his eyes flickered open, he looked up to see Calliope sitting by his bedside.

"Good morning, Baba," she said.

Lucius looked around, but Adara and Phoebus were not there.

"They are at Dagon and Briana's. A letter came from Einion in Dumnonia."

Lucius sat up.

"Here," Calliope said, handing him a cup of water. "Drink. How do you feel?"

"I feel good," he said, a moment of hope entering his mind and making him look at his arm. *Still a monster,* he thought as he looked upon his burned skin.

"I didn't want you to wake up alone. When they left, I was practicing some of the healing Etain has taught me. Do you feel it?"

Lucius felt guilt then, for the darkness he had nursed the night before. His daughter was so good and pure, and he felt like he had taken a few steps away from her with his new-found determination.

"Yes. I do feel it. Thank you, my girl."

Calliope hugged him and then took the pot of resin and fresh linens from the table nearby. "Let me change your bandages, and then we can go and see what the letter from Einion said."

She got to work, removing the previous day's bandages, spreading more resin over Lucius' burned skin, and then wrapping him in fresh linen.

"What did the letter from our grandparents say?" Calliope asked as she worked. "Are they well?"

Lucius did not answer immediately, but spoke after a few seconds. "They are well, and they miss you terribly."

"I wish we could see them," Calliope said, and the thought must have been pleasant to her because she began to hum.

The tune was one Lucius recognized, for his sister Alene, before she was murdered, used to sing it to Calliope and Phoebus as babies. Calliope had absorbed the melody and it had become a part of her.

"They would all love to see you, my girl," Lucius said as she finished wrapping his limbs and helping him put on his tunic. "Let's go find the others."

It was a sunny day and the birds were loud and joyous in the air about Ynis Wytrin.

Lucius found himself enjoying the walk with his daughter as they went, and he tried to linger in the feeling. However, no matter how hard he tried to ignore it, he found himself constantly harassed by perceived threats, even in that blessed isle, thoughts of the outside world and the anger and rage and worry that accompanied those thoughts. His enemies were still out there, the people who had sought to kill him, his wife and children, and his friends.

In some cases, those enemies had succeeded.

He thought of the letter from Publius and Delphina again and worried for his mother, brother and sister, and Emrys too. Why had they not written?

He squeezed Calliope's hand as they walked and she held him close to her side as they rounded the animal pens and cut through one of the apple orchards toward the peaked thatch roof of Dagon and Briana's home.

Lucius and Calliope found the others sitting on logs outside of the roundhouse.

"Anguis!" Dagon waved when he saw Lucius and Calliope approach, rising to greet them.

"Dagon," Lucius said as Calliope ran to play with Antiope who held her arms out to her.

"Adara told us about the letter from her parents."

"It was sent a long time ago," Lucius acknowledged, shaking his head beneath the black wool of his cloak. He had a faraway look in his eyes though, and Dagon noticed this.

"What is it? What are you thinking?"

Lucius looked at his old friend. He wanted to tell him what he was thinking, what he wanted to do more than anything since their visit to the hillfort. But he could not. *No,* Lucius thought. *He needs to pull away from me, for his own good...*

Dagon looked at Lucius for a moment, recognizing the dark look in his burned features. He was about to press him for more details, but decided to leave it. *Not now,* he told himself. "There is news from Einion in Dumnonia."

They joined the others.

"What news from Einion?" Lucius asked, feeling more panic and worry creeping in.

But Briana smiled. "All is well there. The land thrives, and Gwendolyn is with child." She had begun to speak the words excitedly, but then remembered that Adara was beside her, one hand upon her scarred abdomen. Briana clenched her fists, angry with herself. "Forgive me... I..."

Adara stretched out her hand and touched Briana's arm. "Don't be. We've had enough guilt and anger to last a lifetime."

Briana gripped her friend's arm and leaned over to hold her close.

Adara smiled, feeling the weight of months of anger slowly lifting like a morning mist rising when the sun and sea breeze work in concert. She looked up at Lucius. "Isn't it wonderful news, Lucius?"

He forced a smile. "Yes, may the Gods bless them." It was difficult for him to picture Dumnonia in any other light but a dark, red one, for all that had happened to him there.

"There's more," Dagon said. "Briana, read it to him."

Briana held up the scroll she had received and read a part of Einion's words. "'Dragons have come into our land,' he says. 'Many of them. They have been shunned in every other part of Britannia, but I have welcomed them in Dumnonia. Lucius and Dagon would be amazed to see them.' That is all he says," Briana finished.

Dagon's eyes were wide as they looked upon Lucius, hopeful. "I dare not believe it," the Sarmatian said.

Lucius could see the tears forming in his eyes. "The land did not thrive under the wyrm we met in battle."

"No," Dagon said with absolutely certainty. "It did not."

They stared at each other, but neither gave voice to the thoughts and hopes they then entertained.

"I haven't seen my brother in so long," Briana said.

"Why don't you go to him?" Adara asked. "Antiope could meet her uncle at last."

"It isn't safe enough," Lucius said darkly. "The ordo of Lindinis might have men out looking for any of us."

They all looked at him, confused and disappointed.

"Is it worth the risk?" Lucius asked.

"Perhaps it is?" Dagon said, thinking of what Einion had written. "I too would love to see them. We'll think about it anyway."

Lucius felt very alone then, felt the pull of dark memory once more, of Lunaris dead upon the moors of that land, of blood and chaos, and of unimaginable pain in a dark forest grove where he fought for his life, and the even more painful truth.

If that truth is real, then why am I still afraid? he yelled at himself inside. *Why do I sit still while evil men continue to roam the world?*

"Baba?" Phoebus' voice broke into his thoughts as his strong, young hand gripped Lucius'. "Are you unwell?"

Lucius shook his head and snapped out of his dark reverie. "What? Yes…I'm fine. I… I think I'll go to the Well of the Chalice."

"I'll come with you," Adara said, beginning to stand.

"No, no!" Lucius interjected. "I will go myself. You stay. Enjoy the sun. I…I just want to be alone for a time."

Without another word, he was gone, leaving the others to watch his dark form cut through the crops on the other side of the field where some of the priestesses were at work.

"I just don't know what to say to him sometimes," Adara said sadly as she sat down again beside Briana.

"He'll come around," Briana said.

"It was not an easy journey we made," Dagon added. "But I think the most difficult part of it was the belief that the villagers still had in him… in all of you."

Adara looked up at that, a deep, shuddering breath expanding her chest. "If only he held that belief in himself."

The deep green court that surrounded the Well of the Chalice pool was quiet when Lucius arrived. He found himself standing at the pool's edge, staring down into the cool, red water, and as he did so, he remembered faces looking

down at him, the faces of Love, and of Apollo, but then the wavering faces of
Weylyn, Etain, Gilmore, Aaron and Rachel. The latter had been at the forefront, their hands laid upon him, helping to pull him from the red depths and
into the world of suffering as he had tumbled from the heights of Olympus.

"Did I make the wrong choice?" Lucius asked himself, thinking of
what he had glimpsed, the brief, painless joy he had felt beneath the
branches of that shimmering olive with the Gods beside him.

The water looked suddenly too attractive to resist. He let his black
cloak fall to the ground and removed his sandals. Crouching carefully,
Lucius slid into the pool and allowed the healing water to envelop him,
soak through his bandages to touch his burned skin. He lay back slowly,
suddenly very close to a desperation that he had been holding at bay
since he had emerged from his fevered dreams.

He lay back and allowed the water to swallow his shoulders...his
neck...and then his entire head.

All I have to do is inhale.

But he held his breath, and found that he could do so easily for some
time, and in that time, the faces of his family shimmered before him in
the light high above.

You are not finished in the mortal world, a voice said in Lucius'
mind.

Lucius tried to ignore it, the voice of his father, but like the sound of
a single, beautiful note upon a mountain hillside in summer, he could not
shake it from his consciousness.

Lucius' mind stepped to the edge of breathing, of gazing into the
mirror at yellow eyes set in a charred face, but in that moment, his pain
receded even more, and he felt his muscles flex and relax, pulse with the
sun's light. He opened his eyes beneath the water's red surface and saw
the forms of three people standing over him.

Gasping, he shot up out of the water to see the children, Rachel and
Aaron sitting at the edge of the pool. Both had their hands immersed
deep in the water, and behind them, watching keenly, was Father
Gilmore.

"It would be a great sin to carry out the action you are entertaining,
Lucius Metellus Anguis," Gilmore said, his voice firm.

Lucius wiped his face so that he could see better, and looked at the
two children. He wanted to ask them what they had done, but it felt
invasive to ask, ungrateful. And there was a part of him that did not

want to know. "The waters are healing to my skin," Lucius said, though he knew the explanation was weak and insufficient for the priest.

"The pool of life gives clarity to all, and the blood of the Christus should not be darkened by death." He turned to the children. "Go now, Rachel and Aaron. I will meet you in the chapel shortly."

The children looked once more at Lucius and smiled.

He smiled back and they left the green of the garden. When he looked back at Gilmore, his expression darkened once more as he climbed out of the pool.

"I see what you are thinking," Gilmore said, "what is in your heart."

"Oh, do you, priest?" Of all the people Lucius had met in Ynis Wytrin, Father Gilmore had always made him the most uneasy. Though he had been kind to Lucius' family, Lucius felt that toward himself, Father Gilmore held too much suspicion. "I am not Rome, Gilmore."

"No. Perhaps not. But you are turning to something darker. Has Death himself come to the Isle of the Blessed?"

"What do you mean?"

"Weylyn and Etain continue to believe in the good you can bring to this world, this land, but all I see since you came out of the darkness like Lazarus, is anger and hate, and a thirst for violence."

"You know nothing of what I have been through," Lucius said through gritted teeth.

"I know that you have dipped your hands in rivers of blood, and that those rivers will become oceans before you are finished with this world."

Lucius turned more quickly than he could have imagined, hoped for, and found his fists balled in the brown cloth of Gilmore's robes.

But Gilmore stood his ground, his eyes unflinching in the face of Lucius' sudden rage. "You see? You cannot control this anger. This hate. You, the Roman Dragon, who has been blessed with such a family. How can you keep them safe when you are so easily drawn into violence?"

"Not even your Christus has seen and suffered what I have," Lucius growled.

Gilmore remained calm. "Oh, he has suffered, and he did so for us all, the Son of God." His features softened and he sighed, as if realizing something for the first time. "Perhaps that is why I dislike you so…why I have fallen prey to such jealousy? I resent you, Roman, for being close to Him in a way that I could never be. For having a divine father, but shunning the purpose that could give you." Gilmore stepped back then. He seemed confused, torn.

Lucius did not know if the priest was speaking to himself now, or to the god he so fervently believed in.

"How can one be so gifted, but ignorant of the purpose and potential of his own life?"

"I know my purpose!" Lucius said. "I tried to help the world, but evil men got in the way."

Gilmore shook his head. "Not evil men, Lucius Metellus Anguis. Yourself! You say you know your purpose, but do you truly know yourself? You have travelled far, but not travelled at all. The Christus suffered in the desert of his mind with singular purpose, and emerged with purpose. You...you have emerged with hate and anger, and you will burn us all if you continue in this way."

Lucius felt rage building inside, and it scared him. *Leave now, Gilmore!* he thought, and a moment later, he found himself alone, staring at a spot of brilliant sunlight upon the ground beside the pool where it filtered in from the sky above.

"I know my purpose," Lucius said as he bent to pick up his cloak and sandals. "I will make it right."

That evening, Dagon and Briana invited Lucius, Adara and the children to eat with them in their home, in an attempt to mend the perceived rift between them, to begin anew like the first green growth in a field that has been burned.

Adara had been feeling the closeness of friendship like a healing balm and had accepted the invitation without a thought.

Phoebus and Calliope too were keen to go, but as they all prepared to leave the guest house, Lucius declared he was not going.

"But why, Lucius?" Adara asked, disappointed. "They'll think you don't want to be with them."

Lucius was silent a moment, wondered if perhaps a part of that were true. When he looked upon Dagon and Briana's child, he could not help but be reminded of the child he and Adara had lost. But that was not the main reason. "I'm exhausted by the journey to the hillfort the other day. I just want to sleep."

"But it is not yet dusk," Adara countered. "Come for a short time at least."

Lucius shook his head and stepped toward her. "You go," he said, his voice low as he leaned in to hug her. "I love you."

She looked at him, confused, but returned the embrace.

Lucius turned to Phoebus and Calliope. "Good night. Take care of your mama."

"Baba," Phoebus said. "There is no danger here in the blessed isle. Just you rest."

Lucius smiled. "I will." He looked at Calliope who was staring up at him strangely. "I'm just tired, my girl."

She did not say anything, but nodded and went out the door.

"You'll be missed," Adara said, going with Phoebus after Calliope.

Lucius stood in the open doorway, watching them walk toward the great oak tree where orange light spread across the ground. It was peaceful out, birdsong filling the air which was devoid of wind.

When his wife and children were out of sight, and no one else was visible, Lucius went back inside to the table. He pulled back the cloth that covered the weapons and found the pugio he had taken with him to the hillfort. He took the cingulum and sheathed the blade when it was secured about his waist, beneath the loose black folds of his cloak.

He found himself feeling nervous and took a few deep breaths to calm himself. *I can do this. I've waited too long now.* He extinguished the lamp upon the table and went outside.

Lucius walked slowly across Ynis Wytrin, acknowledged by some of the priests and priestesses, but spoken to by none. They had become accustomed to his shadow amongst them, his dark presence. They were also wary of it.

He wanted them to ignore him anyway. He wanted to be invisible.

Soon he arrived at the animal pens and spotted the white pony that had led him and Dagon through the marshes. It cropped at the grass among the goats and sheep, but looked up at Lucius' approach.

From beneath a small overhanging shed beside the pen, Lucius took a leather harness and a carrot from a basket that was used to treat the animals. He clicked his tongue, and the pony trotted over to the gate, using his bulk to press through the goats who had gathered to look up at Lucius.

"Will you help me tonight?" Lucius asked, holding out the carrot. He

opened the gate and the pony came out as Lucius pushed a couple of the
goats back in. He handed the carrot to the pony and, after it finished
chewing, began putting the harness about its head, holding the reins in
his hand. He looked around to see if anyone was watching, and then
began walking toward the southern part of the isle and the path they had
taken only a couple days before.

As he prepared to go into the outside world again, Lucius felt his
heart racing, his breathing loud in his own ears. He paused at the edge of
the forest path and looked back at the peace of Ynis Wytrin one more
time.

"I am dead to the world outside of this place," he said to himself.
"This will be a new beginning…"

With that, he leaned upon the pony's side and swung slowly and
awkwardly upon its back. He had not sat on a horse in a long time, and it
felt strange to do so, but riding bareback would be easier in his state than
in a saddle.

As the pony set off down the path, into the dark of the forest, toward
the marshes, Lucius thought he could hear Xanthus neighing loudly
behind him.

From the shadows of the nearest orchard, like an evening mist when
the air cools, the grey-white form of Weylyn watched Lucius disappear,
feeling his heart sink as he did so.

The pony had moved more quickly and nimbly without the weight of a
wagon behind him. It was still light when they reached the end of the
hidden path and the line of the road heading south toward Lindinis.

Lucius searched his charred memories for any recollection of the
way, and found a vague memory of a country road leading off of the
Fosse way, located just south of the ancient hillfort where they had
helped Olwyn Conn Coran so long ago.

The road was not busy, and the few wagons and riders that passed by
ignored Lucius, taking him to be a hermit of sorts.

When Lucius reached the country road, he reigned in and looked
around. When he had travelled that way before in a wagon, he had only
had eyes for Adara.

But now, he sought something else. "This must be the way," he said
to the pony, pulling on the reins so that they turned right down the road

that wound its way over rolling hills beneath the bodies of looming trees.

Lucius began to wonder if he had taken the wrong road, and was about to turn around when the sound of voices reached his ears. He reined in and listened, looked. It was getting dark now, and he slowed the pony. Then, he spotted it, the start of the stone wall along the side of the road.

The air carried with it the faint smell of woodsmoke and roasting meat, and farther down, there were torches marking a break in the wall, the entrance to the compound.

"That's it," Lucius said beneath his breath. He looked around, feeling suddenly very exposed upon the road. He dismounted and pulled the pony off to the side, into the forest for a short distance. "Will you stay here?" he asked the animal. "You need to take me back." He tied the reins loosely around a fallen log so that the pony could crop at the grass upon the forest floor. "I won't be long," he said, the timbre of his voice dark, determined.

Slowly, Lucius crept through the forest, his feet noiseless upon the new growth, not yet dry from the summer heat. His eyes scanned the wall as he went, and the field beyond where he had stood that night, so long ago. He could see the forms of the slaves moving about the grounds, and he searched for a way that he could slip in unnoticed.

There were no guards, and Lucius could tell that there was little worry about intruders. Complacency was often a flaw of the arrogant.

Just beyond the reach of any torch or light, Lucius crept around the perimeter of the compound until he was on the other side of the court-yard at the end of the bathhouse wing. He listened for the sound of splashing or talking, but it was silent within except for the gentle echo of water upon the painted walls.

Lucius looked around at the fine villa, the grand home, and felt bitter hatred rise within an extreme urge to see it all destroyed, to feel the satis-faction that that would bring.

With a glance at the noisy slave quarters at the north end of the compound, he entered the bathhouse from the first door beneath the peri-stylium. Inside, he moved slowly through the tepidarium and where it met the caldarium, he found a three-headed oil lamp upon a table set with strigils and phials of oils.

The hypocausts were not lit, and so Lucius could see through the room of the caldarium down toward the frigidarium. He looked upon the walls painted with country scenes and seascapes, and among the trees, satyrs peered at him questioningly, wondering what he was doing amongst them.

Lucius looked back at the table, and the lamp, and then unhooked it from the bracket so that he held it in his hand. With his other hand, he poured one of the phials of oil all over the table.

When he touched one of the lamp's spouts to the oil, the fire took immediately and spread upon the surface.

Lucius jumped back, taking another of the glass phials and moving to the next room where he set a slave's stool alight. An orange glow and smoke began to pulse behind him as he went, leaving a trail of oil.

In the frigidarium, he spotted the mosaic with Aeneas and Dido at the bottom of the water, as if they were drowned. He remembered sitting in that pool, remembered the attack before.

Stepping to the final door, he looked upon the wood surface and there, at the base of the door, he dropped the oil lamp he had been holding so that the flames erupted from the floor upward, licking in deadly earnest, working their way up.

Lucius listened for voices, for shouts of alarm, but none came for none had noticed the fires that were burning within the tiny windows of the bathhouse. He slid through the apodyterium to the corridor of the main house and stopped to gaze the length of it. Lamps hung upon bronze stands every ten feet or so, and Lucius was about to set the corridor alight when he heard voices.

He felt his heart begin to race, his blood pound within his ears.

It's him, he thought as he looked ahead and to the right at the door to the tablinum. Lucius crept along the wall and around the first lamps, listening like a desert lion with its head cocked to the expanse. He drew the pugio slowly from its sheath and stopped to listen.

"Do you smell that?" a snarling voice said.

Lucius had a vague recollection of the voice, knew it was not the one he had come to see.

Suddenly, there were rushed footsteps and the form of Nolan Phelan burst out into the corridor.

"Smells like a fire!" the man said, and as he turned back to the tablinum door, his eyes fell upon Lucius' dark form standing there with his blade drawn. "Who are you?" he said, more shocked and surprised than concerned.

Lucius lunged for the man, and plunged his pugio up beneath his chin without a thought.

Nolan Phelan's eyes shot wide and froze as blood dripped out of his shuddering mouth.

"What did you say, Nolan?" came the voice of another man, and a moment later, Serenus Crescens stepped into the corridor.

Lucius spun and kicked out as best he could, sending Crescens sprawling back upon the floor inside his tablinum.

"Help!" Crescens yelled, but the words barely escaped his throat before Lucius was upon him like a fury, clawing at him, punching him. "Who...are...you?" Crescens cried between blows. "Help!"

"Don't you recognize me, Serenus Crescens?" Lucius growled. "You watched me burn....you watched my home burn...you watched my world burn!" Lucius felt strength returning to his limbs with every stroke of vengeance then as he pommeled Crescens with his fist and with blunt end of the pugio.

"No! It can't be!" Crescens yelled. "I saw you die!"

"I did!" Lucius yelled, but as he was about to strike again, he felt clumsy, frightened hands grasping at him from behind.

"Dominus!" one of the slaves grabbing at Lucius yelled. "The domus is on fire!"

Lucius stabbed wildly behind him and felt a connection. There were screams as one of the slaves grabbed at his eyes. Lucius turned as the second slave pulled him to his feet, about to strike with a club. Before the blow came, Lucius thrust his pugio into his throat, once, twice, and then kicked so that the body fell flat upon the blinded one.

Crescens backed away toward his desk, horror upon his face as Lucius looked wildly about the room, then went to the corridor where he threw oil lamps in both directions, blocking off the path to any other slaves who would rescue their hateful master.

Crescens had found his feet when Lucius returned, and held a dagger pointed toward him. He squinted, uncertain of what he looked at, shaking his head in disbelief through the blood that ran over his eyes.

"Serenus!" came his wife Sabina's voice from the upper floor. "Help! I can't get through!"

"Your wife is calling for you, Serenus!" Lucius growled. "You should help her."

"Please, Metellus!" Crescens begged, unable to use the blade he held in his hands as he faced Lucius. "Claudius Picus forced me!"

"Oh he did, did he? And you obliged. You destroyed everything, and you killed my child!"

"No, I didn't!" Crescens shook his head wildly, no longer the certain, arrogant ordo member he had always been, but a man fearful for his life, of the vengeance that stared him in the eyes, of the furies who stood behind Lucius, whispering in his ears. "I lost my son!"

"Your son?" Lucius thought of the hateful youth that had been Crescens' son. Of the pained look that was imprinted upon Phoebus' face having had to kill to protect his sister. "Look at me!" Lucius yelled, his eyes wild, his blade steady. "Your son deserved to die! And this is the end of you and of your world, Crescens."

Crescens' face hardened then, and out of sheer desperation, with his wife's screams and those of his slaves echoing throughout the burning house, he lunged.

Lucius' blade lashed out and cut the wrist of Crescens' dagger hand, making the man cry out in pain. Lucius pushed him back so that he stumbled into his table, knocking over the oil lamp that had been burning there.

Scrolls instantly began to burn and fire ringed Crescens' head. He screamed as the flames licked at his hair and ears, as his tunic began to glow and then burst into flame.

Lucius grabbed him, ignoring the burning feeling upon his hands.

"To Hades with you, Crescens!"

Lucius stabbed him in the gut first, and then the groin, and then the chest. Faster and faster, his hand went in and out, plunging the blade deeper and deeper each time, more violently as he cried out among the flames, uncaring of Crescens' cries of anguish. He took in the sight of the bulging eyes, the pained expression, and with every look, all Lucius could see was fire and his burning home, all he could hear were the cries of his family, his wife and children, his friends. The dead called out to him, and with every stroke, he offered them blood and vengeance.

After a few moments he released the limp, bloody corpse to fall upon the floor as it burned.

Lucius turned, his pain bringing him back, and looked for a way out of the fiery, scream-echoing domus. He leapt for the doorway into the hall and saw fire everywhere. Across the way he spotted the double doors to the triclinium and made for them.

Inside the room, the tables had been set for a dinner, but no one was there. Lucius strode across the room, to the doors that opened up onto the field beyond and before going out, he kicked over one of the burning braziers so that the coals spilled across the mosaic floor to set the tables and couches alight.

Outside, the slaves' screams could be heard everywhere, but the dark was Lucius' friend and he walked away in full view, a shadowy wraith full of anger and blood. At the edge of the field, beside the road, Lucius turned to watch the burning villa, to take in the sight of what he had been dreaming of.

And he enjoyed it.

He enjoyed the sight of flames rising up into the night sky.

Sabina Cresca's screams echoed even louder then as she appeared at one of the upper windows, unable to escape the conflagration.

"Help me!" she yelled to the slaves that had gathered in safety below, but none of them dared approach.

She was on fire now, and Lucius could see her climbing out of the burning cubiculum in which she and her body slave had taken refuge. She hung upon the edge, her legs dangling from a height, and as the flames licked at her arms she let go. She tumbled head first to land with a crack upon the garden wall below.

Lucius watched for a little longer before turning from the scene. As he went into the darkness of the forest to find the pony, he felt stronger than he had in a long while.

"I'm coming for you," he said through gritted teeth and pain.

V

IRAE SANGUIS

'The Blood of Anger'

The early morning light was only just cracking on the horizon when Lucius arrived at the edge of Ynis Wytrin to find the way blocked by a woman upon a brilliant white stallion.

She looked upon him, and there in her starry eyes Lucius saw a deep sadness and regret.

What have you done? Epona asked him.

Lucius reined in the pony, blood from the night before spotting its white coat. He slid off and approached the goddess. "What needed to be done."

Epona looked upon Lucius and tried to reach out to him, to ease his suffering with her divine touch, but he turned his head away.

"You have helped me so many times before, lady. But you cannot help me in this. It is my own task, my own decision."

The path you are choosing will affect more than just yourself, she said, trying to sway his mind, his heart.

Lucius looked down at his cut and bloody hands. "I know. It is what I do."

And yet you will continue? She stepped forward and held him by the shoulders. *Please don't, Lucius Metellus Anguis. You are more than this. So much more…*

Lucius removed her hands. "Lucius Metellus Anguis is dead. He is now anger and fury. He is vengeance." With those words, Lucius stepped around her, leading the bloody pony in his wake.

Epona watched him go and felt her divine heart bursting with sadness and despair, for she could not sway him, that son of Apollo, or douse the fires of hate that were burning more brightly than ever within him.

Apollo and Venus, all you gods who have ever watched over him...I beg you to help him now...

And with that, she mounted her horse and disappeared into the greenwood and morning light.

Lucius' dark form moved slowly across the grass like a wolf that had just sated itself on a kill, eyes wide and staring, his senses slow, numb. As he approached the animal pens, priestesses came running to meet him, followed by Weylyn and Etain, but when they saw the state of him, they stopped short, their voices caught in their throats.

Some of the priestesses cried out in fear, but Etain and Weylyn looked at each other and then back at Lucius.

"Take them away," Weylyn said to Etain, nodding toward the priestesses. "I'll take care of him."

She looked at her old friend and shook her head. "I did not see any of this."

"I'm sure no one did. Go. I'll cleanse him."

Etain began to usher the priestesses away, and Weylyn went directly toward Lucius.

"What have you done, Dragon?" the Druid said to the Roman.

Lucius stopped, and Weylyn noticed that his eyes were looking somewhere else, somewhere beyond the grass at their feet, the trees, and the bleating animals in the pen behind them.

"Lucius...my friend..." Weylyn said, more tenderly. "How did you come to be here in this state? The way should have been blocked to you and the pony."

Lucius' eyes focussed now and he turned to Weylyn. "I walked."

Only immortals can come and go from Ynis Wytrin as they please, Weylyn thought. *Of course.* "You seek vengeance for all the pain you have suffered. That your family has suffered. The Gods know, I have bled enough enemies in my youth for the same reasons. But you have sullied this sacred place, Lucius. We must cleanse you. Come."

Weylyn led Lucius away toward Wearyall Hill, hugging the edge of the lake and marshes until they came to a path that led out into the water where the mud and grass squelched beneath their feet as they went. It was a spit of only a few feet wide, and led far out to a circular island that was hidden from sight of Ynis Wytrin by tall reeds and rushes.

There was no birdsong in that spot, only dim light and solemn silence.

"What is this place?" Lucius asked, suddenly very tired.

"It is a place of purification," Weylyn said, pointing at a rocky altar where a blade rested beside a dark patch of charred grass where a fire had been lit long before. "I must get some things. Wait here for me."

Lucius nodded and Weylyn rushed back the way they had come.

As he walked, Weylyn tried to remember the last time he had performed the ceremony, the last time so much blood of anger had been brought to Ynis Wytrin. *When I came here in my youth...* Up ahead he spotted Morvran waiting for him at the end of the path. "Morvran, please help me."

"Yes?" the young man said through his deformed mouth, great concern in his eyes. He had come running when he heard the screams of the priestesses.

"Quickly now. I need to you get me a tinder box, some dry grass, and a jug of water from the Well of the Chalice. Do that while I go to the Dragon's family."

"What ha...hap...happened?"

"Angry blood has been spilt and brought here."

Morvran yelped.

"Quickly now, Morvran!" Weylyn said and the younger man ran to carry out the Druid's bidding. Meanwhile, Weylyn walked quickly to the guest house and knocked.

Adara opened the door, her face a mask of worry. "What is it?"

"He is back. Do not fear," Weylyn said. "But you cannot see him yet. I must cleanse him."

"Why? What's happened?"

Weylyn stopped himself, knowing she deserved an explanation, that she needed one. "He killed someone last night, and returned to Ynis Wytrin with their blood still upon him and the animal he took."

"What?" Adara began to shake. "Who? Who's blood?"

"I do not know, but I must cleanse him or else you will all be expelled from this isle immediately. Please, lady. Give me one of his clean tunics and another cloak if he has one."

"Of course..." Adara turned and went inside to rummage through a trunk that was on the floor near Lucius' bed. She removed a white tunic, and then went to the fire where Lucius' second black cloak was drying before it. She folded them quickly and handed them to Weylyn. "Can I see him? Can I help?"

"No!" Weylyn said quickly, then closed his eyes, stopping himself. "Forgive me. It is best you stay away for now, that you keep the children away. I will carry out the cleansing ritual. It will not take long, but no one else should be there."

"Very well," Adara said. "Thank you, Weylyn."

"Do not worry, lady. All will be well." With that, Weylyn turned and rushed back to the other side of Ynis Wytrin where Morvran was waiting for him with the tinder box, a bucket of dry grass, and the jug of water.

When Weylyn was gone, Adara closed the door, relieved to know Lucius had returned, but now terrified at what he had done. They had been awake for the entire night after returning from Dagon and Briana's, worrying about where he was. Calliope had been unable to see anything except that Lucius was alive, but it still left them all in sleepless uncertainty.

Adara stared at the table where the swords were laid, and noticed that the pugio was missing.

"What have you done, Lucius?"

When Weylyn came back up the sodden path, he found Lucius standing with his back to him, staring out at the calm, dark water of the marshes, gripping the pony's reins so that it could not escape.

The animal seemed flustered as it stood there, covered in an outsider's blood, and Weylyn felt for it.

It knows.

He stopped, and set down the clean clothing and jug of sacred water just outside of the circle of the small island. Then he stepped forward with the dry grass and tinder box, noticed that Morvran had included some dry wood as well. "Remove all of your clothes," Weylyn said as he set about starting a fire.

It took a while for Lucius to do so, but by the time the fire was going, all of his bloody bandages, his tunic and cloak were removed. The cingulum with the bloody pugio was set down beside it.

Weylyn took the reins of the pony and pat the animal's shaggy head, soothing it. He turned to Lucius to see his massacred body standing before him, away from the fire. His healing skin had torn in places, no doubt from whatever struggles he had undergone in the night, but he did not seem to notice or feel much.

"Are you in pain?" Weylyn asked Lucius.

"Yes," Lucius said, but his voice was calm as if the thoughts he mulled over distracted him from the sensations that tore at his consciousness.

Weylyn nodded. "Let us begin."

The Druid turned to face East, South, West and North alternatively as he said the words he had not spoken in a long while.

"Spirits of Earth, and Wind, and Water, and Fire... Spirits of this world, and the next, above and below... Hear me now... Cleanse this warrior...this Dragon...that he may yet walk the sacred grounds of this blessed isle. Accept his actions, and forgive the blood he has brought here..."

"Forgive?" Lucius blurted angrily.

Weylyn held up his hands for silence and continued.

"Accept the blood of this innocent instead, and be appeased...let this offering cleanse the dragon among us. Bless him..."

Weylyn then turned to the pony and led it to the rock where he picked up the blade that had lain there and held it over the fire for a few brief moments.

With a swift, sure action, the Druid cut the pony's throat and held its head above the rocky altar so that the blood dripped upon it.

The animal's eyes rolled in its head and it fell upon the altar as its lifeblood ran in a thick stream over the rock and then away to the edge of the marsh, into the water.

Despite the shock he felt at the quick action, Lucius did not flinch or balk at the sight of the dying animal. In fact, as he stood there, naked in the breathy breeze of the marshes, he felt more alive than he had in a long while.

Weylyn bent over the body of the animal and closed his eyes with his hand over its head. "May your spirit be free now, and may you know our gratitude for your sacrifice..."

After a moment, Weylyn stood up and turned to the pile of Lucius' clothes. He picked them up and threw them on the fire where they smoked and shortly after, began to burn as the flames licked at the blood-stained fabric and bandages. He then picked up the pugio and held it in the flames, turning it over to ensure that every inch was touched, and when he was finished he threw it expertly to land outside of the circle beside the clean tunic and cloak that Adara had given him.

"Now," he said to Lucius. "Step into the water on the North side."

"But I'll sink!" Lucius said, looking at the murky depths.

Weylyn shook his head. "No, you won't. Just do it."

Lucius stepped to the edge of the water and tentatively placed one foot in so that the water rose to the height of his waist. He stepped in with his other leg and then turned to Weylyn.

"Turn North. And wash yourself completely so that your head goes beneath the surface. Then do the same facing East, South and West."

Lucius followed the Druid's command, and as he did so, the blood of his enemies was washed away from his skin to disappear in the black waters around him.

"Now…step out of the water and stand before the fire."

Lucius emerged from the water, feeling cold and clean now, and he stood before the flames, uneasy in such close proximity, but daring to nevertheless.

Weylyn then poured some of the water from the pitcher over Lucius' head, shoulders, hands, legs and feet. When that was finished, he held the pitcher over the fire where the clothing was just burning to its final embers. He poured the remainder of the water over it and the fire hissed and fizzled as smoke rose into the sky and surrounded him and Lucius before being blown away from the shores of Ynis Wytrin.

Weylyn stood with his arms outstretched and faced the cardinal directions once more.

"Spirits of the Earth, of Wind, of Air, and of Fire… Spirits of this world… We honour you, and thank you for blessing and cleansing this warrior that he may walk sacred ground once more…"

Weylyn was silent for a moment as he faced West, his eyes closed as the words echoed in his mind, as he relived memories of blood and vengeance from his own life, and grappled with the understanding of what Lucius had done, and the compassion he had for him. *It is no easy thing, a dragon's life…*

"Are we finished?" Lucius asked.

Weylyn turned to look at him and nodded. "We are." He pointed to the tunic and cloak that were upon the ground of the path leading back to Ynis Wytrin.

Lucius put on the tunic slowly, and then wrapped himself in the cloak.

"You must leave the sandals and cingulum here," Weylyn said, "but you may take the dagger."

Lucius nodded and then felt a sadness come over him as he looked upon the pony's lifeless body.

Weylyn put his hand upon his shoulder and sighed. "Do not worry for him. He knew what he was doing when he took you there. It was destined." Weylyn looked up at the sky. "It is midday. Your family will be worried for you. Come. We may return now."

Together they walked back, passing through the shielding mist that had formed as if to protect the isle from the ceremony that had been performed, from the blood that had been shed.

When they stepped onto the green grass of the fields once more, with Wearyall Hill rising up to their left, Weylyn finally asked what had been on his mind.

"Whom did you visit last night?"

"Serenus Crescens."

"I see," Weylyn said calmly. "And has your thirst for vengeance been fulfilled?"

Lucius did not answer immediately, but both of them knew the answer to the question.

Weylyn felt an uneasiness in his gut then, for he knew that this was just the beginning. He had travelled such a road before, long ago, and so had his son after him. *Now, it is the Dragon's turn.*

Neither of them spoke again on their walk back.

When the door of the guest house opened, Lucius found Adara sitting by herself before the hearth. He closed the door behind him, Weylyn having gone to see Etain and Gilmore.

Adara did not turn when she heard him enter, but the tone of her voice was full of fear and anger.

"What have you done?"

Lucius did not speak right away, but went and sat down on the stool beside her to stare at the flames in the hearth instead of her eyes. He knew she wept, that she would not understand.

"Answer me, Lucius. What did you do last night? I heard Father

Gilmore shouting at Etain about us, saying that we cannot stay here any longer." Adara 's eyes then turned to Lucius and, despite the anger and rage he had felt, was feeling still, it broke his heart to see her so desperately sad and worried.

He reached for her hand, but she withdrew it, her hands wringing each other in her lap. "Weylyn had to purify me."

"Why?"

He could feel his patience at an end. He was tired, and full of pain again and, when he thought about it, he felt his actions had been justified. Lucius stood and looked down at his wife.

"I went to the villa of Serenus Crescens," he said, his voice as cold and hard as the edge of a gladius blade. "I killed him. I drove my blade into his body over and over. I killed that viper, Nolan Phelan too. He was visiting at the time."

Adara's face was buried in her hands, her body shuddering with silent sobs.

"I burned their home to the ground about them. All of it. From the darkness, I listened to the screams and watched as his wicked wife fell from the upper storey to break her neck on the ground below."

Adara looked up then, rivulets wetting her cheeks. She barely recognized Lucius in that moment, the contorted and burned features, the cold, removed look of a murderer in his eyes. She tried to see the face of the brave, wounded beast that he was, but all she saw were the eyes of a killer, and those eyes terrified her as much as Claudius Picus' ever had.

"How could you do this? By the Gods, Lucius! You were so much better than that!"

"They deserved it!" he said without reservation. "Crescens, along with his son and Claudius Picus, watched me burn! They came to our home to kill you and our children. They burned our world, and they killed our unborn child!!!"

Lucius' shouts exploded from within the guest house, and beneath the arms of the great oak outside, Phoebus and Calliope sat with Rachel and Aaron, weeping to hear their parents' shouts, their father's rage and anger made clear in that one-time place of peace.

Lucius continued now, kneeling before his wife, wanting her to understand. "You and our children are everything to me! How could I let them live?"

"We had a chance for a new beginning!" Adara said. "A new life!

And now that you've done this thing, this murder, you've pushed us back into their world. I was finding happiness again, Lucius. Here, in this blessed place. And you've taken that away from me, damn you!"

Adara stood abruptly, pushed him aside, and fled from the small domus.

When the children saw their mother emerge from the guest house, Calliope stood and ran after her.

Phoebus sat staring at the guest house, Rachel holding his hand and speaking soothing words to him as he imagined his father within those stone walls, brooding like a dragon trapped within a cave.

"At least he is back," Phoebus said softly.

"I don't think Father Gilmore will allow you to stay now, Phoebus," Aaron said, a great sadness in his voice. "I will try and speak to him."

"We both will," Rachel added.

Weylyn, Etain, and Father Gilmore stood in conference upon the back of Wearyall Hill, beside the gentle tree that Joseph of Arimathea had planted so many years ago. They had wanted to be out of earshot of everyone else in the isle, and that was perhaps the quietest place, a place sacred to all of them.

When Weylyn finally found Etain, Gilmore was already making his case against the Metelli, for their expulsion from Ynis Wytrin.

As he spoke, Gilmore paced back and forth before the flowering hawthorn as Etain and Weylyn listened with patience to his pleas.

"The Isle of the Blessed is sacred to all of us. To this entire land and every Briton who draws breath. And the Roman has soiled it with his violence and blasphemy! They cannot stay here any longer."

"You speak out of fear, my friend," Weylyn said. "You worry for your charges, for Rachel and Aaron. But the dragon is no threat to them. Their safety, and the safety of what they represent, would be protected by him and his children."

"I thought you were more intelligent than that, Weylyn. Can you not see? He is a menace. He is even turning on his own family. He won't be happy until waves of blood wash upon these sacred shores."

"Don't be ridiculous!" Weylyn said, waving his arm angrily. He had had quite enough of Gilmore's sanctimonious talk. "The Gods have blessed Lucius Metellus Anguis…he is one of them!"

"There is only one God! And it is not Apollo or Lucius Metellus Anguis!" Gilmore growled.

"Enough." Etain's voice was calm, but she knew she had to stop the argument. "Lucius is a good man, and discovering the truth about oneself is never an easy thing. He has yet to understand and fully deal with that truth." She turned to Gilmore. "Even the Christus disappeared for a long time to come to terms with the sacrifice he had to make, the mission he had to undertake. Did he not?"

"He did," Gilmore said, straightening his robes as the wind picked up.

"The Dragon, though he has suffered great loss and pain, though he has burned in the fires, has not yet come to terms with his truth. He sought to better this world and to help us, and for that he was made to suffer. Is that not worthy of thanks? Should we turn our backs upon him for feeling angry at all that he has lost?"

"Serenus Crescens and the ordo of Lindinis would have overrun Ynis Wytrin if not for Lucius," Weylyn said. "He has already saved Rachel and Aaron. All of us."

Gilmore was silent. He thought of Phoebus and Calliope, of how much Rachel and Aaron loved them, how their young hearts had been open to them from the moment they met. He had always tried to see what they saw in people, in the world about them, but the goodness in the Metelli was perhaps the most difficult to see.

"I will not expel the Metelli from Ynis Wytrin," Etain said.

Weylyn breathed easily in that moment, glad of her decision.

"But-" Gilmore began, but Etain reached out to take his hand.

"Nor will I prevent them from leaving. The Dragon and his family are welcome here whenever they so chose. They are now a part of this place as much as you or I, for in saving it, they have made it their home."

"And what of the blood upon his hands?" Gilmore asked. "That stain can never be washed away."

"The men who fight for more than just themselves always have blood upon their hands," Weylyn said, his knowledge of blood more intimate than Gilmore could ever understand. "It is their curse to come to terms with those stains in the aftermath."

"Lucius Metellus Anguis will make his own decisions," Etain said, "and I have made mine. He may stay, or he may go. Ynis Wytrin will always be a place where dragons are welcome."

Gilmore nodded reluctantly. "As you wish, my friend," he said to her. Gilmore touched the tree one more time and then turned to go down the hill toward the chapel.

The air was growing cool, with a breeze rushing in from the distant sea as the sun began to dip in the West.

As he walked down the slope of Wearyall Hill, Gilmore saw Rachel and Aaron walking briskly toward him. When they reached him, he stopped and held out his hands to them.

The children took his hands and walked with him.

"You know what has happened, children?"

"Yes," Aaron said. "The Roman has killed a man."

"He has killed many men in his life. This time, he murdered a man."

"A wicked man?" Rachel asked.

"Does it matter?" Gilmore asked. "Only God may take a life."

"Perhaps other gods have different rules for men?" Aaron said.

Gilmore stopped walking and turned to his young charges. "How can you say that? You, of all people, know there is only one, true God."

"Yes, Father Gilmore," Aaron said. "But we also remember all that you have taught us about compassion and understanding."

"You taught us about helping others, even our enemies, in their time of need. That we should love them," Rachel added.

"I did, yes," Gilmore acknowledged.

"The Metelli are not our enemies," Aaron said. "They are our friends."

Gilmore, humbled once more by his two charges, began to walk again with Etain's voice and wisdom in his head. "They are. That is why they are not being expelled from Ynis Wytrin."

The children smiled, and he felt their hands grip his more tightly as they walked.

From the top of the hill, Etain and Weylyn watched as Gilmore, Rachel and Aaron walked back to the chapel.

"His anger is assuaged for now," Weylyn said to her.

"It is," Etain answered. "But we must acknowledge his worries. Those children are his own family, and he has caught a glimpse of a man who has almost lost everything. Gilmore is not immune to fear, and neither are we."

"Will the Dragon remain here?" Weylyn asked. "What have you seen?"

"The end is too far distant for my sight," she said. "And only Lucius himself can see the road ahead."

"The road is never what one expects," Weylyn said, smiling sadly.

"No. It is not."

It was nearly dark, and the night was calm and clear like the Middle Sea in summer, a shade of deep indigo pocked with stars that whirled in the heavens.

Lucius lay upon his back at the top of the Tor, wrapped in his cloak and looking up. He had wanted to sleep that evening, but after his conversation with Adara, sleep had eluded him.

He wondered how many more times he would have the opportunity to sit in that place and allow his mind to drift.

Could we have made a new life in this place? Lucius thought as he looked up at the sky. "Father... You are the God of Prophecy, and yet the future is barred from your own son's sight..." Lucius stopped himself abruptly. He had told himself he would not speak with the Far Shooter. His anger was focussed on other faces in his mind.

He sat up and cocked his head at a sound from behind him. He was alone, but the air shimmered strangely in a spot at the top of the Tor. Lucius stood and stared.

A circular space of light began to form, as if a pool of water was laid before a dim sun.

He looked upon it and felt that if he were to walk through it, his pain would fade away and his anger would dissipate and be forgotten.

But something held Lucius back.

His mind raced over the previous night. He had finally killed one of his great enemies. Crescens had caused his family much pain, or so he had thought. The act had brought a fleeting moment of satisfaction, but not an end. As Crescens had begged for his life, the doubt had begun, even as the blade had plunged into his flesh, over and over again.

"I know that look, Dragon," a voice said from the other side of the light.

Lucius stepped back, almost falling down the steep slope of the Tor, but he caught himself. He watched as the light shifted and shimmered, and then someone emerged from it. "You?"

The Boar of the Selgovae stood before Lucius. He appeared strong and vibrant, and his smile was easy as he walked just three paces toward Lucius, unable to distance himself too much from the light at his back.

Lucius shook his head and rubbed his eyes with his rough-skinned hands.

The Boar still stood there, and laughed. "You're not dreaming, Dragon."

"What are you doing here?" Lucius stepped closer, the light from the Boar illuminating his face more.

The Boar looked upon him and his smile faded. "You are still wounded, I see."

"It was fire," Lucius said, his eyes closing.

"Hmm. Fire. The realm of dragons…"

Lucius opened his eyes again. "What do you want?"

"To help a friend. I sensed it when blood was brought into the Isle of the Blessed, so near to the gates of Annwn."

"That is Annwn?" Lucius pointed to the light.

"Of course. You remember it?"

"I will never forget it." Lucius sighed. "I remember how you helped me to come back here."

"Do you regret it?"

The answer might have been easy once, but now, Lucius was not so certain. "In part. So much has happened…"

"I think the pain you are feeling stems not so much from the burning you endured."

"You have no idea!"

"Perhaps," the Boar said, "but have you ever recovered from the wounding truth you learned in Annwn from the lips of the Gods themselves?"

Lucius was silent.

"I envy you that truth. What one could have done with that knowledge!" The Boar had a wistful look in his eyes as he spoke the words, shaking his head in wonder. "You can do anything."

"I am not a god."

"Not entirely. But a part of you is. Have you thought about what that means?"

"All I have thought about is vengeance upon my enemies."

"I know." The Boar tried to reach out to touch Lucius' shoulder, but he stopped short. "Believe me, Dragon. I know what it is to seek the death of one's enemies. I bathed in rivers of their blood, but it was not until I met you, and felt true compassion and understanding that I understood the length of that rocky road." He shook his head.

"What are you saying?"

"I only speak of the truths I discovered for myself. You have your own to discover. What I am saying is that not all truths are to be found beneath the blood of one's enemies. You can wipe it away without end, but the full meaning will always be hidden."

"They must pay. *He* must pay."

The Boar nodded. "I understand. And so it seems that you must go on a long hunt."

Lucius nodded, but he could not speak.

"You must slay the great beast to feel it is done...to start anew."

"Yes," Lucius said. "It is the only way now."

"I look forward to hearing about it," the Boar said with a hint of sadness in his heart. He then looked back at the light were it began to shimmer again and grow a little fainter. "You know...you're a hero there. It is a place where the Dragon would be welcome. You could be a lord of Annwn!"

Lucius looked at the bright gateway and found that a part of him was tempted to walk through, to stop the pain of the world in which he found himself, to stop the torment he was heaping upon those he loved.

"I can't. I'm not finished. I can't leave them."

"Of course. The hunt." The Boar turned to go back the way he had come, but turned one more time to Lucius. "We all have to leave. The manner of that leaving, and what we do after it, is each man's decision." He smiled and placed his fist over his heart. "Be strong, Dragon."

A moment later, it was dark again.

Lucius stared at the spot where the Boar had emerged and it was as if nothing had happened. He looked around and found the world a bit clearer, even in the darkness.

He decided then and there that he did not regret killing Serenus Crescens. *He deserved it.* But he knew that the satisfaction he felt was false. *I'm not finished,* he thought, deciding in that moment to step onto that long road to see where it would lead.

"It is time to leave Ynis Wytrin..." Lucius said as he took the path down the back of the Tor.

.   .   .

It had been a difficult night for Adara, for her dreams had rippled with sadness and worry, like a still lake into which pebbles had been repeatedly tossed. Only at the time of deepest dark, her exhaustion had overtaken her and she had found a measure of peace in all the worry, a place to lie down in her mind.

But when the cock crowed in the misty morning, she found herself unwilling to rise. She was tired and scared of what the day would bring, of looking her husband in the face, a face she no longer recognized. And so she held her eyes shut for as long as she could.

However, Lucius' voice crept into her forced reverie and she turned to see him sitting upon a stool beside her bed.

"Adara?" his voice said, low and broken, no longer soft and melodious as it had been before the burning. "My love?"

They were the words she had longed for since he had come out of his endless sleep, and there was indeed love behind them. Her eyes opened wider and she looked upon him, sitting there with the hood of his cloak back, his head and face bared.

"What is it? Are you unwell?" she asked.

"I'm sorry. I did not mean to hurt or scare you yesterday."

She was confused, for he had been so adamant about what he had done, so certain. Now, it seemed, there was some understanding behind his eyes. "You frightened us, Lucius. We didn't know what had become of you."

"I know. And I know that I have threatened our life in this sacred place. It's just that... Are we finished with the world outside yet? I am not, but if you are, if you say to me that you are finished with thoughts of our family far away, and that you are ready to stay here forevermore with our children, then I will understand..."

"You can't place such a decision upon my shoulders, Lucius. It's not fair." Even as she said the words, Adara was already imagining seeing her mother and father again, one last time perhaps, of feeling the sun upon her face and swimming in a turquoise sea. "What are you saying?"

"I can't regret what I did. I don't. But I do regret what I have done to you. If you want to, we can make our way to our family. Since that letter, I can't help but think that they need us."

"It's too dangerous. They'll be looking for you. For us. You were attacked nearby. What's to say they won't be looking for you elsewhere?"

"I know. But no matter where we go, nor where we hide, some things we can't escape. I can't stay here any longer, Adara."

She felt fear creep in upon her once more as she looked up at Lucius, for there was a different man behind those eyes. She knew, however, that he would never feel still or whole if his mind was constantly longing for something else, for somewhere else. She thought of seeing her mother and father again, of holding them tightly and watching them with Phoebus and Calliope.

Adara found herself nodding even before she decided. "Yes," she said. "We will go." *And perhaps the thirst for vengeance and all the painful memories of this land will fade away if we leave it?* It was a hope she began to nurture inside from that moment. "But how will we get out of Britannia?"

"I have an idea."

It was late morning when Lucius walked up to the roundhouse to find Dagon sitting outside with Antiope upon his knee before a small fire. He stopped to watch them from a short distance away. He remembered the peace he had been given when his own children were small, when they had had those years in Etruria together.

That time had perhaps been the happiest of his life, a time when their family had been together. He had been young and strong...and whole. Life had pulsed with a vibrance he had never before felt upon that ancestral land, and there had been great hope for the future, his and that of his children.

Sadly, even then, a part of him had longed for war, to lead men into blood and chaos, to hear his name chanted by thousands. The poison of hubris had crept into his veins then, so long ago, and he had not had the acuity to see it.

He watched Dagon, one of the greatest warriors he had ever fought alongside, hold his daughter, kiss her cheek as she giggled, laugh together, share precious moments that, to Lucius, seemed far out of reach.

You don't have to go from this place, Lucius.

He felt the warm touch upon his shoulder, and the voice of a soft melody singing in his ears as she spoke.

Lucius looked up, and found himself standing beneath the limbs of an olive tree, not in Ynis Wytrin, but in a place of sunlight and warmth, with the gentle lapping upon a pebbled beach in the background.

Venus stood before him, her eyes full of love, of kindness and of worry.

Before, Lucius had fallen to his knees whenever she had appeared to him, awed by Love's presence. Now, however, he stood before her, angry and ashamed of what he had become, but determined not to be swayed from his chosen course.

"I do have to leave, lady," Lucius whispered. "I am not wanted here."

You have no idea, do you? These people need you, and your family. Your family has a destiny here in this land. You cannot walk away from it.

"I did not stay on Olympus with you and my father for a reason," Lucius said. "I must finish what I came back to do."

You came back to this life of pain for love, Lucius, not vengeance. The goddess' voice shuddered then, and a golden tear fell from her eye. *Think of your wife and children. Honour yourself and who you are!*

"Myself?" Lucius laughed bitterly. "A cursed son of Apollo? Not even he cared to visit me here, did he?"

He cares more than you can imagine. He always has, young one.

"Then why did he lie to me the whole of my life? Where was he when my sister was slain? Why did he not protect me when I bled to death upon the green grass of Annwn? Where was he when the fires consumed my body and left me looking like this?" he shouted.

Venus remained still and her hand reached up to touch the side of Lucius' burned face.

He felt his anger calm for a moment, regret creeping upon him for having yelled, but it was only momentary.

Love withdrew her hand when she saw him so resolute, despite her attempts. *You forget all of the times he was there for you, guiding you, giving you the strength you needed in battle, and as you walked the corridors of the blessed life you have led. You forget how he tried guide you away from danger, and how you ignored him, just as you ignore me now.*

Lucius crossed his arms and stared into the goddess' star-whirling eyes. "I know what I need to do, and if my divine father wishes to say something to me, he may seek me out."

For the first time in an age, Love felt herself turn cold, for as she looked into Lucius' eyes - a man she had watched over since the day they met on the banks of the Tiber, long ago when he was a child - she saw only the defiant and grim determination of a man who is torn between worlds, his soul shattered by experience. She knew that Lucius had yet to learn who he was, and what that meant.

I wish you had remained here with us, Venus said, the song of her voice more melancholy than Lucius had ever believed possible. She looked at the olive tree that shaded them beneath the sun, the sea beyond, and the slopes of Olympus above them. *Perhaps, one day, when you have discovered your own truth...*

"It is the truth that has set me upon this path!" Lucius snapped.

Love was gone, and Lucius was back in Ynis Wytrin, beneath the limbs of the apple tree, watching Dagon and his daughter play before him.

"Anguis!" Dagon waved the moment he saw him, setting Antiope down and walking over to him.

Lucius stepped forward to meet them.

"Are you all right, Anguis?" Dagon said. "You had everyone worried!" There was anger in his voice.

Lucius waved it off. "Are you and Briana still going to Dumnonia to see Einion?"

"We were thinking about it. Why?"

"We're coming with you."

"What?"

"We're leaving Ynis Wytrin."

VI

IPSEM EXSILIUM

'Exile of the Self'

"Antiope, can you go and help your mama inside?" Dagon said to his daughter, not taking his eyes from Lucius.

"Yes," the girl said, releasing Dagon's hand and running back to the roundhouse where she disappeared into the darkness of the doorway.

"What are you talking about, Lucius? Leave Ynis Wytrin? This is the safest place for all of us."

Immediately, Lucius could sense, see, the familiar fear of loss in Dagon's eyes. He had had that same fear many times before. It was a fear not of losing one's own life, but of losing those one loved, or of leaving them behind, adrift without protection from the world. That fear stifled action when action was needed.

Lucius knew, however, that the action he needed to undertake did not, could not, involve Dagon. Their paths had led across the grassy plains of life in parallel for many years, but the time of their separation was, perhaps, approaching.

"Can we sit down, my friend?" Lucius asked.

"Of course," Dagon motioned to the logs by the fire and they sat. He stoked the fire with an iron bar and waited for Lucius to speak. "Tell me what happened," he said, looking back at the house to make sure Antiope was not listening. "Where did you go last night?"

There was a definite edge in Dagon's voice. He had kept Lucius safe when they had visited the hillfort just a short while ago, and then Lucius had gone off by himself, at night.

Lucius saw that Dagon would not look at him at first, but stared into the fire which he poked and prodded.

"I went to the villa of Serenus Crescens."

Dagon looked up. "Why?"

"To kill him."

Dagon felt his heart sink. To kill a man, to kill hundreds, in battle was one thing, but to murder a man in the dark of night...there was no honour in that. "And did you?"

"Yes," Lucius answered quickly, clinging to the rightness of the act he had performed, forcing himself to see the flames that had consumed him while Crescens watched, likening them to the flames that had burned away Crescens' villa. "I looked him in the eye and killed him, as well as that other ordo member, Nolan Phelan."

"I don't know who that is," Dagon answered.

"He was just as terrible." Lucius stood and walked around to the other side of the fire opposite Dagon. "I burned their entire home to the ground, and I watched it burn." He did not mention seeing Sabina Cresca's body falling to the ground.

"Why didn't you ask for me to come with you?" Dagon stood to face Lucius. "You took a great risk leaving here at night. How did you get out?"

"I took the white pony." Lucius pulled the cowl closer about his head and face. "I knew you would try to stop me. I had to do it."

"The man already lost his son. Did he not suffer enough for his crimes?"

"No."

Dagon rounded the fire and came to stand before his friend. "Lucius. I'm afraid. This isn't you. This isn't the Dragon we followed."

Lucius stared at him, but he could not find the words to explain fully, could not find the will to make Dagon see what was so clear to him.

Dagon rubbed his beard. "But why do you have to leave Ynis Wytrin?"

"We have to. We're not wanted here anymore. Father Gilmore-"

"Father Gilmore is stubborn, but he is a good man," Dagon said. "He will listen to Etain and Weylyn."

Lucius shook his head. "Not this time."

"All right. Let me rephrase the question... Why do you *want* to leave Ynis Wytrin?"

"There are things I have to do."

"What?"

"Are you going to be insubordinate now?" Lucius asked, annoyed at being questioned.

"Insubordinate?" Dagon looked around and shook his head. "Lucius, in case you haven't noticed, the Ala III Britannorum is no more. The dragons are dead or cast to the winds. My people are no more. Don't pull rank on me. I'm your friend. Now tell me what you plan to do!" Dagon's voice was raised now, the sound of tenderness and friendship, of understanding, swallowed up with fear, impatience and frustration.

Briana's form appeared in the doorway to watch the two men, but she said nothing. *How has it come to this?*

Lucius looked Dagon in the eyes. "I want to find out what has happened to my family, and then I'm going to kill the man responsible for all our suffering. Only then will I feel any sort of peace."

Dagon reached up to hold Lucius by the shoulders, though he feared to do so. "Anguis...my friend...don't do this. You will never get to him. If you need to blame someone, blame me for not being there for you...or for Barta. Do you think you're the only one who is tortured day and night with thoughts of failure?"

"You have no idea. You live at peace here, whole in body and mind with your wife and child in your arms-"

"And you have your wife and children!" Dagon snapped. "Do not, by all the Gods, hold it against me that our child survived!"

Lucius stepped back, his breathing ragged, his eyes looking for a way out, like an angry, cornered animal.

Dagon softened his voice. "I'm sorry... I... I understand how being in this place can be both a blessing and a torment for men like us...for you...but I beg you, Lucius, if you want to keep your family safe, take a different path to the one you are gazing down."

Lucius breathed deeply and looked about them at the trees, the birds flitting from branch to branch, the sound of animals and their children playing somewhere beyond the orchard. He calmed himself before speaking again. "I will think about what you've said."

"That is all I ask," Dagon answered. He knew that he could not be sure of what Lucius said now. He was a changed man, a man full of bitterness and anger, and though he tried to understand, it frightened him.

"You and Briana spoke of perhaps going to Dumnonia. Are you still considering it?"

Dagon looked back at the house and saw Briana standing there. He waved her over. "Yes. We would like to go, but have been wondering how best to travel there. The ports will be watched, and we don't know any trustworthy sea captains who would take us."

"They'll be watching every major port for you, Lucius, and for Dagon and his countrymen," Briana added. "I want to see my brother more than anything, but I don't know how it would be possible to do so safely."

"Lucius Metellus Anguis is dead," he said, looking at Briana. "And so is the man who helped Claudius Picus kill him." Lucius shook his head. "No one will be looking for us, or you. We'll travel by road to Isca Dumnoniorum, and then over the moors to Einion." He turned to Dagon. "The route we took before."

"It might work," Dagon said.

"What if it doesn't?" Briana added. "Perhaps Einion could come here?"

"I need to leave, Briana," Lucius said to her. He saw the sadness in her eyes, that brave Briton who had come to his aid in Caledonia so long ago with her brother, who had saved his life and the lives of his wife and children. It would hurt just as much to leave her as it would Dagon, but he could see little choice in the matter.

"Adara told us about the letter from Graecia and what it said." Briana nodded slowly. "I'll ask Etain if she sees any danger upon the road for us if we go to Einion."

Dagon looked at Lucius and felt the fear acutely then, not for himself, but for his friend. He could see Lucius' mind was set and wondered in that moment if vengeance was the only thing that could bring Lucius back to himself. He knew he did not understand Lucius now, nor the burden of his true identity. *He is lead by a daemon that I cannot comprehend.* "Then it's settled. We'll travel to Dumnonia together." *And we will see what dragons dwell there now…*

"I will make preparations," Lucius said.

"So soon?" Briana looked around.

"Why wait?" Lucius added as he began to walk away. "Besides…we don't have much time here now…"

Briana and Dagon watched him as he left, crossing the grass toward the apple orchard, his black form disappearing among the lithe trunks and flowing branches.

"What does he mean?" Briana asked.

Dagon looked at her. "I'll tell you later," Dagon said as he spotted

Antiope running toward them from inside the roundhouse. He gathered his daughter up in his arms and held her tightly. "My concern is that you both are safe. That's all that matters," he said as he kissed his wife and daughter.

The prospect of leaving Ynis Wytrin left Lucius feeling confused and a little empty. He felt confined there now, restless and uneasy, especially as he pondered what he needed to do, where he needed to go. He was not the warrior he had been before. He was still healing, he knew, and it angered him without end. But what angered him even more was that the one man responsible for all their pain was still out there, unaccountable for the suffering and death that he had caused.

Son of a god... What good has that done me!

"Are you truly leaving?" a soft voice said from the end of the orchard.

Lucius looked up and saw Etain standing there, alone, waiting for him while she watched the children playing with the animals in the pens.

"Forgive me..." Lucius said, feeling awkward. "I did not see you there, lady."

"You were not expecting me." Etain smiled and reached out to take Lucius' arm. There was no fear in her eyes, nor discomfort in her voice.

Lucius was constantly amazed by the strength exhibited by the head priestess of Ynis Wytrin, her tenderness and ability to understand.

"I am sorry for frightening the priestesses," Lucius said, remembering the cries when he had appeared bloody upon the sacred grounds.

Etain nodded and laced her arm through his as they walked together. "The act, and this place, have been purified," she said. "Weylyn knows the ritual well."

"He does."

"He also understands the hunger for vengeance."

Lucius did not answer.

Etain stopped and turned to face Lucius. "I know what drives you at this moment. I also know that it blinds you. No, please...do not leave," she said, holding his hand. "I also know that sometimes we can only fumble in the dark before we find what we are looking for."

"I know Father Gilmore does not want us here anymore. Adara heard him speaking with you."

"Gilmore is a good man, a trusted friend and advisor, and protector of those children over there." She looked toward Rachel and Aaron who laughed with Lucius' own children. "But he cannot force you to do anything."

"I must go," Lucius said.

"I know," Etain answered.

Lucius looked at the priestess directly and her bright eyes stared back at him.

"When you leave, you must carry it with you in your heart that you and your family are always welcome here, that you will always have a home here. Promise me that, Lucius Metellus Anguis."

Lucius nodded, unable to say anything.

"And though you perhaps feel unworthy of it, know that this land needs all of you."

He looked at her, confusion written upon his face, but he said nothing as she smiled back at him.

"I will ask the priests and priestesses to prepare a wagon to take both your families to Dumnonia," she said. "Einion will be happy to see all of you."

Lucius watched Etain go and wondered at her skills with the sight. When she was gone, he turned to watch his children playing with Gilmore's charges. He felt a new guilt creeping upon him as his son stopped to smile at him, but it was not enough to deter him from the course of action he had already decided upon.

Phoebus stopped running with the lambs with the other children to wave at his father whom he had seen speaking with the priestess, Etain. He had been worried earlier when they heard his parents arguing. He had not been able to stop thinking about it. Thankfully, Rachel and Aaron always found a way of making him and Calliope feel better about the world, a way of helping them to find joy in even the smallest of things, things like the soft coat of a mewing lamb.

He had had another dream that night about killing the boy back at the hillfort. It had been very real, the feeling of the sword plunging into his gut, the scrape of the blade against bone.

Calliope had awoken to comfort him in the night, as she always did, by humming the song their aunt had sung to them as children.

Phoebus envied his sister her memories of their aunt, and wondered at how Calliope was able to remember such things as they were only babies when she was slain.

As they broke their fast, Calliope mentioned that she thought they might leave Ynis Wytrin, that their father was restless and needed to travel a long road.

When Phoebus asked her what she meant, she only said that she had been seeing their family leaving for a time and that they should be prepared to go. But Phoebus was not sure he wanted to go. *It is so much safer here, and the world...is a cruel place...* he told himself. *I have killed a man, and I don't want to have to do it again.*

"Phoebus?" Rachel's voice brought him around. "Are you all right?" she asked, taking his hand in hers and squeezing.

Phoebus looked back at the young girl, her long dark hair and large, brown eyes, and smiled sadly. "Just thinking."

"About what?" Rachel asked.

"I don't want to leave here."

The girl's eyes grew watery, but she did not cry. *Father Gilmore tells us not to cry.* "I don't want you to leave either," she said. "But if you have to, we will be waiting for you."

"That's right!" Aaron said as he and Calliope joined them. "Just remember..." he said, breathless from running, however serious his voice was in that moment. "We will meet again. Your parents are to be cherished. They have not abandoned you...as ours have..."

Rachel touched her brother's shoulder, and he smiled.

"The greatest gift you can give to them," Rachel continued, "is forgiveness and love. Your father especially needs it."

Phoebus smiled, and felt strength again. He squeezed Rachel's hand tightly and together they ran among the lambs and goats with Aaron and Calliope, their laughter pushing back any darkness that may have crept in upon the isle.

The next morning, after Adara and Calliope helped Lucius spread the resinous ointment over his wounds and applied fresh bandages, they sat down as a family to a light meal of fresh bread, cheese and honey.

Adara looked across at Lucius. "Your skin is healing faster, it seems."

Lucius nodded. "Yes, though it is extremely itchy, and I don't yet have feeling everywhere." He stared at the table as he ran his hand over his face and short, patchy hair.

"I still see you, Baba," Calliope said, placing a hand upon his arm and smiling.

Lucius smiled back at her. *I would slay the world to keep you all safe.*

Calliope frowned a little, as if she heard the thought, but then continued eating.

Adara looked at Lucius and nodded. It was time to tell them. After Lucius had told her, she had been up all night thinking about the impending journey that had come about as a result of their near exile from Ynis Wytrin. A part of her was reluctant to leave, for she knew the great danger they were placing themselves in. However, another part of her longed to see her family, to feel the life-giving heat and see the brilliance of the colours of Graecia. She had been torn thinking about it, but in the end, Lucius' actions had all but guaranteed that they would have to go.

Lucius cleared his throat. "There is something we need to discuss."

"We're leaving Ynis Wytrin, aren't we?" Phoebus said. He looked up from his food which he had barely touched.

Lucius looked back at his son. "Yes. We are."

"I don't want to leave," Phoebus answered. "I want to stay. It's safe and we have friends here."

"We cannot stay here any longer, Phoebus," Adara said softly.

"Because Baba killed someone?"

"Where did you learn that?" Lucius asked, sadly. He had hoped to keep it from his children.

"I'm not stupid. You didn't come home the other night. And then I heard Father Gilmore arguing with Etain and Weylyn. You're the reason we have to leave."

Lucius did not know if the children would ever forgive him for making them leave, at least Phoebus would not. But when he looked at Calliope, he knew that it was something else haunting her thoughts. *Did she see me kill Crescens?* He hoped not.

Adara spoke up, reaching out to her son. "Listen Phoebus... I know it is scary, leaving this place. You had hoped to grow up here, with your friends, to be safe. But we have not heard from avia Antonia in a long time, nor have you seen avia Delphina and avus Publius since you were very small. Would you not like to see them all again and make sure they are safe?"

"People aren't trying to kill them though, are they?" Phoebus stood up and his stool fell backward to clatter on the floor. "They're trying to kill *us*, and the moment we leave this place, they'll have their chance."

"They won't remember us, Phoebus," Lucius said. "And our enemies think I'm dead."

"Like the man at the hillfort who was waiting for you?" Phoebus snapped. "Or Serenus Crescens?"

"He cannot harm us anymore," Lucius said.

"But there are others, aren't there? When will it end, Baba?"

"I will do all that I can to keep you safe," Lucius said.

"Safe?" Phoebus laughed. "When were we ever safe? As babies in Numidia when amita Alene died on top of us? On the road here in Britannia surrounded by the liars of the empress' court? We weren't even safe from *you* in Caledonia!"

"Phoebus, that's enough!" Adara cried.

"Why, Mama? If even a son of Apollo can't keep us safe, especially from himself, what hope is there?"

"There is always hope, Phoebus," Calliope said, reaching out to touch her brother's arm.

But he pulled back. "I'm not leaving here! You'll have to go without me!" he shouted.

"Why?" Lucius asked. "So that you can become a Christian acolyte of Father Gilmore's? By the Gods, you will not! You're coming."

"To Hades with you!" Phoebus shouted. "Why couldn't you have just died!!!" And with that, he stormed out the door, slamming it loudly behind him so that the morning peace of Ynis Wytrin was broken.

"I'll go after him," Calliope said. She got up to go and stopped at the door to look back at her parents. "He doesn't mean what he said, Baba. It's just that he thinks about the boy he killed, all the time. He doesn't want to have to do it again."

I will do it for him, Lucius thought as the door closed and Calliope went after Phoebus.

"Are you sure you want to do this?" Adara asked as she gathered the clay plates and set them on the table beside the covered swords. Her fingers reached out to linger on the hilt of her own sword, but she withdrew it. "Will we take these?" she asked as she looked at the row of blades.

"We will take most of our possessions since we don't know how long it will be before we return," Lucius said.

"If we return," Adara added, staring at Lucius.

"If."

"Lucius..." she was about to speak, but she stopped herself.

"What is it, Adara?"

"I feel like I'm losing you, like you're slipping away from me. I don't know what the Gods have told you...what they've shown you...but if I trust you in this, trust you with our children's lives, and anything happens to them..." Her once-bright, green eyes focussed on him intensely. "If something happens to them, you will never see me again."

As Lucius looked upon her, he knew she meant it with all her being. He could not believe they had come so far, only to have their unified hearts torn asunder. *My enemies have even taken my family's love from me!* He walked over to Adara to stand before her. Once he would have held her fast in his arms...kissed her...reassured her of his love for her, but something had changed in her, and her heart was shelved where he could not reach it. "Nothing will happen to them, or to you. I'll make sure of that."

"Then we had better start packing."

Later that afternoon, Dagon came to see Lucius. They sat together at the top of Wearyall Hill, beneath the lithe branches of the Holy Thorn, looking out at the verdant green world of Ynis Wytrin.

"Briana is excited to go to Dumnonia," Dagon said. "She was missing Einion very much."

"They've always been close," Lucius said, but his voice was sad.

Dagon plucked a few blades of grass and rubbed them between his fingers as he stared at the ground. "Adara and the children are angry with you?"

"I don't know anymore. I only ever wanted to keep them safe, but then it seems I've only ever done the opposite."

"That's not true, my friend. Even as you were near death, you rode to their aid. I don't want to think of what would have happened to Adara and the children if you hadn't stopped Claudius Picus."

"I'm losing my family, Dagon," Lucius said, his voice full of regret and anger, but mostly of sadness and despair. "I've done so much in this life, but to what end? What good is it all if I lose that which I cherish most? I can make do with this burned corpse I now inhabit, but only if I have their love. If I don't, what is the point?"

Dagon looked out at the misty levels around Ynis Wytrin and remembered similar thoughts from his uncle. "Mar used to despair at times. When I was young and our entire family had been slain, I remember him praying aloud to the Gods, asking them what the purpose of all the loss and suffering was. A part of him wanted to die, to end it all... I knew that at times, it was only my existence that kept him going, me, his sister's son. But it was also some deep belief he held in his role in the world. He told me once, when I asked him, that he did not know what his purpose in this life was beyond being a symbol of a dying nation. He said that he had come to believe that in the great story of the world, his life, whatever it may entail, was a piece of that story and that it was his duty to see it to its completion. He believed he had to live his part, even though he did not know the end to which he contributed."

"He was a wise man, your uncle. But what are you getting at, Dagon?"

"I'm not entirely sure, but what I do know is that we all have some role to play in the great story of this world, whether as god, man, or even beast. You may believe in a specific role for yourself, Anguis, but what if you're wrong about it? What if it's much simpler than the role you've placed upon yourself? You were not meant to be emperor, but perhaps you're not meant to be avenger either?"

"Then what am I? A cripple? A failure?"

"To all of us, you are *the* Dragon. But what really matters is what you are to yourself. If you don't know perhaps, like my uncle, you just need to have faith that you're fulfilling your role simply by living. Let the story play itself out."

"You've become philosophical in your parenthood," Lucius joked.

But Dagon did not smile. "It has made me think of many things."

The time for their departure arrived, and the preparations to leave for Dumnonia were complete, each of them having finished their tasks before leaving the next morning. It felt as if there was a certain finality to every action. The Metelli had spent so long in Ynis Wytrin, each with a different experience, each having travelled that experience with a different set of emotions, that it felt once again like they were quitting their home.

Rather than leaving of their own free will, Phoebus and Calliope felt as though they were being forced to leave.

As for Adara, the last couple of weeks, all she had been focussed on was seeing her parents once again and confirming that they were indeed safe.

For Lucius, he knew it was he who was leaving the isle, that sacred place where he had come back into the world, born of pain. It was a pain that he still felt acutely, deeply, and which he sought to resolve, once and for all, no matter how long it took. And now he stood on the threshold of that journey as he looked down at the few possessions his family had left to them - clothing, scrolls, military decorations, coin and his and Adara's swords.

His skin felt hot and he removed his tunic to stand only in his short bracae, his mottled and burned skin bared and open to the summer breeze that came in at the door and window. His fingers grazed the branded dragon upon his chest and he was surprised to feel the muscles once more beneath the surface of his body. *Apollo has given me healing, at least...* He pushed away the bitterness and continued.

Lucius looked down at the items, all that they owned, which fit upon the surface of a single table. It saddened him, made him feel like a failure, and yet, the sight added to his anger, an anger he would cling to for however long it took.

He had decided to leave the strong box in Ynis Wytrin for safekeeping, for it was too heavy to bring with them, and if they ever did return, it would be safest there. Inside the box, he placed a third of the pouches filled with gold aurea and silver denarii, all of his military decorations, the deed to the hillfort, and a few of the scrolls Diodorus had left him.

Phoebus had asked to bring along the copy of Arrian's account of the campaigns of Alexander, and Adara had expressed her wish to read Longus' story of *Daphnis and Chloe* once more, a wish, Lucius thought, to think of happier times in their life.

He set those two scrolls aside, as well as the deed to the lands in Etruria, and then picked up the paper of safe passage that the emperor had given him years before. He had almost burned it, and now, he pondered bringing it along, for anything that could identify him or his family was a danger.

But what if I need it at some point? he wondered. *I can hide it well enough, and then use it after when...*

"Lucius?" There was a knock at the door and Dagon appeared on the threshold.

"Dagon. Come in," Lucius looked up briefly and then back at the table.

"You almost ready?" Dagon asked, coming to stand by him, looking down into the chest and all that had been packed. "Are you bringing that?"

"No. The chest is staying here for safekeeping. Etain said that I could leave it with her."

Dagon looked at the pouches of coin, the scrolls, and the decorations. He then looked at the rest of the items upon the table, the remainder of the coin, a couple of scrolls, and the weapons. "Lucius, you can't take the swords with you, especially yours."

"Travel without a sword? I'm going to need it."

Lucius' voice sent a chill through Dagon. "You're well-known for that weapon. There is none other like it, as well as your ancestral gladius. Any man who has seen you as tribune or praefectus will recognize it."

"Then they will get a blade in their guts," Lucius said harshly. He shook his head and grasped the handle of the sword Adara had given him when they were married, so long ago it seemed. "I won't travel with them in the open."

Dagon put his hands up. "All right, but I think they would be safest here."

Lucius turned on him, his chest with the branded dragon rising and falling quickly. "Did you come to annoy me?" he snapped.

Dagon stood back, observed his one-time friend, and knew then that the gap between them was widening with every passing day. He felt for Lucius, but he also knew that it was his decision to leave. "Forgive me, my friend. I forget how much you have on your mind, and it's a long road to Dumnonia still. I came only to see you."

Lucius relaxed, and suddenly he appeared exhausted.

"Does it hurt still?" Dagon asked, looking at the image upon his chest.

"It burns all the time, like a dagger is permanently planted there,"

Lucius answered. He then turned to the table and picked up the cloth in which the image of the dragon - all that survived of his armour - was wrapped. He pulled back the folds and looked upon it. "This has been with me always in battle, and now it goes everywhere with me."

Dagon looked down at the unblemished metal that had survived the fire with Lucius and felt that it was a thing alive that was held before him. "Men will also recognize that if it's found on you."

Lucius nodded. "Yes, they will." He wrapped it up again and gently placed it inside the strong box with all the other items he was leaving behind. "There. The rest, we shall carry...clothes, scrolls, coin, and these." He placed his hand upon the three swords and the pugio. "Do we have a wagon for the journey?"

"Yes. Etain has arranged for two of the priests to meet us on the other side of the marshes with a large, covered wagon drawn by two horses. It will fit all seven of us." Dagon paused. "Are you sure you still want to bring Xanthus along?"

Lucius nodded, sadness coming over his face. He had neglected the stallion, his friend, but he knew it was for the best. "Yes. I know what I need to do."

Dagon nodded. "He can follow behind the wagon. No one can ride him anymore."

"Any word from Einion?" Lucius said, a little abruptly.

"None." Dagon paused, and looked at Lucius again. "Are you going to be all right...going back there?"

"Where?"

"Dumnonia. So much happened there, Lucius. I worry that-"

"I'm not the same man I was when we were there last." There was a finality to his voice and the words he spoke.

No, you are not the same man, Dagon thought, and that thought gave him great sadness.

"Lucius...there's something I wanted to say..."

"What is it?"

"I wish I could go with you...all the way...but-"

Lucius shook his head and tried to smile. "I know...I know. You are my friend, and you have always ridden at my side into danger. But things are different now. You must protect your family. You must stay. I understand."

As Lucius looked into Dagon's eyes and gripped his shoulders tightly, Dagon felt tears begin to burn his eyes, for in that moment, he glimpsed his true friend once more. It was not the wounded warrior, nor the angry son of Apollo, but rather the man he admired and whose friendship he had always cherished.

All Dagon could do was nod. "Do you want me to take the box to Etain?" he finally asked.

"No," Lucius said, withdrawing his hands and standing back. "She said to leave it in here." He looked around the room. "I don't know why, but I think she believes we'll be back in no time."

"Maybe you will?" Dagon said, his voice slightly hopeful.

But Lucius knew better. *Much has to happen before that day comes.*

The remainder of that final day, Lucius and Adara spent their time roaming familiar paths about Ynis Wytrin - Wearyall Hill, the Well of the Chalice, the avenues of oak and yew, and the path to the top of the Tor itself from which they looked out at the isle. From there, they spotted Phoebus and Calliope sitting in one of the orchards with Aaron and Rachel, the friends who, more than anyone, had got them through the immediate trauma of the past.

"We will need to be there for our children now, Lucius," Adara said as she leaned against him. "Now that it comes to it, I'm afraid to leave here."

"Perhaps that is why we need to leave," he said.

She did not understand, but she did not press him either. She saw him staring at the children. "You know, Rachel and Aaron have been their saviours. While you and I were healing, they were there for them. They've formed a special bond."

"I know," Lucius acknowledged. "And I know how the two of them have also helped you and me. They are special, despite Father Gilmore."

"He is not so bad as you think. He bears a great burden."

"How so?"

"You know those children are not…well…normal. From what little lady Etain would tell me, the only place in the world in which they are safe is here. They too are hunted by Rome."

"Those two children?" Lucius said, surprised at the revelation.

"Why do you think Gilmore is so vehemently protective of them?" Adara squeezed Lucius' arm. "One more thing Etain told me, perhaps to comfort me in my situation, is that their parents did not desert them."

Lucius turned to look at her.

"They were murdered by Rome." She felt Lucius tense and turn his head to the sky, his eyes closed.

"Rome has much to pay for…"

"Lucius…my love…"

The words brought Lucius back, for a part of him had been longing to hear them again. He looked at her, the green of her eyes framed by her black and greying hair.

"Let us live for each other now, and for our children. In death… perhaps we have been given a gift? A new beginning?"

How could he tell her the thoughts he had been nurturing, the plans, the pathways of blood he had been walking in his mind's eye? He could not. She needed hope of a different kind, and he knew that he must not destroy that hope, or disillusion her of it.

"It *is* a new beginning, my love," he said, and with those words, he pressed his burned lips to hers and felt her tears there, wetting their embrace.

The morning of their departure was calm and misty, as if a shroud of grief had been spread over the isle at their leaving.

The Metelli, Dagon, Briana and Antiope stood with their belongings upon the small quay at the foot of Wearyall Hill while some of the priests loaded their belongings and Xanthus into the hulls of the two shallow craft.

Etain, Weylyn, Father Gilmore and Aaron and Rachel had come to bid them farewell, as did Olwyn Conn Coran and some of the other priestesses who had aided in their healing.

As Lucius looked over the group of them, he realized fully how very much they had helped them, that they had truly saved them.

Etain hoped that Lucius knew that the aid was not one-sided, that he and his family had a part in helping Ynis Wytrin, and that that help was not yet at an end. She stepped forward to speak with Lucius and Adara.

"You are always welcome here. This is your home, no matter what befalls you."

For perhaps the first time, Adara saw tears in the priestess' eyes and she stepped forward to hug her. "Thank you, lady...for everything."

Etain held her tightly. She had had a glimpse of Adara's road ahead, and knew that it would not be an easy one. Her heart ached for the younger woman who had already come through so many trials in her life. When Adara released her grip, Etain looked her in the eyes. "You must come back here with your children when you are ready. You have a home here."

Adara looked a little confused, but agreed. "I...I will, lady. Yes."

"Good." Etain smiled and turned to Lucius. "Whether you believe it or not anymore, Lucius Metellus Anguis, the Gods are with you upon this road." She stepped forward to kiss Lucius on either cheek. "Come back to us."

"Lady..." Lucius said, his voice shaky. "Thank you." He could not say more to her. He did not need to, for in her eyes he saw that she understood. Lucius then turned to Weylyn.

"Come back to us, Dragon," the old Druid said, his eyes twinkling in the morning light. "We will be waiting, and watching over you from afar."

"My friend...thank you for everything." Lucius grasped Weylyn's hand and squeezed. He had perhaps more in common with the old Druid than with anyone else among them.

"May the Gods guide you on your journey," Weylyn said.

Lucius then turned to Father Gilmore. "I am sorry for being a disturbance to you here."

The priest looked back at Lucius not with dislike, but with regret. "I too am sorry, for not being so gracious as I should have been. You have protected this isle in the past."

"And I will continue to do so," Lucius said, looking at Rachel and Aaron. "Do not fear."

The gratitude upon Gilmore's face changed him, and Lucius felt in that one look that he understood, finally, the urge he had to protect those two special children. It was the same burden he carried in feeling, more than anything, the need to protect his own.

As Phoebus and Calliope thanked Etain, Weylyn, and Gilmore, each of whom embraced and blessed the children in their own way, Lucius and Adara knelt in the grass before Rachel and Aaron so that they could look them in the eyes.

"Thank you both for helping us," Lucius said. "I know you may not understand why we have to leave, but I hope you know that you will always have our love and gratitude."

"We'll be back," Adara added, and that brought a smile to their faces.

Then, Rachel stepped forward and placed her hands upon Adara's cheeks. "God go with you, lady."

Adara felt warmth rush through her then, a sense of peace to calm her even in the darkest of times. When she opened her eyes, the smile before her was genuine and heartfelt.

As Lucius watched, he remembered Rachel and Aaron's faces hovering over him as he lingered at Death's threshold, the light that they had held out to him in the dark, and the healing touch that had awakened him. Had they stood beside the Gods themselves to bring Lucius back? Whatever the feeling was, whatever the reason or cause, he felt gratitude as he took their hands. "Thank you," he told them.

"Farewell, Lucius Metellus Anguis," Aaron said. "Please take care of them."

Lucius looked at Phoebus and Calliope who stood there with tears in their eyes as they looked upon their friends and rushed into their arms one more time.

"Be careful upon the road," Weylyn said to Dagon. "Send word if you need anything."

"We will," Dagon answered. "And we'll be back home soon."

"This *is* your home, Dagon. Never forget that." Weylyn stepped aside to bid Briana farewell, and Etain approached.

"You will be warmly received, Dagon," Etain whispered so that only he could hear her. "Feel guilt no more. It is a time for joy at last."

Dagon looked at the priestess and nodded, a lightness of being filling his heart.

"And you, lady Antiope," Etain said as she bent down. "Enjoy seeing new things and meeting your brave uncle."

"I will," Antiope said, reaching up to hug Etain with her little arms.

As the Metelli, Dagon and Antiope got into the barges, Etain turned to Briana. "Be careful. Let me know when you arrive at Din Tagell."

"I will. Thank you." Briana wiped the tears away from her cheeks.

"Why do you weep?" Etain asked, holding her close.

"Leaving here is like leaving my heart behind. I will miss you."

"You will be back soon," Etain soothed. "And your heart now goes with you." She smiled and her long fingers gently wiped the tears away. "You have been strong for so long, my dear. Now, it is time for you to have the peace that you have waited for. You deserve to be happy. Know that."

Briana smiled sadly, but there was certainty in that smile, a knowing that could only be had in Ynis Wytrin. She let go of Etain's hand and followed the others into the barge to sit beside her husband and daughter.

As the priests pushed off the shore with their long poles, Lucius, Adara, Phoebus and Calliope, along with Dagon, Briana and Antiope, all waved to the others upon the shore, their friends, their family in a way. The emotions each of them felt as they left the Isle of the Blessed swirled around them as much as the mist through which the barges cut.

Soon, the shore was hidden from their sight, the silhouettes of the Tor and of Wearyall Hill, and all they could see was mist and shadow and morning light above the dark depths beneath them.

Adara sat cradling Calliope who wept silently beside her in the boat. She looked up at Phoebus who was sitting with Xanthus, stroking the stallion's leg to calm him as the boat rocked gently in its forward progress toward the far shore.

"Will we ever return, Mama?" Calliope asked, her voice softened in the mist.

"We will see, my love," Adara answered. "The Gods will guide us."

In that moment, Lucius could not bring himself to look back, for all he saw now was the road ahead. He could not promise his family that they would return to Ynis Wytrin, and he could not tell them that the only thing he saw was the promise of blood and of the vengeance he had thought of while healing in paradise.

VII

LACUS SANCTUS

'The Sacred Pool'

The summer rain upon the road south was incessant at first, but for the Metelli and Dagon's family it was a blessing, for it cloaked their passage.

In the past, whenever Lucius had travelled the roads of the empire, he had done so with a retinue of his warriors, been recognized and lauded by the men of the legions, men who had come to know the 'Dragon of Rome' and be inspired by him.

If Lucius was honest with himself, those were good days indeed.

There had been times of course, when he had journeyed in secret: once when he had fled for his life from Leptis Magna, in North Africa, and more recently when he had last travelled to Dumnonia to help Einion reclaim his father's throne. But even on those occasions, there were many who would have, and did, come forward to help him - soldiers, veterans, and even the empress herself.

Lucius thought about Julia Domna for a moment as the wagon trundled along the rain-soaked slabs of the Fosse Way toward Isca Dumnoniorum. The empress had helped him in the past, but she would not do so this time. She could not be relied upon for protection on this next journey. No.

Now, as Lucius travelled the arteries of the empire, there would be no help. The friends and family that were left to him in the world would be holding to the shadows themselves because of their proximity to him, the 'Dragon'.

From the darkness of the wagon, Lucius looked at Adara and Calliope who dozed on and off, holding each other, while Briana stroked Antiope's hair beside them. Upon the driver's bench, Dagon sat with

Phoebus beside him gazing out at the countryside, eyeing the occasional traveller headed to Lindinis.

Lindinis had been their first challenge, for if any of the ordo members had been present, they most certainly would have recognized Adara and the children, if not Lucius in his wounded state. Thankfully, it had not been the market day, and with the rain pouring out of iron grey skies, most had taken shelter indoors.

But Serenus Crescens isn't a threat anymore, or Nolan Phelan... The thought gave Lucius satisfaction as he watched the town pass by from the back of the wagon where Xanthus trotted along in tow. Lucius remembered shopping in the centre of the town with his family, going to the baths, facing off with Crescens, and even meeting Terdra, the mysterious smith who had forged Adara's sword.

Lindinis was a town of ghosts to him now, and as it faded into the mist behind them, Lucius thought forward to Isca Dumnoniorum. *I hope it is not market day in the agora when we arrive.* The thought worried him, for it would be the first test of his faceless self, to pass in front of the eyes of Rome's warriors without being recognized.

"He's looking at you, Baba," Calliope said as she opened her eyes.

"What, my girl?" Lucius looked at her.

"Xanthus," she said, waving to the great stallion behind them. "He is sad."

Lucius turned to look at Xanthus and saw the great, dark eyes observing him from beneath the fringe of that long, black mane. "Hello, boy," Lucius said reaching out to the stallion.

Xanthus trotted forward to keep apace with the wagon and stretched his massive head forward to Lucius' hand.

"I'm sorry I haven't been there for you as I should have," Lucius said. He felt a great sadness inside at his neglect of Xanthus, for the stallion had saved his life on several occasions, and without him, Adara might not have been sitting there. "I've failed you, my friend." Lucius rubbed the soft, black muzzle and felt the hot breath upon the palm of his hand. "But I'm going to make it up to you. You will love where we're going."

"Baba," said Phoebus, looking back from the driver's bench.

Lucius put his finger to his mouth, indicating Adara where she slept, and Phoebus waved him forward to switch places with him. They each crawled along the bottom of the wagon and Phoebus settled at the back to pat Xanthus while Lucius tried to climb up onto the bench beside Dagon.

"Everything all right?" Lucius asked.

"No. I don't know how we're going to get through Isca," Dagon said as he flicked the reins. "You may not be recognized, but I will be."

Briana came forward then to talk with them. "I've been thinking the same thing. Who are we all? We will need to tell them something."

Lucius thought about it for a moment. They were right. If they were questioned at the gates of Isca, they would need to identify themselves. He looked at himself, his black cloak, tunic and sandals, and then at Dagon and Briana.

"Say that you're going back to your family farm in Dumnonia, now that you have heard the plague is no longer present there."

"Where was I?" Briana said.

"With your husband here," he said, patting Dagon's shoulder, "Marcus Petronius. He's a veteran of the VI Victrix in Eburacum. His term of service is done and he is retiring to Dumnonia."

"'Marcus Petronius'?" Dagon chuckled. "Sounds like a sort of clown!"

"That's the point. You don't want to sound like a great warrior, and certainly not a Sarmatian," Lucius said.

"What about your story?" Dagon asked.

"They won't look too closely at me. If asked, tell them I'm Briana's cousin...a seer... I've been sick. They won't want to look too closely at me. This is my wife and children."

"And that will be enough?" Briana asked. She was more and more nervous about this expedition. Not only would they have to pass through the Roman town, but she had not been back to Dumnonia for years.

"It should be." But Lucius was not sure of anything anymore, and he began in that moment to realize more fully the danger he was putting his family in.

They spent a night in a small, nondescript inn along the road, and departed at dawn the following morning, eager to cover as much distance the following day as possible. However, it was slower going with a wagon than on horseback, as they had travelled that road before.

People paid them little heed thankfully, and many distanced themselves from Lucius, some mistaking him for a leper when they glimpsed his face and bandaged limbs.

As Adara watched, she struggled with her fear of all of them being caught, but also at the way in which people recoiled from her husband. On that long, quiet journey, she found herself falling victim to waves of nostalgia. *I used to be so proud...* she thought, wanting at times to weep. *Now, all I see is an angry, wounded and bitter man, a man I don't know anymore.* Of course, she knew she was being unfair, but she also knew that Lucius was not telling her everything. *And he won't!* She focussed instead on the coming reunion with her parents and the joy she would feel at sitting with her children in her parents' triclinium on the slopes of Hymettos, with the sound of cicadas whirring in the day, and the scent of jasmine in the evenings. She tried to picture her mother's frescos upon the walls, and wondered what new creations she had adorned the family home with. She tried to imagine her sisters married, and wondered whether or not they might have children yet. These thoughts entertained Adara, but mostly they were a distraction from fear and the long road ahead.

When the walls of Isca Dumnoniorum came into view on the third day, everyone in the wagon tensed, and they held their collective breath as they followed the flow of people, litters and wagons into the town.

It was market day.

The press of people on the streets of Isca was thick and loud, and they all flowed toward the forum where the main market was thronging with locals and outsiders, traders from Britannia, Gaul, and other parts of the empire.

Lucius had settled himself in the back of the wagon, while Adara and the children huddled in the darkness within. Upon the driver's bench, Dagon sat at the reins with Antiope between him and Briana, a family heading home.

It took some time to get through the town, and Xanthus' bulk at the back of the wagon drew curious looks from passers by who gave him a wide berth for fear of being kicked. The passage went smoothly enough, and the troops at the northern gate had paid them little attention, wanting only to keep the crowds moving and avoid chaos at the gates.

An hour later, the wagon approached the southern gate that faced the river crossing, beyond which the lands of Dumnonia opened up.

Dagon drove the wagon forward slowly, clicking his tongue at the horses and trying to look relaxed. "Gods no!" he hissed.

"What is it?" Lucius asked from the back.

"It's Flaccus! The trooper who helped us through last time. What if he recognizes me?"

Lucius could tell there was absolute panic in Dagon's voice, and he knew it was warranted. Lucius may have looked different, but Dagon did not. Before he could give much more thought to the situation he heard the centurion's commanding voice.

"Hold!" Flaccus said, stepping into the road to block the wagon with his hand up.

Dagon quickly observed ten troopers around the gate, four of them flanking their centurion. Even had they wanted to, they could never push their way through. They were too slow and cumbersome. Dagon breathed deeply and nodded to the centurion.

"Where you headed?" Flaccus asked, not looking directly at Dagon yet, but observing the wagon and the horse at the back.

"Going to see my wife's family in Dumnonia, near Din Tagell." Dagon fingered the thick leather of the reins but forced himself to stop when Flaccus came to stand beside him, looking up.

The other troopers were surrounding the wagon then too, and when one of them came to the back, Lucius half-shut his eyes and tried to appear ill.

"And who are you?" Flaccus asked Dagon, and in that moment, the centurion looked directly at him. His eyes widened for a tense, fleeting moment.

Dagon swallowed. "My name is Marcus Petronius. I'm a veteran of the VI Victrix in Eburacum."

"Eburacum? What are you doing down here?" Flaccus asked, and as he did so, his eyes went to the left and right where his men were looking inside the wagon.

He knows! We're done! Dagon thought. "My term of service is over. We've come to settle on my wife's family farm. Time for a quieter life now, eh?" Dagon said.

"I understand," Flaccus said. "We all want a quieter life." He looked inside the wagon. "And who are these people?"

Briana spoke up then. "My cousin, Ludo, and his family" she said. "He's a seer, but he's grown sick. He's coming to live with us. It's too cold in the North for him."

"Hmm." Flaccus leaned over and looked inside to see a woman and two more children sitting in the middle, and beyond them the seer. "He doesn't look well," Flaccus said.

"He's been better," Dagon added.

"Sir!" one of the troopers called from the back of the wagon.

Flaccus went around the back. "What is it?"

"This horse is no pack horse, sir. Look at the size of it! See the scarring on its hide?"

"What about this horse, seer?" Flaccus asked Lucius.

Lucius' opened his eyes a bit more and the centurion looked closely at him, his burned skin and the bandages about his arms and legs.

Lucius' heart was pounding in his chest. A part of him wanted to yell out who he really was, to defy the world and step from the shadows, but he knew that could not be. They were in real danger, and he needed to get his family and friends through. With a weak voice, he said, "The horse…is a gift for Lord Einion of Din Tagell. My cousin's family live upon his lands."

Flaccus looked at the horse and nodded. "A worthy gift…for a good lord. Einion has been a friend to the men of the legions here," Flaccus said. "Always sends us the best wine from his trade shipments. Isn't that right, lads?" he said to his men.

"May the Gods bless him!" one of the men cried happily, setting off laughter among the others.

Flaccus looked once more at Lucius, and nodded. "Safe journey to you…seer." Then, he went to the front of the wagon to speak to Dagon. "You may pass, and tell the lord Einion we are grateful for the wine!" He leaned in closer. "And have a care…Marcus Petronius… Word is that dragons have returned to this land. Dangerous creatures. More dangerous than any wyrm, unless you know how to speak to them."

Dagon wanted to thank the man, to let him know that he was grateful for his secrecy. He longed to tell him that the Dragon of Rome was in the wagon, that he had been wronged. But he could say nothing. And it was a comfort to see the look in Flaccus' eyes that told him he would say nothing either, to anyone.

"You have my gratitude, Centurion," Dagon said, bowing his head.

Flaccus nodded, and waved his vinerod. "Move along!" he called out loudly.

Dagon flicked the reins and the wagon creaked on through the gateway and down the road that led to the river crossing.

No one spoke as they crossed the bridge and the fast-flowing waters of the Exe below. As they reached the other side, the sun emerged from its hiding place behind the clouds and the green and rocky lands of Dumnonia stretched out before them.

"I'm home," Briana whispered, grasping Dagon's sweaty hand.

In the back of the wagon, Lucius looked to see the form of the centurion in the gateway at the top of the road. *There are still some good men left,* he thought.

The last time Lucius had seen that land of expansive moors and rocky tors, it had been for a very different purpose. Dumnonia had been a land of mystery and danger, an enemy land.

Now, it was to be their sanctuary, at least temporarily.

The sun shone as the wagon rolled along the old, unkept Roman road, until it turned to dirt and rock. Their progress slowed, but as the sun was shining, and it was summer, the journey was a pleasant one.

Briana and Adara had taken down the canvas canopy of the wagon so that they could be open to the sky, and as they drove, Briana pointed out the many marks of beauty of her homeland, a land she had not seen in many years.

Adara and the children listened to her speak of the wind and rain like they were old family members, of hiding behind yellow gorse, and riding upon their ponies over the heathland to the ancient stones along the highway across the moors. They listened to her warnings about the bog mosses that grew over deep black waters in colours of red, green and brown.

Dagon smiled to himself as he listened to his wife remember. Dumnonia, it seemed to him, was a much more beautiful land this time, and he found himself excited to see Einion and the others whom they had fought alongside to reclaim the latter's throne. He looked at Lucius, however, and wondered how he was feeling about being back.

"Are you all right, Anguis?" Dagon asked.

Lucius pushed back his cowl for the first time and felt the wind and sun upon his head, his eyes closed momentarily for all the brightness.

"I feel strange," he said. "You know what happened last time we were here. It's different now."

"It is indeed," Dagon said, looking around. "We helped to put the rightful king upon the throne, and look at this land now!" There was a hint of longing in Dagon's voice.

He misses being a lord of his people, Lucius thought. *But better that than not being yourself anymore.* He felt like he was betraying Dagon by thinking it, but he could not help the bitter sentiment.

If Dagon wanted to settle in that land with Briana and his child, he could. But Lucius knew that he and his family would not be staying long, that Dumnonia was the only port far enough from Rome's reach where they could safely find a ship. Lucius left those thoughts behind for the moment as there were other pressing matters at hand.

"You notice the tracks upon the road?"

"Yes, I did," Dagon said, leaning over to look down at the dirt as the wagon passed overhead. "Horses…lots of them."

"Last time we came here, there was nothing at all. Not a soul upon the road."

"Maybe Einion sends hunting parties out?"

"This far from his fortress?" Lucius shook his head. "And these are rather fresh tracks."

"We're not alone then," Dagon said, touching the hilt of his sword where it leaned against the bench beside him.

"No. We're not." Lucius looked back to see Xanthus trotting along behind them, and he felt the sadness coming on him again. The time was approaching. It would be soon, and he did not know how he would bear to do it.

The stallion seemed alert, and held his head higher, prouder, than he had in a long while.

Soon, boy. Soon, you will see. Lucius thought as he looked forward down the long swaying road to the tors and distant copses of trees of the Dumnonian expanse.

For three days, they travelled across the moors, making slow progress with the wagon, and for three days, Briana enjoyed her homecoming like a slow reintroduction to a long-lost acquaintance. They stopped early in the evenings to bivouac by the roadside, or against the stony sides of rocky outcrops that jutted out of the green landscape. Briana had to smile at the sight of thriving life upon the moors, for it meant that Einion had indeed successfully taken up his role as leader of their people.

Despite the green comfort of that land and the shining sun that lit the road before them, Lucius and Dagon took no chances when it came to sleeping at night, and took it in turns to keep an armed watch beside a bright fire while Adara, Briana and the three children slept.

There were no huntings in the darkness, however, no banshees' cries, frightened nymphs, or wyrms anymore... The land was quiet, and safe. But still, Lucius felt an uneasiness being there, like they were being watched from a distance. He wondered if someone had followed them from Isca, whether Rome's spies knew the dead walked again, or that Lucius Metellus Anguis sought to strike at the heart of the empire.

He looked up at the stars that peeked out from behind soft, flowing clouds in the night sky. He had forgotten their beauty, had forgotten a lot of things. *Maybe one day, when it is done, I will be able to see beauty again...* He sighed inwardly, turning over the hilt of his sword and looking at it in the firelight. It felt strange to him in his hand now, and even though he had grown stronger, was now able to hold it and wield it, there was something about it that felt wrong, something about himself.

He remembered long ago when Apollo had appeared to him in the desert at night and shown him that sword before casting it across the firmament. When Adara had given him that same sword after their marriage, Lucius had felt sure of his destiny.

But all that had changed. *I cannot see so far now,* Lucius thought, and a sorrowful feeling came over him once more. He had felt purpose long ago, and he had purpose now. The difference was that his current purpose did not inspire him the way it had in his previous life. No. His current purpose was more like a mad hunger that needed to be sated so that he could feel normal again.

He stood from the fire and stretched his body. His bones and muscle felt well enough, but his skin itched and burned as he had not applied the resin for some days. Trying to ignore the discomfort, he walked over to where Xanthus was tied loosely to a log.

The stallion's dark form turned toward Lucius as he approached with his hand out to stroke his neck.

"We're almost there, boy." Lucius reached up and hugged the thick neck, let the dark mane fall over him so that he could almost hide beneath it. "We've both changed since that terrible night, haven't we?"

The thudding of Xanthus' heart was loud and strong, and Lucius stood back to look at those dark eyes.

"We'll be there tomorrow. And then, you'll see…you'll be happy again…"

When the sun rose on the moors the following morning, it cast an orange and pale pink light across the land, revealing herds of deer gathered in the mist, their ears alert to any sound, their bodies ready to shift and bolt at the first sign of a threat.

Lucius had not slept, had let Dagon go through the night. He was standing looking out at the moors and morning light when Calliope approached him.

"Good morning, Baba," she said. "You didn't sleep, did you?"

"No. I can't, my girl. Did you?"

"Yes. It's beautiful and calm here."

It wasn't always like this, Lucius thought, but he did not want to dash her view of the place. "Yes, it is," he said.

She gripped his hand and looked up at him. "Are you really going to do it?"

Lucius looked down at her. "Do what? What are you talking about, Calliope?"

"Xanthus," she said, her eyes watery as she looked up at him. "He is part of our family."

"He is. And he has been one of my truest friends. That is why I have to do it."

She nodded. "Goddess Epona says the lady is expecting us."

Lucius turned to his daughter. "Epona came to you?"

"Last night."

"What else did she say?" Lucius asked. *And why did she not speak to me?*

"Only that I shouldn't worry about Xanthus. I stopped crying about it after she came to me."

Lucius smiled and touched his daughter's cheek. "Then that is a good thing." He put his arm around her and together they watched the deer move across the moor, even as the others started to wake up behind them.

They travelled far that day. In the summer sun, the view looked different, especially as there were no more trees, and for miles around the land was covered in boulders, bog moss and the familiar verdant green of the moors.

Briana sat on the driver's bench with Dagon and Antiope, her eyes scanning the countryside in search of a familiar landmark.

"Do you remember the way there?" Dagon said to her as they went.

She shook her head. "It's been so long...I...I can't seem to find it," the Briton said, frustrated with herself.

"Can you speak to her the way you do with Etain?" Dagon asked. "Perhaps she can guide you."

Briana sighed. "No. I can't." The truth was that the priestess and water nymph had unnerved her when she had last seen her in flight from Dumnonia. She had been kind and helpful, but there had been something about her and her knowing that was different to Etain.

Lucius came to the front of the wagon and looked out with them. The wagon jarred him and he almost fell backward. Gripping the wood of the bench, he tried to scan the world ahead with his eyes. *We're close.* "Stop the wagon," he said. "Let me down."

"Why?" Dagon asked as he pulled on the reins.

"Trust me." Lucius said, going to the back of the wagon where he untied Xanthus. "Phoebus, help me."

The boy jumped quickly down out of the wagon to help his father.

"Take him and follow me," Lucius said, handing him Xanthus' bridle and walking around to the front of the wagon.

"Lucius, is everything all right?" Adara asked.

"It's fine," he answered without looking back. "We're just lost."

Adara and Calliope went to the front of the wagon to watch with the others as Lucius, Phoebus and Xanthus walked slowly ahead upon the ancient trackway.

"I should know my own land!" Briana said.

"It has been long, as you say," Dagon said, his hand upon her arm. "Were I to return to Sarmatia, I would not know where to go either. So much has happened since I was last there."

Adara thought for a moment what it would feel like to her when they returned to Athenae, for it will not have been so long since she was there. *I know every tree and rock of my family's home,* she thought. *I can see it now.*

Lucius walked forward with his son and Xanthus as the wagon creaked along behind them. It felt strangely familiar now, though it had been a long time since he had last been there, and in a wounded state no less.

Keep going.

Lucius stopped and looked around. The voice was soft at the edge of his consciousness, but it was there. He looked up at Xanthus and the stallion's eyes too were looking, his ears cocked forward to listen to something.

They walked along a bit farther, passing various small paths that flowed up and away from the trackway, paths used by goats and deer, and by the wild moor ponies.

Lucius stopped then at a path that went downward. "This is it!" he called back to Dagon. "Will the wagon get through?"

Dagon leaned forward to look at the turning radius he needed and the width of the path. "Only just!" he said, slowing the wagon and turning the horse team sharply to follow Lucius. "I recognize the scent," he said to Briana.

"As do I," she answered, smiling. "I remember now."

The ground began to rise higher and higher on either side of the path as it went down, eventually almost hiding the entirety of the wagon from outside eyes. Then, they heard it: horses.

On either side, swift-running teams of wild horses cantered upon the peat and clover ground as if accompanying the newcomers.

"Mama, look!" Calliope said excitedly.

"I see them, my girl. Are they wild, Briana?"

"Yes," Briana answered, smiling broadly. "But much more than that."

Lucius and Phoebus turned again, the latter holding on tightly to Xanthus' bridle as he looked to the left and right to observe his wild brethren.

"Easy, Xanthus," Phoebus whispered. "They're friendly."

There was a trickle of water then, and Lucius and Phoebus looked down to see the path was running wet, even though the sun was out and it was summer. The air was pleasant-smelling, their nostrils filled with the damp scent of peat, clover and wet rock.

The wild horses ran up a rise and then disappeared downward again, and the pathway followed.

"I remembered wishing you had been with me the when I first saw this place," Lucius said to his son.

"What is this place?" Phoebus asked.

"A safe place. We can get help here."

"Do we need help right now, Baba?" Phoebus started to look worried, but Lucius put his hand upon his son's shoulder and smiled.

"No. Not now, Phoebus."

As the path rose and fell a little more sharply away before them, the lake came into view.

"There it is!" Briana said from behind them.

Lucius reached up to pat Xanthus' neck as they walked. "We're here, boy."

"What is this place?" Phoebus asked.

"A sanctuary."

Just then, the sound of horses' hooves faded away and at the edge of the still, black lake, a tall woman in white priestess' robes and a black cloak appeared, the lake water soft at her feet. She seemed to smile as the group approached, the braids of her long, black hair swaying in a gentle breeze.

Xanthus pulled on the bridle, wanting to go ahead, but Phoebus held him fast.

"It's all right, Phoebus," Lucius said.

Phoebus let go and the stallion trotted forward eagerly.

Xanthus went straight to the priestess who reached up to him with soft, pale hands to stroke his head and neck.

"Who is she?" Phoebus whispered to his father.

"She is a water nymph…a priestess and guardian of the sacred pool."

"And protector of the wild herds," the priestess said as Lucius and Phoebus approached, followed by the others as the wagon came to a halt behind them. She smiled at Phoebus. "I am Elana."

"I am Phoebus Metellus Anguis."

The priestess smiled at the boy. "Welcome, Phoebus." Then she turned her eyes to Lucius and there was great sadness in their blue depths. "You have returned, Dragon."

"Yes," Lucius answered, stepping closer to her.

"But…much changed…" Her voice was like a sad song played late at night when the fires are dying down. "What has happened to both of you?" she asked, looking from Lucius to Xanthus and back.

"Lady…" Lucius said, his voice brittle for a fleeting moment. "Much has happened to all of us…" he turned to reach out to Adara and Calliope who approached. "This is Elana," he said to them. "She helped to heal me when…when last I was here."

Adara looked upon the priestess and stepped forward to grasp her hands. She felt drawn to her, though she did not know why. For those who have been harshly treated by the trials of their lives, kindness is always a beacon. And Elana was kindness itself.

"The Dragon's family is always welcome," Elana said, gripping Adara's hands and holding them fast. "Always."

"Thank you," Adara said, forcing herself not to weep, for what she did not know.

"Is this your lake?" Calliope asked, stepping to the water's edge.

"I am its guardian. Just as I watch over the sacred herds. Look." She pointed across the broad, still lake to the other side where horses were running along the water's edge.

"They're beautiful." Calliope turned to her brother. "Phoebus look! Did you see?"

Phoebus stepped forward to stand with his sister.

Elana smiled at the children, turned, and walked past Lucius and Adara with her arms out. "Briana," she said, her voice full of emotion.

"Lady," Briana said, unable to speak further as she fell into the priestess' arms.

"You're home," Elana whispered to her. "All is well now."

Briana remembered it all again, arriving in that place, tired, hungry and terrified for her and Einion's lives. They had seen their family slaughtered before them, and the world had felt like it was falling apart.

Elana had provided comfort and refuge for them. She had saved them.

"How you have grown," the priestess said as she released Briana to look upon her. She turned to Dagon and smiled. "I am glad to see you return."

"It is good to see you, lady," Dagon replied, holding Antiope's hand.

Elana looked at Briana and smiled. "You are a mother now?"

"This is Antiope," Briana said, smiling. "My girl, this is Elana. She's a very good friend."

Elana crouched down to greet the child. "Greetings, Antiope."

"Hello," Antiope answered shyly, moving behind her father's leg.

Elana smiled and stood to look at all of them. "Come. You must be tired after your journey. There is food and a warm hearth for all of you." She glanced at Lucius and began to walk with Briana and Antiope back to the roundhouse where she lived, followed by Dagon who led the horses and wagon after them.

"What is this place, Lucius?" Adara asked, feeling a calm wash over her as she looked at the far shore, the wild horses cropping at the grass, and her children standing arm in arm at the water's edge where the sky was perfectly reflected.

Lucius looked up at Xanthus, and then back at Adara. "Sanctuary," he answered.

As evening began to fall, the summer sky clear and ornamented with myriad stars, the group sat around the hearth inside the roundhouse. Elana had fed them bread and hot broth, and now handed them all cups of tea brewed from the healing herbs she had drying in bunches that hung from the rafters of her home.

For some time, Briana told Elana of all that had happened to her, of Ynis Wytrin and the news there. She also asked after Einion, for she had not received many letters from him.

"As you can see, the land is thriving under your brother's rule," Elana said. "The healing has taken place in Dumnonia. The people are happy, and the wild herds can roam safely without fear of the wyrm, or the dark Hunter."

Lucius looked up at that, and Elana met his gaze immediately.

"He has left us all alone, Dragon, thanks to you."

"The Dark Hunter?" Adara asked. "The one whom you fought when-"

"Yes," Lucius answered, taking a deep breath. "The same."

"And Einion said something about dragons returning to the land?" Briana asked.

Elana smiled, and looked at Dagon and Lucius. "Yes. They are elusive. But Einion will know where to find them."

"Mama," Calliope said. "I'm tired."

Adara looked at her daughter and son and nodded. "You may sleep. Come," she said, taking both of them to the blankets that had been laid in the dark along the wall of the roundhouse. "Sleep now, my loves," Adara whispered, kissing their heads as they lay down and quickly fell into peaceful sleep beside Antiope, who was already dozing soundly.

"They are very special, all of them," Elana said to Adara and Lucius, Briana and Dagon. She sat straight on the other side of the fire, gazing from the flames to each of the four adults. She had been happy to see them all, but every time she looked to Lucius, her smile faded and sadness threatened to overwhelm her.

Lucius noticed this, knew she understood, that she could see.

"It feels strange to be back here," Briana said, looking around the dwelling and then back at Elana. "The last time I was here, it was-"

"A time of terror for you," Elana finished. "You and your brother had just experienced a great trauma. You feel you should be sad coming back here to the sacred lake, seeing me, seeing this land again?"

"Yes," Briana said. "But I'm not. I'm coming home with my husband and child." She reached out to take Dagon's hand and he smiled at her, the fire casting a warm glow over his bearded face. "We thought all was lost when we arrived here, tired and bloody, with nothing but the clothes upon our backs and the swords in our hands." She looked back to Elana. "I can never thank you enough, Elana."

"No matter how dire the circumstances are, you need to know that the Gods will always be there for you. They led you here, to me, and then guided you down the road."

"I don't know if the Gods always care as they should," Lucius said. There was bitterness in his voice, familiar to the others, painful.

Elana looked at Lucius then. She barely recognized the man on the surface, true, but the man on the inside, the one who had helped put the rightful king back on the throne at the risk of his own life, that man was much-changed. "The Gods guide us, Dragon. They push us at times, but the choices are always our own."

"And what do they do for a nymph who lives between worlds?" Lucius said suddenly.

"Lucius?" Adara looked askance at her husband, embarrassed.

Elena remained calm, her hands in her lap as she looked across the fire at the burned and broken Roman. "It is more difficult for those who are caught between worlds. As you know."

Lucius stared at her. He felt his anger rising, not with Elana, but with everything. He wanted to be allowed his anger, to wallow in it, for it gave him the strength and determination he would need in the time to come. *They don't understand!*

There was a loud neighing of horses then, coming from outside, and the sound brought Lucius back. He looked at the fire, then at Elana. "I'll check on the horses," he said, standing and going out into the darkness of night.

When Lucius was gone, Adara turned to Elana. "I'm sorry, lady. So much has happened to him, to all of us..." She sighed, and the sound was near to weeping. "I fear he may never be the same again."

Briana moved to sit beside Adara and put her arms around her.

Elana looked at the two women and then at Dagon who leaned on his knees staring into the fire. "I will check on him."

Outside, Lucius walked directly to the edge of the lake. The summer moon was bright, and nearly full, illuminating the water with a silver light. He looked around to see the wild horses on the other side, their still shapes like sentries around the perimeter.

He heard another sound too. Not far to his left, Xanthus was standing there, gazing across the water at the herd.

"You like it here, boy?" Lucius said.

The black stallion trotted over to Lucius' side.

The air became very still, absent of breeze. There was no sound either, as if every horse around the lake had held its breath.

And then, Lucius saw it. A light emerging from the middle of the horses on the other side. It should have been too far to see, but he could, and when the light came forward from among the animals to stand on the shore opposite to Lucius, the latter gasped.

It's him! Lucius thought. *It's impossible!*

On the other side of the lake was a bearded man in leather armour. And there was a dragon upon his chest. In his left hand, he carried a small sort of shield with a bear upon it. But he had no sword.

Lucius pushed back the hood of his cloak and stepped into the water so that it lapped around his ankles, sending ripples across the lake. *In Annwn...it was you?*

The man stared back at him, the palm of his empty right hand out to Lucius as if pleading for help, for some explanation of how the world had thrashed his hopes and dreams.

Lucius recognized that look all too well, and his heart ached for the apparition. He wanted to give the man a weapon for his empty right hand, to tell him all would be well, that he needed to fight for it. He wanted to give the warrior hope, but the hand lowered slowly, still empty.

A moment later, the man backed away, his light fading, into the midst of the still, dark horses on the other side.

All there was again was the smooth surface of the lake, and the wind in the reeds at the water's edge.

"Are you not well, Dragon?" Elana said as she approached Lucius.

Xanthus went to her side immediately, his great head looking back at Lucius.

"He is worried for you," Elana said.

Lucius turned back to her from where he stood in the water. "I saw..."

Elana gazed across the water at the horses but saw nothing. "What did you see?"

Lucius shook his head and rubbed his eyes. "I must be tired. I saw a man who does not exist, standing on the other side."

"How can he not exist if you recognized him? For I see recognition on your face, Dragon." Elana reached out to touch Lucius' arm and pull him gently out of the water.

"I...I saw him in Annwn."

Elana's eyes widened. "Yes?"

"A warrior with a world of sadness. I had seen him back when..." Lucius shook his head. "He just appeared, but seemed even more vulner-able...and he was without a sword...my sword."

"Was it you? Did you see yourself across the mirrored lake?" Elana was intent now.

Lucius looked directly into her watery blue eyes. Even in the dark, they seemed full of vibrancy and colour. "No. It wasn't me. But he was like me in a way. He bore a dragon upon his chest. But upon his shield was a bear."

Elana was at a loss. She studied Lucius for a moment. *He is not mad, but he is lost. To go from Annwn and then into the fires as he has would drive any man into madness. And yet…he is not…*

Lucius reached up to pat Xanthus who had edged closer to him.

Elana decided to let it be. *The Dragon's visions are his own,* she thought, but she also knew that what he had seen felt right and true for some reason, though she had no idea why. And that rarely happened to her.

"We've been through so much," Lucius said to Xanthus. Elana joined him in patting the stallion.

She could feel the sadness in the animal, could feel that he was tired of battle and of blood. He had given everything to the son of Apollo who stood beside her. "He has nothing more to give," she said softly.

"I know," Lucius said, and his voice was full of sadness and regret once more. "He saved me many times. And even when I came out of the fires, he carried me to battle again."

"His journey is ended, Dragon. He cannot go farther."

Lucius looked down. "I know." He looked up at Elana then. "That is why we are here. Will you take care of him? Can Xanthus remain here at the sacred lake with you?"

"I think he has already decided that for himself," she answered. "But yes, he may stay for the remainder of whatever days are left to him."

Lucius nodded, but found he could not speak. He simply leaned into Xanthus' bulk to feel his warmth, and the strong beat of his heart.

Elana felt tears burning at the rims of her eyes as she stood there in the moonlit dark beside the horse and rider. Never had she seen such a bond, nor such a difficult parting. *But it is necessary for both of them.* "You may see him again," she said softly as Lucius turned to walk back to the roundhouse.

He stopped to look back at Elana where she stood beside Xanthus. "Perhaps," he said, and in that moment, a star shot across the sky above, its reflection cast across the lake to seemingly land on the other side where the man had stood. *By the Gods,* he thought, and then he remembered who he was. "Perhaps," he repeated, and then went inside.

"Gods can weep as much as men," Elana said to Xanthus. "And more so. You are noble to let him go…"

Inside the roundhouse, Lucius could see by the light of the fire that

Einion and Briana lay asleep beside Antiope, and that Adara lay beside Phoebus and Calliope.

It was peaceful inside, the crack of the hearth soothing.

But Lucius was restless, as if some decision pressed his mind with urgency, though he was not sure to what end. He picked up the bundle that contained his and Adara's swords, and the ancestral gladius, and sat down by the fire. There, he pulled back the folds of the woollen blanket at one end to reveal the gathered hilts.

The gold glinted in the firelight as he ran his fingers over the images of dragons, and the eagle upon the pommel of his old gladius, the one Phoebus had used to kill that night. The blades had seen much blood and death, even the one he had given Adara. They were special, and unique. *They are recognizable,* Lucius thought, and he knew in that moment what he had to do.

The morning was misty and still, like the sea at midwinter.

Elana had already built up the fire in the hearth when her guests began to stir. A scent of cooking oats filled the roundhouse.

Once they were fully awake, the children all went to join Elana about the fire where she handed them each some tea and wooden bowls into which she ladled some of the oats.

Calliope helped Antiope to eat while Phoebus kept the younger one from getting too near the fire.

While the adults packed up their belongings, Elana sat with the children. She could not help but smile at them, how mature they were, how they worked in concert together at the task.

Phoebus looked up at her while, Calliope fed Antiope. "Are you really a nymph?" he asked.

Elana smiled, but the expression was not devoid of sadness. It could be a lonely existence, being a guardian. She nodded. "I'm the guardian of the sacred pool here, and have been so for a long time."

"You don't…look old…" Phoebus said shyly.

She chuckled. "My kind live longer than mortals."

"I see."

The nymph observed the Dragon's child then. She could tell that he had seen the Gods before. As had his sister. *That changes a person. It leaves a mark of light,* she thought. *I see it on them both.* "Do you like it here, young man?"

Phoebus looked at the nymph, her brilliant blue eyes, and the long black hair falling over her shoulder. She was a part of the place. "Yes. I like it very much here," he said. "It's peaceful and safe."

"And the world is not always so, is it?" she asked.

"No," he answered quickly. "It isn't."

"Well, Phoebus... Just as this place offered sanctuary to Einion and Briana long ago in their time of need, it can also be a place of peace for you and your sister. You are always welcome here. Know that."

Phoebus nodded, his brow creased as he wondered why she was making such an offer. *Are we in danger? Will our parents be slain?*

Elana reached out to place her hand upon his arm, immediately calming the rising panic she could see in his face. "You need not worry," she soothed. "Sometimes, we only need a place to go to. A place to think. Do you think you could find this place again if you needed it?"

"I don't know," Phoebus said. "I will mark the way as we travel today."

"Yes. Do."

For a brief moment, it seemed to Phoebus that Elana's face shimmered and changed to that of Venus. He rubbed his eyes.

She smiled. "The Gods are with you. Remember that on your travels."

"What should they remember?" Adara asked as she came to sit with them.

Elana rose and hugged her warmly. "I was telling your son that you are always welcome here should you need it."

"That is very kind of you," Adara said. "We have few friends these days. My husband is hunted."

Elana took her hands and squeezed. *No,* she thought. *He is the hunter now. I see it.* But she could not bring herself to say it.

Lucius, Dagon and Briana joined them around the fire then and each ate and drank their fill.

While Briana spoke of seeing Einion and wondered how far along Gwendolyn was in her pregnancy, Elana busied herself with a mortar and pestle upon one of the tables beneath a window. She had risen early to prepare a new resin for Lucius' burned and healing skin. When she was satisfied with the mixture, she scooped it into a clay jar, and then called Lucius over.

"Yes?" he said, coming to her side.

"I have prepared this resin for you. It will help speed the healing and ease the discomfort you feel."

"Will it mend my skin fully?" he asked.

"No," she said. "Nothing can do that. But it will help you mend so that you can feel the kiss of the wind again, or a gentle touch."

"That is something, then. Thank you."

Elana looked back at the fire and the children sitting there. "Your children are quite astonishing."

Lucius looked at them. "I've failed them in many ways," he said.

"No. You love them, and want to keep them safe. You have not failed them. Just do not forget them."

Lucius said nothing, but looked into her liquid blue eyes, bright like a turquoise bay in the Middle Sea.

"Have you told them yet?" she asked.

"No."

"Do. They are quite attached to Xanthus and need their time to say farewell, as does he."

"I know. Another disappointment for them."

"He will be better here. He cannot go where you are headed. And he is tired."

Lucius nodded and went back to the fire with the clay pot in his hand. He sat down beside Adara and leaned forward to look at Phoebus and Calliope.

"I need to tell you something."

Phoebus looked up and Calliope handed Antiope to Briana.

"Yes, Baba?" Calliope said as she and her brother looked at him.

"It's about Xanthus."

"What about him?" Phoebus asked.

"He is going to be staying here."

The children were silent, and in their eyes, Lucius could see disappointment once again.

"But why?" Calliope asked.

"He needs to rest now. He has fought long and hard." Lucius felt Adara place her hand upon him and looked at her. She understood. He looked back to the children. "He will be happy and safe here with the others, and Elana will take very good care of him."

Calliope looked up at Elana and smiled through her tears.

"You can go out and say goodbye to him if you like," Elana said. "He is waiting by the water for you."

Without another word, the children stood and went out the door, their hands clasped, their heads hanging.

"I'll go with them," Adara said, but Lucius held her back. "Just a moment." He looked at Dagon and Briana.

"We'll go with them," Briana said, picking up Antiope and going out with Dagon.

When Lucius and Adara were alone with Elana, Lucius stood and went to where he had slept to pick up the bundled blanket. "There is something else I would leave with you, lady, if you will agree." He sat back down beside Adara with the bundle across his lap. "I think we all feel safe here with you, that this place is special to our family." He looked at Adara and she nodded, her eyes going to the bundle.

I know what he is doing, Adara thought. *It is right.* She nodded to Lucius to continue.

Lucius folded back the blankets to reveal the hilts of the three swords beneath, and their golden light reflected onto his and Adara's faces. He looked at Elana.

"These blades have seen much blood. But they have always been wielded in defence of good. They are the Dragon's blades. The one, my ancestral gladius, and the other two…they…they were forged by the Gods."

Elana's eyes widened as she looked upon them, for she could see the divine craftsmanship in them, the destiny written upon the blades, and as she observed this, she heard the voice of Apollo himself calling to her.

Be the keeper of these weapons, and be tied to the Dragon's line for all time.

Far-Shooting Apollo, All Seer… I shall do as you bid. Willingly, I pledge myself to the Dragon's family. Elana nodded to Lucius. "I will keep these weapons safe for you and your family."

Lucius' eyes were wide then. "Did he just speak to you?"

Elana nodded slowly.

Adara tried to figure out what was being said, but she had learned that some things were better not explored or explained.

"Do you agree with this, Adara?" Lucius asked. "I do not want to part with them, but wherever we go, they will draw attention and put us in danger."

"It is best," she said reaching out to touch the handle of the blade Lucius had given her, the blade she had killed Claudius Picus with. Her hand stopped short of the hilt. "I have wielded it enough."

Lucius stood and placed the bundle in Elana's lap.

She looked upon the three blades, the dragons, the Pegasus, and the eagle. "They will be safe here until they are needed again."

"Thank you," Lucius said, taking one last look at the blade Adara had given him long ago, the blade that he had wielded in battle without fail.

Elana folded up the blanket and set the muffled blades upon the table by the window. "You should leave if you wish to make Din Tagell by nightfall."

"Will we be able to make the journey in one day?" Lucius asked.

"The wyrm is long dead, and the plague has passed," she said. "Yes, you will."

Lucius and Adara found the children standing with Xanthus farther along the shore of the lake.

The children wept as they leaned into his bulk, and as Lucius and Adara approached, Xanthus' neck turned to watch them.

Adara felt tears in her eyes now. "So much is changing again," she said.

Lucius gripped her hand as they walked. "It's inevitable now."

She released his hand and walked forward to meet the children.

Lucius stopped to watch. To his left, he saw Dagon preparing the wagon and horses to depart while Briana and Antiope pet some of the smaller ponies that had come up to them, curious about the newcomers. As he looked around the lake, Lucius' eyes searched for any sign of the man he had seen the night before, but all he could see was the rising sun upon the rippling water, and the herds of wild horses running upon the green slopes on the other side of the lake. He breathed deeply of the cool morning air and, perhaps for the first time since he came back from Death's door, it did not pain him to breathe so deeply.

Soon, the wagon was loaded and ready to depart, and Elana stood outside the roundhouse to bid farewell to all of them. She preferred her solitude, most of the time, but in that moment of farewell, she knew she would miss the Dragon and his family, and Briana and hers. It was not her destiny, she knew, to be among others, to be happy in company. *I am a guardian,* she reminded herself. *This is my realm. And now I am custodian of those sacred weapons.*

Briana approached Elana and wrapped her arms about her. "It was so good to see you again!"

"It is my joy, Briana, to see you happy," Elana said from the falls of Briana's blonde hair. "Come back to see me."

"I will. When we return to Ynis Wytrin."

"You may not return there for some time," Elana said. "Come then, or before. This is also your home." She turned to see Dagon and Antiope approaching.

"Thank you for welcoming us again, lady," Dagon said, taking her hands in gratitude.

"You are always welcome." She knelt to look Antiope in the eyes. "And you, young lady." Elana smiled. "You are very special."

Antiope smiled and reached out to put her arms about Elana's neck.

When they had said their farewells, Phoebus and Calliope approached with Adara.

"Remember what I said," Elana looked at all of them. "You are always welcome here. This is your sanctuary." *You may need it after the long road down which you are departing,* she thought, her heart constricting at the things she had seen in the mists of her mind. "I am here for you."

"Thank you," Adara said, as the children hugged Elana in turn. "And thank you for what you are doing for us," she whispered.

Elana smiled, but as she looked at Adara, her expression shifted and her eyes brightened in the morning light. "Gods can weep as much as men...and more so...let him go...and he will return..."

Adara looked at her, confused, scared, unsure of the meaning of what Elana had just said. The words sent a cold shiver down her back.

Elana looked surprised for a moment, then rallied herself for the woman before her. "All will be well, Adara. It will."

Adara released her hands and stepped back to take the children's hands. "Thank...thank you, lady, for everything." She turned to Lucius who was standing behind them. "We should go."

"Yes," Lucius answered. "I'm coming," he said as he watched Adara and the children climb into the back of the wagon where Xanthus was leaning his head over the side to say farewell one more time. He turned to Elana. "Thank you."

"I am here for you, Dragon. And I will keep your weapons safe."

"I am grateful for it."

"Now…you must go while the sun is upon the moor." Before Lucius could turn, Elana stepped forward quickly to place her hand upon his chest where the dragon was burned into his flesh. It writhed between hot and cold. "The Gods are with you, Lucius Metellus Anguis, but you must also be with yourself."

She pulled back and bowed to him.

Lucius bowed back, confused, his hand still upon his chest. He then turned to Xanthus and looked up at the stallion. "Farewell, my friend." Lucius took him by the bridle and led him to the water's edge. "This is your home now, my friend." His throat was tight as he spoke, for he had not thought enough about this moment, the actual parting. "No more fighting…no more pain. Live and be at peace, and know that I am eternally grateful to you, no matter what befalls me."

Lucius reached up and hugged the stallion around the neck one last time, their breathing and heart beats unified as they had been in their greatest hours together.

Epona, please watch over him for me, Lucius prayed, and in his mind, the goddess smiled and nodded.

I will, her familiar voice said.

Lucius reached up to unbuckle the bridle that was still around Xanthus' head, and removed it. "Farewell, my friend."

Xanthus looked at Lucius one last time and then trotted away around the edge of the lake.

His heart a little broken, Lucius went back to the wagon and climbed in to sit in the back. "Let's go," he called to Dagon who was sitting on the driver's bench.

The wagon lurched forward then, moving away from the roundhouse and up the watery track, away from the lake.

Phoebus, Calliope and Adara sat with Lucius at the back of the wagon looking toward the lake where Elana stood with her hand in the air bidding them farewell, and in the background, on the other side of the lake, they could see Xanthus running and rearing among the other horses who dwelled there in peace and safety.

With his daughter weeping quietly beside him, Lucius raised his hand to the guardian nymph one last time.

Elana stood there watching the wagon until it disappeared over the hill and into the summer sunshine where it was beginning to burn away the mist.

She was alone again, but for the horses about her.

It is different now, she thought, and her mind went back to the bundled blanket upon her table. *I must hide them. I must keep them safe.*

She walked back to the roundhouse and entered.

Inside, the fire in the hearth was still burning, low and steady. She looked around and felt that her home was empty. *So it is.* She then found what she had been thinking of - two leather satchels that had been waxed on the outside and oiled on the inside. She used them on the rare occasions when she travelled across the moors, but now they would serve a new purpose.

Elana took the bundled swords in the blanket and slid them into the first satchel. She tied the open end as tightly as she could, and then slid the entire thing into the second satchel, tying that end as well.

She looked over the thick bundle, every seam, every inch of wax, and was satisfied. "It will hold well."

She then set the bundle down and removed her robes so that she stood naked in the firelight.

She had been there so long, in that place, and yet she had not aged. *Ever beautiful, but always alone...* She used to be bitter about it, about the Gods' plan for her, but she had come to accept her destiny. *It is a worthy one,* she thought as her fingertips strayed to the space above her breasts where the dragon had burned itself onto her soft skin so long ago. It was a brand of solitude, she knew. She then picked up the bundle and walked outside. She stood there, the air tingling her bared skin as she gazed out at the still water beneath the blue skies.

Elana walked toward the water's edge and looked down to see herself there, holding her destiny in her hands. *Yes. This is right.* She looked up from her shimmering reflection and saw a point of light out in the middle of the water. *There.*

She waded into the water, farther and farther out until the surface rose above her hips and stomach, and then above her breasts. After a relaxing breath, she dove and swam freely with the bundle until she was at the appointed spot.

Down and down she swam until she found the ancient altar at the bottom and there, upon the algae-covered bowl of the altar, she placed the bundle and fastened it with the rope. She stood back, her arms and legs fluttering gently so that she hovered in that familiar, watery realm, her hair spread out around her like a dark, rayed sun.

Until you are needed again.

She bowed to the altar, turned, and swam back to shore.

When Elana emerged from the depths, her body dripping, revived, she turned to look out at the lake, her lake, and smiled.

May the Gods treat you well, Dragon.

VIII

DUX DRACORUM

'The Leader of Dragons'

It was fortunate that it was early when they left the sacred pool, for Briana had forgotten how long a journey it was across the moor to get to her ancestral fortress. She had not seen Din Tagell in many years, but she could still picture it in her mind, hear the way the winds rushed about the castle rock, smell the salt-sea air everywhere. It was a dream, as was travelling over the great moor to get there.

"This land is unlike any I've ever seen," Adara said to her as they drove along the ancient highway over the moor.

Briana smiled "This was where Einion and I rode and hunted as children. We always found something new to explore. That was before any plague, and the wyrm was simply a story."

As she spoke, Lucius looked ahead to the place where he, Dagon and Einion had discovered the awful truth of that, where they had battled the wyrm and nearly died for it. *Are you out here, Lunaris?* he wondered. Another stallion that had bled for Lucius.

While Adara and the children marvelled at the forms of the giant, rocky tors that towered in the distance like brown, green and grey titans, with Briana remembering the names of each, Lucius and Dagon rode at the front in silence.

"Maybe we should spend the night, Lucius? It will be dark by the time we arrive there."

Lucius shook his head. "I don't want to spend the night out here. It's too exposed."

Dagon flicked the reins and the horse trotted a little faster. "You know…Lunaris sacrificed himself for you willingly."

"Many have, Dagon." Lucius stared down at his burned hands, now without even a sword to wield.

"The men all did so willingly too. They were more than aware of the risks they ran. We all knew that an attempt to set you upon the imperial throne was to stare Hades square in the eyes."

"Are you telling me that you feel no guilt or anger that your countrymen have all be slain or scattered to the winds of this world?"

Dagon looked at Lucius. "How can you even suggest I don't? Of course I do, but I've learned to live with it. So should you."

I will do more than live with it, Lucius thought. *I'm going to do something about it.* But he felt badly for prodding Dagon. Of course he knew the guilt that Dagon felt. In fact, he had, in a way, admired him for his ability to move forward with Briana and their child, to find some measure of happiness in the detritus of all that had happened. Then the bitterness crept in again. *But his child survived, and he is whole.* He looked back at Adara and saw her staring at him, wondering what he was thinking. *His wife adores him still.* "Forgive me, my friend. This journey is not an easy one for me." He put his hand on Dagon's arm and squeezed.

"Gods know it, Lucius. We didn't expect it to be," he said as he and Lucius looked to the North where, in the middle of the moor was a green mound surrounded by ancient stone slabs for walls. "I can still hear the echoes of that battle in my mind."

And Lunaris' screams, Lucius thought as they watched the site pass by, a short distance from the ancient highway.

Dagon flicked the reins again and the wagon lurched forward a little more quickly to follow the line of the ancient road and the standing stones that marked its progress over the moor.

As they went, Lucius looked around, his eyes scanning the landscape for any signs of man or beast, and he longed for the weapon he had left behind. He could feel someone watching them, from somewhere at the base of the tors, but he could see nothing but the wavering grass, moss and wildflowers dotting the moor, and the site where Lunaris had died.

Keep going, Lucius... he told himself. *Keep going...*

The Gods had blessed their passage that day, for the rains that usually assailed that land never came. The sun's chariot shone brightly all the way as it progressed across the sky taking them into a purple evening.

"How much farther is it?" Adara asked Briana.

Briana looked around. "We should reach the coast in about an hour. We're lucky the ground has not been soft or muddy. The wagon has rolled much more smoothly and quickly than I expected."

"Why is the fortress called 'Din Tagell'?" Phoebus asked as they watched the evening sky stretch out to the North.

"It means 'fortress of the narrow entrance'," Briana answered. "It refers to the landward passage."

"Is it easier to defend against an enemy?" Phoebus said.

"Why yes! Good, Phoebus. Before, this land was full of various kings all vying for power, and our ancestors sought to protect Din Tagell against them. They used the natural landscape to their advantage. The fortress itself is an island rock."

"How do we get across?" Calliope asked.

"Very carefully," Briana smiled. "There is a bridge."

Adara half listened to the conversation, but her mind was tired and she worried about what they would do next. She knew they would not remain in Dumnonia long, but was not sure how they would leave it either. There was apparently a lot of trade along the coast, but who could they trust? They lived in a world where most men would betray them for a few denarii. One utterance of the name 'Metellus', and they would be done for. *Lucius and I need to discuss that.*

It grew darker and darker, and just as they began to regret not stopping for the night, the smell of salt filled their nostrils.

"We're here," Briana said, moving to the front of the wagon and changing places with Lucius. "Come, Antiope. Let me show you!" She felt her heart beating quickly as they rolled along the road toward the narrow, torch-lit gatehouse of the landward fortress.

"Einion has done some work," Dagon said, pointing to the new stables lining the road before the entrance. "The gatehouse is similar to the one back at-" He stopped himself from saying more. "There are guards."

"What's that sound?" Antiope asked as the wagon slowed before the oncoming torches.

"That's the sea, my girl," Briana answered, her voice shaking a little as the realization that she was finally home came crashing upon her.

Dagon reached out to touch her arm and smiled. "You're home, Briana."

She nodded silently, wiping a tear away from her cheek and breathing deeply of the sea air.

"Hold there!" one of the guards said as he and another stepped forward. Both men wore matching grey woollen tunics and cloaks pinned with round, bronze brooches. They each carried a round shield and long spear with a leaf-shaped blade, and had gladii belted around their waists. "Who are you?"

"Lucius, it's Arthrek!" Dagon called back, remembering the young Dumnonian who had fought so bravely at their side the night they had taken the fortress. Dagon smiled and called back. "Arthrek of Dumnonia, is that any way to greet your mistress, Lady Briana, daughter of Cunnomore and Queen of Sarmatia?"

The guard was stunned briefly. "Queen of... Lady Briana?" he rushed forward as Briana was stepping down out of the wagon. "I'm here to see my brother, Lord Einion."

"By the Gods, lady!" Arthrek said. "He'll be overjoyed to see you! And Lord Dagon, you've returned!"

"I have," Dagon said, dismounting and reaching up to take Antiope into his arms.

Lucius, Adara, Phoebus and Calliope watched as the introductions were made, and proceeded to get down out of the wagon themselves.

Behind them, along the road, more men were emerging from the stables and the makeshift tavern to see what the talk was about.

Lucius pulled his cloak over his head and walked forward with Adara and the children to join Dagon and Briana.

"I can't believe you're back," Arthrek was saying, his official demeanour having crumbled. He felt joy at seeing Dagon again, and awe meeting Briana for the first time, after all the stories he had heard of her prowess in battle. "Lord Einion has told many tales of your battles around the hearth fire of the hall at night, lady."

Briana laughed. She felt good. "Exaggerated, I'm sure," she said.

"Never!" Arthrek added, brushing aside his shaggy blonde hair. "Is the Dragon not with you?" he asked, seeing the black-cloaked stranger approaching from the wagon with a woman and two children.

Lucius stepped forward so that the torches caught his features. "I'm here, Arthrek," Lucius said.

The Dumnonian could not speak in that moment. He could only stare, try to comprehend the sight before him, the changes that had been wrought on the great warrior who had slain more of Caradoc's men than any other, the man he had seen chase a god from the halls of the castle rock, risking everything for their rightful lord.

"Lucius Metellus Anguis…" Arthrek whispered, his head bowed. "Is it really you?"

"Yes, Arthrek. It's me, but barely." Lucius reached out to take the young man by the shoulders and hold him up straight. "Stand tall before your mistress. You're a warrior."

Arthrek nodded, gulping audibly at the sight of Lucius' disfigurement. He looked at Adara and the children.

"My family," Lucius said. "My wife, Adara, and my son and daughter, Phoebus and Calliope."

"An honour," Arthrek said, bowing to them.

"Where is my brother?" Briana asked, trying to draw the awkward attention away from Lucius who had pulled his hood closer about his face.

"In the hall upon the summit, lady. Come, I will take you to him." Arthrek looked beyond them to the wagon and the other guards who had come to listen to what was being said, whispering that the Dragon had returned. "Quickly now! Three men to bring their belongings across the bridge. And another to stable the horses and stow the wagon!"

"Yes, sir!" one of the men said.

Soon, three men laden with their satchels were walking ahead and passed beneath the wooden gates of the entrance to the fortress.

"We can carry our belongings," Phoebus said, not wanting to appear weak before the young captain.

Arthrek smiled at him. "You will need both your hands to cross the bridge, young man."

After passing the gates, which were closed behind them, they walked along the narrow passage between the tall rock embankments, until they reached the black abyss of the chasm. The crashing of the sea was loud in their ears, and the new rope bridge that Einion had built swayed a little in the darkness, the ropes creaking with every step.

"Mama, I'm afraid," Calliope said, looking down.

If she was honest, Adara was too, but she could not say so before the children. Even Phoebus, usually somewhat more daring, was hesitant to set a foot upon the bridge.

"It's perfectly solid!" Arthrek called back. "Just hold on with both hands while you cross!"

Briana went first, followed by Dagon who had Antiope clinging about his neck like an oversized torc, her eyes shut.

"I'll go first," Lucius said to Phoebus and Calliope as he pushed his hood back the better to see. "Stay close behind me and don't look down. Just keep your hands on the ropes." He looked at Adara. "Are you all right?"

"Yes," she answered. "Let's just go."

Together, they followed the dark forms of Dagon and Briana, slowly at first, and then a bit more quickly once they grew accustomed to the swaying of the bridge. Soon enough, they were on the other side in a small courtyard where the others waited for them.

Lucius stopped to look back the way they had come. He remembered running after Gwyn ap Nudd that night, across the bridge they had just crossed. He could still hear the taunts, his rapid breathing, and the gallop of the horses' hooves as he pursued the hunter onto the moor. *Would any of what has come to pass had happened if I had not come here in the first place?* he wondered. He knew, of course, that the knowledge he had gained in Annwn would not have affected the actions of Rome against his family. *Am I any better for knowing? Would I have even tried to take the throne if I had not known?*

Lucius pulled his cloak back over his head as he stared at the bridge and the abyss below it.

"Lucius?" Dagon was at his side.

The others watched, curious, from the torchlight of the courtyard where they waited to follow the path up to the summit.

"My friend?" Dagon said. "I'm remembering too."

Lucius looked at him, and Dagon stepped back a little upon seeing the anger etched upon his face.

"A lot of blood was spilled here, I know. And I can still see you running from that hall after him… It was one of the bravest things I've seen any man do, to run after a god like that."

"Sometimes, I wish I hadn't," Lucius said. "Things might have been different."

Dagon shook his head. "You know that's not true. You made a truce with at least one enemy that night."

"But there are more," Lucius said, walking forward to join the others, not waiting for Dagon. "There are always more..."

Arthrek, with Briana beside him, led all of them up the small road, and as they went, the sounds of laughter and of singing rang out above the sound of the crashing sea.

Briana smiled to herself at how good it felt to be there, to hear laughter and joy again where she had thought it gone forever.

"This is where we got into the fortress," Dagon said to Briana, pointing to the postern gate door that led down to the beach.

Arthrek stopped. "I remember it well, Lord Dagon. I had to get that door open for you, Lord Einion, and the Dragon." He looked back to see Lucius coming up from the rear, a shadow at their backs. The young warrior cleared his throat. "Caradoc's men didn't make it easy to get in."

"I see you carry the scars upon your face," Dagon said.

"And I wear them with pride!" Arthrek continued walking up and around the curve in the road as it climbed higher.

Phoebus hung back to wait for Lucius. "What happened here, Baba? You've never really told me."

Lucius looked at the doorway that led to the beach far below. He did not want to revisit that night anymore, but the look in his son's eyes made him realize that while he was so lost in his anger and remembrance, he was forgetting how confused, and even lost, his wife and children must be. They were in a strange place, preparing perhaps to set out on a long and dangerous journey. In his mind, Lucius knew what he intended, how he saw their journey playing out, but they were ignorant of the path. They trusted him.

"Well..." he began. "Dagon, Einion and I, along with Einion's queen, Gwendolyn - she's an excellent archer - we came up from the beach far below, the place they call 'the Haven'. The tide was coming in and there were guards down there. After we took care of the guards, we climbed up the very steep and dangerous stairs to this door. Arthrek had to fight three men to get to the door and open it in time for us."

"And did he?" Phoebus asked.

"Yes. We came in here and then, hidden beneath our cloaks, we walked up the way the others are going now." Lucius began to walk with Phoebus, following Adara and Calliope as they rounded the turn in the road. "It was a blood moon that night, and there were banshees in the sky above."

"Did they attack you?" Phoebus sounded scared, but his curiosity was stronger. He looked up at the dark sky as they went.

"No. But Caradoc's men did. They were everywhere, but they were busy receiving offerings from the villagers." Lucius looked around and saw the scattered bonfires upon the plateau where people gathered and sang. Up ahead, he saw Arthrek and Briana slow down as a group of older women who remembered her came to offer their greetings and marvel at Antiope who clung to her mother's arm.

The people appeared overjoyed to see the returned daughter of Cunnomore and her family, to know she was back at her brother's side.

They also greeted Dagon, some of the men recognizing him as they passed and calling greetings.

When the Metelli passed, however, there was silence. It was as if the joy and laughter were suddenly sucked out of the air.

Calliope grasped her mother's hand, and Phoebus walked close beside Lucius.

"Why are they staring at us?" Phoebus asked.

"I don't know," Lucius said, but in truth, he did. They did not recognize him. The warrior they remembered had been young and strong-looking. The one who walked before them now appeared old, and ruined.

"It's all right, Baba. They don't know," Phoebus said.

Lucius looked ahead to where Adara walked, obviously feeling awkward. "Let's join your mother and sister." Lucius and Phoebus came even with Adara and Calliope as the ground flattened out before the stone hall and a gathered crowd of warriors and villagers.

Warm light poured out of the hall onto the ground outside, inviting them in.

"So many people," Adara said.

"Where are they?" a loud voice burst out from within the hall at that moment, and they all recognized it and relaxed. "Where is my sister and my friends?"

At that moment, Einion appeared in the doorway of the fortress hall, a wide smile upon his face. He wore a simple circlet about his head, and was dressed in a dark blue, wool tunic bordered with a line of gold thread, matching breeches, boots, and a cloak of dark grey which was fitted with a large round brooch. About his neck was a thick, twisted torc, the symbol of his lordship.

But he was the same Einion they had all known and loved, and as he stepped toward them, he threw his arms about Briana and the crowd cheered all around them.

Adara felt tears coming to her eyes at the sight of brother and sister reunited, the warmth of the greeting Einion gave to Dagon, and his first look at his niece as he knelt down to look Antiope in the eyes. She had never seen Einion so happy. The weight of the guilt and worries that he had carried on his shoulders for years, and since the day she had met him for the first time, seemed to have disappeared. But she did not weep for that, she knew. *Will I ever see Lucius so happy again?*

As Einion stood up again, he paused to look at the Metelli, and the crowd grew quiet around all of them. He stood there, noble and proud and full of emotion as he looked upon them.

Behind him, Lucius heard some of the people whispering.

"Pen Draig," said one person, and the word name was repeated by others.

Lucius ignored them.

Einion opened his arms and walked forward. "Phoebus...Calliope... You've grown!"

They had been nervous to see Einion again, but as soon as they were face-to-face with him, they rushed to him.

"I've missed you both so much," he said, and he meant it. One might have thought that the king of that land would not show such emotion, but such was Einion as lord that he did not hold back when it came to those he loved, for he had fought for them all, and cherished them all, cherished that place.

"Adara," he said, taking her hands and kissing her cheek. "I'm..." He saw the tears in her eyes that she was holding back, and forced himself to stopper his own. *What has happened to you my friends?* he thought, but instead of speaking more, he squeezed her hands and touched his forehead to them.. "It is so good to see you."

"And you, Einion," Adara said, steadying her voice. "It's been so... so long."

"I know... I know," he answered. "But you are here now. You are safe." He released Adara's hands and then stepped toward Lucius who came forward to meet him within the circle of firelight that stretched into the darkness from the hall entrance.

Lucius could see Einion's shock at his appearance, his great sadness as he looked upon his burned face and thin hair.

They clasped hands briefly, their eyes locked, and then Einion pulled him in and wrapped his arms about Lucius tightly. "My friend..." he whispered. "What have they done to you?"

Lucius squeezed back and knew that of all the people in the world, Einion most of all would understand the thoughts that were running through his mind, the anger, the thirst for vengeance.

Einion tried to smile, but he could not. Instead, he raised his arms to the people gathered round. "My friends! Not only has my sister, her family, and my dearest friends returned to us this night. But Lucius Metellus Anguis - the Dragon! - has returned. If not for his courage and skill, I might not be standing here with you today, for that night of the Blood Moon would have been death to us all had he not chased the Dark Hunter from our hall." Einion then turned to face Lucius, and bowed. "My home is yours, dear friend."

Lucius wanted to fade into the dark, to disappear then, feeling unworthy of the attention in that moment, but the smile upon his children's faces forced him to stay where he was. He bowed back to Einion.

"Come!" Einion shouted. "Drink and eat with us!" he turned to go with Adara and the children into the hall behind Briana, Dagon and Antiope.

Lucius followed them, but was hampered by people gathering around him, reaching out to him, touching his cloak and whispering.

"Pen Draig... Thank you... Pen Draig..."

Lucius managed to pull away and entered the hall. He stopped short once inside and remembered the blood that had run deep upon the floor, the bodies piled high, the screams. He forced himself to focus on the laughter now, the bright, warm light, the garlands upon the walls instead of guards, the joy that spread throughout the room.

Just then, two more of Einion's warriors came up with Arthrek to greet Lucius.

"By the Gods, Lucius Metellus Anguis..." said one. "Do you remember me?"

Lucius looked at the man and forced a smile. "Of course," he said. "Edern, how are you?"

"Well, sir. As you can see. Life is very different here now than it was that night so long ago." The warrior adjusted his cloak and sword.

Lucius looked at the weapon.

"A gift from Lord Einion. He presented one to each of those who had fought for him that night," Edern said.

"Do you remember me, sir?" said the other warrior.

"Yes. Ewella. You are much changed," Lucius said, immediately realizing how ridiculous that sounded. No one had changed more than him.

But Ewella had the grace not to say anything, but reached out to take Lucius' arm. "It was an honour to fight beside you that night, sir. To fight beside the Dragon."

"The honour was mine," Lucius said. He looked around the hall. "The world is much changed here."

"The land thrives, and so do we," came a woman's voice. "Welcome back, Lucius Metellus Anguis."

Lucius turned to see Gwendolyn standing before him, surrounded by the women who had been her friends, and who had fought alongside them as well that night.

She stood tall and beautiful, her long black hair flowing down over her shoulders in a thick braid to rest upon her swollen belly. Her bright, grey eyes looked upon Lucius with kindness and a measure of disbelief.

"The Gods have truly blessed us with your coming," Gwendolyn said, her hands taking his. "I have just met your wife and children. Such a family. I am sorry to hear of your ordeals."

"Some things cannot be undone," Lucius said, trying to stop that conversation. "But I see your family is growing." He looked at her belly and smiled. "May the Gods bless you and your child."

Gwendolyn smiled and caressed her swollen belly. "It is near time. This child, I feel, is strong like its father."

"Einion is fortunate to have you beside him, lady." Lucius looked at the three women who stood beside Gwendolyn and bowed to them. They had all risked their lives that night, and he found it strange that they should look up to him so much, a seasoned warrior, when they, who had never fought before, had waded into the fray of their own accord. "Caja, Ebrel... Melwyn... It is good to see you all well."

"Thank you, lord," they said, almost in unison.

"I am no lord," Lucius said his hands up.

Gwendolyn leaned in at that moment. "Please know...you are so much more to us and our people than a 'lord'. You must remember that."

Lucius nodded and Gwendolyn took his hand and led him through the crowd to the front of the hall where Adara and the children sat at a long table with Dagon, Briana and Antiope. Behind them was the stone throne that they had fought for, and beside it, a matching one made of oak from the land.

But Einion did not sit above them all in that moment, but alongside them at the tables laden with food, pitchers of wine and water. He rose when Gwendolyn approached with Lucius, and gave his seat to his friend, the Dragon. He then took his wife's hand and kissed it.

"My friends!" Einion called out to the hall. "Tomorrow night, we shall have a great feast in honour of my sister's return home, and to honour my brothers-in-arms and the Dragon's family! We have much to celebrate!"

The hall erupted with cheers that rang out into the night, no longer the screams of lost time, but of joy and life in a prosperous land.

Across the table, Lucius looked at Adara, but she would not meet his gaze. He wanted to reach out to her, to wipe away the stream of tears that she was trying so desperately to hide, but he could not.

Even surrounded by joy in that moment, their children smiling and laughing with Einion and Gwendolyn, Adara was distant, and so was he.

They were in the midst of someone else's joy, and that only made them taste their regret more bitterly.

After the hearth fire began to burn down and the people dispersed to their dwellings either upon the fortress rock or on the mainland side of the bridge, Arthrek took the Metelli to one of the stone guest houses on the northern side of the plateau.

Einion wanted them to stay up the night to talk, to tell him everything that had occurred, but the journey had taken its toll upon Lucius and Adara.

"Arthrek," Einion said. "Take our honoured guests to the main house on the northern side. They'll be most comfortable there." He turned to Lucius and Adara. "It's warm and safe. I'll come to you in the morning."

"Thank you, my friend," Lucius replied, and Einion hugged him tightly, uncaring of the burns covering his body.

"Rest, my friends," Einion said, before Arthrek led them out. When they were gone, he turned to Briana and Dagon. "Tell me all that has happened."

. . .

Outside, the sky was dark and the moon hidden behind a cloak of clouds. The Metelli were led along a grassy path, following Arthrek's torch as they went. The sound of the sea far below was a constant, but apart from that and the wind, there was little else.

"Lord Einion built these guest houses with you and Lady Briana in mind," Arthrek said as they approached a small gathering of squat stone structures with slate rooftops. They were partially set into the ground so as to shield them from the winds. "There are other buildings like this across Din Tagell's fortress, but these are the nicest." He smiled as they arrived and he opened the door.

Lucius, Adara, Phoebus and Calliope followed him inside, ducking under the lintel. The room was of similar size to the guest house at Ynis Wytrin. In a small hearth, a fire already burned brightly to warm the house, the smoke escaping through a small chimney that poked out of the slate roof. Thick, warm blankets had been laid upon two wide beds with fresh straw mattresses, and upon a single, pedestal table, there was a pitcher of water from the fortress well with four clay cups.

"It's simple," Arthrek said, "but it is warm and dry. Everyone eats in the hall with Lord Einion and Lady Gwendolyn. Caja and Ebrel are excellent cooks. You'll see." Arthrek smiled. "Do you need anything else?"

"No, thank you, Arthrek," Adara said. "This is perfect."

"Very well. Until tomorrow." He bowed and went to the door where he turned back to them. "It really is an honour to meet all of you," he said. He looked to Lucius. "Without you...none of us would be here." Arthrek smiled slightly. "Goodnight."

When the door was closed, Lucius bolted it. He and Adara turned to Phoebus and Calliope only to see that they were already asleep upon one of the beds. They smiled.

"They're exhausted," Adara whispered, going over to cover them with two of the thick blankets. She turned back to Lucius to see him struggling with his tunic which had stuck to his skin. "Let me help you."

Lucius turned to her and ceased his efforts to rip off his clothing. He had felt suffocated in the crowded hall and was eager to get his clothing off.

"Einion seems to have found his place in the world," Adara said. "And Gwendolyn is kind and beautiful. Their people love them well."

"That they do," Lucius said as the tunic finally came off. "The land thrives under his rule, just as Elana said."

Adara hung his tunic over a wooden stool by the fire. "It must have looked very different when you were here."

Lucius stood still and thought about it. "It was." He sat on the edge of the second bed and bent over to remove his sandals. "His uncle was a tyrant, and the people were sick and hungry and full of fear."

"Einion seems different too. He's truly happy," Adara said, sitting down beside Lucius.

He did not answer right away, only stared into the fire opposite. "The crushing weight upon his shoulders was lifted after he slew his uncle. Vengeance healed him."

Adara stared at the floor. "Vengeance does not heal or erase all ills, my love."

My love... Lucius repeated the words in his head.

"Helping those in need, knowing you have done so to the best of your ability…that could also be a salve for the soul." Adara placed her hand upon his shoulder, her fingers touching him gently. "Arthrek said it himself. None of them would be here without your help."

Lucius nodded absently. He did not want to talk of everyone else's happiness in that moment. For the first time in a while, he looked upon his wife, remembered her beauty and, for a moment, remembered the passion that had once burned so brightly between them. His fingers stroked a long strand of her dark curls and traced her shoulder down to her breast.

Adara reached up to touch his face with the palm of her hand and she leaned forward to kiss his rough lips. Nervous, she sat back and slowly pulled her tunica up over her head so that she sat naked beside him.

Lucius looked at her soft skin, traced with scattered scars above the thicker, red one across her abdomen. He leaned over to kiss that scar and then together, they lay down beside each other.

They were awkward together, unsure, and it was as if they were two youths at the dawn of their life, taking those first, tentative steps of intimacy.

As Adara's hands ran gently over Lucius' ravaged body however, they both realized that he had been robbed of much more than his appearance.

His face contorted and he pulled away. "Leave it," he said, his rage burning violently inside. He wanted to scream, to punch the stone wall beside them, but instead he lay down and turned his back to her. "I'm sorry."

Adara pressed herself against him, refusing to let go. "It's not your fault, my love. At least we are together and alive with our children. That is our gift."

Lucius did not reply as he lay there, eyes shut while she stared at the back of his head and shoulders, tears running down her cheeks as the wind and waves howled outside in the darkness.

When morning came, a thick mist hung about the fortress of Din Tagell. The sound of sea birds perched and nesting in the crevices and ledges of the high rockfaces echoed all around, a cacophony atop the deep rush of the waves far below.

Phoebus opened his eyes to see his mother and father sleeping upon the same bed. It was the first time in a long while that he had seen them sleep together, and the sight of it made him feel a sliver of happiness. *Thank you, Gods,* he thought.

He felt the cold sharply then, for the fire had long gone out, and so he rose and went to the hearth to add more kindling and wood shavings. He took a tinder box from the floor beside the hearth and set about lighting the fire. Soon, the flames leapt and smoke began to rise up and out into the sky above the house.

Phoebus looked at his sister to see if she was awake, but all he could see were strands of blonde hair sticking out from beneath the edge of the warm blanket. He looked again at his parents.

Adara still slept, but Lucius lay there with his eyes open, gazing at the fire. He looked up at his son. "Thank you for starting it, Phoebus."

The boy smiled at his father. "I couldn't sleep any more. The birds are so loud," he whispered.

Lucius nodded, and slowly sat up, covering Adara with the blanket. He stood and walked in his breeches to the table by the fire where the clay pot that Elana had given him sat. "I'm sorry..." he said to Phoebus. "Will you help me with this? My skin burns today."

"Of course, Baba," Phoebus said, taking the clay jar and removing the lid.

The contents smelled very strongly, and he could not tell what it was, only that it was very slick.

Lucius sat down on the stool by the fire.

Phoebus began to apply the mixture to the skin of his back, shoulders and then his arms and chest, covering the dragon last. "Does it hurt very much still?" he asked, looking at the angry brand upon his father's flesh.

"Sometimes," Lucius said, reaching for his tunic. "Help me with this?"

Phoebus set the jar down and wiped his hands upon a rough cloth that was there. He then took the tunic and carefully placed it over his father's head, so that it fell down as Lucius stood.

Phoebus then looked around the room, a slight panic in his eyes as he began searching.

"What is it?" Lucius asked.

"Someone has stolen our weapons!" he said, a bit too loudly. "They're gone!" he hissed.

"No…wait, Phoebus. They're not gone. They're safe."

"What?" The boy looked at his father, a rising anger evident.

"We cannot take them where we're going. They'll be recognized, and that will put us all in danger."

"What do you mean? Where are they?"

Adara and Calliope were now stirring.

"I left them with Elana at the sacred lake, for safekeeping," Lucius said, his hands up and reaching out to his son.

But Phoebus pulled away. "You what? You had no right to do that!"

"Quiet yourself," Lucius said.

"No! How are we to defend ourselves if we have to? You gave me that gladius! It was mine. It helped me to defend myself and Calliope. I must have it!"

"Phoebus…please…" Lucius forced himself not to get angry, for he could see the panic in his son's eyes. "I too left my greatest weapon with her, as did your mother. It was necessary. If we take them, they may be taken from us, but if they remain with Elana, they will always be there for us when we need them."

"What if we don't come back?" Phoebus said.

Lucius could not answer. He knew in that moment that perhaps they never would come back to Britannia.

"The Gods curse me!" Phoebus said before opening the door and slamming it behind him.

"What's happening?" Calliope said from her bed.

"It's all right, my girl," Adara said, going to the bed and lying beside her daughter. She looked across at Lucius.

"He was looking for the swords. I had to tell him."

"We should have told him sooner," Adara said before closing her eyes again, trying not to think of what happened the night before.

Outside, Phoebus scanned the surrounding area to see the grassy surface of the fortress rock and, jutting out of the mist, the low stone walls and slate rooftops of a few other buildings. He walked for a short time up the path, but stopped when he saw someone approaching.

The cloaked figure walked directly toward him, but he could not see who it was, only that they carried a longsword at their waist.

Phoebus felt distinctly unarmed in that moment and began to look around desperately for a weapon of some sort, a branch or farming implement, anything he could use. His heart began to race and he thought about running.

"Phoebus wait!" An arm reached out and grabbed him.

It was Einion.

"It's me, Phoebus!" Einion said. "What's wrong?"

It took a moment for the boy to register who it was, and when he did, he fell into the older man's arms, shaking.

Einion held him tightly. "It's all right, lad. Easy...easy now... You can't go running around the fortress. You'll fall off the cliff and there are deep crevices on the surface. You must stick to the paths."

Finally, Phoebus relaxed, looked up, and nodded. "I'm sorry. I thought you were an attacker."

"You're safe here," Einion said, feeling great sadness at the changed look in the boy's eyes. "It was a look he recognized from himself when he was young, when he had escaped death at the hands of his uncle. "You're among friends here."

"My father gave away our weapons, his sword, Mama's, and the gladius he gave to me. We're defenceless now."

"What did he do with them?" Einion asked.

"He gave them to the nymph at the sacred lake to keep."

"Elana?" Einion said. "They will be safe with her. You needn't worry. She'll keep them for you."

Phoebus shook his head. "You don't understand...we're leaving and never coming back!" He pulled away and ran back toward the guest house, rushing past Lucius who had come out to look for him.

"Phoebus!" Lucius called, but his son did not stop.

Lucius watched the door close and was quiet for a moment before turning to walk toward Einion.

Einion found it difficult to speak at first, seeing Lucius in the light of day. He found it hard to believe that that was Lucius Metellus Anguis.

Lucius saw his eyes. "I know...say it."

"Say what, my friend?" Einion answered, snapping out of it.

"How hideous and weak I look."

"I could never imagine you weak, Lucius," Einion said. He shook his head. "Briana and Dagon told me what happened...all of it."

"And?"

"And what?" Einion said, his hand upon the hilt of his longsword. "If you want, I'll help you hunt down and slay every last one of them."

Lucius looked at his friend and knew that he meant it. There was no hesitation in Einion's words. He had travelled a similar road and was now happier than he had ever been, it seemed. It made Lucius smile for the first time in a long while. He looked up at the sky where tufts of white cloud could be seen beyond the mist. The sound of the crashing sea was loud in his ears, just below the cries of gulls and cormorants. "I know you would," Lucius said. "You're the only one who understands."

"Of course I do. Sometimes, vengeance is the only remedy."

"Thank you, Einion. Truly. But I cannot ask it of you."

Einion looked at Lucius then, unarmed, burned and thin. "You can't do such a thing on your own."

Lucius gripped his arm, and for a moment, Einion saw light blazing in his friend's angry eyes. "I have to."

"Then, let me help you however I can, Lucius."

"Thank you," Lucius answered as they began to walk.

"Come," Einion said. "Walk with me around the fortress."

.   .   .

As the sun and wind dispersed the mist that had blanketed the seaside fortress of Din Tagell, Lucius and Einion walked along the paths to the southern cliffs, passing gatherings of small, stone dwellings, and followed the western edge northward.

"When I was here last," Lucius said, "I didn't realize how vast the plateau is, and how many dwellings there were."

"It is vast, but I rebuilt many of the dwellings. My uncle did not allow anyone else to live here, except for his personal guards," Einion said, his voice betraying the hatred he still felt toward Caradoc.

"You've done a lot of work."

"Much. We've been rebuilding around Dumnonia, for the people, not at their expense. The mines are working again, and we have a lot of trade."

"What are you mining?" Lucius looked out at the broad, bald coastline. It stretched southwest from where they stood, to the green lands beyond that led to the moors.

"Tin, mostly," Einion answered. "Romans can't get enough of it!"

Lucius stopped walking and turned to Einion. "Are there Romans here?"

"There have been a couple of prospectors showing interest. They came to me for permission to survey some areas. I had to give a little, so I allowed it in areas to the south."

"Don't let them in, Einion. You know what will happen. Slowly, they'll take over your lands and push you out."

"I know, but I have my people to think about. If I resist any interaction with Rome, they'll come with troops, won't they?"

Lucius nodded slowly.

"If I sell some land to a couple of merchants to build villas, then there's more of a chance that that will suffice." Einion saw that Lucius seemed doubtful. "Besides, most of the trade comes from outside, and I hold the majority of the mining operations for my people."

"You have a lot of traders coming through?"

Einion smiled. "Almost every day, there are ships coming here to trade goods for our tin, many of them from the Middle Sea."

Lucius looked up quickly. "Really?"

Einion nodded and continued to walk. "I trade for Samian wares from Gaul, olives, oil and wine from Italy and Graecia, and even garum from Iberia and Africa Proconsularis."

"You hate garum!" Lucius said, remembering Einion's face the first time he had tasted the Roman fish sauce.

"True," Einion laughed. "But the Romans at Isca Dumnoniorum can't get enough of it!" He stopped and looked out to sea. "Look! See those three ships to the northwest?"

"Yes."

"They're coming here on their way back from a trip up the coast to the end of the Roman wall," Einion said. He spotted the dolphins upon the sails and smiled. "Those corbita belong to captain Creticus."

"Creticus?" Lucius stared out at the oncoming ships, their sails bulging as they sped toward Din Tagell. "Is he Greek?"

"Yes, but he lives at sea. Even has his wife and children on board with him at all times. The larger ship is their home."

"Do you trust him?" Lucius asked as they continued to walk around the northern edge of the fortress.

"Absolutely. He has no love of Rome. He only deals with the empire insofar as he must. Sometimes he brings me items that...well..."

"What?" Lucius asked.

"Things the authorities would frown on."

"Like?"

"Weapons, mainly. Gladii, spathi, and the occasional falcata. Even some north African bows. Weapons intended for the legions in the North." Einion looked sheepishly at Lucius, but the latter smiled.

"Interesting. Will this Creticus stay here long?"

"He usually stays a few days to await the tin shipment from the moors - he likes to load up as much as possible to return to Italy."

They completed their circuit of the fortress at the northeastern edge where they looked down on the harbour, known as the 'Haven', far below. On the steep slopes, there were a few stone warehouses beside a quay that appeared to be carved out of the fortress' rockface.

Einion pointed down the cliff. "That's the 'Iron Gate'. The ships will dock there and unload the cargo into the first warehouse, and then they'll load up the tin we trade with them from the second warehouse. If the sea is rough, they have to wait to make berth." He looked out at the bay and the waves in the Haven. "Creticus will have to wait a couple of hours before he can dock."

"I'd like to meet him," Lucius said.

Einion turned to him. "Phoebus said you are planning on going away…and never coming back… Is that true?"

The change in Einion's voice was sudden. There was a sadness there, and it touched Lucius, but not enough to sway the course he had set in his mind.

"We do need to go away." He explained the letter they had received from Adara's parents and how he was worried for his own mother and siblings since then. "Whether we will come back…I don't know."

"This land needs all of you, Lucius," Einion said. "And I think that you need this land in a way. It's become a part of you."

"It nearly killed me." Lucius turned away.

"No." Einion stepped around Lucius to face him again. "Rome almost killed you. You have friends here, Lucius. More than you think."

"I also have my own labour to complete."

Dagon and Briana had told Einion what they thought Lucius was planning, and when he heard the news, it filled him with fear for his friend. *It's not possible,* he had told them. *It's suicide!* He did not want to speak of it then, for fear that any talk of it might encourage Lucius. He had meant it, of course, when he offered to help. He even understood the reasoning behind it. But some battles could not be won.

"Can I meet the captain or not?" Lucius asked, his voice hard and unyielding.

"Of course, Lucius. We'll hold a feast tonight in the hall. You can speak with him then."

"Thank you."

They began to walk toward the hall, and ahead of them they saw Adara, Phoebus and Calliope going in as well.

"There are some other people I would like you to meet too," Einion said, waving to Phoebus who looked back at the two men.

Phoebus looked, but did not wave before entering the hall.

Lucius sighed. He knew he would have to speak with Phoebus to help him understand. But there was something more important in that moment. "There is one more thing, Einion."

"Yes, my friend," Einion answered, his arms crossed as he turned to Lucius.

"I would ask that you don't use our full names when introducing us to the captain or others. The fewer people who know who we really are, the better it will be."

.   .   .

When Einion and Lucius entered the hall, they were met with the scent of fresh bread and woodsmoke from the large hearth fire.

At one of the large trestle tables toward the front, before the thrones, Adara, Phoebus and Calliope sat with Gwendolyn, Dagon, Briana and Antiope.

Einion approached them all and rounded the table to kiss his wife and touch her belly. "Creticus' ships have just arrived. We shall have wine and olives for tonight's feast!"

Briana laughed.

"What is it?" her brother asked.

"You!" she grinned at him as he sat across from her. "Look at you! So lordly...receiving trade shipments from around the empire...a father-to-be...and now you're eating olives and drinking wine!"

"What's wrong with that?" Einion said, unable to hold back his own smile.

"You used to hate olives and preferred beer to wine."

"Since meeting Lucius and Adara, I developed a taste for them." He winked.

Adara smiled and looked down to the end of the table where Lucius had seated himself to eat across from his son.

Phoebus would not look at his father, and when Lucius reached across the table to touch his son's hand, he pulled it away quickly.

"Phoebus...please... Let me explain."

"What's to explain?" the boy said loudly.

Gwendolyn's women, Caja and Ebrel, set down some fruit and cheese in that moment, but then hurried away to the kitchen, along the east wall of the hall.

Lucius looked at everyone. "My apologies."

Phoebus turned on him, his eyes looking up from his plate. "You should be apologizing to me, Baba! That sword was my birthright. I used it in battle. I killed a man with it!"

"Mama," Antiope said to Briana. "Why is Phoebus shouting?"

Briana hushed her daughter and fed her more of the oatmeal Caja had prepared.

"Phoebus, don't shout, please," Adara added.

"You knew about this too? How could you?"

"Enough!" Lucius slammed his fist and his horn cup of water tipped to spill over the edge of the table. "The decision was not yours to make. We are hunted, Phoebus. Do you understand what that means? It means that any person out there," Lucius pointed out the door, "would be willing to plant a pugio in our backs for a few denarii. We will be travelling as a simple family. We could be searched at any time by Roman authorities. We could be killed and left for dead on the side of the road!"

"Baba!" Calliope cried, unable to take the argument anymore, seeing the frightened look in her brother's face beside her. "Stop it, please!"

"Those swords are unlike any others, Phoebus," Lucius said, forcing his voice to calm. "They would be recognized, or at least raise questions, and so draw attention to ourselves on our travels."

"But why do we have to travel at all?" Phoebus asked. "Can we not stay here, or in Ynis Wytrin? Or even live back at the hillfort or in the village with Paulus and his family? Why do we have to run?"

Lucius stopped and stared at his son, pushing his hood back to reveal his burned face and head. "We're not running, Phoebus. We're going to see our family. To make sure *they* are safe. And I have to-"

Lucius stopped himself from saying more. He could not tell them. His family was afraid enough as it was. *I can never tell them,* he thought.

"You have to what?" Phoebus pressed.

"I have to see that my mother, brother and sister are well too."

"Have you had no word from them at all, Lucius?" Einion asked.

"None," Lucius said.

"Culhwch and Alma had a letter that a courier brought from Graecia from my parents," Adara said, "but nothing from Antonia, Caecilius or Clarinda."

No one said anything, and the adults there did not give voice to the thoughts that were going through their minds, for they were too dire to think on.

After a few seconds of silence, Einion looked at Phoebus at the other end of the table. He knew what Phoebus was feeling, the fear that was gripping him more and more tightly with each passing day with the uncertainty that lay ahead. That, coupled with the fact that he had been forced to kill a man at such a young age, was enough to unnerve him permanently. *And Lucius is dealing with his own demons now,* he thought. He cleared his throat. "You know, Phoebus, I have an armoury of simple weapons. If you like, you can pick one to take with you."

Phoebus looked up quickly, his face incredulous.

Einion looked at Lucius and Adara. "That is, if it is all right with both of you?"

Adara nodded to Lucius. "We cannot be defenceless," she said.

"You should all have something," Briana added, looking at her brother who nodded in agreement. "You can't travel unarmed."

"Very well," Lucius said to his son. "What do you say to Einion?"

"Thank you!" Phoebus said, the aura of fear falling away from him momentarily.

Einion stood. "Come! Let me show you." Einion waited for Lucius and Phoebus to join him, as well as Adara.

"Are you coming, Calliope?" her mother said to her.

Calliope shook her head and slid over to sit beside Briana. "I don't need one, Mama."

Adara laid her hand upon her daughter's head. "I understand, my love." She kissed her head and followed Einion and the others to the back of the hall, beneath a curtain that led through what she presumed was Einion and Gwendolyn's private chambers, to a door at the far end.

Einion unbolted the door and pushed it open. Taking one of the oil lamps nearby, he went first. "I had this built onto the hall when the chamber was done," he said. "I needed a more private place to store the weapons from Creticus, and didn't want the few Roman traders who came here to see what I had."

They entered a large square, stone room and from the faint light of Einion's lamp, they could see that the walls were lined with longswords, axes, cudgels and gladii. There were simple leather cuirasses, chain mail shirts, round shields and spears as well.

Einion touched the lamp to a brazier in the middle of the room and it ignited right away, illuminating every blade and piece of metal armour.

"You could arm a turma of men with all of this," Phoebus said, his eyes scanning the walls and a smile coming to his face.

Einion turned to face them. "I won't be caught unawares like my father was," he said. "If anyone dares to threaten my family, they'll regret it." His eyes met Lucius, then he turned to Phoebus and put his hand upon the boy's shoulder. "Pick any weapon you like. It is my gift to each of you."

Phoebus scanned the walls where the weapons hung. He picked up a falcata and pulled the curved blade from its sheath. It was much heavier than what he was used to.

"You should have something that you are trained with," Lucius said. "Something that can be concealed."

Phoebus scowled over his shoulder at his father, but put the falcata back. He knew he was right in what he said, though he would not admit it. He walked over to stand beside his mother where she stood looking at the range of gladii, some with long, straight blades, and others with a longer, taper that ended in a deadly point.

Adara took down one of the latter, stepped back from the others and twirled it in her hand deftly. She stabbed out, cut up, and thrust again. It was a shorter version of what she was used to, but it would be easily concealed, and she knew Calliope could wield it as well, if she had to. "Thank you, Einion."

"You're as much a warrior as the rest of us, Adara," he said.

She slid the gladius back in its sheath.

"Here," Einion said, taking a small pugio from the wall. "Take this too, for Calliope." Both weapons had simple, wooden handles, hilts and pommels. "They're plain-looking, I'll grant you, but they are very well-made."

After staring at the wall, Phoebus took down a gladius similar to the one Adara had chosen, except the wood had a more reddish tinge, as if it had been stained with blood. The sheath it had was of a deep, crimson leather, and he ran his fingers along it. He looped the scabbard over his right shoulder so that the sword hung at his left side, and then he drew it.

In that moment, the face of Serenus Crescens' son appeared before him, and Phoebus thrust his blade out quickly, once, twice, three times, reenacting the scene that haunted his dreams in an attempt to make it go away, to become accustomed to it. He spun the blade, parried, and thrust again.

Lucius watched his son staring into the space before him and wondered what invisible enemies he slew. He remembered playing at soldier by himself along the banks of the Tiber when he was a child, but never could he have imagined killing someone at that age, the way Phoebus had been forced to. "It suits you well," he said to his son, sadness in his voice.

Phoebus turned to them. "Thank you, Einion." He slammed the

gladius home in the scabbard and looked at Lucius who had not yet chosen.

Lucius turned to the wall, his mind going back to days when he had commanded men, fought beside his brothers. He could hear the clang of steel and the rush of cavalry as his eyes ran along that wall. No sword could ever replace the one he had left with Elana at the sacred lake, but he needed one that was reliable and strong, one that would be the tool he needed to defend his family as long as he could, at least until he had completed the task that was etched upon his now-stony heart.

His eyes came to rest upon a simple gladius in the style legionaries used. Its long, straight blade was extremely sharp and cut his finger when he touched it, and the hilt, handle and pommel were all of black walnut wood. He took down the blade and tried it, thrusting and cutting, and though he felt the strain upon his muscles, it felt right, light, and accurate. He spun the blade one way, and then the other way, and thrust again. *It will do.*

Einion handed him the scabbard of black leather. "May it serve you well, my friend."

Lucius accepted it and slid the gladius slowly into it. "It will," he said as he hung it over his shoulder the way his son had. "Thank you."

While preparations were being made in the hall of Din Tagell for the feast that night, Lucius, Adara, Phoebus and Calliope roamed the fortress together and gazed out at the vast sea from the cliffs. The sun emerged from behind intermittent banks of cloud to warm their faces as they walked.

While Calliope strolled alongside her mother, Phoebus managed to find open spaces of grass, away from any villagers who were present, to practice his sword skills again. It had not felt right to do so in Ynis Wytrin, but at Din Tagell he felt compelled, especially on the brink of a journey such as the one they were planning.

"Do you think this sea captain can be trusted?" Adara asked Lucius as they looked down on the three ships being unloaded at the Iron Gate far below the eastern cliffs.

"I don't know," Lucius answered. "Einion thinks so." His left hand released its grip on the pommel of the black gladius that now hung at his side, and gripped Adara's. "I've been thinking about something..."

"What?"

"Our name. We can't use it on this journey. Perhaps ever again."

"What name should we use?"

"I don't know, but it can't be Metellus, or even Antoninus. It's too dangerous."

Adara was silent as she looked down to the ships and the sailors going to and from the warehouses perched on the side of the fortress rock. "Everything is changing." Her voice was sad, tinged with despair.

"Everything *has* changed," Lucius answered.

The day passed slowly, and the tide came in and swept out as the Metelli wandered the heights of Din Tagell, stopped every so often by villagers who had come to find Lucius, to thank him and Dagon, the returned heroes who had helped place their rightful lord back upon the throne.

As dusk began to fall and the sea began to grow still, torches and fires were lit about the fortress, along the paths leading to the hall where garlands were hung and the sweet smell of roasting meats wafted out into the evening air.

After cleaning up in the small house where they had slept, Lucius, Adara and the children emerged to make their way to the hall.

Lucius and Phoebus wore their gladii beneath their cloaks, but Adara and Calliope went without for the time being. Their clothes were simple wool, for all that they used to possess had burned in the fires of their home long ago. As they walked together toward lord Einion's hall, they looked more like a family of Britons than Romans, and that endeared them all the more to the people they encountered at every step.

Lucius was relieved that Phoebus had begun speaking to him once more, and he wondered if it had only been his fear that had made him so angry toward him. Now that he had a weapon again, he seemed more relaxed.

"Baba?" Phoebus asked as they walked behind Adara and Calliope along the path. "Why do the villagers keep calling you 'Pen Draig'? What does it mean?"

Lucius had been wondering the same thing, though he did not know the answer. "We'll have to ask Einion what they mean by it," Lucius said.

"Yes…" Phoebus seemed thoughtful, and he stood a bit taller as he walked now, his fist upon the pommel of his gladius. "There is something about the words…they sound right for you for some reason. I don't know why."

Lucius' smile faded as they approached the hall and the gathering of people outside around the fires. He noticed that sometimes he would actually forget the state of himself, the wrecked and burned body he now inhabited, and how his appearance made people uncomfortable. Quickly, he pulled his cloak over his head, just as Arthrek waved them over.

"Lord Einion is waiting for you, sir," Arthrek said as he turned and began to lead them inside to their places.

The crowd of villagers parted for them and they made their way into the warmth of the hall.

"Pen Draig!" some people called to Lucius as he passed, confusing him even more as to the meaning of it, the reason they used it. He supposed it was better than if they called out his true name. There were many people there, and he could not be sure they were all loyal to Einion, though it did appear that way. *Relax, Lucius,* he told himself. *You're among friends.*

As if feeling his discomfort, Adara reached out to take his hand as they walked. The crowd around the throne was thick, and it was difficult for them to see above all the heads of people standing and at table.

Then, they saw Dagon who, as soon as he spotted them, came directly toward them. His eyes were red, as if from weeping, and Lucius felt an icy prickle of fear come upon him.

"Oh, no," Adara whispered. "What's happened?"

Dagon stopped before them, filling the path and view ahead.

"What is it, Dagon?" Lucius asked. "What is it?"

"By Epona, Lucius," he said, his voice shaky, his hands trembling. But then he smiled, so broadly and with such relief that Lucius thought he had perhaps gone mad.

"What?"

"Elana was right. The dragons have come to Dumnonia!"

"You're not making sense!"

Dagon smiled and stepped aside, and behind him stood Brencis and several others of his Sarmatian countrymen.

Lucius felt his throat tighten, and Adara gasped beside him, her hand upon her mouth as the hall went silent.

In that moment, Lucius felt as though he was looking the dead in the face, observing their tattooed arms and necks, their long, braided hair, and the leather and mail of their clothing. But they were not dead. They were alive.

Brencis smiled and approached first, but slowly, his eyes taking in what he had only heard of, the burned person of their praefectus.

"But how?" Lucius stuttered, and looked to Einion beyond the men where he stood in front of his throne, smiling down at the gathering of warriors.

He remembered them all - Brencis, Akil, Deva, and even Boas who had spoken so well outside the walls of Eburacum. *I thought they were all dead!* Lucius cried inside. Magar was there too, and Dima, Shura, Hipolit, Barna and Taboras. Lucius stepped toward them, his hood falling back as he did, but he did not notice. All he saw were his long lost men, Dagon's countrymen.

"Ave Anguis!" Brencis said loudly before saluting Lucius. The others behind him followed suit. "Hail the Dragon!" they called, and the hall erupted in applause and cheers as Lucius stepped in amongst the men to greet each of them personally.

Dagon watched with tears in his eyes, and met Briana's gaze where she stood holding their child and watching the scene. "Never could I have imagined such a thing," Dagon said to Adara who was standing beside him with Phoebus and Calliope.

Adara watched as Einion came down from the dais to join Lucius, while Gwendolyn waved her over to join her and Briana at table with the children. Adara stepped forward, the Sarmatians bowing to her as she passed, greeting each of them. *They too, are our family,* she thought.

Lucius turned to Einion as he joined him, Brencis and Dagon. "But how is this possible?" he asked. "Brencis, what happened?" He was gripping the younger warrior's shoulder tightly, wanting to make sure he was real, that the men around them were real.

Brencis' face darkened. "After that night in Eburacum, we were scattered. Caracalla's Praetorians were hunting us down ruthlessly. For months we rode across Britannia in small groups, but I had given quick orders to pass the word that men should aim to make it here, to Dumnonia and Einion, since I remembered you had helped him reclaim his lands."

"Over the past year, they've been trickling in," Einion said.

"Lord Einion and his people have given us sanctuary," Brencis said.

"We've been blending in among the people, living in different places across the moors."

"And they've helped me to fight off some of the Hibernian raiders that sometimes attack our shores!" There was gratitude in Einion's voice.

"I can't believe it," Lucius said. "I feared you all dead."

"Most of the men were slain," Brencis added, draining his cup. "So many of our brothers…hacked down by the Praetorians or betrayed by those seeking favour with Caracalla."

Lucius felt his anger again, a cloud to pass over the joy he had so recently felt.

"But some of us have survived, Anguis. We live in secret peace in Lord Einion's lands."

"Is this all of you?" Lucius asked.

"No," Brencis said, his smile returning. "Some of us made it north to Lord Afallach in the Votadini lands. We are Sarmatians no more, but rather Dumnonians and Votadini."

"And you're all alive!" Dagon said, hugging his cousin tightly.

"And we're alive," Brencis echoed.

"To the Dragons!" some of the villagers called out, raising their cups and toasting the Sarmatians. "And to Lucius Pen Draig!"

The hall echoed with joy that rebounded off of the garlanded walls as wine flowed and platters of meat and cheese were brought out and set upon the long tables.

Lucius turned to Einion as the men all began to seat themselves and start eating. "I've been meaning to ask you… What does 'Pen Draig' mean?"

Einion smiled. "Since your men, the dragons, have come here, since they have helped protect us against the raiders, the people have said that dragons have returned to Dumnonia. They *are* the 'dragons'."

"And 'Pen Draig'?"

"It means 'Head Dragon'. My people remember you helping me reclaim and save this kingdom. They tell stories of how you chased the Hunter from this hall. They know that you led these men in battle… And so, you are the Pen Dragon to them. A mighty leader of great warriors."

"Pen Dragon," Lucius repeated the name, nodding as his mind turned the words over. There was something that echoed true in the name, though a part of him felt that he did not deserve it. Still, as he stood there with Einion and walked to sit among the men, the people in the hall continued to call it out, to raise their cups of wine and beer to him where he sat.

"Looks like you have a new name," Dagon said to Lucius where they sat.

"Seems that way," Lucius answered, nodding to Dagon and then looking across the table to Adara.

She reached across the table to grasp his hand, her green eyes searching his in the firelight, looking for some sign of how he was feeling with everything that had happened. Therein, she saw confusion and anger, relief and rage, and in that moment, she knew that his mind was still set. *At least I will see my family,* she thought. "Pen Dragon..." she said, looking at Lucius and then to Phoebus and Calliope beside her. "It is a good name, I think."

Lucius nodded, and smiled sadly. *I'm leaving a part of myself behind, but I am not myself anymore...* "As good a name as any," he said.

Phoebus and Calliope understood what was being said in that moment. They all had to change for the journey ahead, and in their minds, they tried out the new cognomen.

"Baba," Calliope said, her face thoughtful as she stared at him. "Anguis and Pen Dragon...they're the same in a way."

Lucius smiled at his daughter. *So wise.* "Yes, my girl. They are."

The evening wore on as more food and drink went around, and more wood was added to the hearth and fires outside.

Throughout the evening, Lucius could see that the men were taking turns observing his disfigurement, that they too felt anger at what had been done to him and his family, to their countrymen at Rome's hands.

At one point, when Lucius stood to stretch his legs before the dais, Brencis and Boas came to join him.

"So, Anguis?" Brencis said. "When are we going after them?"

"After who, Brencis?" Lucius asked.

"The bastards who did this to you. We all want vengeance! Blood for blood!" There was anger and resentment in his voice, a determination that was shared by the look in Boas' eyes and the eyes of all the other Sarmatians there. "We almost had them in Eburacum. We'll get them again."

"Claudius Picus is dead," Lucius said.

"But not..." Boas lowered his voice and stepped closer. "But not Caracalla."

"That is not your concern, my friends. You've bled enough for me."

"How can you say that?" Brencis growled. "We are pledged to you, until death. Or have you forgotten?"

"No. I haven't forgotten, Brencis. But in a way, you have died," Lucius said. "You have been reborn and have a chance for peace now."

"We don't want peace, Anguis. We want vengeance for you, and for our slaughtered countrymen!"

Lucius grabbed Brencis' arm tightly, the mottled flesh of his face turning red. "Listen to me. It's finished for all of you. That is my last command. I want you to live. Your allegiance is to your king, Dagon, not to me."

Brencis laughed. "You can't dismiss us!"

"Listen to me. Vengeance is not within your grasp. You are hunted, and will be across the empire. This is the only safe place for you. Take the gift the Gods have given you." Lucius turned to Boas. "All of you."

"And you?" Brencis said. "Dagon tells me you're leaving Britannia. Where are you going to go? You're hunted more than any of us!"

"We go to our families."

"Really? And what else?" Brencis stared at Lucius intently. "We want to go with you, Anguis."

"You will always be my dragons," Lucius said, softening his voice. "And I will get vengeance for all of us." With that, Lucius turned and went to see Einion who was sitting on the throne as he and Briana spoke.

"Lucius 'Pen Dragon'… It suits you!" Einion said.

"Where is the captain you spoke of…Creticus? I would speak with him."

Einion leaned forward. "Arthrek just brought word from the Iron Gate that Creticus is determined to finish unloading the cargo tonight. He'll be up here in the morning with his family. You can meet him then."

Lucius balled his fist.

"What is it, Lucius?" Briana asked. "Aren't you happy to see your men alive?"

"Of course I am," Lucius answered quickly. "It's just…" He took a deep breath. "Never mind." He turned to walk back to Adara and the children. *We don't belong here.*

.   .   .

That night, as Lucius lay in bed, sleepless beside Adara, he thought about all that had happened that evening.

Seeing the Sarmatians again, seeing them alive, was truly a gift from the Gods, he knew. He had never thought to see them again, any of them. Or to see Dagon so full of joy and relief. But in seeing them, he had been frustrated too, for knowing that they were there, and alive, and loyal to him still, after everything, had layered more guilt upon his already guilt-ridden mind. He felt his own resistance to his plans, and it galled him. He knew he needed to reinforce his resolve, to leave Din Tagell soon. And the only way he could do that was to take ship with Creticus.

He only hoped that the captain was trustworthy.

Tomorrow, I'll find out.

The morning was still and misty, the air absent the crash of waves. The muted cries of gulls on the cliffs could be heard more clearly, as could the creak and pull of the corbita and their rigging down by the Iron Gate of Din Tagell.

Lucius was up before his family, and rather than wait for them to administer the resin to his skin, he dressed himself and went out to walk the clifftops and look down on the dolphin-sailed ships below.

To his surprise, the seamen, who had unloaded cargo the previous night, were already loading up the tin that they had traded for with Einion. Lucius looked to see a small group of people making their way up from the quayside, along the path that climbed up past the warehouses to the summit of the fortress. They made slow progress, but as they got closer, Lucius could see a man, woman and two younger men making their way up.

"Must be the captain and his family," Lucius said to himself. "Apollo...make them kind and trustworthy." He began to make his way to the hall where he knew Einion would be receiving them. As he walked, he checked the gladius that hung at his side. He did not know the newcomers. He needed to be ready for anything.

Arthrek and Edern were standing outside the entrance to the hall when Lucius arrived. They were speaking with Hipolit and Barna about the latest Hibernian raid on the southern coast.

"Anguis!" Barna saluted.

"You don't need to salute me anymore, Barna," Lucius said, trying to smile at his former decurion.

"We will always salute the Dragon, sir," he answered without pause.

"Arthrek," Lucius said to Einion's man. "Is your lord awake yet?"

"Yes, sir. He's always up early, no matter how long we drink into the night. Besides, today, he wanted to see captain Creticus early."

"I think I saw the captain and his family on their way up just now. May I go in?"

"My lord and lady said this is your family's home, sir. You may go where you wish."

Lucius nodded and went into the hall, his eyes adjusting to the darkness within. The fire had been lit, and rather than the raucous chorus of celebration that had occurred the previous night, what Lucius heard was the sound of a family united.

Antiope's young voice echoed in the hall as she asked questions of her uncle, Einion, about the bulge in Gwendolyn's belly.

Dagon sat there too, his arms around Briana as he straddled the bench beside her. They watched their daughter with her tiny hands upon Gwendolyn.

"I felt it!" Antiope said, a look of wonder upon her face.

"That's your cousin speaking with you," Einion added, kissing Gwendolyn upon the cheek and also placing his own hand beside his niece's. "You will be great friends."

Lucius suddenly felt like he was intruding. He stopped, still hidden in the shadows, but Dagon heard the shuffle of his footsteps and turned.

"Lucius, come join us!" Dagon said.

Einion stood. "Yes, come, Lucius. There is food!"

Lucius walked up to the small group. "I'm sorry to disturb you," he said, his eyes turning to Gwendolyn.

"You are family to us all, Lucius Metellus Anguis" Gwendolyn said.

Lucius approached the table, putting his hand upon Dagon so that he sat back down. "There is something I must speak with you all about. The sea captain and his family are on their way up."

"Good," Einion said. "That man's crew is efficient, I'll give him that. I'll introduce you."

"That is actually what I wanted to talk to you about." Lucius looked back to make sure they were still alone. "You cannot introduce me as Lucius Metellus Anguis, or any of us as 'Metellus'."

"But that is your name," Gwendolyn said. "A proud name, especially in these lands after all that you have done."

"It's not safe for me or my family anymore. We are hunted...*I* am hunted."

"Lucius, I don't think you should go on this journey," Dagon said, standing now to face him. "Please don't go. This is the safest place for you to be. Adara and the children will be safe here."

"Rome will find us."

"Rome thinks you are dead still," Einion said.

Lucius shook his head. "That is why we must go now. We need to see if our families are safe. They're in danger because of me."

"Is that the only reason you're going?" Dagon said, his brow creased in worry and frustration. "You can't do this!"

"Do what, Dagon?"

"Kill the emperor!" he said, his voice low so that Antiope would not hear.

But the others did.

"What?" Gwendolyn's face paled and she looked at Lucius as if he were a threat in the middle of her home. "That's not possible."

Lucius looked back to the entrance of the hall to see if the captain had arrived. "Please...just... Do not call me Metellus anymore. My family must travel under another name."

"What shall we call you then?" Einion asked, standing as voices began to come in at the doors at the far end of the hall.

Lucius looked at Dagon and Einion. Call me 'Lucius Pen Dragon'. Our family is now 'Pen Dragon'."

The group was silent, but he could see Dagon nodding. "It is right," the Sarmatian said. "You are the leader of dragons, Lucius. 'Pen Dragon'," he tried it out.

"That is what our people already call you, Lucius," Einion added, coming around the table as the sea captain's family was led slowly into the hall by Arthrek. "If you are ever asked, you can say that you are Dumnonian. You are my own family."

"And that also, is true," Briana added, coming around the table to take Antiope into her arms. "We are all family."

Lucius looked upon them as the captain's footsteps approached. "Thank you."

"Captain Creticus!" Einion said loudly. "Welcome once more to Din

Tagell!"

Lucius turned to see the new arrivals.

Captain Creticus was short and stout for a Cretan. He had black hair and keen, stormy eyes that were used to squinting into the distance. His skin was like leather, weathered from so many years at sea, but it suited him and matched the brown leather jerkin he wore beneath his thick grey wool cloak. He gripped Einion's arm eagerly, greeting him as if greeting an old friend.

Behind Creticus was a taller woman whom Lucius presumed to be his wife. Beneath the long fringe of her brown hair were lively grey eyes. Strangely enough, she also had weathered skin, which was unusual for a woman, for rarely did men bring their women on board ships, considering it bad luck.

Creticus' sons were older than Phoebus and Calliope by a few years. They were tall, lean and strong with long, curly black hair that appeared to be oiled. Their eyes were dark but they smiled readily when Einion greeted them.

"Ah…" Creticus said, looking around the warm hall. "Din Tagell is always our favourite port, Lord Einion!" He smiled, waiting for Einion to introduce the others.

"Captain Creticus, this is my sister, Briana of Dumnonia, her husband, Lord Dagon, and my niece," Antiope jumped into Einion's arms at that moment, "Antiope!" He hefted her so that she was nearly taller than everyone else.

"An honour." Creticus bowed politely to Briana and Dagon. "You have your brother's look about you, lady."

"We are twins," Einion said.

"As are our boys," Creticus' wife said, smiling. "How are you feeling Lady Gwendolyn?" she asked.

"I feel well enough, thank the Gods," Gwendolyn smiled. "But I am ready to hold my child in my arms, and not inside."

"Such is the feeling toward the end," the woman said.

Creticus turned then to Lucius, and his smile faded slightly, though he did not appear threatening or worried, merely observant of the silent stranger in their midst.

"May I also introduce our good friend…Lucius…Pen Dragon."

Lucius did not step forward or extend his hand, and Creticus did not reach for it. Both men bowed slightly.

"This is the man whom you spoke of last night, Lord Einion?" Creticus asked.

"Yes. He and his family are our dearest friends and allies." Einion came to stand beside Lucius.

Creticus turned back to Lucius. "And you require passage to Italy? Just yourself?"

"Myself, my wife, and two children," Lucius answered. The more he spoke with this stranger, the more exposed he felt. *But if Einion trusts him, so can I.*

"You want to go to Ostia, or to Brundisium?"

Lucius thought about it a moment. Both places would be too dangerous. "Pisae, if your route takes you there."

"It can, for a fee, of course." Creticus put up his hands. "But we can speak of that later." He smiled. "For now, I am pleased to meet a friend of Lord Einion's."

Lucius could see Creticus looking at him, his injuries, but the man had the good grace not to say anything.

"This is my wife, Nerissa."

Lucius bowed to the lady.

"And our sons, Castor and Pollux."

Lucius nodded to the young men.

"We are a family that lives by the sea, and at sea. Our ships are our homes, and we do not invite strangers onto them easily. But...as Lord Einion is a good friend - and client - you and your family are welcome to sail with us."

"I thank you, captain," Lucius said.

"Please, sit," Einion said. "Eat."

Gwendolyn stood to leave. "I'll have Caja and Ebrel bring more food and drink."

"Our thanks, lady," Creticus said, taking a seat at the long table, followed by his wife and their sons who sat themselves at the end. He turned to the older boys. "Don't go eating Lord Einion out of hearth and hall."

"No, Father," the boys said, smiling in unison.

"I will go and see where my family is," Lucius said, turning to leave.

The group watched Lucius leave the hall.

"By the Gods, those are bad burns," Creticus observed.

"He has been through much," Einion said, his voice severe.

"Excuse me," Dagon said, leaving the table to go after Lucius.

Outside, the sun had begun to burn away the clouds, and the green of the grass upon the fortress plateau was bright beneath their feet.

"Lucius, wait!" Dagon said, walking past Hipolit and Barna.

Lucius stopped, his hands upon his hips, his face turned to the sky above. "What is it, Dagon?" he said without looking at him.

"Are you sure you want to leave?"

"You keep asking me that, even though you know the answer."

"I don't have a good feeling about this." Dagon's voice was pleading, and full of worry. "I know what you want to do. I can sense it. And I know you have the Gods' ear, that you know things I could not fathom, but this is madness. Stay here. Send Creticus to bring your families back here instead. Let them make Britannia their home."

Lucius turned to Dagon. "You think the Gods are helping me in this? You think I'm privy to some great mystery? I'm not, Dagon. Until a couple of years before, I wasn't privy to the origins of my own life, and now that it is branded upon my very chest, I still don't understand it!"

Dagon stopped. He could see the anger coming back, the redness rising up from Lucius' neck to fill his scarred face. "I'm sorry...I...I don't want to see you go. The men don't want to see you go, not again. Lucius you have no idea how relieved they all are to see you and your family again. You're as dear to them as I am."

Lucius turned to Dagon and hugged him tightly. "I know...and I am grateful for it. I thank the Gods that some of them survived. But I have to leave. I will never be able to rest or allow myself even a small measure of happiness until I see this through, until I finish it."

"Will it ever be finished?" Dagon asked as the wind picked up and swirled around them, pulling at their cloaks.

"One way or another, it will be finished," Lucius said, his voice calmer, resigned. "It's been the greatest honour of my torn life to lead your countrymen, but our paths must now diverge. You have a life here with your family. You have to keep Briana and Antiope safe."

"And what of Adara, Phoebus and Calliope?" Dagon asked, his voice louder and more angry.

"They will be safe."

"You don't know that. No one can!" Dagon turned to see Adara and the children walking along the path toward them from the guest house near the northern cliffs. "Let them stay here with us. We'll protect them until you return."

"No, Dagon."

Dagon stood back and stared at Lucius. He had never known him to be so absolute, so reluctant to hear reason. He shook his head and turned to go back to the hall. When he reached Hipolit and Barna, he stopped. "Tell the men... Anguis is only to be called 'Pen Dragon'...Lucius Pen Dragon."

"Not Metellus?" Hipolit asked, chewing on a crust of bread.

"No. Lucius Metellus Anguis does not exist anymore. They are the Pen Dragon family."

Barna nodded. "It's the Gods' will then."

Dagon looked at Lucius. "Yes. It is."

Adara watched as Dagon walked determinedly away. "What's wrong?" she asked Lucius, his cloak and cowl pulled tightly about him.

Lucius looked down at his family and in that moment, he felt doubt again about his decision to bring them, to put them yet again in harm's destructive way. *Maybe they should stay here?* He shut his eyes and shook his head.

"Baba? What is it?" Calliope asked, reaching out and hugging him with her lanky arms. "Did you and Dagon have an argument?"

Lucius opened his eyes to look at his family, and he felt a great sadness then. They wore everything they owned. They were refugees, not of the hillfort, or Rome, or Athenae, but of the world itself. *How has it come to this?* he asked himself for the thousandth time without the satisfaction of an answer.

"Do you all wish to stay here, while I sail with Creticus' ships?" he asked.

"You ask us that now?" Adara asked, the displeasure written clearly on her face. "Do not ask it again! I wish to see my family, Lucius. I need to see them, to see my home again!"

"Mama," Phoebus said. "It's all right. Baba is just asking a question," he turned to Lucius, "weren't you, Baba?"

Lucius stared at Adara, and she at him.

"Make up your mind," Adara said evenly.

As they stood there, in the middle of the fortress plateau, the gulls swirling in the wind overhead, the sea a deep, writhing blue in the distance, Lucius' mind explored their options. He did not want to be separated from his family. The truth was, he did not know if he would come back, and Adara would resent it if she never saw her family again.

"We will go," he said.

"Fine," Adara answered.

Phoebus and Calliope closed in on each other, holding hands. They were less prepared to quit Britannia's shores, but they trusted their father still.

"All will be well," Lucius said to them. "But we have to change our name," he said to the children. "Inside is the captain and his family who will take us. They appear nice, but we don't know them. Einion trusts them," he said to Adara. "But still...from now on we have a new cognomen, a name that is more Briton than Roman."

"What is it?" Phoebus asked.

"We are the 'Pen Dragon' family. You two are Phoebus and Calliope Pen Dragon. Mama is Adara Pen Dragon. And I am Lucius Pen Dragon."

"What does the name mean?" Calliope asked, tucking a strand of her golden hair behind her ear.

"It means 'Head Dragon', or 'Dragon Leader'."

"I don't want another name."

"I know, Phoebus," Lucius said. "But we can't risk anyone knowing our true identities. That includes the captain and his family whom you are about to meet. Do you both understand?"

"Yes, Baba," they said.

"Good. Shall we?" Lucius led Adara and the children back to the hall, and when they entered, more of the Sarmatians were seated at tables.

They stood to greet Lucius, Adara and the children, but Lucius waved them back down to their seats upon the benches, not wanting Creticus to see the honour the warriors paid him.

"Captain Creticus," Lucius said. "I'd like to introduce you to my wife and children... Adara Pen Dragon, Phoebus and Calliope."

Creticus smiled and stood along with his wife, followed slowly by their sons.

"Ah..." Creticus said, his keen eyes taking in the newcomers. "I'm pleased to meet you, lady," he said to Adara.

"Captain," Adara said, placing her hands upon her children's shoulders. "Thank you for taking us aboard your beautiful ships."

"Think nothing of it. As I said to your husband, any friends of Lord Einion's are welcome." He turned to his wife and sons. "This is my wife, Nerissa, and our sons, Castor and Pollux."

"Are you twins?" Calliope asked the older boys.

"No," said Castor, smiling. "He wishes he were like me." He elbowed his brother.

"Settle down, boys," their mother said, smiling. She turned to Adara. "They always get agitated when on land."

"We do not!" Pollux said to his mother, pushing back his black hair.

"Of course you do," Creticus laughed. "You're both mad!"

Adara chuckled. She could see they were a close family. *They seem trustworthy enough.*

As they talked, Lucius watched Creticus and his family for any sign of doubt, any question that surfaced in their minds and features about who he was, who his family was. Creticus seemed straightforward enough. Honest. As such, Lucius knew he would not appreciate being lied to, so it was essential they maintained the facade of their new identities.

As they all sat to continue eating, Lucius noticed that Dagon was no longer there. He turned back to look around the hall, but did not see him with the other Sarmatians who were gathered around Brencis, Arthrek or other Dumnonians, at the far end of the hall.

"So, Lucius Pen Dragon," Creticus suddenly asked. "What is it you do? I make it a point to know about a man before I invite him onto the deck of our wayward home. You understand, of course."

"I do, yes," Lucius said, but things had moved so quickly, he had not thought through the entirety of his story. "I was in the legions…a long time ago. I did my service, and then became a venator, finding animals for the amphitheatre in Londinium."

"How long did you do that?" Creticus asked, dipping a chunk of bread in the bowl of broth he was eating. "That's not an easy job."

"True enough," Lucius said. "I didn't do that for long."

"Was that because of your accident?" Creticus said, looking at Lucius. "I'm sorry…I couldn't help but notice your injuries."

Einion stepped into the conversation then. "Lucius was here, hunting on the moors last year. It was a dry summer. You remember?" he turned to Gwendolyn who nodded. "A fire started in one of the villages near Rough tor. There were children inside one of the house that had caught. Lucius rushed in to help. He saved the children, but…did not escape injury himself, as you can see."

"How terrible!" Nerissa said, her look softening, less suspicious.

"It was terrible," Adara said, placing her hand upon Calliope's, sensing the girl's rising panic.

"Then you are a hero," Creticus said. "Were the Sarmatians fellow hunters, then?" He smiled sheepishly. "I couldn't help but hear them speaking. When you travel the empire as much as we do, you become adept at reading people's backgrounds."

"We are all of us friends here," Einion said. "All are welcome in my lands, as you know, Creticus."

"Of course, Lord Einion!" The captain smiled. "I always say to Nerissa and the boys that yours is the only real, warm and welcoming house upon our northern sea route."

"And what news of the empire, Captain?" Adara asked. "We've been in the countryside for so long as my husband healed, we know little of the latest gossip."

"Yes, Creticus," Einion added. "You always bring me news of strange goings on. What has happened in the wider world since you were last here?"

Creticus finished chewing his bread and then drank the rest of the water from his horn cup. "I have much to tell you, Lord Einion." He looked around the table. "This has been a strange time indeed…across the whole of the empire!"

"What has happened?" Einion put down his cup and glanced at Lucius.

"First of all, it seems that we are all now citizens of the Roman Empire."

"What do you mean?" Lucius asked, baffled by the man's words.

Creticus smiled and nodded, his hands out to the side. "I learned about this only a short time ago, before leaving Brundisium. It seems that the emperor passed an edict - the Constitutio Antoniniana, I think it's called - that makes every free man within the borders of Rome's empire a true, Roman citizen, and grants every free woman the same rights as a Roman woman."

"I don't understand," Einion said, leaning forward over the table. "Are you telling me I'm a Roman citizen now?"

Creticus nodded and chuckled. "Yes, lord Einion. And every man here, except you, Lucius Pen Dragon. I assume you were already a citizen if you were in the legions."

Damn! Lucius thought. *He knows more than I gave him credit for. Maintain the illusion.* "And now we all are," Lucius said.

"Why would they pass such an edict?" Adara asked.

"I don't know, lady," Creticus said. "Political motives are beyond me. I only know what I've heard."

"And what have you heard, Creticus?" Einion asked.

"Some say the emperor passed the edict so that he could tax more people. Others say that the edict will make many more men eligible to serve in the legions."

"But men used to sign up for the auxiliaries because they were granted citizenship at the end of their term of service," Lucius added. "If they are already citizens, then the motive for enlisting is gone."

Creticus shrugged. "I only know what I hear. Perhaps the emperor has plans? There are whispers of some big campaigns coming up in the East. I know, because some of my clients fear what will happen to their shipments if war should break out again."

"You mean 'emperors', don't you?" Adara said, pointing out the words that had also caught Lucius' attention like a thorn as one brushes past a gorse bush. "Both Caracalla and Geta are the emperors."

Creticus glanced at his wife and she stared at her plate. He looked at each of their faces around the table, his eyes wide at the fact that they had not heard the biggest piece of news. He turned to Adara. "Why, no, lady. I mean 'emperor'. Early last year, Emperor Geta was slain."

"H...how?" Adara asked.

"Why, by his brother...Emperor Caracalla." Creticus picked up his cup and drank again. "Some say that Geta was plotting against Caracalla and attacked him, but most suspect the older of the two."

Lucius heard a ringing in his ears. The news was shocking. A part of him had been thinking that perhaps Geta might have been useful, not least because half of the power and decision-making was his. *No more.*

"Some say that the emperor slew his brother in his mother's arms in the palace," Castor said from where he was hunched over his bowl, eating.

"That's enough, boy. You're scaring Pen Dragon's children," Creticus chided his son.

Lucius looked at Phoebus and Calliope and saw that their eyes were wide. Such an act as fratricide was utterly foreign to them.

"Forgive me," Creticus said. "With all that I hear, I sometimes forget that the ways of the world are not meant for younger ears." He inclined his head. "Perhaps that's why we like being at sea? When we are riding Neptune's waves on Oceanus' current, we are as far as possible from the madness. Nothing like a sea journey to clear the mind!"

Lucius did not say anything more, but looked down the table to Einion. If there was danger in Lucius' plan before this news, then now, it was increased tenfold, for it meant that Caracalla was sole ruler, and that he would stop at nothing to protect his rule. He had breached the confines of his sanity.

"Captain," Lucius cleared his throat. "Would you be able to make port in Pisae?"

Creticus sat up. "I always do," he said, his smile returning. "I have friends there, and I always make it a point to pick up a shipment of Etrurian wine. Of course, we have good wine on Crete, but Etrurian vintages are catching on. Good money to be made."

Lucius nodded. "When can we leave?"

"We can leave tomorrow, if the weather's fair," Creticus said. "Sooner the better, if you ask me. That way my sons can stop acting like land-locked Cilicians and get back to normal!"

The young men stopped eating, looked at each other, and then at their father before going back to eating.

"We'll be ready to leave," Lucius said, standing from his untouched plate of food. "I have some things to do. Excuse me."

They watched Lucius walk past the Sarmatians and Dumnonians, and go outside.

"Is your husband not well?" Nerissa asked Adara.

"He's fine. Just nervous about seeing family after so long, what with his injuries and all."

Creticus and his wife said nothing to that, but carried on conversing with Einion about the next time they would return.

Adara did not listen to them, but sat there between her children, wondering what Lucius must be thinking.

. . .

Later that day, after wandering the clifftops of the fortress, digesting the news that Creticus had brought, Lucius found Einion and Dagon alone in the hall.

"Where is Creticus and his family?" Lucius asked as he approached Einion and Dagon where they were seated around the hearth.

"He's preparing the ships to leave tomorrow. Says the weather will surely be fair enough to leave," Einion said.

Dagon looked up from the ground at Lucius as the latter sat across from him. "You're really going to leave?"

"Dagon...I-"

"It's fine, Lucius," his friend said, his hand up. "I understand. I don't agree, but I understand."

Lucius nodded.

"I've drawn up some papers saying you're a representative of my mining operation here in Dumnonia," Einion said to Lucius. "You'll need a better cover than that of retired legionary." He leaned forward to hand Lucius a rolled papyrus with a red seal depicting a series of circles that looked like battle standards upon it. "I'm hoping it looks somewhat official."

"Thank you," Lucius said. "I'll only present it if I have to. I don't want to attract unwanted attention to you."

"Especially now as you can be taxed more," Dagon said.

"Einion told you?"

"Yes. So, we're all citizens now," Dagon said.

"Except none of us besides Einion and Briana are supposed to exist anymore," Lucius said.

Dagon stared at the flames, shaking his head. "This is madness."

"I know," Lucius agreed.

Dagon looked up quickly, a glimmer of hope in his eyes that quickly faded.

"But we have to go," Lucius added.

Dagon nodded. *There is nothing more I can say to try and dissuade him.* His face was a mask in that moment, but inside, he was weeping for the loss he knew would come, for the farewell he would have to say.

As Lucius sat there with his friends, he felt the sting of impending loss. *They have been there for me in so many ways...and now I have to leave them.* He cleared his throat and pushed back the hood of his cloak.

Einion handed Lucius a cup of wine and the three of them sat staring across the flames at each other.

"You know," Lucius began, "this is probably the last time we three will be alone together." *Stay strong. Say what you have to say, but don't change course!* A part of him wanted to change plans, to tell them they were not leaving, that he would remain in Dumnonia and make a life for his family, a life of peace. But he knew he would never rest, that the voice of Nemesis would always be whispering in his ear. "I just want to say that…" his voice caught, but he cleared it again, "…that you two are the greatest friends a man could have." He held up his cup to Dagon and Einion. "It's been an honour and a blessing to fight and live alongside you both, and I will never forget all that you've done for us."

The other two men were at a loss. Lucius Metellus Anguis was saying goodbye, and there was a finality about the words, the look behind his eyes, and in the expression of his burned features.

Einion raised his cup to Lucius. "I drink not to the Gods, Lucius, but to you. To all that you are, and all that you have done. May Apollo guard you along the road."

Dagon too raised his cup, but he could not speak. For so long, they had fought alongside each other, saved each other's lives. They had become family. "To the Dragon," he finally said, and they all three drank. This time, Dagon did not hide the tears that streamed down his cheeks. *May the Gods keep you, Lucius…*

The feast that night was going to be a smaller affair than the previous one.

Captain Creticus and his family said that they would stay on their ship that night, making their offerings to the Gods for a safe journey. Before going down the long, steep path to the Iron Gate and quay, Creticus had told Lucius that they would be setting out with the tide at first light.

"Besides," the captain said, reading the emotion that was as thick in the air as a morning fog at sea, "I think you and your friends need some time. Farewells are never easy. I should know, I've had many."

"We will see you in the morning then," Lucius said.

"Listen for the horn. That will tell you we will be leaving soon."

Lucius watched the captain go back down the path, and when he was out of sight, he made his way back up to the guest house. "Creticus says we're leaving first thing in the morning."

Adara, Phoebus and Calliope all turned to him from where they were filling their satchels and checking that they were not forgetting anything. But they were quiet, and Lucius could see that the journey weighed heavily upon them, especially the children.

Adara's movements were harsh and angry as she finished tying off things. She turned to Lucius. "I just don't know anymore. I want to see our parents, to make sure they're all right… It's been too many years… But, is this wise? Is it too early to leave Britannia?"

Lucius breathed deeply. He did not want to have this conversation again. He could see that Adara and the children had been arguing about it, that Phoebus and Calliope most of all did not want to go on this journey. He swallowed his anger and frustration. *It is not the time to be divided,* he told himself.

Instead, Lucius sat down on the stool by the fire so that they could all see him.

"I know we're all scared of this journey. So much has happened." He turned to his children. "I know you feel safer here with Einion and Dagon, with the Sarmatians… So do I. It feels like home in a way, being among friends, doesn't it?"

Calliope nodded.

"Yes. It does," Phoebus said.

"I know you're angry too. But we have family elsewhere in the empire. Don't you want to see your grandparents and aunts and uncles?"

"We don't even know them!" Phoebus said, and as Lucius saw Adara tense, he wondered if that was what they had been arguing about.

"What if they're dead?" Calliope asked bluntly, her face full of worry and fear.

Lucius breathed deeply. *Then I will avenge them,* he thought, but pushed the darkness away. "What did Etain teach you about using the Sight?" he said to Calliope. "When you are calm…do you see such a thing happening?"

Calliope looked at the ground and shook her head. "I've been trying. I asked the Gods to help me see, to show me."

"And?" Lucius knelt before his daughter.

"They are alive."

"Good."

"But they are so sad..." she looked up, directly into Lucius' eyes.

He did not know what to say to her, but only felt the apprehension seeping into him as she wrapped her arms about his neck.

"If they are sad, then we should go and help them, shouldn't we?" Lucius said.

Calliope nodded as she hugged him, and Phoebus too agreed as he stood from the edge of the bed and went to hug his mother.

When Lucius stood, the orange light of the setting sun lit upon his chest from the small window at the end of the guest house. "Come," he said. "Let's make our offerings to the Gods for a safe and successful journey. And then, we will feast with our friends." He then took up a small pouch that lay beside his satchel on the table.

The four of them left the guest house, their cloaks wrapped about them against the summer wind. Lucius led the way along a path to the western cliffs where a rocky altar looked out at the sea and the Dumnonian coastline to the southwest, the way they would sail with Creticus.

In a small, stone-lined chamber, there was wood, dry grass, and a tinder box.

"Einion comes here to make offerings," Lucius told them as he placed grass and dry kindling upon the altar.

Adara, Phoebus and Calliope stood back a little as Lucius lit the fire, their prayers already echoing in each of their minds as they unburdened their wishes to the Gods. The wind made it difficult for the fire to take, but after a few minutes, the flames leapt up and swayed in the dusky light.

Lucius stood then, looking down at the fire with his family standing beside him.

"Gods..." he began, his palms out and facing up. "We have been through much. Please grant us a safe journey to see our families. Protect us upon the road. Keep our families safe. Let us be reunited."

Lucius looked out to the sea far below, that great roiling blue kingdom, and closed his eyes. "Oh Janus, Lord of Beginnings...look favourably upon our journey so that we come safely through the other side. May this be a new start for our family..." Lucius pulled a small piece of incense out of the pouch he carried, and placed it in the fire. The incense caught, and its sweet smoke began to rise into the air. He continued...

"Great Neptune, may we pass safely through your realm to our destination. Grant us peace and safety upon the sea, and may your guardians guide us along the way. We honour you." Lucius placed another piece of incense upon the flames so that it burned and smoked alongside its twin.

Lucius then looked up at the sky, unable to speak for a moment. He felt Adara's hand upon his shoulder, could hear his children's breathing beside him.

"Far-Shooting Apollo...Father... We honour you...and we trust you." Lucius closed his eyes, feeling a great light and welling up of emotion inside. When he opened his eyes again, Apollo stood on the other side of the altar staring directly at him. His sky-blue cloak billowed strangely about him, unaccountable to the winds, and his star-whirling eyes gazed deeply into Lucius' own.

You don't need to go, Apollo said to Lucius. *I will watch over you here...in this land... You are the Pen Dragon now...as was always intended...*

Lucius felt his jaw tighten, and his anger grow. *More riddles and secrets...*

No! Apollo said. *Truth!*

Give us your blessing... I go to make things right! Lucius said, the full force of his iron-bound will behind it.

The light in Apollo's eyes changed, flickered in colours that only came at dusk on Olympus, as he gazed upon his vengeful, angry son.

Lucius continued his prayer, feeling Adara's hand squeeze him, urge him to finish the prayer. "Oh, Apollo," he continued, his eyes looking to his father. "Shine your light upon the road ahead that our true path may be lit. Protect my family on this journey that we may find our way in the darkness, and return home."

Lucius took a third piece of incense from the pouch and placed it in the fire, his eyes never leaving his heavenly father's.

The stars in Apollo's eyes spun faster and faster before he closed his eyes and nodded. *Very well.*

And then he was gone, all that was left was the swirling smoke of the offerings, now carried away on the wind in his wake.

Adara, Phoebus and Calliope raised their hands and bowed to the flames, their own silent prayers upon their mute mouths as Lucius finished his own.

Lucius turned to them. "All will be well," he said, reaching out to grip his wife's hand.

"We should go to the feast now. They'll be waiting for us," Adara said, looking back to the hall on the other side of the fortress where smoke was rising into the evening air.

"You go ahead with Phoebus and Calliope," Lucius said. "I'll follow in a moment."

Adara nodded and smiled, a little sadly. "Speak to him, Lucius. He is your father. Make peace."

Lucius nodded and watched them go back to the hall across the green expanse of the fortress plateau. He then turned back to the flames, stared at them for a time, listening to the wind, the beating of his heart, and the crackle of the offerings upon the fire.

"Oh Nemesis, dread daughter of the Gods, grant me the vengeance I seek... Help me to avenge the crimes committed against my family." Lucius' features hardened with the words, twisted and changed the same as a piece of flesh tossed upon a fire, a fire he could still feel burning him as he prayed.

He held his breath for a moment now. He had not prayed to his uncle for a long time. Indeed he had refused to do so at first, since when he first bloodied his gladius upon the field of battle.

But now, Lucius sought a different kind of battle, and as he drew the black gladius at his side and laid it before the flames, he spoke the words. "Mars Ultor...oh great Avenger... I know that I have not often honoured you. The fault is mine. I know you have made me pay for it dearly. And I have paid. But now...now...I need your help. Stand beside me in the months to come. Walk this bloody road with me, Uncle... Help me to obtain my revenge. I cannot sleep, I cannot eat, I cannot believe in anything until it is done."

Lucius found himself shaking, tears burning his eyes and anger raging within like a fire with pitch thrown upon it, as if there was a war already raging, two opposite sides pulling at each other.

He reached down to take the gladius. He slid the blade across the side of his hand so that a thin red line appeared. The line grew redder and blood began to drip. Lucius held the hand over the fire so that his lifeblood fell into the flames. With his other hand, he reached into the pouch and produced a small phial which contained some water from Ynis Wytrin. He poured it over his hand so that the water and blood were offered up.

"May my blood, the blood of the goddess, and of the Christus seal my pact and ensure vengeance upon my enemies. From this day forward, I am Lucius Pen Dragon…"

Lucius listened and watched, and on the wind, he could hear it, a faint laughter, and the deep thrumming of the drums of war echoing across the sea.

He looked down at his hand then to bind it, but to his surprise, the skin had sealed itself. He looked upon the water in the phial and replaced the stopper, wondering if it had healed him, or if the gods had refused his offering. He turned to leave, but stopped suddenly.

Why are you doing this? Epona asked, her face close to his, her fiery hair blowing in the wind about them. *You cannot leave. Not now.*

"I must," Lucius answered. He could see her so clearly, like a bright green shoot in spring, or the sunrise on a clear morning.

Please stay, the goddess said. In her eyes there was true feeling, and it began to wear at Lucius' resolve. *I watched you die once before. I don't wish to do so again. Stay here in this land that needs you. You belong here.*

"I cannot, lady," Lucius said.

Then stay with me, in Annwn where there is no pain.

"No pain?" Lucius said. "I felt my greatest pain in that place."

It will be different, Epona said, and she stepped closer to hold his hands. *I…I love you, Lucius. I always have.*

Lucius felt his heart race, found that he was unable to pull away as the goddess leaned forward and pressed her lips upon his. His eyes closed and he felt a lightness of being that he could not have imagined possible for his shattered self. The grass grew greener about their feet then, and summer flowers bloomed in a circle about them. *I love you too, oh goddess, but I also love my wife…my love…*

Then why do you lead her into danger? Epona asked, her lips still upon his.

Lucius pulled back and opened his eyes to see Epona before him, radiant as the sun upon a field, bright as the moon upon a calm expanse of water.

"I honour you," he said, bowing his head before looking into her eyes once more. "But I must go."

A stream of tears fell away from the goddess' eye. *I cannot go with you this time.*

"I know." Lucius reached for her hands, and she did not pull them away, but gripped his in farewell.

I will watch over them here, she said, looking back toward the hall where Dagon and the others feasted. *You are all my warriors,* she said, before releasing his hands and placing her palm upon his cheek. She walked away from Lucius then, and in that moment, he felt a great loneliness.

Lucius looked once more at the fire and saw that the flames were dying away, that all had been consumed.

He walked slowly back to the hall.

When he entered, a cheer rose up from the Sarmatian and Dumnonian warriors there present.

"Pen Dragon!" they called to him, reaching out to touch his arm and pat his back as he passed down the centre isle to the head table where Einion, Briana and Dagon waited for him.

Adara met his gaze from where she sat with their children, and in that gaze was sadness and trepidation.

Another journey for our family, he thought as he was greeted by their dear friends. *But this will be the last one...this...the last farewell.*

They ate and drank into the night with their friends, each of them trying to set aside their pain, sadness, and nostalgia, and instead enjoy being together a last time by the light of a warm hearth.

When the dawn's rosy light crept in at the curtain of the small window of the guest house, it was to reveal a day that promised clear skies and a bright sun. The wind whistled around the fortress as it grazed the stone surface of the small house. The gulls were out too, soaring along the heights and bobbing upon the surface of the water far below.

Lucius and Adara lay back to back in the bed, both with their eyes open, both contemplating the step they were about to take.

Though they had not yet had the opportunity to talk about it, the news that Creticus had brought them of Geta's murder hung heavily upon them. Not because either of them had known Geta particularly well - in truth, Lucius had never really liked him - but if the rumours were true about his brutal murder, then Caracalla was more unpredictable and dangerous than ever.

However, it was the immediate leaving that preoccupied both of them as they lay there.

Would they ever see their friends again? What would they find when they arrived in Italy, or in Athenae?

Adara tried to inspire her determination by thinking of her childhood home, of her mother's paintings upon the walls of their domus, of the scent of summer pine upon the slopes of Hymettos, the brilliant light of the sky above the Middle Sea. But her worries and fears betrayed her. Were they tempting the Fates by leaving?

Lucius' thoughts were of a different variety. While he welcomed the prospect of going back to Etruria to see his mother, brother and sister, his focus was of a darker bent, his goals largely dependent on finding out more information than he had. *One step at a time, Lucius,* he told himself.

"Are you awake?" Adara asked Lucius as the light travelled up the wall in front of her.

"Yes, my love."

She had once loved hearing those words from him, more than anything. But as she stared at the wall she realized that they now sounded different, like he was speaking to her from a place far away.

"We should wake the children," Adara said, sitting up.

They both rose and the blanket fell away to reveal Lucius' torso.

Adara looked him over and touched his skin. "Does it hurt today?"

"It's dry, but the pain has been receding."

"That's good at least. Let me put some of the mixture Elana gave us on you." Adara stood from the bed in her loose tunica and walked to the table to take up the small clay pot. On the way back to the bed, she stopped and gently nudged the children who mumbled incoherently at her touch. "Phoebus...Calliope...time to wake up. We have a long journey ahead of us."

"I'm up! I'm up!" Calliope said, quickly and groggily as her brother rubbed his face and sat up slowly.

Lucius stood up and spread his arms wide so that Adara could apply the resinous mixture. His skin soaked it up, and he felt great relief as the stretch of his skin eased and cooled.

"You seem to be healing more quickly," Adara said. "Apollo has aided your healing, I think."

Lucius did not say anything to that, for he still saw the Far-Shooter's face across the flames the previous night, warning him, telling him he did not have to take this journey.

"There. Finished." Adara wiped her hands on a rag and replaced the lid of the clay pot which she then placed in one of the satchels.

The children began to dress themselves in layers, as they had discussed, for it would be colder at sea. When Phoebus was finished, he hung his gladius about his shoulder, beneath his cloak.

Calliope, reluctantly, tucked the pugio Adara had picked for her, into the cingulum about her waist. "Do I have to wear this?" she asked.

"Yes," Adara said. "We don't yet know the captain, his family, or the crew."

"Everything you say now scares me," Calliope said, stopping to look out of the window by the table.

Adara walked over to her and hugged her. "I'm sorry, my girl. Truly. I suppose I'm scared too...of the unknown, of such a journey. But some journeys need to be made."

Calliope turned. "We've travelled so far already."

"I know," Adara whispered.

"And Baba is different," Calliope said, glancing over Adara's shoulder to the far end of the house where Phoebus was helping Lucius put on a thin tunic before the thicker woollen one. "I see darkness wrapped around him, Mama. Not fire or wolves, just darkness...dark like the wood of the weapons he now carries all the time."

Adara hugged her daughter close, Calliope's head resting upon her shoulder now as they were almost of the same height. "All will be well, my love," she whispered.

When they were all dressed, their satchels packed, coin securely hidden within each of them, apart from a small pouch at Lucius' waist, they left the guest house and made their way to the hall.

As they walked, laden with their only possessions, Lucius listened for the horn that Creticus had told him would sound when they were ready to sail. However, the only sound was the crash of water upon the beach of the Haven below, and the cries of sea birds on the cliffs.

There was an excitement in the air, however, and as Lucius listened more closely, he could discern the sounds of songs coming up from the Iron Gate below as the sailors prepared the rigging and finished securing the last of the cargo.

Smoke was wafting up into the morning sky from the roof of the hall, and the scent of fresh bread met them as they approached the double doors and entered.

Phoebus and Calliope were immediately greeted by Antiope who had been waiting for them to arrive. She flung her arms about their legs and pulled at their hands. "Sit with me!" the toddler said, leading them down the hall to the table where her parents sat with Einion and Gwendolyn.

Dagon stood and walked to greet them, noting the packed satchels. "This is the day then."

Lucius nodded. "Yes, my friend."

Dagon sighed. A part of him had been hoping that Lucius would change his mind at the last minute, but it was not meant to be. "Come. Eat. Einion thinks Creticus will want to set sail soon."

They walked together down the length of the hall, behind Adara who went to sit with Briana.

"Do you trust this sea captain?" Dagon asked.

"To an extent. He seems honest enough, but I'll be on my guard. Don't worry."

"Of course I'll worry. I can no longer watch your back, Lucius." Dagon's voice trembled, and he stopped, turning Lucius to face him. "Promise me something."

"What is it?"

"That if you need me, or the men...you will send for us. Send for us, and we will come...wherever you are...we *will* come to you."

Oh, Dagon, Lucius thought. *I would not tear you away from your well-deserved happiness for all the vengeance that I seek.* "I thank you with all of my heart...my brother." He hugged Dagon then, tightly, with every ounce of sincerity he possessed. "For that is what you are to me, Dagon...a brother."

"I fear that Dagon will never be the same without Lucius," Briana whispered to Adara as they sat at the table. "Nor will I without you," she said, grasping Adara's hands.

Adara felt the sadness welling up again, like a fresh spring that has broken stony ground. She turned to look Briana in the eyes, her hands squeezing back. "No matter what happens, we will come back. This land is our home now, and you are our family. I would stay as far away from Rome as possible."

"And Lucius?" Briana asked.

Adara looked away, stared at the oak beams of the table. She had no answer for that, for she knew that whatever her husband now had in mind, wherever his thoughts drifted to, it was apart from her and her own wishes. She felt Briana hug her tightly, and she closed her eyes beneath the blonde strands of her friend's hair.

They ate heartily, the talk more of a distraction than a focus, but such is the time before a leaving, especially when one does not see to the other side. Between the silent pauses, and saddened looks, there was some measure of joy, of hope, with the sound of children's laughter, and squeals of delight at Gwendolyn's churning belly.

"Someday," Einion said, "perhaps our four children will be dining together in this hall, just as we have?" He looked to Lucius, Dagon and the others and smiled sadly.

"We can only hope for such a glorious day, Brother," Briana said.

Lucius was about to speak, to say that he too shared that hope, though he had hidden it far back in the caverns of his mind for the moment. The sentiment felt right though, as he watched Phoebus and Calliope playing with Antiope beside Gwendolyn whose smile was radiant in their company. He was about to express that hope when a solemn call reached their ears.

From down at the Iron Gate, the sound of Creticus' horn rang out. It was time to depart.

They all fell silent.

"My lord!" Arthrek came briskly down the aisle of the hall toward Einion. "Captain Creticus says they are ready to leave. The tide is with them."

"Thank you, Arthrek," Einion said. He turned to Lucius and Adara. "Don't worry about Creticus. You can trust him. I would never have sent you with him if that were not the case."

Lucius stood. "I know."

Gwendolyn propped herself up on the table to stand, and Phoebus helped her. "Thank you, Phoebus." She pat his shoulder and turned to Adara. "Early this morning," she said, breathing a little heavily. "I sent extra food stores down to the ships with clear instruction that they were for the four of you only. Some dried meat, cheese, and nuts. Creticus said that he has food for all of you as part of your passage, but I wanted you to have more." Gwendolyn smiled at them. She did not yet know them well, but she know how much they owed to Lucius. She walked around the table to Adara and hugged her warmly. "I wish you were here for the birth. I think it will be soon." She held her belly.

"I will pray to the Gods that you have a safe one, and that your child is healthy," Adara said.

"Thank you...Lady Pen Dragon." Gwendolyn winked. "It actually does suit you all." She turned to Lucius then. "I will not come down to the Iron Gate with you, Lucius. I'm too unstable upon my feet at this point."

"I understand," Lucius said. "Take care of yourself, and look after that one." He winked and nodded toward Einion.

She smiled, and hugged him. "Thank you again for everything you have done for us and for this land, Lucius. May the Gods bless you and guide you."

Creticus' horn sounded again.

"We'd better go down," Einion said. "The tide moves quickly enough here."

Lucius, Adara, Phoebus and Calliope picked up their satchels, and Einion, Dagon, Briana and Antiope joined them.

They followed Arthrek out of the hall, down the path to the stairs that led to the Iron Gate and quayside. The air was cool and breezy, but refreshing, and Lucius filled his lungs as they went, feeling the cleansing sea air.

"Which ship are we going to be on?" Phoebus asked as they reached the moorings.

Captain Creticus turned from speaking with one of his sailors to meet the group.

"Good morning, Captain!" Lucius said. "Permission to come aboard?"

"Of course!" Creticus said, extending his hand to Lucius, and turning to Phoebus who had asked the question. "You'll be on the larger corbita, the Europa! She's the beauty at the end of the dock. There's a small cabin for you, plus plenty of food and fresh water."

Lucius and his family looked down the quay, past the first two cargo ships, both sitting low in the water, toward the larger of the three. It too was low in the water, but its deck was higher, the mast reaching into the sky.

The Europa was a massive, one-hundred and twenty-foot corbita, solidly-built of oak beams fastened end-to-end, with the hull sheathed in smoothed lead. Its vast, billowing sail donned a leaping dolphin, the same as the two other ships of Creticus' personal fleet, and at the stern of the deck, near the steering oars, a carved and painted dolphin seemed to jump up from the stern post.

"It's so tall!" Calliope said.

"Yes it is!" Creticus said proudly. "And she's sturdy and swift if the wind hugs her just right." Creticus pointed to the top of the mast where the crossbeam held the sail. "Look up there! Who do you see?"

Phoebus and Calliope looked up to see Castor and Pollux waving down at them from on high.

"Our own Dioscuri can fly when they're at sea," Creticus said, laughing and waving back.

"Don't they get scared?" Phoebus asked, fingering the pommel of his gladius beneath his cloak.

"No. They're more at home up there at sea than upon green grass." Creticus looked around. "I hate to rush you all in your farewells, but we really must get going. I'll leave you to it." He turned to Einion. "Lord Einion. Always a pleasure doing business with you and seeing you and your men. I will see you next year."

"I look forward to it, Captain Creticus." Einion walked with Creticus a little so that they could speak. "Remember, I will pay for anything they need. Just be there for them. They are my family."

Creticus stared him in the eyes and nodded firmly. "Rest assured. They will be safe. I always keep my word."

"Thank you," Einion said, grasping his arm and watching him go up the gang plank to board the ship. He waved to Nerissa who was awaiting them on the deck. That done, Einion returned to Lucius and the others. "You're all set. Creticus will look after you and take you wherever you wish to go. You can trust him."

"Thank you, my friend," Lucius said. "I…ah-"

"There's nothing to say, Lucius. Gods willing, we'll meet again." Einion pushed back his long hair and breathed deeply. "I hope being a father is much easier than this goodbye."

"You'll be fine," Lucius said, hugging his friend. "Take care of Gwendolyn and your child."

"I will." Einion stepped aside and Briana approached after having bid farewell to Adara and the children.

She wiped the tears away from her cheeks. "I don't know what to say, Lucius. It seems like so long ago that the Gods led me and Einion to you, and now, they lead you away."

Lucius looked at the Briton and smiled sadly. "Thank you for being such a good friend, Briana."

She hugged him tightly, and for a moment, Lucius felt like she was the sister he had lost so long ago. "Don't stop believing in yourself, Lucius. Do what you have to do, but come back with your family. You are a part of all of our lives." She pulled back, the tears flowing freely now.

"I will," he said, uncertain whether he was lying or not, but the words seemed needed in that moment. "Take care of Dagon." He smiled.

"I will," Briana said, taking Antiope's hand as she approached them.

Lucius bent down to speak to the child. "Farewell, princess."

Antiope smiled shyly.

"Your mother and father are great warriors and they love you very much. They'll need your help."

"I help them," she said.

"Be good," Lucius said, touching her cheek.

Antiope pulled away at the roughness of his hand and ran back to hug Phoebus and Calliope.

"Time to go, Lucius Pen Dragon!" Creticus yelled from the stern of the ship as the other two corbita pulled away from the quay to make their way out into the bay.

"There's never enough time," Dagon said, as he approached Lucius. He looked back to see Adara and Briana hugging once again, both weeping. They all began to walk toward the gang plank.

Lucius turned to Dagon and hugged him tightly. "My brother…"

Dagon turned to look up at the cliffs and smiled. "Look Lucius."

Lucius looked up and there, at the edge of the cliffs, stood the Sarmatian and Dumnonian warriors, all of whom had fought alongside Lucius.

Brencis was at the forefront of the group and as he drew his sword, along with all the others, he yelled. "Pen Dragon! Pen Dragon! Pen Dragon!"

The cries of those proud warriors echoed over the cliffs, the bay, and out to sea, drowning out the sound of the gulls overhead.

Lucius felt a chill run through his body then as he looked up to them and drew his sword in salute back. *Farewell, my warriors. May the Gods keep you.*

Beside him, Dagon wept to see such a sight. He turned to Lucius. "Come back to us, Anguis. No matter what happens, promise you will come back."

Lucius grasped Dagon's forearm and touched his forehead to the other's, his eyes closed. "I promise. One way, or another, I will come back."

Dagon nodded, wiped his tears and pulled away as Creticus made a final plea for them to board.

Adara, Phoebus and Calliope began to ascend the gang plank, and Lucius followed. As soon as they reached the top, they went to the rail to watch, to listen to the continued chanting of their new name as the gang plank was brought in and the ship's sail fully lowered to immediately fill with wind.

"It's like our new name signals a new beginning," Phoebus said, inspired by the sight of the warriors upon the cliffs. He drew his gladius and saluted them and they roared even louder back.

Calliope clasped her brother's hand. "Maybe it *is* a new beginning, Phoebus?"

Adara came to stand beside Lucius and together they waved to Einion, Dagon, Briana and Antiope.

The shuddering in each of their hearts in that moment was strong, full of apprehension and uncertainty. They watched the cliffs of Din Tagell fade away, the shores of Dumnonia and Britannia shrink in the distance, while the sea spread wide before them like a wholly new, unexplored realm.

"This must be what Odysseus felt like leaving Ithaca," Adara said, still holding Lucius' arm.

Lucius smiled sadly. "With hope, we won't be gone for twenty years," he said.

As Adara went to check on Phoebus and Calliope who were standing before their cabin amidships, Lucius walked to the prow to stand alone.

He drew his gladius and pointed it to the spot on the horizon where the sky met the sea.

"Gods," he said, his voice lost on the wind. "Lead me to vengeance…"

Part II

FAMILY

A.D. 214

IX

IN MARE

'Upon the Sea'

The open sea casts a spell upon the uninitiated, those who are unfamiliar with the ways of that wine-dark realm. If one is already lost in thought, the gentle rocking of a ship, especially a large vessel, can hold one such that it is difficult to break free of the reverie.

For the Pen Dragon family, such was the case upon the deck of the Europa. For the first few days, as Captain Creticus' three ships swung around the Dumnonian cape, crossed the Mare Britannicum, and began the descent down the coast of Gaul, they said little.

At first, Creticus believed they were only adjusting to the sway of the sea, that they felt ill.

"They only need to find their sea legs, husband," Nerissa told him.

But he was not so sure. Of course, he could see that the Pen Dragons felt a great sadness having said goodbye to their friends in Dumnonia. *But why did they leave in the first place?* he wondered. He decided he would give them a bit more time before trying to engage in any meaningful discussion, but it could not wait long. A group of ghostlike passengers caused unease among the crew, and as the days wore on, Creticus sons informed him that members of the crew were growing wary of the newcomers.

"They move like sad shadows around the deck, or don't come out of their cabin at all!" Castor said.

"Maybe we can put the boy, Phoebus, to work? Teach him something about sailing?" Pollux suggested.

"That's a good idea," Creticus told them. "But let's give them another day or so. I'll approach Lucius Pen Dragon first."

His wife touched his arm. "Be kind, husband. It seems to me that they have seen great tragedy recently. Things are not always as they seem."

Creticus looked into Nerissa's large, pale, grey eyes, those eyes that always spoke truth to him as if some oracle lay behind them. "I will," he said. "They seem like good people. There's just something about them though that, makes me uneasy, especially when the father stands alone at the stern, talking to himself."

Nerissa looked up at the dusk sky to see the light of the first, kindled stars. "He may not be talking to himself." She looked down. "If we help them, perhaps the Gods will favour us?"

"Maybe," he said. "And maybe not..."

Those first days at sea were not easy. While Adara and the children wrestled with sadness and doubt after the painful farewells, their hearts still sitting upon the quay of Din Tagell, Lucius withdrew it seemed, deep within, to ponder the road ahead.

Adara was sure there was something he was not telling her, but she had to focus on the children.

Phoebus was wary of every sailor who crossed his path, including the Dioscuri, the sons of Creticus. He kept his gladius close at all times.

Meanwhile, Calliope, in addition to her heavy heart and the tears that often came as she lay upon her pallet, felt the swaying of the sea more acutely than anyone else. She had, of course, crossed the channel from Gaul before, but that had been nothing compared with the open realm of Oceanus with its infinite expanse to the West.

Lucius, more often than the others, walked the deck of the Europa, his hood pulled over his head as he gazed out to sea. He knew that he made the crew uncomfortable, but he was all right with that.

He heard the crew whisper about the 'Pen Dragon' in their midst, but said nothing. It felt strange to go by the name of Pen Dragon, but it also felt right, somehow familiar, like a suggestion someone has made, but that one has never considered before. It suited not only him, but also his family.

What are you telling me? he asked Apollo one night as he stood upon the quiet deck, the sound of the creaking rigging above him as he looked to the starry sky to see an arrow shoot across the heavens from his father's silver bow.

It saddened Lucius to be stripped of his identity, but he wondered if perhaps there was something more to it. Perhaps 'Metellus' had been the true mask, and only now was he shedding it?

While the children slept, Adara watched her husband from the open door of their small cabin, his dark outline just visible in the pale moonlight. She turned to look at the children where they slept, and sighed. She could not bring herself to leave them with so many crew members about at all hours, but she knew she had to get to know them, just as she had done on her travels to Caledonia. *It's safer to get to know people, than to be silent,* she reminded herself. She remembered how it had been at the empress' villa outside Rome, just before the death of Plautianus, how she had befriended the staff there. But that was not a pleasant memory. She did not want to go back to Rome. A part of her feared that Lucius wanted to.

She focussed her thoughts on seeing her family, for that was her comfort during those first days of the voyage. Every time she found herself doubting the purpose of their journey, pondering the risk they were all taking in leaving that far corner of the empire behind, she thought of her mother's smile as she touched her face with her paint-stained fingers, or of her father's open arms as he welcomed her back home.

She took a last look at Lucius before going to lie down for another swaying sleep at sea, her gladius beside her instead of her husband.

It was a sight to see, the sun's chariot bursting over the edge of the world to light the indigo expanse of Oceanus.

On their seventh night at sea, Lucius had stood upon the deck the entire night, unable to sleep as usual, filling his eyes with the light of the stars and moon, and then with the brilliance of the sun. It was strange to be on a ship without oarsmen, for the only sound of passage to be the flapping of the giant, square sail above his head. After a few days, it had become soothing.

"Beautiful, is it not?" Creticus' voice came from behind Lucius as he was looking to the rising sun.

Lucius turned to see the captain smiling at him, a chunk of bread and a cup of water extended in each hand.

"Please," Creticus said. "Eat. Drink." He handed the cup and bread to Lucius.

"Thank you."

"You've been here all night," Creticus stated.

"I don't sleep much anymore," Lucius answered, tearing his eyes away from the sun. "I find it easier to think out here than in the cabin."

"I understand that," Creticus said. "Especially when in close quarters with my sons. They do nothing but fart in their sleep!" he chuckled.

Lucius could not help but smile. He remembered such things from his time in the legions, sharing a tent with seven other men. "They seem like good boys, Captain."

"The Gods have blessed us. They are healthy, strong, and kind, our Dioscuri. Your children are twins are they not?"

Lucius nodded. "Yes. They are very close."

"I can see that." Creticus was quiet a moment as he watched the coast a couple of miles to the East. "We're coming up on Aquitania now."

"It's a long journey."

"Yes. But it is quiet, and summer is a good time for sailing this route. You wouldn't want to do it in winter. Neptune is full of anger in winter." Creticus looked sideways at Lucius. "Over land through Gaul is usually easier for most people who are unaccustomed to the sea."

Lucius said nothing, and finished drinking the water from his cup. "I know we haven't touched on it fully, but what payment do you require for our passage?"

"Nothing."

Lucius turned sharply toward him. "Nothing? Come now. There is no free passage, Captain. Even I know that."

"True enough. Four people is a lot of space taken up on a ship, even one this large. But Lord Einion paid me in full for your passage, with more promised for future services to you and your family, including a return voyage."

"He did?"

Creticus nodded. "He's a good man, and he obviously cares a great deal for you and your family."

"We are family, in a way," Lucius said, still incredulous at what Einion had done.

"Listen, Lucius Pen Dragon…" Creticus moved to stand in front of

Lucius. It was time to speak candidly. "A man's business is his own, to be sure. And any friend of Lord Einion's is definitely a friend of mine."

"That is good to know," Lucius said, feeling his fingertips search for the pommel of his gladius beneath the folds of his black cloak.

"I don't know what you are running from, or running toward... I don't want to know. I just need you to tell me if you are a threat to my family, my crew, or my business. Am I endangering everything by taking you aboard? Tell me truly."

Lucius looked at the man before him and knew that, were he in Creticus' position, he too would be wary of Lucius. "We are not a danger to you, Captain. Rest assured. We are, however, going to help family who have perhaps had trouble with the imperial authorities. We won't know until we get to Etruria."

"Are the imperial authorities looking for you?" Creticus asked the blunt question. "You seem to have very little to your names, but then you do not have an impoverished air about you. None of you do."

Lucius looked him in the eyes. "I swear to you, the Pen Dragon family has no dealings with the imperial authorities at all. We're only going to see family whom we have not seen in many years. There was a rift, and that is why we appear so thoughtful. We also don't know how long we will be away, and that is why we were reluctant to bid farewell to our friends in Britannia."

"I'm glad to hear it," Creticus said, nodding and seeming to breathe more deeply then. "Now that's settled, I should tell you that the crew are nervous having you all aboard. They don't see or hear much of you and your family, and they are growing worried. You know how superstitious sailors can be?"

"Yes."

"If you could get your wife and children moving about more, it would be good for the crew, as well as good for them. My sons have offered to teach your son - and your daughter if she wishes it - a bit about sailing. And my Nerissa would love some more female company if your wife is willing to spend time with her. As you can see, the days upon the water are long and lonely."

"I'm sorry if we've been recluse these first days at sea, Captain. Leaving Britannia was not easy for us, and we're nervous about seeing our family."

"Families will do that to you, I suppose. You miss them, and yet they weigh you down."

"True." Lucius smiled. "I'll speak with Adara and the children. Looks like a nice, sunny day to be on the deck."

"Good man. Thank you," Creticus said. "Now, if you'll excuse me, I'll rouse the crew and get them to work. We'll make for the port of Condevincum tomorrow and I need to ensure the correct cargo is ready to offload. They do love Caledonian wool there!"

Lucius watched Creticus walk away, and breathed deeply to calm himself. The direct questions had taken him by surprise, but he could understand why the captain had asked him. But he was even more surprised by the fact that Einion had paid for their voyage, and wondered what he had promised Creticus upon their return. *If we return.*

Lucius stood there for a while longer, watching the sun rise higher and higher, lighting the green, Gaulish coast in the distance as it stretched out beyond sandy beaches and dark, rocky cliffs, like fair hair atop a rugged face. But it was the sea to his right that mesmerized Lucius. It was an endless expanse of water that led to only the Gods knew where. It was calm and still in the morning light of summer, but he could not help but wonder how terrible it might be in winter, when the waves could swallow a ship whole and drag it to the bottom of Neptune's realm.

The seven crew members of the Europa began to move about the deck then, rising from where they slept beneath thick blankets on deck, or coming up from the hold below where a few slept among the amphora, bundles of wool and piles of lead pigs they had picked up in Dumnonia.

Lucius walked back to the cabin amidships and slowly opened the wooden door, the sound of which blended in nicely with the constant sway, creak and groan of the massive corbita. Inside, through the increasing light of the awakening sun, Lucius could see Adara lying upon the fleeces spread over fresh straw.

Phoebus and Calliope lay to either side of her, both soothed by the rocking.

Lucius was relieved to see they had adapted to the sway of the ship, for it would have been a long journey indeed had they not. He almost did not want to wake them for fear of disrupting their peaceful dreams. *Maybe they're dreaming of Ynis Wytrin?*

Phoebus certainly had expressed his longing for that hidden sanctuary, the place that had saved them all. He smiled sadly as he looked upon his son. *So young still, and yet eager and ready to become a man...forced to.*

He turned to look at Calliope then, but as he did so, she opened her eyes and smiled.

Good morning, Baba, she mouthed silently.

Lucius waved back, and she smiled and stretched again. He motioned that he would wait for her outside, and she nodded.

After a few minutes, the cabin door opened and Calliope came to where Lucius stood at the base of the thick mast.

"Good morning, Calliope!" Nerissa called down to her from the quarter deck above the cabins. She smiled broadly to see the young girl, as some women who have only been blessed with sons are wont to do.

"Good morning, lady!" Calliope called back, smiling at the woman. She turned back to her father. "Mama and Phoebus just woke up. They're coming."

Lucius hugged his daughter and she squeezed him tightly.

"You didn't come to sleep last night, Baba."

"No," Lucius said, his smile fading and his eyes going to the sun. "My mind races round like a chariot in the circus."

She placed her hand upon his arm, her breathing calm and deep. "You need rest."

"I know," he replied, noticing something in her eyes, as if a thought flashed across them. "What is it?"

"The Gods have sent me strange dreams of late. I don't know if it is grandfather speaking to me, or even Etain - she and I have been... well...talking."

"You have? From so far away?"

Calliope smiled. "This distance is not so relevant. Only if we make it so."

"What did you see?"

Calliope began to walk toward the bow of the ship to where Lucius had been standing all night. He followed her as she looked up at the dolphin sail and one of the sailors climbing to the highest point to gaze out at the world. When she saw they were alone, she turned to her father to speak.

"I saw an island...I think it was Britannia, but I'm not sure... Black waves were crashing upon the shores of the island, and in the middle of the island was a bearded man with the dragon upon his chest. He was standing alone." Calliope's eyes gazed as if she were seeing the man again. "He was so sad, Baba. I've never seen anyone so sad and desperate, but so full of strength...apart from you."

Lucius looked at her and she gripped his hand tightly.

"But it wasn't you I saw...though there was something about him. He had your sword...the one Mama gave you, that you left with Elana."

"He did?" Lucius felt himself pulled back to Annwn, that realm of forgotten life and living dreams. As she spoke, he could see the man she spoke of, and he too felt the sadness creep upon him. He saw that tears were forming in Calliope's eyes then and he took her into the crook of his arm as they looked out to sea.

"I don't want you to be so sad as that man, Baba. I worry that all dragons are meant to be thus."

Lucius stared at his daughter, unable to give voice to the whirling thoughts she had given rise to with the description of her vision. He hugged her and stared out to sea.

A moment later, Adara and Phoebus came to join them on the deck near the prow of the ship.

"What a beautiful sun," Adara commented, placing her hand upon Lucius' shoulder, and looking at Calliope. "Are you all right, my girl?"

"I'm fine. I was just telling Baba about a dream I had."

Calliope did not explain further, and Adara did not ask. The latter had learned long ago not to press her daughter when it came to her dreams or visions, for she always spoke of them in her own time.

Lucius saw Creticus and Nerissa standing on the upper deck above the cabins and remembered what the captain had said to him.

"I spoke with the captain early this morning," he said to the three of them. "It seems we are making the crew uncomfortable by always staying in the cabin."

"But we're out of their way," Phoebus said.

"I know. But sailors are odd," Lucius said. "They worry about who comes on board. Creticus asked that we come out more and that you," he turned to Adara, "try and interact with Nerissa a little. Seems she is happy to have some more female company on board."

"Of course, I can do that," Adara said. She looked around to make sure no one was near to hear her. "When I hear them speaking in Greek, I'm tempted to speak it too."

Lucius thought for a moment. "It's fine. We can't completely hide who we are," he whispered. "We don't necessarily look like Britons. You can speak of growing up in Athenae, just not your father's name or what he does."

Adara nodded. It was difficult to keep track of lies once told, but she knew Lucius was right in what he said.

Lucius turned to Phoebus. "Also, Castor and Pollux have been asking if you would like to learn something about sailing. I think they're eager to show you around the ship. You too, Calliope."

Calliope smiled, but Phoebus frowned. "I don't want to make friends with them." He gripped the pommel of his gladius beneath his cloak.

"I know," Lucius told him. "Believe me. But we need to be able to trust them, and we need them to trust us. If we hide in the cabin the entire time, they will be eager to be rid of us. We have a long journey ahead still."

Phoebus was quiet, but eventually nodded. "Fine. I'll do it."

Lucius knew how his son felt. All he wanted to do was to be alone with his thoughts, to retreat inward so that he did not have to deal with the rest of the world about him. But they were out in the world again, and that demanded interaction with others.

He was about to hold Adara close as Phoebus and Calliope moved to the prow of the corbita to look down at the waves when there was a shout from Pollux who was at the top of the mast.

"Cetus!" the young man yelled from his high perch, waving his arms excitedly and pointing out to sea.

"Cetus?" Adara said. "Does he mean-"

"A sea monster," Lucius turned to see Creticus and Nerissa rushing toward them.

"You must see this, all of you!" Creticus was saying, pointing in the direction his son was indicating from on high.

Castor, the other son, could be seen climbing nimbly up the mast to join his brother, and together they both pointed, broad smiles upon their faces.

"This is a treat!" Nerissa said as she came to stand beside Adara. "Look dear!"

Adara, Lucius, Phoebus and Calliope all stared in the direction the captain's wife was pointing, but all they could see was open sea beneath a blue sky.

"I don't see anything," Phoebus said.

"Wait for it, lad," Creticus said, as there were more shouts from the other two corbita of Creticus' small fleet. "There!" he shouted, pointing.

Then, they saw it, a great grey beast that breached the surface of the water to writhe and turn, suspended in the air before landing upon its side and sending up a great splash.

Then, other titans of the sea performed the same acrobatics, this time moving nearer to the cutting ships.

"One, two, three..." Creticus said, counting them all. "Seven of them!" he called out. "Look," he said to Calliope. "There is a calf with its mother!"

Calliope smiled broadly and turned quickly to look at the mother and calf. "He's beautiful!" Then she frowned and turned to Creticus. "You're not going to kill them, are you?"

"Absolutely not!" Creticus said quickly, as if the thought were unimaginable to him. "The cetus is a creature of the Gods, and they do us no harm. Herakles and Perseus may have slain them, but we've no need. Some captains order them slain so that they can sell the fat at port, but its messy work to do so. Besides, were we to do battle with a cetus our ships would incur a lot of damage."

"We just like to see them up close," Nerissa said.

Adara turned to the lady. "I've never seen anything quite like it. So enormous, yet so graceful."

"The sea has many secrets," Nerissa said, her awe of that water world evident, even after so many years at sea.

The crew members were all cheering now as the pod came closer to the ships, some breaching the surface again, others arcing in the water so that their dorsals emerged and then dove, only to be followed by a wave of their great black and grey tails.

"I saw its eye!" Phoebus yelled. "By the Gods!"

"Exactly boy," Creticus said. "There is a world of wisdom in the eyes of those beasts.

Lucius moved to stand on Adara's other side at the rail and placed his hand upon hers. "Incredible."

She turned to him and smiled, for in that brief moment, Lucius had something of the awe she had once loved in him, and she was able to see past the burns and scarred features. "It is," she said, looking from him to the ranging sea titans.

For some time, they watched the group of ceti cutting through the waves before they all rose and disappeared into Neptune's deep.

"That was the best sighting yet!" Castor said as he and Pollux ran up to the group and their parents at the bow of the ship.

"It seems the Gods have blessed our voyage with you on board," Creticus said to Lucius and Adara. "I will make offerings," he pointed to the bronze tripod that was fastened to the deck between them and the thick mast.

"Do you want us to show you both around the ship?" Pollux said to Phoebus and Calliope. "You don't have to climb the rigging if you don't want to. But we can show you the hold, how to tie the best knots, and how to fish from the deck."

Phoebus looked at his father, and Lucius nodded.

"Just be careful," Adara added, and the children followed the Dioscuri.

"They're thrilled to have other young people on board," Nerissa said to Adara. "Are you hungry, lady? I've made some fresh bread."

"Please, call me Adara. That would be lovely."

"Come," Nerissa said, smiling and taking Adara by the arm to lead her to the upper deck at the stern of the ship.

When they were gone, Creticus turned to Lucius. "You have a beautiful family."

"Thank you," Lucius said, fighting the suspicions that always seemed to arise now when strangers came close, or commented on his family.

"You can trust us, Lucius Pen Dragon." Creticus touched him on the arm. "I've seen enough of the world and men around the empire to know that worried, distrustful look in your eyes. Sometimes it is warranted, but there are times when it is not. Lord Einion is my friend - a good one - and as such, so are you. I just want you to know that."

Lucius looked at the captain, his eyes did indeed appear sincere, as did the smile that creased his leathery face. "Forgive me, Captain. It's a force of habit. I've had too many run-ins with people who wear masks easily."

"I understand. But there are no masks here, Lucius. At sea, the Gods don't tolerate falsity." He smiled. "And I too have a family to protect."

"Understood." Lucius smiled.

Creticus looked at the broad shore of Gaul in the distance and scanned it for landmarks. "We should be reaching Condevincum by evening. It will take a couple of hours to unload the cargo and then take on more, so, if you and your family want to explore the port, you can. The baths there are decent."

"Thank you, Captain," Lucius said. "I'll speak with my wife to see if she wants to go ashore."

"Excellent. In the meantime, if there is anything you need, you just let me or Nerissa know. Now, I need to go over some of my accounts before we offload."

"Not to worry, Captain. Please go about your business," Lucius said.

When Creticus was gone, he stood once more at the bow of the ship searching for the ceti, but he saw none. He shook his head, preoccupied now with the thought of going ashore. *It's too dangerous,* he thought, and determined to convince Adara and the children of the same.

That evening, as Creticus' crew unloaded the cargo and took on a new one in the port of Condevincum, Lucius, Adara and the children stayed aboard the ship, watching the bustle of activity from the quarter deck, above the cabins, so as to allow the passage of the sweating crew and slaves as they carried off bundles of Caledonian wool, and loaded more lead pigs.

"More lead?" Lucius asked Creticus as the ship was tied up.

"Yes. Big demand for it in Rome. There are so many building projects at the moment, especially the finishing touches on the emperor's bath complex. It's taken years to build the thing."

"I've heard," Lucius said, remembering when the project was announced so many years ago.

Creticus saw the change in Lucius. "Are you sure you and your family don't want to go ashore for a couple of hours? Might do you some good?"

"Not this time, thank you," Lucius said.

"Captain!" one of the crew called to Creticus. "The port magistrate is here!"

"Excuse me. I have to go down and speak with him," Creticus said to Lucius, taking a scroll from his table on the deck and climbing down the ladder.

"Are you sure we can't go into the market or to the baths?" Adara asked Lucius. "It does't seem that busy."

"It's busy enough," Lucius said, his voice low. "And look. Creticus is speaking with one of the Roman officials there. What if they've had orders to look out for us?"

"I don't know if we're that important to them, Lucius."

Lucius turned to her. "Adara…" His voice was low, intense. "I was a usurper to the imperial throne. I wish we weren't that important."

"That was a long time ago now, and they think you're dead. That we're all dead."

"We can't let our guard down," Lucius stared at his wife for a few uncomfortable moments, but then turned when he heard the tramp of soldier's boots in the port below.

They watched as the troops marched to another, smaller ship farther down the dock and pulled a man from the deck. There was a scuffle, some shouting, and then the troops closed in on the man and dragged him away, cutting through the crowd that had gathered to see what the fuss was about.

By then the children had joined Lucius and Adara at the rail and watched beside them.

"Nothing to worry about!" Castor called up to them from the dock directly below. "He was a smuggler! Happens every once in a while at port." He turned to go to his father's side where Creticus was finishing up with the magistrate.

Lucius turned to look at Adara, but she said nothing to him. He could see she already regretted leaving Britannia, that the ship was now their prison.

They waited for another hour as the remaining cargo of lead was loaded, after Creticus had paid the appropriate merchant's tax to the authorities, and soon the ship was being prepared to set sail with the moon lighting the water.

The sounds and smells from the port and nearby market had been tempting, especially for Adara and Calliope who had wanted to go down and explore, but they had silently given up their wish after the smuggler had been arrested.

Phoebus, on the other hand, had been unwilling to leave the deck. He had enjoyed the day exploring the ship and learning about its workings from Castor and Pollux, but the prospect of going down into the crowded marketplace had been too much for him to contemplate.

Lucius noticed that his son's hand never left the pommel of the gladius that hung at his side, his thumb constantly fingering the polished wood and bronze rivet at the end. It made Lucius sad to see, but he understood. We'll deal with it when we have to get off.

"Everyone all right?" Creticus said as he climbed back onto the quarter deck.

"Seems busy," Lucius said.

"It is tonight. Not always, however. The presence of the soldiers made things a bit more exciting than usual. The imperial authorities have been looking for that man for a long time. Someone must have snitched on him for a good sum. If you don't pay your port taxes, they'll hunt you down eventually, and he was one of the worst. I never miss a payment, so my business runs uninterrupted." Creticus turned to call a few orders and looked out to sea again. "Going to be a beautiful night of summer sailing again," he said, smiling.

Over the coming weeks, the triad of dolphin-sailed ships made a smooth passage down the coast of Gaul to the port of Burdigala, where they took on a cargo of wine, which Creticus would sell in the markets of Ostia. From there, they hugged the coast of Hispania, stopping at Brigantium for a shipment of gold, and then Olissipo for silver. The last two places were highly secure because of their industry, and procedures were highly regulated.

Lucius could see that his family was getting tired and ragged of the same routines, of being relegated to the ship. Washing with sea water and sponges had become a dreaded routine in the confines of their small cabin, and the sight of the endless horizon to the West had lost its allure.

The captain's and Lucius' families had fortunately grown close over their weeks at sea, eating together on deck, sharing the odd bit of humour and listening to Creticus' stories of his travels around the empire. All the while Lucius had said very little of their own history, not only out of self-preservation, but also to keep Creticus and his own family safe, for if they knew who Lucius was, they too would be in danger.

I'm done with endangering the lives of friends, he told himself.

One day, before making berth at the port of Gades, Creticus approached Lucius when Adara and the children were out of earshot.

"Lucius," Creticus said, leaning on the railing at the prow of the corbita. The sun was bright and hot, and Lucius wore only his tunic, his bare, scarred arms exposed. "May I speak candidly?"

"Of course."

"I like you, and your family is now like family to ours. When we first set out, I told you we don't take just anyone onboard. I don't really need the extra coin. We do well enough. I'm glad you came aboard, but…"

"What is it, Creticus?" Lucius asked, turning to the captain, his arms crossed. Lucius was feeling stronger by that point, having exercised regularly on deck, trying to build his muscle once more.

Creticus looked at the burns on Lucius' arms and the edge of the dragon where it peeked out at the hem of his tunic. "I'm no fool. I can see when a man is hiding something." Creticus put up his hands quickly. "And don't misunderstand me… Everyone has their secrets! Far be it for me to pry into a man's personal affairs. It's just that, I see a deep fear in the eyes of your wife and children. And in yours, there is a fire burning that seems fuelled only by anger. I've seen it in men's eyes before, and it has never come to any good."

Creticus stared at Lucius who could only look back at him, speechless, wanting to tell him, to confide in him.

I can't tell him, Lucius thought.

Creticus continued. "I hear stories in every port. In the port of Luguvalium, near the end of the wall in Britannia, I also heard stories."

Lucius felt his heartbeat increase, but tried desperately to keep calm. He did not want to hurt the man before him.

"I heard stories about dragons in that mysterious land, about brave men who were invincible against the barbarians. I also heard about a certain praefectus who made to challenge the emperor. The troops I spoke with talked of him in whispers as if he were a shade. They said he was blessed and cursed by the Gods." Creticus looked out to sea and sighed. "You know the stories soldiers and sailors tell. Fantastical tales, they are. Tales to rend the heart sometimes. Philotimo has many faces."

"What did you say?" Lucius asked.

"Philotimo," Creticus repeated, turning to face Lucius again. "To us Greeks, it means that everything we do, every one of our actions, is honourable, and for honourable ends. It means that what we do in life, betters not only our lives, but the lives of those around us."

Lucius looked at the planks of the deck, his hand upon his chest and the dragon beneath it. "The love of honour," he whispered.

"Yes. That's it." Creticus reached out to touch Lucius' arm. "I don't know what haunts you, Lucius Pen Dragon, but I wish nothing but peace and joy for you and your family, and if you need help, you have only to ask it."

Lucius looked at the man before him, and thought that he had rarely met a man of such honesty. "Thank you."

"Even I can see that the Gods bless you. The curses in our lives, I have noticed, are more often of our own making." Creticus turned to leave, but stopped and turned back to Lucius. "Those stories of dragons were inspiring. They were stories of hope." Creticus grinned, his leathery face bright and friendly in the afternoon sun as he walked away to prepare to make port. "I believe in dragons."

That evening, they made berth at Gades so that Creticus could pay the way tax required to pass through the Pillars of Hercules and enter the Mare Internum the following day.

At dawn, before setting sail, Creticus and his crew made offerings at the seaside to Hercules and Neptune. As the smoke of their sacrifices swirled and rose into the air, they thanked Neptune for granting them safe passage thus far, and then prayed to him and to Hercules for safe passage through the Pillars, the gap the hero had created on his tenth labour to capture the cattle of Geryon.

Lucius, Adara, Phoebus and Calliope prayed too from the deck of the ship as they watched Creticus and his crew honour the Gods.

It was strange to think of entering the Middle Sea again after so long, but they were not there yet. The passage between the Pillars could be treacherous, and Lucius and Adara definitely noticed a change in the crew as the time approached for them to make the journey. There was an apprehension there, something approaching fear, as if they were passing through Scylla and Charybdis.

With the taxes paid, and the Gods honoured, Creticus' three corbita, led by the Europa, left the port of Gades and made for the Pillars.

Almost immediately, the sea became rougher, the current stronger, as if the ships were being sucked into the throat of a great beast. The rigging groaned more loudly and the dolphins upon the great sails stretched and strained with the winds.

"Hold on tightly!" Creticus yelled from the bow where he clung to the railing, his eyes scanning the waves as he pointed to his left or right to indicate which way Castor and Pollux should steer from the portside and starboard rudders.

The faint cries of the crews of the other two ships could be heard on the wind as they followed the path cut by the Europa.

Nerissa stood at the door of the cabin with Lucius and Adara while Phoebus and Calliope crouched inside for the rough passage. "Don't worry, friends," she said. " Creticus has done this many times. Neptune favours our ships. Hold on! This is the roughest part!"

Calliope screamed unintentionally as the ship rose abruptly and then fell, skimming a steep wave like a dolphin playing in the surf. At the bottom, however, the ship sidled roughly to the starboard, pushing the Europa toward the Mauretanian coast.

For a moment, Lucius thought the ships would not be able to pull back, but that they would be forced onto the rocks to the south.

But Creticus and his crew were skilled seamen, and just as the ship slowed in its starboard arc, he raised his left fist high and, with his sons steering, the Europa sailed smoothly back to the port side to come out of the channel and ease itself into the open sea ahead.

"That was rougher than usual!" Nerissa said, turning to Adara and the children. "Are you all right?"

Adara nodded from where she knelt beside Phoebus and Calliope, her own stomach threatening to heave as she cradled their heads. "Only once have I experienced rough seas like that, but that was in winter."

"You would not want to make this voyage in the winter months," Nerissa said, pressing a wet cloth to Calliope's forehead while Adara did the same for Phoebus. "You all did very well. Most passengers have their heads in the bucket during that part!" She went to Lucius who was standing on deck just outside the cabin door. "And you, Lucius? You seem to have managed well enough."

Lucius turned to her. "It was thrilling," he said, his eyes locked onto the blue sea.

"Perhaps you're a sailor at heart?" she laughed and went to join

Creticus at the bow where he was making an offering in the tripod on the foredeck.

Lucius stood there for a few more minutes, and then went to the rail to watch the rocky coastline sail by, the Pillars of Hercules behind them now. *What must it have been like when he first came here?* he wondered, thinking of the son of Zeus in that wild place. Lucius actually found himself smiling then, but not at the thought of the ancient hero. Rather, it was that he had survived what had felt like another brush with death. There had been a moment when, as the ship fell away, he thought that perhaps the end was near. But he had stood there, in the door of the cabin, staring out defiantly at the rising walls of sea water around them with a sense of calm. The only fear he had felt had been for his family in the cabin behind him. Any care for himself seemed to have been burned away with the past.

"Lucius," Adara called. "Can you help us?"

He turned quickly, suddenly realizing that he had not checked on them. When he entered the cabin, he found Adara holding Calliope's head and hair as she vomited into a bucket, while Phoebus sat green-faced in the corner, his eyes closed. "What can I do?" he asked.

"Bring some fresh water for her to drink!" Adara snapped.

Lucius went out and came back with a small pitcher of water which Adara put to her daughter's lips.

"I'm fine now, Mama," Calliope said, falling back to lean against the wall of the cabin.

"When can we get back on land?" Phoebus groaned.

"Yes, when can we, Lucius?" Adara said. "We've not been off this ship for weeks. I want to have a proper bath. It's summer now, and we're in the Middle Sea, wearing wool!"

Lucius felt apprehension at the thought of getting off of the ship but the sight of his wife and children in such a sweaty, sickly state gave him pause. "I'll speak with Creticus about the next ports. Maybe one of them will be safe."

Adara did not look up at him, but continued to help Calliope drink.

Lucius went back outside and found Creticus on the quarter deck above the cabins. He climbed up the ladder to join the captain who was signalling to the other two of his ships.

Creticus turned when Lucius approached, wiping his brow with a cloth he had tucked into his belt. "The others are all right, thank the

Gods!" He slapped Lucius on the shoulder. "That was a crossing, I tell you!" He glanced at the floor below. "How are your wife and children faring? I hope they don't feel too ill."

"They may not stand for a while yet," Lucius said.

"Understandable. Even I had a time of it!" He turned his palms over to show Lucius the abrasions he had endured by gripping the wooden rail at the bow so tightly. "The Gods looked after us on that one, no doubt about it." He saw Lucius' concern, but waved it off. "Nothing a little sea water won't mend." He saw the look linger on Lucius' face. "Is there something else bothering you?"

"Adara and the children are desperate for a bathhouse, and we need to buy some new clothes. Is the next port…safe, so to speak?"

"In a few days we'll stop at Carthago Nova, and yes, it is one of the safer ports we stop at. Mostly garum suppliers there, and the factories are dotted along the coast outside of the city. We're taking on a shipment of garum, so we'll stop, but most ships bypass it, as do landward travellers."

"Because of the smell?" Lucius asked, remembering encountering the stench of garum production along the coast of Africa Proconsularis at one point.

"'Smell' doesn't quite describe it. More like the stench from a titan's anus! Frankly, I don't know how Romans eat so much of the stuff, but I'm glad they do. They pay a fair price for it. That's the only reason we take it on board."

"It's not my favourite either," Lucius said, "but it sounds like we could safely visit the baths and market for some new clothing."

Creticus nodded. "Yes. You can do that. We'll make enough time for it. Just watch for the cut-purses. They're vicious."

"We will."

"You have a couple days yet, so tell Adara and the children to hang on. Soon, they'll have solid land beneath their feet!"

Creticus was right. A stench like no other clung to the city of Carthago Nova but, despite this, it appeared to be a large, thriving polis.

As Lucius and his family stood on the deck watching the approach to the port, holding their breath as much as possible, Lucius remembered Diodorus' lessons. He had spoken of the city that had been secured by

the Punic general Hasdrubal, brother-in-law of Hannibal, during the first
Punic War. It was later taken by Scipio Africanus at some point during
the second Punic War. Then, it had held strategic importance, and
yielded silver, but now its main commodity was garum.

Lucius tried to imagine Hannibal and Scipio's forces upon the land
before him, as well as his own Metellus ancestor who fought alongside
Scipio. *Not really* my *ancestor*, he thought, but the smell was so overwhelming as the ship approached its berth that he quite forgot what he
was thinking about.

"It's a big city," Nerissa said as she approached them, "but the streets
will be empty and quiet at midday. It's too hot, and the stench drives
people indoors."

"That's right!" Creticus said, joining her. "Carthago Nova comes
alive at night, but during the day, it's deserted."

"But you should find some clothes in the market. The sellers still
come out in the hopes that one person will stop to purchase something."

"Are you coming with us?" Adara asked.

"I'll come to the market with you, but not the baths. The smell really
is too much," Nerissa said.

Carthago Nova was a good-sized city with a perimeter wall and tile
rooftops stretching back from the sea. The port appeared to be the main
point of entry with the cardo maximus stretching away from it and
leading to the heart of the city. Along the eastern wall was a theatre and
an amphitheatre, and beyond the western wall was a lake that was
crossed by an aqueduct that fed the city, including the baths and homes
of wealthy merchants and garum producers. Temples stood on several of
the hills around the city perimeter, their white columns glinting in the
blinding sunlight.

It was somewhat eerie to walk in the light of day while the city
streets were as quiet as if it were the middle of the night. Despite the
smell, and how hot she was beneath her wool tunica, Adara felt life
coming back into her body as she enjoyed the warmth of the sun upon
her face and the familiar sound of cicadas fill her ears.

When they had stepped off of the ship, Lucius, Adara and the children had almost fallen over. They had become so accustomed to the sea,
that land had proven a bit too still for them. After a few minutes, they
had their land legs back and were walking with Nerissa up the cardo
maximus to the forum and market at the heart of the city.

A few people were about, but most were slaves running midday errands for their masters who did not want to go out of doors at such an hour.

"Here we are!" Nerissa said as they turned to walk beneath a colonnade and head into the forum. "Now, let's find you all some proper summer clothing."

Lucius walked with Phoebus behind Nerissa, Adara, and Calliope. He noticed his son fingering the pommel of his gladius and put his hand upon his shoulder. "Don't worry. We're safe here. Not even the troops want to be out in the day."

"It stinks," Phoebus said.

"Yes, it does," Lucius agreed. "Let's just find some clothing, take a bath, and get back to the ship."

There were three clothing sellers in the forum, each with broad, colourful awnings that allowed would-be customers to browse comfortably in the shade. They approached an Egyptian merchant who had incense burning at every corner of the stall. He waved them over to where he and his wife and daughter were waiting in the shade of the awnings. He did not speak, but did indicate that they should look at his stock.

For the women, there were racks of linen and silk stolae and tunicae, some in solid colours and others with brocade borders in gold or silver thread.

For the men, there was a wide array of tunicae of similarly varied colours and patterns.

For himself, Lucius chose a plain, dark grey, linen tunica that was belted and hung loosely down to the knees. He also picked a straw hat to protect his exposed head from the intense sun and to hide his face.

Phoebus chose a similar linen tunica in dark blue with a single red line of thread around the hem. Both his, and his father's, came with matching summer cloaks.

Adara and Calliope on the other hand were having trouble deciding on what to get.

It broke Lucius' heart to do so, but when he saw them picking up the more elaborate stolae, he walked over to them. "We can't wear anything that will draw attention," he told them. "Please choose only simple tunicae and cloaks."

Adara turned to him and the look in her eyes was gut-wrenching. She had been excited to shop with Calliope, not because she wanted to spend, but because it provided them with a shared moment, because by putting on a stola once more, she could feel some sort of normalcy.

"I'm sorry," Lucius said when he saw the look in his wife's eyes. "It's not safe."

"What should we buy then?" Adara asked.

"Just pick a thin tunica. There are some linen and silk ones over there." He pointed to a rack of plain coloured tunicae without brocade or other ornamentation.

"So we can dress like peasants?" Adara said.

"Please," Lucius said, his voice low. "For safety's sake."

Adara knew he was right, but she still felt gutted putting back the bright blue stola she had been holding up to Calliope's body. "Come love," she said to her daughter. "Your father's right."

Calliope did not seem to mind so much, and picked a long, silk, gap-sleeved tunica of light green, the colour of spring grass. It too came with a matching summer cloak.

Adara nodded as she looked her over, and then for herself, she picked a floor-length tunica of pale, sea blue that was belted just below the breast. It too had gap sleeves with simple knots, and a matching cloak.

Lucius walked over to her, but Adara pulled away a little.

"We also need new sandals," she said, "or will footwear draw too much attention?"

"We have many sandals!" the merchant's wife said from the other side of the racks where she was showing Nerissa some jewellery.

"Yes. Let's get some," Lucius said, thinking of the long road ahead and how he would need some more rugged footwear.

While Adara and Calliope chose some sandals for themselves, Lucius and Phoebus decided to look over the caligae.

"Won't these dig into your skin, Baba?" Phoebus said, looking at Lucius' burned feet.

"Yes, but I'll oil them and wear them only for a couple of hours a day at first." He knew it would hurt, but he wanted something sturdy. He picked a dark brown pair with hobnails that were made of softer leather, and Phoebus chose similarly. "Let's check if your mother and sister are ready. We've lingered too long."

Lucius looked around the market to see more people roaming about, emerging slowly from their midday slumbers.

"We should go if we want to get to the baths," Lucius said to Adara.

"We're finished," she said, holding up two pairs of light-coloured sandals for her and Calliope.

They carried the clothing and sandals to the merchant's counter and his eyes widened at the sale he was about to make.

"Are you sure the ladies would not like a couple of stolae to go over the tunicae?"

"We're sure," Lucius said curtly. "How much?"

"Or perhaps some jewellery to show off your wife's beautiful neck?"

"Nothing more. Tell me how much," Lucius said, leaning forward so that his burned face stared at the merchant.

The Egyptian glanced down at the black pommel of Lucius' gladius, beside which hung his leather purse. He gulped. He scanned the items the family had chosen, and added in his head. "Six aurea for the tunicae and cloaks, and four for the sandals. Ten aurea in total."

"That's preposterous!" Lucius said.

Nerissa, who often visited the sellers began to move away a little, embarrassed by the display.

Lucius felt he was back in Africa. He had grown unaccustomed to haggling, for it was not so common in Britannia, and he had not shopped in a market for well over a year.

He removed his purse and looked inside. "I'll give you six aurea for everything. Take it or leave it."

The man glanced at his wife, and then at the piles of clothing and sandals. He sighed, knowing full-well he would not make such a large sale that day or any other day in Carthago Nova, for the locals favoured the local Iberian and Latin sellers.

"Yes. Is good!" he said, putting on a smile that revealed a row of yellowing teeth. "Good deal!" he said, looking to Nerissa who smiled back at him and nodded her thanks.

Lucius fished out the six gold coins from his purse and placed them on the counter while the merchant's wife and daughter bundled the clothing and sandals together with twine.

"Thank you," Adara said as they turned to leave. "Do we still have time for the baths?" she asked Nerissa.

Nerissa looked up at the sun and nodded. "Plenty of time. Do go now before it gets too busy. I'll show you where they are, and then head back to the ship. I need some fresh sea air." They walked south a few streets and then Nerissa turned to point down a street to the right. "They are straight ahead where the smoke is rising. These baths are not segregated, but it won't be busy at this hour, so you can all four go through without issue. The slaves are pretty good here about watching your things, but you may want to promise them a few extra bronze ases so they don't rifle through your things. Enjoy! I'll see you back at the ship in about an hour?"

When Nerissa was gone, Lucius, Adara, Phoebus and Calliope walked with their new clothes in hand to the bathhouse. Each of them was imagining how wonderful it would feel to bathe in warm water, to oil themselves and scrape away the dirt that had built up over the past weeks on the ship. Sea sponges did an adequate job, but there was nothing like a strigil and oil.

The bathhouse was large enough, and the apodyterium cubicles spacious and clean.

The slaves looked Lucius and Phoebus over apprehensively, frightened by their weapons, but more so by the burned appearance of the man.

"If you keep a close watch on all of our things, and don't touch, there will be two ases for each of you."

The slaves' eyes bulged and they bowed. "Yes, dominus!" they said in unison as the family passed into the tepidarium.

The one slave turned to the other. "You sit there in front of their things, and don't let anyone near them. Two ases each!" He picked up the family's dirty clothes. "I'm going to give these a quick wash and put them out in the sun. Maybe they'll give us three each then?"

It felt luxurious to bathe again. Lucius, Adara and the children had the run of the place, no gawkers or boy-lovers, no dandies approaching Adara or Calliope. They made their progress through the rooms, getting wet in the tepidarium, and then oiling and scraping their skin in the caldarium.

Adara sighed to herself as she felt the grime wash away from her body. Her fingers traced the scar on her abdomen, however, and she felt a great loneliness wash over her as Phoebus and Calliope splashed each other and jumped into the pool of the frigidarium, their voices echoing off of the high ceiling.

"Are you all right?" Lucius asked, coming to stand beside his wife.

"No. I can't help but think of our child every time I see this scar." She looked at him then, standing naked, his burned body changed beyond recognition, in the sunlight that was angling its way in from the windows in the roof. "And every time I see you, I think of what they did to you, what they did to our home."

"I know. I'll make it right, Adara. I promise." He touched her shoulder and kissed her forehead.

"How, Lucius? You keep saying that, but you can't 'make it right'. It's done. The damage is done. They've taken everything."

I know. And I will make them bleed for it. But Lucius said nothing. Even being in a bathhouse reminded him of the one they had built upon their land at the hillfort, now all but ash in the mud and grass.

"We'd better stay with the children," Adara said suddenly. "I didn't like the way those slave boys were looking at Calliope."

They went into the frigidarium, and felt the heat of the day fall away, the cool, mountain water that fed into the baths from the aqueduct invigorating and soothing.

Soon enough, it was time to leave, for they had been there for over an hour. When they returned to the apodyterium, Lucius checked over their things to make sure all was accounted for. When he saw their old clothes missing, he wheeled on the slave boy.

"Where are our clothes?" he demanded, his hand up.

The boy looked frightened and shocked, stumbling upon the ground to get words out.

"Lucius!" Adara said.

Lucius looked at his hand and the boy grovelling on the ground. He remembered helping a slave boy at the baths in Cyrene years before, and it jarred him to think of that man as separate from the one he was now. He quickly lowered his hand and calmed his voice.

"Where are our clothes?"

"He went to wash them for you."

"I didn't ask you to do that."

"Here they are!" said a breathless voice as the other boy came rushing back in with the clothes folded neatly in his arms.

"Forgive me, dominus, but they smelled of sweat and were stained with salt from the sea. I washed them quickly in fresh water and put them in the sun. They are mostly dry now." The boy bowed his head, not looking Lucius in the eyes.

"Very well," Lucius said, as he placed the clean clothes upon the bench beneath the cubicles and reached for his purse. "You didn't touch anything else?" he asked, looking at his purse, weapons and other items.

The boys shook their heads.

"Good." Lucius reached his fingers into the pouch and pulled out some coins. "Here are four ases each. Hide them so no one takes them from you."

"Thank you, dominus!" they cried, smiling broadly. "We'll leave you alone to change, but if you need anything else, just call for us!" They went away to the entrance of the baths gazing at the coins in the palms of their hands

As Adara, Phoebus and Calliope put on their new clothes, Lucius slid his new tunic on over his head and belted it with his cingulum. He then tied on his old sandals, waiting until the new ones were oiled before trying them. When his gladius and pugio were belted on, he turned to see his family in their new clothes.

To think that new clothes could change one's demeanour so. It came as a surprise to him, but Adara, Phoebus and Calliope all smiled more.

"You look beautiful," he said to Adara and Calliope. "And you," he said to Phoebus, "you look quite noble. Strap on your gladius and pugio and let's go. We're late."

They gathered the remainder of their things and went out onto the cardo maximus and back down to the port. As they were walking, Lucius could feel the eyes of the locals on them, as if staring from dark doorways and upper floor windows.

Then, he heard them: hurried footsteps. The sound was determined and quick, and as the Europa came into view at the end of the cardo, Lucius felt his heart beating more quickly.

"There's Creticus," Phoebus said, looking ahead to see the captain waving to them from the deck.

"Phoebus can you carry these for me?" Lucius asked, handing his son his clean woollen clothes.

Phoebus took them and went forward to join his mother and sister as they began to make their way up the gang plank.

"Don't they look lovely?" Lucius could hear Nerissa say to Creticus.

As Adara and the children reached the top of the gang plank, the footsteps were coming nearer and faster.

Lucius reached beneath the linen of his new cloak for this gladius and just as the sound almost reached him, he spun quickly, his gladius drawn.

The Egyptian merchant cried out, his eyes wide with fear as the entire crew on the deck of Europe, and Lucius' family, turned to see the deadly tip of Lucius' gladius pointed at the merchant's throat.

"Why are you following us?" Lucius growled.

"Baba!" Phoebus said, dropping the clean clothes on the deck and rushing to his father with his own sword drawn.

"I…I…I…" the terrified merchant could barely speak, but with a shaking hand he raised a straw hat to the side. "Please… You forgot this."

Lucius looked at the hat he had purchased, hanging from the man's shaking hand. He felt the stares of every person there, the crew, their hosts aboard the ship, the slaves and other merchants on the quayside. They all stared at Lucius.

As Lucius lowered the gladius, the man held out the hat to him. The moment Lucius accepted it, the man turned and ran away.

When Lucius turned, it was to the shocked faces of Creticus and his wife, sons and crew, but Adara was gone.

Phoebus sheathed his gladius quickly and went to his father. "It's all right, Baba. Simple mistake. Come. Let's get aboard."

They walked up the gang plank to Creticus and Nerissa, who were standing behind Calliope.

"All is well?" Creticus asked.

Embarrassed, Lucius nodded. "Yes. Just…just a misunderstanding."

"Remind me never to sell you anything, Lucius Pen Dragon!" Creticus said before bursting out in friendly laughter that was echoed by the crew.

Only Nerissa did not laugh as she placed her hands upon Calliope's shoulders and looked to the cabin to which Adara had fled.

"Weigh anchor!" Creticus called to the crew.

As the men moved about the deck, Lucius, Phoebus and Calliope went to their cabin to get out of the way.

The corbita bobbed gently as it moved out into the broad port, followed by the other two ships. The sound of Creticus' commands, and the cries of the gulls and sailing songs of the crew, were drowned out by the pounding in Lucius' head and the sound of Adara weeping gently within as her children tried to comfort her.

Lucius stood outside the cabin door, unable to go in, to face her. His impulse had ruined their outing, and he hated himself for it.

It took them six days of hugging the coast to the northeast to reach Narbo where Creticus had one last shipment of wine to pick up. The late summer journey was smooth and pleasant. To the port side, broad sandy beaches where waves crashed, stretched out before their eyes. Beyond, low rocky cliffs the colour of pale red and tan, rose up to grassy plains or marshes, and in the distance, the hazy hills of southern Gaul were like a dreamy landscape.

It should have been soothing for Lucius and his family, but the tension between him and Adara overshadowed that summer brilliance, darkened further still by Lucius' anticipation of their arrival on the Etrurian coast at Pisae in a few days.

At the bustling port of Narbo, they waited aboard ship as an enormous cargo of wine amphora was loaded onto the Europa and the other two ships.

"I suggest you don't go ashore, Lucius," Creticus said as they watched the unloading from the bow. "It's very busy here. A lot of troops, if you know what I mean."

"I do." Lucius had not said much since leaving Carthago Nova, and Creticus and Nerissa had felt the tension between him and Adara acutely. The crew had gone back to muttering, waiting for them to be offloaded in Pisae.

"I don't have any business in Pisae," Creticus said, conversationally, "so, we'll just drop you off and get underway."

"I'm sorry about what happened," Lucius said. "I thought he was following us."

"I don't mind myself, Lucius. But perhaps you should say that to your wife? I know it's none of my business - Gods know I'm not a perfect husband! - but honesty and the ability to admit fault between a man and his wife is the only foundation for a happy life. Being aboard ship most of the year with mine has taught me that. When all you have is right before you, that is when you should realize it."

Lucius looked at the old sailor and nodded. "You're right, of course."

"Of course, I'm right. I'm the captain!" Creticus smiled and turned to look to where Castor and Pollux were showing Phoebus and Calliope how to tie more knots. "Your boy was right there with you."

Lucius nodded but did not smile. "Yes. He was. He's been through a lot."

"Seems like he's had some training."

"We all have," Lucius said.

"Of course..." Creticus said. "A venator leads a dangerous life, and so does his family if they travel with him."

Lucius saw the knowing look in the man's eye. "Yes."

"Well, when you are done in Etruria...if you need passage again, to Graecia or anywhere else you are headed, we'll be in Ostia selling some of this cargo, and then in Brundisium at the markets for a few weeks. Keep that in mind. We're there for you, my friend. If you ever need to get word to me, just leave a message at the offices of the merchants guild in any port, and I'll get it." Creticus placed his hand upon Lucius' shoulder and smiled.

"Thank you," Lucius said.

"There's your wife," Creticus said, seeing Adara emerge from the cabin and climb up onto the quarter deck above. "May be a good time to talk." He began to walk away. "Nerissa!" he called. "I need your help with something!" he said, leaving Lucius to speak alone with Adara.

The five days from the port of Narbo to Pisae went quickly by, and during that time Lucius and Adara spoke openly about what had happened in Narbo.

Adara could see the constant tension in Lucius' eyes, the worry, anger and fear, and it was that which upset her, not the fact that he drew his sword on a merchant.

"What worries me, Lucius, is the change in you," she said, holding his burned face in her hands and looking into his transformed eyes. "There is a part of you that I cannot know, a part that only you and the Gods can know, and I glimpsed it when you turned on the Egyptian. It scares me to think you are slipping away from me."

Lucius held her tightly then, felt her tears upon his neck as he squeezed her. *I am not changed,* he wanted to say. *I will always be with you.* But he could not mouth the words. He knew she was right in what she said, and it frightened him too.

Upon that last leg of the sea voyage, they also spoke of the days to come, and of their apprehension. They had not returned to Italy for many years, and however much a part of Lucius might have been excited to see Etruria again, to see his mother, brother and sister, to walk the rich soil of his ancestral lands once more, there was a part of him that feared what they might find.

They would have to go cautiously into Etruria, they knew, and as the port of Pisae came into view where it sat at the mouth of the river Arnus, Lucius and Adara felt the anxiety in their guts. They had to be extremely careful now.

This time, only the Europa made berth while the other two ships bobbed at anchor out in the bay.

"They say Nestor of Pylos founded this port after the Trojan war," Creticus said to Phoebus as they all stood at the rail, waiting for the ropes to be tied off. He could tell that the boy was nervous, fiddling with the pommel of the gladius that hung at his side. "Just offloading passengers!" Creticus called to the harbour master below.

The man waved back and moved on to the next ship.

"You can hire a wagon over there on the other side of the Arnus," Creticus said to Lucius and Adara, pointing to the stables alongside the river. "The via Aurelia will take you south."

"I know it well," Lucius said absently, his mind already on the road ahead.

"Listen," Creticus said, his voice low, for Lucius and Adara only. "They will want to check your papers here. "It is Italy, after all. You have the papers Einion gave you, saying you're his representatives?"

"Yes," Lucius said, alert now, forcing his mind back to the present moment. He turned to Creticus and Nerissa. "Thank you both, truly." He clasped Creticus' forearm. "We may see you in Brundisium, but if not, farewell."

"With hope, we will see you all again," Nerissa said, hugging Adara. "Take care and may the Gods guide you safely."

"Thank you," Adara replied.

"Practice your knots!" Castor said to Phoebus and Calliope as he and Pollux stood beside their parents.

Grasping their full satchels, Lucius, Adara, Phoebus and Calliope made their way down the gang plank onto the busy quayside of Pisae. They turned one last time to wave to Creticus and his family, and then disappeared into the crowd.

"Will they be all right?" Nerissa asked her husband.

"I honestly don't know, love."

Pisae was indeed an ancient port, and rather than the polished marble and limestone buildings of ports such as Narbo, the muted sandstone, brick, and tile structures of Pisae spoke of an earlier age.

The crowd rang out with various dialects of Latin and Greek, accented here and there with Phoenician. Everyone was busy, ensuring various cargoes were offloaded or loaded, fair prices agreed upon, and good deals struck.

They did not have to go into the city to leave Pisae, but to exit the port by way of the bridge over the Arnus, Lucius and his family had to pass through a guarded archway.

Three armed men from the local vigiles questioned people before they were permitted to go through.

Lucius and his family joined the line and waited. "Let me do the talking," he said to Adara and the children, clutching the papers from Einion in one hand, his satchel slung over his shoulder with the other.

Soon enough, it was their turn and Lucius, his heart racing, stepped up to the guards.

"Who are you and what is your business in Italy?" the guard said. He was shorter than Lucius, his eyes searching. His hands were calloused and scarred from fighting, likely breaking up brawls in the port.

"My name is Lucius Pen Dragon. I represent my employer in Britannia who is a lead merchant. I'm here on business."

"Strange name." The guard took Lucius' papers and looked them over. Then, he looked behind Lucius at Adara and the children. "You bring your family with you on such a long journey?"

"We always travel together," Lucius answered. "I want them to see the beauty of the empire."

The man laughed. "The beauty of the empire?" He looked back at the other two soldiers, and then at Adara and Calliope. "Looks like you've got enough beauty right here!"

Behind Lucius, Phoebus gripped the pommel of his sword, but Calliope discreetly gripped his hand to calm him.

The soldier smirked through broken teeth, his rank breath reaching out to Lucius as he looked closely at him. "What happened to you anyway? Why are you so ugly?"

Lucius forced a smile, willing himself with all his strength not to draw his gladius. "Smelting accident."

"Where you going anyway?" the soldier asked, stepping back again.

"Sena Iulia. My employer wants me to contact someone there about a mine."

The man turned back to his fellows. "Any lead mining near that shit hole?" he said, swatting a fly away from his face.

The other two soldiers shrugged, and so did he.

"Hmm. I thought it was just wine and pigs down that way." He handed the papers back to Lucius, glancing past them to see the building line behind them. "Get you going."

The guards stood aside to let them pass, their eyes taking in the sight of Adara and Calliope as they walked ahead of Lucius with Phoebus in front of them.

"Next!" the guard called down the line.

When they were over the bridge on the other side of the Arnus, they paused to breathe.

"Why were they so mean, Baba?" Calliope asked.

Lucius hugged his daughter. He could see that she was unnerved by the looks they had given her. "Small-minded men with a little power think they can treat others however they wish, my girl. Don't worry. I would never let anyone hurt you."

"I know," she said.

"I'm hungry," Phoebus added, seeing the stalls of food sellers along the road.

"We'll need provisions for the journey," Adara said as she looked along the cypress trees dotting the straight line of the via Aurelia, the main road south along the coast and into Etruria.

Lucius turned to look and spotted the place where he could hire a wagon and mule. "Calliope, you can come with me to get the wagon. Phoebus, you go with your mother to gather some food for the journey."

"Yes, Baba," Phoebus said.

"Be careful," Lucius whispered to Adara. "I have a strange feeling."

She put her hand upon his arm. "It will be fine, Lucius. Don't worry so much," she said as she turned to Phoebus and led the way.

"You want to pick the mule?" Lucius said to Calliope.

She smiled. "What if the mule picks us?" she replied, laughing.

Within an hour, they had a four-wheeled wagon pulled by a sturdy brown mule with a white muzzle. Lucius drove with Phoebus beside him on the bench and Adara and Calliope sat among soft fleeces and fresh straw with their belongings in the back.

As they began their journey down the coastal road, they ate some of the bread, cheese and dried meat that Adara had purchased. Food had never tasted so good as it did then, and the taste of that simple Etrurian fare brought back long ago memories for Lucius.

They joined the flow of traffic along the via Aurelia, the green and brown hills to their left, and the turquoise sea on their right.

Lucius thought about how he could not wait to taste the food and wine from his own estate, but despite the brilliant sun and the Etrurian beauty surrounding them, he had a sinking feeling in his gut. In two days, he would see his mother, brother, and sister again. He wondered what they would be like, if they were well. And he wondered how they would perceive him after so long away. Much had changed.

X

IMPERII CINIS

'Embers of an Empire'

R ome's empire was not only a stage upon which the Gods played, but one to which they gravitated as an audience to see the great comedies and tragedies of mortal existence play out. There was some truth to the thinking that the immortals manipulated and coerced, but even the Gods had to admit that most often, it was mortal choices that led to some of the greatest loves, battles, and bloody ends that played out upon that great stage for the pantheon's pleasure.

The beginning of the reign of Caracalla was no less bloody and tragic than others that had come before, but mortal and immortal alike had to ask themselves if it was not more displeasing than others. There was little of heroism upon the scene, and in that play, the main character was, as far as anyone could tell, a villain.

A song of fratricide still rang through the streets of Rome, was whispered about in dark corners of the Forum Romanum. Two years after the empress' younger son died in her blood-soaked arms, those who were brave enough to point out the truth referred to Caracalla as the 'kinsman-killer'.

However, after the initial storm during which he hid in the Praetorian camp, the emperor had gone into the curia to declare to the senate that he was the equal of Romulus who had slain his own brother, Remus, for the good of Rome.

"This is a new beginning for Rome!" Caracalla had declared.

And he was right. It was a new beginning for Rome, a beginning in which he bathed the world in blood.

The proscriptions had begun almost immediately, like an archaic blood rite to fulfill a secret vow of the emperor's. Some said that the blood had begun to flow in faraway Britannia, but it was in Rome where

THE BLOOD ROAD

it was truly felt, for in the first wave of proscriptions, after Geta's murder, over twenty-thousand supporters and friends of Severus' younger son were slain. Among the victims were some senators, popular athletes, singers, dancers, and even infants of those with some thin tie to Geta. All were butchered, and bodies were tossed outside of the city walls to be burned or left to rot. The deaths were so violent, the victims so many, that there were portions of Rome's walls where none dared to venture for fear of the angry shades that now lingered there, especially those of the slain children.

Caracalla even slew Lucius Aurelius Commodus Pompeianus, the son of Lucilla, sister of Emperor Commodus, who had been a great general of Rome and had set up a great altar to Septimius Severus at Lugdunum in Gaul, where the latter had won a massive victory at the beginning of his own reign.

None were safe, not Caracalla's wife, Plautilla, who had been living in Sicily, nor even certain Vestal Virgins whom he believed to be unchaste.

He continued to attack Geta beyond the grave as well with the erasure of his very memory all across the empire. Any image of his brother, any inscription or mention in texts or histories, was ordered removed, chiselled away or burned. It was as if, thinking himself a god, he had taken it upon himself to strike out his brother's existence.

This act, upsetting enough to the Roman people, was only to be over-shadowed by another of Caracalla's - his Constitutio Antoniniana.

Across other parts of the empire, free barbarians and commoners alike may have been happy at receiving Roman citizenship, but in Italy and in Rome itself, the people felt alienated. Their Roman citizenship, once a point of pride, was now commonplace. They were no longer special, as if their appointed father had taken another mistress and fathered other children to take their place, to drown out their voices and take the food from their plates.

Rome became intolerable for Caracalla, for he could do no right by the people. He was protected only by the fact that the troops remained loyal to him, both the Praetorians and the men of the legions, for he had enriched them greatly.

And then, as if the Gods figured Caracalla had done enough to Rome for a time, the drums of war began to thrum once more across the empire.

In Germania, the Alamanni and Carpi decided to take advantage of the chaos at the heart of the empire to rebel and make yet another attempt to throw off the yoke of Rome's oppression. Not only had they, as dediticii, tribesmen beyond the Danube frontier, been denied the universal citizenship that had so recently been granted across the empire, but they had also grown tired of living beneath the boot of lesser men.

The Germanic tribes tossed the bones to fall where they may, and so, Caracalla and his legions crossed the Danuvius once more with fire and sword and brutal war upon the mountains and hillsides, in the forests and fields.

Eventually, winter came, and with the snows in the north came the end of the campaigning season and the return of Rome's emperor caput mundi.

The city was quiet, as if holding its breath in fearful anticipation of another wave of bloody proscriptions with Caracalla's return.

When the streets remained free of blood, however, the people gave silent thanks in their prayers before the altars to their household gods, offered whispered wishes for either a new, more learned emperor, or a quick end to his rule before the cancer spread.

Never was Septimius Severus more loved, or missed, than during that time when Caracalla sat silent and sullen within the imperial palace complex built by his father in the heart of Rome.

It was then the Gods watched the scene again, of a solitary man at his table, alone upon the stage, his head in his hands, haunted by all that he had done and would do, for if the choices of one's life made the man, then he was truly damned.

How did my father do it? Caracalla asked himself as he sat there among the scrolls and unfurled maps upon the broad, red marble table in his rooms in the palace. He had thought it would be soothing to return to Rome, that the people would have welcomed him after campaigning in Germania, but such was not the case. Instead, he stayed within the palace as Macrinus, his Praetorian Prefect, suggested.

The blood of the proscriptions was still wet upon the paving slabs of Rome's streets, and sometimes the mob, no matter how many games one put on, found it hard to forget.

Caracalla hated it when he began to feel sorry for himself. *I am emperor!* he told himself. *And this world is mine! It exists to serve me!*

He looked up from his hands to gaze about the sprawling room, his mantra dry upon his lips. The smoke from the numerous sticks of incense jutting from the bronze tripod a few feet away wafted up into the air. Nearby, the marble bust of the god Serapis stared back at him. From beneath the modus which the god wore upon his head, and the thick, full beard, those eyes gazed into Caracalla's very soul as if asking him, *What do you intend to do? Self-pity is for the weak.*

But it was not just his own self-pity that irked Caracalla. It was Geta.

Every night when he lay down to sleep, no matter how much he had drunk, fought, or sated himself with women, his brother's shade continued to come to him. He would find him standing beside his bed staring down at him, or standing in a corner pointing at him. Caracalla would shout at the shade or draw his gladius and slash at him, but nothing made it stop or go away.

He had taken to killing a prisoner or slave every time he had one of those nightmares in the hopes that the Gods would remove the shade from his presence and send it to the realm of the dead where it belonged, but not even the blood of those sacrifices had helped.

Holding his golden-hilted gladius adorned with eagles, Caracalla paced the room and came to stop before the bust of Alexander, his own hero.

"How did you get the people to give you their hearts so willingly?" he asked those vacant eyes. "Was it your victories across the world into Asia? Was it power and fear? Was it your willingness to do anything?" He lowered his head before the son of Zeus. "My father was no god such as yours, but he was a great man... How did you achieve all that you did? Did you set fear aside? Did it even exist for you?" Caracalla stood back, gazing at Alexander. "How alone did you feel when you reached the pinnacle of power? Did the shades of Cleitus, Parmenion and others haunt you as my brother does me?"

Caracalla walked over to his armour upon the stand along one of the walls, and looked over the black cuirass that displayed a large lion head. His fingers traced its outline, ran along the leather strips of the pteruges, and played upon the high, horsehair crest. He already missed the field, for if he felt welcome anywhere, it was when he was with the men of the legions. They had accepted him as he was, their momentary lapse in

Britannia having been due to the treachery of their legates and not the men themselves.

He walked over to the large open balcony that overlooked the Circus Maximus and gazed down at the sprawling sands where the slaves were busy raking the surface prior to the morrow's races. He used to love the races, to race himself, but now it only reminded him of Geta.

"Sire," one of the Praetorians appeared at the edge of the balcony.

"What is it?" Caracalla snapped.

The soldier, who had been on guard outside the double doors of the room, saluted. "Your mother and Praefectus Ulpianus are here."

"Bring them in."

The man saluted smartly and turned to go.

Caracalla stared out at the grey, overcast world a little longer. He did not want more bad news from his mother and the Praetorian prefect, but he knew they would not leave him be. He breathed deeply, his fists gripping the marble railing and then stood tall, his cloak wrapped about him as the wind picked up.

As he walked back inside, past the slaves who were building up the fire in the nearby braziers, he saw Julia Domna and Ulpianus sitting upon the stools on the other side of his table.

They stood and bowed as he approached.

"Mother. Ulpianus. What is it?"

"It is time for our daily update, sire," Ulpianus said.

Julia Domna was quiet, silently observing her son, noting the look of disaffection upon his frowning face. *You begin to reap what you have sown, I see,* she thought.

Ulpianus cleared his throat. "The provincial governors continue to write with word about the effects of the Constitutio, sire."

"Yes?" Caracalla looked up from the map to finally meet their eyes. "And how are things proceeding? How do the people of the empire feel now, being granted Roman citizenship?"

Julia Domna stared at her hands, waiting for Ulpianus to answer.

Ulpianus cleared his throat and adjusted his toga. "People are ignorant, sire. They do not understand. They only see that they are expected to pay more taxes and-"

"What are the governors saying?" Caracalla stood and leaned forward on the table top, looking down on Ulpianus.

"In general, people are not happy. There have been riots in places."

"Riots?" Caracalla's eyes widened in disbelief. "Riots because I granted all freedmen in the empire Roman citizenship?"

"Yes, sire."

Caracalla slammed his fist on the table sending styli and papyri onto the floor.

A slave began to pick them up immediately, only to be kicked by the emperor and sent sprawling onto the floor several feet away.

"Damn the ungrateful bastards!" Caracalla screamed. He pointed at Ulpianus. "*You* suggested I increase the criminal powers of the provincial governors! Why can't they use those new powers to calm things down and prosecute...no, execute the rioters?"

Ulpianus fidgeted with his papers, but beside him, Julia Domna remained calm, removed, looking upon her son in his torment.

Maybe now you understand what it is to rule, she thought.

After a moment, Caracalla turned on the two of them again.

"Can't the people of the empire see what I am trying to do?" He pointed to the bust of Alexander. "I have brought his dream to fruition! I've turned our empire into a communis patria, a common homeland for all citizens. I've made the provincials equal to Italians! No longer are the Italians superior to the people of Africa Proconsularis, Syria, Iberia or Britannia in the eyes of the law. I have made them equal, given them rights! We now have a universal state! What have they to complain about?" he roared, his voice echoing off of the marble walls.

Ulpianus said nothing. He could not reason with Caracalla. He never could converse with him the way Papinianus used to with Severus.

As Caracalla seethed silently before them, Julia Domna spoke at last.

"My son... In his time, Alexander was misunderstood as well. His people turned against him for bringing barbarians into the fold, just as you are. History will remember you for what you have done, but it is the fate of a ruler to be..."

"To be what, Mother? Tell me!" Caracalla's voice was thick with sarcasm.

"To often have his actions misunderstood. You must be patient with the people. Give them time, and in the interim, give them victories. They understand war and riches more easily. You give them that, and then later will come their understanding of the pan-Roman world you want to create."

"In their letters, do the governors at least understand?" Caracalla asked, for Julia Domna had been put in charge of important correspondence while he was away in Germania.

"Most do," she lied. "But it takes longer for the people to achieve understanding."

"And what am I supposed to do in the meantime? Do either of you know? Tell me! Do I let the people riot? Do I wait for the mob to attain understanding?"

"We would not presume to tell you what to do, my emperor," Ulpianus said.

"I am *asking* you, you idiot!" Caracalla fumed now. In the past, Ulpianus had been forthcoming with advice, but now, he spoke little and only when pressed. "By the Gods, Ulpianus, you are excellent at drafting laws and making an argument in the senate, but when it comes to action and decisions of martial consequence, you're absolutely useless! Thank Serapis and Sol for Macrinus in such matters."

Ulpianus pursed his lips. "As a former gladiator, hunter, and postal courier, I'm sure Praefectus Macrinus would have more advice of a physical and martial nature. I do but try to understand the mindset of the people, for in doing so, we may better predict outcomes before slashing at them with a sword."

"You are no oracle, Ulpianus, to be sure." Caracalla sat back down again, his breathing slowing, deepening. He stared at his mother and once more, he spied the changed way in which she looked upon him. He remembered how they used to sit and talk, how he could always rely upon her council. They had been closest when they had a common enemy in Plautianus, but things were different now. Even had he wanted to speak in confidence with her, he knew he could not. "Leave me, both of you," Caracalla said. "I need to be alone."

Ulpianus inclined his head, gathered his papers and stood. He bowed to Caracalla and departed without waiting for Julia Domna.

She stood but remained there for an uncomfortable moment, looking down at her son. A small part of her felt pity for him, but the moment her heart began to soften toward him, the moment she almost reached out to hug him, she remembered her younger boy bleeding to death in her arms, and the tenderness she felt turned to bitter ice.

Caracalla looked up at her then and, for an instant, the deep crevices in his brow began to flatten out. His lips parted as if he would say something, but with the sound of a harsh voice out in the corridor, snaking its way into the room, he shut his mouth and leaned back in his fur-draped chair.

Julia Domna inclined her head to her emperor, turned, and walked away through the cloud of incense smoke that hovered at the centre of the room. As she left, she saw the Praetorian prefect, Marcus Opellius Macrinus, coming toward her, his gruff voice disturbing the peace of Caesar's sanctuary.

Macrinus was fully armed, as usual, in his military regalia, the dark brown cuirass and matching greaves adorned with the she-wolf suckling the babies, Romulus and Remus. His black horsehair crest made him appear two heads taller than Julia Domna, and it wavered as he walked, like a cockerel in strut.

Julia Domna inclined her head as she passed. "Praefectus," she said, her hatred of the man veiled politely. *How history does repeat itself,* she thought as the man's narrow, bearded face turned toward her.

"Augusta," Macrinus said as he passed without stopping on his way to Caracalla.

Julia Domna walked on, joined by her ladies-in-waiting who had been lingering in the corridor and joined her as soon as she emerged, to go back to her own apartments in the palace.

As the doors closed behind him, Macrinus saluted Caracalla sharply. "Caesar."

"Macrinus. Well-met. I was tiring of my mother's company."

"Wine, sire?" Macrinus asked, holding up his hand for one of the slaves to come and pour for both of them. Two golden cups were filled and the slave handed the first to Caracalla who took it without looking. Macrinus took his and waved the slave away. They both poured a little on the floor and drank. "I saw Ulpianus leave before her."

"Yes. They decided it would be a good time to lecture Caesar."

Macrinus sat opposite, removed his helmet and set it harshly upon the ground.

Caracalla looked directly at him then.

"What did they presume to lecture you about, sire?" Macrinus leaned back.

Caracalla's fists balled and released a few times before he spoke. "It seems that the provincial governors have been writing to complain about the Constitutio Antoniniana. The people are unhappy and there are riots in places."

"What are they unhappy about?" Macrinus asked, his face an image of disgust. "They don't want to be Roman citizens?"

"They don't want to be taxed even more. Citizenship is secondary to the lightness of their purses, it seems." Caracalla stood and picked up his gladius again, swinging it in thought. "What they don't realize is that if they wish to have the security and protection of this empire and my legions, they need to help pay for it."

"It is only common sense, sire," Macrinus said. "Distract the people with games, and execute the ringleaders to silence the opposition."

"I quite agree!" Caracalla said, turning to face the prefect and slamming his fist on the table. "I have done millions of people across the empire a great service! I mean, look at yourself! You came from a poor family in Mauretania. You've been a gladiator, a venator, and a courier... and look at you now! You are Praetorian Prefect!"

Macrinus bowed his head. "By your good graces, sire."

"Exactly. And by granting people Roman citizenship, I have elevated them and given them the opportunity to better themselves." Caracalla stood before the bust of Alexander again, his hands clasped piously before the Greek king. "I'll see it done, Macrinus. I'll create a pan-Roman world greater than the pan-Hellenic one Alexander envisioned. You'll see."

"I believe you, sire. It will be glorious."

Caracalla was silent for a few moments before turning to look at Macrinus. "What news have you for me?"

Macrinus sat up, having drained his cup. "There were a couple of winter raids along the Danuvius since we left the front, but the legions took care of them. The barbarians will, however, be ready for another fight come the Spring. So, after Winter, we will need to go and finish them off."

"I can't wait! I'm already bored of Rome and my skulking mother."

Macrinus barely concealed his smile.

"What about our proposal to Artabanus V of Parthia? Have we heard back from him yet?"

"Not yet, sire. But I expect we should within a couple of months. The Parthians are slow to decide such things."

"They're bitter about their defeat at my father's hands. Soon enough, they'll realize what an honour I'm offering them."

"Of course, sire."

Caracalla thought about what it might be like to have another wife, and though a Parthian one might not have been his first choice, he returned to the thought that if it was good enough for Alexander to marry an Asian, it would be good enough for him, a way to secure peace in the East. *Plautilla never gave me a child,* he thought bitterly. *Perhaps the Parthian would be more fertile?*

"Tell me Macrinus... How does it feel to be home with your wife and son again?"

Macrinus smiled, and were Caracalla not so blind, he would have seen that it was perhaps the only time true sincerity crossed the man's face. "It is good to see them. Nonia and I get along well."

"And your son..."

"Diadumenian, sire."

"Yes. How old is he now?"

"He is seven."

"I can see you love him very much," Caracalla's look was wistful, as if he wished for a son too, an heir to treat better than he had been treated.

Macrinus observed Caesar then, and the look he saw there was one of great anger and resentment. He knew that he had to tread carefully when Caracalla got such a look in his eyes.

"Sire... The Parthians will accept your offer and you shall have an heir you can be proud of, just as Alexander and Roxanna did."

Caracalla smiled and nodded. "I'm glad you, at least, understand, Macrinus. You're a new man with new ideas. And that is what's needed." He took his wine cup and drank it in one draught. "Now that my enemies are all dispatched, there is nothing to stop me. No more looking over my shoulder. I can look to the future."

"As your Praetorian Prefect, sire, I will look over your shoulder for you so that you can focus on the world you wish to create."

Caracalla walked around the table and placed his hand upon Macrinus' armoured shoulder. "We'll do great things, Macrinus. You'll see."

On the other side of the imperial palace, back in her private apartments, Julia Domna walked slowly about her large room. She circled like a cat before picking a place to sit for a while in contemplation of a world she was not yet used to, nor ever would be. The wind from out of doors was bitter and cold, seeping in from the interior garden that was her own within the Severan palace complex.

Long, thick curtains of burnt orange wavered in the breeze they tried to block out, and the many braziers set about her rooms flickered and leapt, their light and heat as unreliable as the world around her. She had changed the apartments several times since Geta's murder, in an attempt to escape the scene that replayed itself tortuously in her mind, but her attempts had been futile. No matter how much she changed the physical appearance of the rooms, nor how many frescoes she hid, she could still see the blood upon the floor at her feet, in her lap.

"Leave me," she said to her body slaves who had been waiting by the door.

The two women rose and left the room. They were used to the Augusta's frequent need to be left alone.

When they were gone, Julia Domna walked to one of her dressing tables and picked up a polished bronze mirror with a jade handle. She looked at herself in the shimmery reflection and, as ever, was shocked to see the face looking back at her. Her once smooth olive skin was now pale and permanently creased with worry, her tightly-woven hair more brittle and grey where once it had been as smooth and dark as Tyrian silk. But she did not care much anymore for peacocking the way her sister did. Her clothing, and her demeanour, tended more toward darkness.

She walked a few paces to where couches were set around a central table beside a pigeonhole shelf filled with scrolls.

"This is my sanctuary," she said to herself, running her hands along the shelves so that they brushed the rolled papyri, played with the silk ties around them that hung from their niches. She closed her eyes and breathed deeply, feeling herself growing calm again. Then, she turned and went to one of the couches where she had been re-reading *Heroicus*.

As she unrolled the scroll, her mind carried her away, the words a raft to take her to safety and forgetfulness.

The light that had been angling its way into her apartments from outside was gone when Julia Domna opened her her eyes. She had been covered in furs by her women, and a bright, warm brazier had been set behind each of the couches, except not before the shelves of scrolls.

Upon the table before her, a platter of fruit, vegetables, and cheeses had been set alongside a pitcher of warm, spiced wine, and two cups.

Why two cups? she wondered, her mind still hazy from her repose. She looked down at the scroll she still grasped and remembered. *Philostratus is supposed to be here tonight.*

As if hearing her mistress' thoughts, one of the slaves approached her. "Domina... Philostratus is here." The slave bowed.

"How long has he been waiting?" Julia Domna sat up, and rubbed her eyes, thanking the Gods she felt rested, for she did not like to engage in philosophical discourse when tired. It was precious time wasted.

"He arrived only a few minutes ago," the slave answered. "He insisted we leave you to rest."

"Help prepare me."

The slave waved to the other and together they went with Julia Domna to her dressing table on the other side of the room, hidden behind flowing curtains. There, they combed and pinned her hair more neatly, touched up the minimal makeup she wore upon her face.

Julia Domna looked at herself in the mirror and nodded. "That will do for philosophical discussion," she said. "You may show him in."

As the slaves departed to get the Sophist waiting out in the corridor, Julia Domna stood looking out at the cold moonlight of the garden. She now lived for the times when the members of her salon would attend upon her to discuss their latest works, or plumb the ideas and theses that had occurred to her in her reading. Intellectual adventure was all that was left to her now. She had no need of young lovers, or of court gossip the way so many women her age did, the way her sister did. Philosophy was her poetry and song, papyrus the silken sheets beneath which she writhed with pleasure.

"Divine Augusta. It is a joy to see you again."

Julia Domna turned to see Lucius Flavius Philostratus standing before her, bowing as her eyes met his.

The Athenian was dressed, as always, no matter the season, in a plain, grey toga. His right arm was folded over his chest, and his left, lean and soft, hanging down at the side. He wore no ornament, and yet, to Julia Domna, his intellect dressed him like a friend-king. His hair had receded upon his forehead, but grew wispy at the sides, long so that it fell to blend in with his beard.

Julia Domna stepped forward to take his hands and he smiled at her touch as if he had been looking forward to their converse for an age. "You should have had my servants wake me, for every moment of time in discourse with you is precious, Philostratus."

"You are too kind, Augusta," he smiled, his appearance not at all marred by his crooked teeth.

"Please, sit," she said, indicating the couches. "Have food and hot wine to take off the winter chill."

"There is no chill in your presence, lady," he said as they each took a couch and reclined.

When they had settled and were served food and wine by the slaves, she looked at him across the low table.

"So, tell me of your recent travels. Where have you been?"

Philostratus set down his cup and wiped his fingers on a cloth napkin that had been placed there. His eyes widened and seemed to grow brighter as if, like a plant starved for water, he stood taller with his patron's attention.

"I was in Cyrene for part of the summer. Such a beautiful place, ancient and inspiring. Daily I would make offerings at the temple of Zeus and then, in the shade of towering palms, I would sit and discourse with my Socratic colleagues from the renowned school there."

"And did they appreciate you as much as I do?" she asked, a smile forming at the sides of her mouth.

"No, my lady. None do."

"And then where did you go?"

"To Alexandria."

"Of course. To the library?"

"Daily," he said, a look of mock guilt upon his face. "It will take lifetimes to read all that is there."

"But were you to read all those revered tomes, you would not have time to write, and that would make the Gods weep."

The philosopher blushed most sincerely, and Julia Domna smiled to herself and his humility. "Now, now, such humility is hardly Sophistic, is it?"

"When it is sincere, lady, I would say it is."

They both laughed before he continued.

"I also visited the tomb of Alexander, recently reopened by the emperor, your son."

Her face darkened, but she set those thoughts aside the moment they threatened to overtake her. "And how was it, visiting the tomb of the hero again?"

"Inspiring…" Philostratus seemed to be looking far off to a time not of battles or of conquest and kings, but to his imagined moments when Aristotle had been granted the gift of teaching the young Alexander, unknowing even himself of how high the young prince would fly, the heights to which he would aspire, the glories he would achieve. He looked Julia Domna in the eyes. "I am not ashamed to say, lady, that I wept before his tomb. Such a man! Such a king!"

"A true hero," she said. "Greater than Achilles himself."

"Yes!" Philostratus sat straighter. "He was, without a doubt. Men feared Achilles, but they loved Alexander."

"My son strives to emulate Alexander," she said suddenly.

Philostratus' smile faded slightly, but he nodded. "A most worthy idol, to be sure. They whispered of Caesar's wish for a pan-Roman world in the streets of Alexandria."

"You mean they rioted at his wish for more taxes," she corrected.

"You have heard, then?"

"Of course." She was silent, and the philosopher felt discomfort at her sadness and faded light.

"The Gods will show the way, and the stars will continue to shine, lady."

"That is my hope," she said, her voice betraying the deep sadness that ran along the pathways of her soul.

Philostratus felt his heart tighten at the sight of his empress, such a brilliant woman, so beset by sorrow that it hung on her permanently, like an invisible shroud.

"I see you have been reading the *Heroicus* again?" he said, smiling and nodding toward the scroll he had given her, written in his own hand upon the very best Nile papyrus.

Her large brown eyes brightened again as she looked up at him, and her smile returned, though not fully. "Yes. It is my escape from the confines of this scented and conspiring world of the palace."

Philostratus looked around the room and he too saw the luxurious surroundings as she did - as a prison. "Tell me what you liked about it, lady…"

In that moment, without looking at the scroll or touching it, Julia Domna closed her eyes…

. . .

"Echo, dwelling round about the vast waters beyond great Pontus,
my lyre serenades you by my hand.
And you, sing to me divine Homer,
glory of men,
glory of our labours,
through whom I did not die, through whom Patroklos is mine,
through whom my Ajax is
equal to the immortals,
through whom Troy, celebrated by the skilled as won
by the spear,
gained glory and did not fall."

As she spoke the words, the dead passed before her, Patroklos, and Ajax, and Achilles himself, their forms changed to the faces of her husband, her son, and other heroes who had passed through her life only to leave her in solitude. When she opened her eyes again, Philostratus was kneeling on the floor before her, grasping her hand, tears in his eyes.

When Julia Domna awoke the next morning, she felt revived, as if her time with Philostratus had given her the strength she needed to get through the days to come. There was always hope in philosophy and epic, potential for change in learning.

After waking and reading the first parts of a draft of Philostratus' *Life of Apollonius of Tyana*, she sat for a time in the morning sunlight. The draft was more of a sketch, initial thoughts on the character of Apollonius, a noble and magical man, not unlike the Christus of the Christians. She had heard of the Christians of course. She had even spoken with some. It was an odd religion, a belief in only one, merciful god. Then again, it was not unlike the followers of the Sun. The former was merciful and kind, the latter one of terror and beauty, to be respected.

She allowed her mind to wander those intellectual paths for a time before deciding that it was time to get to work. There were more letters to read and reply to, more instruction to give so that the empire thrived, not for her son, but for the memory of her husband who had fought to build it. She did not want to let the dead down.

But even as Julia Domna passed the hours writing letters and reading missives from all corners of the empire - the purpose Caracalla had given her - her thoughts grew more depressed and dark. There were problems behind problems, layers of disappointment and neglect, so much so that she began to wonder what the world would have been like if Papinianus' plot to put Lucius Metellus Anguis upon the imperial throne had succeeded.

"Another dead hero," she thought sadly, surprising herself. "At the time, she had fought to keep her cousin, Papinianus, from carrying out his plan, but now when some ethereal end stared her in the face, she regretted it.

When Caracalla had told her of the death of Lucius Metellus Anguis and his family, Julia Domna had wept privately, and prayed to the Gods that he and his family should be looked after in Elysium.

She had protected her sons by countering Papinianus and Metellus, but at what cost? The thought was too much to bear.

"The world would have been better," she whispered to herself, reminded herself, before returning to the work of her 'penance', as the Christians put it.

Marcus Opellius Macrinus sat in the tablinum of the praetorium, in the heart of the Praetorian camp, just behind the Quirinal and Viminal hills of Rome. It had been a long day, long weeks in fact, and as he rubbed his temples and bearded jaw that felt as tight as a vice, he wondered how long he would have to endure the role he played, even whether he could for as long as was needed.

After only a few weeks in Rome, the emperor had become intolerable, and dangerous. The combination of Caracalla's own boredom, blood guilt, and the rejection of the things he was trying to do across the empire, all combined to frustrate him to no end, and it was those closest to him who were dangerously near the sword edge.

Macrinus removed his armour and placed it upon the stand nearby. It felt good to remove it once he was in his private quarters for the night. He had never had to wear full armour before, even when in the arena.

How far I've come, he thought as he looked upon the polished cuirass and crested helmet of the Praetorian prefect. *Even farther than Plautianus.* He sighed. *But he wasn't patient enough. I must be patient.*

Macrinus did not mind serving, but it had been easier with Severus, and even as a legal advisor under Plautianus. That was when it occurred to him that perhaps the most powerful role in the empire was that of Praetorian prefect, especially when one had a weak emperor.

But, he knew nothing was certain, and Plautianus had lost sight of that. *I've worked too long and hard to get to where I am,* he thought, remembering the hovel he and his family lived in when he was a child in Mauretania, a place stinking of camel dung and goat urine.

He looked around the ornate marble room, the painted walls, the bronze lamps and braziers that lit up the tablinum and nodded.

Caracalla had offered him rooms on the Palatine hill, and Macrinus had accepted them, but only as a place for him to spend the night when he was up late with the emperor. In truth, he preferred to live in the Praetorian camp with his wife Nonia Celsa and their young son, Diadumenian. He wanted them farther away from Caracalla. They were safer in the Praetorium, surrounded by men to whom he had given even larger bonuses than the emperor had.

True, he had to travel across the city to get to the Palatine every time the emperor called for him, but he liked that, whether walking, riding, or being carried in a litter, for wherever he went, the people were made aware of who he was. They did not laud him as he passed, but they did fear and respect him. *One day, they will cheer.*

He smiled at the thought.

Patience.

There was laugher from the peristylium where Nonia played with Diadumenian, chasing the boy along the pathways through the garden where dried leaves scraped upon the mosaic floor.

Macrinus moved to the doorway where he leaned against the frame to watch his wife and son playing.

Nonia too, had experienced hardship in her life, just as he had, and that fuelled his vision for their future.

She too deserves to live upon the Palatine.

His smile disappeared when he saw one of the Praetorian messengers from the palace coming along the colonnade toward him.

The man stopped before him and saluted. "Praefectus!"

"What is it?" Macrinus said.

"The emperor calls for you."

Macrinus felt like telling the man to go back to Caracalla and tell him it was late, that he was with his family, but such words and thoughts would get him nowhere. *And I've come too far.*

"Tell the emperor I will come with all haste."

As the messenger saluted again, turned, and left, Nonia approached Macrinus with her son trailing behind her.

"Our evening will have to wait, my dear," he said.

She looked around before speaking. "Can he not do without you for one evening? We barely see you." She placed her hand upon his chest.

"He is restless. And I'm the one he trusts most."

"He treats you like a caretaker still!"

"Shhh!" Macrinus hissed, stepping closer to her and looking around as he gripped her shoulders. "You mustn't say such things out loud."

"You're hurting me," she said, her face contorting slightly.

His eyes widened and he released his grip quickly, before turning to go back into his tablinum. "I will see you in the morning," he said, leaving a moment to kneel and open his arms to his son.

Diadumenian ran to his father, his shaggy black hair bouncing as he came to him. "Good night, Father!" the boy said.

"Good night, young one. Get some rest now. I will see you tomorrow." He kissed his son's cheek and sent him back to Nonia. "All will be well," he said to her before she turned and led their son to the triclinium on the other side of the garden.

"Looks like we'll be eating alone tonight, my boy," he heard her say as their voices faded away.

Macrinus turned from the door and went to the stand with the armour upon it. He sighed loudly, his fists balled, before putting it all back on again.

"Prepare my horse!" he yelled so that the guards at the far end of the peristylium could hear.

"Yes, Praefectus!" one of them replied.

"Time to attend upon Caesar," he mumbled.

It was not yet Saturnalia, but the air of revelry was already running through the streets of Rome, up the slopes of the Palatine and into palace complexes. Fires burned at every corner, as if to warm the outside air as well as inside, and light the pathways for the sandalled feet of the imperial family.

In the old house of Livia, Julia Domna dined with her sister, Julia Maesa, and the latter's daughters, Julia Soaemias, and Julia Mamaea.

Servants moved in and around them, bearing trays of food and pitchers of wine, while others ensured the braziers remained fed and bright. The frescoes of illusionist architecture, painted fruit and flowers, provided a peaceful backdrop to their conversation, but Julia Domna had no illusions about her sister and nieces. Though she enjoyed their bi-weekly dinners, she also knew that they were, all of them, ambitious.

Her nieces, both in their thirties, had two children each of their own now. They were no longer the young, smiling girls she remembered playing beneath towering palms in Leptis Magna, but rather Roman matrons, each with complaints about their husbands, their chosen lovers, and wishes for the future of their sons and daughter.

And watching them proudly, was their mother, Julia Maesa, who had taught them all she knew about survival at court and how to wield power.

And I taught her, Julia Domna thought as she watched them all around the lamplit table, laughing, smiling, gossiping and sipping their wine.

All of her nieces' children showed potential: Julia Soaemias' son, Bassianus, was the oldest, but Julia Mamaea's son, Alexander, even at seven years of age, displayed a keen but hard intellect that would make him a formidable ruler should he ever have the opportunity.

As Julia Domna watched her sister and nieces, and thought of their own families, she wondered if the stars would decree that she should live long enough to see what would become of them all. She was not sure she wanted to see it. She remembered the sheer optimism she had felt when her sons were young, not yet ten, and thought that she and Septimius would shape a new world that their dynasty could be proud of.

Those dreams had turned to ash, and as the memories of blood and tears passed across the horizon of her mind in the triclinium of the old palace, she thought of her son, alone on the other side of the palace complex. He had done terrible things, and perhaps would do more, but he *was* her son. He was all she had left.

"What are you thinking about, Sister?" Julia Maesa asked while her daughters were engaged in their own conversation about the latest young equestrians to make a name for themselves.

Julia Domna put on a thin smile and shook her head. A few of the slaves had just entered with the next course of salads, roasted vegetables, and steaming bread, while another slave ensured all of the lamps were still lit. When they were all gone, she spoke again.

"I was thinking about the emperor."

"Surely here," Julia Maesa said, "we can call him by his name?" There was a bitter edge in her voice. For so long, she and her sister's son had been so close, but since the death of Geta, Caracalla had withdrawn from his aunt's attentions, either out of guilt, or some other reason she could not fathom, or care to discern. She had observed that those close to Caracalla were no longer faring very well, and so she had withdrawn to watch from a distance until the Gods cooled his mind, if they ever would. "How is my nephew since he returned from Germania?"

Julia Mamaea and Julia Soaemias grew quiet and looked up across the low table at their aunt too.

Staring at her plate, wishing she was back in her apartments reading, Julia Domna pushed some of her food around, revealing the silver relief of a dining scene beneath. "He is tired and withdrawn. He misses war, I think."

"Winter quarters never agreed with him," Julia Maesa put in, her eyes watching her sister keenly.

"He is not fond of Rome."

"And Rome is not fond of him," Julia Soaemias added. She had always been fond of her younger cousin, Geta, and had felt his loss acutely, though, she had now hardened herself to the thought of it.

Julia Domna looked up, her large eyes holding Soaemias' gaze. "For your own, safety, Niece, please do not speak thus. We are in the desert without shade now."

"And will not the Sun protect us, as it always has?" Julia Mamaea said.

"Or burn us to cinders," Domna replied calmly. "The emperor has much on his mind, and I do not think he will remain in Rome for the entire winter. The time between the beginning of Janus' month until the month of Mars is too long. He does not relish Rome, as I said, and he will be eager to go back to Germania where the barbarians are still quite rebellious."

"Where can he go that people are not angry with his new taxes?" Julia Maesa asked, knowing the answer.

"So long as he is at war, alongside his legions, he is secure. He has also mentioned Parthia in passing, if he does not receive a favourable reply from Artabanus."

"He loves war so?"

"It's what helps him to forget," Julia Domna answered.

They were silent again. They had all been quietly angry with Caracalla and what he had done to their family, but none of them could voice that opinion. They had had to carry on as if nothing had happened, or as if Geta had deserved the death he had received.

My sister did not deserve to have her son die in her arms, Julia Maesa thought as she reached over to comfort Julia Domna. "My poor sister," she said, unusually sincere.

Julia Domna looked up at her sister and nieces, her own hand squeezing Julia Maesa's. "Do not pity me," she said. "I played my part and did not see how far things would go. My son's blood is also upon *my* hands." *And I suspect your children will cause you similar pain in the years to come,* she thought, looking across the table at her nieces. *None of us is safe from such things.*

XI

UMBRAE ET MANES

'Shadows and Shades'

"What do you remember of the estate?" Phoebus asked his sister while they sat in the back of the wagon as it drove along the via Aurelia. The coast was passing slowly by to their right, and the rolling green hills and forests of Etruria to their left.

Calliope smiled, but it was a different sort of smile, sad and weighed down by something. "I remember playing there in the grass by the river, near the lady with flowers in the field."

"I don't remember a lady with flowers playing with us," Phoebus said.

"She was there, I'm sure of it." Calliope played with a piece of straw and leaned back to look up at the sky. "What about you?"

Phoebus looked out over the hills as if trying to see the estate. "I remember running through the vineyard and riding to the top of the hill to see the ancient tomb. I loved doing that." Phoebus craned his neck to look at Lucius where he sat on the driving bench beside Adara. "Baba, do you think we could ride up to the tomb at the top of the mountain?"

Lucius turned to look at his children in the back of the wagon. "If you like, yes," he said, a little absently.

Adara put her hand upon Lucius' thigh and squeezed. She had sensed his tension, the deeper they went into Etruria, the closer they got to their one-time home. "What are your happiest memories of that place?" Adara asked, trying to get him to focus his thoughts on something else.

Lucius stared ahead at the empty road. They were surrounded by green and brown fields, and hills that swept away from the road, leading to scattered forests where boar roamed. In the distance, the faraway peaks of the Apennines rose up, shielding that fertile, ancient land. The sound of cicadas still filled the air from dawn until dusk, bringing him back to halcyon summer days napping beneath the upper loggia of the villa, his children nestled in his arms while Adara sang softly nearby. He remembered roaming the estate lands in the autumn, the air scented with soil-covered truffles, and the vines in the vineyard heavy with bunches of grapes, their leaves a riot of colour like a blanket cast over the hills. He could still see the peasants working in the fields, gathering hay for the winter. He used to help them cut, dry and rake the hay before gathering it.

"Lucius?"

"Yes," he smiled and squeezed Adara's hand. "Sorry. I was just thinking of the haymaking time. I remember standing in the middle of the field on a sunny day as the hay was cut and tossed. They air was filled with it. It seemed to stay suspended in mid-air, and I remember thinking that it was like the Gods made time stand absolutely still in that moment."

"That was your favourite thing?" Phoebus asked, surprised.

"No," Lucius said, ruffling his son's hair. "Being there with all of you is my favourite memory."

Adara saw his hand grip the reins tightly so that his knuckles whitened in the afternoon sun. She knew then that there was much he did not want to think about when it came to the estate - his father, Alene's burial, and his last fight with Argus. "Much has changed since we were last here, Lucius," she said. "You know more about yourself now."

He looked at her and nodded. "You're right. I'm not the same person I thought I was then."

At the beginning of that day's journey, Adara had noticed Lucius relaxing to an extent, enjoying the sibling banter from the back of the wagon as they drove with the sun upon their faces. She thought that finally, Lucius was allowing himself to consider being happy returning to Etruria, that the worries about not hearing from his mother were unfounded. "Letters get lost all the time," Adara had told him. And he had agreed.

However, Adara also knew that any childhood memories Lucius had of the place had been poisoned by the man he had thought was his father. And then, there was the looming presence of Rome to the South. *One step at a time,* Adara thought.

"There it is!" Lucius said, looking around at the landscape

surrounding them. "That's the turn-off." He pointed to a smaller, minor road that led east, away from the via Aurelia, and drove inland.

Phoebus and Calliope got up and knelt behind their parents to look ahead with them at the golden hills covered in vineyards and crowned with clusters of cypress trees.

"Are we almost there?" Calliope asked.

"We should arrive before nightfall," Lucius said as the wagon turned and he clicked his tongue at the mule pulling the wagon.

Lucius felt a familiar excitement in his stomach as the landscape spread out before him, for he had always loved going there after the congested chaos of Rome, but then, just as the tide of his childhood joy came in to the shore of his mind, it ebbed away to reveal the deep anxiety he had been feeling beneath the surface.

Gods, let all be well...

As the sun began to fall away, setting the landscape to brilliant orange about them, they followed the gentle flow of the small river on their left. The sound of the water drew them on, and in that soft gurgling, it was as if the local nymph laughed along with them, as she had when Lucius had been young, and as she had always done with Phoebus and Calliope who now hung over the edge of the wagon looking down at the play of water upon the sand and rock.

Along the roadside, silver birch trees stood like an honour guard to either side of the wagon, still clinging to their leaves which now had only just begun to yellow, waving in the evening breeze like twinkling stars in a cold sky.

"It's so quiet," Adara said as she sat beside Lucius, looking at his face now and then to discern how he was feeling.

"I forgot how beautiful this place is," Lucius finally said, taking a deep breath of the cool, early evening air. "We should be smelling the olive press soon," he added, bracing himself for the sting of that pungent smell.

But the air remained fresh and silent, accented only by the laughter of the water nymph running alongside them.

Lucius slowed the wagon. "There's the bridge," he pointed to the stone arch that crossed over the water, just fifty feet or so from the milestone that marked the road they were on.

All of them looked ahead, their view of the villa and hill hidden by the trees.

Adara turned in her seat to look at Phoebus and Calliope. "Your grandmother will be so happy to see you both," she said, smiling. But her smile faded when she saw her children's faces.

"Mama look," Phoebus said.

As Lucius turned the wagon onto the bridge, he first spotted the apple and plum orchard. Where the trees should have been weighed down by fruit nearly ready for picking, there were only hacked limbs or fallen trunks devoid of fruit and flower. He looked for the grazing animals that usually dotted the field on the other side of the drive, and only saw overgrown grass, brown and brittle, the orange of evening muted and sad.

They were all silent as the wagon reached the other side, and once they did, the sound of the river was more like weeping in their ears, dreadful, exhausted and constant.

"No!" Lucius said, pulling hard on the reins and jumping down to the ground where he stumbled beside a pile of rocks overgrown with grass. "Ahh!" he cried.

"Lucius!" Adara handed the reins to Phoebus and went after her husband where he fumbled clumsily in the dead grass, grasping at the stones, his hands brushing away dirt and filth to reveal the face of a woman. "Alene!"

All about him, the monument that had been erected to Alene Metella lay in cracked and burned pieces, the gentle curve of the marble scrolling hacked away, the flanking warriors who had represented Lucius and Alerio crushed into the dust, and the flowing stola of Alene herself, walking among field flowers, broken such that a jagged crack ran through her body down into the ground.

A serpent that had been sleeping in the crack quickly slithered away into the grasses beyond as Lucius' fingers swept around the broken monument.

Adara stood behind Lucius, her own tears running down her cheeks as she laid her hands upon him, tried to pull him up.

Lucius found the edge of the bronze tube that had jutted from the earth, and through which Alene's shade had received offerings. It had been bent, and folded into the ground, but his desperate fingers found the edge and he pulled at it, slowly bending it back upward as if it would resuscitate the dead.

"Calliope wait!" Phoebus suddenly called.

Lucius and Adara looked up through their tears to see their daughter walking slowly up the drive, her gentle form standing before a backdrop of utter destruction.

Phoebus jumped down from the wagon, his gladius sliding out of its sheath in his right hand, while in his left he pulled the mule along by the reins. "What happened?" he said, his few childhood memories of the place suddenly blurry in his mind.

Lucius and Adara both drew their gladii and walked forward to join their children. When they all reached Calliope, they stopped and stared, unable to eject themselves from the nightmare that had swiftly engulfed them.

What once had been a sight of comfort, of sanctuary, was utterly gone. The olive groves and fruit orchards were hacked and burned, and the vineyards lay wild and unkept. No animals, apart from a few serpents basking in the last sun of day upon the road, were there.

Lucius felt his reluctance to look on, to see the proof of his suspicions up the hill, but he forced himself, channeling his feelings in that moment to the vats of anger he had been fermenting for many months.

Beyond the caved-in ruins of the servants' quarters, stables and outbuildings, the plateau where the Metellus villa had once stood now only played host to a pile of charred rubble and scattered roof tiles. The smoke had long since drifted away, but the black intent that had been etched upon every single inch of their ancestral home was written plain for all of them to see.

Phoebus handed Calliope the mule's reins and began to walk around, his keen eyes searching the fringes of the property for any sign of mortal life, some peasant to question, a neighbour, or even a thief, but there was no one.

Lucius led the way up the drive, toward the ruins of his home, his gut churning, expecting to see the bodies of his mother, brother and sister. As his eyes picked among the fallen stone walls and deteriorating plaster, the rotting farm implements and rusted iron of nails and scythe blades, he looked for jutting bones, for skulls and ribs picked clean by the carrion birds that dwelt in the shadowy, distant treetops.

All was quiet, but for the grinding of the wagon's wheels upon the gravel drive, and the soft sniffling of his daughter.

"Gods..." Lucius said, his voice low. "Why have you allowed this? Where is my family?"

They reached the plateau before the villa, the only things standing being the cypresses that had been there for an age.

Lucius felt as though he were a Trojan, returned to the ruins of his city, not having had a chance to fight, to spill enemy blood in defence of his kingdom. The villa and estate had indeed been his kingdom, his tie to the past, to youth, to the memories bitter and sweet that had made up his perceived self, and yet, once again, that perception had been burned before him like brittle parchment.

"Who has done this?" Adara said, but even as the words left her mouth, she knew the answer, and the look in Lucius' eyes confirmed it.

"They take another home from us, as if to ensure there is no place in the world where we can go."

"This is not the Gods' doing, Lucius," Adara said, touching his arm only to have him pull away.

"Not the Gods," he growled. "Phoebus!" Lucius said suddenly, looking to where his son was picking his way over fallen walls into the ruins of the villa. "Come back here!"

Phoebus did not listen, but walked slowly forward, the point of his gladius out in front of him as if he were sneaking upon prey in a wood.

There was a sudden cry, and then the smacking of steel upon wood from within.

"Phoebus!" Lucius rushed forward as he heard his son's angry voice ringing out.

"Thief! I'll kill you!" Phoebus yelled.

"Leave us be!" a woman's voice cried out.

There was the clash of steel and wood again, a yelp of pain, and then Phoebus emerged dragging someone by a ragged tunic, the point of his blade at the person's throat.

"They were inside, Baba!" Phoebus said, throwing a short, bald man into the dust at Lucius' feet.

The man swept up with the broken piece of wooden handle he had been wielding, but Lucius parried it right away, sending it flying from the man's hand, and just as he was about to raise his sword to bring it down, the scene of destruction urging his rage on, a woman came stumbling out of the ruins to throw herself upon the man at Lucius' feet.

"Leave us be!" she cried, her tears covering her face, her eyes wild with fear.

Lucius stayed his hand, his breathing quick, his heart beating furiously. "Who are you?" he demanded.

The man and woman looked up at him and screamed when they perceived death standing above them, his features burned by the fires of Hades, his eyes full of hatred and a thirst for blood.

"Kill us quickly then, and be done with it!" the man said, his arms wrapping about the woman as they both closed their eyes.

"Lucius, wait!" Adara said, rushing to his side and staying his hand as if holding back the dread character waiting in the wings of a tragic play. "Look at them!" Adara stepped forward, and knelt beside the couple. She reached out her hands to their shuddering bodies, her own tears falling into the dirt between them. "Numa? Prisca?"

The man and woman looked up slowly, unable at first to contemplate the people before them for all their fear and suffering, but then recognition dawned as they looked into Adara's eyes.

"M...mi...Mistress Metella?" the man said. And then he looked up at the dark, cloaked figure of Lucius and began to weep violently as he lunged for Lucius' legs and grabbed onto them, sobbing, as if he were a man lost at sea, newly washed upon a friendly shore. "Master! You've come!"

Calliope stepped forward to help her mother and together they raised the woman to sitting, her own sobs joining her husband's.

Lucius looked down in shock and stunned silence at the people who had always been a part of that place, who had kept it running over the years for as long as he could remember, who had taken care of him and his family in their time spent there. They too were family and now, it seemed, they roamed the ruins of that place like forgotten wraiths. Lucius sheathed his gladius, pried the man's arms from his legs, and knelt in the dirt to hold him. "Numa...my friend... We're here now... we're here..."

Night fell quickly after their arrival at the villa, and as the foxes screeched in the neighbouring fields, and a sounder of wild boar grunted and nosed in the dirt of the surrounding forest, Lucius, Adara and the children sat around a small fire flanked by the broken walls and splintered beams of the ancient villa. Through a makeshift roof of cedar and ivy above them, the stars and moon of that dark night shone down upon them, but it was the glow of the fire that lit Numa and Prisca's horror-scarred faces before them.

"We thought the Gods had abandoned us," Numa said, his voice still shaking, his hands going constantly to his face where he attempted to hide the angry knife slashes that had been inflicted on him.

Beside him, his wife Prisca held his other hand as if to lend him the strength he needed to tell of all that had happened, to relive for the head of their familia all that had led to the destruction of that one-time paradise.

"What happened here, Numa?" Lucius asked, unable to wait any longer. "Where are my mother, brother, sister and Emrys? Are...are they all dead?" He needed to know that first, above all else.

"They escaped, Master Lucius," Numa said.

Lucius felt his ability to breathe return at that, as if he had been holding it in anticipation of bad news. "Thank the Gods," he mumbled. "Where are they?"

"We don't know exactly, master," Prisca said. "Everything happened so quickly. They left in such a hurry... Lady Antonia...as she fled with the others...said that if you ever came back, we should tell you they've gone to Athenae." Prisca turned to Adara. "I assumed she meant to your family, lady."

Adara reached out to take Prisca's shaking hand. She could tell that Prisca had also suffered greatly, though her wounds were unseen.

Meanwhile, Numa reached for a small platter of scavenged mushrooms, half-rotten apples, and some olives, and tried passing it to Phoebus and Calliope, smiling through broken teeth.

Lucius felt his heart tighten at the state of the two people who had always been a point of kindness and light growing up, during his visits to the villa. He passed on the food. "Phoebus, go to the wagon and bring the food we have. There is some bread and cheese left."

"Yes, Baba," Phoebus said, taking up his sword and picking his way among the ruins to go out.

"They've grown so much," Prisca said, trying to smile as she looked from Phoebus' departing form to Calliope who was sat beside her mother at the fire.

Lucius turned to Numa again. "Tell me... What happened? I need to know, my friend."

Numa stared into the fire and shut his eyes against the images he needed to relay. As he rallied his courage to tell the tale, a stream of tears flowed down his dirty, cut cheek. Then, he began.

"We've been living like this for a long time," he said, his eyes opening and looking around the fallen walls of the villa he had spent his life caring for. "It was many months ago, over a year?" He looked at Prisca, but she did not recollect either.

"It is difficult to know what day it is when you are just surviving from one to the next," she said before she looked down at the ground.

"It's all right," Lucius said. "Go on..."

Numa cleared his throat. "Many months ago...it was day... I was doing my rounds of the fields, taking stock, giving direction to the workers - the usual - when, down by the river, while I was in the orchard, a procession of Praetorians arrived. I recognized the scorpion banner."

"How many?" Lucius asked.

Numa shook his head. "Maybe sixteen of them. I asked them what their business was, respectfully of course, and they said that the villa and all these lands were now the property of the emperor. I said there must have been some mistake, that the lands belonged to one of Rome's greatest warriors, Lucius Metellus Anguis..." Numa shut his eyes briefly.

"They said...they said... They laughed and said you were dead." Numa began to weep, but caught himself. "Before I could tell him he must be wrong, his men began killing the workers who were with me in the orchard. I slipped away and had one of the younger lads run up to the villa to tell Lady Antonia and the others what was happening and that they should get out, make for the mountain."

"And did they?"

"Yes," Numa nodded. "Master Caecilius, Gods bless him, always has horses saddled and ready to go. The four of them, your mother included, rode for the tomb just before the soldiers made it to the villa. They were destroying everything as they came, torching the orchards, killing the animals, burning the outbuildings. I ran-"

Prisca came around the fire to sit beside her husband as his shaking began.

Lucius looked at Adara and the children, Calliope weeping silently out of empathy for the couple, for they too understood what it was to see one's home destroyed before their very eyes.

"I ran up to the house," Numa continued. "I wanted to get Prisca and the deeds to the property and lands so as to have proof, but I wasn't fast enough. The Praetorians arrived and held the two of us while they killed the rest of the slaves and workers who had not escaped into the fields and forests. I tried to reason with them, to say it was all some terrible mistake. I told them you and the emperor knew each other well, but they only laughed at that. I told them the empress was a friend of the Metelli, but they only spat at her name. When I tried to stop them from going through the domus, they beat me and then..."

Prisca began to sob, unable to be strong for her husband any longer, and so he placed his arm about her and whispered for her alone. Then he looked Lucius directly in the eyes.

"They ravaged my poor Prisca and made me watch with a dagger pressed to my face." He pointed to the horrible cuts on his cheeks, weeping silently as he looked upon the head of his familia.

Lucius' fists balled tightly and he knelt in the dirt before the two of them, his arms wrapped around them.

"I'm sorry I wasn't here," Lucius said to them. "I'm so sorry." Lucius stayed there for a few moments, holding them until their sobs ceased, then he sat again. "When did my mother and the others leave?"

"Not long thereafter. They remained hiding in the tomb for some days, and then, when they were sure the Praetorians were gone, they gathered what they could, what had not been destroyed in the fire, and left for Brundisium to get a ship to Athenae. Emrys said he knew people in the port who would help them."

"Did they make it there? To Athenae?" Adara asked.

Numa shook his head. "I don't rightly know, lady."

"Why didn't you go with them, Numa?" Lucius asked.

"Your mother...she asked us if we would come with them, but I said we should stay here...in case you ever came back. And you did, Master Lucius, you did." Numa remembered wanting to die that night after the Praetorians arrived. He could not forget lying in the dirt, beaten, holding Prisca after her terrible ordeal, watching as the villa burned fiercely and fell before them. He had hoped in that moment that the burning beams would fall onto them and end their misery, but the Gods had spared them for whatever reason. He coughed.

"How have you survived this long?" Lucius asked, amazed that they should have done so.

"After your mother left, the servants from the neighbouring estates snuck us food and clothing when their masters weren't looking. None of their masters ever treated their familia as well as yours, so they could only do so much."

"Did none of our neighbours help my mother?" Lucius said.

Numa shook his head. "They were all too afraid of Caracalla. The proscriptions had already been underway. People were being killed for far less in Rome."

Lucius wrung his hands as he stared at the fire, his anger breaking new boundaries within. He could feel Numa and Prisca's eyes upon him, hear the questions upon their lips that they were too timid to ask. But he needed to know more.

"And you've heard nothing since, from anyone? I would have thought that Caracalla would have given the estate to one of his followers."

"No one has tried to live here, Master Lucius," Prisca said. "They came only to destroy this place, and nothing else."

That made Lucius even more angry, and he was about to scream when Numa spoke up.

"The only strange thing that happens occasionally is that...well... from time to time, two men come to look around the place."

"What men?" Lucius asked.

"They say they work for one of the neighbouring estates, but after so long, I know a Praetorian spy when I see one."

"Spies?" Phoebus asked.

"Yes," Numa said. "They come every month or so. Threaten Prisca and myself, look around the ruins, and then leave."

"It's as if they're trying to make sure of something," Prisca added.

"We're not afraid of them anymore," Numa said. "The troops had done their worst."

"What do they want?" Lucius said.

"They ask where you are, Master Lucius."

"Where I am?"

"Like Prisca said. It's as if they're trying to make sure of something. To make sure you are dead."

"And what do you say?"

"Though we had prayed to Apollo that it was not true, when they come, we always tell them that you are dead in Britannia, just like the soldiers had told us."

Lucius nodded. "I almost was."

They were all silent. Lucius looked across the fire to where Phoebus was holding his gladius in his hands, and where Calliope had allowed herself to nod off against Adara's shoulder, as if she had escaped into sleep so as not to relive her own traumas.

"What did happen to you, Master Lucius?" Numa asked softly, taking in the sight of Lucius' burned features and arms.

Lucius thought back to that night in Eburacum, the darkness and the clang of steel as he and his men had scattered into the night. He thought to tell Numa that the legions had wanted to make him emperor, but to know such a thing would only endanger the two of them even more. *And their pain is my own fault...*

"Caracalla's men came after us as well. One of his men tried to burn me alive and... I almost did die. Then they attacked our home in Britannia, and burned everything to the ground. My men, and our friends and neighbours, fought to save us and slew Caracalla's men. But then we all scattered. We escaped Britannia by way of Dumnonia."

"Master Emrys' homeland?" Numa asked.

"Yes," Lucius said. "The lord of Dumnonia is a good friend."

"How did you survive the fires?" Numa said, but Lucius only looked at him.

How can I tell him who my real father is? Lucius thought. *How could he even comprehend all that has befallen me, all that I have learned? He can't.* "The Gods' will, I suppose. I was meant to come back here to see you, to find my family."

"And I will thank the Gods for it, always," Numa said. "I just don't understand why the emperor would turn on your family...after all you've done for the empire."

"Don't worry about it, Numa," Lucius said. "You're both safe now. I'll make sure of it."

After a while, with the fire built up for the night, everyone slowly nodded off to sleep from the sheer exhaustion of the journey, from the telling of the tale.

Only Lucius lay awake as darkness spread deep and silent around the ruins of his childhood home. He lay away from the fire, in the shadows, his blade resting across his lap.

What did I expect to find, coming here? he thought. *Caracalla would slay and burn the world to keep himself safe.*

Lucius had thought that their lives could not get more painful after what had happened in Britannia, but that was not the case. There was plenty more pain to be had, and as the charred ruins of the estate had come into view, as Numa and Prisca had relayed the horrors that had befallen them, new wounds had been opened up in the flesh of Lucius' soul, new hatreds born.

I will have vengeance like no other, he told himself. *Caracalla will wish that he had never taken the throne.*

At dawn, Lucius had only slept for a short while, but his exhaustion had been so complete by that point, that he had drifted into a deep sleep. It was the time of half-light, but the estate no longer awoke prior to that dreamy period of the day, no longer began with the rousing of the workers or the crowing of the cock, for they were all dead or dispersed and there was no work to be done.

The group of them lay sound asleep among the ruins of that ancient villa, the damp and dew adorning their sleeping forms where they were huddled around the cold fire pit.

Except for Lucius in his dark corner, for as he slept he heard it, the thrumming of a deep drum within the earth. He found himself walking in a stubbly winter field covered in morning mist. He could not see far, but felt the cold creeping up his arms and legs. His feet squelched beneath him, but the mist was so thick that he could not see where he stepped.

Then he stopped walking, for a form began to take shape in the mist before him. It was a warrior, tall, armoured and red-cloaked, carrying a great spear and shield. The crest upon his helmet was tall and bristling. Lucius felt his gut tighten, but he did not turn to run.

Instead, as the chiselled and bearded face turned to him, there was no aggression in the eyes, but rather pity. The eyes gazed toward Lucius' feet.

Lucius looked down and saw blood and dirt rising above his ankles, pulling him downward. He could not scream, he could not move.

The warrior extended his shining hand to Lucius, willing him to take hold of it and be saved, but Lucius did not reach. He only sank lower and lower, until the blood was up to his chin, the scent of iron strong in his nostrils, and then...

"AHHH!" Lucius screamed where he lay beneath his cloak in the dark corner he had chosen to sleep. His eyes shot open to find the freshly kindled fire a few feet away where his family sat with Numa and Prisca, eating sparingly of the dried meat and cheese they had brought, as well as some figs that Phoebus had scavenged from trees at the edge of the property.

Calliope was beside him in a moment, her hand pressed to Lucius' sweaty forehead. "It's all right, Baba."

Over his daughter's shoulder, Lucius could see Numa and Prisca watching, worried looks upon their faces as he tried to slow his breathing.

Calliope helped him, her hands upon his head and chest, just as Etain had shown her. "Did you see him?" she whispered.

Lucius looked up at her face, still trying to pry himself from the one world into the other, and nodded.

"I saw him too. It was your uncle, the Avenger."

Lucius could see that Calliope was not scared or weighed by any worry of the sight.

"Did you speak with him, Baba?" she asked.

Lucius felt strange, his daughter questioning him thus, so calm in the face of such a sight. Maybe he appeared to her differently.

"You must speak with him," she added. She stood up. "Come, Baba. You need to eat."

Light was angling its way into the ruins then, casting the place in a whole new light. Lucius looked up at the light and tried to feel it fill him with strength. Upon the highest-standing piece of wall, a mourning dove sat, its head turned toward the rising sun as it sang, and in that moment, it seemed the estate grew into a place of hope around them, rather than of despair.

"Things feel different today," Prisca said as she watched the dove and smiled.

"Of course they are," Numa said, patting his wife on the shoulder. "The Dragon has come home."

"How long are we going to linger here, Lucius?" Adara asked as they walked around the ruins of the house later that morning. Her eyes were ahead, on the children as they picked among the remains of the house, looking in vain for anything that had survived. "If Captain Creticus is going to be at Brundisium, we don't want to miss him. We can get to our families in Athenae."

"I know. We can't stay here long," Lucius said, but in his mind, he still saw the warrior standing before him in the field. "We can go in another day or two. There must be something we can do for Numa and Prisca. They've lost everything because of me."

"Because of Caracalla, Lucius," Adara said. She stopped then, looking back at the old couple on the other side of the villa where they tidied up as if their lives carried on as normal, as if the dishes were being cleared and the tile floors swept. "Why don't we bring them with us?"

Lucius shook his head. "We can't. It would arouse too much suspicion." Lucius rubbed the rough skin of his face. "I'll think of a way to help them."

They carried on walking with the children, and stood in what was the front courtyard of the u-shaped villa.

"We spent so much time here," Lucius said to Adara and the children as they surveyed the place, "and it's all gone." He kicked at a blackened wood column that had been part of the peristyle. "I don't recognize it."

"There's nothing left inside," Phoebus said.

"No. There wouldn't be," Lucius answered his son. "The soldiers probably took anything of value, and then the place was picked clean by scavenging peasants."

"No, Master Lucius," Numa said as he and Prisca came to join them. "It's those two spies that come. Every time they came at first, they would pick through the remains, looking for anything that would fetch some coin." Numa looked at the ground. "I tried to stop them, but they just beat me for it. I'm sorry...I...I just gave up in the end."

Lucius turned to Numa. "You have nothing to be sorry for, my friend. Please don't say such things." He then turned to look down the hill toward the river. "Come, there is something we do need to do." He turned to Phoebus. "Go to the wagon and get my satchel."

"Yes, Baba," Phoebus said, going to where the mule had been unhitched and was tied to a nearby tree.

When Phoebus returned, the group began to walk down the drive toward the river. It was quiet and peaceful, but the beauty around them was haunted by the destruction that had been wrought there, and even more so than the ruins of the villa, Lucius was reminded of that destruction by the broken monument to his sister, Alene Metella.

They stood before the cracked and broken remains in silent grief once more, as if Alene had only recently departed the mortal world.

Adara stood between her children, grown and healthy now, her hands upon their shoulders, and thought of how they stood there only by way of Alene's courage. She could not help but weep, and Phoebus clasped her hand as she did so, himself grabbing at any thread of memory of his aunt.

As Lucius stepped forward from beside Numa and Prisca, Calliope began to hum the earliest tune she knew, the longing tune that, as it happened, her aunt used to sing to them as babes-in-arms.

Lucius stared down at the pile of broken marble and thought of when Alene had been taken from them. Those too had been Praetorian spies. *And now they've done this,* he thought as he bent to pick up pieces of the heavy marble. He knew, of course, that he could not fix it; he had not the skill or the tools. Only Emrys, could have done that, but he was in Graecia with Lucius' family.

As Lucius brushed away the dried grass, aided by Phoebus and Numa who quickly bent to help, the pieces with writing upon them revealed themselves, and they laid them together upon the ground as best they could.

Here lies Alene Metella
Daughter, Sister
Beloved of Apollo
Alas too young to leave...

It was as if they were burying her remains all over again, as if Emrys had only just finished the monument and pulled back the silk covering to reveal the lifelike representation of Alene, walking in a flowery field, mourned by the kneeling warriors to either side.

With the destruction of the monument, however, the otherworldly skill with which Emrys had brought the image to life was no longer present. Rather than appearing at peace in Elysian fields, the image of Alene, cracked and broken in several places, was now faded and lifeless. Her eyes were blank, her smile faded. It was as if she were now frozen in grief upon that desecrated monument.

They finished placing the pieces as best they could, flat upon the ground, and then Lucius bent to clear the bronze tube jutting from the ground with a stick. Dried dirt fell through to mix with her remains, and it made Lucius' eyes burn. He persisted and eventually the tube was straightened. When he finished, he stood and looked around. It had once been a beautiful place, but now there was nothing left.

Phoebus handed his father the satchel, and Lucius pulled out the incense and tinderbox he had brought.

In the broken bowl of the altar, which now lay flat upon the ground before the monument, Lucius placed a smoking chunk of incense. Then, he turned to Prisca who gave him a cracked jug of water.

Adara, Phoebus and Calliope closed in around Lucius, along with Prisca and Numa, and they all bent their heads as the smoke of their offering to the dead wafted around them and up into the sky.

Lucius closed his eyes, his mind trying to reach out to his sister, wherever she was. "Alene…" he began, and felt Adara's hand upon his shoulder. "Wherever you are, we hope that the Gods have blessed you…and Alerio, my friend. May you both be at peace in Elysium with Apollo's sun full upon your face. May you be free always of the pain and torment of this world. We miss you…I miss you…" As Lucius' voice wavered, and Adara wept quietly at his side, he poured the water down the tube to feed his sister's shade, and fell upon his knees before her broken image.

Had he looked up from his despair, he would have seen her then, his sister, standing on the other side of that monument, looking down at him, reaching out to him to provide ghostly comfort.

But Calliope did see her, and she stepped forward to place her hand upon her father's shoulder, looking up at the shade of her aunt. She smiled through her tears and her song.

Tell him I am well, the shade said to her.

I will, Calliope answered in her head. *Thank you for saving us, Matertera.*

The shade smiled and looked down at Lucius. *Be strong, Brother… We are all with you…*

Lucius looked up quickly, and for a fleeting moment, he saw the bright light that covered the monument before him. He felt an easing of his sorrow, and it gave him the strength to rise from his knees. "May the Gods keep you, Sister."

He looked down at his daughter then, and saw her smile up at him.

"She is well, Baba. I know it," Calliope said.

Numa and Prisca stepped forward with bunches of wild flowers clutched in their shaking hands, and placed them upon the bowl beside the burning incense. The flowers had always been Alene's favourite, and in the years since the monument had been erected, they had offered them to her.

The sun was high by the time they finished, and so, for the next hour, as Numa and Prisca went back to the ruined house to lie in the shade of their makeshift home, Lucius, Adara, Phoebus and Calliope wandered the remains of the stables, the wine production building, and baths to survey the destruction.

Nothing was left of anything.

Any wine and oil vats that had been there had been taken or smashed, the earth soaked with their precious contents. No animals dwelled in the barns among fresh-cut hay. The servants' quarters were gutted and empty, and the hypocausts of the bathhouse were clogged and cold.

"There's nothing left at all," Lucius said.

"I'm sorry, Lucius." Adara took his hand as they walked toward the vineyard and the wild tangle of vines that now twisted in a chaotic mesh-work of green, yellow and gold.

Phoebus and Calliope each picked a bunch of dark grapes they found and began to eat. They handed some to their parents to eat too, and they all continued to walk around the back of the house.

Lucius looked up the hill to see the tip of the cypress tree that crowned his ancestors' tomb. He paused, staring up at the place that had held so much dread for him as a child, but which had come to symbolize something greater as the years and responsibility had worn on. Though he had never understood why, he felt as if the place was meant for more than the mere remembrance of dead Metelli ancestors.

Approach...

Lucius blinked and rubbed his eyes. "Did you hear that?"

"Hear what?" Adara said.

"I thought I heard... Never mind." But as they turned to walk back to the ruins of the house, Lucius stopped and looked back up at the hilltop. "I...I need to go up there," he said.

"To the tomb?" Adara asked. "Why?"

"I...I just..." He shook his head as if trying to clear his thoughts. "I haven't been up there for so long. We may not come back here."

"We're not splitting up, Lucius," Adara added quickly. "You heard what Numa and Prisca said. Those spies could be back at any time."

Lucius' face darkened. "Then let's go together. There is enough daylight left to go and come back." He turned to his son. "Phoebus, run to the house and ask Numa if he has a torch we can use."

"Yes, Baba."

A short time later, Phoebus retuned with a thick stick wrapped with a dirty cloth on the end that appeared to be mildly damp with oil.

"This is all Numa had," he said.

"It'll do. Come," Lucius said, looking up the path that led into the forest and up the hill. "We'd better get going."

Lucius thought that the forest never seemed so dark as it did then, despite the brilliance of the sun overhead.

They walked with their gladii drawn, with Lucius out in front, his eyes scanning the trees. Snakes skittered out of the way as they approached, leaving the sun-dappled spots upon the path where they had been lying. Not far off, they could hear a boar nosing at the earth, but there was little else in the way of sound.

Halfway up the hill, Lucius began to feel a fluttering in his stomach. In his mind, he thought he could hear whispers, and so he stopped frequently to look around the trees, his sword point out before him.

Adara and the children looked with him, but they saw and heard nothing, only the speckled sunlight and the distant sound of cicadas.

When they reached the top of the path, a crow cawed loudly from one of the trees, startling them. They stepped out of the trees to stand before the grassy mound topped by a giant cypress that reached skyward as if stretching to touch the chariot of the sun as it passed overhead.

Lucius paused to catch his breath, and looked upon the ancient tomb.

"Are you sure you want to go in, Lucius?" Adara remembered the time they had found that someone had been living in the tomb, the last time they had seen Argus, who had come to kill them. "I don't like this place."

Approach...

Lucius turned quickly at the voice in his head, but saw no one but his family standing about him.

"They want you to go in, Baba," Calliope said, turning her wide eyes upon him. "You have to."

"How do you know this, Calliope?" her mother asked.

"I just do." She reached out to hold Adara's hand. "It will be fine."

Lucius stared at his wife and daughter and nodded. He then reached into his satchel to remove the tinder box and lit the torch that Phoebus was holding out to him. Once it was lit, he took it and gave the satchel to his son.

"Do you want me to come with you?" Phoebus asked.

Lucius shook his head. "I'll go alone. You keep a watch out here. Call if anyone approaches."

Phoebus nodded, his eyes already scanning the surrounding tree line, his sword drawn.

"Come, Mama," Calliope said. "Let's sit in the grass."

But as her daughter sat in the long grass, Adara followed her husband to the tomb entrance, her eyes meeting his one more time before he turned to go into the darkness, following the light of his torch as he went.

Lucius looked back one more time at Adara, silhouetted by the sunlight at the entrance to the tomb, and then turned to go in, the weak light cast by the torch choked by the darkness.

The interior of the tomb smelled musty and damp as he went, looking into each of the ante chambers on his way to the main room at the heart of the mound. He remembered the layout of the tomb, but somehow, this time, it felt different. If Lucius had been asked to explain what happened in that moment, words would have failed him.

As he passed the ante chambers, the painted terracotta faces of men and women upon their deathly dining couches stared back at him from out of the darkness and, despite his faint torch, he could see them...and hear them. His head filled with whispers he could not decipher, some in tongues he could not comprehend.

Then, something strange happened. Each of the ante chambers became a world unto itself. In one he saw a vast desert plain where two great armies faced each other, dust rising to the heavens where eagles soared high above on thermals, watching a momentous battle. In another room, a warrior was climbing to the top of a mountain where a lone temple stood at the top of the world. In another room, two ancient warriors, one male, one female, stood shoulder to shoulder against a horde of barbarians, placing themselves between a village of mostly women and children and an enemy they could not possibly defeat.

The corridor of the tomb seemed to go on and on, impossibly so, revealing different ages and battles in which various warriors stood proudly in the fray, either victorious or on the verge of desperate defeat. The sights made Lucius shiver with excitement or feel a deep sorrow. He stopped at one of the final ante chambers to look more closely at a lone warrior whose eyes locked onto his, and in a split second, light exploded in the chamber, causing Lucius to stumble backward until he dropped his pitiful torch and rolled in the dirt in the middle of the main, central chamber of the tomb.

He felt light-headed and cold for a moment, and then his body began to shudder. He was about to speak, but his jaw tightened like a vice and his vision blurred. The room spun and it seemed to him as he looked at the roof of the chamber that the walls and ceiling blew outward to reveal a brilliant, star-pocked sky.

It was a sky he had only seen in one place before, in the eyes of the Gods themselves. He shut his eyes, but still, the stars whirled in his vision, darting through radiant clouds of colour and light, the constellations moving before him. It was then he realized the stars spun in his own eyes, and just as he felt like weeping, fearing himself finally dead, there was music. It was a music that he had never heard before in his world, or the otherworld. It filled him with light, and strength, and fed his will like a thousand healing wells.

A part of Lucius wanted to scream, worried that he would fall forever in that place, but instead, he stopped, breathed deeply, and felt every fibre of his being strong and calm, his own heartbeat like a gentle, reverberating string upon a lyre.

Lucius... a voice said.

The sound startled him, but he somehow recognized it.

The stars began to fade and the walls closed in. He felt the hard ground beneath his back, and slowly Lucius opened his eyes. As he did, he gasped, his hand scanning the ground for the gladius he realized he had dropped.

You are among friends, Lucius, the voice said again. *You are among brothers and sisters...*

The chamber was filled with a pale, pure light, and Lucius found himself surrounded by warriors, men and women, each of them of a different place and time, but each of them familiar in some way, proud in their bearing. They all looked toward Lucius, their bright eyes keen and kind, full of understanding as they looked upon the torn man in their midst.

A part of Lucius wanted to weep, but whether it was from fear or joy, or from the deep sense of unity he felt then, he was uncertain. His eyes scanned the ranks surrounding him, the dragons emblazoned upon each of them, and then his gaze fell upon the eyes of a tall, strong warrior who appeared as confused as he was. He recognized the man, but saw the mingled sense of hope and deep sadness upon his face as he looked about the chamber as if in a dream.

From Annwn, Lucius thought, but then his gaze moved on.

Stand among us, my boy, the previous voice spoke again.

Lucius turned to see a warrior in a simple, red legionary tunic step out from among the other warriors, his hand extended. Lucius took the hand and was pulled lightly to his feet. "Grandfather?"

The warrior nodded and smiled. *You've come so far,* the shade said. He was proud, but there was great sadness in his features. *We have all been made to suffer in our time,* he said, looking around at the others who nodded, *but none of us as greatly as you have.*

Lucius turned in a circle to look at all of them. He was no longer afraid, but rather comforted by the kinship he felt. "The Dragon..." he said.

Avus Metellus Anguis smiled. *We are all dragons...but none so much as you. You are the bridge between worlds and ages, Lucius.*

"The bridge? I don't understand." Lucius stepped toward his grandfather, but the shade shook its head. "Explain to me...please."

That is for your father to decide.

"Quintus Metellus betrayed us all. He killed my sister."

Not him, the shade said. *It was never him.*

For a brief moment, Lucius saw regret and dislike in the shade's eyes, and he knew again, with absolute certainty, that Quintus Metellus was never his father. He remembered the last time he had seen the hateful man in otherworldly Annwn, sad, pathetic and raging, alone in the afterlife.

Not him, the shade repeated. *The secrets were in part revealed to you in Annwn.*

"I must go back there?" Lucius asked, feeling a little dread.

In that moment, the light around the chamber began to slowly fade as some of the shades disappeared, saluting Lucius before departing. Only the lone, confused warrior lingered, straining to look and hear as he was pulled away with the rest.

"Wait!" Lucius looked around. "Please!" He locked eyes with Avus Metellus.

You need not decide to go there yet. But Britannia needs you, Lucius Pen Dragon. It needs your family.

The lone warrior stopped at that, appeared to cry out, but there was no sound, and Lucius was only vaguely aware of him as he disappeared.

Avus Metellus then placed his pale hand upon Lucius' shoulder. *You have a long road to travel, and many decisions to make.*

"Revenge," Lucius' said, his features hardening. "Britannia can wait."

Avus Metellus looked down, a great sadness shrouding his features. *That is your decision.* He stepped back then, ready to depart. *We are our decisions, Lucius. And dragons always have the most difficult ones to make.*

With those final words, Avus Metellus pointed to Lucius' chest, turned and faded into the stone walls of the chamber.

For a moment, Lucius stood alone in the centre of the chamber, his hand upon his chest and the dragon brand beneath his tunic.

Apollo… What have you shown me? Lucius thought, but there was no answer, only a feeling that his father was indeed waiting for him.

Lucius looked down to see the torch and his gladius lying upon the stone and dirt floor. He bent down to pick them up, remembering that Adara and the children were waiting for him outside. He sheathed the gladius and walked back the way he had come, the distance feeling much shorter than it had on the way in.

.   .   .

He reached the entrance to the tomb and stepped into the sunlight to see Adara, Phoebus and Calliope sitting upon the grass.

"I'm sorry I took so long!" Lucius said, rushing toward them.

Adara looked back at him, confused. "Long? You just went in!"

Lucius stopped and looked at his family. "What do you mean? I was gone for more than an hour!"

Phoebus and Calliope looked at each other and then to their mother.

Adara walked toward him, and placed her hand upon his brow. "Are you all right, Lucius?"

"I feel well," he said.

Adara could see the brilliance in his eyes, as if merely stepping in and out of the tomb had cleansed him of something, as if some heavenly breeze had blown away the clouds that had hovered before his eyes. But she also saw that he was confused, that his body was still desecrated and burned. "We should get back to the house," she said.

Lucius nodded absently, turning to look back at the dark entrance to the tomb and the towering cypress that rose into the sky. He looked up to the blue above, and for a moment, he thought he could spy stars in the heavens, and the writhing draco constellation.

"Lucius?" Adara said. "Come." She led him by the hand and, together, the four of them left the clearing to go back down through the forest to the ruins of the villa.

As they went, Lucius felt in his heart that he would never see that place again, and he knew that things were as they should be.

That evening around the fire with his family, Numa and Prisca, Lucius went over the day's events in his mind, or at least he tried to. Over and over again, he revisited what had happened in the tomb, or what he thought had happened.

Adara and the children had sworn that he had only been gone for a minute or two, and that caused Lucius even greater confusion.

Still, he had felt comfort in what had happened to him. The face of his grandfather remained with him, kind and encouraging, but also saddened by Lucius' decision to carry on down his chosen path.

And that is what bothered Lucius most. Self-doubt began to chip away at his anger and determination, the only things that had kept him going since he came back from the brink of death. He looked around the fire at his family. *I must keep them safe at all cost.*

"Numa…Prisca…" Lucius turned to face them, sitting forward toward the fire, somehow no longer bothered by the heat and light. "I've been thinking… There is nothing left for you here. It is not safe."

The old couple looked down, the fear clearly etched upon their faces. They had wanted to go with Lucius and his family, but now, they could see that that was not an option.

Lucius waited until they looked up before he began speaking again. "We need to head south tomorrow, to Rome. And then we need to find my family and Adara's." Lucius paused. "You cannot go with us, though I would gladly bring you. It would raise too much suspicion, and I cannot be recognized. None of us can."

"Master Lucius," Numa said, his eyes panicked. "Do not go to Rome. They will kill you!"

Lucius could feel his family's worried eyes upon him. He knew that it was extremely dangerous, and if he could find a way to go on his own he would. *Caracalla will be there, after all.* "I am not abandoning you. When this is all over, we may be able to return here and rebuild, but for now, you are not safe. You should not have to endure the abuse and violence and harsh winter." Lucius reached into his satchel and pulled out one of the pouches of coins, one containing a few aurea and denarii, and handed it to Numa. "Take this. Go to Pisae and get an affordable place in one of the tenements there over the winter. When spring comes, you wait for a ship called the Europa. It is owned by a man we trust, a captain called Creticus. I will let him know to pick you up. He will take you to Britannia and safety and, if it is the Gods' will, we will meet you there too."

"Britannia?" Prisca burst out, the land conjuring images of howling barbarians in her mind, of northern winter weather and danger around every corner. "We cannot go to Britannia, Master Lucius."

Numa placed his hand upon his wife's arm to calm her panic and nodded. "We are grateful, Master Lucius, truly. But we are old and we cannot possibly make such a journey."

"You cannot stay here, living exposed and in the open," Lucius said. "It's obvious our neighbours are reluctant to help you, or defend you in my absence. You are a part of my familia and it's my duty to ensure your safety." Lucius looked down and nodded to himself. "But you are also free, so, I will leave the choice to take the ship up to you. Take this money and go to Pisae for the winter. Be safe and warm. And then you can decide whether or not to board the Europa when she comes for you in the spring. Can you do that?"

Numa smiled at Lucius and looked around the fire at the children and Adara. "How have the years passed, Master Lucius? So much has changed. It is not fair."

"I know," Lucius said. "But I've discovered that, despite our best intentions, life is often not at all fair." He looked at Adara, Phoebus and Calliope, and felt the wounds of all that had happened to them. *We were so happy!* he thought, wanting to scream it, but he was calm as he turned back to Numa. "Do you accept?"

Numa looked at Prisca, her ragged, abused face and body, and nodded, tears falling from his lids as he did so. "We do. Thank you, Master Lucius. May the Gods bless you." He accepted the pouch from Lucius and placed it on the ground before him.

"May they bless us all," Adara added, smiling at the couple.

"We should all sleep now," Lucius said. "We have long roads ahead of us."

Each of them settled about the fire then, and slowly, one by one, they allowed Hypnos to take them.

All but Lucius succumbed to the weariness of dusk, for in his mind, he could still see his grandfather, still feel the presence of the other warriors in the tomb, especially the one who appeared so out of place and confused. But he shook his head and tried to focus on other matters, such as what he would do when they got to Rome.

Will Caracalla even be there?

Eventually, even Lucius could not withstand sleep's whispers, and slowly, his eyes closed and cast a curtain before the orange light of the fire.

Night passed, the symphony of the countryside lulling all of them as the stars twinkled and the moon passed overhead.

Lucius' eyes fluttered beneath their lids and shot open in the early dark. He looked around to see his familia laying still, asleep and peaceful, and then rose himself, taking hold of his gladius. He picked his way out of the ruins. The smell of damp earth and woodsmoke tickled his nostrils, shielding him from the scent of burnt plaster from the ruin of his home. He felt like he was back at the hillfort again, picking through the remains of his family's life, and the anger surfaced once more.

He walked a little, trying to wrest the stiffness from his joints, rubbing his chest where it burned and itched around the dragon. He continued down the hill to the southeast, picking his way through the carcasses of the ancient olive trees that had provided sustenance for generations.

Lucius stopped and looked around, overwhelmed by anger and grief. He wanted to shout, but as he was about to open his mouth, a loud thrumming reached into his consciousness and the air about him oscillated between dark and light. His heartbeat grew quick. He then realized what was happening, stopped, and turned slowly to look up the hill to where a tall armoured warrior stood looking directly at him. Upon his head was a great crested helmet, and in his thick, strong hands were a long spear, the tip of which shone in the dawn light, and a great round shield upon which images of men and horses charged and did battle. The warrior's beard was thick and his jaw hard-lined. His muscular arms to either side of the shining cuirass were solid, as if wrought of stone. But it was the eyes that caught Lucius' attention more than anything, for in them he saw blood and battle and the whirling of the starry skies of autumn. He also saw an unexpected kindness as he approached the warrior.

The scent of the damp, rich earth, tanged with the scent of iron and blood, grew strong in Lucius' nostrils as he came before the warrior.

"Uncle…" Lucius said.

Mars nodded, set his shield down, and removed his crested helmet to tuck it beneath his left arm. He then smiled, a smile as Lucius had never received from the headlong God of War. *I've been waiting for you,* Mars said.

"You heard me in Britannia?"

You called on the Avenger.

"Yes. I did. I know that I have not often asked for your help, that we have been at odds sometimes but-"

Is that what you think, Lucius…Pen Dragon? I have done nothing that your choices have not led you to.

"My choices?" Lucius bristled. "You have hounded me all my life!"

Rather than grow angry, Mars' face softened. He looked with pity upon Lucius. *Am I only war and blood to you? Vengeance?*

"We are who we are!" Lucius snapped back.

Mars nodded and, to Lucius' surprise, looked saddened. He dropped his helmet and spear onto the ground and knelt in the soft, dark soil. *I am not Ares, though battle and blood are sometimes my realm.* He reached down and dug his thick warrior's hands into the earth to bring up two handfuls. He looked at the soil in his hands and admired it, saw the potential in it, and even as Lucius looked at his uncle, he saw green shoots rise up out of the soil in his hands.

I also take pleasure in rich, dark earth and green growth. Life must be nurtured in order to fight on. The two go hand-in-hand, Lucius. You have lost sight of this truth.

"What truth?" Lucius snapped. "That while I am fighting, my life will be burned down around me with no chance of growth? My unborn child was slain! The home I built was destroyed. And now this!" Lucius waved his hand to show the land upon which they stood.

Your life and home is not dead, just as this land is not. Mars gently laid down the earth he had been holding, now shot with green, upon the ground and stood. He looked Lucius directly in the eyes like he had never done before.

Lucius blinked, shocked by the tenderness and concern he saw there. "You are not the Avenger."

I am many things, just as you are. You have been given so much, Lucius. You and your family have so much potential, but you must choose which side of yourself to nurture. Will it be that? Mars pointed to the green shoots that continued to rise out of the earth. *Or will it be this?* He touched the black gladius Lucius grasped in his hand. *At this moment, I see that the path you are set upon is fraught with pain and blood. Is that what you want? Or do you wish to plant roots for the future?*

Lucius knelt to take a handful of soil and let if fall through his fingers. No green emerged from the blackness in the palm of his hand. He could only smell blood and charring, and so he dropped the rest of the soil. "Some blood must be shed before I can finally be at peace. I want vengeance, Uncle…Avenger… I will not be able to rest, to replant my life until I punish those who took it from me."

Mars closed his eyes, and it seemed to Lucius that he sighed deeply, sadly, a sound of despair and reluctant acceptance. When he opened his eyes, they were hard once more, determined and full of fury. He bent to take up his helmet and placed it upon his head. Then, he took up his shield and spear, and stood tall and full of strength and menace before Lucius.

If that is your choice, Nephew, then so be it. Give me blood. Take up the mantle you were meant to wear - that of a killer.

A part of Lucius wanted to step forward and ask Mars for more advice, to have the god reiterate his choices, even to convince him not to pursue his chosen course. But his stubbornness and pain prevented such a weakness. He stood tall, his chest out, and held his gladius firmly in his hand.

Mars nodded, the crest of his great helmet bristling in an unknown breeze. He then turned, and walked away over the far-reaching fields.

When he disappeared from Lucius' sight, a scream rent the morning air.

For a moment, Lucius believed it was the departure of War, the sound of his own anguish and anger inside that he heard. But the scream erupted again, and fear stabbed at his gut.

"Calliope!" Lucius said, bursting into a run, up the hill toward the ruins of the house.

The men came upon them as they were eating, calm and at familial peace about the fire. They came like wraiths, their footfalls hidden by Adara's voice as she described their life in Britannia to Numa and Prisca.

One moment, Adara and Phoebus were sitting across the fire from Numa and Prisca with Calliope beside them, holding the old woman's hand to calm her. But the next terrible second, a rough, dirty hand was grasping Calliope by the hair, its owner a black-cloaked man who held a razor sharp gladius to the girl's neck.

Calliope screamed.

Phoebus and Adara jumped up, their gladii drawn.

Numa and Prisca stood clumsily, looking at the man and his companion who howled with laughter to see the surprise on their faces. The two men who had tormented them for months were back, and now they had others to torment.

"Let her go!" Adara yelled.

"What you gonna do, sweetheart?" the second man laughed, looking at his fellow holding the squirming, crying little girl. He then turned to Prisca. "Sweeter meats await us this time, don't they my pretty?" He reached for Prisca's chin, already wet with tears, her face full of fear for the knowledge of what those men were capable of.

They backed away, out of the ruins and into the courtyard before the rubble of the villa.

Phoebus and Adara followed, their swords still up.

Phoebus scanned the ugly, rough men quickly, and saw that they were well-armed, both with sword and dagger.

"Looks like we have others to talk with on this visit, eh?" the man holding Calliope said, craning his neck down to lick her cheek.

She screamed even more loudly and punched at him, but he only chuckled.

"When we're done with her, we'll give you some attention then," the other said to Adara.

Phoebus stepped out in front of his mother. "I'll kill you before you touch either of them!"

"Don't worry, boy! You can have a turn too!" the other man said, both of them laughing. "But first, let's have a chat." His face grew dark and he too drew his dagger. "Who are you and what are you doing here with these two?" He pointed his blade at Numa and Prisca.

"We're travellers on the road," Adara said, trying to steady her voice as the man held her daughter's life in his hands. "It got dark, and these two people gave us shelter."

"Shelter?" the one asked Numa. "You call this shelter? Not very hospitable of you now, is it?" He looked around the ruins. "This was a nice place, but orders is orders."

"Speaking of orders," said the man holding Calliope. "You wouldn't know a Lucius Metellus Anguis now, would you?"

Calliope shook her head quickly.

"You sure, little one? I have ways I can make you talk. Nice ways." The man shot a look at Phoebus who had crept a little closer. "You stay there, boy! Or I'll stick her!" He pressed the blade into Calliope's skin and a droplet of blood trickled down to be soaked up by the hem of her tunica.

The other man turned to Adara. "This Metellus, he might have been travelling with a woman and two children." He looked at the three of them.

"Lucius Metellus Anguis is dead! How many times have I told you?" Numa shouted, his old, tired voice echoing off of the ruins around him.

"Shut up!" the man yelled, slapping Numa so that he spun off of his feet to the ground.

Prisca ran to her husband's side, but the man kicked her as she went and she fell hard upon the earth.

The man holding Calliope looked at Adara. "Now here's what's going to happen. You're going to tell me where the traitor Metellus is, and then I'm going to have a little fun with your children while you watch. Or, we can have the fun first and make it last. It's up to you. Either way, we'll get it out of you."

"We're just travellers," Adara said. *Lucius where are you?* "These people helped us out. That's all!" Adara's voice was growing frantic now.

As she spoke, Phoebus caught Calliope's eye and he subtly tapped the pugio that was tucked into his cingulum at his right hip, staring at her captor's own hip.

She stilled herself, stopped struggling, and nodded minutely.

Phoebus began counting by lifting fingers on the handle of his gladius so that she could see. *One...two...* Calliope's hand slid back and *...three!*

Calliope pulled the blade free and stabbed blindly, jamming it into the man's thigh. In the brief second his grip loosened, she spun sideways out of the way and ran.

Phoebus charged in and his sword met the man's as he howled, grasping at the blade in his thigh.

The other man made to lunge at Phoebus to hack him down, but as he stepped, Numa slammed into him, knocking him to the ground.

Prisca screamed.

The man and Numa rolled in the dust.

"I've had it with you, old man!" the attacker said, gaining the upper hand and then quickly driving his pugio into Numa's chest five times in quick succession.

Instantly, there was blood everywhere.

Adara and Phoebus fought the first man, but he was fast despite his wounds, and when the other joined him, they began to back up, all along Prisca's screams piercing the air as she threw herself upon her husband.

The men were about to press their advantage with Adara and Phoebus getting dangerously close to the ruined walls when a loud shout came from behind them.

The men turned quickly to see a burned man in a grey tunic running at them with a black gladius. The first of them turned to face him as he leapt over Numa's body.

Lucius attacked like a fury, his gladius stabbing in and out, over and over, trying to find an opening like an enraged viper, but his opponent was skilled and he parried wildly, moving to a more open space away from the ruins.

The other man went to join him, but Phoebus and Adara ran after him.

"Are you him, then?" one of the Praetorian spies said as he slashed at Lucius.

"You're going to regret this," Lucius growled. "Caracalla's going to regret this."

The man's eyes opened wide, and then he smiled. "Oh, you *are* him!"

The two men were back to back now, one facing Lucius, the other, limping, facing Adara and Phoebus.

"After we kill you, we're going to do things to your wife and children that will make these hills echo with their screams. It's a shame you won't be here to see it." He lunged suddenly, furiously, and caught the side of Lucius' arm.

Lucius cried out briefly, but he was ready and countered with his own thrust to the man's thigh, sending him to one knee. He raced in, hacked off the man's sword hand and fell on top of him so that they struggled like animals in the dirt.

As the man's companion turned to help, to cut at Lucius, Phoebus sprang beneath his blade and slashed at his hamstrings from behind, sending him onto his stomach, raging in agony.

Lucius and his opponent scratched at each other's eyes, punched and kicked.

Lucius ignored the searing pain in his left arm, straining to get on top of the man. Finally he did and his fists began to pound away at his face, over and over and over, staining them with blood. The man's teeth broke audibly, and as his eyes rolled in his stunned head, Lucius had the chance to reach for his fallen gladius. Just as he raised it to bring it down, he felt another stabbing pain in his right shoulder as the other man thrust from where he lay upon the ground.

Phoebus was on top of him, his blade planted into his back, even as Lucius turned and slashed at his face, cutting a swathe across it.

Lucius, gasping for air, turned and plunged the tip of his gladius into the gaping throat of the man he straddled, feeling the top of the spinal chord sever at the back of the neck, making the body go limp beneath him.

The world spun then, and Lucius turned to see that Adara and Phoebus were all right. His eyes searched for Calliope and just before the world went dark, he spotted Calliope coming out from behind a wall, her pugio in her hand as she plunged it into the back of the man who had threatened her.

It was the sound of Prisca's wailing that roused Lucius. He was lying propped against one of the walls. For a moment, his head lolled atop his shoulders, but then he found his balance and his eyes stopped spinning.

Calliope was holding his hand, her tear-stained face full of worry and fear.

"Are you all right?" he asked her, and she nodded. He could tell though that she was still feeling the grip of terror. He looked at his arm and the bandage where the blood was seeping through. "Did you do this?"

"Mama and I did," Calliope said. "Baba...you didn't even flinch when we pressed the hot blade to your skin. I thought you were dead."

"I'm fine, my girl." He put his arm around her and pulled her close. It had been the longest run of his life to get to them from the far field. He had almost been too late. Then he registered the new screams and turned his head to see Prisca bent over Numa's body.

Adara sat beside her, trying to comfort her while Phoebus stood in stony silence, his bloody sword resting on his shoulder as he stared down the drive to the river below.

"Help me up," Lucius said to Calliope, and she strained to get her father to his feet.

Phoebus ran over to them to help. "Baba, are you all right?"

"I'm fine, Phoebus. I've had worse." Lucius could not rip his gaze from Numa's body as he walked toward them. When he reached them, Adara stood.

"He saved Phoebus," she said, tears in her exhausted eyes. She hugged him and Lucius could feel the deep shudder in her body. She pulled away and stepped aside so that Lucius could speak with Prisca.

"Prisca…" Lucius said, kneeling slowly and putting his arm around her. "He was a wonderful man. The Gods will bless him for his courage."

She shook her head and through her tears, spoke. "I don't know what I will do without him. He is everything to me…everything!" She fell upon the body again, and would not be moved for a long while as the sun crossed the heavens and the shadows grew long.

While Prisca slept upon her husband's body, Lucius and Phoebus busied themselves with the Praetorian corpses.

"What do we do with them, Baba?" Phoebus asked. The boy's face was hard to read.

On the one hand, Lucius thought he was in shock, but then, he seemed to be quite lucid. *Children should never have to see or do such things,* Lucius thought to himself, the guilt building higher and higher upon his shoulders. *Mine have seen enough for a lifetime already.*

Lucius thought of all that had been done to his family, to Numa and Prisca, to their homes and friends and others, by Caracalla and his henchmen. His face darkened as he looked at the Praetorian bodies and then to the wagon. "Help me load them into the wagon, Phoebus."

When Prisca awoke, Adara and Calliope were there for her, and helped her to clean Numa's body.

While they did that, Lucius and Phoebus were down by the river on the far side of the bridge.

"What are you going to do?" Phoebus asked once they had taken the bodies out of the wagon and lined them up on the drive.

"Get those broken scythe handles from the wagon, Phoebus."

As Phoebus went to do as his father asked, Lucius turned with a sword he had taken from one of the bodies, and looked down on the Praetorians. He glanced up at the red sun in the distance where it was beginning to set.

"I offer these hateful men to you, Mars Ultor. May I find my enemies and make them pay." With that, Lucius swung down hard to sever the neck of the first body, and then laid into the second one.

"What are you doing?" Phoebus asked as Lucius took one of the scythe handles.

"Sending a message," Lucius said. He then took a handle and drove the splintered end into one of the heads so that it stuck there like a grisly piece of meat for the fire. The eyes of the dead man gaped in shock and horror at them, but Lucius did not care. He did not even look when Phoebus vomited at the side of the river.

Lucius drove the stake into the ground where the road met the bridge, and then dragged the body to rest at the base. He then proceeded to spit the second head and propped it up likewise on the other side of the bridge beside the road. With that body laying prostrate before its pale, blood-stained face, Lucius stood back.

"No one will come here now," he muttered.

Phoebus approached his father apprehensively. "Baba...what are we going to do now?"

"Tomorrow, we'll bury Numa, and then we'll go to Rome." Lucius turned to look at his son briefly and then mounted the wagon. "Let's get back to the house."

Phoebus struggled to recognize the look he then saw in his father's eyes. He had seen it before, but it was a look from a much darker time, a time, it seemed, that had returned. *Gods, please help us.*

After a night of pain and shuddering hearts, a red dawn emerged to see Lucius, Adara, Phoebus and Calliope taking Prisca down the hill to bury her dead husband in the grass beside Alene.

As they drove, Adara spotted the heads Lucius had mounted, confirming what Phoebus had told her the night before. It sent a chill down her spine, and added to her fears. *I want to leave this place,* she thought, looking around at all the death and destruction, *but will Rome be any better?*

Lucius and Phoebus had dug a hole in the ground earlier, and as the wagon carrying Numa's body pulled alongside, the dark depths of that hole opened before them.

Prisca continued to weep, unable to stop touching her husband's body. "Don't leave me," she kept saying to herself, over and over again.

Lucius placed his hands upon her shoulders. "Prisca. We need to bury him. The Gods will look after him. He died a hero and he will have his entrance into Elysium."

She nodded through her tears and stepped back to allow Lucius and Phoebus to pull Numa out and lay him as gently as they could in the ground. They then shovelled the earth back into the grave, slowly, respectfully, until Numa disappeared beneath.

As Adara, Calliope and Prisca laid flowers upon the earth, Lucius lit the last of his incense and the smoke swirled about the grave.

"Gods," Lucius began. "See this brave man safely to Elysium. Keep him well..." he found his voice shuddering, the previous day's events finally getting to him. "Watch over this kind man. May he have the peace he so richly deserves." Then, he spoke lower, to himself as the others said their own words. "Father... See that this man who saved your grandson is sped quickly to the Afterlife. Ease his suffering and that of his wife. I ask you."

Lucius felt the sting of sadness and grief as he finished, and looked down at the grave one more time through the smoke of the offering.

Prisca wept loudly then, held close by Adara and Calliope who joined her in grief.

When they were finished, Prisca rested upon the mound of soft, rich earth, and they left her alone for a while to weep, to mourn, and to remember.

When yet another day dawned, Lucius knew that it was time they left, but he worried about Prisca.

"We can't take her with us," Lucius said to Adara.

"Lucius, she's all alone!" Adara said to him. "She has no one left in the world but us."

As they were speaking, they did not see Prisca coming toward them, her cheeks cheeks dirty and tear-stained. "I won't endanger your family further," she said to Lucius and Adara.

Lucius looked to her, saw the children over her shoulder where they were packing things into the wagon.

"You can't go to Pisae alone!" Adara said to Prisca, putting her arm about her.

"I can, and I will," Prisca answered. "Those men only wanted you dead. All of you. As you said, it would raise suspicion for you to have servants. I will do as you said and go to Pisae to await the ship."

"Are you sure?" Lucius asked her.

Prisca looked down the hill to her husband's dark grave. "I am." She wiped her face. "Numa died trying to keep you safe. It wouldn't do for me to endanger you more."

"It's my fault, Prisca," Lucius said.

But she shook her head. "It's not your fault. Evil men will always sow pain, and the emperor is such a man."

"He'll pay for it," Lucius said, and Adara looked at him quickly.

"The Gods have their ways," Prisca said. She straightened her dirty, blood stained tunic and sighed deeply as if mustering her courage. "Now. I will take one of the horses left by those horrible men, and go to Pisae. You are right. There is nothing for me here now."

"Will you be all right?" Adara asked, hugging her.

"I'll be fine dear. Numa will look after me." She pat Adara's hand and looked at the children waiting in the wagon. "Such fine children. So brave." She looked at Lucius then, as if taking him in one more time. "You are a good man, Lucius. Never forget that. The Gods do love you, despite all that has happened." She placed her hand upon the burned skin of his cheek. "I'm happy you came back, happy to see you are alive after all."

"I'm so sorry," Lucius said.

Prisca shook her head. "No more apologies, Lucius. Go. Find the rest of the family, and I will see you in the Spring."

"Here," Lucius said, handing her the pouch of coins he had given to Numa. "Don't forget this. You will need it."

She accepted it and kissed his cheek. Then, she turned to hug Adara. "Take care of each other, lady."

"We will. Be safe, Prisca. In Britannia, we'll have a new start."

Prisca nodded, but said nothing. She then walked over to the wagon to see the children. "You are both very brave," she said. "I am very glad to have seen you again. Be strong, and trust in your parents."

"We will," they said, leaning over the side of the wagon to hug her.

"Be safe, Prisca," Phoebus said.

She smiled sadly at them and, as they turned, she subtly placed the pouch of coins into the back of the wagon. "Go now! All of you. You should reach Rome in a few days."

Lucius climbed into the wagon with Adara, and turned to Prisca.

"Take both those horses, Prisca. When you get to Pisae, sell them. Then wait for Captain Creticus in the Spring."

"I will. Now go…go!" she said. "May the road be kind to you!"

Prisca waved as the wagon went down the path to cross the bridge and pass the deathly threshold of the drive.

From the wagon, Lucius stopped to look one last time at the ancestral lands of the Metelli. "I don't think we'll ever come back here again," he said.

"Do you want to?" Adara asked him.

All of them looked at the ruined fields, and the charred remains of the villa. Alene's broken monument stared back at them, and the cypress tree upon the tomb at the top of the hill stood still and quiet. The voices within it were silent then, the music of the nymphs of the river and groves no longer to be heard. It was indeed a place of death.

"I don't know," Lucius said. "Maybe some day, there will be life here again." *It's up to me whether or not we can safely come back here,* he thought.

"Will Prisca be all right?" Calliope asked as she saw her walking slowly down the drive.

"I hope so, my girl," Lucius said. "For now, we have our own road to follow."

Adara looked at her husband, unsure of what he was thinking, wishing she could get through to him, but with all that had happened in so short a time, he was unreachable yet again.

Lucius took one last look at his lands - the tomb, the villa, the river and dead crops - the place where he had played as a child, where his children had played, the place that had been his family's sanctuary. It was time to bid farewell to it, and as he flicked the reins, he felt a heated, stabbing emotion in his sternum. *Breathe, Lucius. Breathe…*

As the wagon rolled away, none of them saw the newly green and sprouting olive tree in the eastern field, rising up out of the ground where Mars had planted it. They did not see the God of War leaning against its lithe limbs, watching them as they drove away, down a road he had warned against.

.   .   .

When the wagon was out of sight, Prisca wept, her hands shaking. "May the Gods guide you all," she said, looking down at the rope she had taken from the ruins before walking down the hill toward the river. "Numa…my love…you can't leave me like this."

She reached the grave where only the day before, she had buried her husband. They had spent their lives on that land, caring for it, nurturing it. She would not leave it. "Mistress Alene…" she said as she ran her hand along the piled, broken marble of the monument to one of the kindest women she had ever known. "I won't leave either of you alone here." Prisca smiled, at the image of Alene Metella in that flowery field, and then turned to her husband's grave.

She knelt in the dirt and lay upon it, touching her lips to the soil and the body of the man beneath it. "My love…" she whispered, no longer afraid. After a few minutes, she got herself up, took up the rope, and fastened it to the highest point of Alene's monument. "Hold me mistress…" she said, and in the refracted light from the river opposite, she thought she saw Alene's smiling face.

Prisca then placed the loop of the other end of the rope around her neck, and pulled it tightly. She sat down to lean against the broken marble of the monument so that she could look at the earth where Numa was buried. Prisca smiled to herself through the tears that fell from her weary eyes, and then closed them.

As she did, she saw sunshine and fertile fields. She heard songs around the hearth fire and her husband's laughter. She looked into his twinkling, youthful eyes, so full of love for her that she felt her world the greatest gift from any god. *Numa, my heart…my love…*

No one spoke as the cart sped along the minor road, through the Etrurian landscape, to join the via Cassia to the East. Pain and sadness sat heavily among them like passengers they could not be rid of, and uncertainty dogged their thoughts with every diminishing mile on the way to Rome.

Adara wanted to speak with Lucius, to plumb the depths of his no doubt raging mind, but she knew that her children needed her. They lay in the back of the wagon, each child leaning against her as Lucius drove the cart onward, whipping the mule every time it slowed to eat or drink.

Calliope had not spoken much at all since she was attacked, and

Phoebus stared at the blood upon his hands, his gladius still gripped in his fist.

The sight of them broke Adara's heart, even as she felt her own body shaking with the trauma of what had happened. They had come so very close to horrible deaths at the hands of the Praetorian spies. *So close…* The reality of it robbed her of speech, and it was all she could do to sit there, gripping her children and kissing their sweaty heads over and over again as the cart bumped along violently.

For Lucius, he could not get away from the villa quickly enough, for another part of his world had been consumed by flame and blood and poisoned memory. He tortured himself with guilt over not having been there to protect his family, and in his mind he could still see the bastard's hands upon his daughter, hear the clang of steel on steel as his son fought desperately to defend Calliope and Adara in Lucius' stead.

And now? I'm taking them to Rome to hunt down the man responsible for all of this! Lucius cursed himself for not being better prepared, for bringing his family along, for putting them in harm's way, for having taken them from the safety and peace of Ynis Wytrin. The list of his failures was long and he played them over and over in his mind as the gold and green hills of Etruria rolled by. That beautiful, fertile and fragrant world could have been a desolation of ash for all he noticed as he drove toward the rising wall of the Apennines.

Eventually, Adara moved to touch him on the shoulder. "Lucius," she said, her voice hoarse. "Lucius we need to stop. The children need to wash in the river."

Lucius seemed not to hear her for he kept driving.

"Lucius!" Adara finally yelled. He turned quickly to her, his eyes wide and angry, but she would not be dissuaded. "They still have blood all over them! We need to stop so they can wash and change, or we will draw too much attention. Do you hear me?"

He nodded, and slowed the cart. They had been driving for hours and the sun had long ago tipped over midday. A short time before they had joined the via Cassia where it ran along the river Arnus across the plain. To either side, groves of olive and fields of wheat swayed in the hot breeze, and to their left, the river snaked its way among them, the banks shielded by linden, oak and elm.

Lucius turned the cart off of the road and made for the riverbank, his eyes scanning the area. No one was about, but that could change quickly enough. He had seen the city of Arretium where it sat upon its steep hill not far away. When the wagon stopped, he took a deep, shuddering breath, and then turned in his seat to look at his family.

Their bloody and bedraggled state stabbed at his heart, for they were pale, blood-covered, and fearful. When Adara looked up at him, it was with pity and frustration, anger and disgust.

Lucius forced himself to snap out of his own miserable state and got stiffly out of the wagon to help them.

"The mule will be no use if it drops dead," Adara said, pointing at the foaming creature hitched to the wagon. "Untie it and let it drink and eat. I'll take care of the children."

Lucius turned away from her, and went to take care of the beast. It breathed raggedly, and pulled away from him when he approached, but Lucius calmed himself and spoke softly to it. He had treated it badly, and he knew it. "There, there. I'm sorry. Time to eat and drink your fill." After unhitching the mule, he led it by a rope attached to the bridle down to the river where it could drink and eat the rich green grass that grew there. Once the mule was settled, Lucius went back to the cart.

Adara was pulling out their previous clothes for the children to change, and so that she could try to scrub away the blood stains in the river water of the Arnus.

When Lucius approached her, she pulled away. He could see her hands shaking as she led Calliope to the riverside where they sat down and proceeded to scrub at the blood upon her face, neck, hands and arms. Lucius watched as Calliope finally began to weep and leaned into her mother's arms.

"I will never let anyone harm you again, my love," he heard Adara say to her as they sobbed together.

Lucius turned to Phoebus who was leaning against the base of a tree trunk, his gladius across his lap as he stared at small fish darting in the sun-kissed river water.

"You fought very well, Phoebus," Lucius said, kneeling before his son.

The young man's eyes were tired and stared blankly into the space before him. After a moment, he focussed and turned his eyes on his father. "Why does this keep happening to us?"

What can I say to him that will make him feel better? Lucius wondered. *Shall I tell him I have led us to this? That the Gods have abandoned us? That it is all Caracalla's fault?* Lucius closed his eyes for a moment. *I don't even know if any of that is true!* He wanted to shout, to rage, but he knew none of it would help. His son needed him, needed reassurance.

Lucius took the sword from his son and laid it on the grass beside him. He tried to hold Phoebus' gaze before speaking. "I'm sorry, Phoebus. Truly. I didn't want any of this for you." He reached up to touch his son's cheek. "But I do know that the Gods have not abandoned you, your sister, or your mother."

"And what about you, Baba?" Phoebus looked at his father's face, the scarred skin, the short, patchy hair spattered with blood. "Have they abandoned you?"

Lucius was silent. He did not know how to answer that. Did the Gods ever truly abandon someone? Or was it people who abandoned themselves? It had come to the point where Lucius wanted it all to be over, to give up. But then he thought of the reason why he had left Ynis Wytrin, left Britannia. It was that one purpose, that one bloody goal that kept him alive. He may have ruined his family's life and chance of happiness and peace, but he would not give up until he reached the end of the road he was now walking down. He looked back at his son and shook his head, a poor smile on his hard lips. "I'll be fine."

Phoebus turned away and said no more. He stepped into the river water, removed his blood-stained tunic and tossed it onto the grass. He then knelt in the shallows and began to scrub the blood away from his hands, arms and face, using some of the sand from the bottom to scour himself.

Lucius stood and watched as Adara and Calliope also scrubbed themselves in the waters of the Arnus, the blood still clinging stubbornly to their faces and arms, only slowly being erased to flow away with the current, unlike the memories of all that they had endured, images and experiences that would continue to haunt them when the blood fully faded. He looked at his family and knew then that the sight before him was completely unnatural. It was wrong. *And it is all my fault!*

By the time they were cleaned and changed, their clothes drying on the low-hanging branches of the surrounding trees, the sun was already close to the horizon.

"It's too late to travel any more today," Lucius said to Adara.

"Can we stay here the night? Is it safe?" she asked.

"I looked around while you and the children were washing. We're hidden from the road, and no one else is about. We should be fine for one night. I'll light a fire and keep watch while you sleep."

"We're almost out of food."

"There are villas and estates along the road. We can stop and buy some on our way south."

Adara nodded and looked around the small clearing to see where the children were sitting on the riverbank, leaning against each other. She could hear Lucius' ragged breath, his burned lungs struggling as they had ever since that horrible night long ago. She turned to him and saw the deep sadness in his eyes, the blank despairing stare as he watched their children. The blood of others had dried upon his desiccated skin, gathered along the rough edges like pollution in a dried-up river. "Phoebus and Calliope can start the fire. Let me help you wash."

Lucius simply nodded.

"Phoebus…Calliope?" she said. "Can you start a fire? I'm going to help your father clean up."

"Yes, Mama," they said.

Adara then took Lucius' hand and led him to the water where she removed his tunic and began to wipe carefully and methodically at his skin. "We need to apply the resin. It's been too long."

It took some time, but eventually the blood was mostly gone, and the tincture of what remained only blended in with his already red and angry skin. Once his tunic was washed and drying, Adara applied the resin that Elana had given them.

Lucius felt his skin soothed immediately upon application, and felt as though he could breathe again.

Adara then helped him to slide his clean tunic over his head and then they sat together for a moment while the children finished coaxing the fire to life with wood they had gathered along the river.

"Lucius… I'm so sorry about Numa and the estate. So much has happened…I didn't fully realize how hard the destruction must have been on you."

"That estate was our family's livelihood, and now it's gone."

"I know." She put her arms around him and her head upon his shoulder as he watched the flames rise up from the wood before them. She waited for him to say more, but he did not, and it worried her. They had lost another home, a place that had belonged to dragons for generations, a place of history and of secrets. And Lucius had little to say about its destruction. "Perhaps we can rebuild it one day?"

Lucius shook his head slowly. "It's gone, Adara. Another home, destroyed. Caracalla has taken it as well." He craned his neck to look at her. "We'll never go back there."

The night passed without incident, and though Adara and the children slept uneasily, they did rest. All the while, Lucius kept the fire burning, his gladius gripped in his hand as he watched the darkness surrounding them, his mind churning over the horrors that had befallen them.

He had not had the chance to think fully on the destruction of the Metellus villa until then, or to register the horrors that Numa and Prisca had undergone at the hands of Caracalla's henchmen.

I'll make him pay...I'll make him pay... he repeated to himself through the long night as his family slept.

He knew that he had to find Caracalla to do so, however, and he needed a plan. But, the more he thought of it, the closer Rome got, the realization that he had no plan became more ridiculous. He could not afford to be reckless, not while his family was with him. *I've failed them enough for a lifetime.*

Lucius thought of any friends he might have left in Rome, any he could call on for help. But who would help him to get close to the emperor? Who would risk their lives to consort with an enemy of the state, even if that enemy were presumed dead long ago?

Lucius thought that he could perhaps approach Senator Dio, but he knew that would be impossible. Caracalla was likely keeping such men under close watch. He thought then of Numonius. He had, after all, helped Lucius in the past. *But what good can an offering seller do when it comes to this?* He shook his head to himself. *No. Numonius already risked too much in the past. I can't ruin another life.*

By the end of the night, as the sun began to colour the sky with faint breath, and as Lucius stared at his wife and children sleeping side by side before the fire, he began to feel panic. He knew, almost with absolute certainty, that only death awaited him before the gates of Rome. He had six days of travel to figure something out.

.   .   .

Travelling through Italy felt strange to Lucius. Under other circumstances, he would have felt a kinship, a familiarity with the land along
the road to Rome. He had journeyed that road many times in his life after
all, but now, as the line of the Apennines passed on their left, and the
broad, fertile plains, forests, and hills of that land rolled along on the
right like some unending, softly shaded fresco kissed by sunlight, he
realized that it was not familiar at all anymore. Where once he would
have smelled rich soil, crisp air and the occasional tang of olive presses,
he only caught the scent of burning and death. Where once he had been
Lucius Metellus Anguis, the carrier of a family name that meant something in Italy, he was now Lucius Pen Dragon, an unknown refugee in
his own land.

How has it come to this? He thought, realizing the absurdity of his
own question. He knew the answer, of course, and he longed to put an
end to things so that he and his family might get on with some
semblance of a life. *I owe them that much, at least, for all the pain I've
caused them.*

The question was, where would that hoped-for life be? What would it
look like glimpsed through the floating ash of two homes destroyed by
Rome?

From the outskirts of Arretium, it took them two days to get to
Clusium, the walled city that rested upon a hill overlooking the Clanis
river, one of the tributaries of the Tiber, and the large lake nearby. They
did not dare to enter the city, but kept to themselves as they travelled,
only stopping at the occasional villa estate to buy food before continuing
on their way.

From Clusium, it was another day and half to the Etruscan town of
Volsinii. As they neared the settlement, they passed the ancient tombs
resting in the shadow of rocky outcrops, the names of their long-departed
occupants inscribed upon the lintels of their dark doors.

Lucius could tell that Adara and the children would have liked to
stay the night in one of the inns of Volsinii, but he could not bring
himself to lead them within the city walls. After resupplying at a farm,
their wagon carried on down the via Cassia, skirting the forested banks
of the immense lake outside the city.

With Volsinii behind them, Lucius remembered a story he had heard
long ago about the settlement.

"I remember learning something about that town," he said, glancing over his shoulder at the walls and tombs fading into the distance.

"What story, Baba?" Calliope said, climbing onto the bench beside him to rest against his shoulder. As the days passed, she had grown more talkative, her resilience helping her to put the trauma of what had happened at the villa behind her.

"Volsinii was once a rich, Etruscan town. But somehow, they angered the Gods."

"How so?"

"I don't know exactly. But I do know that the God Mars was so angry with them, that he loosed a bolt of lightning at the city and it burned up completely. They had to rebuild, and that is the city you see now."

Calliope was silent as she looked thoughtfully at the lake water passing by. "Did we anger Mars too, Baba?"

Lucius felt his heart tighten, shook his head and gripped his daughter's hand. "No, my girl. We did not. Mars is our friend." Lucius pictured the god he had often misunderstood in the past, standing before him in the field only days before. He could hear his deep, resonant voice trying to guide him to another path.

But Lucius' mind was already set, and now he travelled with his family toward the city of Mars' own people. *I am no longer one of them,* he thought.

"Baba?" Calliope said. "Are you all right?"

Lucius cleared his dry throat. "Yes. I'm fine, my girl."

"Calliope, please sit with your brother in the back," Adara said behind them. "I'd like to speak with your father."

Calliope turned and climbed into the back to settle in the hay beside her brother while Adara climbed onto the bench in her place.

"Not a very good story," Adara said.

"No," Lucius answered. "I'm sorry. I didn't think."

"I hope you're not thinking of taking us into Rome," Adara said abruptly. She had been worrying over Lucius' plan for days by then, ever since they had left Arretium.

"I had thought about going into the city." He could not look at her.

"Are you mad?" she asked. "Would you put our lives in danger again? Rome is a wolf's den, and we would be torn to shreds. Someone is bound to recognize us."

"You don't know that, Adara. Look at me." He pointed at his face and held out his arms. "Who would recognize this?"

"What about the children? What about me? Would you have us burned beyond recognition too?"

Lucius turned on her, horrified.

Adara shut her eyes. "I'm sorry... I'm just scared, Lucius. Until we're out of Italy, we're not safe. What would you want to go back to Rome for anyway? The old domus was sold years ago, and anyone who was a friend thinks you're dead, or would be too afraid to help us if you revealed yourself."

"I don't know, Adara...I just..."

"What, Lucius? You can't do this to us. The children have suffered enough, haven't they? We can't avoid remote inns along the road, and then go traipsing into the city to stare Death in the face."

What if I *am Death?* Lucius thought, but did not dare speak it. He could not tell her he did indeed want to enter the city, to get inside the imperial palace if he could...to finish things once and for all.

"I see this look in your eyes, my love," Adara continued, her hand upon his arm, "and it terrifies me."

Lucius stared down the road that stretched into the distance ahead of them. He knew that Adara and the children were exhausted and uncomfortable, and that they could all use a good night sleep beneath a proper roof. They had endured much, he was well-aware. He also knew that Adara was right about Rome. *But how can we come so close and not enter? I could finally end this!*

"It's three more days to Rome," Lucius said, avoiding the other conversation. "We can find an inn tomorrow night."

Adara took her hand from his arm and sighed. "That is something, at least," she said.

The following day, as Rome loomed in the distance, they stopped for the night at an inn called The Raven. The yard before it was nearly empty, but for a few merchants' carts and one other family, all of whom were travelling to Rome and the markets there.

The innkeeper - a man named Horatius - was an older veteran with scars criss-crossing his arms and a paunch that he had developed later in life. He had been running the inn for twenty years along with his wife, two grown sons, and their families. The fields behind the inn also belonged to Horatius and provided additional income.

When Lucius entered, to ask about a room for his family for the night, Horatius and his wife looked warily upon him.

"You're not a leper, are you?" the veteran asked bluntly.

Lucius felt like shouting at the man, but breathed calmly before answering. "No, sir. I was burned by fire in a smelting accident."

The man seemed unconvinced until Adara stepped forward with the children. "My husband suffers from his accident. We are travelling to the sanctuary of Asclepius in Graecia for his healing. We're on our way to Rome and then to Brundisium to get a ship."

Horatius nodded slowly, his eyes taking them all in, including the weapons they carried.

"What are those for?" he asked, nodding at the gladii.

"It is a long, dangerous road," Lucius said, his eyes locking on the other man's from beneath his cowl.

"Where you from?"

"Gaul," Lucius said.

After an awkward moment of silence, the innkeeper nodded. "You can have the large room upstairs. That'll be four semis, and it includes the evening meal. Add an as for us to take care of your mule."

Lucius fished in the pouch that hung at his waist and took out a dupondius. "I'll give you this for all of that, a meal in the morning, and some supplies for the road."

Horatius' features softened almost to the point of smiling. "Far be it for me to refuse a man and his family upon the road." He pat Lucius' shoulder. "Sorry for assuming you were a leper."

"It happens," Lucius said, resting his hand upon his gladius beneath his cloak. "We'll just get settled then."

The innkeeper and his wife watched as Lucius, Adara and the silent children walked out to get the rest of their things from the wagon.

"They don't sound Gaulish," the wife said.

"What do you know, woman? So long as their money's good. That's all I care about."

. . .

The room was simple but clean. The floor boards were thick and sturdy with no cracks to reveal the tavern beneath, and the ceiling was solid with inset, plastered beams that had been recently painted.

Once they were settled in their room, Lucius, Adara and the children made their way downstairs for the promised warm meal and were shown to a table in a corner by one of the front-facing windows that looked onto the twilit courtyard outside.

Shortly after they sat down, jugs of water and wine were brought to them, along with four clay cups. Then, four plates of beans and boiled greens, roast boar and fresh bread were set before them.

In a second, Phoebus and Calliope were eating away as if they had been starving for days.

Lucius and Adara watched their children for a minute before tucking into the food themselves to savour the flavours.

"We've been eating dried meat and cheese for so long, I feel like I've forgotten the taste of hot food," Phoebus said through a mouthful.

Calliope elbowed him for his manners and they giggled together.

Lucius marvelled at his children, able to laugh and joke, even after so much hardship and horror.

"Everything to your liking?" Horatius asked after they had been eating for a few minutes. "Caught that boar myself this morning."

"It's delicious," Adara said, smiling. "Thank you."

"It's no trouble, lady. And again, I'm sorry for my harsh greeting when you arrived." He looked at Lucius who sat up straight, and pulled a chair from the table beside. "It's been strange days the last year and a half."

Lucius could see that the man was a talker and, from his own experience, the owners of roadside taverns were often ready with gossip. "Strange how?" Lucius asked.

The man leaned in. "Everybody's so jittery and worried. I've noticed that the folk who stop here are either too scared to interact with others, or are secretive and hiding something."

Lucius smiled. "Well, it's not easy to hide this now, is it?" he pointed to his own face.

"Ah! You're a good man, I can tell!" Horatius said, patting Lucius on the shoulder. "Not everyone is though."

"What are people worried about?" Adara asked.

"Well, no doubt you've heard the rumours about the emperor and his brother, and all that happened there?" He was whispering now, checking over his shoulder at the rest of the room. When he looked back, his face was serious. "Terrible thing that happened, but emperors is never perfect, is they?"

"I suppose not," Lucius said evenly. "We did hear something about it."

"Madness. Folks say he was so fed up with talk behind his back in Rome that the emperor went campaigning in Germania again. Germania!"

"Is he still there?" Lucius asked, leaning in.

"In Germania? No. Actually, he passed through here with his Praetorians not a few weeks ago. I heard that he wanted to come back to Rome early for winter quarters, but also to take care of some enemies, if you know what I mean?"

"Enemies?" Lucius asked.

"Folks that was talking against him while he was away with the troops. Long proscription lists…"

"I see." Lucius took a sip of his wine to clear his dry throat. He could see that the children had stopped eating, that they looked afraid. "And is the emperor still in Rome?"

"Why? You want to meet him?" Horatius laughed and slapped Lucius' back.

"No, no. I just wondered if there might be some games we can go to. Maybe something in the Circus Maximus."

"I don't know about that," Horatius said. "But one traveller who came through here two days ago said the emperor was going back to Germania early, that he preferred living with the troops than with the palace vipers."

"He's not in Rome now?" Lucius asked, a bit too vehemently.

Horatius sat back. "I don't know if he's still there. Likely not from what that traveller told me." He stood and put the chair back at the neighbouring table. "I'll give Caracalla one thing in that he prefers the company of soldiers. An emperor who bows to Mars is better than one who bows to Bacchus!" He winked. "Although, I prefer the latter to visit my establishment!" he laughed. "I'll get you some more wine."

When Horatius was gone, Lucius and Adara looked at each other.

She wanted to ask what he was thinking, but more people came into the tavern at that moment.

"Is everything all right, Baba?" Phoebus asked.

Lucius could see that the talk of Caracalla was worrying them. "Everything is fine. Nothing to worry about." *Gods!* he thought. *Please make Caracalla still be in Rome!*

The next morning, the wagon was once again rolling down the via Cassia toward Rome.

Horatius had given them plenty of provisions for the journey, and fresh hay for the back of the wagon, but the entire time he blathered on to them, all Lucius could think about was finding out whether or not Caracalla was still in Rome.

The miles passed by as they drove on, and as Adara watched her husband, a deep-set fear invaded her. Lucius seemed obsessed with Caracalla and his whereabouts.

At every chance he had, whenever it seemed safe enough, Lucius would now try to strike up a conversation with fellow travellers or farmers, trying to ascertain the emperor's whereabouts, to discover if he was still in Rome.

Every time, the answer was the same: the emperor and his Praetorians had left Rome for Germania once again.

There was a lightness in the people's voices when they spoke about it, as if Italy had become safer once more with Caracalla gone, though they would never have said as much. The crucified bodies that began to appear along the roadside made sure of that.

"Why are we here, Baba?" Calliope asked, hiding her face from the gaping mouths and crow-pecked eyes of Caracalla's victims lining the road.

"We need to by-pass Rome on the way to Brundisium," Lucius answered.

"Phoebus...Calliope..." Adara said, looking around at the more crowded road and the bodies of the punished that so mesmerized her children. "Put your cloaks on and cover your faces. Lie down in the back of the wagon as if you are asleep."

"Why, Mama?" Phoebus asked.

"Just do it, Phoebus!" Adara snapped.

Both children nodded and lay down, but while Calliope hid her eyes,

Phoebus gazed up from beneath the fold of his cloak's hood at the passing corpses set against the blue sky.

Adara sat beside Lucius. "What are you doing? How can you bring us here, and make them look at all of this?"

Lucius turned to her as he flicked the reigns and the mule trotted more quickly. "We have no choice. We need to go around Rome to get to Brundisium."

"By the Gods, Lucius, if you take us into the city, if you risk the lives of our children any more, I'll never forgive you."

Lucius turned to look at his wife and there he saw her emerald green eyes ablaze with worry and rage. Despite that, and the words she spoke, he merely set his jaw and rolled on.

Soon enough, the walls of Rome came into view.

Lucius and Adara paused their silent argument as the wagon rolled past groups of travellers coming and going from the city.

After the world of Britannia, Rome's walls appeared larger and more menacing than ever, stretching out to either side of their view. It appeared impregnable and dangerous, yet majestic and inviting.

Lucius pulled the wagon onto the side of the road beneath one of the towering cypress trees on a knoll where the city was more visible. He looked at the mausoleum of Hadrian along the river, spotted the dome of the Pantheon, the mass of the Colosseum, and the hills of the city of his birth with the Palatine in their midst.

"It's all right," Adara whispered to Phoebus and Calliope in the back of the wagon while Lucius stared ahead. "We're just stopping for a moment."

Lucius gazed at the city, the way the evening light highlighted it from the West, the flights of birds soaring over it, how pockets of smoke hovered over the walls and monuments like colonies of soft clouds.

He had wondered how he would feel coming back to Rome, seeing it again after so many years. It was terrifying and attractive at once, and he, like so many was drawn to it as a moth is inevitably drawn to a bright and dangerous flame.

"Caracalla's not there," Lucius said to himself, but Adara heard him.

"Thank the Gods for it, Lucius. Your father watches over us." She placed her hand upon his arm and sighed. She had not thought of what it would be like for him to come back. "Are you all right?"

He shook his head. "No."

Adara felt that he wanted to go into the city, but she also knew that it would be the end of them if they did, felt the truth of it in her gut and bones. "Please, Lucius. Think of your family, our children. Let's go around and press on to Brundisium."

"It will be dark by the time we reach the southern side of the city and the via Appia."

"Then let's do that and find an inn there," she pleaded. "Just don't take us into the city."

Lucius did not answer, but continued to stare as the traffic passed their wagon at the roadside. *What if he is there?* he wondered. *I could end this once and for all!*

Lucius was about to flick the reins of the mule, to press on directly for the gates of the city, no matter how much his wife pleaded, nor how precious the cargo they carried, but in the moment he raised his hands defiantly to do so, a light on the Palatine hill stood out in his field of vision, like a beacon or warning light, and Lucius knew that it was his father's house, the temple of Apollo.

Do not proceed to the city! the warning came in Lucius' mind. *Go around, Lucius...my son. Do not enter Rome!*

Lucius paused and looked at his hands clutching the reins before lowering them slowly. He turned to Adara and saw the pleading in her eyes, and turned to see his children looking up at him from where they were hidden in the hay in the wagon bed behind him. He nodded acquiescently, and without saying a word, flicked the reins to cross the road to join one of the minor ones that circled the city.

"We should be able to find an inn by nightfall," he said.

Adara exhaled and gripped his hand. "Thank you."

But Lucius said nothing.

It took them a long time to circumvent the walls of Rome, keeping a safe distance from the gates as they drove the wagon on, but no one bothered them as they went. There was always traffic from travellers and farmers around Rome, like colony ants around a hive.

They passed the eastern side of the city, crossing the via Placina and others as they travelled quietly in the dusk behind the silent masses of the Quirinal and Viminal hills.

When the dark mass of the castra Praetoria came into view, set into the walls on the eastern side, Lucius grew silent, unable to take his eyes from it.

The fortress built by the Praetorian prefect, Lucius Aelius Sejanus, during the reign of Tiberius, represented much of the pain and suffering that his family had endured ever since the time of Gaius Fulvius Plautianus.

Lucius wondered how often plots against his own family had been discussed within those solid, high walls and battlements. He thought also of Argus and wondered in vain what had happened to him within the Praetorian camp that had encouraged such deep hate. It all seemed like another lifetime, and yet, the threat that emanated from the fortress, from Rome itself, seemed all too real and present.

Eventually, the castra Praetoria faded from view and they passed around the back of the Esquiline hill, and then the palaces and gardens of the Sessorium.

By the time they reached the via Appia it was dark, and the shadows cast by the monuments, umbrella pines and cypress trees in the occasional torchlight of a passer-by were like claws reaching out to the cart as they went.

Soon, they found an inn and stopped for the night.

It was with great relief that Adara and the children stepped down out of the wagon to speak with a kindly innkeeper who emerged from the main building to greet them.

While Adara spoke with the man about lodgings for the night, Lucius stepped onto the thick cobblestones of the road to look back at the walls of Rome where the city glowed like a fire in the night.

He felt a hollowing in his chest as he looked upon it. He had asked others where the emperor was as they drove around the city and, yet again, the answer had been the same.

The emperor had gone back to Germania.

People had smiled as they said so. It was only Lucius who did not.

As he turned back to go into the inn with his family, Lucius felt like he might have understood how Hannibal felt after years of war with Rome, to finally fight his way within reach of her mighty walls, to finally have the chance to take his vengeance for all the pain Rome had caused him, and yet to have to turn his back on it at the last moment.

It was as if, in the matter of a few moments, victory had been turned to defeat, and such a feeling only served to enflame Lucius' anger even more.

They had to press on...he had to press on...down a road that, in Lucius' mind, ran with a crimson current about his feet. He did not even acknowledge the innkeeper as he handed over the coins for their stay and supplies, did not even speak to his family as they ate the hot food that night before sleeping.

All Lucius could see was the road ahead to Brundisium, the ship he hoped would still be at anchor in the port there, and the continuation of his family's journey tempered with the hope that he would find his mother, brother and sister safe in Athenae. It was difficult to fathom what lay ahead, however, especially when the road behind them was riddled with ash and death and a past that was utterly lost to them.

XII

ODYSSEA

'An Odyssey'

I t felt good to be at sea once again, to feel the wind and to taste the salt spray as the Europa cut across sun-sparkling Ionian waters toward the coast of Graecia.

For Lucius, there was a lingering sense of loss as he left Italy behind. That feeling had accompanied him as they travelled south along the via Appia from Rome, transited the Alban hills, and then crossed the Pontine marshes on the way to Capua. The weather had been fair for the entire journey across the broad-skied landscape of southern Italy, from Beneventum to Tarentum, amidst sweeping hills covered in olive groves. A part of him doubted if he would ever return to Italy, though he kept this sentiment to himself.

The only time he had paused was when they passed the tomb of Caecilia Metella along the road. In his youth, he had thought the woman, Sulla's wife, had been his ancestor. He had even defended her name with his fists. He now knew, as he looked upon the white tower that commemorated her, that she was of no relation. His ties to that land were thin, his ancestry on his true father's side something beyond borders, something far-reaching like the light of the sun itself.

While the wagon rolled quickly on, it was as if the mounting miles between Lucius and Rome were cutting away at an abscess. By the time the hazy skyline of Brundisium came into view, set against the backdrop of the sea, he was thinking more clearly, more determinedly than ever to see his plans through.

As the two titanic columns that marked the end of the via Appia came into view, Lucius, Adara and the children drove the wagon straight for the inner harbour to search for the Europa. They were questioned upon entering, but it helped to have known the name of the ship and to adhere to the story that Lucius was seeking healing at the sanctuary of Epidaurus in Graecia.

They panicked when the Europa was not at berth in the inner harbour, but pressed on to the outer harbour, relieved to see her floating at anchor, low in the water, waiting to set sail with the other two ships of Creticus' fleet.

Castor, who had been sitting in the nest atop the main mast, happened to see the wagon coming toward the ship, and called down to his father that the Pen Dragons had arrived.

"It sure is a relief to see all of you!" Creticus said as Lucius approached him. The sea breeze rustled the branches of a wavering palm nearby as if the winds were picking up in that moment, ready to set them on their journey. "We were going to leave soon!" Creticus grasped Lucius' forearm. "I'm glad we didn't."

"You have no idea how relieved we are to see you, Captain," Adara said, smiling as she held Calliope's hand, with Phoebus standing quietly beside them.

"You must be exhausted after such a long journey," Nerissa said. "Come. Your cabin is ready for you."

Creticus turned to his sons who were smiling down from the deck. "Castor...Pollux... Come help with their belongings!"

The boys set to and helped Lucius empty the wagon.

It had been that moment when he looked closely at the back of the wagon that Lucius later remembered with great sadness as he stood at the prow of the ship upon that blue sea: the extra pouch of coin that he knew he had given to Prisca should not have been there. *Why, Prisca?* he wondered as he stood in the sunshine at the back of the wagon. But he knew the answer. When he showed the pouch to Adara, she too knew what had happened, and in the quieting light of dusk as the ship cut across the waves toward Graecia, she wept for the kind woman.

When Lucius, Adara, Phoebus and Calliope had come aboard the Europa, it was obvious to Creticus and Nerissa that something grave had happened to them. The captain and his wife did not want to pry, and so they let them get settled within their cabin to sleep and, they suspected, to feel safe once again.

Creticus watched Lucius standing at the prow of the Europa, alone. After a day or so, he approached him with two cups of wine and handed one to Lucius.

"To the Gods," Creticus said, tipping some of the wine into the sea.

Lucius followed suit, and they drank together.

"Is your family all right, Lucius? Nerissa heard your wife and daughter weeping, and your son has said little of anything since you boarded. What happened on your journey?"

Lucius sipped his wine and stared out at the gentle rise and fall of the deep blue waves, the hazy coastline in the distance. "We... When we arrived at our home, we found it destroyed. Completely."

"I'm so sorry, my friend," Creticus said.

Lucius could see that the captain meant it. "We were attacked by...by brigands while we were there, and an old friend was killed."

"Gods. That is no homecoming."

"No. Worse still, my son was forced to kill a man, one of the attackers."

"By the Gods, Lucius. No wonder he's silent. To have to kill a man?"

"I know. He saved his sister's life. My children have lived a lifetime before reaching adulthood, Captain. It isn't right."

Creticus could see the deep regret in Lucius' eyes as he looked out at the sea. He had more questions, of course, but he dared not ask. He stood beside Lucius at the rail and looked out to sea with him. "You know... they say a sea journey is cleansing in a way. To travel the waves of Neptune's deep, to see the sun rise and fall and feel the wind and spray upon one's face is a way to leave things behind. Maybe that's why, deep down, I love it so much. You can feel like a new man with every journey. Italy is behind you now, as is Britannia... You can only go forward."

Lucius nodded, said nothing. It was an idealist's view, what Creticus said. He wished he could believe it, but as he watched the water from the prow of that ship, he knew that it was not so simple. He was not ready to leave the past behind, for there was too much unfinished business.

"Of course," Creticus continued, "a man has to have the desire to move on and forget and forgive the past. Remember Odysseus. He too was a wanderer with hardship, but he eventually found his home."

Lucius smiled sadly and looked at him. "You're a philosopher, Captain."

Creticus chuckled and finished his wine. "Every Greek is a philosopher. We can't help it!" He looked at the water ahead, the sun, the coast, and seemed to breathe it all in with a deep inhalation. "We have at least six more days until we reach Piraeus and Athenae. You can be calm,

Lucius Pen Dragon. See to your family and let the journey ease your troubled minds." He laid his hand upon Lucius' shoulder. "You are among friends here. I promise."

"Thank you," Lucius said, draining his cup and handing it back to him.

As Creticus left, Lucius turned his gaze to the long coast of the island of Corcyra as it passed slowly by. The treed cliffs and turquoise coves beneath looked inviting, like a place that one could get lost in. The captain said a sea journey was a way of moving forward, of forgetting, but Lucius knew that he had travelled this route years before. "I've come full circle now…"

"It feels like that, doesn't it?" Adara said, appearing at his side.

Lucius turned to his wife.

"Phoebus and Calliope are sleeping," she said. "I'm so relieved."

The truth was that both children had been having nightmares since Etruria, and so had avoided sleeping as much as possible in the hopes of not recalling the terrible visions that seemed to be returning over and over again.

"I'm worried about them, Lucius," Adara said. "How can their young minds hope to decipher all that they've seen and felt already in their lives? Did you at their age? I know I didn't." Adara looked at the water, and spotted a dolphin charging ahead of the ship, playing in the sun-glinting waves.

"At their age I was learning from Diodorus, swinging a wooden sword on the banks of the Tiber, and running around the forum with Argus."

"And I was dancing in the olive groves around my parents' home with my sisters, watching the performances of the Panathenaea in the theatre of Dionysus, and riding my horse, Phoenix. The taste of Hymettos honey and orange was always on my lips."

Lucius felt an acute sense of failure then. When he had met Adara, when they were married in Rome during the Ludi Apollinaris, he had had such dreams of the future he wanted for them, and the children they would one day have. *Such dreams!* It was a deep hurt that the reality of their life looked nothing like what either of them had imagined.

It would be easy to put the blame solely on others, Lucius thought as he saw the sparkling sunlight reflected in Adara's green eyes as they looked longingly at the water. *But, in the end, I was the one who made the choices that led us to this. I have to make it better.*

Then Adara smiled at a memory, though her lips were touched by a stream of tears.

"I'm sorry, my love," Lucius said. "I know this isn't at all what you imagined our life would be together."

"I'm not thinking about that," she answered. "I was thinking of the last time I was in Athenae. Alene was with me. I had been missing you so much, wishing you were with me to see everything I was showing her." She wiped her cheek. "She loved it, the light and colour, the smell of orange and jasmine and wild thyme that tinged the air. She loved the agora too! She and I were closer than I ever was with my own sisters. I remember thinking that if only you were with us, everything would have been perfect."

"I wish I had been with you too. To see Athenae with you and Alene. My only time there was when I first joined the legions." Lucius remembered visiting the Roman agora and the brothels with his old friends, with Alerio and Argus, Antanelis, Maren, Eligius and Garai. *Different times then. And we were different men,* Lucius thought. *The world ruined and corrupted us all.* Lucius realized then that he was the last one alive of that original group of friends. *And most of them met their end because of me...*

"Will you let me show you Athenae now, Lucius?" Adara asked, scattering Lucius' dark thoughts. "This is something we can share with our children at last. Something familiar, and safe."

"I would like that," Lucius said, but in his heart, he knew that no sea journey would cleanse him of the thoughts that tortured him. He did hope, however, that it would perhaps help to heal his children.

Adara looped her arm through his, and together they watched the sun fall to the west, over the water, both thinking of the way ahead, both trying desperately not to dwell too much on the past.

The next day, Phoebus and Calliope were out on the deck of the Europa. They had slept better the previous night, as if the sea were washing away their worries, the lull of the waves and the cry of gulls helping them to forget the horrors of weeks' past.

They were passing between two islands then, the shore so close they could see the pebbles upon the beach of the smaller island to the port side.

"What islands are these, Castor?" Calliope asked one of Creticus' sons as he passed.

"On the starboard side, the larger island is Cephallenia, and the smaller one here is Ithaca."

"Ithaca?" Phoebus said excitedly.

"Yes!" Castor replied. "Home of Odysseus!"

Phoebus and Calliope stood and went to the railing to watch the island pass by.

"It's small, isn't it?" Lucius said as he came up behind them.

Calliope turned and hugged him, squeezing so very tightly that he thought she might burst into tears. Her eyes were dry however, as they looked up at him.

"Is everything all right?"

"I just needed to do that, Baba," she said, smiling a little before going back to the railing with her brother.

Lucius stood with them, watching the coastline of the small, but legendary island pass by, its rocky shore caressed by clear, turquoise water, and the rugged slopes that led upward to the blue sky above.

Phoebus turned to his father quickly, his eyes wide. "Can we stop there and explore, Baba? I want to see it. I want to see Odysseus' home!"

The corbita bobbed up and down on the waves, and Lucius gripped the railing to steady himself. Normally, it would have been a smooth passage between the two islands, but at that late date in the year, it was starting to get choppy. Lucius turned to see Adara coming toward them. "Phoebus would like to stop and see the island."

Adara smiled at her son but shook her head. "I'm sorry, Phoebus. I just asked Captain Creticus if we could stop, but he says that we need to make up some time. If we don't get around cape Malea soon, it could be very dangerous." It broke her heart to see the sad, longing and disappointed look in her son's eyes, but she knew that Creticus was quite serious. "Perhaps on our return journey we can see it?"

"If we have a return journey, you mean," Phoebus said, quietly turning back to watch the island.

Lucius thought of Odysseus and his great journey and his twenty years away from his home and family. *I have my family with me, and yet I feel like I will be wandering eternally.* It was a strange and frustrating thought. *At least Odysseus had a home to come back to.* "I passed this way before," Lucius said to his children.

"You did?" Phoebus asked.

"Yes. When I first joined the army. I was in III Parthica legion and we came to Graecia to recruit more men. I wanted to stop then too, but wasn't allowed."

Phoebus looked annoyed, but Lucius pressed on. "You've read *The Odyssey*, Phoebus. What do you think it is about?" Lucius could remember Diodorus asking him the same question in his youth, and how difficult it was to pick out one thing that it was about.

Phoebus shrugged. "About how a man should respect the Gods."

"What else?"

"It is about life."

"How so?" Lucius countered. He could see Adara smiling at him as she held Calliope and watched the shoreline before them.

"How difficult it can be."

"And?"

"I don't know, Baba!" Phoebus said, frustrated. "I just wanted to see the place. I don't have a Diodorus to teach me these things, do I?"

"I'm sorry, Phoebus. You don't, you're right." *And I've not filled that role for you at all,* he thought sadly. "Your answers are not wrong, Phoebus. Life is difficult. Odysseus had many trials after the war at Troy. He was prevented from coming home because of his hubris. For so long he was a wanderer, but despite the hardships he experienced, he eventually did come home, back to Ithaca."

"But he needed revenge upon the suitors before he could be happy at home with his wife and son," Phoebus said, turning to Lucius and staring him straight in the eyes.

The look made Lucius cold, for in it there seemed to be an awareness, an unspoken understanding of the darkness Lucius was trying to shield his family from.

"The story is about not losing hope, Baba," Calliope said, as the wind twirled her hair about her face. "No matter how hard things get, we mustn't lose hope."

"That's right, my girl," Lucius said, surprised.

"Mama used to tell me the story too," she said turning back to watch the southern end of the island pass. "Odysseus had Athena watching over him, but we have Apollo, don't we?"

"Yes, my girl," Adara said.

"All will be well then," Calliope added, absently, a note of positivity in her voice that humbled Lucius.

Phoebus did not seem convinced though, and Lucius could tell that his thoughts leaned darker, just as his own did. "Maybe we still have something of a journey ahead of us, Phoebus, before we can set foot upon Ithaca?"

"Maybe," Phoebus muttered, pulling away from Lucius and making his way to the Europa's stern to watch Ithaca fade away behind them.

Over the next days, the Europa and Creticus' other ships plied their way along the western coast of Graecia, past the mouth of the Alpheus river that led to Olympia, and then along the rock and sand shores of Messenia. Once they passed Pylos, the sea grew worse, and as they journeyed on toward the southern tip of Laconia, it was as if Scylla and Charybdis awaited them.

The ships rose and fell upon the waves and the clouds darkened, though no rain yet fell to soak the decks of Creticus' small fleet.

Before attempting the passage between cape Malea and the island of Cythera, they made offerings to Aphrodite, who was said to have emerged from the sea foam on the shores of that island which belonged to her for ages.

As they stood around the bronze tripod that was fastened to the deck of the Europa, perfumed incense rising from the bowl, Lucius, Adara and the children each dropped garlands of flowers upon the foamy waves that lapped against the corbita's hull as it rose and fell at the goddess' feet.

Oh divine Goddess, Adara prayed. *Guard us on our journey. Bring us safely to my parents' home. Let them be well, and may our own family remain strong in the face of the trials to come.*

As the pink and white flowers rose and fell upon the sea swells, Adara clasped Lucius' hand, and he took Calliope's, and she Phoebus' so that they formed a garland such as the one they had offered the goddess.

It was then that the clouds broke and sunlight streamed down to light the deep.

"The goddess speaks!" Creticus called from the tripod up to his sons where they balanced upon the cross beam of the mast. "Unfurl the sail!"

The dolphin sail fell downward with a rush and the ship lurched forward toward the straight between the island and the cape.

The Europa pulled ahead quickly, as if time were against it, as if the goddess urged it on to safety.

"Lucius!" Creticus called from the helm. "Get them inside the cabin! It's going to get rough!"

Lucius nodded and the four of them went back to their cabin.

From inside the cabin, they could see the crew holding fast to the rigging and railings as the sky came in and out of view with the rise and fall of the ship. Water splashed over the sides and they could hear a howling on the wind.

"The goddess will look after us," Adara reassured the children, holding them to her.

Up and down the ship went, driving onward through the waves and wind and sea spray that covered everything and reached their nostrils inside the cabin. It had begun so quickly that they had not really known what happened, for the opening the goddess had given them was short and treacherous.

But Creticus was as skilled a seaman as any, and as quickly as it had begun, it ended and they were safely through the straight, making their way north toward the Argolid peninsula and the pine-scented island of Pityussa where they would check the ships and resupply before crossing the Saronic gulf for Piraeus, the port of Athenae.

As they crossed the blue depths, bald and rocky headlands jutting out of the hazy distance, Lucius remembered that the gulf was surrounded by several entrances to the Underworld. The thought gave him pause, for he would not yet step through those dread thresholds, not with his family.

Apollo, I know that some day, I may have to for all that I have done and will do, but let it not be yet. Let me finish my own odyssey.

Lucius could not see his father then, nor hear the shuddering of his breath as his son spoke of the Underworld, the place from which few heroes returned.

My son... Apollo said as he gazed down from the slopes of distant Parnassus, *you must be strong. It is only beginning.*

It was early in the morning two days later that the broad port of Piraeus came into view beneath a cloudy sky that heralded the coming of colder days. The sun in that land, however, somehow refused to be muted, and as Creticus' ships bobbed up and down on the swells, waiting for their turn to press on into the commercial harbour, the shadows drew back to reveal the mountainous land around the bowl of distant Athenae.

The ancient, long walls of Themistocles still stretched out from the port to that bright and shining polis, a little battered and less imposing, but their line could still be seen.

"There she is! The city of Athena! Go and see!" Creticus said to Lucius and his family, inviting them to go to the prow of the ship while he took the helm. "Go and see for yourself!"

Lucius, Adara, Phoebus and Calliope walked to the prow and watched as the ships moved slowly toward the sprawling, commercial harbour and the city only just about six miles beyond.

"Mama, what is that shining in the distance?" Calliope asked, pointing.

Adara smiled and felt herself feeling lighter as she saw it, her hand upon her daughter's shoulder. "That is the statue of Athena upon the Acropolis of the city. You can see it from any direction. It is a beacon to draw us home."

"I feel it calling to us," Phoebus said. "Can we go and make offerings to the goddess? I feel like she asks it of us."

"Of course," Adara said, and in that moment, she began to feel as if she could breathe again. "I hadn't realized how much I missed my home."

Lucius' hand reached out to take hers. "We're here, my love." *You'll be safe here,* he thought as he looked around, remembering the last time he had been in Athenae. They had docked in the military harbour that time, when he arrived with his friends to begin recruiting for the newly-formed Parthica legions. It felt strange to be travelling as a civilian, but the anonymity was something of a comfort to him, for there would no longer be superiors barking his name at him for all the world to hear. He no longer had to prove anything as a soldier, as he did in those early, idealistic days, at least not to himself. *Now, I only have to see my family safe and carry out my own, private mission.*

The Europa began to steer toward a berth that would accommodate all three ships, but even so, Lucius marvelled at the skill with which Creticus and his crew manoeuvred the large corbita toward such a small space. The docks were crammed with countless ships of many sizes, with smaller vessels darting in and among them carrying crewmen to the shore where people moved like ants around a great mound. Some men carried unusually-large or heavy loads upon their backs, and others dodged in and out of the crowds to press on and get out of the port to make for the city beyond.

"It's so busy! Even more than Ostia!" Phoebus said.

Lucius could see that a part of his son was excited by the prospect of visiting Athenae, but that another part of him was reluctant to wade into such a large gathering. Phoebus' fingers fidgeted with the pommel of his gladius again. "It will be fine, Phoebus. Everybody here has their own business to attend to. And yes, it is busier than Ostia. The only port I've ever seen that is perhaps more so, is Alexandria."

Phoebus nodded, but said nothing.

Lucius looked to Adara and he could see that, beyond the hem of her cloak's hood, she was crying. "What is it?" he whispered to her.

She turned to him, her eyes utterly changed in the light of her home. "I've missed it so much. I've missed my family. I just can't believe we're here at last, after everything."

Lucius put his arm around her and pulled her close, the children standing in front of them. "I should have brought you here long ago."

Adara shook her head. "We're here now, Lucius. That is all that matters. That, and the safety of our families." She wiped her eyes and smiled. "I can't wait to show you everything," she said to Phoebus and Calliope.

"Can we go into the temple of Athena?" Phoebus asked again.

Adara nodded as he turned to look at her. "Yes, and the temple of Olympian Zeus, and of Hephaestus. We'll go shopping in the agora, just as I did with your matertera, Alene."

"She must have loved this place," Lucius said.

"She did. She had a smile upon her face everywhere we went. And even Ashur and Carissa enjoyed it for a time...that is...until we visited the temple of Apollo."

"Is that where-"

"Yes," Adara said quickly. "Things changed from that point on."

Lucius felt guilt for some reason when he thought of Ashur. It had been so long since they had seen each other. Not since Julia Domna had kept them in the villa along the Tiber before the fall of Plautianus. *So long ago...* Ashur and Carissa had gone off to live their own life together in a self-imposed exile. They had not written to Lucius since. *Maybe Emrys will have heard from them?* Lucius wondered, thinking of Carissa's former mentor, the Dumnonian sculptor whose work had once been the talk of Rome, and who now was Antonia Metella's partner.

The family stood together at the prow as Creticus' crew slung enormous ropes to the men on the jetty, and the rooftops of the customs buildings and warehouses rose up to block out the view of Athenae beyond. Soon, the Europa was tied off, lengthwise against the moorings, and the gangplanks were put in place, one for the passengers, two more for the cargo that was already being carried out of the hold. Some crew members called out to friends they recognized on the quayside. It became noisy all of a sudden, like when one approaches a hillside beehive after a silent walk in the wood.

Creticus and Nerissa waited until all three ships were safely moored, and then they came to see Lucius and his family. "Well, Pen Dragons? Welcome to Piraeus and Athenae!"

"Is everything all right, my dear?" Nerissa said to Adara, observing the longing look in her eyes.

Adara caught herself. "I'm fine." She cleared her throat, and turned the children to face their hosts. "We can't thank you enough for everything."

"It has been our pleasure!" Nerissa said, stepping up to hug her. "I hope we will see all of you again."

"That's right!" Creticus said. "Lord Einion wishes me to bring you all back to Britannia when you're finished with whatever it is you're doing!" He laughed. "We can't disappoint him!"

"No, we can't," Lucius said, smiling. "When we're ready to return to Britannia, Captain, how can we reach you?"

"I always winter in Piraeus, and leave my itinerary with the collegium of merchant captains here." He pointed to a narrow, two story building farther down the port, adorned with the image of a trident. "You can leave a message with them and they will get it to me."

"We can't thank you enough, Captain," Lucius said.

Beyond Creticus, Castor and Pollux arrived, sweaty and smiling from their labours on deck. They chatted briefly with Phoebus and Calliope while their parents spoke with Lucius and Adara.

"Where are you headed now?" Creticus asked.

"Into the city to visit with friends," Adara said.

"We just need to rent a mule and cart," Lucius added, his eyes scanning the quayside.

"There are plenty of places to rent or buy a mule and cart here," Creticus said, "but the most trustworthy one is Mucius. His place is located where Piraeus' walls meet the long walls to Athenae. Tell him you're my friends, and he'll give you a good deal."

"Again, thank you," Lucius said. "We won't forget your kindness, Captain. Nor yours, Nerissa."

"As my husband said, you are always welcome. If you need us, just leave a message and we'll take you where you need to go."

Lucius smiled at them and nodded. "I should go and get our things from the cabin. I'll be back. Phoebus, come help me."

Phoebus nodded and went with Lucius to the back of the ship to help gather their belongings.

As they went, Nerissa glanced the sword hanging beneath Adara's cloak. "Are you sure you will be all right?" There was worry in the seawoman's voice. "Your husband seems...well...more serious as he is about to set foot on shore."

"We'll be fine. We haven't seen our...friends...in many years. He's just nervous about it."

"I'm sure it will be fine," Nerissa said, hugging Adara. "Athenae is not Rome."

"No, it isn't," Adara said, feeling that great sense of relief once again that she had felt upon seeing Piraeus and the Acropolis of Athenae in the distance.

After another round of farewells, Lucius, Adara, Phoebus and Calliope plunged headlong into the crowded port to find the cart and mule business of Mucius. They felt a reticence in leaving Creticus and his family and crew behind, but also knew that it was necessary. The thought of seeing their family at last, that evening, drove them onward.

Unlike at Ostia, there were far fewer troops around the commercial port of Piraeus, and that gave Lucius some comfort as they pressed through the crowds. Cut-purses were the only real threat, but still, he knew he needed to stay vigilant. Praetorian spies could be anywhere at any time, gathering intelligence.

Lucius scanned the crowds of merchants, seamen, and students who had come from all corners of the empire to learn from some of the greatest minds. There was a buzz in the air, a feeling of hope that rose above the sense of oppression that had been prevalent in Italy. But Lucius knew that his second visit to Athenae would differ greatly from his first.

"I can't wait to see everyone!" Calliope said, feeling the excitement building.

"Me too!" Phoebus added, relaxing as they made their way out of the thickest part of the crowds.

"There it is!" Lucius said, pointing at the business of Mucius.

True enough, as Creticus had said, the muleteer and wagon seller named Mucius gave Lucius a very good deal on a four-wheeled cart and a sturdy, well-tempered mule.

"This is my best team," Mucius said to Lucius. "Any friend of Creticus is a friend of mine!"

"Thank you," Lucius said, dropping a denarius into the man's hand. "We'll take good care of both."

The man smiled and sent them on their way with a couple of goat cheese and honey pies that his wife had just finished making.

By midday, they had left the towering palms, tiled rooftops and temples of the port behind and were driving between the long walls toward the Piraean gate of Athenae.

The ride did not take long and would have been even faster if not for all the pedestrian traffic along the road. Lucius was surprised to find so many walking from Piraeus. Merchants mostly opted for wagons to take their wares to the city, but groups of young men deep in discussion went on foot, slowed by their own discourses.

There were few women around, and so Adara and Calliope kept their hoods up. There was no need to draw unwanted attention to themselves, but even so, Adara could not help but sit at the front of the wagon with her children behind her, gazing ahead at the city, and the shining temple of Athena Parthenos atop it.

"It's more beautiful than I had imagined," Phoebus said to Calliope.

"Mama said that it has been there for ages, and that there is an olive tree upon the Acropolis that Athena herself planted when she competed with Poseidon for the patronage of the city."

"It's still there?" Phoebus asked.

"That's correct, my son," Adara said, turning in her seat to look at them. "There is so much I want to show you. And wait until you taste the olives and honey from our farm! They're the best you will ever have!"

Phoebus felt his stomach rumble and rubbed it. "I am hungry! Do grandmother and grandfather have a good cook?"

Adara smiled. "I don't know if they do anymore, but your grandmother is an excellent cook herself. It's good you're hungry, because you won't be able to stop her feeding you!"

Lucius chuckled beside Adara on the driving bench as he flicked the reins. He found himself looking forward to seeing Adara's parents too. They had always gotten along well; Adara's father, Publius Leander Antoninus had always been understanding of Lucius. Lucius hoped that his father-in-law would have information about the emperor's plans for the near future. However, more than anything, Lucius looked forward to seeing that his mother, brother and sister were safe. *There are worse places to be exiled,* he thought as he looked around.

The air was fragrant and dry even though the autumn rains had already begun. Beyond the walls to either side of the road, and over the city walls directly ahead, one could see rocky outcrops and tiled roofs flanked by brilliant splashes of bougainvillea, jasmine, and night flowers. Palms bristled in the breeze alongside winking olive and sturdy orange trees. All around them the mountains rose up, like a natural fortress about the city of the goddess, with the pine-clad slopes of mount Hymettos where Adara's family lived, ahead and to their right.

Traffic began to slow as people and wagons came to the Piraean gate of the city. It was not as large and accommodating as the Dipylon gate to the North that led to the Kerameikos cemetery and the Panathenaic way that led all the way to Eleusis.

Lucius began to feel a slight panic as the crowds closed in, and men walked alongside their wagon, glancing into the back at his children and their belongings.

Phoebus felt it too and gathered their satchels close to him, even going so far as to reveal his sword.

"Don't draw it, Phoebus," Lucius warned. "Only if absolutely necessary." Lucius turned to Adara. "Do we need to go through the city to get the road to your family's villa?"

"No. We can avoid the Piraean gate if we take the small road that runs along the Ilissos river, past the shrines..." Adara remembered the place where she had spent time with Alene and Ashur, the gathering of shrines along the river below the massive temple of Olympian Zeus, where the ancient temples of Kronos and Rhea were located, as well as to Pan, the nymphs, and of course Artemis and Apollo. *Where Ashur broke with him...* She would never forget the look upon Lucius' friend's face as he came out of the Far-Shooter's temple. It had been a look of deep sadness, anger, and of total abandonment. "Here is the road, Lucius," she said suddenly, just as they crossed the bridge over the Ilissos. "Turn right here."

Lucius looked and the wagon forced its way to the right, causing a few of the pedestrians to shout behind them, waving their arms in their wake.

"Tourists!" someone shouted. "Idiota!"

Lucius heard Phoebus' blade slither as the wagon pulled away along the smaller road. He turned to see his son pointing the gladius at a group of young men who stared after them.

"Put that away, Phoebus!" Lucius shouted. "We don't need that kind of attention."

"But they were shouting at us, Baba!" Phoebus said, his voice angry and defensive.

"Phoebus, everyone shouts here. Don't worry about it. Don't draw your weapon unless absolutely necessary."

"Yes, Baba," the boy said, his sister patting him on the shoulder as the sound of the gurgling river reached their ears.

"Maybe we should stop at Apollo's temple and make an offering there?" Adara asked, still thinking of her last time there.

Lucius shook his head and pushed back his cowl. "No. We need to press on to your family's home. I don't want to be on the road as the shadows fall." He looked to either side of the road, the river on their right and the rooftops of the ancient temples to their left, hidden as they were by sweet-smelling pines, cypresses and olive trees. Statues stood among the temples, like silent adherents of the Gods.

There was a squawking in the trees that flanked the length of the temple of Apollo Delphinios. Among the branches of a tall pine tree, a crow of deepest black called out, his dark eyes watching the passing wagon.

Lucius looked at the bird, his father's messenger. It flapped its wings and dropped out of the branches to glide to the ground before the temple and when Lucius saw where it landed, he stopped the wagon.

Apollo stood there among the sentry trees before his temple, the crow pecking at the ground about his sandalled feet. He stared directly at Lucius, his blue cloak wavering gently in the breeze like the curtain before a window looking out onto the world.

Do not stop here, Lucius, Apollo said. *You must keep going. I will see you soon.*

"Baba?" Calliope said. "Is that…grandfather?"

Adara and Phoebus both looked at Lucius and Calliope, and then at the silent grove around the temples.

"Lucius? Shall we stop and make an offering?" Adara asked.

"No," he said. "We need to keep going." He looked at his daughter. "You see him?"

Calliope nodded, her eyes wide and full of sunlight. "Keep going, Baba," she said, and Lucius flicked the reins and the wagon rolled on, up the hill toward the ancient stadium and the slopes of Hymettos.

Adara felt her childhood memories flooding back as they climbed the gentle rise among the olive groves and vineyards of Hymettos toward her family's villa. How many times had she taken that road to and from Athenae on trips to the agora or the theatre, to the temples of the Gods? How much of her life had she spent riding her horse, Phoenix, among the groves and thyme-tinged air on hot summer evenings in the fields around her home?

She could feel her excitement building as she gave Lucius directions as to which paths to take. They had missed the summer, and swims in the sea that year, but there was still time to taste the last of the black and green figs that adorned the trees on their family farm, to pick at juicy pomegranates, or to show the children how to bring in the olive harvest; she could still hear the thwacking of the long, sinewy canes they used to coax the fruit from the gnarled trees. But what she looked forward to the most was seeing her mother and father. It had been many years, and Adara had missed just sitting with them by lamplight in the triclinium, the walls illuminated by her mother's paintings as they talked of art and the latest philosophical trends to be tested out in the alcoves of the schools there, still living and breathing long after the Roman dictator, Sulla, had destroyed them.

"We're almost there!" Adara finally said, excited as the familiar rise

in the land came into view. The cart wended its way around a slight bend
to reveal the stone walls that surrounded the two-storey villa that was her
home. Jasmine bushes hovered like wild, green clouds all along the tops
of the walls, blocking the view of the tiled rooftop. "Looks like my
mother has decided to allow the jasmine to grow wild," Adara mused.
"Phoebus, Calliope, you'll love the smell in the evenings. There's
nothing like orange and lemon in the day, and jasmine in the evenings."
She put her arm around her daughter and squeezed, her own smile broad
as she felt all their past worries melting away. She waited for that first
glimpse of home through the rows of fruit trees that they would get as
they came to the arch in the walls. She could feel her parents' arms
around her, and anticipated the happiness that would bring.

Lucius could not help but smile with relief at his wife's excitement as
he drove on toward the arch that led onto the villa grounds, but as he
turned the last corner onto the drive, the mule balked at something in the
drive just beyond the gate.

A sound of flies was suddenly everywhere, and lacing the orange and
lemon-scented air, was a scent of sun-drenched death.

"Whoa!" Lucius pulled on the reins hard and the mule stopped
abruptly.

"What is this?" Adara began to say, shaking her head. "That's…
that's one of my father's Thessalian horses!"

Lucius handed the reins to Phoebus and jumped down off of the
wagon after Adara, drawing his gladius.

"No, no, no, no…" Adara muttered as she looked down at the
animal, and then noticed other corpses of goats and sheep at the bases of
the fruit trees. "NO!" Adara cried out, running on down the path.

Lucius ran after her, turning to his son as he went. "Bring the
wagon!"

Phoebus flicked the reins hard, forcing the mule to go around the
equine body in the drive. "We're too late," he said to his sister.

Calliope did not answer.

Lucius' eyes scanned the trees, searching for any sign of intruders,
but all was quiet. When he caught up to Adara at the end of the fruit
grove, he found her on her knees, tears streaming down her face as she
gazed at the blackened ruins of her family's villa.

"No… NOOOOOOO!" she screeched as her nails dug into the dry
dirt and she wept before the ruined home.

Lucius stepped in front of her to observe the devastation. It had been done some time ago it seemed, for nothing smouldered, and weeds had grown up around the broken masonry and cracked and dusty plaster. There was nothing left. The vultures had done their work. Lucius felt his heart breaking anew for his wife, and a sudden wave of worry swept over him as he thought of her parents, sisters, and his own family who had supposedly joined them. *Are their bodies lying among the ruins?* He began to panic but caught himself. *Adara needs me now!* he told himself as he put his hand on her shoulder.

"Don't touch me!" Adara yelled.

Lucius removed his hand. He could hear Calliope weeping as she and her brother approached them from behind. He turned to Phoebus who had his sword drawn. "Stay with them. I'm going to take a look."

"Yes, Baba," Phoebus said, bending to hug his mother as Calliope already was.

Lucius walked forward cautiously through the sprawling detritus. It was like reliving a nightmare over and over again, only this was his waking life, and the pain of his family was all too real.

Whatever the villa had looked like before, it was unrecognizable now, even beneath that brilliant sun that heated the mountainside. It had been a paradise, Lucius could tell, for the trees and fields around it were still intact. If they had been set alight, the entire mountain would have gone up in violent flames in the dry heat of the Athenian summer. The destruction of the villa, he noticed, was complete and quite deliberate, as if it had been taken apart piecemeal and then slowly, methodically, burned. It was a message, a signpost that Lucius felt had been left for him alone to read, no matter the destruction it wrought on others' lives.

As he searched the debris, he found pieces of coloured plaster among the broken tiles and dust, the fin of a dolphin, the brown tones of summer skin, and delicate silver-green of olive limbs. *It must have been so beautiful,* he thought sadly.

"My mother's paintings," Adara suddenly sniffled behind him as she stared through watery eyes with her children to either side of her.

Lucius turned to look at them, and then went back to his search.

They picked their way among the destruction, and after a time, Lucius stopped and looked up at the sky. *Thank you, Apollo.*

"What is it, Baba?" Calliope asked, seeing the strange look of relief upon her father's face.

Lucius stepped forward to take Adara's hands.

"Adara...there are no bodies. Your parents, sisters and my family must have got away."

"They did," a voice said from behind one of the trees nearby. "But you won't!"

Lucius turned quickly to see a lean-muscled shepherd emerge with a thick club in his hand. He stepped forward to stand in front of his family, but as he did so, six more such men stepped out.

"The Romans told us you might come back here," the first man said, smiling through yellow teeth.

Lucius could smell the man from several meters away, but that was not what bothered him as she shed his cloak. They were all armed, all staring from him to his wife and daughter and son. "What Romans? Who?" Lucius asked, buying time as he moved to a flatter area free of debris, with Adara and the children following him.

"How should I know?" the shepherd said. "All's I know is that they had plenty of coin."

"Were they soldiers?" Lucius pressed, but the men were closing in, not answering.

"They also said that there would be double the money if we brought your heads." There was a slight pause, and then the shepherds closed in quickly like a swarm of Suburan thugs in a street fight.

"Stay back-back-to-back!" Lucius hissed to his family.

There was no time for the nervousness or the fear that comes before a battle. There was only rage and a will to survive.

The shepherds surrounded them as if penning in a flock of sheep, hooting and waving their staffs and cudgels as if it were sport.

Lucius looked at them with cold, removed anger. "You cannot pen in dragons."

Adara was the first to draw blood, her fury overwhelming her as she lunged, parrying a club and thrusting her gladius into the throat of one man.

Calliope stayed at her side, dodging another swing and screaming as she jammed her pugio into another's gut, sending him backward onto broken wall remnants.

Phoebus tried to stay with his mother and sister, but was forced to move quickly to avoid the two men who came at him.

"Put that sword down, boy. We'll be good to you!" one of them said, but without another word, Phoebus' gladius snuck in beneath the swinging cudgel and stabbed upward under his chin only to be pulled out quickly and plunged into the gut of his second attacker.

The three last men surrounded Lucius, more cautious of the older, man with the massacred skin.

"Caracalla sends you to take care of me, does he?" Lucius laughed. "Take your last look at the sun." He then stood still and waited for them.

The men looked at each other, confused, then smiled and rushed at once.

Lucius felt strength fill him then and he parried and spun, hamstringing one man and flowing in to parry a second before plunging his gladius into his side. The third, however, bore down on him quickly and Lucius readied to take the sweeping blow of the staff, but it went wild as Adara's pugio took the man in the side of the head, sending him sideways into the dust.

Lucius stood and spun to make sure there were no more. It had happened so fast. They had not been prepared, and yet, they were still alive. "Are you all right?" he asked his children, who nodded quickly, panting from the sudden fight. He then turned to Adara who stood with her bloody gladius looking at the surviving men writing on the ground.

"I want to kill them, Lucius," she said. "They destroyed my family's home. They threatened my children..."

Lucius looked upon her, and in that moment, he saw not his wife, but a warrior, an Amazon returned to an empty, destroyed home, thirsty for vengeance, a vengeance he understood all too well.

Together, they walked over to the first man Lucius had struck. He was grabbing at his side, blood pumping out between his dirty fingers.

"Where are the people who lived here?" Adara demanded.

"When were you ordered to watch this place?" Lucius said, his gladius pointed at the man's eye.

The shepherd spat at them, and without a moment's delay, Adara slammed her gladius into his chest. His eyes shot wide, their incredulity almost comic, like the masks hanging on the walls of the theatre of Herodes Atticus down in the city.

There were more cries as Phoebus went round finishing off the other men, but before he could run the last survivor through, Lucius caught his hand. "Phoebus, no! We need to ask him." He turned to the man who gripped at the guts that had begun to slither out of the cut in his abdomen.

Calliope turned away from the horror to vomit, and her brother rushed to her side.

"Tell us what you know, and I'll make it quick," Lucius said to the dying man.

The young shepherd shook his head. "Men in black came...offered us money to kill a man...a woman...and two...two children if they ever came. More coin than we could ever imagine."

Lucius felt his rage coming back like a tidal wave of anger, and he would have reached out to tear him apart with his bare hands were it not for Adara beside him, standing there, staring down at him through her tears and blood-spattered face.

"What else can you tell us?" Lucius asked.

"That's all I know, by Pan and the Nymphs, I swear!"

Lucius began to raise his gladius to dispatch the man quickly, but Adara stayed his hand.

"No!" she said, staring from Lucius to the man. "You destroyed my family's home. It was all we had left."

The young man shook his head as blood trickled from the corner of his mouth, even as his bladder emptied.

But Adara continued to stare. "You dare invoke the Gods for your actions? We'll not make this fast." She knelt down so that her eyes were level with his. "Die now, and know that the Gods will not help you where you're going."

He began to weep as the woman looked into his eyes, and the burned man stared down at him like some ghostly apparition. His vision blurred and then all was darkness.

Adara stood when his eyes finally closed, and went to Phoebus and Calliope. "Come away from here. Now." She led them back to the area that had once been the front courtyard where the mule and cart stood. "I'll check if the well is still functioning," she said.

After Lucius checked to make sure every one of the shepherds was dead, he made his way back to the children. "Where is your mother?" he asked them.

"She went to get some well water," Phoebus said, his arm around Calliope whose eyes were closed, her dirty cheeks streaked with tears.

Lucius looked to see Adara walking away among the trees, carrying a bucket she had found on the path. The sight broke his heart. She had been so excited as they had driven up the lower slopes of Hymettos, to see her family, her home... And now, where she had no doubt walked as a child, with her sisters, chains of wild flowers held gently in their hands, she now walked in torn and stained clothing, holding a burned bucket and bloody sword. *Gods, let me not lose her to this tragedy,* he prayed, but he feared she was already gone.

Adara walked in the direction of the well as if in a daze, a waking nightmare from which she could not escape. The sword in her hand felt heavier than ever. She could feel her despair acutely then, feel it pulling her mind away from her body as she began to weep.

She forced herself to look up, to look around at the trees of the olive grove where she stood, leaning on the well head. She could see the bench among the trees where she used to sit, where she was sitting when Apollo and Venus had appeared to her all those years ago when Lucius was in Numidia.

"Gods... Where are you now? Why have you allowed this to happen to my family?" She looked down into the well and her tears fell to commingle with that sweet water of her youth. She closed her eyes then, as if doing so would erase the pain that stabbed at her heart. She tried to imagine the villa intact, sweet-smelling after a summer rain with arches of bougainvillea rustling in the hot, mountain breeze. She remembered the golden glow of lamplight upon the walls painted by her mother, of forests and bull leapers, of dolphins and the olive harvesters. Those walls had been adorned with her mother's joy, had been the skene of her life before she had bound herself to Rome...to Lucius.

The thought made her weep more, and the sound of her weeping filled the grove that had once only known her laughter.

"A..Adara?" a weak, hesitant voice said from among the fruit-laden trees.

Adara looked up quickly, dropping the bucket in the dirt at her feet. She raised her blood-caked gladius, wiping her eyes as she did so. "Who's there?" she demanded.

"Adara Antonina?" the voice asked, followed this time by a hunched woman in a torn black tunica. She emerged from behind one of the broad-trunked trees like a timid wood-nymph, reluctant to approach, but when she got a better look at the weeping woman at the well, she stumbled toward her, ignoring the blade pointed at her. "You've come home!" the woman said. "Thank Athena!"

Adara stared at the woman through her watery eyes which suddenly widened in recognition. "Kaleos?" She suddenly remembered the woman who had been a part of her familia, who had helped her as a child, been at her mother's side through so many memories from Adara's childhood. She had been so majestic, so kind and wise, and now, she appeared ancient, world-weary beyond recognition. "Kaleos what are you doing here?" Adara dropped her sword and rushed to the old woman, her hands reaching out to grasp the gnarled, arthritic knuckles that clung tightly to her bloody hands.

After a few moments of convulsive crying, the woman looked up at Adara, her fingers gently brushing her soft cheeks to wipe away the tears, just as she had done when Adara was a girl.

"Mama? Are you all right?" Phoebus said as he, Calliope, and finally, Lucius, came up the path through the trees to find her. As soon as he saw the old woman clinging to Adara, he lowered his sword, as did Lucius. "We heard you crying."

Adara turned to her children. "It's Kaleos!" Adara said, turning to look at Lucius. "She was my nursemaid when I was a child. She's part of our familia." She turned back to the old woman and led her to the stone bench in the grove where she sat with her.

Kaleos continued to grasp Adara's hands, mumbling gratitude to the Gods over and over again for her safe return while Lucius, Phoebus and Calliope watched. The old woman looked up at the grown children and then back at Adara, a smile spanning her weathered face even then. "Such beautiful children!" When she turned to look at Lucius, she scowled deeply. "Romans!" she said, spitting in the dirt.

"Please, Kaleos," Adara said, understanding the woman's anger. "Lucius is my husband. He too is hunted by Rome."

"I know! He is the reason the emperor's assassins came and destroyed our home...our beautiful home..."

Lucius stepped forward and bent on one knee before the woman and, as if with new sight, she saw the devastation wrought upon his body, the burns that made him look almost as old as herself but for the solid muscle beneath the scarred skin.

With one of her hands, she reached out to grab Lucius' hand, her other still clinging to Adara's.

"Kaleos," Lucius said softly. "What happened here? Where is everyone?"

The old woman released their hands and clasped hers in her lap. "They came early one morning. Soldiers in black-"

"Praetorians?" Lucius asked.

She shrugged. "Violent men on horses. They all looked the same." She turned to Lucius. "Your mother, brother, sister, and the sculptor had only been here for three weeks. They had arrived here in haste, with almost nothing." She turned back to Adara. "It was early in the morning. The young man...Caecilius... He was awake with one of his headaches sitting in the front courtyard watching the sunrise. He heard horses and harsh voices, then saw the torches. He rushed into the house to wake everyone. There was panic, but somehow," she said to Adara, "your father was prepared. He and Caecilius had had a wagon with supplies and horses ready to go at the outbuildings up the mountainside."

Kaleos stopped suddenly in her recollection of that day, closed her eyes and shook her head. "They could have burned the whole mountain with everyone upon it, things were so dry, but after searching the house, they began to take anything of value and then to destroy the walls with heavy hammers swung by slaves they had brought, and men they had paid with the emperor's coin. It took a whole day. They took their time, as if doing so would lure your father out."

"Did Baba approach them?" Adara's worst fears ebbed at the shore of her consciousness, and she waited for a great wave of grief to crash upon her. "Did he?"

"No, child. Everyone watched from up the mountainside as the sound of crashing walls rose up to meet them. We watched our home destroyed, and couldn't do anything about it. They then lit the fires to burn the house." Kaleos shook her head. "The flames ate everything and would have swept through the trees in moments had not the Gods intervened. Father Zeus gathered his clouds for us and a downpour began just as the first tree began to burn."

"Where did the men go?" Lucius asked. "Did they search the mountainside?"

"They left. Back to Athenae. But they did send the shepherds afterward...those horrible men!"

"Did they harm you?" Adara asked, putting her arm around Kaleos.

"No. I knew all the hiding places. They were not Hymettos shepherds, so they were not familiar with the mountain. They stayed around the villa with orders to wait for you, should you ever come. But we were not sure you would come. We heard the soldiers in black say that you were all dead, but that they would destroy the villa in case you were not." She kissed Adara's hands, uncaring of the blood. "Thank the Gods you are not."

Calliope sat on the other side of the old woman then and held her hands to calm their shaking. She remembered her mother speaking of Kaleos a few times, but she had never thought to meet her.

Kaleos felt herself calm, her shaking stop, and she looked at the young girl with wide, rheumy eyes. "You have the gift, child."

"I am Calliope, lady."

"And I'm Phoebus."

Kaleos looked at both of them and smiled. "Such fine children. And strong! I saw how you all slew the shepherds."

"Lucius trained us all," Adara said.

Kaleos looked disapproving for a moment, but when she thought about it, she thought differently. "It is as well he did. You are hunted and need to protect yourselves." She looked up at Lucius. "But a child should not have to kill."

Lucius looked at her, but said nothing as he stood back up, nodding slowly.

Adara grew quite serious then, unable to hold back the question that had been harassing her mind ever since the old woman had appeared. "Kaleos...my family...are...are they dead?" *Please Gods, let them be safe.*

"I believe they are safe, child," Kaleos said, patting her hands.

"Where are they?" Lucius asked. "You said they had a wagon and horses? Where did they go?"

Kaleos grew silent, her eyes then searching the olive grove for unfriendly eyes. When she felt certain it was safe, she paused and looked up at Lucius. There was, however, a sudden change in her aspect, as if her eyes cleared and stared more deeply into him than they had up until that point. Her voice was clear and quiet, like the soft string of a lyre plucked in the night. "They have gone to your father's high-peaked home, Dragon, to the navel of the world..."

Adara released Kaleos' hands and sat back, unnerved by the sudden change in her demeanour. She and Lucius exchanged looks.

When Kaleos looked at them again, she said, "I believe they are safe."

Lucius closed his eyes and turned his head to the sky. *Father…is this your doing?*

"We will find them, Kaleos," Adara said to the old woman, her daughter on the other side. "We will take you with us."

Kaleos shook her head. "I am too old to travel now, my dear. I was raised on this mountain. I raised you here." She smiled sadly. "I will die here with the sun on my face and the sound of Hymettos bees singing in my ears."

"We can't leave you," Lucius said.

"You must. And you must keep moving to keep your family safe. You must reach sanctuary, by the Gods you must!"

They spent the night upon the mountainside, but not in the family home that Adara had dreamed of and missed for years. The destruction was too complete, and Kaleos felt certain there may have been other shepherds in Rome's employ, watching the estate.

Lucius was not too sure about that. Seven had been plenty for such a task, but he was not willing to take chances at that point.

After washing at the well, and wandering about the scattered pieces of Adara's childhood home, they all got in the wagon and made their slow way through the groves and up the mountainside to the outbuilding where Kaleos had taken refuge.

Inside, there were barrels of cured olives and the last production of soaking goat's cheese before the herd was slaughtered by the Romans.

As the children sat beside a small cooking fire with Kaleos, Lucius approached Adara where she sat on a short stone wall looking down the mountainside toward the villa, and the city and sea beyond.

"I had so many happy memories here…" Adara said, the orange light of the setting sun lighting up her face, lighting her hair which she had let down to wash. "It's all gone now…"

"I'm sorry, my love-"

"Don't. I don't want any more apologies, Lucius. After Etruria, I hoped that would be an end to the blood. But now, here, in my childhood home, I saw my children stain their hands with more blood. My children!" Adara gagged at the thought, the memory of the fight, and Lucius thought she would vomit. "I don't want this anymore, Lucius. I can't do it."

Lucius breathed deeply of the pine-scented mountain air, and let out a long sigh. "I know, my love. You have no idea how deeply I regret doing this to all of you. This is not the life I envisioned for our family."

"Then let us build a new one together," Adara said, turning away from the burned villa below to look at her husband. "You and I, together with our children and our families if they are still alive. Let's leave the world behind and start anew. We have to, or we'll drown in blood."

I can't, my love, Lucius thought, his own heart cracking as the thought came to him. *Not until it is done. They will never leave us alone, unless I finish it.* As he looked at her, the desperate hint of a hopeful smile at the corner of her mouth, willing him to agree, he felt himself falling away from her, away from all of them. He was falling through the air with no place to land or cling to.

"Kaleos has fallen asleep, Mama," Calliope said as she and Phoebus approached them.

Adara turned from Lucius to look at her children, inviting them to sit to either side of her. "Kaleos is old and tired. She's been through much."

"She's very nice," Calliope said, holding her mother's hand and looking at the sun far away over the sea.

"This is not how I wanted to show you my home," Adara said.

"We know, Mama," Phoebus said softly.

"I can picture it in my mind though," Calliope said, trying to smile, trying to forget the blood that had once more stained her hands. "I can see it...and it's beautiful!"

"It was in that olive grove down the hill where the Gods told me I would have you." Adara smiled sadly, wiped a tear from her cheek, and felt grateful once again that, despite all, her children were still with her, still safe. *But how long will that last?* she worried. The anxiety of that thought was constant, and draining.

Lucius stood up and walked down the rock and root slope a little to stare out at the villa, the city, the sea and mountains beyond. He felt the waning sun upon his face and tried to breathe it in, to assume some strength from its gentle glow. He would need it.

"Are our grandparents still alive?" Phoebus asked quietly, giving voice to the worry that had been on all of their minds. "It wasn't Kaleos who spoke to us earlier, was it, Baba?"

Lucius turned and shook his head. "No. It wasn't."

"Are the Gods telling us that our family still lives?" Phoebus asked again.

"Please, Baba?" Calliope said. "Please tell us they are all alive."

Lucius felt the weight of who he was then, the expectation of a son of Apollo. But he had not the sight, no gift, it seemed, other than to provide pain and suffering. *I must get them to sanctuary. Then, I can finish it!*

"Where are we to search for them, Baba?" Phoebus asked, sliding off the wall to go to Lucius' side.

Lucius put his arm around his son and turned to face Adara and Calliope.

"What did she mean by 'your father's high-peaked home', the 'navel of the world'?" Calliope asked.

Lucius looked at his children and then to his wife. He imagined the long journey ahead, and felt tired just at the thought. But it was necessary. It was the place to take them…to sanctuary.

"It means that we are going to Delphi."

XIII

ASYLUM

'Sanctuary'

They left Athenae behind them, like a tarnished gem they could not bear to look at any longer. It was a place that held nothing for them now, except for faded memories that brought only pain in their recollection.

As the wagon rolled north over the Eleusinian plain, Adara was quiet, contemplating the cruel illusion that her childhood now felt like. She began to feel cold, the damp from the sea to their left creeping in slowly with Winter's approach. While Lucius drove the mule on at a quick pace between crowds of pilgrims on their way to Eleusis from the city, in the back of the wagon, Adara gathered her children, grown as they were, into her arms. *I will protect them no matter the cost,* she thought. And she meant it. She meant it with every fibre of her being. They had nearly lost everything, and she would be torn by wolves before she let anything happen to her children, for they were her world, and in that moment, nothing, nor anyone else, mattered.

The sun was high as they travelled, the wind steady, as if a god in some cave whistled steadily, enjoying the play of his breath over the rocky landscape. Soon, they reached the sprawling sanctuary of Eleusis, the place where the great Mysteries had been carried out for ages, on the spot where the goddess Demeter had lost her daughter, Persephone, to Hades' greedy grasp.

It was crowded without the walls of the sanctuary, where pilgrims gathered to enter and make their offerings to the goddess, even though September, the month in which the Greater Mysteries were celebrated, had passed. Beyond the walls, Lucius could see the newly-built arches and propylaea erected by Rome's Hellenophile emperors Hadrian and Marcus Aurelius. As ever, Rome had tried to put its mark on the world.

Once, it would have given Lucius a sense of pride to see it, to be a part of it, but now it only angered him.

Rome's mark is a poison, he thought, his fists clenching the reins as he drove alone at the front of the wagon.

But it was the great mass of the telesterion that caught the eye, the massive, square hall where only initiates of the Mysteries were permitted to enter and take part.

Lucius was curious about what happened within the confines of that sprawling hall. It was rumoured that initiates, after taking part in the Mysteries, were supposed to be relieved of their fear of death. *I have already died,* Lucius thought.

As the smoke of offerings wafted into the senses, the wagon slowed as the crush of traffic became thicker.

"We're going to need to get some more food and warmer clothes," Lucius said over his shoulder to Adara. "Shall I stop so we can visit the agora?"

"No!" Adara said suddenly, startling Phoebus and Calliope who had gone to the opposite edge of the wagon to watch the people and try to spy some of the sanctuary beyond. "Please, no, Lucius." Adara felt her heart contracting at the thought of going there, of being anywhere near the place where a mother had lost her child. "I can't bear to be in this crowd now...this place."

Lucius turned to look at her, and when he saw the panic in her eyes, the worry, he understood.

"We can make it to Thebes by this evening. It will be less crowded and we can get supplies and wool and fur clothing there."

"Then let's keep going," Lucius said, seeing her relax at once, kneeling as she joined the children to watch the sanctuary pass by.

Goddess, please watch over my children always, Adara prayed, even as the sky darkened overhead and the wagon plodded on into the rocky lands of Boeotia in the distance.

With the sea behind them, they travelled over the rocky road of that ancient, war-torn land toward the crumbling remains of Thebes. The distance was not great, but the road seemed to go on forever, hugging the pine and scrub-clad cliffs above sprawling valleys until they could see the long finger of the settlement with the Cadmea, the ancient fortress rock, at the centre of Thebes.

"Is that it?" Phoebus asked, sitting beside Lucius on the driver's bench. He searched the landscape as if looking for more. "There isn't much there."

"Seems that way," Lucius said. "I remember Diodorus telling me about Thebes, the home of the great poet Pindar and the Theban Sacred Band. They chose the wrong side in many conflicts and paid for it."

"Alexander destroyed the city, didn't he?" Phoebus asked.

Lucius nodded. "All but Pindar's home, apparently." The wagon rolled directly toward the small settlement then, across the plain. "He regretted his actions, it's said, and always treated Thebans with respect and reward thereafter. Cassander, one of Alexander's successors, rebuilt the city but it never achieved the greatness it had once enjoyed. It's been five hundred years…" Lucius' thought trailed off.

"I can't imagine the world so long from now," Phoebus said, "I wonder if Rome will end up looking like Thebes?"

"Only the Gods know," Lucius answered, and he found that he did not really care, for in his own mind, Rome had sided against him. If he could, in that moment, he would have razed Rome to the ground, just as Alexander had devastated sad and lonely Thebes. "It'll be dark soon," he said. "Let's find an inn."

There was not much to Thebes - crumbling walls, a couple of roadside tabernae, and a single inn that looked respectable enough to accommo-date a family of travellers. It seemed to Lucius that the only thing that kept Thebes alive was its location on the road to Delphi which had a steady flow of pilgrim traffic for most of the year. Otherwise, the settle-ment was a way point for shepherds, hunters, and traders coming down out of Thessaly and into Attica.

People observed them silently, but let them be, assuming that they were pilgrims on their way to Delphi like so many others, and that the burned man travelling with his family was in need of Apollo's ministrations.

Despite this, Lucius, Adara and the children carried their weapons beneath their warm cloaks, for they had seen too much of violence already to become complacent among strangers. They picked their way among the scattered market stalls of the sad agora, purchasing food and thick woollen blankets, and two bear and wolf pelts for the mountain cold they knew was coming. Then, they sought accommodation.

The inn was on two levels with the stable to one side, just off of the road, with a courtyard between the two structures. The cool air smelled of burning, of leaves and wood and meat over hot coals. It was crowded inside, with several pilgrims and traders gathered to eat before continuing their separate journeys the following day.

Lucius wasted no time in finding the taberna owner, procuring a room and stable space for the mule and cart. He had no wish to make niceties with anyone, and his appearance aided him to that end, for none wished to make eye contact with a man the Gods had obviously struck down.

Let them believe what they will, he thought as he dropped the appropriate amount of coin on the counter, *so long as they leave us alone.*

"Up the stairs outside and to the left," the innkeeper said as he swept the coins off the counter into the palm of his blackened hand. "Food's included with the room. You eat in here."

Lucius turned and went outside with the man watching his back and eyeing the pommel of the black gladius that jutted from his side. As Lucius closed the door behind him, the man made the sign against evil on his forehead.

With the mule and cart taken care of for the night, and a hot and hearty meal in their bellies, the Pen Dragon family, as they were now known, settled down to sleep on straw mattresses in the simple room. Exhaustion gripped them round the heart and head, and it did not take long before Phoebus and Calliope were sound asleep beside each other.

Adara sat watching as Morpheus took them, Calliope with a hand upon her brother's crown, and Phoebus with a ready hand upon the handle of his gladius, as if to protect her should the need arise in the dark of night.

"I remember when he slept with a wooden horse, and she with a jointed doll," Adara said, the side of her face lit by the small, burning brazier in the centre of the room to ward off the chill of night. "Now they sleep with swords."

"The days of dolls and toys are long gone," Lucius said, his voice cold. "We'll leave early so we can have a chance of reaching Delphi by nightfall."

Adara said nothing at first, but stared at her husband. Every since the destruction of her childhood home in Athenae, the distance between them had widened, and his anger had grown stronger, strengthening each and every brick in the wall Lucius had been building between them. What saddened her most was that she did not have the will or the strength to tear down that wall as she had in the past. *I'm so tired,* she thought. *Gods, how much longer can we endure this?*

As Lucius refused to look at her, lost in his own tremulous thoughts, she took one of the blankets they had and lay down beside Calliope, wishing for a deep and forgetful sleep, and if she did not wake, there was a part of her that really did not care.

When Adara was asleep, Lucius watched the three of them breathing deeply with exhalations of their complete physical and emotional exhaustion. His guilt ate silently away at him. *I've failed them... It's my fault everyone's homes are gone... They're in danger because of me.*

"All greatness comes to ruin," he mumbled, thinking of his own hubris. He shook his head and thought of how true that was, how the very place in which they found themselves was a prime example.

Thebes... He had learned so much from Diodorus who had used that sad polis as an example of wasted potential and wrong choices. They had sided with the Persians against their fellow Greeks, and then they had not understood the vision that Alexander had for their world, how they could have been a part of it.

Somewhere in the ruins of that city of bygone greatness was the house of the epinikion poet, Pindar. Alexander had ordered it spared while the rest of Thebes had burned down all around it.

Lucius remembered Diodorus teaching him some of the odes, but at the time, he was not so much interested in poetry, preferring the history of battles to words. However, he did remember one line from those archaic poems of praise...

If any man expects that what he does escapes the notice of a god, he is wrong.

Lucius had taken that to heart for the whole of his life, and it had always been a comfort to him, driven him, filled him with philotimo.

Now, however, Pindar's words haunted him. Lucius had much blood upon his hands, and he was seeking to soak them in it even more. And now, they were journeying to his father's home on the slopes of Parnassus, one of the most sacred places in the whole of the empire.

Lucius did not know what to expect, nor whether his family would be welcome at the navel of the world.

He thought of Hercules himself having gone to Delphi in ages past to receive his penance from the oracle for the crimes he had committed against his wife and children, through no fault of his own, that long-suffering hero. The thought made Lucius panic, for he had willingly committed the acts others would perceive as crimes, and though his wife and children yet lived, they still suffered, and greatly. His heart began to race and he breathed deeply to try and slow it. At the back of his mind, he could hear Love whispering to him, willing him to receive her thoughts, her warmth, but Lucius shook his head as the image of the goddess emerged from the dark mists clouding his mind.

Whatever happens, whatever punishment I am to endure, I am ready.

And as he dozed off to uneasy sleep, it was to the faint sound of heavenly weeping.

When morning dawned over the sad Theban plain, Lucius and his family were already speeding toward the distant, snow-capped mountains marking their destination. The air was fresh and cold, with a promise of brilliant light throughout the day, the only darkness upon their path cast by their own thoughts as the mule trotted quickly on.

The land rose gradually, and the temperature began to drop little by little, ever so slowly, but enough to chill the bones. Very slowly, the slopes of sacred Parnassus came into view, but even as the red sun began to melt away behind the mountain's screen, it appeared no closer than before. It was as if the Gods intended all theopropoi, those who wished to consult the oracle, to have ample time to think of why they were there, why they were intending to set foot on that supremely sacred ground with all of their worries and crimes following them.

But Lucius was not there as a suppliant. He wanted to find his family. It would, however, not be for another day, for darkness began to fall quickly as the cypress and pine-flanked road they followed approached the settlement of Karyai.

"We won't make it today," Adara said as she sat beside him on the bench. "There are plenty of inns here."

"There are fewer pilgrims than I expected," Lucius said, gazing into the doorways and windows of the structures that replaced the deep green of the trees and the rich soil of the earth to either side of the rocky road.

"We're on the verge of the winter months when no oracles are given," Adara said.

"What? Why?" Lucius asked.

"Your divine father-"

"You don't have to call him that."

Adara placed her hand on Lucius' arm. "He is your father, Lucius, and he has brought us here safely." Lucius shook his head, but she continued. "He is not here during the three months of winter. They say Dionysus comes in his stead while he is in the land of the Hyperboreans."

Though he did not want to admit it, Lucius felt a deep sadness at this. A part of him had known this from what Diodorus had taught him, but it saddened him nonetheless for after all the blood and despair, with more to come, the child in him might have longed to see his father's face before setting out.

"But our families will be here, Lucius. For that, we can be grateful."

Lucius looked at his wife and marvelled still at her belief that all was well, despite the destruction of so much.

Adara closed her eyes and breathed deeply of the cool mountain air. "Tomorrow, we will see them."

.

The village of Karyai was made up of inns and houses made of rough mountain stone and timber. The smell of woodsmoke was everywhere as people kindled their nighttime fires, and the sound of wolves crept out of the distant woods that rose up on the mountainside beyond.

They soon found a place to stay with a warm hearth, hearty food, and a room that overlooked the valley far below. It was strange, but they all felt it, that sense that all would be well, a lightness of being.

Lucius, however, fought the feeling of calm and repose that crept in upon his heart and mind, just as he had fought it in Ynis Wytrin. There could be no rest until he had done what he had set out to do, that which his heart was set on. As he thought of this, looking beyond the balcony window to the cold, starry sky beyond, Adara sat with the children by the fire, each of them cleaning themselves so that they did not arrive in Delphi in disarray and dirt.

"Mama," Phoebus asked. "What is the sanctuary like? How long ago were you here?"

Adara smiled, a little sadly, but then turned to face her son and daughter. "I was here before you were born, with your aunt..."

"Matertera Alene?" Calliope asked.

"Yes," Adara forced back her sadness and smiled again. "She loved it here, and she wrote to your grandmother about it." She saw Lucius look at the floor then. Alene's death had been like the first thread that had begun the unravelling of their world. Now they clung to that single thread, it seemed. *But if Theseus could find his way out of the darkness of the Labyrinth clinging to a single thread of hope, then perhaps we can too.*

"Grandmother is from Delphi, isn't she?" Phoebus asked.

"Yes, she is. She was in training to be one of the Hestiades."

"Hestiades?" Phoebus asked. "What is that?"

"They are the Delphic maidens who, along with the Pythia, keep the immortal flame burning in the temple of Apollo."

"Like the flame in the temple of Vesta in Rome?" Calliope put in.

"In a way, only this flame is the light for the entire world, not just Rome."

"Why did she not join the Hestiades?"

"She fell in love with two things."

"What were they?" Calliope sat up straighter.

"Painting, and your grandfather."

Calliope sat back. "I can't wait to see them."

"If they are in Delphi at all," Phoebus added darkly. He turned to his father who was watching them from where he leaned against the wall beside the balcony. Lucius let fall the thick curtain he had been holding aside.

"Do you think the emperor sent his men after them here?" Phoebus asked.

"Shhh!" Lucius hissed suddenly. "Not so loud!"

"Sorry, Baba. I'm only worried that-"

"I don't know," Lucius said, pushing back worries that had been building. "We will find out tomorrow." He and Adara locked eyes, and her chiding look signalled the end of the conversation. "I'm sorry. I'm just tired from the journey. Let's get some rest so that we can leave early to find them. It won't take long at all to reach Delphi from here."

As they settled in to sleep another night, each of them imagined what it would be like to see Delphi, and how the family would react to seeing them.

It felt like they were coming out of the desert to a welcome oasis, but they were unsure of what lurked in the trees of that oasis.

Lucius could not stop the waves of worry that greeted him behind his closed lids. Too much time to think could be a curse for him, for his thoughts were often dark, made up of the worst outcomes he could imagine. *What if they are all dead? What if Caracalla's assassins are there, waiting for us?* he wondered. *If they are, I'll be ready.*

For herself, Adara lay there beside her grown children, watching the flickering flames in the hearth and thinking of how surprised her family would be to see them, how all they had lost would be worth it if everyone was safe in Delphi. *Phoebus and Calliope will lift their spirits after all that has happened,* she thought, even then weeping a little for the lingering image of her destroyed home in Athenae.

Dawn came bright, clear and cool upon the mountainside. Though he could not explain it, Lucius felt something in the air, anticipation mingled with reticence. He pulled the curtain aside and stepped onto the small balcony. The broad valley sprawled beneath a sky of pink clouds, the sun's orb already burning over the edges of the mountains opposite, as if their rocky screen were a piece of slowly burning papyrus.

Adara came to stand beside Lucius and, together, they watched in silence as the sun fully revealed itself. "How do you feel?"

His hands gripped the iron railing as she placed her hand upon his back. "In truth, I don't know. I've never been here, and I don't know what to expect."

"This isn't a battle, my love. This is your father's sanctuary, the place where he has been guarding our families."

Lucius turned to look at her. "How can you be sure? Men could be there waiting for us, as they have elsewhere."

Adara removed her hands. She did not want to fall prey to Lucius' determined darkness, his unceasing need to see threat everywhere. She knew he could be right, of course, but she desperately wanted to believe it was otherwise, that the Gods had not abandoned them entirely. "I just feel it," she said. "We'll be safe here." She looked out over the valley where the ancient groves of olive far below were slowly revealed by the spreading light, the sun's heat warming her face. "Come, let's get ready. I'll put what's left of the resin on your skin. We haven't done so in many days."

Lucius looked at his hands and arms, the roughly-scarred surfaces of his body. "Thank you," he said, suddenly taking Adara into his arms and hugging her tightly.

For a moment, she was stunned, but then her arms wrapped themselves about him and she squeezed hard in return. "They'll be there, Lucius. You'll see."

It was a little more than seven miles from the village of Karyai to Delphi, but that final stage of their journey was a slow one, for the road was crowded, and perched precariously in places upon the rocky slopes. The morning chill quickly faded away as the sun rose higher to reveal the deep green of the pines, their sweet scent released as the sunlight caressed their outstretched limbs.

Lucius and his family rode in silence, just as most of the pilgrims upon the road did. The approach to that ancient place was an exercise in contemplation of the world, of oneself, for at Delphi it was as if the living too could be weighed in the Gods' scales and then given a chance to make things right before the end. Lucius flicked the mule's reins and watched people's faces as the wagon rolled past.

There were families, couples, the old and young. Some had looks of hope etched upon their faces, others of dread and desperation. Some of the pilgrims walked quickly, their feet light and determined to get to the Delphic sanctuary as quickly as possible. But there were some who walked slowly and methodically, pausing now and then to catch their breath or simply to wait, as if the inner burdens they carried slowed them down and sapped their will. If the oracle could lay low a hero like Hercules, what then could it do to a mere mortal such as the shivering, sandal-footed pilgrims they passed on the road?

And yet the oracle and Apollo have gone for the winter! Lucius thought. However, seeing the bundles people carried, he realized that they intended to spend the winter months there. They would wait for Apollo's return from Hyperborea so that they might be some of the first in line to see the oracle, after those with first rights, promanteia, and the Delphians themselves.

The pine trees suddenly thinned out and the edge of the road dropped away to the sprawling valley below. The wind swept through the olive trees, making them dance and sway, as if the resident nymphs shook their silver-leaved branches in the shadow of the high, snow-dusted mountains to the right. Then those trees seemed to have climbed up the slopes to the edge of the road. The air was scented with olive, pine, and sacred laurel, casting a spell over all who arrived.

"We need to stop," Adara said rather suddenly. "Turn to the left, Lucius." She pointed down a rocky path that led off of the main road, downward to a small, shaded area where pilgrims had lined up.

Lucius turned the mule, very slowly, for there was not a lot of space to manoeuvre, and as they turned, groups of altars and temples, including a beautiful tholos, came into view. The cart came to a stop beneath an olive tree and the four of them dismounted, carrying their satchels with them. They stood and stared at the site.

"Is this the sanctuary of Apollo, Mama?" Calliope asked.

Adara took her daughter's hand. "No, love. This is the sanctuary of Athena Pronaia. When people come to Delphi, they must stop here first. We're here to thank the goddess for bringing us to Delphi safely."

Lucius and Phoebus stepped forward to join them. They all walked down along a path among the trees, just outside the sanctuary's retaining wall. A small bridge over a cool mountain stream led to the western entrance of the sanctuary.

"It's beautiful!" Calliope exclaimed, stopping to look up at the ancient temple of Athena that stood directly before them.

"It looks very old," Phoebus added.

"It is," Adara answered. "But this is the newest temple. There was another, older one, but it was destroyed over seven hundred years ago."

The children and Lucius looked at her and she smiled sadly.

"My mother grew up here. She told me all she knew about this place." Adara stepped forward, passing the pilgrims who were gathered in small groups about the sanctuary.

The temple of Athena's walls were of solid marble, and though they were worn with time, they appeared sturdy. The Doric columns were thick and unyielding, and supported a red tile rooftop that peaked in a painted finial. The air smelled sweetly as smoke from offerings wafted out of the darkness of the cella within.

Adara stood there before the steps leading up to the temple and paused.

"What shall we offer the goddess, Mama?" Phoebus asked.

"Whatever we have," she answered, reaching into the linen bag that contained some of their food supplies to pull out an untouched loaf of bread. She turned to Lucius. "Can we offer some coin?" she whispered, and he nodded.

The sun was high by then, the light bright and the world about them bursting with brilliant blues and greens, yellows and reds.

Lucius felt himself relaxed in the sanctuary, as if the goddess were guaranteeing their safety for a time, and so his hand slipped away from the pommel of his gladius. As Adara prepared the offerings to the goddess, and tied a red ribbon Calliope had around the loaf of bread, Lucius turned to look at the other parts of the sanctuary.

The most striking structure was the round tholos temple with its soaring doric columns supporting a two-tiered, tile rooftop adorned with a tall acroterion, and ringed with lion heads. Smoke, and a steady chanting emerged from within the tholos, but Lucius did not understand the language. His feeling was that it was ancient and not to be disturbed, but he could not pull his eyes away from the metopes of the temple depicting the battles of the Amazons and of the Centaurs. The warriors were frozen in time, their pain, their glory etched in marble and faded pigment for all to see. He did not know why, but it saddened him to see it.

"Lucius," Adara said from behind him. "Shall we go in?"

He turned and together the four of them went up the steps into the temple.

Inside, it was dark, and there was little ornamentation. Silks and garlands and ancient offered weapons hung from the walls that led to the cella, where the altar stood before a statue of the goddess.

All sound was sucked out of the world about them, and their eyes were inexorably drawn to the altar at the goddess' feet.

When the pilgrim before them was finished and departed through the smoke, Adara, Lucius and the children stepped forward. Together they stood before the altar looking up at Athena.

The goddess had her helmet resting upon her head with her shield against her left leg, and the shaft of a mighty spear in her right hand as if she were guarding the entrance to the sanctuary.

Adara raised the loaf of bread in her hands. "Oh Goddess Athena Pronaia...thank you for bringing us safely to this sacred place. We honour you and place this offering upon your altar in gratitude." She laid the loaf among the other offerings left by pilgrims - glass phials of oil, bundles of herbs, decorated vases, and bronze and clay votive offerings in the form of animals and other objects - and then stepped back with her hands turned so that her palms faced upward as she prayed.

Lucius stepped forward and placed a denarius there upon the altar, hidden among the other offerings so that it might be found by the priestesses of the temple. For a fleeting moment, he saw a tall woman in a brilliant peplos standing beside the statue, and he felt his heart beat wildly as she smiled at the four of them. She then disappeared, and there was a loud flapping above their heads where a white owl had come to land in the rafters high above.

Adara looked up and smiled. "Thank you, Goddess." She breathed slowly. "We can go now." They emerged from the dark of the temple and descended the stairs to the ground below. Without speaking, Adara led them around the sanctuary as if the walk soothed her, as if she had come home, such was the peace of that place. They passed two ancient treasuries, and then the ruins of another temple where people gathered to sit, and where they still laid offerings to the goddess.

Opposite to the older temple ruins, before the treasuries, Lucius stood beneath the gleaming bronze statue of one of Rome's emperors. To him, it felt out of place, an invasion of sorts.

"Who is it, Baba?" Phoebus asked.

"Hadrianus. He loved Graecia and did much for it. It must have been erected after his tour of the empire."

Phoebus said nothing, but rested his hand upon the pommel of his gladius and continued to walk to join his mother and sister.

Lucius took one more look at Hadrianus, the fellow Roman in their midst, and carried on to join the others.

Beyond that first, larger temple of Athena Pronaia, they came to a series of altars, some to Athena, one to Zeus, and another to Hygeia. Once they had made a circuit of the sanctuary, they made their way to the path leading back up the hill to their cart and the road above.

They walked slowly, especially Adara who seemed to be in a contemplative state.

Lucius caught up with her and put his arm about her. "Is all well?"

"I don't know. I'm nervous now about going to see our families. What if they're not all right? What if something has happened?"

"I saw her in the temple," Lucius said suddenly.

"Who?" Adara asked, looking to where the children had arrived at the wagon ahead of them.

"Athena. She appeared to me in the temple...before the owl."

Adara felt sad then, for she would have liked to see the goddess. But it was not to be. "Did she speak?"

"No. But she did smile...as if to say all is well." He paused. "Maybe it is?" He was not sure he believed it, but he knew Adara needed to. One way or another, they would know if their worst fears had become reality.

Adara stopped walking and turned to her husband, her hand resting against the side of his head where his hair was still short and thin, his cheek scarred by fire. He had healed much with the help they had received from their friends faraway, but there was still much unseen, wounds that only he could mend. She hoped that being there would begin that mending in earnest. "Come. Let's find them."

Soon they were back in the cart, the mule straining at the harness to pull them up the slope back onto the road.

A silence fell on them as they reached the bend in the road above the gymnasium below, the grunts and shouts of the athletes training fading away into the thick green growth upon the mountainside. Then, as the road turned, flanked by wild olive, towering cypresses, and thick laurel, Adara pointed directly above them at two soaring cliffs.

"There they are," she said to Phoebus and Calliope, "the Shining Ones...the Phaedriades..."

Lucius too, looked up as he drove, the wagon moving very slowly.

Adara was pointing to two towering limestone peaks that jutted out of the earth to reach for the heavens above. They emerged from the green undergrowth at their feet to shine like beacons kissed by sun-fire. From the cleft between the Phaedriades, high above the world, a waterfall as brilliant as quicksilver fell down to the rockface and trees below.

"They're beautiful," Calliope said, straining her neck as the wagon got closer and closer.

"The water that pours into the world from between them feeds the sacred Castalian spring which all pilgrims must wash in before entering the sanctuary. Even the Pythia must cleanse herself with the sacred water before carrying out her duties."

Lucius set his eyes back upon the road as it bent away from the dark green shadows that hid the Castalian spring within. The thought of the oracle made him nervous, for the Sibyl's voice followed him everywhere since Cumae years before. What then should he think of the Pythia? Would she too have words for him, words that would haunt him further, the rest of his days?

The wagon rolled on, but Adara was still gazing up at the mountain peaks when she spoke next. "'Parnassus' pathless peaks grow bright with welcome to the new-born day.'"

"What is that from, Mama?" Phoebus asked.

"The words are from Euripides, Megas Alexandros' favourite playwright."

"They describe it perfectly," Phoebus added, holding his mother's hand as his eyes took in the scene. And then he gasped.

Glimpsed between the trees rising up the hill, the four of them spied a gleaming vision of sunlight and fire, of marble, gold and bronze. It was the sanctuary of Apollo, impossibly-perched upon steep mountain slopes like an earthly Olympus.

They were silent as the cart came to a standstill upon the dirt path, staring up at a layered world of colour and brilliance, of temples and soaring columns, gleaming statues and spear tips, stoas and the ancient treasuries. Fires burned in great tripods that smelled of sweet summer herbs and cedar, despite the fact that winter was upon them.

"I never expected to see this place," Lucius said, his voice nearly a whisper. He felt Adara's hand on his shoulder.

"It's your father's earthly home, Lucius. We've arrived." Adara sighed and wiped the stray tear from her eyes, remembering the last time she had been there, when she and Alene had walked slowly up the Sacred Way to the temple, arm in arm like sisters.

Lucius thought of Apollo, the battle he had fought there upon the mountain before creating that great place of beauty and inspiration. *A beauty born out of blood.* In a way, the thought gave him hope.

"I want to see our family," Calliope finally said, breaking into all of their thoughts.

Adara looked down and nodded. "Of course, my love." She shook her head as if coming out of a dream. "We must. It is time."

Lucius flicked the reins, and the mule began to pull away.

"The village is just a little farther down the road," Adara said.

As they drove, Lucius felt his chest hot in the place where the dragon was burned into his skin, as if being so close to the sanctuary had tethered him. He felt excitement and relief at being there, but then as the rooftops of the village came into view, he worried that they would only be met with more misery. *Apollo, let them be safe…*

The village was not far from the sanctuary itself, but in leaving the latter, it felt as though they were leaving the sun behind. The road dropped away to their left into a rocky abyss. The bottom of the valley was filled with the sacred olive groves which, from those heights, appeared as silver-green waves crashing upon the mountainside, their branches thrashed by the valley winds.

To the right of the road, the terrain was flatter and they could see the first rooftops among the hovering smoke of hearth fires and trees. Flocks of goats dotted the road and pathways up the mountain, and high above, an eagle soared toward its eyrie overlooking the village and neighbouring sanctuary.

"How do we find them?" Phoebus asked, now sitting on the bench beside Lucius.

"I'll have to ask someone," Lucius said.

"We can't use our name though," Phoebus said, his hand again seeking the handle of his gladius.

"We will use our new name."

"Let me ask that group of women over there," Adara said, pointing to five women who sat talking in the sunshine beneath an olive tree. She slipped down from the back of the wagon and walked ahead.

Lucius noticed her gladius lying in the back of the wagon, and rolled to a stop. The mule, it seemed, wished to announce their arrival and let out a raucous call as Lucius set down the reins and got down with Phoebus and Calliope.

Adara approached the group of women who had now stopped talking to observe the newcomers. "Kalispera sas," Adara greeted them, smiling as she walked up to the group. As she did so, she had a strange feeling of familiarity, of safety.

The women were all middle-aged or older. From their demeanours, they could have been nobles or peasants. From their speech, which Adara had overheard as she approached, they may or may not have been educated. They were not field labourers, and yet they were, it seemed, a part of the land. They held themselves well, as if they were as rich as Croesus, but they did not balk at Adara's travel-worn appearance. They were all beautiful, and yet not the sort of beauty that would have driven men mad with desire.

"Kalispera to you, dear," the woman in the midst of the others said. She was dark-haired with blue eyes, of medium height, with a wool tunica and cloak that reached down to hide her feet. Her hair was wound simply atop her head, the better to reveal her broad, kind smile and the simple golden earrings in the form of a raven that hung from her lobes. "Can we help you?" she asked, stepping forward to meet Adara. She looked over the newcomer's shoulder to see the children and the hooded man standing by the wagon.

"I...ah..." Adara stumbled with her words at first, unsure suddenly of how to ask after her family. The woman before her, and the other four behind, who were all now standing and listening, observed her, Lucius, Phoebus and Calliope closely.

The first woman's eyes widened and locked onto Lucius for a long moment, her smile fading, before she shook her head ever so slightly and looked back to Adara.

"Forgive me for interrupting your conversation," Adara said, "but we've come a long way."

The woman reached out and grasped Adara's hand as if to steady her upon her feet.

"You did not interrupt us. How can we help you?"

"I'm looking for a family whom I have been told now lives here."

"There are many families living in Delphi, and I know all of them. What is their name?" She looked again at Lucius and then back to Adara.

Adara's eyes looked to the women behind and then to the one before her. Her voice low, she asked, as if relating a secret. "We're looking for the family of Publius Leander Antoninus."

The woman's eyes immediately locked onto Adara's and stayed there for an uncomfortable few moments. The wind picked up then, and several wisps of her dark hair fell down to frame her face.

"I'm sorry, they must not be here," Adara suddenly said, turning, but as she made to retreat from the woman's gaze, she felt her hand lock onto hers again.

"Forgive me, but...who are you?" the woman asked. "Most strangers go to the sanctuary and don't bother with our humble village.

"I am Adara Pen Dragon, and this is my family." Adara did not want to say all of their names. She was feeling desperate now, just wanted to know if the worst had come to pass. "Please...we've come a long way. If the family we're looking for is not here, do tell us if you know where they have gone to and we'll be on our way."

"They are here," the woman said, now grasping Adara with both hands. "Pen Dragon, you say?"

"That is correct," Lucius said, walking up to stand beside Adara. "We would appreciate your help, lady."

The woman looked up at Lucius, her eyes taking in the sight of his scarred face and hands beneath the dark cowl of his cloak. "I am Theia."

"My name is Lucius Pen Dragon, and these are our children, Phoebus and Calliope."

"Calliope...and Phoebus..." the woman repeated, smiling. "Lucius Pen Dragon... I will take you to the family you speak of. They live just at the top of the village." She did not point but looked up and away into the trees beyond the clay rooftops of the first stone houses. "I will take them, and see you later," she said to the women behind her, before turning back to Adara and Lucius. "Come. You will need to walk your mule and wagon, for the way is steep in places." She then turned and went up the narrow street that climbed up from just beyond the tree where she had been sitting.

"Follow your mother," Lucius said to Phoebus and Calliope as Adara began walking with the woman, glancing back at them over her shoulder. He could see Adara was relieved, holding back tears, having heard that her family was there. Lucius clicked his tongue as he took the mule's reins and urged the animal forward.

The path they took up through the village was a winding one, and from windows and doorways, eyes watched them as the woman led them on.

Lucius gripped his sword with his left hand. It felt like the perfect place for an ambush if there were to be one, but they were too far along now to change their minds, the streets too narrow to turn the wagon around or to back up. The only way was forward.

Soon enough, the small houses gave way to an olive grove. Trees rested upon level, raked earth about their variously-sized trunks. The air was sweet in the more open space without the village.

"I would not have guessed there were more houses up here," Adara said as she followed the woman in front of her.

"That is the intent."

"How long have you lived here?" Phoebus asked the lady.

Theia paused and turned to face Adara and her son. "All my life. Come," she smiled again. "We're almost there."

They walked a bit farther through the olive trees until they emerged from the grove to stand before a tall, wide, stone perimeter wall. In the middle of the wall was a single arched door made of oak and iron. Above the door, set into the masonry, was a single eye of brilliant blue enamel to watch over the place, to ensure no evil was brought over that secret threshold.

"Are they...are they all home?" Adara asked.

Theia turned and placed her hand upon Adara's arm. "Most of them." She then reached up and knocked three times upon the hard door before stepping back and waiting.

It took a few moments, but soon enough, the sound of an iron bolt sliding could be heard. The door creaked inward and a woman of about Adara's age stood there. She wore a plain, long-sleeved tunica and had pale, shoulder-length hair. "Good day, Ambrosia," Theia said. "These travellers have come a long way to see Publius Leander and his family. I brought them straight here."

"Ambrosia?" Adara said, stepping forward.

The woman looked confused for a very brief moment, and then recognition dawned and her hand began to tremble.

"Not here, Ambrosia," Theia said quickly, taking her hands tightly. "Bring them inside."

Ambrosia nodded quickly as she looked at the rest of the new arrivals. She looked over the children, her eyes incredulous at the sight of them, and then to the man behind them, standing beside the mule.

Lucius could not bring himself to look at her directly and pulled his hood forward a little. Though it was obvious she did not recognize him, he certainly recognized her, the former slave who had been Argus' lover all those years ago. He fought back the rising anger he suddenly felt, for he remembered that she too had been betrayed by his foster brother, and that she had been a loyal servant to his mother thereafter. *Where is everyone?*

"Please, come inside," Ambrosia said, turning to go into the compound. "You can leave the wagon. No one will touch it."

Adara, Phoebus and Calliope followed her through the doorway, and when they were gone, Theia turned to Lucius who was getting Adara's gladius and their satchels from the back of the wagon.

"You need not worry here, Lucius Pen Dragon," she said. She looked up at Lucius' face where it hid in the shadow of his cowl, her blue eyes searching the darkness for his own. "You have come to sanctuary at the navel of the world."

"Who are you?"

She smiled again. "I will see you again soon," she said before looking through the doorway one more time and turning to leave.

Lucius watched her go slowly downhill, through the olive grove, her hand reaching out to touch the trees as she went, her head tilted toward the sun and blue sky above as if she enjoyed every moment of her existence. There was something truly familiar about the woman, but Lucius had no time to dwell on it any longer, for his thoughts were interrupted by a chorus of exclamation and crying. He turned to go through the doorway in the wall.

Beyond the wall was a world of peace and serenity. Directly ahead was a square, stone domus that centered on an interior courtyard which was reached by way of a narrow passage in the wall. Lucius could see Adara and the children within, but before following, he scanned the surroundings a little longer. Within the walls of the compound, a few stray goats and sheep wandered among almond trees to the left, and to the far right, around a fenced-in garden where vegetables grew. Beyond the olive trees, could be seen the leaves of an oak tree and the spear tips of a few cypresses. Smoke from a nearby hearth hovered around the grounds, and there was a distant sound of chiselling.

But the cries grew even louder and Lucius was drawn into the courtyard of the clay-roofed domus directly before him. He emerged from the shadow of the corridor into a courtyard with a single olive tree in the middle. There he saw Adara enfolded in her parents' arms, her sobs audible over their vocal gratitude. Beside them, a young woman was kneeling before Phoebus and Calliope, tears streaming down her face as she looked up at them.

When Lucius stepped into the light and put down the satchels that had been hanging from his shoulders, the people all turned toward him in stunned silence.

The young woman with Phoebus and Calliope stood and walked slowly toward him.

"Clarinda?" Lucius said.

Without a word, or even a shudder at his appearance, Lucius' younger sister rushed into his arms.

It felt strange to be met with such emotion, for Lucius had never been very close to his younger sister, and he had left for the legions when she was but a little child. And yet now, here she was, grown and world-weary.

"I can't believe you're here," she said, stepping back and wiping her eyes after a few moments. "I...I just..." It was then that she seemed to finally notice his changed appearance, and it made her weep all the more in that moment.

"Children!" Publius Leander Antonius, Adara's father, now turned to Phoebus and Calliope, along with Delphina, Adara's mother, and together they embraced the grandchildren they had been missing for so many years. "Thank the Gods, you're safe!"

Delphina was too overcome with joy to speak, for she had dreamed of that day for what felt like an age, how she would embrace her daughter tightly and tell her she loved her more than anything, how she would inhale the scent of her grandchildren and never let go again. It was to be a moment she could never capture in charcoal or pigment, for it was too overwhelming even in her daydreams, let alone the reality of it.

Clarinda continued to wipe the tears from her eyes as she looked upon the scene of reunion, and as Publius and Delphina embraced Phoebus and Calliope, Adara turned to come to her and take her in her arms. "Thank Apollo, you're safe!"

Adara wiped her own eyes and looked to Lucius who stood beside them with shock and worry upon his face. "You're a woman now!" Adara said to Clarinda. "Has it been so long?"

Clarinda nodded. "It has."

"Where are Caecilius and Emrys?" Lucius asked suddenly. "Where is my mother?"

His voice was like a dark cloud, a rumble of thunder settling over the courtyard.

Publius Leander had always loved Lucius like he was his own son, but after all that had happened to his family, all the loss, he had never felt like striking a man more than he did in that moment. He stood before Lucius wanting to be angry, to unleash all the grief and frustration he had locked upon inside, but when he looked upon his daughter's husband, it became apparent to him that of them all, perhaps it was Lucius who had suffered most. Without a word, Publius Leander stepped forward, took Lucius by the shoulders, and held him close in a fatherly embrace. "What have they done to you, my boy?"

Delphina too stepped forward, seeing Lucius through her watery eyes and reaching out a trembling hand to touch his rough, scarred cheek. "Thank the Gods you've come back to us."

"Forgive me," Lucius muttered, unable to say much, knowing that there was little he could do to make amends for all the pain he had caused them.

Delphina shook her head and wiped her eyes. "You're here now. That is all that matters." She gripped his hands tightly and in earnest, and he remembered how much he had loved them like he did his own mother.

"My brother and mother..." He had to ask. He had to know. "Are they..."

"Caecilius is hunting on Parnassus," said a thick voice from the doorway of a cubiculum off the courtyard.

"Emrys?" Lucius released Delphina's hands and strode to the burly, oncoming form of the sculptor.

Tears streamed down Emrys' cheek to get lost in his thick beard as he threw his arms about Lucius. "By the Gods, Lucius. You're a sight!" He looked at Adara, Phoebus and Calliope and smiled before looking back at Lucius.

"Emrys...where is my mother?"

"She's here Lucius. She's..." Emrys swallowed hard, but dared to look Lucius in the eyes. "She's been unwell. She had a dream about all of you...such dreams..." He turned to look at a doorway from which Ambrosia had just emerged. "Come. Your arrival will lift her spirits."

Emrys glanced at Publius and Delphina who nodded to him, and he led Lucius to the room at the far left corner of the courtyard.

Ambrosia stood outside the door, her head bowed to Lucius as he approached.

Lucius paused and laid his hand upon her arm. She looked up and as she did so, he smiled his thanks to her. She smiled back, but it was obvious something was not right, not least because of the bloody cloth that was hidden in the clay bowl Ambrosia held in her hands.

"Let Baba go alone, children," Adara said to Phoebus and Calliope as she watched Lucius disappear into the dark doorway of the cubiculum. She turned to her parents. "Is she very ill?"

Publius and Delphina turned to each other, and the look they exchanged made Adara's heart sink.

As Lucius entered the cubiculum, it took his eyes a few moments to adjust to the darkness and dim light. He stood in the doorway for a few moments, his heart pounding, as he watched Emrys' thick form disappear farther into the room. After a few moments he was able to see two simple, bronze braziers burning in two corners for heat and light, and several furs laid upon the stone and earth floor. A trunk along the far wall was all there was for the storage of possessions. There was no ornamentation, and little colour, creating something of a sadness in the air.

The smell of sickness was there too, like a ghostly presence, invisible and full of menace, and it drew Lucius' eyes to the centre of the back wall as he went farther in to see the low, wide bed where his mother lay in the middle with Emrys sitting upon a stool to lean over her.

The sculptor, who had been her companion for many years since the death of her husband, Quintus Caecilius Metellus, whispered softly to her sleeping form as Lucius waited, his hood still covering his head.

A bowl of incense smoked on the bedside table and hovered around the room like an early morning mist in the olive groves without, but when Emrys stood and came over to Lucius, the smoke swirled and Antonia Metella's form came into focus.

Lucius could not help but gasp, for his mother now appeared as an old woman, her once lustrous hair completely gray, and her skin withered and hanging off of her bones. Her breathing was ragged, a wheezing sound flowing in and out. Her eyes however, as they opened, sought the dark form of her returned son, and when they found him standing there, like a shadow or shade, her thin arm reached up.

"Lu...Lucius? By Apollo... Is it you?" Her voice wheezed more loudly with the effort of speaking, and she began to cough.

Emrys rushed back to her side and pressed a cup of water to her lips. "Drink, love. Yes. It is Lucius. Your son has come back to you." He looked up at Lucius, knowing that the sight of him would shock Antonia even more than it had shocked him.

"I can't see him, Emrys. Lucius? Come closer. Remove your cloak."

Lucius wanted to shed his cloak, for it was very warm inside that room, but he feared what would happen when his mother saw him.

"Come, Lucius," Emrys said, stepping aside so that he could take the stool beside the bed.

Lucius took a deep breath and pushed back the hood of his cloak and let it slide off of his shoulders so that it fell onto the floor.

Antonia was silent as she looked upon the massacred form of her once-beautiful boy, her son who had meant everything to her. She said nothing, but held her arms out to take his hands, even as the tears streamed down her cheeks in the dim firelight.

Lucius quickly sat down and took his mother's trembling hands.

She pulled him close and wrapped them around his neck. "Oh, my boy," she said in his ear, her voice tremulous with grief and rage. "What have they done to you?" Her fingers touched his thin hair, and she ran them over the rough surface of his face, neck and arms like a blind woman trying to see. "Thank Apollo you've come. You are safe now... you are here in this place."

Lucius sat straighter, his hands still gripping hers. "Yes, Mother. I'm here now. All will be well."

Antonia shook her head and managed a smile. "You still cannot lie well, my good boy." She coughed again and he took the cup Emrys had set upon the table and gave her a drink. "I was afraid that you were... dead...for the longest time. I...I despaired."

"I'm so sorry, Mother. I let hubris possess me, and now look at all that has happened. We've lost everything."

Her eyes shot wide at that. "We have not lost everything. All my children are safe. Our friends...our loved ones," she smiled sadly at Emrys. "Villas can be rebuilt...crops regrown... But our loved ones, our

children...once gone, they cannot come back across the dark river...
Alene..."

As Lucius sat there, he watched his mother break down and weep,
still, after many years, at the thought of his sister's murder. *Her murder
at Rome's hands!* he thought, seeing the faces of all who had wronged
their family.

Antonia collected herself and looked to him again. "I miss her still,
but the Gods tell me she is in Elysium with her love, and that is a blessed
thing."

Lucius nodded though he could not say anything, his throat blocked
up with the grief that surfaced whenever he thought of his sister.

Antonia pulled at his hands and he leaned closer so that he looked
into her eyes. "None of this is your fault! Do you understand? None
of it!"

"I thought I could change the world. I was wrong."

Antonia's eyes widened and looked skyward, as if she were seeing
the possibilities. "And what a world it would have been, Lucius... Something worth fighting for."

They sat in silence for a few moments.

"Lucius...the Gods had other plans, and that is all right. So long as
you and your family are safe. We are all here now, together, and that is a
blessing beyond price." She sighed, a great sound of relief. "The people
here are good. They watch over us."

"You live in squalor now," he said, looking about the room, ignorant
of the hurt the comment must have caused Emrys.

But Antonia shook her head. "Not squalor... Simplicity gives us clarity. It sheds light on the things that truly matter. I have you and Adara
again, and Emrys is here..." She looked at him and the tears forming on
the edges of his swollen lids. "Do not cry, love." She turned back to
Lucius. "I have Caecilius and Clarinda, and my friends, Delphina and
Publius. And now my grandchildren... Are they well?" She tried sitting
up. "Let me see them..."

Lucius stood and made to go, but his mother held him fast.

"I'll get them, Antonia," Emrys said, leaving the room and coming
back a few moments later followed by Adara, Phoebus and Calliope.

Adara approached the bedside opposite Lucius and knelt beside her
mother-in-law. "Antonia..." she said, forcing herself not to weep or look
shocked. "It is so good to see you. The Gods bless us."

"They do, my dear," Antonia reached out to squeeze Adara's hand. "Still so beautiful and kind... I've missed our talks."

"We will have many now," Adara said, feeling her eyes blur.

"Do not weep for me. I am well now." Antonia turned to look at the two tall youths standing at the foot of her bed, and it was then that she wept aloud. "By the Gods! Has so much time elapsed?" She held out her arms and slowly, Phoebus and Calliope came around the bed where their mother had been, and knelt beside Antonia. "I've missed you so much!" Despite her weakened state, Antonia pulled each of them into a tight embrace.

"Are you ill, Grandmother?" Calliope asked, holding Antonia's hand, kissing it.

Antonia looked at her hand in surprise. She felt a pulsing strength returning, though it was ever so faint. She looked up at her granddaughter. "You have the gift...I can feel it."

"I'm here for you now," Calliope said, and despite all the blood and horror, in that moment she felt better than she had in a long while, as if she was where she was meant to be.

"We'll help you, Grandmother," Phoebus said beside his sister, and Antonia's eyes lit up with pride.

"You look so like your father when he was young. Taller even."

Phoebus smiled and looked proud in that moment, but tried not to look at Lucius across the bed.

Antonia noticed this and shook her head. "He has fought long and hard for all of us, your father has... Honour him. Help him. For the relationship between a father and his son is one that should not be neglected. The world needs good men." She squeezed Phoebus' hand tightly. "And you *are* good, my boy. I can see it as clearly as the sun upon these mountains."

To everyone's surprise, Phoebus leaned forward and burried his head in the furs that covered his grandmother.

"There, there," Antonia said, stroking his smooth dark hair. "We're all together now." She turned her neck and looked at Lucius. "We're together," she repeated, smiling more than she had in a long while.

A moment later, Antonia sighed and her lids became heavy. "I'm tired now, and must rest. We will talk more later."

"Yes, Mother," Lucius said, silently indicating the door to Adara, Phoebus and Calliope.

The three of them went out into the daylight and fresh air.

Lucius turned back to his mother. "I cannot leave you."

Antonia chuckled. "You are not. You are going to eat and rest. Speak with Delphina and Publius... They have suffered much..."

Lucius looked at Emrys, but the sculptor said nothing, only watched the woman he loved lying there abed.

As Lucius stood, Antonia smiled to look at him.

"I remember that day long ago...the light...the beauty of it... It was a light that blinded..." Even as she smiled, she closed her eyes and fell asleep.

At the doorway, his cloak over his arm, Lucius looked back one more time to see Emrys bend over Antonia to kiss her on the forehead as he settled back down on the stool beside her.

Lucius and Adara were given the room in the southwest corner of the small domus, and Phoebus and Calliope the one beside them where, if the door was open, the frame was filled with the sunlit olive tree in the quiet courtyard. The rooms were simple like Antonia's, sparse of ornamentation. What furniture there was appeared to be newly hewn from trees upon the mountainside, mostly pine. The beds consisted of simple straps of interwoven hide with sheep skins laid overtop, for there was very little hay available.

From what little they had seen of the rest of the domus, everyone else's cubicula were similarly appointed. The days of silver and bronze lamps and wall hangings, brightly frescoed walls, and furniture carved such that it came alive, were all distant memories. The priority in that home for their families was warmth and survival.

While Phoebus and Calliope settled into their own room, Lucius and Adara sat in theirs.

"Are you all right?" Adara asked as Lucius sat on the edge of the wood bed, his head in his hands. He had been silent ever since he had left Antonia's room. Adara sat next to him. "She was very happy to see you, all of us. She'll get better now, you'll see, now that we're all together."

Lucius looked at her. He could not bring himself to say what he was thinking. "Look what I've brought everyone to. My family and yours...

They each had their own homes, generations old and filled with beauty, and now, it's all gone."

"They're happy enough, Lucius. Don't lose sight of the Gods' blessings now. Our families are alive! After Athenae, I feared…" Adara shut her eyes and put her hand to her mouth, "…I feared that we would find them all dead."

"They're living like shepherds, Adara."

Adara had to admit that she had been shocked too to see how they were living, but she could not lose sight of what was important. She also knew that Lucius was feeling his guilt more acutely than ever. *There isn't anything I can do about that,* she thought a little bitterly.

"We have to see life here as a good thing, Lucius, for now at least. My mother grew up here. The people are kind and welcoming to our families. They won't betray us to anyone. Not here."

Lucius looked up at his wife where she now stood before him, her arms crossed as she leaned against the wall facing him. Beside her, the open doorway looked onto the dusky courtyard where the tree swayed in the early evening breeze. He had to admit to himself that he felt something of emptiness in that place. He had hoped that Apollo would be there, that they would finally be able to speak, but it was not to be. The Far-Shooter was in Hyperborea for the winter. *How long will I have to stay here before I can finish what I set out to do?* Lucius wondered as he fingered the black gladius handle where it leaned against the bed.

"Lucius?" Adara said. "I don't know what you're thinking anymore. I used to, but not now. Please…" She squeezed his hand to stop him touching the weapon. "Be here with me and our children, our family. We're all safe now."

He looked up at her green eyes, and a part of him remembered how they had sparkled so keenly when they were young and free of the worries that would soon entangle about their limbs and necks. He did not care for himself anymore, for pain and hatred had become a part of him, but it did occasionally break his heart to see what he had done to the woman he had loved so deeply and still loved.

Lucius set the sword down and brought Adara's hand to his lips.

"Mama, Baba?" Phoebus' voice came in at the doorway. "Grandmother says that food is ready in the triclinium across the courtyard."

"We're coming," Adara said, smiling at her son over her shoulder. She turned back to Lucius. "Come. Let's enjoy a meal with our family."

· · ·

The triclinium was the largest room in the domus, but despite that, it consisted of a simple amalgam of stools and chairs around a few low, rough tables. Bronze braziers fizzled with fire and heat at either end of the room, shedding light upon the plain white walls around which Delphina had painted small red acanthus leaves.

Lucius was silent as Publius Leander sat across from him with Adara, sipping his wine from an olive-wood cup, smiling as he watched Phoebus and Calliope with Clarinda.

Lucius could see that Publius - once so warm and welcoming to him - now found it hard to look at him. He wondered whether it was because of all that had happened, or because of Lucius' appearance. Either way, Adara's father had spoken very little, but he did continuously hug his daughter and grandchildren, his lips moving in silent thanks to the Gods each time for their safe delivery.

Delphina had busied herself with preparing a meal for all of them, moving to and from the kitchen and food stores at the front of the house, and then bringing in platters and bowls of simple fare to the triclinium with Ambrosia's help.

"Mother," Adara said. "Please let me help you."

"Nonsense!" Delphina answered. "You've just arrived after a great journey. Sit and rest. Ambrosia and I will join you soon."

When she had gone back out to the kitchen, Publius leaned toward Adara. "Let her do this today. She has missed you so very much. Tomorrow, you may help."

"I would like to as well!" Calliope said.

Publius smiled broadly, his eyes watery in the firelight. "Of course, my girl! Your grandmother would love that."

"Does my mother… Can she join us too?" Lucius asked.

For the first time since they had sat down, Publius looked directly at his son-in-law. He shook his head. "I'm sorry, Lucius. Your mother has been too weak to leave her bed for many weeks now."

"She just stays there alone in her cubiculum?" Lucius asked.

"No. We take it in turns to watch over her, and the medicus comes once a day to check on her."

"What does he say?" Adara asked her father.

Publius shook his head. "He does not know what is wrong. She is no older than any of us, but...he suspects her grief has been too great." He looked at Phoebus and Calliope again. "But that may change now with you here."

Lucius wanted to reach across the table to his father-in-law, to thank him for all that he had done for Antonia, but what passed his lips was something different. "Publius... I... I'm sorry for all the pain that I've caused your family. I didn't ever think that-"

"Think?" Publius cut in, staring into his cup. He chuckled darkly, the visage of the kind man he was giving way to one of bitterness and despair, like a man who has been thrown out of Elysium. "You didn't think, I suspect, of what would happen, of who would be affected by your actions."

"Baba," Adara said, her voice pleading. "Lucius did what he thought was right." Even as she said the words, she knew her voice sounded half-hearted. "The legions' legates, the troops...they all wanted him to take the throne..."

"Such supreme power is not easily taken, Daughter." He turned to look at Lucius. He had thought of all that he had wanted to say since their nightmare began, but it all slipped away in the face of the destroyed man's appearance before him. "And it is always at great cost." Publius drained his cup and set it harshly on the table. "We are all paying for your arrogance, Lucius."

"Grandfather stop!" Calliope said, jumping up from her stool to stand beside Lucius. "Can you not see what Baba has been through? And it is much more than his fire-burned skin! He has been to places, seen things that no mortal could-"

"Calliope, stop," Lucius said softly, his hand upon his daughter's shoulder, his heart swelling with pride as she, and then Phoebus came to stand at his side.

"No," Calliope answered. "They need to know what you've been through. It's so much more than a burning house!" Her voice wavered. "There was so much blood! So much!" In that moment, his daughter's arms wrapped around his neck and Lucius held her close as she sobbed, the rest of the family staring dumb-founded at the two children standing beside their father.

Lucius closed his eyes, and willed what strength he had to feed his daughter and son who stood by him, who yet, after all the horrors, seemed to believe in him.

Through her tears, Adara looked across the room to see her mother in the doorway, weeping as she looked upon the scene, as she processed all that she had heard of the conversation.

"Forgive me, Lucius," Publius Leander said. "These have been difficult months."

Slowly, Calliope released her arms from Lucius' neck, and before speaking, Lucius wiped her tears and kissed her cheek.

Phoebus led Calliope back to her stool beside Clarinda, and Delphina walked in to hug her granddaughter tightly.

Lucius cleared his throat. "No apology is needed, Publius. I know what I've done, and I'm aware of the pain I've cause all of you. I'll make things right, by the Gods I will."

Publius stood and walked around the table to stand with Lucius. He reached out and took his son-in-law's arms. "You already have, Lucius. You've brought my daughter and grandchildren safely here. That is all that matters."

They ate quietly at first, allowing the intensity of the previous conversation to fade before they could speak of generalities and of what was happening outside of the pain they had all experienced.

In days long gone, in Rome or Athenae, they had had kitchen slaves to cook delicacies, to gather a rich array of foods from the fora and agorae, and the money to do it. But as they ate, Lucius was aware of how much that had changed. Now, Adara's mother had prepared the meal, with help from Ambrosia who had been freed some years before and had chosen to remain at Antonia's side. The meal they ate consisted of boiled field greens and lemon, beans in oil, fresh bread, goat's cheese, and the meat from one chicken for all of them. Simple though it may have been, to Lucius and his family, it felt like a feast to be eating thus in safety and with family.

As the food and watered wine took effect, they relaxed and eased into each other's company again. The initial awkwardness of such a long absence slowly faded away.

Lucius looked at his much younger sister and marvelled at how much she had grown. She was a young woman now, plain but beautiful in her own way. He hoped the horrors of her childhood had faded from her memory, but suspected that they were buried deep down, and that thought made him sad. He had not been there for her, ever, nor for his younger brother, Caecilius, who still had not joined them.

"Clarinda," Adara suddenly said, looking across at her sister-in-law. "Your tunica looks much like a priestess' robes. Is it a new fashion here?" Adara knew the question sounded absurd, but she had had enough of the silence. She wanted to know what had happened to everyone in their absence.

Clarinda smiled and shook her head. "No, Sister. They are priestess' robes. I am an initiate at the sanctuary now. I serve Apollo."

Lucius looked up. "Is that what you want?"

Clarinda turned to her brother. "It is safe," she said sadly. "And yes, it is what I want." She set her piece of bread down upon her clay plate. "When we arrived here, we were desperate and tired. We saw our home destroyed in Etruria, and then, after fleeing to Athenae, saw that home destroyed as well. We were lucky to escape."

There was an awkward silence around the room as everyone watched Clarinda speak, her words salting their still-fresh wounds like a piece of meat upon the table.

"We arrived in Delphi, and I was deep in despair, such that I wanted to jump from the cliffs and end it all." She paused, overcome with the remembering of such a time. "I...I was washing at the Castalian spring - the pool at the base of the Phaedriades - and I just wept. I was there, alone for some time when Theia found me there."

"The woman who brought us here?" Phoebus asked.

Clarinda smiled at her nephew. "Yes. She saw my despair and was so kind. She somehow knew who I was. She knows Delphina."

Adara and Lucius looked to Delphina where she sat beside her husband.

"It's true," Delphina said. "We grew up together. I moved on, but she remained to serve Apollo. She is...very special."

Clarinda continued. "Theia felt that I would make a good servant of the Far-Shooter here in the sanctuary. With all that we had lost, it seemed like the best option for me."

"Will you not marry someday?" Calliope asked.

Clarinda shook her head. "I've seen what men do in the world. I've no wish to be tethered to that. Besides, the sanctuary here is the only place where I've ever felt truly peaceful and happy." She looked across at Lucius and he felt that he could not hold her gaze. *Another person whose life I've destroyed.*

But Clarinda smiled at her brother and, seated between her niece and nephew, she did appear to be truly happy.

"And tell us of your journey here, Lucius," Emrys said, as he settled down on a stool to take some food, having been relieved by Ambrosia who was now sitting with Antonia. "By the Gods, how did you get past the Praetorians and Caracalla's spies to get here?"

"It's been a long road, Emrys. We left from Din Tagell where our dear friend is now lord."

"Not Caradoc?" Emrys had heard of the slaughter that had been done in his Dumnonian homeland years ago when the tyrant had taken the throne in the ancient hall. "Tell me you're not his friend!"

"No. I mean Einion, the son of Cunnomore. We helped him take back his father's throne."

Emrys' eyes widened in disbelief. "I knew Cunnomore. A firm but good man. And his son?"

"A greater one," Lucius said, suddenly missing Einion. "Einion and his sister, Briana helped me greatly in Caledonia, and so I helped him, along with Dagon."

"I remember Dagon," Clarinda said, "when he came to you in Etruria with all those men."

"Are they still your men?" Publius said.

Lucius was quiet. "No. We were betrayed and many are dead or scattered to the winds. They were my brothers…"

Adara reached out to Lucius.

"But many of them," Lucius continued, "came to Dumnonia where Einion gives them sanctuary. And Dagon, who is a king among his people, married Briana, Einion's sister."

Emrys sat back and smiled for the first time. "Then hope is kindled in my homeland."

"There is," Adara said, smiling to him. "There is also hope in Ynis Wytrin."

"You've been there?" Emrys asked.

"That is where we were all this time," Phoebus said. "Since the destruction of our home. They wait for our return." He looked at his father then, but Lucius stared at his plate and the half-eaten food lying there.

"We have heard rumours of what happened in Eburacum," Publius said, but tell us how you got here.

Lucius looked up. "Well...we are no longer the Metelli. We are the Pen Dragon of Dumnonia. It was a name given to us by the people there, and as such we travelled by ship from Din Tagell..."

Over the next while, Lucius and Adara recounted the tale of their travels, of the trusted captain Creticus and his offer of help whenever they needed it, of the ports where they had stopped, and of their tortuous journey through Italy after seeing the destruction of their home. Their heavy-hearted account of what had happened to Numa and Prisca brought tears to Emrys and Clarinda's eyes, for they had loved them well.

As Lucius spoke, Publius knew that much was left out, that he would have to ask him later what had happened with Caracalla, of the last days of Severus, and of the so-called support he had had from the legions. However, every time he looked upon his son-in-law's physical state, he decided it was no use. *What is done, is done. There is no going back,* he decided.

"You should have seen our home on the ancient hillfort you gave to us, Baba," Adara said when Lucius had finished telling his tale. "It was beautiful, and the people thereabouts," she turned to Emrys, "the Durotriges, were our friends and allies."

"They still are, Mama," Phoebus said. "They also wait for us to return."

Adara wondered if she should dispel with the thought immediately, seeing that it caused her parents some discomfort, but she decided against it. If the thought gave Phoebus hope, then that was just as well. "They do, Phoebus. You are right." Adara decided to change the subject and turned to her parents. "And what of my sisters? You've not told us of them."

Publius and Delphina looked at each other and what little joy they seemed to have leached away.

"They both married merchants' sons, brothers actually, and they now live in Ephesus."

"Do you hear from them? We haven't seen them in years! Do they write?" Adara asked. "Do I have any nephews or nieces? How are they?" She turned to Lucius who had noticed Delphina's look as Adara plied her with questions.

"We do not hear from them," Delphina answered. "They have abandoned us."

"What? How do you mean?" Adara's face contorted in confusion.

Publius looked at his daughter, and then at Lucius. "When Severus died and rumour of the events in Eburacum spread like wildfire across the empire, Hadrea and Lavena's husbands decided they would move them permanently from Athenae to their family home in Ephesus. Caracalla's proscriptions were brutal and he was seizing all he could. So, to avoid being associated with...with the Metelli...Hadrea and Lavena's husbands forbade them to ever have contact with us, or you, again."

Delphina's features hardened with the obvious hurt that that must have caused her. "We will never see them again, Adara," she said through thin, unmoving lips.

Lucius set his wine cup down and stood. "Again...I am sorry..." He turned to leave.

"Baba, don't go," Calliope said.

"I just need some fresh air," he replied before going out into the courtyard.

"I'll be back," Clarinda said before rising and going after her brother.

Outside in the courtyard, while Adara told her parents and Emrys more of all that had befallen them, Lucius stood beneath the limbs of the lone olive tree looking up at the cold, clear night sky where it seemed a million lamps had been lit. Not since his days in the desert had he seen such a sky. He felt an arm slide through his and turned to see his younger sister standing beside him, leaning against him to look up at that same, star-pocked firmament.

"It's beautiful, isn't it?" she said. "I never tire of it."

"It is."

"Don't worry about Publius and Delphina, Lucius. They do love you like their own son. Lavena and Hadrea's departure has just hit them hard, but seeing you, Adara and the children has already lifted their spirits, I can tell."

"And what of our mother? I've never seen her in such a state, even after Quintus Metellus beat her. Will her spirits lighten with our arrival, or will she only be reminded of lost time and lost lives?"

Clarinda turned to stand before her brother, looking up at him. "Our father was a monster, Lucius!"

Then she does not know, Lucius realized.

Clarinda grabbed his hands. "Despite all the loss we've experienced - our homes...Alene...and more, Mother has been happier since Father's...death. I wonder sometimes if it was Apollo's intent that we should come here all along, to cleanse ourselves, and be healed of the past?"

Lucius wanted to tell her that however much the Gods - Apollo - loved and protected you, pain and torment would still find you. As he looked upon his sister though, and saw the hope in her young eyes, he found he could not dispel her perceptions, for she was embarked upon her own journey to heal and help others. *And that's more than what I have done for those around me.*

"Perhaps you're right," he said. "I've just never seen our mother so frail and weak."

"You'll see. She'll be up and about tomorrow," Clarinda said, "strengthened by your arrival. She was sure you would come, you know. She said she knew, that Apollo had told her."

Lucius thought about telling Clarinda the truths he had learned about his own father in that moment, in that quiet, dark place lit by starlight, but then there was a solid pounding on the front gate. Quickly, Lucius reached for his sword, but found that he had left it in the cubiculum.

Clarinda smiled and made to rush to the doorway, but Lucius grabbed her.

"No, don't!" he hissed. "They've followed us!" Lucius then bolted across the courtyard to the cubiculum and emerged with his gladius in hand. "Clarinda, no!" he yelled as he saw her opening the door.

"It's fine, Lucius," she said as she swung the solid door inward.

Firelight spilled into the courtyard and as Lucius arrived, pushing his sister out of the way, he was faced with a mass of a man holding a torch in one hand and something large slung over his shoulder.

"Get out or I'll kill you!" Lucius said, crouched with his gladius at the ready.

"Lucius, stop!" Clarinda yelled, jumping in front of the man. "It's Caecilius!"

Lucius squinted in the flickering torchlight to see the man standing before the pointed tip of his gladius.

The man was stout and covered in a thick wool tunic and breeches with furs over his shoulders so that he looked like some kind of beast. Hobnailed boots covered in mud made him stand taller, and thick strips of leather with hunting knives and a sword hung about his waist and across his chest. Over his shoulder was slung a mountain boar, its head lolled, tongue out, and on the arm that held the torch aloft was slung a great recurve bow, the sort the nomads used in Africa Proconsularis.

Lucius remembered that bow, but he struggled to remember the man before him, peering through the thick beard and hair to try and catch a glimpse of his younger brother in the rough hunter standing before him. "Caecilius?" Lucius lowered his sword and stepped forward.

Clarinda took the torch from the man and he dropped the boar onto the earth with a thud, stepping forward.

"Lu...Lucius?" he said, his eyes watery in the light. He quickly wiped his eyes and continued to stare at his older brother. "You're alive?" He observed the missing hair and scarred face and arms of the brother he had always looked up to, from whom he had always sought approval and attention. "What has happened?"

"They took everything from us."

"E...everything?" Caecilius' lip began to tremble. "Gods no...the children?" He was about to yell out when Phoebus and Calliope came running out of the triclinium into the courtyard, followed by the others.

"Uncle!" they called as they ran toward Caecilius and their father.

"Thank the Gods," Caecilius whispered hoarsely as they rushed to him. He opened his arms and received them, squeezing hard with gratitude. After a few moments, he let go of them and looked around the circle of family who had arrived. "Sister?" he said to Adara who hugged him tightly. "You're here?"

Adara stood back. "We are. All is well now, Caecilius. I wouldn't have recognized you. You've changed so much!"

Caecilius glanced at Lucius and then back at Adara.

"Around here," Publius said, "the people call him Teucer, after the archer-brother of the Greek hero, Ajax."

Caecilius smiled, a little embarrassed. "I like to hunt in the mountains. It helps me think."

"I see you still have the bow I gave you," Lucius said, his hand on his brother's shoulder.

Caecilius nodded. "It is always with me." He turned to Delphina. "And I've brought tomorrow's dinner!"

"So you have, my boy," Delphina said. "You are such a help."

Caecilius smiled.

"Caecilius has done so much for us," Publius added. "He helped Emrys and me build this domus, and all of the furniture within it."

Suddenly, the poor, plain trappings of that sad home of exiles took on a new lustre to Lucius and, in a way, he felt strange to have not been a part of it.

"How is mother?" Caecilius asked Clarinda. "Does she know they are here?"

"Oh yes," Clarinda said, leaning against her brother's fur-covered shoulder. "She's very happy."

"Thank Apollo," he said, nodding as he looked around the gathering of their family's faces. "I can't believe it…"

"I know," Clarinda whispered.

But Caecilius had trouble feeling the full measure of the joy he might have done at Lucius' family's return, for to look upon his brother was as painful a sight as the distant burning blaze of their family's home in Etruria. He knew Lucius was not the same man, that there was a darkness hanging over him, Adara, and even the children. It wrenched his heart. He could almost smell it, the death that hung around them, just as the deer in the mountain woods can sense danger on the autumn breezes.

"Come inside and eat, Caecilius," Delphina said. "There is plenty of food left."

Caecilius unslung his bow and turned to them. "I'll be along shortly. I just want to check on my mother. Please, return to your meal. I'm coming."

Delphina and Publius smiled and turned to go back to the triclinium with Emrys, followed by Adara, Phoebus and Calliope who glanced back over their shoulders at their uncle.

A moment later, the three siblings stood together, alone again in the courtyard.

"I want to know everything that's happened, Lucius," Caecilius said, reaching out to place a hesitant hand on his older brother's shoulder.

Lucius nodded slowly. "I'll tell you. First, go see mother so she knows you're home."

Caecilius rubbed his temples, and looked at Clarinda who smiled sadly back before he went to their mother's cubiculum where Ambrosia was waiting and watching from the door frame.

When he disappeared inside the dimly-lit room, Lucius turned to Clarinda. "He's so changed."

"As have we all, Brother." She sighed. "But Apollo has brought us all together again here, at the centre of the world."

"Does Caecilius still have his headaches?" Lucius asked, remembering the reason he had given him the bow in the first place; it was a quieter weapon than steel, easier for him to use as he suffered through the unbearable headaches caused by the beating Quintus Metellus had given him long ago.

"All the time," Clarinda answered sadly. "I keep hoping being here, in Delphi, that Apollo will help rid him of the pain he suffers from... But there are some hurts that not even the Gods can rid a man of. Go now. Join Adara and the others. I'll check on Caecilius and mother."

Before Lucius could say anything, his sister was walking across the courtyard, leaving him alone in the dark beside the body of the slain boar.

Lucius looked at the sky and felt the wind pick up, its touch gentle upon his face and in the shivering leaves of the olive tree behind him. The night was strangely still and quiet, but for the jingle of bells upon the necks of the goats in the groves without the walls of that newfound domus.

When Quintus and Clarinda did not emerge from their mother's room, Lucius turned and went back to the triclinium to join the others. It was strange for them all to be under the same roof but, he thought, stranger still for him to be among them. It was a feeling he could not relinquish.

Morning in Delphi brought with it a feeling of strange calm that crept in at the door of Lucius and Adara's cubiculum. It was as if all that could be, was, but also as if all in existence - the people, the trees, the rocks, the wind - were listening. Outside, it was still and cool, and just as the sun began to break the distant ridges of the world, swifts, larks and kestrels plunged from their nests to sing, whilst the eagles in their high thrones looked down upon the sanctuary of the son of Zeus.

Lucius had tossed and turned through the night beside Adara who had slept soundly after several cups of wine to calm her nerves. He looked at her as he sat up, and had an urge to kiss her soft cheek, swollen with sleep, but he did not wish to wake her from the comfort of her tangled curls. He rubbed his eyes, remembered sleeping in fits and starts, and the sight that had greeted him behind his closed lids.

At one point in the dark of night, Lucius had found himself in a narrow gully flanked by fern-covered cliff faces. Among the rocks, eyes had been staring out, eyes that betrayed the entire range of mortal emotion - love and loss, exhilaration and terror, anger and unimaginable sadness. Up above, beyond the darkness of that grim cut in the earth, was brilliant sunlight, a fire in the sky. Lucius had wanted to reach up to it, to fly in it, but he would have had to scale that hoary rockface.

Then, he had looked ahead of him to see the tall, muscular form of his father.

Apollo had stood there, his bow over his shoulder. He turned to Lucius and smiled.

Where are you going? Lucius asked.

Apollo smiled, but did not come close. *To my winter realm in the North.*

Can you not stay?

The Far-Shooter shook his head.

What of my mother? Can you heal her?

Those star-whirling eyes looked upon Lucius. *You already have, my son. Speak with her. Learn more from her memories.* He turned his head to look in the direction he had been walking, the way out of the crushing walls. *I will return when Kore wakes.*

The eyes in those walls widened and stared, bore into Lucius who felt like he had no place to go where they did not see him, suspect him, seek his death. From those hidden eyes that fell back into the hard edges of the world, there was no hiding...

Lucius had slept little after that, and when morning released him from night's cage, he rose, took his gladius and cloak, and went silently out of the room and into the courtyard.

It was peaceful, the lone olive tree shivering in the cool air, clouds falling from the mountain heights overhead to be swept out to the distant sea. For a few minutes, Lucius walked around the courtyard, feeling the aches and stiffness that plagued his limbs loosening up, surprised that they should ease so soon. After so long, after so much pain, it was strange to live with so much less of it.

"Good morning, Brother," Clarinda whispered as she approached from her cubiculum at the back of the courtyard.

Lucius turned to see his sister walking toward him. She was wrapped in a thick white cloak, the colour of her priestess' robes. The hood covered her head with only a few stray strands of her pale hair jutting out to frame her face.

She went straight to him and hugged him tightly. "Did you not sleep?"

"Only a little." He stood back as she released him, the better to see her. "Where are you going?"

"To the sanctuary. I must clean the altars before the rites begin."

Lucius was silent. It felt very strange to see the little girl who had dwelled within the walls of their childhood home, grown, dressed in such a way. "You really have found your calling in this?"

She smiled. "I have. Apollo watches over our family and protects us."

"That isn't a reason."

Her smile faded, and she sighed. "When we arrived here, in Delphi, I was full of anger and fear. You know our childhood, the horrors that our father wrought on our family? From the moment I washed myself in the waters of Castalia, I felt a peace I had never felt before. And the more we lived here, built a life here, the more enveloping that peace became, the more I embraced that feeling rather than flee from it. I decided then that I wanted to live in that peace for the entirety of my days."

Lucius took her hand and squeezed. "That is a reason then, I suppose."

Clarinda smiled.

"There was such a peace for us in Ynis Wytrin."

"The place you told us of last night?" she asked. "It sounds like another world."

"It is. It was."

"There are many worlds upon this earth that we can choose to dwell upon. We just have to pick one. When we find the right one."

"How did you get so wise, Clarinda?"

She laughed quietly, knowingly. "Theia taught me that last, but it rings true, doesn't it?"

"It does."

She looked at the sky and the brightening sun. "I must go now, but I will be back before dusk. Caecilius is awake already. You can both eat the bread and honey that is in the small kitchen."

Clarinda turned away and went to the door where she unbolted it and went out.

Lucius followed to lock behind her, but not before a stray goat plunged into the courtyard, its strange half-eyes gazing blankly at him for a moment before darting away to lie down in a nearby corner.

"I see you've met Tiresias," Caecilius said, laughing to himself as he came up behind Lucius.

"You named the goat after the blind prophet?"

"We thought it fitting with those disturbing eyes. He also knows the moment that the front door will open."

They both turned to look at the black and white goat standing in the corner, staring blankly at the world around it.

"Come, help me with the boar," Caecilius said. "Then we can eat and you can tell me everything that has happened."

Caecilius led Lucius out of the villa walls and around to the back of the walled compound.

"I can't believe all of this," Lucius said as they walked along the path that led between the domus walls and the small grove of cypress and young oak trees in the middle of which was a small stone altar.

"We've been busy since arriving. The baths at the back here are just a single room with a pool, but the water comes from a mountain source, so it never fails. It's even a little warm!" Caecilius spoke with pride about all that they had built, pointing as they walked. "Emrys has a small workshop on the other side, just behind the garden where we grow what food we can."

"You enjoy living here too, like Clarinda?" Lucius asked.

Caecilius stopped at the boar which he had hung from a hook in the back wall of the compound, in a spot hidden by olive trees. He shook his head. "No. I feel like I'm hiding."

"We are all in hiding now," Lucius said, seeing the disappointed look on his brother's face.

"We're safe here, but at what cost? So that those who have done this to us can carry on as they please?" He drew the hunting knife from his cingulum then and plunged into the hanging boar's exposed belly.

Lucius stood back, as his brother made short work of the animal.

"Hand me that bucket?" Caecilius said, pointing with a bloody hand at a wooden bucket beneath one of the trees.

Lucius handed it to him and he placed it under the boar. With a few flicks of his blade, the guts and offal slithered out to fall into the bucket, the animal's blank eyes staring at the ground where its blood pooled.

Caecilius set the bucket aside when all of the innards had fallen out and then stretched the cavity a bit wider. "There. We'll let it bleed out the rest of the day, and then we'll eat it this evening." He walked over to a stone trough along the wall and plunged his hands in up to the elbows, scrubbing the blood away as best he could before taking a soiled cloth that hung from a peg in the wall and drying. "I'm starving," Caecilius said. "Let's get that food."

A short time later, they were sitting on two logs beside the entrance to the domus, just beyond the outer wall of the kitchen, eating bread dipped in honey, and handfuls of almonds from the trees in the southwest corner of the compound.

Caecilius looked sidelong at his brother in the morning light, better able to see the horrors of his injuries. "Are you in much pain?"

Lucius looked at him. "Some. It was unbearable for a very long time. Now, I just live with it."

Despite Caecilius' beard and strong body, Lucius could still see the young, pained boy who dwelled within as he looked upon him.

"What did they do to you, Lucius? What happened?"

As they ate, Lucius told Caecilius of all that had befallen them in Britannia, more than he had told anyone, for his brother seemed to possess the same anger toward their persecutors as he, and so it was easy to fuel the fires each of them nursed. There was a mutual understanding in that.

What Lucius did not tell Caecilius of was what he had learned of his parentage, for that would have created a gulf between them over which there may not have been a possibility of bridge.

The sun was higher in the sky when Lucius finished, and feeling its burn on his skin, he pulled his cowl over his head.

Caecilius was silent, gazing at the pile of broken almond shells upon the ground. He turned his hands over to look at the boar's blood that still stained them, and wiped them on his breeches. "And so...are we to simply stand by after all they have done to our family? Are we to let them live as if nothing happened?" He stared at the tip of his hunting dagger, glinting in the sunlight.

Lucius did not tell Caecilius of his plans. He could not, for he was needed where he was. "We need to keep our family safe, Brother. More assassins will come, and they may never stop coming...even here."

"And that's why...Lucius Pen Dragon...we should hit them first!"

"Take on the whole of the Praetorian Guard? Is that it?" Lucius was about to explain how he had those same feelings of revenge, that he had plans but that it must be him alone who carried them out, that the others were safer with Caecilius there, that he did not want anyone to suffer along with him anymore. But his brother stood and turned to face him where he sat against the sun-soaked wall of the rough villa.

"You know, I was so angry with you for leaving us. I hated you, Lucius. I did. First you joined the legions - you weren't there when our father beat us and nearly killed our mother - and then you left for Britannia where you took it upon yourself to usurp the imperial throne and put us all in unimaginable danger!" He paced and then turned back, the dagger raised at Lucius. "It's you who lit the torch that burned our homes and our lives to cinders!"

"I'm sorry," Lucius said, standing from the log to face his brother's blade. His eyes met Caecilius', even as the blade rested against his throat. "I need to live a while longer before you do this. Then...I might just welcome what you intend, Brother."

Caecilius stared at Lucius, the deep sadness, anger and despair in his eyes set in scarred skin. He looked upon the thin, patchy hair of his head and imagined the pain Lucius must have endured, that he should not have been standing there before him after such torture.

A moment later, his blade was lying in the dusty earth at their feet and Caecilius wrapped his arms about Lucius, silently sobbing into his shoulder. It was as if he could stop being strong, now that his brother was home, as if he could dare to think that perhaps all would be well now.

"I'm sorry," Lucius said as he held his brother's head in the palm of his hand. He was not sure how long they stood there, but the feeling of

SANCTUARY 429

closeness Lucius felt toward his younger brother was completely new. It was as if they had finally come to an understanding, were able to see through the mist of resentment that had drifted between them the whole of their lives as it was finally blown away.

Caecilius stood back quickly and wiped his eyes, not wanting anyone to see him in such a state, a weeping Teucer in the arms of his brother Ajax. He remembered the story of Ajax and Teucer: how Ajax had gone mad and fallen upon his sword, and how Teucer had protected the body. "I'm sorry too, Lucius," he said, "for doubting you all these years."

Lucius smiled and put his arm around Caecilius' shoulder. As they turned, Ambrosia appeared in the doorway that led onto the villa courtyard. Her eyes were wide and watery.

"No," Caecilius muttered. "Please no!"

Ambrosia shook her head. "Your mother... She's up! She's feeling better!"

They found Antonia Metella standing in the middle of the courtyard supporting herself on an olive tree on one side and Emrys on the other. When Lucius and Caecilius came rushing in, she smiled at them. "My boys," she said first, and then turned to look at Phoebus and Calliope who approached slowly hugged her in turns.

"Mother?" Caecilius said. "Are you sure you should be up and about like this?"

Antonia waved it off. "I've been abed for too long. I need fresh air and sunlight." She closed her eyes and tilted her head as if to feel Apollo's light upon her pale face, breathing it in. When she opened her eyes, she reached up to touch Emrys' bearded cheek and then turned to walk toward Lucius, Caecilius and Adara who stood in shocked silence.

Now that she was standing in the light, Lucius could see that his mother still carried the scars of her life with Quintus Metellus, the limp from her broken bones, and the jutting jaw from her beatings. The sight of it still made him want to weep, but he did not betray it. Lucius stepped forward to take her hands and wrap his arms about his mother's frail form, and in her embrace, he felt a radiant love that was as rare as rain in the hottest desert.

Antonia reached out to Caecilius then too, and he took her hand. "Have you two reconciled?"

They nodded and she smiled, before reaching for Adara and hugging her close. "I've missed you, my dear."

"And we you," Adara said. "But you should rest. Don't exert yourself so much at once."

"Yes, Antonia," Delphina said, coming over. "Come, my friend, let Emrys help you back to bed."

"No," Antonia said to all of them. "I've wasted too much time abed. I must wash and stand in the light of day."

Lucius looked at Emrys and the old sculptor nodded, then took Antonia's arm. "I'll help you to the bath, my love. Then you can sit in the sun beside the altar and your favourite oak."

"Yes," she said. "Ambrosia?"

"Yes, mistress?" the woman said, rushing to Antonia's side. "Please bring my clean clothes and a thick cloak to the baths for me."

"Right away," Ambrosia said, smiling as she glanced at Lucius and Caecilius.

Antonia turned to Lucius as she and Emrys passed. "We must talk later, in the sunlight."

"Of course," Lucius answered a little nervously, for he would now have his chance to ask her about all the doubt and disbelief that had plagued him since he came out of Annwn near death.

The first full, sunlit day in Delphi began to feel like a new life for Adara, Phoebus and Calliope. It was as if they had all emerged from a terrible storm.

Adara enjoyed time with her parents with new appreciation and gratitude for even the chance to see them speaking with her children. She felt as though she had robbed them of years, but she forced herself to set that guilt aside and to simply appreciate the sight of Calliope helping Delphina in the garden on the east side of the domus. Her daughter impressed Delphina greatly with her knowledge of herb lore which she had acquired in Ynis Wytrin.

"You learned all of that in Britannia, child?" Delphina said to Calliope, her hand reaching up to touch her silky hair.

"Yes. I learned so much there, Grandmother. You will have to come with us to see if for yourself, to meet Etain, and Weylyn and all the others. Our friends Rachel and Aaron are wonderful. You feel good just being around them!" Calliope spoke so excitedly that Delphina wondered at all that they had been through and experienced, the people they had met, the lives they had led that seemed so foreign to her own life.

"Mama," Adara said. "Are you all right?" She noticed Delphina looking deeply sad in that moment as Calliope had been talking.

"I'm sorry if I overwhelmed you, Grandmother," Calliope said, now holding the old woman's hand.

"I'm fine. I just...I only realized as you were telling me all these wonderful things, how much time we have lost."

"But we are together now, Grandmother," Calliope said, her smile filling Delphina with such love and light that it was almost impossible to dwell in that fleeting sadness.

"You are right," Delphina said. "Now come. We will prepare all of these beans for cooking."

Calliope glanced at Adara as Delphina led her away, and Adara nodded and waved her off, happy to see them together.

Beyond the garden, at the back corner of the compound, Adara saw Phoebus with Emrys who was showing him how to shape a block of stone with a hammer and chisel. Phoebus looked up and waved at his mother, an enormous smile on his face.

Adara choked back her weeping.

"What's wrong, my girl?"

She turned to see her father standing there, reaching out to her, and she hugged him tightly. "They've been through so much, Baba."

Publius squeezed her, not wanting to let her go, the only daughter he had not seen in years, the only daughter who now wanted to see him. "You've all been through so much. I thank the Gods you're here now."

"This world is no longer recognizable to me. My children will never know the peace that I did growing up. They..."

Publius squeezed his daughter's hands as the pain surfaced in her eyes, the deep sadness he recognized as a parent who feels helpless when their children suffer.

"They both have blood on their hands, Baba... My children, my sweet children..."

Publius closed his eyes and hugged her close again. "I'm so sorry, my girl. This world...this empire... It has grown full of evil. All I can say is that you and Lucius and your children need to stay close. You are stronger together. We all are." He released her and sighed, his eyes taking in the poor home they had built with their own hands. "You also have to let go of the life you once led. We all do, for it will never be the same again. I used to revel in heated debates in the agora, or getting a motion passed in the bouleuterion, a new business deal... But none of that really matters. I've learned to be here, in the moment, with you now..." He smiled and gently wiped the tears from her cheek the same as he did when she fell as a child. "I find beauty in the rising and the setting of the sun when we are here, the taste of an olive I grew and harvested, the sound of the wind as it plays upon the trees and the faces of the Phaedriades. I look upon your mother and know that if she is with me, the Gods are too. Doubly so now that you are here."

Adara smiled and relaxed as she watched her son wield the hammer and chisel under Emrys' tutelage. *This is one of those moments,* she thought. *Remember their smiles and laughter.* She squeezed her father tightly as they watched together.

From a bench in the sun along the wall beside the garden, Caecilius sat and watched as well, with Ambrosia beside him as she wove a new basket with sinuous willow branches recently cut.

"Are you all right?" she asked him.

Caecilius continued to stare at Phoebus and Calliope as they set to work, smiling and laughing, despite all that they had been through. "I don't know," he said. "The last time I saw Phoebus and Calliope, I was almost a child myself. And now...now I'm an uncle, and they are nearly grown. I feel like the Gods have robbed us of time, Ambrosia. I've missed their growing up. I barely know them! And yet...I have a great urge to keep them safe. As though I would do anything to ensure they are well."

Ambrosia set down her basket, the stray branches swirling outward to touch their shins in the sunlight. "You've always been that way, Caecilius. I still remember, when we were in the domus in Rome... I remember you hearing your mother's cries and charging down the stairs to defend her from your father. You didn't hesitate."

As she spoke of it, Caecilius reached up instinctively to touch the spot on his head where the medicus had drilled a hole to release the pressure from the injury his father had caused him.

Ambrosia took his hand and held it tightly, as she used to, to reassure the little boy who had been set aside to stand in the shadows while the sun shone. "You have always been like a brother to me. The Gods do rob us of our dreams, it's true." For a fleeting moment, Argus' face hovered in her mind, but she shook it off and squeezed harder. "But we need to focus on the purpose we have been put here to fulfill. To not do so, would be madness. I have come to love your mother and you and Clarinda as if I were your own family. And I would not change that."

Caecilius turned to her. "You are family, Ambrosia." He smiled sadly, and she looked down.

"And I am grateful for that, for I don't know what I would do without all of you." She raised her head again to look at him. "Your brother has returned, but that does not mean that you must step back into the shadows. Stand beside him, for it seems that now, he needs you as much as ever you needed him. Only you are there for him when he was not."

While the rest of the family sat around the garden and workshop on the eastern side of the compound, all was cool and quiet in the small grove that rose out of the earth on the western side. In the midst of a small circle of young mountain oaks and lean cypresses, Lucius sat opposite his mother. Their offerings upon the short, stone altar smouldered and smoked, casting a momentary haze over their heads before floating away into the Delphic air.

Antonia Metella sat back in a chair with an angled back that Emrys had fashioned for her. The midday sun filtered through the trees to warm her face and, after settling down with the help of her son, she closed her eyes to feel the heat upon her skin. She felt free again, without the walls of her cubiculum. As she sat there, listening to the breeze and her son's ragged breathing, she cast her mind back to the days when Lucius was young and vital, when he was full of optimism and rebellion. He had always been gifted, she knew. *More than most,* she remembered. But after a few minutes, she opened her eyes again to see Lucius in his current state, and she felt her heart tighten.

As Lucius leaned upon his knees staring at the altar, he appeared like a smaller version of the aged Hercules, tired and world-weary, crushed by his labours. *Such is the life of heroes.*

Antonia watched him for a time, the way his shoulders collapsed, the way he bent over as if to weep or vomit.

But Lucius did neither. He was still, silent.

For Lucius, he had anticipated the moment when he could press his mother for the truths he had already learned, to get her perspective on all that had gone before.

"My son," she said, her voice soft, but not weak. "Turn to me."

Lucius turned and she could see the red in his eyes, an echo of the scarring upon his skin.

"Some time ago," she began, "I dreamed of the dragon and fire."

Lucius looked up at that.

"Show me."

She did not specify, but Lucius knew what she meant, that the Gods had shown her his pain and suffering in tortuous glimpses. He shed his cloak behind him and lifted his tunic to reveal his chest.

She closed her eyes immediately, nodding, her shaking hand to her lips as she remembered how his skin had been so perfect and smooth as a child, how the slightest cut upon it had made her heart shudder.

Lucius let his tunic fall again. "I have so many questions."

"I know." She looked up at him. "Now is the time to ask them, Lucius. You've waited long enough."

Lucius stood and paced back and forth a couple times, reaching out to touch the leaf of one of the oak trees. When he looked back at her, he saw her eyes focussed upon him. "Who is my true father?"

"You know that already, my son."

"I want to hear it from you."

"Your father is Light. He is Prophecy. He is Healing. He is the Music you hear wherever you go. He is Strength. And to me…he is also Love."

Lucius looked up at the sky, his eyes closed as he listened.

"Apollo is your father." Even though Antonia knew that Lucius was aware of the fact, Apollo having told her of this, she felt a great burden lifted as she spoke the words to her son directly. "I am finished with secrets," she said. "There is no need for them anymore. Nor regrets."

"What do you regret?" Lucius asked. "Marrying Quintus Metellus?"

"No!" she said. "He gave me Caecilius and Clarinda…and Alene. I could never regret that. What I regret is time lost, for not even the Gods can give that back to us."

Lucius pulled his stool closer to her and sat down.

"Tell me now, Lucius," she said. There was fear in her eyes, in the timber of her voice. "Relate to me the things which you have not told the others."

Over the next while, Lucius spoke of many things, of blades in the shadows, of dark gods, and those who had come to his aid. He spoke of Apollo, and Venus, and of Epona, of the Morrigan, and of a boar and a wolf. He spoke of friends and enemies, both dead and living. He spoke of another world she had never heard of, and of a duel. He spoke of fire and the dragon that had swallowed him whole. He spoke of the glimmering heights of Olympus itself and the pain he had chosen over it. He spoke of the trials his wife and children had endured because of his actions and how, perhaps, that weighed upon him most heavily.

When Lucius finished, his mother's face was wet with tears, for in the listening, she had felt his pain as if each new chapter had been a sword cut upon her limbs. She would have done anything to spare him from all of it, and yet she knew that it was a part of his own private odyssey.

"Tell me of my grandfather, Avus Metellus Anguis." For a long time, Lucius had wanted to know more of the man who had met him in Annwn, the lone soldier who had given him courage and comfort when he was lost and alone in that faraway world.

Antonia smiled at the mention, at the warm memories of halcyon days with one of the kindest, most honourable men she had ever known.

"Avus was my guard...my rock...my truest friend. I loved him with all my heart." Antonia closed her eyes and a single tear fell from her lash, a tear shed for the man who had saved her, whom she had missed since the day the Gods had taken him. "He was a hero, and a humble man of great honour. He too was a dragon."

"How so? Was he a child of Apollo?"

Antonia shook her head. "We are all Apollo's children, for we stand in his light, but no, I don't believe Avus was fathered by Apollo. He was, however, chosen."

"To be a dragon?" Lucius could see the men and women in the tomb in Etruria then, as if they all stepped forward to watch, to listen, as he received the truth from his mother's lips, from she who had borne him, she who had been loved by Apollo, who had given birth to one of their greatest.

"I asked Avus one day, in the years after the great plague. We were alone and I could see that he was weighed down by some great burden. I

knew some of it, from my father and from Avus too, but not all. I asked
him to tell me everything of the Dragon, and what it meant."

"What did he say?"

"He told me that the Dragon is not a blood bond. It is a line of worth,
of strength and wisdom. It is a responsibility, a bond to an ideal. It is a
gift of awareness and skill. It is unwavering dedication to goodness, to
the use of strength for right."

"Then I've failed in that duty," Lucius said, feeling his world fall
away like the sand at his feet upon a wave-churned beach.

But Antonia shook her head and reached out to him. "No. You
haven't. To be so chosen is to feel and experience this life more acutely
than any other mortal. Not only the joys, and the great victories upon the
battlefield, but also the pain and sadness that this life has to offer, the
trials or 'ponos' as Diodorus and your grandfather used to discuss."

"Diodorus did speak to me of such things," Lucius smiled slightly.

"He and Avus were great friends, and that is why he became your
tutor. Because Avus had arranged it."

"I still don't understand how grandfather came to be a dragon." It
was all too mysterious for Lucius, and though he had seen and experienced things no other mortal could comprehend, he yearned for some
solid truths.

"He received a letter one day, an inheritance. The previous dragon
had passed and all his possessions, his entire fortune, passed from him to
Avus."

"Just like that? He became wealthy overnight?"

"He became burdened overnight," Antonia corrected, remembering
Avus tell her everything as if unloading his heavy heart, unraveling the
mystery into which he had been plunged. "But yes. One day he was a
soldier from the Suburra, the next, a moderately wealthy landowner with
a new purpose. That is how it works. The Gods show a dragon his
successor, and then that person arranges for the handing over of responsibility, lands, titles, deeds, everything. Avus inherited the home you
grew up in, a library full of texts and letters with the entire history of the
Dragon."

"A library and letters?" Lucius exclaimed. "Why have I never seen
these?"

Antonia looked down. "After Avus died, Quintus burned them all. He
never understood Avus' ties to the Dragon. He was afraid of it. I tried to

stop him, but couldn't. I did manage to persuade him to keep the armour with the image of the dragon upon it." Antonia pointed at Lucius' chest where the brand was forever present upon his flesh. "That dragon."

Lucius looked down at his chest, his fingers hovering there for a moment, recollecting the pain.

"The image of the dragon that was upon your armour was handed down the line of dragons since Quintus Caecilius Metellus came to Delphi after the great victory at Zama. It was here, in this place, that he received a rock given by Apollo himself to a priestess of the temple, a rock intended for him alone. It was out of that heavenly rock that the image of the dragon upon your armour had been fashioned." She thought of Avus then, how he had revered the image, and wondered if he was saddened, wherever he was, by the loss of that image. "It makes no matter now. The image is gone."

Lucius sat up. "No. It isn't. It survived the fires unscathed, Mother. It was pressed into my flesh, but the priestess' at Ynis Wytrin helped to remove it. It is there, in Etain's safekeeping."

Antonia sighed. "That is good, though it should be with you."

"It wasn't safe." Lucius felt the separation from this ancient relic more acutely now, for so many dragons had held it before him.

"It is a relic of the line of Anguis, Lucius. Your line. It is for you to give to whomever Apollo tells you."

Lucius was quiet at that. He knew whom he would entrust the dragon to, but would Apollo have different plans? He looked at Antonia, for the next question would not be easy to ask. "Mother…how…how do you know I am Apollo's child? I mean, we've all heard the stories of gods visiting mortals, but…"

"I don't have easy answers for you, Lucius. I am sorry. I remember it was during the proscriptions after Commodus took the throne. It was a tense time in Rome. Alene was just a child, and Quintus stayed away more and more."

"Was he with Argus' parents?" he asked.

Antonia paused, her lips tight at the shame. "He spent more and more time with them, and less with me. Silas and Aurelia used people. Her especially. She was cunning, and Quintus fell for her. When Silas was in Hispania." She shook her head, unwilling to revisit such shameful memories. "Avus was not feeling well because of an old head injury, but he was still strong. Apollo showed him something when we went to the temple on the Palatine one day - Quintus was not there - and from that point on, he spoke of the coming of light, and of a Druid haunting his dreams."

"A Druid?"

"Yes. I was worried he was going mad in his old age, but he was in deadly earnest. It was to do with the Dragon. At any rate, he would sometimes come to the temple with me. It was on one of those visits that Apollo told me I was blessed, that I would have hope and strength always." She looked at her son and smiled sadly. "But as I said, it was a dangerous time in Rome. There were riots and fires. I was in the domus with Avus, Alene and the servants. Quintus was at the home of another senator. It was late and Alene was tired, as was I. But Avus stayed awake to keep watch. He was armed. As I said...he was my guard and protector..." She gathered herself for the next part of her story, her eyes staring at the smoke rising from the altar. "That night, men came to kill Quintus, criminals with whom he and Silas had crossed paths. That was the night Argus' parents were killed. They came for Quintus, but he was not there. Your grandfather was, however, and were it not for him, Alene and I would have been murdered in our home."

"What happened?"

"There was a great battle in the atrium of our home. Your grandfather and the servants fought off the intruders. There was blood everywhere."

"Did you hear the battle?" Lucius asked, but his mother only stared at him.

"No...I... It was at that time that your father came to me. I know it now. I can see and feel it. The brightest light I had ever seen, such pain, such pleasure."

Lucius looked away.

"It was like a dream."

"What did grandfather do?"

"He thought an intruder had got past him and come upstairs." She shook her head. "That is not what happened. Avus had protected me. No intruders got by. That night is a haze in my memory now, but I know what happened. Eventually the riots stopped, but Avus was weakened by the ordeal. After that, however, your grandfather and Quintus were reconciled to an extent. Not long after, I discovered I was with child." She looked upon Lucius then, the hint of a smile at the corner of her crooked mouth.

"But how did you know it was Apollo?" Lucius insisted.

"A mother knows. And then there was the light..." she looked dreamy again, as if she gazed far off into the distance at a wonderful memory. "It was a light that blinded."

Lucius did not know why a part of him was trying to deny what had happened. He knew he would surely not wish to be the true son of Quintus Metellus. But at least that would have given him leave to accept the failings he saw in himself.

Antonia leaned forward with a groan and reached for her son's hand. "Lucius, I swear to you, by Apollo and all the Gods, that it is true. You know it is and you need to accept it, for when you finally do, you will truly fulfill your destiny as a dragon - one of the greatest dragons to ever lead and serve the sacred cause." She squeezed his hand. "I am so proud of you...as is your father..."

He wanted to ask her more, to press her for clarity in the face of those confused, misty recollections she had related to him, but as she leaned back and closed her eyes, he knew that exhaustion was taking her. *To hang onto such secrets for so long...* he thought, seeing his mother with an entirely new perspective. He thought of all that had been lost too, the documents and letters of all the dragons who had gone before. He could see the hateful old man in that crumbling tablinum in Annwn. Quintus Metellus had destroyed the Dragons' knowledge, the records of the line of Anguis. The thought filled Lucius with fury.

He felt the dragon upon his chest burning and his hand touched it. *A stone!* he thought. *Given to another dragon in this very place...* It was difficult to comprehend, and Lucius knew that he had much to consider now, not least of which was the fact that Apollo had always been there for him, and the reason for that.

The feeling of loneliness that Lucius experienced in that moment was, he suspected, not unlike the great loneliness that he knew his mother must have felt for most of her life. *Oh mother...* he thought as he looked upon her peaceful form, sitting in the chair of that small grove. *How did you carry such secrets for so long? Why didn't you tell me?*

As if she had heard him, she opened her eyes slowly, the sunlight from above bright in her irises. "I didn't want to burden you. I knew you would be capable of greatness, no matter whose son you were..." Antonia's eyes closed again as Lucius watched, but she continued as if trying to squeeze every thought out before exhaustion overwhelmed her. "My son… I know you blame yourself, that you believe you've done nothing worthy of admiration, that you are leaving nothing good behind… But know this…remember… From all you have said, from what Adara has told me, you have raised and protected a beautiful family…blessed children…your wife…your men and friends… You have given hope to people, especially in Britannia, and no matter how fleeting that hope is, it is a gift to cherish. Lucius," Antonia reached out to him, "you are not death…you are and have always been…hope."

Lucius held her hand in his and felt the fervour in her words as she squeezed, though her eyes were closed.

"Go to your father's sanctuary… it will soothe your soul…begin to heal you…" she said before her thoughts drifted back to that night long ago when Apollo gave to her a son, and when the man she had loved defended her in blood in the atrium of her former home.

Lucius left her there for the moment and went to seek his family. Just as he left, Emrys appeared to sit beside Antonia.

Lucius looked back at the sculptor sitting beside his mother, whispering to her and holding her hand, and he smiled and felt relief that at least, she was with a man who treated her with the honour, love, and respect she truly deserved.

After nearly a month in the compound, Lucius was satisfied that they had not been followed. Their time there, among family, was marked only by happy reunion, some nostalgia and, for some of them, the first glimmering of hope. Together, they did feel stronger.

Antonia's health seemed to steady, though the increasing cold hampered her movement out of doors. She was of good spirits, and daily she spent time with her grandchildren and Lucius. She did not speak again of the intimate secrets she had uttered to her son. Action was in his hands now. Besides, simply by watching Phoebus and Calliope in their midst, she felt that the Gods had indeed answered her prayers.

Adara too settled into a routine with her parents, helping them, busying herself with whatever tasks were needed. She even painted with her mother and daughter, beginning the process of adorning the walls of that humble domus so that with every brush stroke, every creature, every leaf, life was breathed into it.

Despite all of this, Lucius and Adara knew that a visit to the sanctuary to purify themselves and honour the god who had brought them there to safety beneath the protective embrace of those shining mountains, was needed.

Since his first talk with his mother, Lucius considered what he would say and do in the sanctuary at a time when Apollo was said not to be there at all. In winter, it was Dionysus who presided over Delphi, who guarded the sacred ways of that sanctuary, rich in ornament from the statues of gold and bronze down to the very letters inscribed upon the walls of Athenae's treasury. Delphi was a different place in winter, for behind the cloak of howling wind, far below the snow-capped peaks of Parnassus, some nights were filled with the orgiastic cries of Bacchae in the woods upon those mountain slopes.

On a particularly sunny day, not long before Saturnalia, when Caecilius was off on one of his hunting trips to the north, Lucius decided it was time they visited the sanctuary.

"I will take all of you," Clarinda said excitedly one morning as they broke their fast. "There is so much I have been wanting to show you. Such ancient things!" She reached out to touch Calliope's hand and the younger girl grasped it, beaming.

Lucius watched his daughter with his sister and smiled to himself, despite the guilt he felt, for he had told his children to say nothing of his secret to anyone. "They will not understand," Lucius had said, "and I don't want to hamper our healing as a family."

Phoebus had understood, but Calliope felt in her heart that the others had a right to know, that it would give them comfort and even more hope for their collective futures. But she acquiesced to her parents' wish.

As Clarinda spoke about the sanctuary and how, from the high slopes, you could see the world stretched out before you, Phoebus and Calliope's excitement grew. They had, of course, heard the stories from Adara, of how Apollo had battled the great Python and become the victorious ruler of Delphi, of the Pythias who came after and how those mysterious priestesses uttered the god's words.

"Can we go today, Baba?" Phoebus asked. "Can we?"

"Yes," Lucius said. "It's time."

"Is it safe?" Adara asked. She had tried not to think of all that had happened on their journey since they arrived, but now that it was time to venture out, thoughts of evil men and blood began to return.

"I've asked some of the priests and priestesses," Clarinda said, "and none of them have seen any suspicious newcomers arrive in weeks. The sanctuary has its eyes and ears as well."

"We will all go," Publius added. "It has been some time since I ventured into the sanctuary."

"We can look at the art together, children," Delphina said to Phoebus and Calliope who smiled and nodded back at her as they finished off their bread and honeyed cheese.

"I'll stay here with Antonia and Ambrosia," Emrys said as he wiped his hands and made to rise.

"Are you certain?" Lucius asked him.

"Of course. My place is by her side."

Delphina watched Emrys go and smiled. "He is completely devoted to her."

"He's a good man, Emrys is," Publius echoed.

"He is," Lucius agreed, but he could not help feeling sad for Emrys. When they had first met, years ago at the banquet on the Palatine, when his statues were the talk of the court, he had been so vibrant and lively. But ever since his beloved apprentice, Carissa, had left him, the great creative force that had dwelled within him had flickered and faded. Lucius had noticed that despite the joy Emrys obviously felt with Antonia, there was always something in his countenance that betrayed deep sadness. He too, like Publius, had lost a daughter of sorts, and such things leave lasting scars. Lucius stood and walked around the table to Phoebus and Calliope to kneel between them. "Let's get ready to go, so that your aunt can show us all the wonders of Apollo's sanctuary."

They smiled, finished eating, and jumped up to go to their cubiculum to dress.

I must cherish my time with them, Lucius thought, not wanting to give more in that moment to the dread thought that one day, and rather soon, he would perhaps have to leave them.

With Emrys, Antonia, and Ambrosia left behind in the safety of the compound, the rest of the family made their way from the village to the sanctuary along the road that hugged the cliff's edge.

It was a bright, clear day with a gentle wind that rustled the folds of their woollen cloaks and tousled their hair. Uphill, the pines whistled and swayed, beside jutting cypresses, and in the valley below, where the

sacred olive harvest had already been brought in, the trees shuddered and
their silver-green leaves winked at the world.

Lucius caught sight of the brilliant blue of the sea down by the port
of Kirrha, and he wondered how long it would be before he once more
plied the waves. He had found himself easing into a comfortable peace
there, among family, sometimes avoiding thoughts of the task he had set
for himself. But he would not let himself forget, and the painful memories and wounds, the harm done to all of them by others, all of it was
kept in an iron box in his soul to be opened when the time was right.

But it was not yet the time, for as driven as Lucius was, the import of
where they were was not lost on him. As they walked, observed by the
villagers of Delphi from porches, from beneath trees and behind
twitching curtains in windows, Lucius realized that he stood upon his
father's threshold, and that for ages, others had come from around the
world to do the same, to seek Apollo's council.

The pilgrims were fewer then, however, the streets no longer
thronged, though some still came to make desperate winter offerings.

"Do you hear the hymns?" Clarinda asked Phoebus and Calliope as
she led them along the path.

They all listened. At first, it was only the wind they heard, but then,
the first hints of voices were picked up, rising and falling in divine
concert as the hymns to Apollo were sung, accented by the gentle shake
of a sistra, the skilled plucking of a kithara, or the thrum of a skin drum.

"I used to sit for hours and listen to the hymns," Delphina said,
remembering the days of her youth upon those shining slopes.

"You were doing just that the first time I saw you," Publius added,
taking his wife's hand as they walked. "You captured my heart as you
sang along, staring up at the sanctuary."

Delphina smiled and leaned against her husband's shoulder.

This made Adara smile, to see her parents still so devoted to each
other. But it also saddened her, for when she looked to Lucius beside her,
she could only see his focussed frown, the swaying of the sword blade
beneath his cloak, and the determined walk of a man who knows no
peace. She risked reaching out to take his hand, as ever she did, and he
gripped it in return even as he scanned the small crowd ahead of them
near the entrance to the sanctuary.

Clarinda turned, holding Phoebus and Calliope each by the hand.
"We can buy some offerings in the agora, but first, you need to purify

yourselves in the Castalian spring. We have promanteia, so we will not have to wait to wash or to enter the sanctuary." She continued on past the agora on the left, and headed directly toward the darkness of the trees where the road bent.

Pilgrims stood in small groups there, waiting for the priest and priestess at the entrance to tell them when it was their turn.

"The line is small, but during the spring, summer and autumn, when Apollo is here, people can wait for days or even weeks to enter the sanctuary and see the oracle." She slowed to lead the way through the people. "Oh look, Theia is at the entrance today!" She waved at the woman who had brought Lucius and his family to the domus.

Theia smiled and waved back, saying something to the priest and priestess who were flanking the entrance beneath the trees. "Clarinda, Delphina, Publius…" she greeted them warmly, then turned to Phoebus and Calliope, Lucius and Adara. "You are most welcome here." There was warmth in her greeting, but also a sadness.

"I have asked my fellow servants of the god to stop admitting people so that you can perform your ablutions. You have promanteia because of Delphina and Clarinda," she hesitated, "but also because…" Her eyes focussed on Lucius', but she stopped herself. "They are ready for you now."

Theia led the way past those who were waiting in line. Some of them grumbled that they would have to wait longer, and others stared curiously, wondering what manner of people carried the sought-after promanteia, and then looking away as Lucius' gaze raked over them.

The priest and priestess stepped back a little as Lucius passed them, but it was not out of fear, but something else. Once the party had passed, they closed together to prevent anyone else from entering.

Theia led Clarinda and the rest of their small group beneath the dark canopy of trees until they were in a sunlit courtyard at the base of the Phaedriades. The echo of falling water was everywhere, itself like music. It fell from high up the mountain, between the Shining Ones, down into a reservoir in the rock, and then was fed into a large rectangular pool where four lion-headed spouts poured it into the Castalian fountain house.

"I haven't been here in years," Adara said, releasing Lucius' hand and stepping forward.

"It's so peaceful," Calliope said beside her mother, her head tilted back to look up from the tree-flanked courtyard to where the water trickled over the shoulders of the Phaedriades.

"It is peaceful," Theia said, nodding to Publius and Delphina to go ahead and wash their face and hands in the cool water.

Lucius watched as Adara's parents sat carefully upon the steps that led down into the pool to perform their ablutions. Clarinda followed and then turned to invite Phoebus and Calliope in with her.

"No, Clarinda," Theia said abruptly.

Everyone turned to the priestess in shock.

"What is wrong?" Adara asked, suddenly worried.

Theia looked upon her with kind sadness, her lips pursed. She sighed, but was firm in her bearing, as if she were a guard at the gates of a fortress. Theia was suddenly imposing as she barred the way.

"What is this about?" Lucius asked, stepping forward.

"Forgive me," Theia said, "but those who have blood guilt upon them must immerse themselves completely. The face and hands will not suffice."

"But surely the children don't have to..." Delphina's words died as they left her lips, as she looked upon her grandchildren.

Calliope and Phoebus stood beside each other, their heads down, the former silently weeping at the memories, and the humiliation before her aunt and grandparents.

Publius, Delphina and Theia all looked at Lucius where he stood in the shadows, just out of reach of the circle of light in the courtyard.

Is this how you welcome your family, Father? Lucius thought bitterly. He pushed back his cloak and stepped forward into the light, his gladius hanging from his side.

"You come armed?" Theia asked, shocked by the appearance of the blade.

"Always, lady," Lucius answered. "Are you going to prevent us - my wife and children who have suffered greatly - from visiting the sanctuary?"

"No," Theia replied, standing yet taller before Lucius. "But the Gods demand you be cleansed before entering. That is all."

"Lucius, we can do it," Adara whispered, ignoring her parents' incredulity. "Please. Let us do this. It will help all of us."

Lucius turned to the priestess. "No one is to intrude upon us."

"Of course." She left to tell the holy guards at the entrance to the spring.

"Adara, what does this mean?" Publius asked, his eyes darting from his daughter to his grandchildren.

"Not now, Baba," Adara replied.

Clarinda approached with Phoebus and Calliope. "I'm so sorry," she said to Lucius. "But it is Apollo's law." She turned to her niece and nephew. "It will be fine. No one will bother you as you bathe, and you will see...you will feel so much better after. The water is sent by the Gods to cleanse us."

Calliope turned to Lucius. "Like the well of the Chalice, Baba."

Lucius nodded and began to remove his clothing, the others doing likewise.

The family of Pen Dragons - for they were no longer Metelli - stood there in the chill sunlight, naked as they faced the rockface above the pool of Castalia, fires burning in niches set in the rock above, beside small votive statues of Apollo and Athena.

Adara went first, the cool water running up her battered limbs, making her shiver as goose bumps covered her skin. She turned to take Calliope's hand and together the two of them immersed themselves quickly.

Phoebus followed, sliding in at the end of the pool, embarrassed that his grandparents and aunt should see his nakedness, though they had turned away for them to enter the water.

Lucius watched his family submerge and scrub their faces and hands, their limbs, their hearts, as if scrubbing away layers of blood.

"Please, Lucius," Clarinda said. "You need to do it. I will say the prayers once you are in."

He turned to his sister, and she helped him with his tunic, pulling it over his head.

There was a loud gasp in the courtyard as Publius and Delphina saw the severity of Lucius' injuries. However, an even louder cry emerged from Theia as she returned to see Lucius facing them, the image of the dragon she knew so well burned deep and bloody, full of anger, into Lucius' chest.

"Forgive me," Theia said suddenly, bowing her head. "I did not know, but only suspected."

"What are you talking about?" Publius asked, but the priestess did not answer.

Theia turned away, her cloak pulled over her head. "You must enter the water...Lucius Pen Dragon..."

Lucius turned away from them toward the pool and removed his sandals, breeches and bracae so that he stood there naked, every scar and fire-burned inch of his skin visible to the world. He stepped forward and descended the steps into the marble-lined pool. The water was cold and soothing, and he felt his skin revived as if it were entirely covered in the healing resin that he had received in Ynis Wytrin.

As Lucius dipped beneath the surface, Theia turned to watch and gasped aloud at what she saw, for as the warrior submerged himself, she saw the entire pool turn red with blood, a thick, congealing slick that spread around his wife and children and which threatened to overflow from the top of the steps and engulf them all.

"Clarinda, the prayers," she said. "Now!"

Clarinda, shocked by Theia's cries, turned and began to mutter the prayers. "Great God Apollo, Goddess Athena Pronaia, Lord Dionysus who watches over this sacred place in times of darkness...please cleanse this family of blood and guilt that they may enter your sacred sanctuaries. Heal them of their wounds and help them to forget the terrors of the world that they may find peace within. They will heap offerings upon your altars in gratitude. Bless them now. Bless them always."

Adara, Calliope and Phoebus knelt side by side in the pool, the cool air nipping at their senses even as the sun shone down upon them.

Calliope turned to them. "Do you feel it?" she asked. "The Gods are cleansing us." She smiled and looked at Clarinda whose eyes were closed as she continued to mutter muted prayers beneath her breath.

"It is wonderful," Adara said. "I never thought..." she could not finish, for the overwhelming feeling of release she felt was too much to express.

Beside his mother, Phoebus shivered and shook. As the tears began to come, he submerged himself to wash them away, to offer them to the waters. He felt the release, and beneath the surface, he looked to see his father at the bottom of the pool, kneeling, the dragon upon his chest burning with fire, even beneath the calm surface of Castalia.

Phoebus jumped up, gasping for air, and followed his mother and sister out of the pool to where Clarinda held linen towels for them to dry with.

Yet Lucius remained below the surface of the pool, and as his family finished dressing themselves, the Phaedriades began to shake.

There were screams from the group of pilgrims upon the road outside the trees as rock and dust fell from the heights.

Clarinda, Publius, and Delphina huddled together beneath the trees with Adara and the children.

"Baba!" Calliope cried, making to run to the pool where Lucius was still submerged, but Phoebus grabbed her and pulled her back, putting his arms around her.

The tremors increased and the ground shook beneath their feet for what felt like an eternity, though it was mere seconds.

Clouds of dust exploded about the Castalian spring.

"The Gods are speaking! They are angry!" Theia said, stepping forward into the dusty air, unafraid of the chaos surrounding her. She walked to the edge of the pool to stare down into the depths at the still form of Lucius Pen Dragon beneath the water. *You must get out now,* she thought as the bloody water appeared to boil before her eyes. *Do not fight the healing, Dragon. Give way to it...allow it!*

Before her eyes, the red dissipated and at last, Lucius' burned body emerged from the cold depths, his bright eyes meeting hers, the fiery dragon upon his chest doused now, its outline sharp and angry.

Theia quickly grabbed the linen towel from the dusty ground and gave it to Lucius.

"What happened?" Lucius asked as he gazed about the courtyard, and then at his huddled family. "What is wrong?"

The air was calm again, filled once more with sunlight and the trickle of water.

Theia looked at the pool and saw that it was clear once more. She turned to Lucius, her eyes wide with awe. "You...you are the one?"

Lucius looked back at her, his hand upon his chest. "I am no one," he answered his gaze dark and forbidding. "And you must remember that." He bent to pick up his clothes and began to dress.

When Lucius had finished, Adara, Phoebus and Calliope came to him and hugged him, though the display confused him still. "All is well," he said. "What happened?"

"There was-" Phoebus began to say, but Adara cut him short.

"An earthquake. Nothing more."

"Really?" Lucius asked. "I didn't feel anything." He looked at the others and saw the confused and worried looks they all cast in his direction. He then turned to Theia. "May we enter the sanctuary now?"

She nodded, and left quickly and quietly.

"Follow me," Clarinda said, taking her brother's hand tightly in hers.

Once they were away from Castalia, they made their way back up the road to the entrance to the sanctuary and the agora that was located there. In the paved court before a stoa where several stalls were set up, many of the vendors were busy tidying up their wares after the tremors that had occurred only a short time before.

Publius and Delphina greeted some of the traders they knew, while Clarinda, Lucius, Adara, Phoebus and Calliope stopped to purchase offerings such as cakes and incense, olive oil and wine in delicate glass phials.

"Where did Theia go to?" Publius asked his wife as they watched Adara and her family.

"She must have had duties to take care of. She always does," Delphina replied, grasping her husband's hand.

"She was afraid. I saw it in her eyes." Publius stared at Lucius from across the agora, his dark form moving among the groups of pilgrims like a shadow in that bright courtyard. He shook his head. "I don't know what is happening, Delphina, but I'm worried for our daughter and grandchildren."

"It isn't anything new," Delphina said, looking up at her husband. "Their lives have always been tainted with danger. It's as the Gods desire. All we can do is pray for them...pray that Apollo is merciful."

"Mercy?" Publius stepped forward as if trying to get a better look at them. "Have you noticed our son-in-law? Did you not also witness our beautiful grandchildren, and our own daughter, being made to wash their entire bodies in the sacred spring? There is only one reason for that... They have each taken lives!" he hissed under his breath.

Delphina closed her eyes and reached out for him. "I know."

"We're ready," Adara said as they approached, holding their offerings.

Publius and Delphina looked up at her and forced a smile.

"Follow me," Clarinda said, leading Phoebus and Calliope through the main entrance into the sanctuary and onto the sacred way.

Lucius and Adara followed closely behind with her parents after. "Amazing, isn't it?" Adara said to Lucius.

For Lucius, it was like a dream, stepping into that place, that forest of faith, for Delphi was not the richly adorned house of a god, but rather a symbol of the timeless trust which Apollo's followers placed in him.

I would you were here, Father... Lucius thought as he gazed up at the frozen votive statues to either side of him, including the great bronze bull of the Corcyrans, the statues of the Spartan admirals, and the ex voto of the Athenians to commemorate their great victory at Marathon, hundreds of years before. They were all immortalized in Apollo's sanctuary, the great statue of the horse of Troy too, as well as the statues of the famous Seven against Thebes.

Lucius felt something grip his hand and he looked down to see Phoebus there, as awestruck as he was.

"We're walking among heroes," Phoebus said.

"We are," Lucius replied, but at the same time wondered what he was. The men surrounding him were here because of their great deeds. What had he done except cause pain for each of the people around him? He had tried to make Rome a presence for good wherever he had gone, but he had done the opposite. Now, he was in the most sacred place in the world, a Roman, like Sulla and Nero before, both of whom had stripped the sanctuary of statues for their own greedy ends. Did it matter that Domitian and Hadrian had graced the sanctuary with offerings and funds for repairs? Could the deeds of one Roman erase the crimes of another? Was it enough?

The road turned as they came to the first of the treasuries, those small temples which various city-states and islands had dedicated to Apollo and which had been filled with offerings. Sikyonians, Knidians, Siphnians, Poteideans, Magarians and many others were represented, their treasuries drawing the eye with their reliefs of gods and heroes, and battles fought long before Rome ever erected its first brick and marble structures.

When they came to the the treasury of the Athenians, Lucius stopped to look.

"Why is it covered in rusty arms and armour and torn banners, Baba?" Phoebus asked.

Lucius stepped closer to look at the displayed fan of spears and swords, ship prows, shields, statues, altars, tripods and more. They reminded him of Parthia, some of the items, and he realized that some of those monuments and trophies had been there for over six hundred years, spoils from battles hard-won by the men of Athenae. "They are spoils of war," Lucius told Phoebus. "Won at the battle of Marathon and other places."

Lucius looked up at the metopes ringing the top of the treasury, adorned in faded blue and red. He saw Theseus and Hercules immortalized in stone, their deeds intended to inspire others despite the passage of time and the ravages of the world, including the crimes perpetrated by Rome. He longed to feel a connection with those long-lost heroes, to feel as though his own deeds had meant something, but the search for such a balm for the spirit felt fruitless. The waters of Castalia had not cleansed him, but made him more aware of his own shortcomings, his failures.

Lucius watched as his family continued on up the sacred way, past the back of the bouleuterion, and on toward a large rock which had altars before it.

"This is the rock of the Sibyl," Clarinda was saying. "It was here that the first Pythia spoke the words of Apollo."

Adara glanced at Lucius as he approached. The rock made her nervous, for she remembered all too well what had happened in the Sibyl's cave in Cumae, all those years ago, and how the words had haunted Lucius since.

But Lucius gave no indication that the prophetess' rock bothered him in any way. Instead, he walked past it to another rock where there stood a statue of Apollo with his bow drawn.

"Lucius?" Adara said softly as she followed him, leaving the others behind.

Lucius did not respond, but looked upon the rock with trepidation, his hand shaking, reaching out to touch it, and as he did so, he felt fear, and anger, violence and victory…

All of the buildings around Lucius suddenly disappeared, and there was a great shaking deep in the earth.

How dare you? A rocky voice yelled from the depths, accusing, vengeful.

Then a woman's voice... *Slay her, my son! Or we are doomed!*

The earth shook violently then, the sun and moon colliding in the heavens to darken the day.

Lucius looked up to see a woman standing upon the rock pointing, her brow sweaty, her face and arms lashed with blood. Despite this she stood brave in the face of something monstrous, like a general near defeat but unwilling to give up.

Something ran by her, to stand before her and there Lucius saw him, the shining god, his great, silver bow drawn back to its full length. Fire leached from his wounds and his breathing was rapid as his muscles strained with all their might and he took aim. His strength was failing but he would not accept defeat, for in that moment, his entire world was at stake and he had to make a choice.

Lucius could feel that choice, the crushing weight of it. He looked up at his young father and followed the tip of his golden arrow to where it pointed.

The feeling of fear was unlike anything he had felt before, for there, rearing up out of a chasm in the earth was the nightmare itself: Python. The great dragon reared up to a height as tall as any Hesperideaen tree. The air was foul as the gaping jaws opened, their fangs taller than any man or god.

Lucius wanted to reach for his sword, to leap to his father's aid but all he could do was watch as the beast descended with the fury of a storm to devour Apollo who, only as death was upon him, loosed his arrow so that it exploded through Python's head like a bolt of lightning from the heavens.

"Lucius?" Adara was saying, her voice full of concern as she knelt upon the sacred way beside the rock where Lucius had fallen.

People were gathering around them now to look. They whispered that the cloaked man had the falling sickness, that he was touched by the Gods.

Publius and Delphina tried to usher people away from Adara and Lucius, and reluctantly the crowd moved on in various directions.

Lucius opened his eyes and looked up at Adara. He was sweating and felt cold. The rock loomed over him and he backed away from it suddenly, ripping free of Adara's hands.

"What happened, Baba?" Calliope asked, at his side right away. "I heard more tremors."

Lucius looked at his daughter, for she heard something of the horror he had seen.

"Aunt Clarinda says that is the rock of Leto. Did you touch it?"

Lucius nodded, and got to his feet. "I'm fine," he said, but as he looked up he saw the rock, and in the sky above, upon a soaring pillar, the Sphinx stared down at him. *No...please...* he thought, remembering the terror he had felt in Annwn, the threat of death and loss as the question was put to him... *Who are you?*

"Lucius, you're scaring us," Adara whispered. "Please."

He shook his head again, looked away from the rock and the Naxian Sphinx. "Let's keep going so we can make our offerings."

"Are you sure you're all right, Brother?" Clarinda said, reaching out to him.

"I'm fine. Please lead the way."

Clarinda carried on with Phoebus and Calliope with Lucius following.

Behind them, Adara was joined by her parents.

"I'm afraid for you, Daughter," Publius said. "Lucius is not well."

"He's fine!" Adara snapped, and walked quickly ahead to make sure Lucius did not fall again.

Soon they reached a broad staircase leading up to the temple of Apollo itself. Beside the stairs, a magnificent bronze and gold tripod with a great serpent wrapped around it, rose up into the sky to hold aloft a fire of hope, a beacon of sorts. Here, the line of pilgrims who wished to enter the temple began. Many stood in silence as they awaited their turn, gazing up at the leaping flames of that tripod, a votive offering of the Greeks for their victory over the Persians at Plataea.

Higher still were the bronze palm tree, and the colossal statue of Apollo, holding not his bow, but his kithara, now offering beauty to the world in place of death. The throng stood in awe beneath the god they had come from far and wide to honour. They were from all corners of the empire, of differing cultures with one thing in common: that their lives were touched by Apollo's light, and that his music could be heard by each of them.

"Because we have promanteia, I can get us into the temple now," Clarinda was saying.

"No!" Lucius said quickly.

Everyone turned toward him.

"I mean, not today."

"Why, Lucius?" Adara asked. "We've come this far."

"You can go in if you like, but I will not."

Adara looked at her husband and saw the determination in his eyes, recognized the fear there too. "We can come back another day."

"Are you sure?" Clarinda asked as she stood at the top of the steps. "We can by-pass the line."

"I'm sure," Lucius said to her. "Is there an altar where we can make our offerings?"

"Yes. Of course. The great altar of the Chians is just around the corner. Follow me." Clarinda hoisted her priestess' robes and walked, followed by the others, until they reached a small staircase leading up to a broad altar filled with offerings. "This is the main altar in the sanctuary and where those with promanteia may make their offerings," Clarinda said.

The court between the temple of Apollo and the altar of the Chians was busy, for here began the line of waiting pilgrims, but also the gathered priests, priestesses, attendants and acolytes of the god, even though he was not in residence. The priests of Dionysus were there too, walking slowly about the temple colonnade, dressed in their long white robes and crowned with ivy and vine leaves. As they walked, their staffs, adorned with sculpted leopards, tapped upon the marble floor of the temple.

Lucius did not know why exactly, but he felt annoyed at all the people there, even the Dionysian priests who had taken over his father's home. He stood staring at the ramp that led up to the temple, the thick doric columns that had kept the roof aloft for nigh on six hundred years. He remembered Diodorus telling him of the temple, and of Delphi; at the time, Lucius had wondered why his tutor had insisted on instructing him about Delphi. *Did he too know my secret?* Lucius wondered. *He certainly knew of the Dragon.*

He found himself wishing Diodorus were there with him to stand beneath the gaze of the finial sphinxes atop the temple roof. He wished he could hear the old man tell him the tale of the Gigantomachy and of Apollo's triumphant entry into Delphi, displayed upon the temple pediments where those ancient scenes came to life. As Lucius looked up, he could hear the tramp of Apollo's horses as they pulled his chariot, see the fluttering of his father's cloak in the stoney breeze. He could hear lions roar as they tore into stags, and the clash of battle between the Gods and Giants which was, for a moment, deafening.

In a flash, Lucius also saw a different temple there - one of laurel wood, and then one adorned with wax and feathers, and another of wax and bronze. In a matter of moments, Lucius could see the passage of time in Delphi, and he knew that it was a place like no other, that time meant something else there, that it held not only the memories of a people, but of man and the Gods.

"Baba?" Phoebus said to him. "It's our turn to make offerings."

Lucius turned to his son and looked at him from beneath the black hood of his cloak.

"Are you all right?" Phoebus had been silent since the rock of Leto, but now he looked concerned for his father and squeeze his hand hard as if to awaken him. "We won't have to go back through the crowds, Baba. Aunt Clarinda says that there is a path out of the sanctuary in the northwest corner.

Lucius nodded, and looked back at the temple and its large gaping door. For a moment, he thought he glimpsed Theia standing in the shadows, watching him.

"Come, Brother!" Clarinda called to him where she was waiting with Adara and Calliope at the top of the altar steps.

Lucius tore his eyes from the temple and turned with Phoebus to mount the steps leading up to the magnificent altar of the Chians.

The altar was one of the largest he had ever seen. It had a base of blue stone that rose up to be topped by a surface of pure white marble. The short wall that surrounded it gave the impression of silence, cutting off the wind and voices of pilgrims just enough to allow those making their offerings the peace they needed to honour Apollo.

When Lucius arrived at the top of the stairs, he and Phoebus stood beside Adara, Calliope and Clarinda. Publius and Delphina stood at the far end making their own offerings of thanks to Apollo for bringing their family together again.

"Far-Shooting Apollo," Clarinda began, laying a cake upon the surface among the other offerings. "We honour you and thank you for your protection. Thank you for bringing our family together…for healing our mother…for watching over us all wherever we go…whatever we do…"

Lucius looked aside at his sister and felt humbled then, for her words made him realize that perhaps he had been too harsh with, and too expectant of, Apollo. He had glimpsed the responsibility of the Gods, and not only was it an unimaginable burden, it was also terrifying. He looked at Adara's moving lips as she spoke muted prayers above the cake and incense she had placed before her. He observed his children's bowed heads as they prayed to a grandfather they could only dream of, in whom all they could do was believe in, despite the horrors they should never have had to endure.

Lucius then placed his own cake upon the altar, and lit a chunk of the incense which he placed beside it. *Shining Apollo…Father…I would you were here now. I see your struggle, and the trial you underwent. I have always honoured you, but now…recently, I have neglected that duty as your son. Give me the strength I need to keep going, to see my own trial through to the very end that I might give my family peace. I ask only for the strength and skill needed to defeat my enemies and finish this.*

He took a glass phial of oil and poured it over the cake and around the incense so that the golden liquid spread upon the marble like a circle of sun fire in the brilliant daylight. He did not hear or suspect the prayers uttered by his wife and children, prayers dedicated not only to Apollo, but to Lucius' own strength and life, strong prayers of love that could hold back the mightiest of life's tides.

When they had all finished their prayers, their offerings smouldering upon the marble surface of the great altar, they descended the steps back into the court and the priests ushered the next pilgrims forward.

Lucius stood facing the temple again, looking toward the dark interior.

"We will come back," Adara said to him, lacing her arm through his.

"This way," Clarinda said, leading Phoebus and Calliope by the hands.

Together, they walked beneath the gaze of the colossal statue of Apollo, past other votive offerings, including a chariot dedicated by the Rhodians, and the shrine dedicated to Neoptolemos, the son of Achilles. Everywhere they looked, there were votive offerings, not least of which was the massive bronze charioteer that stood in the middle of the sacred way, and the lion hunt of Alexander the Great, a bronze group dedicated by his general, Crateros, which stood behind the stage house of the great theatre of Delphi.

From inside the theatre, they could hear the skilled plucking of a lyre's strings. *It is fitting,* Lucius thought, *to hear such a sound in this place.* And a part of him longed to hear his father play.

"You will hear more music and poetry in the months ahead," Clarinda said. "The Pythian Games are set to take place this summer, and the participants have already started to arrive. They make offerings to Apollo, trying to win his favour in the time before the games."

Lucius looked back to see Phoebus still standing before the lion hunt of Alexander, looking up at the hero he had read so much about.

While the others stopped to listen to the music being played in the theatre, Lucius stood in silence beside his son.

After another minute, Phoebus spoke. "Is it strange for you to be here, Baba?"

Lucius put his hand upon his son's shoulder and sighed. "It is very strange. I have never been to this place, and yet I feel like I have always known it."

Phoebus looked up at that, his face thoughtful. "Alexander's father was an immortal too, was he not?"

"You know from your reading, that Zeus was Alexander's father." Lucius felt the weight of that now. "I always looked up to Alexander as a leader of men, a general. That is how I related to him - as a great leader in war, descended from both Achilles and Hercules."

"Both of them?" Phoebus' eyes were wide as he turned back to the bronze statue.

"But I understand him in a different way now, the burden he carried, his ponos..." And in that moment, Lucius felt great sadness. He understood something of the weight Alexander had placed upon his own shoulders, the vision he had had but that few understood. "It must have been very lonely."

Phoebus turned and hugged Lucius, uncaring whether or not others saw this. "Are you lonely, Baba?" He squeezed hard, and Lucius returned it with all his heart.

"Ye...yes." He felt like weeping then, but fought hard not to. He thought of all that Alexander had done, the empire and the unity he had created, the hope he had kindled. *And yet,* he thought, *even he was cut down, his work destroyed by lesser men.* Lucius took a deep breath as he held his son. *I don't want my children to carry my burden. I don't need to create an empire, only to save one...*

Lucius Pen Dragon, a voice said beside them, *the world is not for you to save. The blood never stops…*

Lucius turned to catch a glimpse of an auburn-haired man in a white and red thorax with eyes as alive as the sun itself. He smiled at the statues there and looked back to Lucius and Phoebus.

That our fathers would have spoken to us more…but pain brings learning…and then… He looked up at the sky, his wild hair falling back as he closed his eyes, and then, he was gone.

Lucius gripped his son tightly. "All will be well."

Phoebus looked up at him and smiled. "As long as we are together."

"Come," Lucius said, his voice hoarse. "Let's join the others."

The music in the theatre had ceased as the musician took a rest in the odeon seats, gazing out at the world, and Adara and Calliope waited with Clarinda for Lucius and Phoebus to join them.

"Sorry," Lucius said. "We were admiring the statues."

"My parents have gone ahead. They said that they were tired." Adara turned to Clarinda. "Shall we go out through the stadium?"

"That was my thinking," Clarinda answered. "First, let's go to the top of the theatre to show Lucius and the children."

Adara smiled. She had always loved the view from there. "Good idea."

They walked up the slope, along the outer retaining wall of the theatre, until they reached the path two thirds of the way up where the upper entrance was. There were no pilgrims present at that time, none but the lone musician who now stood in the orchestra praying for his future victory. As they entered the theatre, the sound became focussed, and before them, the world was laid out in brilliant colour and light.

"It's beautiful!" Calliope gasped as they stood in the middle of the seats.

"It truly is," Adara said, holding her daughter's hand.

Above them, the sun shone down with incredible brilliance from an otherworldly blue sky where soft clouds floated easily by. Every detail of the mountains about them was illuminated, and the vastness of the sacred olive groves was alive with the trees' swaying dance all the way to the distant shore of the sea. And in the midst of that paradise, the sanctuary of Apollo was nestled on the lush mountainside, the navel of the earth.

"I don't know what it is," Clarinda said, "but ever since we arrived, I feel like I've finally come home."

Lucius looked at his sister, surprised to hear her speak in that way.

She smiled. "Strange, isn't it? Rome feels like a distant dream now, and this," she waved her slender arm to indicate the sanctuary about the temple, "this is reality." But then she stopped smiling and looked at Lucius with worry. "We should get you home now, Brother. You look weary."

"Come," Adara said, turning to Lucius and kissing him softly. "Before we miss our chance... The last time I stood here, I was thinking of kissing you here, at the centre of the world."

Lucius gripped her hand and a part of him wished to never let go. They walked together after Phoebus, Calliope and Clarinda, toward the stadium where they made their way to the western end. There, they found the path that wound its way along the mountainside, through the groves to their hidden home, their own private sanctuary.

The weeks passed, and Saturnalia came and went. They celebrated with food and colour and song and shouts of *Io Saturnalia!* upon the mountainside, all to the backdrop of the Bacchanalian revels that took place in the pine woods of Parnassus.

They returned to the sanctuary of Apollo often, Lucius roaming the paths of his father's home, becoming acquainted with it and every dedication that remained, everything not yet pilfered by Rome. The Pen Dragons became known to the priests and priestesses who kept the god's house warm and bright in his absence, and they were allowed to venture where they would. They watched the gentle fall of winter snows from the seats of the theatre, as enjoyable in that place as the plays that would be performed there in the months to come when the odeon seats would be filled to capacity for the Pythian Games.

Though his appearance did not change, his skin still bearing the scars of his trials, Lucius did begin to feel strong again, as if he had drunk of the Gods' healing nectar. He began to feel so much better physically that he and Phoebus had begun to run and train in the stadium at the top of the sanctuary where it was quiet, unlike the gymnasium farther down the mountainside where most of the athletes present were training.

Together, father and son ran around the track, going for hours at a time, or sprinting and wrestling. They had even managed to procure a discus and javelin which they enjoyed practising.

Occasionally, Adara and Calliope would join them for training, as they had in those long-ago days upon the green slopes of their hillfort home in Britannia. Caecilius too joined them.

In the evenings, they would gather for the cena, with the rest of the family, in the triclinium that was now brightly painted and adorned with fabulous forest scenes by Delphina, Adara, and the children who shared their grandmother's love of painting.

Lucius often sat with his mother, brother and sister, but they did not speak of the secrets that Antonia had uttered to Lucius upon his arrival in Delphi. Those were for Lucius and Antonia alone, only to be revealed to Adara and the children when the time was right.

"They have a right to know everything," Lucius said to his mother one evening.

"You are right, my son," Antonia had said. "I see how much pain not knowing has caused you, and they already know the greatest secret. But please don't tell you brother and sister, for it will surely break them."

"I won't, Mother. I swear."

"Thank you."

The winter had been hard on Antonia, however, and their conversations were becoming shorter by the day as she became weary, wishing only for the warmth of her bed and the soft glow of lamplight which Emrys ensured she had.

"She's been through so much," Emrys said one night to Lucius after Ambrosia had relieved him from Antonia's chamber. "I've never seen such a strong woman though," he smiled. "Not even in the warrior women of Dumnonia."

"I know a few Dumnonian women who might take issue with that," Lucius laughed.

Emrys smiled again. "True enough. Ach, it would be nice to see my homeland once again!" He rubbed his eyes and shook his head. "But my place is here now, to be with Antonia and to adorn the greatest sanctuary in the world with my art."

"You may yet see Dumnonia again, Emrys. One never knows." Lucius placed his hand upon the sculptor's thick shoulder.

"It's a pleasant thought, Lucius, but I don't think it's meant to be in this life. And I'm fine with that." He looked up at the stars which were particularly bright that night. "I've accepted that…"

.   .   .

Soon enough, after a winter that was more mild than harsh, the first of the spring flowers began to blossom on the mountainside in bursts of yellow, purple and white.

The sound of lambs was added to the laughter and song of Delphi, and with the departure of Dionysus and his Bacchae, a serenity settled over the navel of the world. The priests declared that soon, Apollo would return to Delphi from Hyperborea, and that the Pythia was readying herself to speak his words to the pilgrims who had already started to arrive in droves from across the empire to put their questions to the god.

It was the first in a series of noticeably warmer days when Lucius and Phoebus were training in the stadium with Caecilius. The air was fresh with the scent of dew, earth, pine and laurel. They had been running about the stadium for close to an hour, stopping only to drink fresh mountain water and dry the sweat from their brows.

Lucius looked at Phoebus who ran, his legs long, his torso more defined than it ever had been. He had grown yet again, and was almost of a height with Lucius now. The father smiled at the sight of his son with his uncle, talking easily of the latest hunt upon the mountain.

"Maybe you can come along on the next one, Phoebus?" Caecilius asked. "If it's all right with your father."

"Can I, Baba?" Phoebus asked. "You can come too!"

Lucius nodded, finding that he too was looking forward to such an adventure. He realized then that he was actually feeling the peace of Delphi finally beginning to seep into him, that it had helped him to slowly forget his anger with the world, or at least to set it aside.

And soon, Apollo will return, and I can finally meet with him, and see the temple.

Lucius had denied himself entry into the temple for the last few months since their arrival, feeling as if it were not fitting to roam his father's house in his absence. But there had been something else that had kept him from passing beneath the threshold of those dark and imposing doors. It was something elusive, but he chose not to dwell on it.

Lucius leaned back against the seats of the stadium and turned his head up to feel the full heat of the sun while his brother and son continued running. He had a few minutes of dreamy peace then, moments free from worrying about knives behind his back, or unfriendly eyes peering at him or his family from the shadows.

"Pen Dragon!" someone shouted from the eastern end of the stadium where the starting gates were located. "Come quickly!"

Lucius' heart leapt and he looked up to see Theia running toward him. The priestess had taken some time to become comfortable around him again, and only recently had she come round to his presence and all that had happened in Castalia a few months previous.

"Hurry!" she cried as she approached.

"What is it, Theia?" Caecilius said, running up with Phoebus.

"It's your mother... Antonia... She's taken a turn for the worst. You must go to her now!"

Lucius met the woman's eyes and there he saw fear and felt dread.

"Go," she said. "Clarinda is already on her way back."

Lucius nodded, gathered his things, and together with his brother and son, they ran toward the mountain path that led to the domus.

"Apollo be with you," Theia said as she watched them disappear into the trees.

XIV

APOLLONIS AMABILIS

'Beloved of Apollo'

They ran as quickly as they could over the rocks and among the trees and rooted earth below the cliffs, following the narrow path to get to the compound. Soon, the stone walls came into view and they ran along the eastern wall.

Adara was waiting outside for them among the olive trees and when she saw them she waved.

They arrived, breathless and sweating, and followed her through the outer gate, directly into the domus.

"What's happening?" Lucius asked her.

"She was fine," Adara said. "She was sitting with Emrys, napping in the small grove near the altar and then all of a sudden she started crying out for everyone." Adara stopped and leaned against the wall.

Phoebus rushed to her side.

"I'm fine," she said. "Go now. Go to your grandmother's side."

Phoebus ran ahead with Caecilius, but Lucius stayed with Adara for a moment, looking into her eyes and seeing that same look he had seen in Theia's a short time ago.

"I fear this may be it, Lucius. Prepare yourself." She gripped his hand tightly and together they strode through the courtyard to Antonia and Emrys' cubiculum.

The entire family was there, crammed into that fire-lit cubiculum. Delphina and Publius stood at the back near the door, hand-in-hand, watching quietly as Antonia spoke with Ambrosia who was kneeling beside her bed, tears streaming down her face.

Lucius stopped to let his eyes adjust, to allow his heart to slow its violent pounding as he observed his mother.

Antonia Metella lay in the middle of that vast bed, her face pale, her body like a sinewy willow branch, the outline just barely visible beneath the furs and fleeces that had been laid on top of her. Caecilius and Clarinda stood to either side of the bed, behind Emrys and Ambrosia, and Phoebus and Calliope both sat at the foot of the bed, watching their grandmother, leaning in to hear every word of what she had to say.

Lucius saw this and wondered at his children's courage at a time when most young ones would have wanted more than anything to be out of that room.

Antonia was smiling at Ambrosia, her loyal servant, and reached up to touch her tear-sodden cheek. "Thank you, my girl," she said, her voice so low that most could not hear her. "You will always be a part of our familia. I am so grateful to you for all you have done for me."

"Mistress…" Ambrosia said through her sniffling. "Don't go. Don't leave me."

Antonia just smiled and caressed her cheek.

Ambrosia kissed Antonia's hand and stood up.

Antonia then turned her rheumy eyes upon Phoebus and Calliope.

The children moved down the length of the bed without hesitation and each took a hand.

This made Antonia smile, and her eyes looked from one to the other of them. "I thank the Gods that they brought you to me when they did. Our time together these last months has been one of the greatest gifts they could have given me."

"Grandmother…" Calliope said softly, leaning in to kiss Antonia's cheek. "Surely Apollo can help you."

Antonia looked upon the girl, the knowledge and wisdom that swam in those still-young eyes. She felt awe looking at her, and her brother opposite. "You must both promise me something…" She took a breath and closed her eyes for a moment, but then continued as the flames flickered in the braziers beside the walls. "No matter what happens…do not lose yourselves. Remember who you are…the great things you are capable of. You are both more than…Roman or Greek." Her voice was so low now that Phoebus and Calliope leaned in.

"Grandmother?" Phoebus said, his voice now slightly tremulous.

Antonia's eyes looked into each of theirs, their faces side by side above her as they leaned in. "You are children of Apollo…such light… such hope." Antonia looked to Adara who stood at the foot of the bed now, and reached for her.

Adara approached slowly and sat beside Calliope. "Antonia, a medicus is on the way."

Antonia shook her head and smiled. "There is no need, my girl. My time is upon me."

At this, Clarinda's weeping broke the silence and Caecilius put his arm around her.

"You need to watch your grandchildren grow," Adara said, her eyes stinging with potential tears as she gripped the bony hand. "We've only just returned."

Antonia nodded slowly. "And it is more than I had hoped for. Thank you for coming into our lives, for being a rock and protectress. You are a fine mother and..." she coughed for a moment, "...and a wonderful daughter to me. I love you like my own child."

Adara leaned down and Antonia placed her hands upon her head, patting the curls of her black and greying hair. After a moment, Adara rose, wiping her eyes, and kissed Antonia's forehead. "Thank you, mater."

Antonia held Adara's gaze for a little longer, flashes of their first meeting in their domus during the Ludi Apollinares coming to mind, how beautiful she was, how happy she made her son, and in that moment she smiled and squeezed her hand the same as when they had first met.

"My children," Antonia now looked to Caecilius and Clarinda who stood on one side of the bed and both knelt to be close to her.

"Mother, please," Clarinda pleaded. "The medicus will be here soon. He is a son of Asclepius...he can help..."

"I am so proud of both of you," Antonia said. "We have been through much together..." Now was the first time, Antonia's face betrayed the great weight of regret she had felt for so long, and a tear rolled down the wrinkles of her face to her crooked jaw. "I am sorry for all that you have been through. I wanted to give you such a childhood..."

"Mother, the Gods blessed us in you," Caecilius said, his voice shaking. "Please, stay. Hang on yet a while longer."

"My boy," Antonia put her hand upon his bearded cheek. "No longer a boy...but a formidable man... Where has the time gone?"

Lucius was now standing on the side opposite his brother and sister, but Antonia did not yet look upon him.

Antonia took each of Caecilius and Clarinda's hands and held them tightly. "You are my heart, both of you, but you must promise me..."

"What, Mother?" Clarinda asked.

"You must remain here...do not leave Delphi. You are safe here. Apollo will protect you. Help each other."

"We will," Clarinda said, her voice cracking.

"There, there, my girl... Do not weep..."

"I will miss you."

"And I will miss you," Antonia said, her tears flowing more freely now, though she smiled.

Caecilius had no words for his mother then, but bowed his head to her hand, which he gripped in his rough hunter's hands, trying to burn the memory of her into his mind. His head began to ache and he squinted through the pain, not wanting it to come.

Antonia touched his head where the hole had been made years before. "My brave boy," she said. "You must continue in courage, as you always have. This is not the end."

Caecilius lifted his head and nodded, and as he did so, Antonia looked at him and Clarinda together and smiled. "I love you both."

It was only then that she turned to look at the shadow of Lucius beside her bed. For a few moments, she did not speak, but forced herself to look upon him, and only then did she reach out to him.

He took her hands in his as he knelt upon the stoney floor. "Mother, I..."

"We have already had our words, my son," she said, swallowing, her lips pursed as she tried to smile, tried to see the young vibrant man he had been before Rome had come for him. "There is always hope, remember... You are never alone..."

"But I am," Lucius whispered so that none could hear him. "I feel so alone..."

"You are not!" she said firmly.

"I will make things right," he said, feeling the anger he had tucked away begin to return. *If our homes had not been destroyed, she would not have come to this, not yet...*

"You must live now," Antonia said. "Protect and care for your family... Remember your family too, those who dwell on shining heights..."

Lucius felt her hand reach up to touch his scarred face and head, and remembered all the times she had comforted him after a fight, or cruel encounter in the forum, after the times Quintus Metellus had lashed out at him for his incomprehension of the world in which he, Lucius, lived.

"You are one of the greatest in an ancient line...as are your children... You must take care...and remember..." Antonia sighed as if to weep, but it turned to a cough as she rallied her strength to speak.

"Remember what, Mother?" Lucius asked.

"Who you are. You must never forget, Lucius. Pass on what you know so that it is never lost. Do not be afraid of the darkness-" she stopped and looked up at the ceiling.

Lucius looked but saw nothing but the white wash of the room.

"The Light..." Antonia smiled and seemed calmer. "Oh my son..."

"Yes?" Lucius leaned closer.

"You must go to him...your father... Go to him at the temple. Promise me..."

"I promise."

"He is your true father, Lucius. He has been there for you as much as the laws of the Gods allow. He too loves you...he is the Light...as you are..."

"Mother the medicus is here," Clarinda's voice said from the other side of the bed.

There was some shuffling as the medicus made his way into the cubiculum, some fussing as he took Antonia's hand, but she pushed him away, and turned to face Lucius once more.

"My son..." Antonia smiled and fell back again, her breathing rapid for a few heartbeats as she stepped close to the edge of her life, her eyes taking a last look at everyone in the room. She lingered on Emrys' form a moment, and smiled. Then, she turned once more to Lucius' wide eyes. "I go to be with Alene now...my girl...my beautiful girl... I am coming now..." She paused and looked to the ceiling once more. "Such a blinding light..."

The last of her breath escaped her lips a moment later, and tears fell about the room as Antonia Metella, beloved of Apollo, departed the mortal world.

As Lucius knelt, still grasping his mother's hand, Caecilius and Clarinda doing the same on the other side of the bed, Adara held Phoebus and Calliope to her breast as they wept for the grandmother they had seen but little over the years, but whom they had always sought in their hearts, feeling her love for them across time and the seas.

Publius and Delphina reached out to Ambrosia and Emrys, each of them weeping for what they had expected, but that for which they had never truly been prepared.

No one heard the medicus make his apologies and depart, having come too late to be of any assistance. He would put it down to the Gods' will.

Clarinda and Caecilius wept openly then, for Antonia had been their rock and comfort the whole of their lives, making of their home what she could, protecting them from the monster her husband had become. Caecilius gripped his head as he wept, and Clarinda soothed him, even in the midst of their erupting grief, for she knew too well his pain after so many years.

Lucius looked up, wiping his eyes, and felt a pain in his chest, as if a dagger had been plunged into his sternum and he could not rip it out. A part of him could feel his wife and children hugging him, holding onto him like sea-tossed refugees upon an unwavering rock, but all he could hear was the inner keening of his heart, and his own voice shouting up at the heavens.

Apollo! Why? Why do you allow this? She loved you! Lucius sniffed and wiped his eyes roughly with his arm to look upon his mother's still form upon the bed beside him as Emrys knelt now to close her eyes and kiss her lips one more time. He reached out to touch the sculptor's shoulder as he too let his grief fall like a burden at the end of a long journey. *Alene, wherever you are...* Lucius prayed, *...take care of her now...as I was not able to...*

That night, the domus, the very air upon the Delphic mountainside, was silent but for the wavering notes of sadness that emerged beneath doorways and in the rooms of Antonia Metella's family and friends.

Theia and other villagers who had met and befriended Antonia since their arrival in Delphi arrived at the house to help wash and prepare her body for the prosthesis. As Clarinda, Adara, Calliope, Delphina and Ambrosia watched the preparations through the fall of their tears, they wept aloud as was proper while the village women took great care with their sea sponges dipped in Castalian water. When that was done, they brushed her hair, and dressed her in a blue stola Delphina had given her, a colour closest to her favourite which had gone up in flames along with their home in Etruria. Lastly, a sprig of laurel from the sanctuary was placed in her hand by Theia.

When all was finished the men, who had been waiting in the court-yard of the small domus, were invited into the cubiculum.

There, upon the bed, Antonia was laid out such that she appeared peaceful, even smiling. The villagers moved to the back of the room to allow the family to gather around, the smoke of incense flowing around them like morning mist in a field.

Lucius, already dressed in black, moved to the bedside with his brother and sister, and together they looked down on her.

Clarinda wept openly, falling to her knees beside her mother, and Caecilius stayed at her side, also weeping along with everyone else about the room.

Only Lucius' eyes were dry in that moment, not for lack of grief, however...no. For he felt the tremors of tremendous, insurmountable grief building in his gut, making his body shudder with every breath, breath that his mother could no longer draw. He wondered at all that had happened to have weakened such a woman as his mother, someone so kind-hearted, vibrant and strong - a favourite of the Gods. *If they had been left alone in Etruria...had her home not been destroyed and she had to flee...this might have been avoided...*

Lucius felt his grief and anger commingle within, and it gave him pause for a moment before his mind set to work on the road ahead. He had forgotten his purpose, during that lost winter upon the shining slopes of Parnassus. Now, as he bent over his departed mother's form to kiss her forehead, he was reminded of it.

"Julia Antonia Valens Metella," Lucius spoke his mother's name aloud so that the Gods and everyone else could hear, and then placed a polished golden aureus in her crooked mouth.

The keening in the room reached a crescendo, and Lucius felt Adara, Phoebus and Calliope at his side. Together, they huddled, along with the remnants of their familia, each muttering prayers to the Gods, and visiting their own remembrances of Antonia.

After a while, Emrys, who had knelt red-eyed upon the floor in the spot where he had sat and slept the length of Antonia's illness, rose and departed the cubiculum to go outside into the night air.

The moon was bright yellow with the growing warmth of spring.

"Emrys," Lucius said, following him out into the night. "Are you all right?"

The big sculptor turned to face Lucius, his face shadowed by the darkness with the moon at his back. "What kind of a question is that, Lucius? Am I all right?" He closed his eyes and sighed deeply, painfully. "I am tired of losing people I love, Lucius Metellus...Pen Dragon..." He looked straight at Lucius. "I am not all right. I was though, with your mother. I loved her more than I loved any other woman, but for Carissa, who was like a daughter to me. Now, both of them are gone from my life and..." He stifled his weeping and turned to grip the trunk of the olive tree beside him, squeezing it with his thick fingers.

Lucius stepped closer. "I'm so grateful for the time you spent with her...how much you helped her... I can never repay it, Emrys. Truly."

Emrys turned his head to look at Lucius, and his tear-soaked lips smiled sadly. "It was she who helped me."

Lucius nodded, and looked at the ground, unable to meet Emrys' eyes any longer.

"Now..." the sculptor said. "I am going to my workshop, for her monument will be the last thing that I create."

Before Lucius could say anything, Emrys was striding out of the courtyard and to the back of the compound toward his workshop. Little did anyone know, Emrys already had the chosen piece of stone waiting there, buried beneath a shroud since Antonia first became ill. In grief, he needed to create, not search for stone. After he lit the lamps in his workshop, he looked about the tables and walls at the implements of his one-time trade.

"Apollo...oh divine Muses...guide me in this final creation that it might be worthy of my love..." As the tears fell from his eyes, he ripped away the black cloth that had been covering the stone at the back corner of the workshop, and set to work with his hammer and chisel.

None of them slept much during the next three nights, for grief had a stranglehold upon the household. That grief was unalleviated by the anger that some of them also felt, particularly Lucius and Caecilius who sat together against one wall while villagers came and went to pay their respects.

"Why do all these people keep coming?" Caecilius asked, his voice a harsh whisper. "They barely knew her!"

"They come out of respect for Delphina, whom they have known since childhood," Lucius said. He would also have told his brother that perhaps they were drawn to their mother because she was loved by Apollo, that they came out of respect for the god, though they may not have known it consciously. But he was not certain of it, nor of Apollo's love for her. *Why have you not shown yourself to me, Father?* Lucius wondered. *All these strangers coming and going, and yet you are absent...*

"I suppose it's good that many have come," Caecilius conceded, tipping back the rest of his wine which he had been drinking from a clay cup. "How are Adara and the children?"

"They're..." Lucius sighed and shook his head. "Honestly, they've seen so much death and blood... At least our mother went peacefully..."

"True enough," Caecilius said, feeling his eyes stinging again. "I tell you, when our time comes, we should be so fortunate to go as peacefully."

Lucius nodded, but inside he thought of flames and excruciating pain, and knew that somehow, it was not for him to go peacefully.

"Where is your family now?"

"They went with Clarinda to the sanctuary to make offerings," Lucius said.

"You didn't want to go with them?"

"No. I...I wanted to stay here..."

"Well...I need to get out of here," Caecilius said, standing and brushing the dust from his bracae. "I'll go and see if I can find Clarinda and the others. I'm worried about her. She's said very little since the other night."

"You do that," Lucius said, also standing. "I'll check with Theia to make sure everything is set for the pompa funebris and sacrifice tomorrow."

The distant sound of chiseling reached their ears then, and they both looked up.

"Poor Emrys," Caecilius said. "He was so good to her, to all of us."

"He hasn't come out of his workshop since."

"Whatever he is making, I'm sure mother would love it. I'll see you later."

.   .   .

The day of the funeral began bright and clear. Sunlight spilled over the slopes of Parnassus, and the birds among the blossoming trees heralded the day with their song, led by the mourning doves that nested among the olive, oak and cypress trees.

The courtyard of the domus was busy with all members of the familia ready for the funeral procession that would lead them along the mountain road, through the village, past the sanctuaries of Apollo and Athena Pronaia to the ustrinum in the eastern necropolis.

All were silent as they gathered, shrouded in their darkest tunicae, stolae and cloaks, their heads covered, the faces tearful.

Adara stood with Publius and Delphina who, to her, looked older than ever. They had loved Antonia very much, and grown even closer in their shared hardships, their distance from their grandchildren. *Now, what will become of them?* She wondered as she held her mother's hand. She looked to the olive tree where Calliope stood beside Clarinda, comforting her aunt with words of the Gods and their blessings, though the older was the priestess.

Clarinda had, perhaps, taken Antonia's death worst of all, and had been unable to perform her sacred duties without weeping, an act that was forgiven thanks to the great sway Theia seemed to have at the sanctuary. She had been excused from her duties in order to mourn her mother.

While Lucius, Caecilius, Emrys and Phoebus loaded the covered tombstone into the back of the wagon, another wagon was brought up to carry the body, its bed filled with spring flowers and branches of olive and laurel.

When they had finished securing the stone in the wagon bed, Lucius turned to see Ambrosia directing the villagers who had come to help where to place the body in the back of the second wagon. She had not left Antonia's side, even in death, and through her tears, she acquit herself well of her duties.

Caecilius and Emrys rushed to help them while Lucius stood back and scanned the gathered villagers. It was strange, he thought, that they did not have to hire mourners for the occasion, as they would have done in Rome. The villagers had come of their own volition, genuinely saddened by the loss of a woman they had known but little, but whom they had come to respect in a short amount of time.

Lucius could see their eyes glancing at him from time to time, quickly turning away when he would catch their gaze, or bowing their heads and going about their business.

"Are you sure you need that?" Publius asked as he came to join Lucius, pointing at the gladius beneath Lucius' cloak. "This is your mother's funeral, not a battle."

Lucius turned to look at him. He did not smile or nod, but looked at his father-in-law with red and weary eyes. "Yes, Publius. I do." Lucius turned to look back at the second wagon where Ambrosia was arranging things about her departed mistress. "There're almost ready."

"Yes," Publius answered. "The walk is not long, but with so many people, the procession will take its time."

"How many people are there?" Lucius asked.

"Have you not been without the compound? See for yourself."

Lucius walked past the wagon and out into the compound toward the main, outer doors which stood open.

Outside, along the path that led down through the olive grove to the village road, there were at least two or three dozen people dressed in mourning clothes, holding boughs of laurel and pine, bowls of incense, or sistra. One of the village men even had a small cornu.

Theia came out of the compound from behind Lucius and put her hand upon his shoulder. "They are ready," she said softly. "Are you?"

Lucius looked upon her, this woman who had befriended his mother when, it seemed, much of the world had been against her. "Thank you for your help in this."

"Do not thank me. I would do anything for your mother. She was... very special... Dwell in your grief for a time, wade through it so that you come out the other side of it, into the light."

Suddenly, the sistra rattled in the olive grove and the cornu sounded a long, doleful note, scattering the birds that had been perched among the new-green branches of the trees.

Lucius turned to see the two wagons coming through the compound gate, followed by his family. He caught a glimpse of his mother, lying peacefully among the flowers, and his throat tightened at the sight. *This is it,* he thought with a sense of finality as he joined his brother and sister immediately behind the wagon carrying their mother.

With Emrys, Adara, Phoebus, Calliope, Delphina and Publius behind, the funeral procession set off. Only Ambrosia walked alone, standing beside the wagon, her hand upon the rough timbers that held her mistress.

As the procession moved through the village, others joined its wake, and the keening that had begun as a low hum among the trees up the hill was now as loud as a chorus' call in a tragedy performed in the odeon of the sanctuary.

Lucius stood between his brother and sister as they walked, Caecilius' face solemn and stern, Clarinda's wet with tears, her body shaking. Lucius held her hand in his as they walked, but it was only when Calliope broke away from her mother to walk beside and comfort her aunt, that Clarinda was able to hold her head high and walk on.

Adara looked ahead at her daughter, and hoped with all her heart that she would have more time with her own children than Antonia had had with hers. She looked back and saw Emrys too, before the wagon carrying the monument, his face raked with deep sadness.

Publius and Delphina smiled sadly at their daughter from where they walked just behind her and Phoebus.

Out front, Theia and the other priests and priestesses who led the procession, came to that part of the road that passed the sanctuary of Apollo, and the keening here, reached its peak, as if to notify the god that death was passing by.

As the sistra rattled and the cornu blew a long, lonely note that travelled up the sacred way of the sanctuary, people within stopped to watch the passage. People either made the sign against evil death and turned away, or craned their necks in curiosity.

"Who are all these people?" Lucius asked Caecilius on his right. "Why don't they mind their own business?"

"They're just curious," his brother answered, "and maybe they're hoping for a bite of the sacrificial sows at the back."

"I don't think so," Lucius answered noticing two workmen who had even stopped their toiling on the slopes of the sanctuary, to keenly watch them pass. "It's not like Rome in that regard. People here seem to care."

"I just want to get this over with," Caecilius said, his eyes fixed upon his mother. "It's too painful."

The procession wound its way past the Castalian spring, and then the sanctuary of Athena Pronaia where the temples and tholos shone in the midday sunlight.

"Goddess Athena…" Adara said beneath her breath as she looked down to the sanctuary. "Guide us and protect us always…"

Phoebus squeezed his mother's hand. "She will, Mama. She will."

Adara wiped her eyes again and pat her son's arm.

Soon after that, the procession turned down a path that led away from the main road to the ustrinum of the eastern necropolis.

In a clearing of spring flowers and grass that sprouted from between the rocks, a pyre had been erected. Logs of pine had been set up in layers, the inner ones painted with pitch. Boughs of cedar filled the cracks between logs, and on top was a layer of laurels and more cedar.

The wagons came to a halt, and together, Lucius, Caecilius, Emrys, Phoebus and Publius all lifted the plank bed with Antonia's body out of the wagon and, as gently as possible, placed it atop the pyre.

Theia and others, including Ambrosia and Clarinda, set to placing the flowers from the wagon about the body as the rest of the funeral procession gathered around in a great circle.

"Lucius," Publius said. "As head of your familia, you need to make the sacrifice before the fire is lit."

Lucius nodded and turned to see the altar at the back of the ustrinum where the two sows were held at the ready upon hempen leads. He could see everyone staring at him, waiting. He turned to walk over to the broad stone altar, its surface stained with blood, its base mossy, as if the earth were reclaiming it.

Beside the altar, set in the ground, was a wide grate where coals burned white hot beneath, ready to cook the sacrifice, the thigh bones wrapped in fat for the Gods, and the rest of the meat for those assembled. There would be no feast in their secretive domus, but the funeral meal would take place in the light of day beneath the sun's brilliant orb.

"Will the paterfamilias step forward to make the sacrifice?" the white-robed priest standing before the altar said. He then indicated to the victimarius that he should bring the two sows forward.

The squat man, dressed in a white chiton and short cloak, handed Lucius the first of the sows.

Holding the lead, Lucius turned to look at the crowd behind him, gathered around the pyre holding his mother. He felt numb as the sacrificial knife was put into his hand, its ivory-handled blade smooth and polished, an instrument of ceremonial death. He looked to Adara, and his children, his brother and sister standing side-by-side, and then turned to pick up the first of the sows.

The animal was strangely calm as Lucius hoisted it onto the altar and poured a handful of mola salsa over its scrubbed head.

"Gods, bear witness to this man's sacrifice," the priest began, his arms outstretched to the sky. "Oh, Far-Shooting Apollo... Oh, Goddesses Athena and Demetra... Gods of the soul's passage from this world to the next... Accept this sacrifice and the words and prayers uttered here upon Parnassus..."

The priest stopped abruptly and turned to Lucius.

Lucius held the sow firmly and looked up at the sky. He paused for a moment, and there, high above on the verge of a white cloud, he spotted an eagle circling, its distant cry reaching him as he held the knife up.

"Gods... Accept these sacrifices and see my mother safely to Elysium... I offer these animals to you..."

The knife slashed quickly and deeply, its keen edge unbelievably sharp. The sow cried out for a moment, her body thrashing as blood sprayed and then poured over the altar. Lucius bent quickly to pick up the other sow which was, by now, crying out like a child in terror. The animal slipped from his bloody grasp, and the victimarius stepped in to help raise the animal to the altar.

Lucius took another fistful of mola salsa and poured it over the wriggling animal and, with his words still on the air, he slashed its throat and held it fast until it grew still beside the body of the first.

With spattered blood upon his face, Lucius turned to the priest's assistant who poured water over his hands and handed him a towel while the victimarius immediately set to work expertly carving up the animals to cook on the fire.

Lucius turned to face the pyre and saw the people fanning out now, away from it. The sun shone down upon the clearing with a brilliance that made it hard to see and his eyes began to water as the moment came upon him. In a brazier set nearby, three firebrands smouldered, their flames more intense by the moment.

Lucius stepped forward and was joined by Caecilius and Emrys. He handed each of them one of the torches, and took the last one up himself as they moved to opposite sides of the pyre to wait for him to light first.

Holding the torch aloft for all to see, Lucius scanned the faces of his family gathered there and felt as if a wall of cloud stood between him and them. The only thing that was in full focus was the pyre holding the body of his mother.

Apollo… Father… Take care of her. See her safely across the river so that she can live without pain or worry, in sunlight and green fields. She has suffered enough…

Lucius stepped up to the very edge of the pyre so that the smell of pine resin, pitch and cedar filled his nostrils. "Farewell, Mother…" he said, his voice raspy then. "I will take care of things. I will make this world better yet for our family. I love you…"

And with that, he shoved the torch into the side of the pyre so that the fire immediately took to the logs and branches. Flame and smoke burst into action as Emrys and Caecilius lit their sides of the pyre. They had to stand quickly back as if putting distance between themselves and a starving wolf bent over a new kill.

As the flames rose up, Lucius joined the others to watch as the body was consumed by the fire, the smoke rising like a dancing nymph up into the sky to be carried away on the wind.

It took some time for the flames to fully consume the departed, for the fires to fall slowly asleep until the ash glowed and cooled, and in that time, the wailing of the people gathered, and the sound of the music upon the mountainside dwindled to a gentle thrum to match the slowing of their heartbeats, a different kind of music to dwell in the ears of the Gods.

As Lucius sat beneath a tree with Adara, Phoebus and Calliope, he could feel the bile in his throat, the taste of burning and of smoke. They spoke little, sitting in silence as the fire had finished its work and cooled. It was warm out, and beneath his cowl, sweat began to bead upon his forehead as he watched a priest and priestess gather his mother's ashes at last and place them in the wide, lidded ceramic dish.

The dish had been given to them by a local artist who made such things. It was reminiscent of what would have been used in Etruria long ago, from the meander about the rim, to the triad of horses atop the lid.

During this time, people stood by, talking in whispers, and occasionally approaching members of the family to offer their condolences.

"Lucius," Caecilius called as he approached. "Come. We need your help to unload the monument. You too, Phoebus."

Lucius stood and went with his son, while Adara and Calliope went to Clarinda where she stood alone, staring out at the valley.

The necropolis lay just a short distance beyond the ustrinum, in a wide, grassy area that stretched to the very cliff's edge with a view of the olive-packed valley far below. Various small monuments and sarcophagi dotted the area, sentries of the dead in that place of peace.

When Lucius and Caecilius arrived, Emrys and Ambrosia were discussing with Theia where it might be possible to place the monument and burry the remains.

"I have convinced the priests that Antonia should be placed here, apart from the others," Theia said as Lucius and his brother approached.

Emrys relaxed visibly, and noticed the confused look on Lucius' face. "Antonia and I walked down here once, and she commented on how this was perhaps one of the most beautiful views she had ever seen. She loved the sunlight here, and the distant trees…" He stopped as his voice grew shaky, then turned to Theia. "Thank you."

Theia placed her hand upon Emrys' arm and smiled. "I'll get the workmen who accompanied us to dig the hole." She left, and Lucius turned to his brother.

"How does she have so much say here?"

Caecilius shrugged and joined Emrys at the back of the wagon which had been brought up. Together with Lucius and Phoebus, the four of them hauled at the covered stone monument in the back.

"We must only hold it at the bottom and top," Emrys said. "Not the sides, or we'll break the ornamentation."

The stone was extremely heavy and all four men strained not to allow it to fall as they carried it to the edge of the grass, a few feet from the cliff.

The workmen then approached to dig in front of the monument which remained covered for the moment.

"Excuse me, sir," one of the workers said to Lucius as he passed close by and looked at him. "Won't be but a few minutes."

Lucius recognized the squat, bulky man, his leather Phrygian cap, as one of the two who had watched them pass by from the sanctuary earlier.

The sound of digging echoed over the necropolis and as the crunch of the shovels and grunts of the workers continued, people began to gather around as one of the priests approached holding the ceramic urn containing the remains.

It did not take long for the workmen to finish, and when they had done, they stood aside, apart from the people, their heads bowed, leaning upon their shovels.

Emrys then stepped forward to untie the rope that bound the dark shroud over the monument. He did so in mediative silence and paused before unveiling it, his final creation. When the cloth was removed, and Emrys stood back, there was a collective gasp around the small gathering.

There, before them, was a monument in stone, but for all that appeared there before them, it might as well have been a living and breathing emulation of the woman to whom it was dedicated.

The family crowded around Emrys, as did others who wanted to see, their hands touching him in thanks for his great skill.

"Emrys," Lucius said, feeling his breath crushed out of his lungs. "You've outdone yourself. I never thought-" He could say no more, for the details begged silent respect of all onlookers.

Before them, standing in the sun above the silver-green sanctity of that valley, was a monument to one of Apollo's favourites.

The peak of the small monument was similar to that of a temple that, instead of finials, had the softly-curled edges of a scroll, a scroll that might have contained many secrets. In the pediment was carved a simple sun with rays of light that poured down and appeared to throb with life-giving energy. Both sides of the monument were made up of twined ivy with delicately-carved leaves that shuddered from the sides as if kissed by the wind.

But it was the central figure that caught everyone's breath, the image of Antonia herself, as she had been when Emrys first met her all those years before. The sight of her brought many to tears, even those who had not known her well. Her long hair fluttered easily about her as if the same breeze that touched the leaves also moved about her. The stola she wore over one shoulder fell in long, sinuous folds beneath her arms, and one hand rested upon her belly, the other by her side, the way she stood when watching a sunset, or observing a piece of art.

The rest of the image faded to blend in at the bottom with the stone itself, no legs or feet, a reminder that she was no longer of this world, a beauty beyond reach.

Upon the broad plinth at the base was a simple inscription:

Julia Antonia Valens Metella
Daughter, Wife, Mother, Grandmother
Beloved of Apollo
May She Dwell Forever in the Light

Many wept openly then, for they realized what the world had lost in the woman whose image would haunt that lonely place.

"Lucius," Theia said to him, approaching from the side. "It is for you now to place the urn in the ground."

Lucius tore his eyes away from Emrys' work, from the image of his mother's knowing smile and lively eyes. "Yes, of course," he said, turning to the priest behind and accepting the urn.

The ceramic was still warm from the ash, and the feeling made Lucius' hands shake.

"I'm here, my love," Adara said beside him.

Caecilius and Clarinda joined him as well and together they bent upon their knees in the dirt and gently set the dish in the ground before the monument, each taking a handful of earth and placing it there.

Lucius then accepted the lead pipe from Emrys and set it in the dirt above the dish before the rest of the earth was pushed into the hole to cover it for all time.

The siblings stood when it was finished, and accepted phials of spring water, milk, and honey which they took turns pouring into the lead pipe as offerings to their mother.

The time passed strangely for each of them as villagers approached to look upon the monument, some laying flowers or boughs of laurel and olive, others nodding and offering a few kind words before accepting their share of the funerary feast which was now ready to be consumed at the ustrinum.

People stood in small groups now, eating and drinking of what was offered while the slow, surreality of what was happening began to weigh down on the family.

Clarinda stood, her eyes closed and teary, her face tilted up to the sun. She had never felt so alone, so sad, not even when Alene had been killed. *I don't know if I can survive this,* she thought.

"I'm here, Sister," Caecilius said to her, holding her shoulders as if to prevent her from leaping over the cliff edge. "We have each other."

She turned to him and smiled. "Yes, we do. And now we have Lucius and his family." They both looked to where Lucius stood by the monument alone, one of the workmen approaching to offer his own, humble condolences. "That is something. Things may yet be different now," she said as her brother hugged her tightly.

Lucius felt a great shuddering inside, the same as the day when his mother had passed, the same as when his sister had been murdered. *Why does loss feel so different, so much more painful than anything else?* It was a juvenile question, he knew, but with the death of his mother, it was as if the child inside him had resurfaced, cut and bruised by life, and questioning everything.

"Erm…" a man cleared his throat nearby.

Lucius turned to see the workman in the Phrygian cap. The man chewed a piece of pork and wiped his beard with the back of his hairy arm.

"I'm sorry for your loss," he said to Lucius as he looked down at the monument. "It is beautiful workmanship, though, isn't it?"

"Yes. It is." Lucius watched as the man bent down to read the inscription.

"Your mother was Julia Antonia Valens…Metella?"

"Yes."

"She was from Rome?"

Lucius nodded absentmindedly, annoyed by the questions.

"And you are Lucius? Lucius Metellus Anguis?"

It happened quickly, for as soon as Lucius heard his name he turned to catch a glimpse of the glinting blade that was rushing toward his gut, his hand only just catching the man's wrist.

"The emperor sends…his…regards…" the man said as he pressed harder. He was strong and it wasn't long before the probing point of the blade was against Lucius' side, their hands locked.

Lucius felt his skin break, but not before he slammed his forehead into the workman's face, exploding his nose and sending him back against his mother's monument.

Clarinda screamed from somewhere in the crowd as the man rushed back at Lucius quickly, pushing off of Antonia's monument.

In a moment, Lucius' black gladius slid up and out of its sheath and across the attacker's face so that they both fell backward toward the cliff edge.

"Die Metellus!" From somewhere in the crowd, the second workman ran at Lucius with a pugio which he pulled from beneath his tunic.

"Lucius!" Caecilius yelled, rushing in with one of the shovels and tripping the second man.

Chaos ensued as the two assassins closed in on the Metelli.

The first rose up from the ground and came at Lucius more quickly and persistently than before, but this time, Lucius was ready and using the man's momentum, he spun and slashed, cutting the back of his neck and sending him over the cliff to break his body on the rocks far below.

Lucius spun, searching the crowd for his family and the other attacker. He spotted the latter running up to the road to try and get away. "Brother!" he called to Caecilius. "He's getting away!"

Together, they ran.

The man was fast. He reached the road above the ustrinum and was running toward a group of horses that had been tied up.

Lucius and Caecilius ran quickly after him, their breathing ragged, the sweat and spattered blood mingled upon their brows.

Caecilius ran faster than Lucius, wielding a hunting knife that he had tucked in his cingulum beneath his cloak.

The man reached the horse, and turned it to ride away, but Caecilius ran like an otherworldly hunter after him, taking aim on the run and let his blade fly free.

The pugio whistled through the air and took the assassin on the side of the head, sending him off the back of the fleeing horse and onto the rocks beside the road.

Lucius and Caecilius were on him immediately, their fists pounding him into stillness.

"Who sent you?" Lucius demanded, though he knew all too well.

Through his swelling eyes, and crushed lips, the man spat at them. "Who'd you think, Metellus?" He smiled a bloody smile.

"Who else is here? Tell us and we'll let you live!"

Caecilius stood back now, listening, watching the horror of what was happening, only now understanding what was at stake. His brother was the hunted.

"We're everywhere. You won't escape. The emperor has put a price on your head... The whole world knows..." he chuckled and choked on his blood. "Your family will all die."

"AHHH!" Lucius cried out, drawing back his gladius and stabbing the man repeatedly in the chest until he slumped like a piece of slaughtered meat.

"We need to get rid of the body, Lucius," Caecilius said, having caught his breath. He looked down the road to see Phoebus and Emrys running toward them, followed by some of the village men. "Quickly!"

Together, they pulled at the body, dragged it across the rocky road to the cliff edge, and tossed it into the abyss. When it was done, Lucius fell to his knees, leaning upon his gladius in the blood-clotted dirt. "I will not rest until he's dead. Mars...Avenger... Oh Goddess Nemesis... Guide me in this, whatever it takes. With or without your help, I will kill Caracalla."

Caecilius heard the words his brother spoke then, just before the others arrived, and he felt an inkling of the fear and anger and rage that his brother had only hinted at until then. *This is the hero's life he's led? He should not do this alone!*

"Baba!" Phoebus called, rushing up and throwing his arms about Lucius.

Emrys reached Caecilius and checked on him.

"I'm fine," Caecilius said. "We got him."

Emrys peered over the cliff to see the tangled, bloody limbs of the assassin far below on the rocks.

"Come...Lucius...Caecilius," Emrys said. "We should get back to the others, in case there are more of them."

Phoebus helped his father to his feet, and they began to walk back, ignoring the gawking villagers on either side of the road, people who only a short time before were offering condolences, but were now retreating from Lucius' presence, making the sign against evil upon their foreheads or behind their backs.

"Just leave us alone!" Caecilius yelled at them over his shoulder as they descended into the blood-stained necropolis.

. . .

"How can you be certain there were only the two of them?" Lucius asked
Theia.

The woman stood before him in the shadows of the domus courtyard
later that night, her face lit only by the flickering brazier nearby.

The night was deathly quiet, unusually so after such a day. The
family had expected to be dining in Antonia's honour, perhaps remembering her smile, discussing the beauty of Emrys' memorial to her and
how much she would have loved it. But instead, they were dining in
silence and weeping, wondering how such a thing could have happened,
how the proceedings could have taken such a turn.

Theia had gone away to speak with the bouleuterion to plead that the
family not be expelled from Delphi. The good news was that the council
was blind to the reasons for the assassins' appearance, that all they saw
was that two workmen had suddenly gone mad, perhaps in their hatred of
Romans. It was deemed that Lucius and Caecilius had defended themselves and their family and that as long as they purified themselves of the
blood, they were welcome to stay.

Theia looked at Lucius and stepped closer, having come only to reassure him. "I asked about the two men. They arrived a few weeks ago to
begin restoration work ordered by the emperor…they say for the slaying
of his brother…"

"They were sent by Caracalla?" Lucius laughed. "I can tell you now
that Caracalla feels no remorse for killing his own brother, or for sending
assassins to kill my family."

"I know this, Lucius Pen Dragon." Her voice was serious, direct.

"How do you know? You did not know me or my family until
recently. You live up here hidden away from the world, safe in the
confines of your little village and yet, out in the empire, terrible things
are happening."

"I know. And terrible things happen everywhere, even here. I also
know that no more strangers other than pilgrims, your family, and those
two men have arrived in Delphi. Your family is safe."

Lucius could feel invisible hands gripping his throat as his worries
increased, as the images of the slain men burst into his mind again,
over and over, their bloody bodies tumbling head over heels into
the air.

"I must return to my family," he said abruptly.

Theia nodded and backed away. "I have asked for your home to be watched," she said. "You can mourn properly now, and sleep peacefully."

"Sleep?" Lucius scoffed "I will not sleep while my family is in such danger." He shook his head and looked up at the sky. "What a fool I was... I thought that at least here, we would be safe."

She reached out and placed her hand upon his shoulder.

It was warm and Lucius quickly looked down to meet her eyes.

"You must go to him in the temple. The time has come."

Lucius stared back at her, but said nothing as she backed away, turned, and went out of the compound back to the village.

"You should be with your family," another voice said, and Lucius turned to see Publius coming toward him. "My daughter and grandchildren are upset."

"We're all upset, Publius," Lucius replied, not looking at his father-in-law.

"How could this have happened?"

"You know the sort of emperor Caracalla is!"

"How can you be sure it was the emperor who sent those men?"

Lucius wheeled on Publius. "You ask me that? After we have been hunted from Britannia to here? After all of our homes have been consumed in fire and blood?" He stepped forward. "The assassin even told me who sent them, that there would be more, and more of them!"

Publius actually backed away, his eyes on the pommel of Lucius' blade where his hand rested.

Lucius looked down and removed his hand, shaking his head. "I only wanted to bury my mother and mourn her properly... Caracalla wouldn't even give me that."

"But he doesn't even know you're alive?"

"It's the chance that I am, lurking in the shadows like death, waiting to come for him. He may not know, but he never was one to take chances."

Publius was sweating then, but he found the courage to say what he was determined to say ever since Antonia's funeral. "My daughter and grandchildren are not safe around you."

Lucius had no words for that as he stared upon the man who had once treated him like a true son. Still, he knew there was truth in that. "You don't think I know that? But if we were not together, they would be used as bait for me."

"You cannot know that. They could remain hidden from the world."

"Hidden? There is no place to hide, Publius." As Lucius said it, he realized that there was in fact one place where they could remain safe and hidden, out of Rome's reach. But they had left that place long ago.

"I heard what Theia said. There were only the two workmen. No more. If you were to leave Delphi, Adara and my grandchildren would be safe here. They could live in peace."

"And me, Publius?" Lucius asked, now deeply hurt that his father-in-law had actually said the words, notwithstanding the knowledge that he was right. "Should I just go away and never come back?"

Publius was silent for a moment, but then he set his jaw and stood straight to face Lucius. "Yes. I don't know what it is about you, Lucius, but ever since our families have been joined, you have been both a blessing and a curse to us. I must think of my daughter and-"

"Baba!"

Publius turned to see Adara standing behind him, her arms crossed, her face contorted in mixed anger and disappointment.

"How could you say such things?"

Publius went to her with his arms out, desperate to hold her, but she backed away.

"Our family has been through worse than this. In fact, you cannot imagine what Lucius has been through. Otherwise, you would not say such things."

"It's because of what you've been through that I do say such things, Daughter. I think only of you and your children."

"Please leave us," Adara said, her voice cold, her nose sniffling from weeping for what the day should have been.

Publius went back to the triclinium where he sat in silence with the others.

"Don't listen to him, my love," Adara said, hugging Lucius tightly. "He's scared."

"He's right in a way," Lucius said.

Adara pulled back and looked at him. "Don't you dare say that!" she shook her head. "After all that we've been through?"

Lucius said nothing, but pulled his wife close and buried his face in her hair, wishing he could just forget all that had happened. The tremor started in his gut, and then moved into his chest and heart, and then, as Adara held him, his tears finally fell. He would never again look upon his mother, nor would his children. She was with Alene then, he hoped, but also a part of him wished that he too was, for then his family might truly be safe. *Not yet,* Lucius thought as his body shuddered. *Gods give me strength…*

It was late at night, after nine days of mourning, that Lucius found himself standing in the courtyard before the Castalian spring. Though he had seen the faces of the Gods many times throughout the course of his life, there was something discomfiting about entering the confines of the temple at Delphi. It was a place and experience that had humbled heroes and kings, so what would it mean for a simple warrior to enter those sacred walls?

But you are no longer a simple warrior, Lucius told himself as he undressed in the moonlit court of Castalia.

He could still feel the assassins' blood slick upon his hands and arms, though he had washed thoroughly after the attack. However, in that place, the blood did not seem to wipe away so easily.

It had to be done, he told himself as he walked down the steps to the trickle of the lion-headed spouts and immersed himself in the dark depths of the spring.

There were no tremors this time, no falling rock or screams. Only silence, as Lucius Pen Dragon, no longer Metellus, cleansed himself before going into his father's home.

He had thought to go with the entire family to the temple, to keep Adara, Phoebus and Calliope close, to give comfort to his sister whose world had crumbled before her eyes with the death of their mother, but he could not. This was something he needed to do alone. So, when Theia had shown up the previous evening to tell him he should come the following night, alone, he accepted that.

As the cold water enveloped him and swirled about him, he realized that he no longer felt the pull and discomfort of his desiccated skin, that he could actually feel the movement of his muscles once more beneath the surface, though his outer appearance continued to horrify people.

And the dragon upon his breast remained red and raw, as if unwilling to fully heal.

Lucius allowed himself to float on his back and look up at the stars twinkling beyond the reach of the pine and cypress trees, and the crowns of the Phaedriades that disappeared in the darkness above. How many times had he stared at that moon and those stars throughout his life? How many times had he wondered about or envisioned the future he would shape? His path had seemed clearer then, before he discovered the secrets about himself. Now, the road ahead, the future, seemed blurry as if standing upon the via Appia in early morning, trying to peer through the impossible mist. There was no way to see ahead, and he knew that he needed to either go forward, or stay where he was hidden, afraid of what haunted those misty shadows.

He caught a movement out of the corner of his eye and stood quickly, the splash echoing about the courtyard.

There, in a patch of moonlight, Love stood before him. Her golden hair floated about her face in an unseen wind, and her peplos invited the moonlight to shine about her such that nothing else was visible to Lucius in that moment.

He bowed to her, but her eyes remained cold and blue, more distant than he remembered, devoid of the pleading and pity he had seen in Annwn.

"Oh, Goddess…" Lucius said.

Your thoughts no longer hold Love aloft like a torch in the darkness.

Lucius hung his head, feeling his skin cold in the night air.

What of your wife? Your children? Such love can overcome the greatest adversity, and yet you push it away, push me away!

"I need to be strong, to keep them safe," Lucius answered, feeling the weight of her gaze and disappointment.

To kill… she said, and the light in the court dimmed as the words passed her lips. *Your anger is undoing you and blinding you. It is what is burning the world around you and your family. What about your desperate urge to make the world a better place? Have you forgotten?*

"I have not forgotten. I will make it a better place!"

Love stood still, staring down at Lucius, and before her she could see the boy, the idealistic young man, the heroic warrior, each of them standing to either side of the shadowy, misguided figure of the half-mortal before her.

Your father awaits you. It is time.

"Why do you come to me now?" Lucius asked, but even as he spoke the words, the hurt in her eyes was like a spear thrust to his heart.

If you need to ask, then I have little hope. Come. She turned to go.

Lucius dressed hurriedly and followed her light as she led him forward out of the tree-enclosed court and along the mountain road to the sanctuary.

The night was spotted with firelight, and there was a silence over the sanctuary that was not present during the day. As Lucius walked up the sacred way, he passed the bronze faces of gods, heroes and generals, their eyes following him. Weary pilgrims slept in corners and against walls, waiting for their turn to see the oracle, and solitary priests or priestesses prayed in the dark before burning tripods, the smoke of which rose to surround their faces. Somewhere in the night, a lyre was being played, its notes snaking their way down and around the sanctuary.

Past the treasury of Athenae, where the metopes shifted and played out the battles of the past, Love paused in her progress and looked back at him. In the darkness behind her, the Sibyl's rock, and the rock of Leto stood silent.

Lucius slowed as he approached them, and he heard a deep growl in the earth then, but it was no quake or tremor. He stopped walking and thought that he could see great, angry eyes in the ground before him. Then, he heard the crushing of stone and looked up to see the skyward column of the Sphinx.

The beast shifted upon its perch and looked down at Lucius with those time-fevered eyes, its claws digging into the marble, its wings slowly flapping.

Lucius thought again of his time in Annwn, but in that moment, the memory of his encounter with that timeless guardian escaped his grasp and made his heart pound. He turned to Love who was staring at him, waiting. She moved on toward the great staircase that led up beneath the titanic tripod which seemed to rain fire down on the altar before the temple of Apollo.

Love stood before the temple then, unseen by the three priests who stood upon the ramp. She stared at Lucius, but said nothing, and he longed for kind and caring words from her lips.

"You are expected, Lucius Pen Dragon," the priest in the middle said.

Lucius looked at the man and wondered at the monotone timbre of his voice, for he did not appear to be fully conscious of his surroundings.

Love continued to stare at him as another of the priests stepped forward with a bowl of water and looked at Lucius' hands.

Lucius extended his hands and the priest poured the water over them.

The third priest then came forward with a platter of pelanon, the honeyed bread that was to be offered to the god before entering the temple.

Lucius took a piece of the dripping bread, turned, and mounted the steps to the great altar before the temple. He looked up at the soaring fire in the Plataean tripod and then set the dripping bread down upon the altar, closing his eyes.

For you, Father.

Lucius turned then to see the priests now standing at the top of the ramp leading into the temple.

His heart sank when he saw that Love had gone, that her light no longer lit the way. The only light lay within the sanctum, and Lucius descended the altar steps and walked slowly up the ramp toward that beacon, following the slow-moving priests with a deep breath to calm his rising fear.

As he passed beneath the temple pediment where Apollo's triumphant horses bridled and neighed as they pulled him, the darkness of the forest of columns closed in on Lucius and he groped as if in the dark to get through the several rows before arriving at the great bronze doors.

He remembered Diodorus telling him of the temple, his lessons on the great Delphic maxims that he believed, if followed, would lead to a life of greatness absent of regret. Lucius looked up and there, lit by fire in the pronaos of his father's home, the words of three maxims jumped out at him.

Surety Brings Ruin

Nothing in Excess

Know Thyself

Lucius found himself mouthing the words, his mind lingering on that last, haunting and impossible phrase. He felt like weeping then, as if the words had stripped him bare and thrown him to his knees in the darkness. Doubt swept over him then, and he longed for the days when he thought he had truly known who he was. The half-mortal who now looked up at those words had been stripped of all his possessions, his lands, his armies, his very name.

Lucius never felt so lonely as he did in that moment upon his father's threshold.

But he walked forward nonetheless as the great bronze doors opened more widely to let him in, closing behind him with a resonant thud.

Once inside, Lucius turned to look around. The feeling was one of reverence, but also of great antiquity. The floor was worn by hundreds of thousands of feet, making it slightly uneven, and the cedar-panelled ceiling was blackened with smoke from incense and fire, even though it was obviously cleaned regularly. It smelled of charcoal and laurel very strongly, but there was also an underlying scent that Lucius could not place, something menacing and unpleasant.

The priests waiting ahead of him did not rush Lucius as he walked forward slowly, looking from side to side at the offerings left by count-less pilgrims - statues of bronze, ivory and marble, frescoes, enormous kraters and tripods that shimmered in the fire from braziers, ornately carved tables where kings might have dined, an array of ancient and exotic weapons, and even a chariot which sat beside the north wall, tilted forward and unused for an age. There were instruments of various kinds, dedicated by victors in the games, crowns of glinting gold, and finally the iron throne which, Lucius remembered from his lessons, the poet Pindar used whenever he had visited Delphi.

Suddenly, Lucius felt a presence somewhere beyond the dim, bejew-elled light that surrounded him, and his eyes searched ahead. He wondered if this was where that Metellus long ago had walked, before he had been given the stone by the priestesses. His hand went to his chest again, as he approached a wide screen of wood and ivory that separated the first chamber from the cella. In the distance, his eyes caught a glint of gold and fire.

Two of the priests opened doors in the screen and Lucius stepped through, following the first. They moved slowly and methodically, but he could see them trying to catch glimpses of him from beneath their mantles.

Lucius stopped and looked around again. Before him was the raised cella upon a platform where a soaring statue of Apollo looked down upon him, muscular and vibrant, an all-knowing Olympian. At his feet was a broad basin full of fire. This was the sacred flame which was never permitted to burn out. The women who moved silently about it, feeding it logs of fir, were the Hestiades, the Delphic maidens specially tasked with maintaining Apollo's sacred light.

Along the walls to either side stood five silent men in white robes and mantles who watched Lucius with great curiosity and expectancy.

Uneasy beneath their gaze, Lucius turned to the nearest priest. "Who are they?" he whispered.

The priest, the youngest of the three, leaned in. "They are the Holy Ones, the descendants of Deucalion whose ark ran aground on the slopes of Parnassus. They have come to see you with their own eyes."

"Me?" Lucius looked around at the shadows quickly.

"Do not be afraid, Lucius Pen Dragon. There is no safer place."

"You must make your sacrifice now," the first, older priest said from where he waited before the great altar with a pure black goat.

Lucius looked away from the younger priest who backed away, and stepped toward the altar. He had to step around to the side to go up, for directly in front of the altar and cella was a dark stairway which led down into the earth. He paused to look at it, not without some dread, for from that darkness came the dizzying smell of anger and of fear. Still, he wanted to descend into that void, but the priests urged him to the other stairs so that he now stood before the great altar.

The goat was hoisted upon the spotless surface and water from the sacred spring was poured over its head.

As Lucius held the animal by the scruff of the neck in one hand, and the knife in the other, it began to bleat and then to shake uncontrollably.

"Apollo accepts your offering," the priest said. "You may perform the sacrificium now!"

Lucius looked at the animal, pulled back its head and slashed at the neck.

The goat shook wildly for a few moments and then its body grew still as its lifeblood poured slowly out and over the white altar.

Lucius' head was bent and his eyes closed for a few moments before he looked up at the stony gaze of his father's face. He looked at the Hestiades moving silently back and forth as they fed the sacred fire, and as they put more incense into a bronze burner in the form of a priestess holding aloft a great bowl like some beautiful Atlas holding up the world.

The smoke grew thicker all about them and Lucius noticed the Holy

Ones, the priests and priestesses looking about. They seemed confused, awed, and a little afraid as Lucius descended the steps and stood before the abyss of the chasm. Though no one had told him, he knew that he was to go there next.

The three priests rallied themselves and made to go before Lucius, as they did with all those who sought the oracle's advice, but in that moment a tremor shook the foundations of the temple and a light kindled in the chasm of the adyton below.

"He must approach alone!" a deep, strong voice ordered from far below.

The priests looked at each other, clearly confused, and the Holy Ones stepped forward, unsure if they had heard correctly.

"Come, Lucius Pen Dragon!" the voice ordered.

Lucius looked at the priests and the Holy Ones, pulled back his hood, and descended the narrow staircase.

The light changed immediately, as if he were miles from the sacred flame. He felt dizzy, for there were fumes in the stone chamber beneath the cella. He did not know how far he had gone, for there was no sense of distance or time in that place. But the light ahead grew brighter and brighter and eventually, the narrow passage gave way to a circular cavern.

The space reminded Lucius of the tomb in Etruria, the place where he had seen the shades of his fellow dragons. He looked around, expecting to see their ghostly faces, but none were there.

There was sound of running water, and Lucius looked down to see a stream flowing through the rock, out one wall, across the room, and then disappearing into the opposite wall. There was also a great crack in the bedrock which he was careful to avoid, and out of this there rose fumes, as if the earth's breath could be seen on a cold winter's morning.

"Father?" Lucius called out, his voice muted on the glistening walls.

"He is here," said a deep, but strangely-timbered voice.

Lucius' eyes followed the crack in the rock ahead to the far end of the chamber and there he saw her, the Pythia.

She sat atop a great bronze tripod and was cowled, covered in a red robe over a white peplos, her pale arms folded across her front. In her hands she grasped a bowl of water and a branch of laurel, taken from the sacred tree that shivered out of the rock beside her. On the other side, there stood the stone Omphalos, the navel of the earth. Lucius could hear a ringing in his ears as he gazed upon it, the carved black stone covered with its agrenon, the wool net held in place by two golden eagles.

Lucius approached the Pythia slowly, daring to search her gazing eyes, rubbing his for the fumes that rose up out of the earth. As he got closer, his breath caught and he felt his heart race.

"Theia?"

"I am the Pythia…" she said with a voice that was not her own, "… all seeing…all knowing…the voice in the darkness…the voice of the Light…"

"Where is my father?" Lucius asked. He felt his anger rising in that sacred place, and the earth trembled again beneath his feet. For a moment, he thought the great Python might have resurrected to swallow him whole and rip him from the world. The memory of Apollo's trial flashed in his mind…the god's fear, the sweat and blood…the dragon…the bow…

"Drink," the Pythia said, raising the bowl to Lucius.

He stepped forward, took the bowl in his two hands, and drank. The cool water soothed his dry throat and he felt relief.

"Eat," she then said, holding out the branch of laurel.

Now he hesitated, but she held it aloft again. He then took a single deep green leaf and placed it in his mouth. The taste was extremely bitter at first but then, something happened. His senses sharpened. He heard faint music. He felt his limbs pulsing as if filled with fire, and the burning of the dragon brand upon his chest soothed and glowed with a cold blue light.

The Pythia slumped suddenly upon her tripod as if she had been robbed of her essence and purpose.

Lucius made to step forward to help her, but then…

"I am here…my son."

Lucius froze, just inches from the Pythia. He could tell she was alive. He did not now how it was possible, but it was. And so, slowly, he turned.

"Father?"

There before him stood Apollo, but not as he had seen him in any other space or time. The stars did not whirl in his godly eyes, nor did the invisible winds about him play with his cloak and hair. But he shone in that dark place, oh how he shone!

And that same light burst forth from Lucius' own chest as he stood face-to-face with his father.

"You've come at last," Apollo said.

Lucius looked up at him and he found he could not speak, only radiate all that he was feeling, the sadness and despair, the anger and rage.

Apollo reached out to hold Lucius by the shoulders and hung his head, a fiery tear falling from his lid into the steaming chasm below.

"I loved your mother very much. I…I felt it when she left. I was there with her. You must believe me."

Lucius remembered his mother speaking of the light as she departed the world, of the smile upon her face.

"You could have saved her," Lucius said, standing back. "You could have saved all of them. You could have stopped the burning of our lives."

Apollo shook his head, wishing for his son to understand, but how does one explain the laws and workings of the universe to one who was raised in the mortal world? "It was not permitted, Lucius."

"Not permitted?" Lucius stood tall then, his anger and frustration giving him strength, feeding his ignorance. "Just as you were not permitted to save me in Annwn as I bled to death? Or as the fires consumed my body?" He ripped open his tunic to reveal his branded chest and the scarred skin of his neck and shoulders.

"I helped you in what way I could," Apollo said, looking Lucius in the eyes.

As never before, Lucius looked back at the god, directly in the eyes, and without fear or pain. But neither did he feel elation or get the promise of a world of possibilities that he had previously glimpsed.

Lucius, and the earth beneath him, shook with his anger and pain, tortuous feelings that Apollo could see written plainly upon his son's mortal body, and which Lucius sought to lay blame for.

"My heart wept when your mother passed from the world," Apollo said, trying to soothe Lucius. "But know that she is now with your sister and that they dwell where there is no pain or suffering, in the green and sunny fields of Elysium. They are well."

"And what of the rest of my family?" Lucius demanded. "Are they to be hunted by Rome the whole of their lives? Until they too burn in fire and blood?" He shook his head, his fists clenched as he looked down at the chasm and inhaled deeply of the fumes rising up, as if he took in the anger of Python.

"Your family will be safe, my son. I promise you. Stay here, upon sacred Parnassus. Be calm and at peace. Hunt long days and into the nights in the vale of Tempe with me. If you will not dwell in Olympus as I once offered you, then live here upon the mountain slopes as free from pain as can be in the mortal world. You will be together with your family. Safe."

Lucius shook his head and looked up at Apollo again, the fumes working upon his senses. "Safe here, in Delphi? As we were when Caracalla's men attacked us at my mother's funeral rites?" He paced then before Apollo, like a caged leopard. "I won't rest until I'm drowning in my enemies' blood! Until there are none of them left!"

Apollo shook his head and felt such sadness at the knowledge that perhaps he had indeed failed in this trial. But he reached out a last time to Lucius.

"Listen to me..." Apollo said. "You are my son. It is true, Lucius. You are. You are also mortal. You are of both aspects, and they are warring inside you. Hear me now... Understand me... Divinity is not about what you can destroy. It is about what you create, how you better your world and inspire and nurture others. You are both mortal and immortal - terrible and good. Which part of your self will you nurture, my son?"

Apollo closed his eyes and in that moment, Lucius could see the words written upon the pronaos of the temple above.

"Know Thyself..." Apollo said. "It is written for a reason. It is one of the greatest trials for man...and god."

"I do know myself," Lucius insisted. "And I know what I must do!"

"You are blinded by your pain and anger. Let me help you."

"Your help has only brought pain."

Apollo stepped forward now. "Your own choices have brought you pain," he said, his divine voice angry, as if a string had broken upon a lyre.

The Pythia jolted on her tripod then as she felt the Far-Shooter's anger.

"You have seen the rock outside this temple," Apollo said to Lucius, and as he did so, they were standing before it. "I slew my enemy there, my family's enemy. And even though I was victorious, I paid for it and dearly. There is payment to be made at all levels of life and creation, Lucius. You are not above it."

They were suddenly back in the adyton.

"And I want to kill my own enemy," Lucius growled, feeling his teeth grind like the rocks in the earth below as another tremor shook them. "The only salve for my pain now is blood. If you won't help me, then at least guide me."

Apollo's sadness then was like an age of rain. There was no music or light in it, only an acrid rain that turned to blood as he peered into the future of his son's life.

"Sometimes the enemies we seek to slay…whom we *need* to slay… are not the ones we see before us." Apollo hung his head for a moment, but then looked up, reconciled to what he was about to do.

"Go to Antioch and the drums of war. Find a friend's truth at the sign of the Golden Bough."

"What do you mean?" Lucius asked, taken aback by the words, his anger dwindling.

"What you do on the road you take is your choice…your will…"

Lucius felt his anger soothed for the moment and he once again stood before his father with awe. He would have reached out to him then, like a child wishing for the embrace of his father, but something stopped him.

Apollo stood back and in his eyes the stars whirled, his hair and cloak writhing in the winds that followed him everywhere.

"There are certain deaths not even the Gods can escape…" he said, and a moment later, he was gone.

Lucius felt the dam of his anger break and give way to great sadness. He fell to his knees in the adyton of the temple, and the Pythia suddenly gasped for breath above him.

When he looked up at the priestess, it was Theia's eyes he saw, and as she looked down upon him, she wept for all that she had seen and heard and felt. She had no prophecy to utter for him, no guiding words or inspiration, for the anger of Lucius Pen Dragon had robbed them both, and the road ahead was dark.

XV

AD SOLITUDINEM

'To Solitude'

Great truths, especially those uttered by the Gods, have a way of haunting mortals. They echo through time and space, are repeated by one's psyche until action is taken. Those who heed these warnings and words can be guided by them to a place of peace in life, to that which is their fate because they chose that particular path.

But what if a man, or even a god, is haunted by conflicting truths? How then does he move forward to ensure the world about him is bettered, that is it safe, not only for him, but for those around him, those who depend upon his honourable action? The choices can be few, or myriad, but either way there can be a sort of madness in indecision. Sooner or later, another step upon the road must be taken.

For many months after his visit to the temple of Apollo, Lucius Pen Dragon remained in Delphi plagued by indecision, knowing what he must do but also what he believed he should do for the family he had brought to ruin.

No more assassins came to Delphi, no more knives in the darkness or day. The veil of violence and grief had been lifted and his wife and children began to feel peace again in that place of light. Apollo did not appear to Lucius again either. Nor did the son of Apollo seek his father out. But the Gods did shield Lucius' family, the innocent who dwelled below the Shining Ones.

Lucius continued to train with his son and brother in the stadium of Delphi, but more often he walked alone at dusk or dawn. If ever a villager met him upon the road or mountain path, they kept their distance but offered their respect. Talk of that night in the temple had run through the population like the waters beneath the mountain.

A son of Apollo was among them.

Despite the safety they now enjoyed, however, Lucius could not hide the urges for vengeance that haunted him. He could not push them away. He could not forget. Every time he closed his eyes, he could see the pained faces of his friends and family, and every time he spotted himself upon the water's surface, he saw only fire. There was a bitter poison in his veins, and though he tried to stanch the flow of blood and hate from his wounds, he remained bent on the revenge he had nurtured for so long.

It was a night in autumn when golden leaves shivered upon Parnassus and the limbs of olives groaned with the weight of their harvest. Adara sat in the olive grove with Lucius, shortly before the chariot of the sun had completed its circuit, and now the stars sparkled like jewels in the heavens.

"It's so beautiful and peaceful here," Adara said as she leaned against her husband, enjoying a rare moment in which they could be alone together and recapture the feeling that they were one, that Lucius was not pulled in another direction.

"It is," Lucius said, holding her close and fighting back the images of their terrifying ordeals. He had become adept at hiding things, despite the turmoil he felt, even in cherished moments such as that.

"But I miss Britannia."

Lucius sat up at that, clearly surprised and shocked by the statement. "But this is your home, where your family is!"

Adara shook her head and brushed her long hair aside. "Not really, Lucius. Yes, our family is together, but this is not our home. I miss our friends in Dumnonia, and the people who joined us in our hall. We were happy."

"We can't get that life back again, my love. Please don't…" Lucius stood and leaned upon one of the olive trees, his face hidden by the low-hanging fruit. *There is only one way we might get our lives back and I have delayed it for too long.*

Adara stood and walked up to him, her green eyes searching for his between the silvery leaves. "The children miss it too," she said, her voice reaching out to him. "They speak often of Rachel and Aaron and of Ynis Wytrin. We could go back there, or we could live in Dumnonia with Einion, Dagon and Briana, safe with your surviving warriors nearby. In our time here, I've realized that the Gods have not abandoned us… Apollo has not abandoned us."

"Don't," Lucius said.

"You've never told me what he said to you that night in the temple. I've not pressed you. I know you have been thinking it over, whatever it is. But we're a family, Lucius. You are my husband. We've been through so much, but the world has forgotten Lucius Metellus Anguis. Can you not also, so that we can live the rest of our lives in peace, among friends?"

"There can be no peace," he said.

"Emrys has been talking about returning to Dumnonia after many years. He's been adrift since your mother passed."

"And your parents? What of them? Would you leave them here and never see them again?"

Adara was silent. She had considered that. In fact, she would have suggested leaving much sooner had it not been for them. "They might come too."

"The only way your father would do that is if I were not there," Lucius said. It saddened him, but Publius had grown distant when it came to Lucius. He could not help but blame his son-in-law for all their ills, for his daughter's and grandchildren's suffering.

And Lucius agreed with him.

Lucius stepped out from beneath the leaves of the tree and held his wife close. After so long, she could still take his breath away. He remembered her in Britannia, how she had trained and fought like some northern Amazon. And now she wore a stola again, and had not held a sword in months. *Perhaps it is a time for peace?* he thought. *But not for me.*

Adara felt his body try to pull away, but she held him fast and looked directly into his eyes. She was still strong, and beautiful. She shook her head. "Don't pull away from me. It's been too long."

"I can't," Lucius said.

But Adara leaned in and kissed him. His burned lips and skin felt strange to her own, but she did not care, for when she closed her eyes, she could see the man she had fallen in love with as clearly as the water in the bay far below. *You are not the broken man you insist on showing the rest of the world.*

Adara led Lucius by the hand, through the trees to a spot beneath a rock wall where they were shielded from the world's eyes. When they reached that spot, she laid her cloak upon the ground and stepped back so that he could see her in the twilight as she unclasped the iron brooch upon her shoulder and let her tunica fall to the ground.

She was naked beneath, and as Lucius looked upon her - the stray battle wounds, the fall of her hair upon her shoulders, and her hardening nipples - he felt himself wanting her as he had not done in a long while.

Adara stepped toward him and unbuckled the gladius he kept constantly at his side. She then removed his cloak, stealing increasingly urgent kisses from him before pulling his tunica over his head. "I have missed you, Lucius," she whispered, as his rough hands reached out to caress her hips and the sides of her breasts. She loosened his bracae and then stepped back to lay herself down upon the cloak. "Come to me, my love."

Lucius felt his body responding to her in a way he never would have thought possible again for all the trauma he had endured, but standing before her in such a way, naked, made him feel like the broken man he thought he was. He hesitated as she looked up at him, her legs open to him.

"Lucius…" she said softly. "Enjoy this moment with me. We are together. We are free… And I am fertile."

His eyes widened. He had never thought to hear Adara utter such words again, to even entertain the thought of another child. He stared at the horrific scar across her abdomen and hesitated.

But she reached up to him again. "Yes, my love. It is time. Come…" She reached out to him.

Slowly, Lucius stripped away the last of his clothing to reveal his severely scarred body, and lowered himself onto his wife as he kissed her neck and lips. As their bodies joined, Adara grasped him tightly, crying out as she did so.

They had forgotten each other, but now Venus graced them. They surrendered to Love's call, the stars the only witnesses to their act.

At dawn, Lucius awoke from sleep to see Adara laying in the bed beside him. He could not remember the last time they had made love in such a way. *Could she also be with child?* he wondered, remembering her words.

As soon as the thought occurred to him, so too did he wonder how he would keep that child safe, for the last one had been ripped from her belly by evil men. *I won't allow that to happen again,* he thought as he leaned down to kiss Adara's brow.

As quietly as possible, Lucius dressed, took up his gladius and cingulum, and went out of the door into the courtyard.

The morning was calm and cool and the light that filtered into the courtyard through the reaching trees was sharp and brilliant.

Lucius stood there for a moment, breathing in that light, trying to calm his racing heart. He should have been calm, he knew, for he and Adara had not enjoyed such a night in a long while. They had recaptured what they both believed had been lost for good.

But how long will that last? Lucius thought, for he knew that such joy was precious and fleeting. It was pain and anguish that seemed to endure. Whenever he was awake, the injustice of that endurance occupied his mind, and he obsessed over how he might change that. *I know what I need to do... I've been hiding from it for so long!*

Just as Lucius was about to fall into another of his despairing episodes, he heard soft laughter on the air, like the trickle of water from the heights of the mountains above him. On the other side of the courtyard, Phoebus and Calliope were walking together, out of the triclinium door toward the passage to the outer compound.

At first, Lucius did not recognize them, for they were both so tall and strong-looking again. He knew he should not be surprised, for they had been in Delphi for a long while now, and he had been distracted while life went on around him. In that moment, he felt as if he was just coming out of an extended dream, that he was awake now, and armed with purpose.

Lucius strapped on his gladius and followed his children outside from a distance as they made their way across the compound to the outer gate that led to the olive grove.

Calliope hummed as she always had done, her long hair trailing in the wind behind her as she walked beside her brother who, Lucius noticed, held his head high again, with his shoulders relaxed.

Lucius thought how much they looked like Alene and himself years ago, in happier, more peaceful days, and he wished his own children could enjoy such peace for longer than he had. He even noted that Phoebus had left his gladius back at the domus, that he was now at ease among the people of Delphi, and in the broader world. It took all of Lucius' own will not to chide him for letting his guard down, to allow his children the time to enjoy peace while they could.

He continued to follow them from a distance until they reached the sanctuary of Apollo and went in, greeted by some of the priests and priestesses, including Clarinda who had been waiting for them in the agora.

Lucius stopped as they went in, refusing to enter, to set foot upon the sacred way. He could still smell the acrid air of the temple's adyton, still hear the reluctant words Apollo had spoken to him, and the thought made him angry once more.

The passage of time suddenly made Lucius feel an urgent need to keep his children and his wife safe, no matter the cost. And that need was as kindling to the fire that had been simmering in his soul through the long months of their Delphic sojourn.

He turned to leave but stopped short when he saw Theia barring his way. He had avoided speaking to her for a long while since that night in the temple. He did not even know why, but that she knew all, had heard all, and he feared every word she would utter as much as he had feared those of the Sibyl at Cumae all those years ago, words to haunt, to drive and dissuade.

"Lucius Pen Dragon," Theia said, her voice soft and full of care. "You are still here."

Lucius looked upon her with trepidation. "Yes," he replied.

"Your children walk freely here," Theia said. "They are safe at last."

"For now."

She stepped closer, her hood pushed back, and made to reach for his hands, but stopped when he pulled back, his right hand fiddling with the pommel of his gladius. "You need not fear me or my words as others do. I am a friend to your family…a servant to your father."

Lucius stared at her and looked around at the changing leaves upon the mountainside, the smoke rising from the sanctuary. "Is he gone from this place again?"

"As he must," she said. "Dionysus is coming once more."

Lucius nodded slowly.

"I know what you are considering," Theia added. "Please think on your father's words, for they are truth. This place is your sanctuary and home, if you will allow it. Your family will be safe here."

"For how long?" Lucius said. "Until another assassin finds his way to my family's threshold? It could be anyone. The jingle of a bag of aurea can be very persuasive."

"If you think that, then you have not really lived here. The people of Delphi are good and loyal, and your family has become a part of them."

Lucius shook his head. He loved his family more than anything in the entire world, more than the Gods themselves, and his heart raged at all that they had been put through. *I would have bettered the world,* he reminded himself as he felt the hard skin on the side of his head.

"You still can," Theia said, and in that moment, Lucius knew that his father was there too. "Take hold of the peace that is offered to you. *Live, Lucius Pen Dragon!*" Theia was now grasping his hands tightly and, for a brief moment, the stars spun in her eyes.

"No!" Lucius wrenched his hands free. "Only death can bring freedom and life now."

"But whose death will it take?" Theia said, her voice high and shrill such that several people nearby looked in their direction.

Lucius pulled away from her and turned back toward the village without answering. He knew she stared after him, her eyes boring into his back as he went and left her question unanswered. He also knew the answer and that, he kept to himself. *There is only one death that will allow my family to live in peace.*

For the rest of the day, Lucius spent his time upon a rocky outcrop of the mountain which had, at times, served as his eyrie away from the world of men. He had often sought solitude, but since arriving in Delphi, it had become an urgent need at times. As he looked down upon the domus in which his surviving family dwelled, the sanctuary far to the left, and the valley beyond the steep-sided cliffs below, he considered a world without him in it. The thoughts he entertained, the course of action, would, he knew, be more dangerous than any other undertaking. He had to be realistic, no matter the help the Gods had given him in the past. Something told him that he would have to do this alone and without aid in the end.

And as the sun began to fall away that evening, Lucius' heart was filled with love for his wife and children, the great sadness that would tear at him for being apart, and the victory of keeping them safe should he succeed.

"Caracalla must die." He said it aloud, as if confiding it to the rocks and trees, and challenging his father to deny him his chosen course of action.

And you will lose everything to bring about that end?

The question was uttered on the fringes of his consciousness, from who, he did not know, but it could have been anyone, man or god. Lucius no longer cared. He was decided, and as he came to that realization, he held out his hand, drew his pugio, and spilled his blood upon the oath, watching the thin trickle of his life spill over the sand-coloured rocks below.

"I need to leave."

That night in the triclinium, the entire family sat around the tables. They talked, and even laughed, and as Lucius watched them, his resolve hardened.

He watched his children sitting with their aunt, and his wife with her own parents, the only family Adara had left. Ambrosia sat in silence beside Emrys who, it seemed, had become a sort of father to her in his time with Antonia, someone who watched out for her. Lucius then caught Caecilius' eye, but his brother looked down at the plate to fiddle with the remaining bits of rabbit meat from the animals he had caught that morning up in the hills.

It still felt strange without Antonia there, but there was also someone else missing. Lucius realized it was himself, that it felt as though he were looking upon the scene without him in it. He was apart from them. But for Caecilius, everyone there was calm, at peace, and he would ensure they could stay that way.

I need to make sure they are never harmed again...

Publius observed Lucius staring at the floor in their midst then. He had begun to regret his words and behaviour toward his son-in-law, for he had always loved and respected Lucius, no matter how difficult it was to let go of his eldest daughter. *But things have changed,* he thought, and without a care for the consequences, he decided to tell them the news he had heard that day. He cleared his throat.

"I heard from one of the members of the bouleuterion today that there has been a terrible massacre in Alexandria."

Everyone looked up at Publius then as a silence fell over the room, dousing the little bit of laughter that had been there.

"Why would you bring up such a thing as we eat, and in front of the children?" Delphina said to her husband beside her.

Lucius stared at his father-in-law. "Did you hear a reason for it? Who ordered it?"

Publius continued eating, and looking at his plate. "There was some civil unrest, as there always is in Alexandria... But the slaughter was ordered by the emperor."

Adara looked at Lucius quickly and the look she saw there frightened her. She could not guess his thoughts but, that afternoon, Calliope had told her she dreamed that Lucius was changed, that something was going to happen.

"Why is he in Alexandria?" Lucius pressed. "I thought he was in Germania."

"That campaign ended last year," Publius said. "It seems he was in Alexandria trying to make approaches to Artabanus V for the hand of his daughter."

"He would marry a Parthian after his father defeated them?" Emrys asked.

"The emperor sees himself as the new Alexander, and like him, he wanted to marry a Persian, well...almost a Persian at least." Publius looked around, unable to stop himself now.

"This isn't appropriate conversation for the cena, Husband," Delphina said.

"Oh, Delphina. It is current events. We get so little of it here." He looked at Lucius again. "Artabanus, however, has rejected the emperor's offer of marriage. It's a great insult to Rome."

"That is Rome's problem," Lucius said.

"True. But it is also the Parthians' problem, for I also heard that the emperor is embarking on another Parthian campaign as a result. The legions are assembling at Antioch."

Lucius felt a sudden ringing in his ears, and his heart began to beat wildly. He could see the family talking again, Delphina and Publius having words, Phoebus and Calliope trying to go back to conversing with Clarinda, and Emrys and Ambrosia rising to clear dirty platters and plates.

Adara and Caecilius both looked at Lucius and might have said something to him, but all he could hear was the ringing in his head and the repeated word... *Antioch.*

Is it a sign from my father? Lucius wondered. The Gods had been painfully silent for a long time and now, suddenly, some bit of news from the agora and that one word had seemingly set the mountain on fire for Lucius.

Lucius had started his first campaign in Antioch, and now he would begin his last there. Without another word, he rose from his seat and went out into the night to get some cool air. The ringing subsided and his feet took him through the courtyard to the passage in the wall and out into the compound. Alone now, he stopped to lean against the outer stone wall, listening to the flickering of the almond leaves nearby as they danced in the cold air. He walked along the wall, feeling the harsh surface of the stone beneath his hand as he dragged it along, the bandage around where he had cut himself catching on it as he went. He was not heading into battle, or to war, but the feeling he had was similar, if not more uncertain.

He pictured Mars standing in the burned out Etrurian field he had left behind, and Love weeping as she looked upon him. And then Apollo as he stood close to Lucius, mouthing the name of Antioch, his expression removed and cold, like the firmament above.

At the altar in the small grove of oak and cypress, Lucius stopped and fell to his knees. There was a part of him that did not want to leave, but he knew that if he did not act, the pain would continue for his family.

"I can't allow them to be hurt anymore," he whispered to the cold, empty altar. It was then that a great feeling of complete loneliness filled him, and knew that he must become accustomed to that loneliness if he was to succeed. Tears streamed down his cheeks as he realized that the time had finally come.

The Dragon had to leave...

Later that night, Lucius knocked on Phoebus and Calliope's cubiculum door.

"We're awake," Phoebus said from inside.

Lucius pushed open the door slowly to see Phoebus reading to Calliope from one of the scrolls they had brought.

"I'm just reading Arrian to Calliope," Phoebus said.

"And how do you find it?" Lucius asked his daughter.

She looked up without smiling. "It's sad. To push oneself and those around you so much, to conquer the world and have such vision, only to be killed by friends or disease…" she shook her head. "I feel sorry for Alexander, and for his mother, wives and son."

Calliope looked different to Lucius in that moment, not only wiser and more mature than her less than fifteen years, but also slightly prophetic. She had possessed the Sight in Ynis Wytrin, and so he wondered what she was seeing now. What was her look telling him? There were no tears in her eyes, only knowing.

Lucius felt his heart tighten as he looked upon his children. *How I've failed them!* he cried out inside, knowing he had left them no home, no safety, and no hope for the future. After all they had been through as a family, after the heights they had reached, they now led a life of refugees from Rome, from Britannia, from the world, it seemed.

Unless I can succeed.

Lucius sat down on the edge of the bed, pushing the clay lamp on the side table a little farther from the edge.

"Baba?" Calliope asked. "Why did you leave the triclinium so suddenly?"

"I didn't want to hear any more of your grandfather's news."

"Grandmother chided him for it after you left."

"And your mother?" Lucius asked.

"She was quiet, and then left to go to sleep," Phoebus added, his voice weighed with a hint of worry that Lucius had come to recognize all too well.

"You're not going to leave us, are you?" Calliope asked.

"Why do you say that?"

Calliope took his hand and squeezed, ran her fingers over his rough knuckles and the torn dressing around his hand as her brother rolled up the scroll. "You know, Baba…we don't care about the legacy you leave us."

"We care about you," Phoebus finished. "You don't have to be an Alexander, Achilles or Hercules. They all had sad ends."

Lucius could see the tears forming in his son's eyes, and he knew then that Calliope had seen something of the future, as she had before, and she had shared it with her twin brother.

"What will happen, Baba?" Calliope asked, almost daring her father to look into the future himself, to tear out their hearts with his own hands.

They were tired, Lucius could see, tired of fighting, of running, of hiding. They stood on the brink of the rest of their lives and they wanted to know, needed to know, that there was something good in the valley before them besides death. Experience had already hardened them, but it was evident by all who met them how very special they were.

They deserve so much more than this, Lucius thought as he looked around the plain, dark room and leaned in to hug them both tightly. As he did so, he knew that he would slit his own throat to keep them safe.

"I'm so very proud of you both, how strong and wise and full of caring you are." He looked down and sighed before looking up again. "I don't know what will happen, but whatever it is...no matter what happens...I want you both to know that I love you and your mother more than life itself. You are everything to me, and if ever something happens to me, I want you to take care of each other and your mother. Do you understand me?"

"Why are you saying this?" Phoebus asked.

"Because, my son... Because I don't know what will happen. No one truly does. And because these things should not be left unsaid. Every night when you go to sleep, I want you to hear me telling you I love you, and to know that I am always with you."

"Because you are Apollo's son, and he sees everything?" Phoebus asked.

"No. Because I'm your father, and that love is stronger than steel."

They smiled as they looked up at him, as if the sun shone upon their faces. And that look tore at Lucius' heart and conscience. "Good night, my wonderful children," he said. "I love you."

"We love you too, Baba," they answered as he kissed their heads and began to leave the room.

"Will you come to grandmother's grave the day after next, Baba?" Phoebus asked. "We haven't been since..."

"Yes. I'll come," Lucius said, and he could see they relaxed at that. He was about to close the door when he had an urge to say one more thing. "Be ready for anything, both of you. And remember the Gods love you...that you are never alone."

They looked at him a little confused, and watched as he closed the door gently, his eyes holding on to the sight of them as long as he could.

When the door was closed, Lucius stood alone in the courtyard. It was later than he had thought, and the moon was but a thin sliver in the blackened sky where the stars were veiled by strips of cloud.

His mind had been racing since the cena, since Publius had spoken of the news from Alexandria and of Caracalla.

"What am I supposed to do?" Lucius whispered to the sky and moon, but all he was met with was silence. "I know what I need to do. It's time." He was determined, but then he looked at the door of the cubiculum where Adara slept, the thin strip of light from beneath that showed she was still awake.

When he opened the door, he could see that she was lying on her side in their bed, the furs pulled up to her shoulder as she stared at the burning lamp upon the small wooden table beside.

"My love..." he said as he walked toward the bed, unbuckling his cingulum with his gladius and pugio and hanging it from a peg in the wall.

Sitting in the corner of the room, he could see his satchel packed with his thick black cloak folded and lain on top.

"What's this?" he asked as he sat on the edge of the bed, his hand upon her covered legs.

Adara did not look at him, her eyes still filled with the withering flame that sprouted from the simple lamp.

"I thought I would pack your things for you...to make it easier," she said, her voice monotone, numb.

"Adara...I..."

"No. Don't. I saw how you reacted when my father spoke of Caracalla. I know what you're thinking, Lucius." It was then she turned and sat up in the bed to look at her husband. "After so many years, and so many goodbyes..."

"I need to make this right."

"And what is 'right' in this instance? Abandonment? Suicide? Because if you're thinking of doing what I think you are..."

"How many times have I ridden off to war and battle? I've always come back."

"This is different," she said, her arms crossed now.

"Is it though? There is an enemy who is a constant threat, that needs to be dealt with."

"Except this time, you have no bodyguard, no cavalry, and no legions to support you. Your men are not here. They are in Dumnonia, getting on with their lives."

"That is what I want too, Adara, for all of us." Lucius turned to face her, and now he could see that her eyes were red, that she had been crying into that singular flame upon the table that represented so much pain and suffering, but also love and hope.

"I don't know what else to say to you. I know that you're set upon blood and vengeance, but as the person who loves you more than any mortal or god, I hope that you will listen to me when I ask you to stay." She sat up and grabbed hold of him, pressed her head against his. "Stay with us, my truest love. Live with us and let the world around us burn away for all I care. You've walked roads alone before, and you almost came to ruin. I don't care where we live, so long as we're together as a family. We're stronger together. Love is our strength, and none but us can break it."

Lucius felt every word she uttered, and he knew she was right. How then was he able to decide upon the course he had set in his mind, to set blood above love? *Or am I to spill blood to save love?* he thought, determined that his children should no longer have to experience such things. He would be their blade and defender, their avenger, even at the cost of his self. He held Adara's face in his hands.

Her glossy green eyes looked back at him, and there he saw the beauty of the life they had created, but also the pain and anguish they had suffered for so long. *She could have had a life of peace and calm, and yet she followed me…she loved me.* "Adara I love you with all of my heart and soul. I cannot say it more plainly. And I'm sorry for the life of hardship I have dragged you into. You didn't deserve all of this."

"Stop this!"

"No, listen to me. I fell in love with you from the moment I saw you, with the Gods whispering into my ear. I wanted to give you such a life! But all I've given you is regret and sadness and anger. I've failed you, my love. Because of me, you've lost every home you ever had…we lost…our child…" He stopped, feeling his chest and lungs shudder with emotion. "And you and our children have nearly lost your lives. I'm not the man I wanted to be for you, and I'm sure that I'm not the man you had hoped for."

"You are more than I could ever have hoped for, Lucius. But no man...or god...is ever a perfect reflection of our hopes and dreams. Those are but beacons to direct us in the darkness. So what if our life hasn't turned out the way we envisioned? Is that not life? But we can't forget each other...our children, who are the greatest gift the Gods have ever given us. They are still here. *We* are still here! I would rather go with you and travel the bloody road you envision at your side, with our children, than be apart from you. Don't you think for a second I haven't felt hate toward those who have harmed us, toward Caracalla. When my father said his name, I wanted to scream! I too wish for vengeance, but my wish to protect the family I have left is greater."

Lucius leaned forward, his face in his hands. The only thing worse than leaving his family behind was, he felt certain, to bring them into a world of greater torment and pain. That was the world he envisioned until his anger was sated. *I can't do that to them. Ever!*

"So, my love," Adara said, her voice soft but firm. "You must decide for us which road we shall take together, for I will never leave your side. You put a sword in my hand, and in the hands of our children and, by the Gods, we will use them if we have to!"

Lucius looked upon her and felt such pride, such deep and unending love...and such shame, for he realized what he must do.

"Then back to Britannia it is."

Adara kissed him, hard and long, her tears rolling down her cheeks to mingle on their lips. "Thank you, my love. The Gods still smile on us. They do!"

"Then let us sleep under their protection for a while longer yet," he said as they both lay down, their arms wrapped about each other as the flame beside them flickered its last before darkness enveloped them. "I love you, Adara," Lucius whispered as she fell asleep. "I will always love you."

He then stared into the darkness, inhaling the scent of her hair and skin, feeling the rise and fall of her body which may have held their unborn child. He imprinted all of it on his memory, in his heart, for he knew that on the road ahead, those images, and the faces of his children, would be the only things to give him purchase in the dark place he sought to go.

·   ·   ·

All but the Gods and stars were asleep when Lucius slipped out of the cubiculum as quietly as he could. His heart pounded and he felt sick in his gut, but the images of fire and blood, the feelings of nursed pain and anger that had been fanned for so long were now burning so brightly that he could feel the heat upon his face.

He looked back at the doors of his wife's and children's rooms, pictured them sleeping silently, ignorant of what he was doing, the same as everyone else he cared about in that mountain domus. He pulled the hood of his thick black cloak over his head, adjusted his gladius and pugio beneath, and slung the satchel over his shoulder, careful not to rattle the pouch of coin Adara had placed in there.

The olive tree before him shuddered in the cold breeze as he passed it on his way to the outer compound. There, he stopped to look up at the stars. They appeared to accuse him, to scream to his family what he was doing, the betrayal he was carrying out.

But Lucius did not care now, for if he did not do this, he knew none of them would ever be safe.

He turned back to the domus from the cover of the trees outside the compound. "I love you," he whispered, as if his wife and children could hear him. "Gods…watch over them, I beg you…" and with that, he turned to follow the path through the grove and down to the main road.

"Where do you think you're going?"

Lucius spun, his gladius unsheathed, and there, beyond the tip of his blade, was Caecilius. He looked him over quickly, and his brother too was dressed for a journey, armed beneath his thick brown cloak and furs, a full satchel over his shoulder.

"I'm going to finish this," Lucius said.

"Going hunting?" Caecilius asked.

"Of a sort. And I'm going alone."

"Hmm." Caecilius stepped forward. "I've watched you march off to war before, Brother. I've waited at home, fought separate battles to yours."

"We all have our own battles."

"True. But this one is mine as well. I too have lost everything." He leaned against the great bow that Lucius had given him years before, and looked up at the sky. "I saw your face when Publius mentioned Caracalla. The look you had was the same one on mine. I want to go with you. I need to go with you."

"It's too dangerous."

"Yes. It is. And that's why I won't take 'no' for an answer. This one time, I want to fight by your side...for our family. Together, we can do this."

Lucius was silent, looking upon his younger brother, broad and strong and willful as ever. Together they had stopped the assassins at his mother's funeral. *Perhaps it is the Gods' will.* He could see the determination in his brother's face, that there was no denying him.

"You won't stop me, Lucius. Not this time."

Lucius stepped forward to face his brother and wrapped his arms about him. "Thank you. Let's go hunting then...for our family."

"For our family," Caecilius repeated, his bearded face smiling in the dark.

As they turned to walk down the path together, a cock crowed upon the mountainside, and the sun's chariot crested the mountains to the East.

The cock crowed again, and Adara woke with a start to see that the sunlight was angling in through the small window above the bed. She smiled, still feeling the lingering warmth and embrace of Lucius' arms the previous night, but then fear entered like a wolf tearing through a nursery.

She turned quickly and felt the space beside her empty. *NO!* her heart screamed. She jumped out of the bed, barefoot, wearing only her tunica, and saw that the satchel, cloak and weapons were gone.

The door slammed against the wall, cracking it, as she raced outside, across the courtyard, and through the compound to the outer door. The ground beneath her feet as she sped through the olive groves was cold, hard and cutting, but she ran on as quickly as she could until she came to the road. She turned left and right, her wild eyes scanning, searching for any sign of Lucius, but he was nowhere to be seen.

She turned and ran westward down the road that led to the cliffs and the paths across the valley toward the distant port only to find the roads empty, devoid of life.

"LUCIUS!" she screamed to the sky and distant sea as she fell upon her knees at the cliff's edge, her tears falling into the icy wind. "Why, my love…why…why…" *How could he choose this over us?* "Why, Lucius?"

For some time Adara sat there, shaking, weeping, for the life they had lost, for the love she had lost. She wept for her children and the last vestiges of her will to live, and suddenly, the cliffs and valley below looked inviting beyond measure.

The pain is too much, she thought as she wiped her eyes and peered into the abyss before her. *I can lose everything, but not Lucius, not my family…* She would have thrown herself over the edge then for her failure to convince him to stay, for the pain she knew she would glimpse yet again in her children's eyes, but then she heard a voice behind her.

"Stay, dear. Your children need you more than ever."

Adara turned on her bloody knees to see Theia standing there, reaching out to her with kind hands.

"You are their light, Adara, their love… Come…"

Adara looked up at the priestess through her watery eyes, but then she felt something else at her side, someone else.

Rise, and be strong, Venus said as she lifted her up and stroked her cold, sweaty brow.

The light of Love filled Adara's burning eyes as she clung to the goddess who supported her.

You are not alone, Adara, Love said. *Not now. Not ever.*

"Why did he leave?" Adara asked as she walked between the priestess and the goddess.

For love, Venus said.

"And for war…" Theia added, her eyes catching a glimpse of Apollo standing upon his Parnassian eyrie, his own starry eyes watching his son's back as he started once more upon the road.

Part III

DESTINY

A.D. 216

XVI

EVOCATUS

'The Veteran'

The sun had not yet risen over the edge of the eastern desert and mountains beyond the banks of the Tigris river when Julius Martialis finished eating his bowl of beans at the small wooden table of his home. Most people were still abed, including his wife and children, but Julius had always risen early, in his youth, and throughout his career as a legionary. He was proud of the fact that he could do this, and he knew that he enjoyed getting up before the Gods themselves so that he could begin his work, but also so that he would not miss those moments of pure quiet.

However, that day would be different. Normally, when he rose and ate, he would head straight out to the fields of his plot of land along the swift-flowing Tigris to check on his crops and herd.

Not today, he thought as he rubbed his short grey hair and adjusted the red woollen tunica he wore more out of habit than anything. He placed his clay bowl upon a counter, and went to the cubiculum where his three children slept in a row upon their beds, his two sons along one wall, and his daughter along another. The room looked like a small barracks, and that made him smile as he bent down to kiss each of them upon the forehead. He had bid them farewell the night before, but he wanted to feel their presence one more time. He still could not believe his fortune that the Gods had granted him such healthy and good children. He took a last look at their sleeping forms, left the room, and went to the bracket in the kitchen wall where his old gladius and pugio hung. He took them down, and strapped them on.

Opening the door of the domus set in the middle of the small, mud brick compound where his family lived, he went out to his favourite spot - a rocky outcrop that jut out into the Tigris river - to watch the sun crest in the East. It was his favourite time of day. To watch the sun's unveiling made him feel like he was party to something secret.

He watched as the first hint of red began, like a fire slowly coming to life. The colour became more and more intense until the sun's orb appeared and the shadows retreated across the distant mountains and desert. The light stretched toward his small farm on the western banks of the river until he felt the heat upon his face. It was warm after the early morning chill, as the light swept past him, over his lands, and beyond.

Somewhere in the pens, a cock crowed.

Julius Martialis looked over his lands, the group of buildings he had constructed that made up his family's home, the millet and corn crops that grew beside the river in rows and splashes of green and white. He felt great pride, and he hoped that he would see it all again.

He thought back to the previous day when a message had arrived from the current legate of IV Scythica, stationed at Nisibis, that some of the legions were mustering there and that the Evocati were being called in.

The message had brought back a lot of feelings and memories of his time in the legions, some of which were good, others not so much. He had served for twenty-five years in the legions, Severus' victorious Parthian campaign being Julius Martialis' last. It had been his service in that campaign that had got him the land he now stood on, the living he now enjoyed and provided for his Median wife, Safira, and their children.

Now, it seemed, Rome was once more going to war against Parthia, this time under Severus' son whom the men called Caracalla.

Julius did not know anything of the former emperor's son, but what he heard from gossip. He took little stock in that. Everyone knew the imperial court was a viper's nest, that it was safer to walk the shoreline of the Tigris and risk the crocodiles and desert cobras than to get involved in imperial politics.

Even the emperor's brother didn't survive! Julius remembered hearing.

The more he had considered the request to come back to service as an evocatus, however, the more he thought it a good idea. The previous year's drought had a bad impact on the crops, and despite the new irrigation systems, he did not have much hope for the size of the yield for the coming year. Also, Parthian raiding parties had been spotted, and had even hit some of the farms of his fellow veterans farther to the south. The extra coin he could earn as an evocatus could help make up for the shortfall in his millet and corn crops, and if he could be enlisted as a centurion this time - after all, he had more decorations and honours that any other legionary in his old century - the pay would be that much better, and his family well-provided for.

Of course, no sane man wanted to go to war, but Julius Martialis prided himself on his past service. *Besides,* he thought, *when Mars calls, a Roman answers!* And no matter what life he now led, he was still a Roman.

The sun was fully visible now, and Julius Martialis turned to see his wife walking along the path toward him, hugging his brown cloak to her chest as she came. She looked sad, and he knew she was worried about him leaving for war, about him stepping into a past that was unfamiliar to her. But he had explained the benefits of serving and how much it could help them and their children.

"Do you have to go?" Safira asked, her big, dark brown eyes glistening in the morning sunlight.

Julius smiled at the sight of her. He kissed her when she arrived and nestled herself in the crook of his arm to watch the river flow by. "Yes. I do. I explained to you how this works."

"Let others fight the Parthians."

He smiled, trying not to let his own worries show. He knew it was a risk to go away, to leave his family alone. He also knew they could use the extra coin and that, if he did serve, it was more likely that the garrison at Nisibis would come to his family's aid if he ever needed it. One needed allies in that remote outpost of the empire.

"It will be a short campaign this time, Safira. Don't worry so much. Our crops are not doing well at the moment and we need the money."

"What if they no give you what you seek? That you fight for nothing?" she asked in her broken Latin.

"They will," Julius Martialis said confidently. "I'm one of their best. The previous emperor always rewarded courage and good service, so why shouldn't his son?"

Safira looked doubtful, but she accepted her husband's decision. After all, he knew Roman ways better than her, and they lived in a Roman world now, and that world was safer than the one she had left, or the one the Parthians would offer.

"I need to go now," Julius said to her after a few minutes.

"I know."

"I love you very much," he said, still feeling a little awkward when he expressed such sentiments.

She smiled and squeezed him. "I know." She then draped his brown cloak over his shoulders and pinned the oddly-shaped, bronze brooch. "I had the slaves prepare your horse for you. There is food in the satchel on the mule."

"Thank you," he said as they walked along the path that led away from the river, among the crops where some of the workers were beginning their day's work. "I will miss you and the children very much," he said as they reached the small dirt court before their domus. There, the horse was tied to a hitching post beside the mule that carried his helmet and lorica, and the provisions his wife had prepared.

Julius Martialis turned to his wife and brushed aside the long strand of black hair that fell beside her face, resting his hand upon her cheek before kissing her gently upon the lips. "I'll be fine, Safira. Do not worry. And I should reach Nisibis by nightfall tomorrow."

"We will pray to the Gods daily for you, that you are safe."

"Pray for a promotion too." He winked before kissing her one more time and pulling himself up into the saddle of the only horse they owned.

She handed him the mule's reins, kissed his fingers and held his hand one more time.

Julius Martialis took a last look at the world he had built and smiled at all the improvements he would make when he returned. Then, clicking his tongue, he kneed his horse's flanks and it trotted forward with the mule in tow.

Safira stood in the middle of the dirt track as the dust rose up around her, waving to him even as his eldest son ran out to stand beside her.

Julius watched them for a few moments before turning to the road ahead with the sun warming his back.

It felt strange to be leaving his wife and children. He had never had to do that before. When Severus had made it possible for legionaries to marry and have children years before, Julius had not wanted that. Focus was key to survival, and he could not focus on surviving every battle should he be worried about a family. But times had changed and now, he was desperate. In planning ahead, he knew that he would not be able to provide for Safira and the children should his crops fail, which they would. Much as he tried, Julius Martialis was no farmer. He was a soldier, and he always would be.

The road west from the Tigris to Nisibis and beyond was busy, for it was the main trade route across the Mesopotamian desert. Long, laden camel trains churned up the dust as they went, but being on a horse with a single mule, Julius was able to pass them by quickly enough and make good time that first day. From what many of the traders were saying, they were trying to make it to the safety of Roman territory before the outbreak of war so that they could sell their wares in either Edessa or Antioch by the sea.

That night, camping in the open beside a fire, beneath the stars above, Julius Martialis had time to reflect on the past, on the ghosts of Nisibis that still haunted him. As he gazed into the flames, chewing on the flat bread and dried meat his wife had packed for him, he sharpened his gladius and pugio which he never allowed to go dull or rust.

He remembered Nisibis all too well, the mountain ridge towering over it to the North, the vast plain to the south, and the river Mygdonius which cut through it. They had almost met their end there, under Parthian siege. He knew that the years since then had been a gift from the Gods, and spilled some of his water into the sand in thanks as he thought of it.

Whenever he thought about Nisibis and the Parthian campaign, he thought of General Laetus, the 'Saviour of Nisibis' as men had called him.

Julius remembered being trapped within the city surrounded by the Parthians. If it had not been for Laetus, they would not have held out until Severus arrived with the legions. He could still see the general atop the walls, his great horsehair crest above the enemy heads as he rallied his men and fought on for days.

It saddened him to think of Laetus' end, sentenced to death for speaking out, and for the actions of lesser men. No one would ever know the truth, but what did it matter then? One of Rome's great heroes had ended up crucified outside the Praetorian camp. That was the only time he had ever thought ill of Emperor Severus. He - and his son by all accounts - had always treated the troops well, but in the case of Laetus, it had been poor compensation for such loyalty and courage.

The man should have been granted a triumph instead.

Julius shook his head as he laid back to look up at the night sky, protected on three sides by his horse, mule, and the brightly burning fire. Italy was a distant memory, another lifetime. He had grown to love the desert, how the Tigris cut through it, and how the water reflected the blazing sun and brilliant stars.

He smiled, his eyes growing heavy now. "Oh, Mars and Fortuna, smile on me in the time to come."

Julius Martialis arrived a little sooner than he expected in Nisibis. The sun still hung above the distant horizon, a brilliant red and orange that lit the walls and streets with evening light. As he rode up to the walls along the main road, he could see various contubernia posted around the perimeter, and men busy upon the walls which still bore the scars of the siege nearly twenty years before.

Apart from the presence of a few traders, guilds, and the tax collector's office, Nisibis was still a military stronghold, and as Julius came close to the walls, his ears were filled with the familiar sounds of army life - the tramp of hobnails, the barks of centurions, and the hammering of smiths upon anvils in the forges as weapons were created for the coming conflict.

It gave him a thrill to be back.

Julius had made sure to wear some of his many decorations - four armillae and a torc - so that there was no mistaking his service. He needed to stand out, he knew, if he wanted to be promoted. His skills, and his knowledge of local customs and language would be, he was sure, an asset.

As he approached the main gate facing the road, he was waved down by the centurion on duty.

"State your business!" the younger man said. He sweat beneath the visor of his helmet after a day in the sun, and his armour and pteruges were dusty. He immediately took in the gladius and pugio at Julius' side.

Julius saluted. "Julius Martialis. Evocatus reporting for duty, sir." It felt strange to salute a man so much younger than him, but then again, he had had to serve beneath young men before. He handed the centurion the paper calling him in for duty. "I'm to report to the legatus of IV Scythica."

The centurion looked the paper over and then handed it back to him. "IV Scythica is still in Zeugma. They should be here in a few days.

Proceed to the principia to see Legatus Aelius Decius Triccianus. He's in command of II Parthica."

Julius saluted and proceeded through the gate toward the principia.

Nisibis was the meeting point, it seemed, for several legions who had detachments throughout the region, in addition to being the winter quarters in the area.

As he led his horse and mule up the via principalis, Julius noticed men from different legions, but none he recognized as yet. There were even a few Praetorians, which meant that the emperor was not far behind if he was not there already.

Soon enough, he reached the principia courtyard and, after checking in with the guards on duty, he tied his horse and mule to a post along the peristylium.

Men came and went from the offices of the tribunes, centurions with new orders, and messengers with dispatches to be taken swiftly in all directions across the desert to rally Rome's men and allies for the fight to come.

Julius looked around and remembered the siege again, the sound of crashing stone, and the screams of men as Parthian arrows rained down on them. It seemed an age since he had stood in that courtyard to hear General Laetus speak.

"You there!" an optio said.

Julius looked at the man. "Yes?"

"What are you doing here?"

"Evocatus reporting for duty. I'm to report to Legatus Aelius Decius Triccianus."

The man looked around in the direction of the main office at the back of the principia. "He's in there." He then looked over Julius. "He's quite strict about appearances. You may want to clean yourself up first."

Julius looked down at his dusty tunica and cloak. He knew the man was right, but he preferred to be prompt. He had just travelled across the desert. A little dust was to be expected. It was everywhere in Nisibis. "My thanks, Optio," he said before brushing himself off and straightening his cloak and cingulum.

He marched across the courtyard and the guards there opened the door to let him through, waved on by the optio.

The room was large, and lit by four braziers that burned in each corner. Several tables were set up where scribes took notes and kept the records for men, supplies, and all the other necessities of the campaign. Everyone was too busy to look up at the newcomer, including the legatus who sat at the largest table at the back with a great pigeon holed shelf the length of the wall behind him. Stacks of papyrus surrounded the legate who was looking more and more annoyed with every word he read or wrote.

Julius was used to men in command, and so he had no trouble approaching.

He snapped a sharp salute. "Evocatus, Julius Martialis, reporting for duty, sir!"

Aelius Decius Triccianus finished writing a few words and then looked up at the older man before him. "You're early. The Evocati are not expected until next week."

"Sir. I thought the sooner I could be here, the sooner I could be put to work."

The legate looked Julius over, his disdain clear upon his features. "You look like you came out of the pig pens."

Julius took a breath before speaking. "Apologies, sir. I came directly here. Just arrived."

Decius Triccianus leaned back in his chair and folded his hands in his lap. "What have you been doing since you retired?"

"I have a farm along the Tigris, sir. Corn and millet."

"Successful crops?"

"Some years, sir. Not this one."

"And so you need some extra coin." He held up his hand. "Would you have headed Rome's call if this year was a successful one?"

"Yes, sir!" Julius said clearly.

"Are you sure?"

"Of course, sir. I fought the Parthians before. I know what they're capable of. I know how to fight them."

"So you want to lead the legions then, is that it?"

"No, sir! I want to serve…as an Evocati centurion if possible. My record speaks for itself."

"Does it?" He looked over Julius again. "Are you in good shape, or have you got fat over the years?"

"I'm fit, sir."

"Hmm. We'll see." The legate picked up his stylus and began writing again. "Well, Martialis. I'm afraid I can't help you. New orders came in just this morning. All Evocati are to report to the Praetorian Prefect's staff who will distribute them as they see fit."

"I see," Julius said, clearly disappointed. "And where may I find them, sir?"

"Other side of the principia. They took over the office of my tribunus laticlavus. He wasn't too happy with that."

"I'll report there then, sir." Julius saluted. "What are their names, if you don't mind my asking, sir?"

"You're to report to the Praetorian tribunes Aurelius Nemesianus and Aurelius Apollinaris. They're brothers."

"Very well, sir. Thank you, sir." Julius saluted again and turned to leave.

"Evocatus," the legate called.

"Yes, sir?" Julius replied, turning quickly to meet his eye.

"Be careful of those two."

Julius felt a chill at the look in the legate's eyes, but nodded his thanks and turned to go and find the two Praetorians. In the courtyard, he paused to take a few breaths. He had thought he could handle the usual interrogations of a grumpy commander, but it irked him to be so treated. *Disciplina, Julius. Disciplina!* he chided himself. *Everyone reports to someone!*

A moment later, he was let through the door into the sparsely decorated room occupied by the Praetorian tribunes. As soon as Julius entered, the two brothers looked up and stood. It was a much warmer reception than he had received from the legatus.

"Evocatus, Julius Martialis, reporting for duty, Tribunes!" He saluted.

"Perfect timing, Martialis," said one of the tribunes.

They were obviously twins, both young and steely-eyed, eager to climb the cursus honorum in whatever way they could. Their black and brown armour was perfectly-kept and polished, but at the same time they were not reviled by the dusty old warrior before them. Both stood and offered him a cup of water before showing him to a seat before their desks.

"I'm Nemesianus, and this is Apollinaris," said the one. "We've been asked by the emperor and the Praetorian prefect to meet with every evocatus who reports so that we can assign them where we see fit."

Martialis nodded.

"So? Are you ready for this fight, soldier?" Nemesianus asked, his warm smile fading.

Julius Martialis emerged from the tribunes' office feeling a little uneasy, but he was familiar with the atmosphere of a base before a major campaign. Still, he had been given a place and assigned a room in one of the barracks blocks where, apparently, he would not have to share with a full contubernium.

The Aurelii tribunes did not promise him a posting to centurion, but they did ask him why he not just ask Caesar. At first, the thought was absurd, but then Julius remembered who he was, felt the weight of his awards upon his wrists, and how Caracalla was said to be as good to the troops as his father had been.

It was then, as if the Gods themselves had heard his thinking, that a chorus of cornui rang out over Nisibis and the desert floor shook with the thunder of horses' hooves.

Men emerged from every office around the principia to stand at attention and there were shouts of 'The emperor is here!' from various quarters.

Thank you, Gods, for answering me. I won't disappoint you! Julius thought as he stood by his horse and mule, watching the gate of the principia.

After a short time, the tramp of hooves and hobnails grew even louder and the cornui rang out again to announce the emperor's arrival. The aquilae of the legions he had brought preceded him, followed by the imagines, vexillia and other standards of the legions, as well as a new-looking banner with a great lion upon it. This last was carried by a burly Scythian with two swords strapped to his back and a great beard hanging from his face.

"Those are the 'Lions'," one of the optios standing near Julius said to another, "the emperor's new bodyguard."

Julius turned to the man. "Surely the emperor prefers the use of Prae-torians for his personal guard?"

The man shrugged. "Not anymore. He uses Scythians and Germans now-" He stiffened suddenly as the emperor stepped upon a dais in the middle of the courtyard.

Julius Martialis strained to see over the heads of the men around him,

past the barbarian bodyguards who surrounded the emperor, to see Caracalla himself.

The emperor was dressed in elaborate black and silver armour with a
long, flowing purple cloak that reached down to the ground at his feet
and bristled in the dusty Nisibian breeze. He removed his tall, crested
helmet, handed it to one of his 'Lions', and turned to look over the
crowd of officers, a wry smile upon his creased face, his short, curly hair
sweaty in the sunlight.

"Men! It's good to be back among you!" Caracalla said. "But it is not
good to be back in Parthia, for we are here to address an insult and to
tame an enemy who should know his place by now!"

Julius looked around at the reactions of the men about him as a few
of them called out and raised their fists in salute.

"Years ago, my father came with thirty-two legions to destroy the
Parthians…and he succeeded at the time. But they're back! They're
raiding Roman lands, stealing Roman supplies. They even offer me
insult by not allowing Artabanus' whore daughter to marry me!" There
was silence, and then he laughed. "I thought I was doing him a favour,
for rumours of her ugliness are far and wide, though she be draped in
gold!"

There was widespread laughter at this, though it was laced with
unease and tension.

"To be sure, she is no Stateira or Roxanna, but after this campaign,
the women of Parthia will be ours to do with as we choose!"

Julius looked around at that and it was then that he knew Severus'
son was indeed not his father.

"I tell you now!" Caracalla shouted. "By Sol Invictus…and by Mars!
We will be victorious in this campaign and never again have to bring our
legions into Parthia. Are you with me?"

"Hail Caesar!" the men chanted. "Hail Caesar! Hail Caesar!"

Caracalla smiled and got down from the dais to walk to the main
offices of Aelius Decius Triccianus near to where Julius was standing.

No time like the present! Julius thought as he cut through the crowd.
"Caesar! My Emperor!" Julius called aloud, even as two of Caracalla's
German companions closed on him with their daggers drawn. "I served
in the last campaign with your father and the general Laetus! Your
Evocati are loyal to you!"

Caracalla stopped suddenly and turned his head to see Julius standing in front of the horse and mule, having been pushed back by his guards. "You see?" Caracalla smiled and laughed. "Even our muleteers wish to fight for us! With old men to carry the bags and booty of our troops, our hands will be free to wield pila and gladii!"

There was laughter all around the courtyard at this, but as Julius shrugged off the Germans' hands and they followed Caesar into the offices, he was not smiling. Far from it. The Evocati had always been highly prized and respected.

It was a poor beginning to the campaign, and Julius began to wonder if he had made a mistake.

"Do not mind, Caesar," said a deep voice beside him. "He is under a lot of pressure with the coming war. He loves to banter with his troops."

Julius turned to see a Praetorian officer in armour nearly as elaborate as Caracalla's. He immediately saluted. "Evocatus Julius Martialis, sir." He looked behind the man before him to see the two tribunes with whom he had spoken only a short time before.

"This is Marcus Opellius Macrinus," Tribune Nemesianus said. "Praefectus of the Praetorian Guard."

Macrinus raised his hand for him to stop, but his smile was genuine, seemingly embarrassed. "Please, Nemesianus. When Evocatus Martialis here was fighting upon these very walls beside General Laetus, I was a mere postal courier."

Julius' eyes widened, and the Praetorian prefect set his thick hand upon his shoulder as if they had been long-time friends.

"We are fortunate to have you in our ranks, Martialis." He looked at his armillae and torc. "I can see you've been decorated several times."

"I'm here to fight, Praefectus. I know the Parthians, their customs and methods, and I can speak with their people. I know the desert too. It will be no easy victory."

"True. It never has been easy for Rome in these parts," Macrinus said. "Your skills will be useful in this campaign, Martialis. I will speak with the emperor about you, and we'll see what we can do about a promotion."

Julius smiled at that, his chest out, his shoulder proudly back. "I'm honoured, Praefectus."

Macrinus pat him on the shoulders and nodded. "In the meantime, I'm happy to have you as an evocatus attached to the Praetorian ranks. The pay is better, and you'll be among Romans instead of 'Lions'."

"Thank you, Praefectus. You won't regret it!"

"I know." The praefectus smiled again, his eyes darting to the office where Caracalla had gone. "Now, I must to the emperor." He turned to the tribune brothers. "The baggage train will be unloaded soon. Tell Martialis where he can get his new armour."

"Yes, Praefectus!" they said in unison.

Julius Martialis stood there, watching the Praetorian prefect walk away, and he felt a great sense of pride. "There is a man who appreciates experience," he said under his breath.

Nemesianus and Apollinaris smiled to each other and turned to disappear into the crowd of officers and baggage crowding the courtyard, leaving Julius alone with his horse and mule.

XVII

AD ORIENTEM

'To the East'

B etrayal and guilt. They are powerful sentiments that can strangle a man, hold him back, or push him to the very brink of insanity.

Vengeance, and the desperate need for it, is even more powerful.

Do the Gods care if a man has betrayed love, or if he feels stabbing guilt? Do they care if his only thought is of vengeance?

They do.

But the Gods have their laws, as do men, even those who are pulled between worlds. And so, each man must travel the road he chooses until the bitter end. At one point on the journey, he will turn and look back. He will see where he has gone and what he has done, and then will he choose to carry on and finish what he has started, or step onto another, unknown path that departs from his perceived course and into the unknown.

Choice can be paralyzing to the weak, but the poison of anger and hatred are a slower, more painful death than can be imagined.

It had been one disappointment or delay after another for Lucius and Caecilius for, having left their family behind to seek vengeance, the brothers were delayed by the Gods at every turn.

From the port of Kirrha, near Delphi, they had travelled across the gulf to Corinth and then to Isthmia to find passage to Piraeus, to seek the Captain Creticus. But when they had arrived in the ancient port of Athenae, it was to find that the Europa and her captain had already set sail for Leptis Magna.

Not wishing to wait, Lucius decided that they should continue their journey regardless, for the talk in the bustling port was that the legions were heading for Mesopotamia for the war with Parthia, and that the emperor himself would soon be in Antioch. Like hounds that have just smelled blood, Lucius and Caecilius became more determined to leave Graecia behind.

The spring seas, however, were unpredictable, and few were willing to risk the Aegean swells.

They did find one private ship owner who was willing to ply the seas for the right amount of coin. He was a reckless Phoenician trader, eager to take advantage of trade with the mustering legions in Antioch and beyond before the drums of war crumbled the roads and passes, and trade became impossible.

The coin spoke for itself, and neither Lucius or Caecilius gave the man their names, nor did he give his. The brothers slept in shifts in the rat-infested cabin of the small but swift trading vessel, always with a blade in hand, no food given and none taken.

After over a week since they had left Delphi behind, they stood on the high prow of the Phoenician vessel on their first day of calm, smooth sailing.

Lucius leaned on the railing, looking out to sea, staring ahead as they moved closer and closer with every nautical mile across Neptune's realm. Upon the deck beside him, Caecilius, who had been sick for the first few days, now slept fitfully beneath the enormous red and white striped sail, among sacks of grain that had been piled on deck.

Lucius smiled sadly as he looked upon his younger brother who, as he slept, had lost his outer appearance of the rough hunter, and yet seemed like the little boy Lucius had known, holding onto his satchel and bow beside him.

Though Lucius had planned to make this journey on his own, he had to acknowledge that he felt better that his brother was there, for Caecilius had become an excellent fighter in a way, though not a warrior. *We are not going to war though,* Lucius told himself. *We are going to kill.*

Still, despite the presence of his younger brother, as Lucius closed his eyes and felt the salt sea spray upon his hardened face and lips, he knew he had never felt so very lonely. The acuity of the great pain and sadness he felt had been tearing away at him. The guilt at his betrayal of Adara and his children was eviscerating him with every step that he took away from them, every mile he sailed. He would not keep his promise to his children to visit his mother's grave together, to pour milk and honey to her shade upon the Delphic mountainside. But it was the pain of all that he may not ever see that tore at his heart - his children grown, the possible birth of their next child, the feel of his wife as he held her in his arms - the past was all he had now, for looking to the future was weakening his mind and resolve.

I must not think of myself, but of them, and of making the world safe for them, he told himself in the dark as he lay upon the creaking ship planks, listening to the waves against the hull. *Lucius Pen Dragon will bring death to his enemies from the shadows.*

Leaving Adara, Phoebus and Calliope was the most difficult thing Lucius had ever had to do, for unlike other times, he could not clearly see a return to them. The road was shrouded in his mind's eye, and there was no going back now.

Antioch was only two days away and, with his gladius already in hand, Lucius began to set aside the weakening feelings of love and loss, and to focus his mind on his sole purpose of blood, fuelled by memories of fire and the screams of all the people he had ever cared for.

Go to Antioch and the drums of war. Find a friend's truth at the sign of the Golden Bough.

Lucius had contemplated Apollo's words constantly in his mind since he had left Delphi, and he wondered what he could expect to find in the Rome of the East. Had his divine father given him a false trail to pursue, or had he genuinely set Lucius on the road he desired? Lucius knew he had also deserted Apollo, and the other gods who had always stood beside him in the shadows of his life.

I'm on my own now, he thought, but then he looked down at Caecilius. *Not completely though.*

Two days later, as the sun rose in the guise of a pink orb, the ship made its final approach to the great harbour of Antioch at the mouth of the Orontes river. The crash of waves as the ship approached the broad coast became audible just beneath the Phoenician captain's shouted orders to his crew.

Lucius woke Caecilius and they gathered their things and went out of the stinking cabin into the fresh air and morning light. The port lay directly ahead, and beyond that, the river Orontes led away from the sea into the green and rocky plains and mountains that surrounded distant Antioch.

"You said you've been here before?" Caecilius asked feeling farther from home than ever before.

Lucius nodded. The last time he had been to Antioch was at the start of Severus' Parthian campaign. He and his friends had all been green recruits then, eager for battle and idealistic about the glories that awaited them on the battlefields of the eastern empire. They were a part of a force of thirty-two legions then, invincible in a way. *They're all gone now,* Lucius thought of them, friends and traitors - Eligius, Garai, Maren, Argus, Antanelis, Alerio and others. Flashes of their battles came as the coast sharpened into focus before the dusty mountains. Lucius was the last of them, but he had now come to Antioch with a different purpose, not to defend Rome's borders, or fight for her glory. No.

As Lucius watched the port come closer and closer, he knew that despite friendship and battle honours, despite the favour of the Gods, he had been burned both literally and figuratively by life itself.

"All that's left is vengeance," he said out loud without realizing he had done so.

Caecilius looked at him and pat his shoulder. "Then let's see to it, Brother."

With nothing but a nod of thanks and the toss of a pouch of coin, Lucius and Caecilius left the Phoenician vessel and captain behind and disappeared into the mobbed port for the baths, some food and supplies, and most importantly, news of the emperor's whereabouts.

But nobody could ever truly disappear, not with eyes everywhere, for there are always others on the hunt. Interested eyes followed Lucius and Caecilius through the port as they purchased supplies, including two mules to carry them across the plains.

As the brothers made their way through the dusty streets and sweaty crowds where sellers reached out to grab at most people, Lucius and Caecilius were kept at a distance, for as soon as people spotted Lucius' hardened face and mottled skin, he became something else to them besides a potential customer. He now was the barbarian, or a leper, someone to keep distant.

"We're drawing too much attention," Caecilius said, and Lucius agreed.

"I agree," Lucius stopped. "Don't look at them!" he hissed.

"Who?"

"Praetorian troops...to our left." From beneath the cowl of his cloak, Lucius observed the black and brown uniforms of the Praetorians, the way they held themselves in a crowd, as if no one could touch them, as if they could do anything. If they found Lucius now, it would all be over. "Come. Let's get out of the port and to the city. We need to see if we can get some information without calling too much attention to ourselves."

Leading their mules laden with some supplies, Lucius and Caecilius cut through the crowds toward the road that ran along the river inland to Antioch. With the sea behind them, they began to make their way to the polis.

They did not see the jackals gathered to watch them leave.

"Those two," said one thief to another.

"Who? The leper and his beggar friend?" answered the other.

"Yes. You see how the satchels are weighed down where they hang from the mule's saddle?"

"Yes."

"I'll wager there's plenty of coin in those satchels. And it's ours for the taking."

The other man nodded, and together they went to get the others to meet at the usual spot along the road.

Despite the frenetic crowding of the port of Antioch, the road between it and the actual city was quiet and deserted in the morning. The road followed the line of the river Orontes for much of the way, leaving its side only occasionally when its smooth bends and curves led too far away for efficiency. The road was another gift of Rome's to Antioch. It passed at times beneath the shaded boughs of trees that crowded the river banks, and also traversed more open, barren ground covered in rock and scrub where travellers were able to glimpse the surrounding mountains and the smoky skyline of Antioch against the sacred mount of Silpius in the distance ahead.

"We should be in the city by this afternoon," Lucius said to Caecilius as their mules clipped along on the road.

Caecilius did not answer right away, too distracted by the world about them, the brilliance of the sky contrasted by the hues of brown and green all around them. He gazed at the trees as they passed too.

"You all right?" Lucius asked as they began to approach the shadows of another copse along the river.

"Shh!" Caecilius hissed, his hand up. He tilted his head to listen. "A flock of birds by the river just shot into the air," he whispered, and as he did so, he unslung his bow from his shoulder and nocked an arrow as the mule continued to move forward.

Lucius drew his gladius, his eyes scouring the trees that now formed up to either side of the road.

On their left, there was a drop down to the river, and to their right, rocks rose up among the trees whose roots clung to them like old fingers.

The mules trotted along as their riders' eyes scanned the trees, and it seemed for a moment that the rocks and trees shifted more than would be usual.

"Are there dryads in this land?" Caecilius asked.

There was a sudden bit of laughter ahead of them and they looked to see a man step into the road before them.

"No," the man said. "But there are jackals."

Caecilius immediately sighted along the shaft of his arrow, but even as he did so, a chorus of yips and roars erupted from all around them, and the man ahead was running at them, startling the mules which began to buck, throwing Lucius off.

"Lucius!" Caecilius cried, loosing an arrow and taking the man before them in the thigh so that he cried out and fell off the side of the road down toward the riverbank.

Lucius felt hands grabbing at him and the glint of a blade caught his eye. His gladius stabbed out once, twice, three times before it bit flesh and another man yelled. He pushed his hood back to see the three men surrounding him, while another was trying to grab his laden mule's reins. "You picked the wrong travellers!" Lucius said as he feinted and then finished off the man he had stabbed the first time.

They were all bald, and dressed in brown, each of them with the rough tattoo of a dog on the side of their heads.

There was a stinging pain as Lucius was hit behind the knees with a staff of some sort, and he went down before another who closed in with a dagger. But even as the man lunged, he was thrown off of his feet by the arrow Caecilius had just planted in his skull.

Lucius rolled aside quickly, almost falling down the steep embankment to the river below, but he caught a protruding root with his left hand and with his sword hand slashed at the heel of the man with the staff, making him stumble and fall over him to the river below where he landed with a splash.

"Ahhh!" Lucius pulled himself up onto the road and ran directly for his mule which was being pulled at by another of the bandits. "Leave it now, or die where you stand!" he yelled.

"Die leper!" the man yelled, releasing the reins and running wildly at Lucius who parried and plunged his blade into his chest twice in quick succession before throwing him to the side.

There was a sudden quiet but for the clip of Caecilius' mule's hooves as he moved around the scene, his bow still drawn.

Lucius looked around. If there were any more bandits, they had melted back into the rocks and scrub.

"You'll pay for this!" a voice yelled from the river.

Lucius and Caecilius approached the edge and looked down to see the man who had stopped them in the road. He was hanging from a root, clinging to the embankment which was red with blood from where Caecilius' arrow had nicked him. He sneered painfully up at the two travellers.

"No one crosses the Jackals!" he said. "To do so is death! By Baal, I'll cut your eyes, ears and noses off and lay them upon his bloody altar!" He grunted in pain, his arm growing numb.

"By who?" Caecilius asked, a smile on his face. "Baal?" he laughed "Never heard of him!" He drew another arrow and pointed it at the man's face.

"You'll both die," he growled through his black and yellow teeth.

Lucius knelt down, his gladius raised. He stared the man in the eyes. "You picked the wrong travellers this time, dog. Dragons eat jackals." And without another thought, Lucius brought down his gladius to cut the man's hand off at the wrist, sending him screaming down the embankment and into the rushing river below.

"You hurt?" Caecilius asked Lucius, helping him up.

"Just a bruise. You?"

"I'm fine. Interesting place," Caecilius laughed, though Lucius detected the nervousness in his voice.

"They must have picked us out in the port. We should keep moving. It will be easier to blend in when we get to the city."

They mounted their mules and, with their weapons still drawn, carried on down the road to Antioch.

It took some time for both of them to calm down after the attack, but eventually the ground opened up and the sun rose higher in the sky to light the road ahead.

"What did you feel like when you first came here?" Caecilius asked Lucius.

Lucius sighed. "Foolishly, I was excited. We all were. It was our first war and we were eager for a taste of battle."

"How did that work out?"

"I survived. But many didn't. I remember seeing my friend Corvus' face explode beside me from a Parthian cavalry spear. One second he was there asking me something, the next he was gone, a piece of meat in the dirt."

Caecilius was silent for a moment. "Different than fighting roadside brigands then, I guess."

"Quite different," Lucius said, still trying to shake the image of Corvus' face from his mind. "I soon realized that war was not glorious. It's gruesome and bloody and soldiers are treated just like that - meat. I set out to be a different commander. I cared about my men..." Lucius' voice faded out as he looked ahead to the city growing before them, remembering the legions encamped on the other side when he first arrived in Antioch. "Even so...in the end, I failed my men too."

"You're too hard on yourself," Caecilius said. "Knowing you, Lucius, you were always at the front with them, fighting alongside them like Alexander."

Lucius looked at his brother and smiled sadly. He knew Caecilius could not understand what he was saying, the guilt he felt, but that was all right if it spared him the painful memories he had himself. *He has his own memories of pain and loss,* Lucius thought. *We all do.*

It was not long before Lucius and Caecilius passed beneath the Daphne gate of Antioch with the rest of the long file of travellers.

Normally, one would face a barrage of questions from the garrison troops at city gates in that part of the world, but in Antioch, trade was the ruler, and as little as possible was done to discourage commerce.

"Reason for coming to Antioch?" the optio at the gate asked Lucius automatically, barely looking him over.

"We come to make offerings at the temple of Jupiter on mons Silpius," Lucius answered.

He glanced at the mules they had. "There are restrictions on beasts in the city streets. You'll have to stable your mules at the eastern gate. Move along," the optio said without looking away from his wax tablet.

"That was easy," Caecilius said as they walked their mules along the colonnaded cardo.

But Lucius did not answer. He pulled his cowl over his head, and from beneath it, his eyes scanned the crowds for any sign of Praetorian troops.

"Lucius?"

"Sorry. It's very crowded here. Let's get the mules stabled and then we can find a place for the night."

"We need to find out if the emperor's here."

"Shh! We will, and the best place to hear gossip is the agora. We'll find lodgings after that. Come on."

Antioch was considered the jewel of the East. It was nestled along the rich river valley between mount Silpius on one side and, beyond the dry plain dotted with villas and olive groves, the snow-capped mountains of northern Syria.

It felt strange to Lucius to walk through such a large polis, for he had not done so in years. He had been living in hiding and isolation like an animal, and now he felt the overwhelm and danger of being in such close proximity to others, to masses who did not know him or care about him. It was a far cry from the friendly villagers he had befriended at the hillfort so long ago.

Those days are gone, Lucius, he told himself. *Press on.*

Antioch was a rich city, founded by the first Seleucus, Alexander's general, over five hundred years before. It was crowded and beautiful with over half a million citizens. Antioch had been favoured by various caesars over the years and, like Rome itself, it had its rich and poorer quarters, places to be admired, and places to be avoided.

The Orontes river passed along the west and northern side of the city, alongside the main agora and the island where the imperial palaces, stadium and hippodrome were located. Residential districts and shops lined the main, colonnaded thoroughfare. On the southern and eastern side of the city were located the amphitheatre, odeon, forum and temples leading up to the slopes of mount Silpius, where the city walls rose and fell along with the mountain curves.

With the mules stabled for the night, Lucius and Caecilius made their slow progress through the thronging crowds of pedestrians and litters riding above them until, at last, they reached the sprawling agora alongside the river.

Even the markets of Trajan did not compete with Antioch's sprawling, myriad-scented agora. The senses were overwhelmed with spice and colour, and the voices of buyers and sellers rang out in all the languages of the eastern empire, including Greek, Aramaic, and Latin. This was a great world beyond Rome's seven hills, and Caecilius could not stop looking around.

"I never thought to see such a place!" he said to Lucius as they walked among the stalls. "Even Athenae wasn't this big."

"I'd forgotten," Lucius said, his hand on his gladius. He was warm, but did not want to remove his cloak and hood. There were far too many troops lining the streets, and he was not willing to risk questioning, for though his black clothing would have called attention to himself in that sea of chaos and colour, his burned complexion would have raised other alarms.

They came to a set of stalls where carpenters sold simple furniture beside fishermen with an array of nets for use in the river below or the sea beyond. All of them were dressed simply in brown tunicae, and bore small, wooden crosses about their necks.

"Who are they?" Caecilius asked Lucius as they passed. "They look so thin, and what are those about their necks?"

Lucius stopped, and as he looked upon them, he was reminded of Father Gilmore. "They're Christians."

"Christians? Here? But there are so many?"

One of the carpenters looked up and smiled at the two travellers. He was not sickly thin, but not bulky either, and he had a thick brown beard that fell to his chest, though he was not an old man. "Come to browse, friends?" he said.

Caecilius did not approach, but Lucius turned to the man, looked to see if speaking to the Christians would arouse attention and, when it seemed they were as much a part of the community as others, he approached.

"Greetings," Lucius said to the man who had put down his mallet and chisel and extended his hand to Lucius.

"God be with you, stranger," the man said. "I am Petrus."

Caecilius stepped behind Lucius, his hand upon his weapons.

The Christian saw this, but did not recoil. There was no fear in his eyes. "There is no need for that here. You are among friends."

"Are we?" Lucius said. "You don't even know us."

"All men are our friends. We are all God's children."

Lucius wanted to laugh at the irony, but the man seemed friendly enough, and he did not want to insult him. "Your work is fine and sturdy."

"Thank you," the man answered. "We do what we can with the tools we have. The work is simple and solid, as is our faith," he said when he saw Caecilius staring at the cross about his neck. He then removed his cross and held it out to Caecilius. "Please, take it. It is yours."

Caecilius recoiled. "By the Gods, no."

"It is the greatest protection you can have," Petrus said. "Not those." He nodded to their weapons.

"They serve us well enough," Lucius said, "but we thank you for your generosity."

The man inclined his head. "What may I do for two travellers?"

Lucius looked around again for any sign of soldiers and, when he saw none, he stepped closer to the carpenter. "Actually, I would appreciate some information, if you are inclined."

"I will speak the truth if asked," the man said.

"How long has the emperor been in residence in Antioch?"

The man seemed disappointed. "He is here no longer."

"What?" Lucius asked, unable to keep his voice low.

"After the terrible events in Alexandria, he came here, his pride calling him to war once again."

"When did he leave Antioch?"

"Some weeks ago. We pay little attention to imperial goings on. The emperor is no great friend of ours, and his universal citizenship has done little to improve our treatment in other cities. The troops come and go from Antioch, and we remain and work and pray."

"Are the legions still encamped outside the city walls?"

"No. The war with Parthia has begun anew."

"Where is the fighting happening now?"

The man looked strangely at Lucius and shook his head. "I've no knowledge of such things, friend. It does not concern me."

"War concerns everyone, does it not?"

"Only if you make it your concern. Wars come and go, but the Lord's love is eternal."

Lucius began to get frustrated with the man's preachy statements, though he was not unused to such talk, having spent some time with Father Gilmore and his priests in Ynis Wytrin. He began to feel deflated. He had hoped to find that Caracalla was in residence in the palace of Antioch, but it was not to be. The hunt would go on.

"Why do you seek the emperor when the Lord is already with you?"

Lucius pursed his lips and shook his head. "That is our affair, not yours." He stopped himself and took a breath. "Forgive me. We are tired from our travels. It has been a long road."

"Most roads are. But do you have a place to stay? You are more than welcome to take shelter with me for the night. My place is humble, but it is warm and dry."

Lucius thought about it for only a moment before Apollo's words echoed in his mind like a plucked lyre string. "You wouldn't happen to know a tavern by the name of 'The Golden Bough'?" As Lucius spoke the words aloud, he felt his heart begin to pound for some inexplicable reason, and as he looked upon the carpenter, the man smiled.

"Why yes. It is near where I live in the Kerateion, the Judeo-Christian quarter of Antioch. Come with me. I will lead you there."

At this point, Caecilius leaned in to whisper to Lucius. "We can't trust this man, Lucius. He'll lead us down a dark alley where we'll be ambushed again. Let's leave now."

Lucius put up his hand and his sleeve fell down to reveal his burned arms.

"Please," Peter said. "I can see you've been through much. I mean you no harm. It is our duty to help those in need."

"We're not in need," Caecilius said.

"Everyone is in need, and the Lord provides."

Just then, a strange sound rang out in the agora, and Lucius recognized it from those misty mornings and evenings in Ynis Wytrin. He saw Peter look up at the sound. "The bells are calling you to prayer," Lucius said as the other Christians around them began to set down their tools, wood and nets and to leave the agora and their wares unattended.

"You have heard them before?" Peter asked, clearly surprised.

"You are not the first Christian to be kind to me."

"Nor will I be the last," Peter said, smiling. "I must go, but you will find the Golden Bough tavern in the Kerateion in the southwest corner of the city, along the city walls just below the mountain of Tauris, on the edge of Silpius. Go there, and you will find what you are looking for." Peter turned to leave, the last to go from among his brethren, but he turned back to Lucius and Caecilius who were now standing alone among the wooden furniture and nets. "Whatever it is you are looking for, I pray that you will find it. God's blessings go with you." And with those parting words, he was gone.

Lucius was silent for a few moments as he watched the Christians file out of the agora, undisturbed by the other traders and citizens as they went toward their place of worship on the other side of the city.

"What strange people!" Caecilius said. "So much talk of just one god. How can you survive with the help of just one?"

"There are worse people than Christians," Lucius said. "Those whom I have met have been kind."

"Speaking of worse, what do we do now? The emperor has moved on."

The mere thought of Caracalla caused Lucius' anger to raise its head from the dark swamp within, reminding him of exactly what he was looking for in that place on the other side of the empire, so far from his family and friends.

"Lucius? You all right?" Caecilius said, placing his hand upon Lucius' arm.

"We need more information about the war so we can find out where the emperor will be." He looked at his brother. "We'll stay a night or two and see what we can find out."

They walked among the empty market stalls of the Christians to the wall walk that overlooked the river below and the island with the imperial palaces to their right. Smoke hovered above the palace rooftops and the sounds of cheering burst into the sky from the hippodrome, but Caracalla was nowhere to be found among that world of gilded stone and tile. They watched the river flowing by far below, the fishermen casting their nets from small boats as larger river barges sailed up river.

"Where can we stay?" Caecilius asked.

"We'll start with the Golden Bough."

"How do you know this place anyway?" Caecilius asked.

Lucius hesitated. "I...I remember hearing about it when I was on my first campaign," he said. "If it isn't any good, we'll just look for another place to stay." They began to walk.

"I don't like the idea of staying in the Christian quarter," Caecilius said.

"Let's get some food," Lucius answered, ignoring the statement.

"Now that's a good idea!" Caecilius said, stopping at a stall where bread and honeyed pastries were sold.

As his brother paid for the food, Lucius turned to gaze across the rooftops of the city toward the mountain and the southwest quarter. *Apollo...where have you sent me?*

"Ready?" Caecilius said through his chewing as he held out a piece of bread to Lucius.

Lucius took it and ate. "Let's go."

It took them some time to get out of the agora, for the sections without the Christian sellers' stalls were as packed as ever, like rows of amphorae crowded in the hull of a ship. Sweaty and tired, Lucius and Caecilius stopped at the great nymphaeum along the main, colonnaded street that cut through the middle of the city. There were in fact, fountains every-where in Antioch that were fed by the various springs of Daphne beneath the city, or by the aqueducts that led down from the mountains to feed the polis' arteries and citizens. However, the nymphaeum was the grandest with an enormous, niched facade rising up from the main street to a pediment that hovered over statues of gods and goddesses who looked down on the mortals passing to and fro.

The trickle of water in Lucius' ears and upon his skin as he splashed his face and neck, was welcome after the sweltering heat of the market. He had forgotten how very hot it could get in the eastern part of the empire, and almost immediately, the smell and dusty air in his nostrils, and the taste of sand grit in his mouth came rushing back.

He had thought to leave thoughts of war behind after so long, after so many other traumas in his life, but it seemed Mars was ever with him, no matter his circumstances.

Caecilius removed the furs from his shoulders, unable to stand the heat any longer. "I can't take this. I thought Graecia was hot!"

"Let's keep moving. We need shelter before the sun falls," Lucius said, gathering up his satchel and going into the crowd on the cardo maximus that flowed toward the Daphne gate like the river Orontes outside the city walls.

Before they reached the gate, Lucius stopped and looked up at mount Silpius where its craggy face jutted out to look over the city. He followed the line of it southward to the smaller face overlooking what the carpenter had told them was the Judea-Christian quarter. "Over there," he said.

"What if that carpenter and his fellows are waiting for us? Could be an ambush, or an attempt for them to…" he leaned in to whisper, "… claim the bounty on you or win favour for their people with the emperor."

"There is no danger." Lucius looked to the lofty pediment of the temple of Jupiter that rose out of the earth to stand above the people against the backdrop of the mountain. *Great father of the Gods, please guide us…*

"How do you know?"

"I just know," Lucius answered his brother as he cut across the crowded street and the square that surrounded the roaring amphitheatre of Antioch. He could not help but wonder at the sad irony that had put the Christian quarter in the shadow of that arena, for it was not that long ago that the caesars had killed many of them in the amphitheatres of the empire.

Everyone suffers under Rome…

They were happy to leave the arena behind them and follow the line of the aqueduct's massive pylons until they reached the narrow streets of the Kerateion where it was pressed between the Roman wall and the mountain.

"It feels strange here," Caecilius said. "I don't like it." He had his hand on his hunting dagger as they walked, his eyes searching every squeezing alleyway where dark figures stood in narrow doorways whispering into the shadows.

The air was rank, only slightly covered by the smell of frankincense that wafted from their hidden temples and homes. Lucius noticed the mezuzot, the pieces of wrapped parchment or clay, marked with sacred texts that were affixed to the doorways of the Jewish inhabitants of the quarter, while others bore the cross of the Christians.

There was a sound of bells once more and the whispers in doorways ceased as people came out into the street again.

The two Romans became uncomfortable in the sudden crowd, but not because of any animosity, for the men, women and children who flowed around them like water about rocks in a stream, smiled and laughed as they continued on with their day. They soon reached what could only be the main thoroughfare of the quarter, for it widened and there were a few shops along the way.

Lucius looked to his left and right for any sign of a golden bough, but he could see none. Then he spotted a man he assumed to be a baker making deliveries, for he carried a sack filled to the brim with flat breads, newly out of the oven. "Excuse me," Lucius said.

The man stopped and, for a moment, seemed that he might carry on when he saw Lucius' appearance and the weapons the two men before him carried. But he did not. "Yes, stranger?"

"I was wondering if you could direct us to a tavern by the name of The Golden Bough?"

"Of course. It's at the southern end of the street on your left. Just look for the sign."

"My thanks," Lucius said as the man continued on his way. He turned to Caecilius. "Come on."

The crowds began to thin out as they reached their various destinations after their prayers. Scents of food began to waft out of windows and rickety balconies above where children played and grandmothers darned with needles and gnarled fingers, keeping watchful eyes over the young.

Lucius stopped in the street suddenly and Caecilius bumped into him.

"What's wrong?" Caecilius said, his hand on his dagger as he turned to look around hurriedly.

"Nothing... I just... I feel..." Then he looked ahead and saw it, a sign that said 'The Golden Bough' above the image of a tree or bush that burned with golden fire. The sign hung from iron brackets over the street, and it swayed gently in the hot breeze, squeaking slightly as iron rubbed upon iron.

But the tavern was closed, dark.

It was suddenly quiet and Lucius felt his heart beat fast and he clutched at the dragon brand upon his chest.

"Lucius! What's wrong?" Caecilius asked loudly, panicking at the look in his brother's eyes. "Are you ill?"

"No. I just…" He shut his eyes tightly.

"Who are you?" said a timid voice from down the street behind them.

Caecilius whipped around, his hunting dagger out, only to find a woman with short, blonde hair staring at them.

Lucius turned too and he felt as if he had been punched in his gut. "It can't be…"

The woman dropped the basket of persimmons she had been carrying and her hands covered her mouth in shock as tears came to her eyes.

Lucius stepped closer to her.

"Who are you?" she asked again, backing away slightly.

"Ca…Carissa? It's me. Lucius…Metellus," he whispered. "What are you doing here?"

"Lucius?" She was shaking visibly now, her tears running down her cheeks. "How can this be?"

Caecilius bent to pick up the fruit she had dropped.

"Apollo has sent me," Lucius said. "I can't believe it…" He looked up at the sign of The Golden Bough. "Do you own this place?"

"No. We live above it."

"We?" Lucius felt his heart racing full force now.

"Yes. Ashur and I."

Lucius felt like weeping and he turned to look once more at the upper floor above the tavern. "Ashur?" Lucius said, and it seemed as if the sound of that plucked lyre string echoed more strongly in his mind as the sunlight lit the sign of that burning tree swaying gently above them.

XVIII

FRATRES

'Brothers'

L ucius could not blame Carissa's fear upon seeing him and his brother standing there in the middle of that Antiochene street. It had been about ten years since they had last met. So much had happened to him, to all of them, and though Lucius could still recognize Carissa, he could tell that the years had not always been kind.

As they followed Carissa slowly up the stairs to the apartment above the tavern, Lucius remembered when they had first met in Rome, how hers and Emrys' work had been the talk of the imperial court. It was she who had captured Ashur's heart and, together, after Alene's death and the fall of Plautianus, they had left the rest of the world behind. They had disappeared.

And now, they were here, in Antioch.

Lucius felt nervous as they ascended the stairs to the unadorned door at the top. It had been so long since he had seen Ashur. They had been close for a time, had saved each other's lives, but the Gods had separated them. He felt sudden guilt for not having thought of Ashur much over the years, for the tide of life had carried his thoughts far away. Now, the Gods had brought them together.

Ashur is alive! Lucius kept saying to himself as the door opened slowly and Carissa went in.

"Stay here a moment," she said to Lucius and Caecilius. "I would speak to him alone first."

Lucius nodded and stood still.

"What is happening, Lucius?" Caecilius whispered. "Did you know Ashur was here?"

"No."

"Lucius," Carissa's soft voice came from inside. "Come in."

They passed the threshold into a rectangular, sparsely-furnished room with a table and two stools around it. To the left, along the plastered wall, was a small kitchen with a basket of various vegetables on one side, and an amphora of oil on the other. Upon the counter were a mortarium and an iron pan and pot. A few wooden ladles hung upon the wall beside dried bunches of herbs.

Lucius touched the table in the centre of the room where Carissa had set her basket of persimmons beside a clay jug of water and two cups.

She turned to him when he did not follow. "Ashur is in there," she said, pointing to a curtain that was drawn across the entire room. She turned to Caecilius. "If you like, sit here and have some water."

Caecilius smiled at her and nodded his thanks. "Go, Lucius," he said. "I'll wait."

Lucius turned to go through the broad, brown curtain and just as he was about to pass through the folds, Carissa grabbed his arm.

"Lucius," she said, her voice very low, tears in her eyes. "Prepare yourself."

He felt a lump forming in his throat as he touched her hand and nodded, for he began to dread what he would find on the other side.

Immediately before him was a small workshop with a few vases upon a table. One sat upon a wheel, half-painted with meander patterns and an image of Aphrodite and Eros, but Lucius' eyes were quickly drawn away to the far left where a couch lay in the light of the setting sun.

"Lucius? Is it you?" called a weak voice. The sound was one of incredulity and sadness.

Lucius approached slowly, the floorboards creaking beneath his feet. "Ashur? I... Can it be?" He let his satchel fall to the ground as he approached the couch.

Ashur Mehrdad lay upon a rough, wooden couch covered in blankets. He faced the window where the orange light could warm his face.

It was not a face Lucius recognized, for before him lay an ancient man whose once taut and muscular olive skin was now mottled and sagging. His eyes were rheumy, and light tremors racked his body as he reached out with a gnarled hand for Lucius.

A part of Lucius thought that the old man could not possibly be his old friend, and yet, he did know it was Ashur Mehrdad. He felt tears stinging his eyes as he looked upon him and fell to his knees at the bedside.

"What have the Gods done to you?" Ashur said, gripping Lucius' hand with all of his strength as he took in the sight of Lucius' burned visage and scarred arms.

"Everything, my friend."

Ashur closed his eyes, his own tears rimming his lids. He had hoped that someday he would see Lucius again, at least one more time. Now that that time had arrived, he felt a supreme sadness at the sight of Lucius, but also gratitude for the chance to bid farewell, one last time.

"Ashur, what has happened to you?" Lucius asked, wiping his eyes and looking at him as he leaned upon the couch.

Ashur swallowed with some difficulty, and then smiled thinly, sadly. "Lucius…I am dying."

Lucius felt the room spin for a moment. *So much time lost… Gods!* He felt Ashur grip his hand again. "But you cannot die!"

Ashur did smile then. "All things must pass, Lucius. Apollo abandoned me years ago, as I abandoned him. I chose love over serving him…and in so choosing, I have come to this… And I don't regret a thing."

"How can you say that?"

Ashur smiled. "I have known a love unlike any other. I can't imagine never having known such a love…a love worth living and dying for." He turned his head to smile at Carissa where she peered through the curtains at them, tears upon her cheeks as she forced a smile for her beloved. He turned back to Lucius. "I have lived for a very long time, Lucius, and I was happy to be free at the end, despite the price I have had to pay."

"Apollo has punished you," Lucius said, his voice full of anger now.

But Ashur shook his head. "No. I have punished myself. The choices were mine to make and…as I said…I regret none of them." His breath was wheezy, and sweat beaded upon his weathered and wrinkled brow, but Ashur Mehrdad yet smiled, more than he had in some time. "I have made my peace with the Gods, and they have granted me this one last request…"

"What request?"

"To see you one more time, Lucius…my brother."

There was a ringing in Lucius' ears then and it seemed that the light of the dying sun in the West grew in intensity as it shone upon them through the small window.

"I have been waiting for you…to tell you…"

"How can this be? Did you know the truth for all these years?" Lucius sat back upon his knees, though it pained him to do so. "You knew, and you never told me?"

"It was not my truth to tell. I also wanted to protect you from the pain of that knowledge. You are a son of Apollo…as am I… But there is a difference, Lucius, and it is burned upon your very flesh."

Lucius felt confused and betrayed, but by whom, he was not certain. His thoughts whirled out of control as he felt his chest burning even then. He let his cloak fall to the ground and pulled the hem of his tunic apart to reveal the brand.

"You *are* the dragon, Lucius Metellus Anguis."

"I am Lucius Pen Dragon now, Ashur." Lucius felt the despair and anger setting in again. "And I've lost everything…"

Lucius slumped onto the side of Ashur's deathbed and, together, they wept for each other, for time lost, and for the painful burden each had carried like a titanic weight across the rocky world.

It was some time before Lucius emerged from behind the curtain to find Caecilius and Carissa sitting together at the table eating a simple meal of lentils, goat's cheese and bread. His brother devoured his food as if he had not eaten in a week, but Carissa ate little, occasionally dipping her spoon into the dark broth.

She had not been able to eat heartily for a long time and, as Lucius could see from the dark rings beneath her eyes, she had not been able to sleep well either.

Such is life when one awaits Death in the darkness of night.

Carissa looked up. "Lucius, please sit, and eat. You've had such a long road." She stood to get Lucius a bowl, but when he stood before her, his arms out, she stepped into them, her body shuddering for all their shared grief, and for the pity she felt for all of them.

Caecilius watched from behind them, but could not stand it and went back to eating. The pain they had all experienced was far too much, and though he had only been young when he had last seen Ashur at their home in Rome, near the forum Boarium, he remembered what a strong, quick man he had been.

"I'm so sorry," Lucius whispered to Carissa.

She stood back and wiped her eyes with a shaking hand. "The Gods have been both kind and cruel to us. It is as it is." She busied herself with getting another bowl, filled it with steaming lentils, and set it on the table for Lucius.

Lucius set the satchel along the wall by the door and hung his black cloak on one of the pegs there beside Caecilius'. Then, he sat down, sipped water from the clay cup she had put there for him, and picked up his spoon, only then just realizing how hungry he was.

"Caecilius has told me all that you've been through, Lucius. I can't believe how much your family has suffered." She stared at him. "And you...I would hardly have recognized you but for your name and Ashur's dreams."

"His dreams?" Lucius asked.

She nodded. "He dreamed he would see you again, before he crossed the river into the Otherworld."

Lucius set his spoon down in the bowl and looked at her across the lamp on the table. "He can't die."

She had no words, but stared into the darkness of her bowl.

"How did you come to be here? How long have you been here?" Lucius asked.

Carissa sat up straighter, and took a sip of her water. "We left Rome shortly after you did, all those years ago. We travelled from place to place...Mauretania, Numidia... Ashur made a living by his sword, helping villages that were being harassed by nomads or brigands. There was a lot of gratitude in his wake." She smiled to herself at the memories. "We ended up in Alexandria for a while, and travelled in Aegyptus. He showed me where he was born and where he grew up, before Apollo took him into his service..."

"And Rome?"

"The only thought we ever had of Rome was of you. In Alexandria, Ashur had news of the war in Caledonia, and he knew then that you were there."

"I was. It was..." Lucius closed his eyes at the memories of blood and battle, of his dead men in trees, and of dark gods. "It was war on many fronts," he finally whispered.

"And Ashur caught glimpses of it," Carissa added.

"What? How?" Caecilius asked, but Lucius put up his hand to stay his questions.

"We had built a home in the south of Britannia," Lucius said to her. "Our friends were many, but Rome burned it and Ynis Wytrin gave us sanctuary."

Carissa's eyes widened. "You have been to the sacred isle?"

Lucius nodded. "For a time, it was our home… But we left. I was not able to stay there because of all that had happened. Rome has been hunting our family ever since, Carissa. We escaped to Dumnonia and Din Tagell, where our good friend is lord. He helped us to take ship from there to Italy."

"You have seen Dumnonia?" There was a wistfulness in her voice then, as if she had not thought of her home in an age.

"Yes," Lucius said, but he would not elaborate on his memories of that place, of his time in Annwn or elsewhere, for the pain was still too fresh, even then. "But how did you come to be here in Antioch?"

"We stayed in Aegyptus for some time, but it became apparent that life there was unsettling for Ashur. One day, he decided we should come here. He could not explain why, but that we should." She looked at Lucius. "Now, perhaps, we know. That was three years ago, and it was about then that his health began to degrade more quickly." She balled a paint-stained fist. "That is when the Gods truly turned their backs on him."

"And why this neighbourhood?" Caecilius asked. "You are among Christians and Jews here."

She smiled sadly at the younger man. "They welcomed us without question. Despite the poverty in these narrow streets, there is great kindness. We needed a little kindness after all those years of travel. Ashur needed a quiet, safe place to rest."

"And you?" Lucius asked. "I saw in the other room that you've been painting."

"I have. To make some coin, I've been painting pottery for one of the local merchants in the Greek quarter. It does not pay a lot, but it keeps a roof above our heads and puts food upon our table. The coin Ashur made during our travels is gone now."

They were all three silent for a time before Lucius spoke up again.

"Emrys misses you, Carissa," Lucius said softly, as kindly as possible. "He knows he disappointed you, and he regrets it deeply."

"As I regret the way I treated him."

Lucius reached across the table to hold her hand. "With my mother gone now, he is more alone than ever. Would you and Ashur consider going to Delphi?"

"Emrys misses you more than he could ever say," Caecilius said softly.

She looked at Caecilius, and then at Lucius, and a solitary tear ran down her cheek. "Lucius... Ashur will not be leaving Antioch." Her eyes became determined, glinting in the lamplight. "He is still hounded by guilt at the death of your sister in Numidia. He has never forgotten it." Carissa suddenly fell to her knees beside Lucius as if she were prostrating herself before a god, and it was then that Lucius knew that Ashur had told her what Lucius truly was. She grasped his hands tightly. "I beg you, Lucius, please forgive Ashur for Alene's death, for he has never forgiven himself."

"Oh, Carissa. It was never his fault. It was Rome's doing. Just as it was Rome who killed all my men and burned our homes. It is Rome who hunted Alene, and who hunts me and my family."

"Please forgive him, Lucius," she asked again.

"Of course."

And it was then that Carissa wept, her tears wetting their clasped hands as if in water-tight agreement.

That night, Lucius and Caecilius slept on mats on the wooden floor in the main room beside the table, while Carissa lay herself beside Ashur on the couch by the window, her eyes closing slowly as they watched the stars' lights flicker out the window above Antioch.

When she had retired, she found Ashur staring out the window as usual, only this time, he was wide awake, as if hanging onto every last minute left to him by the Gods who had so used him.

"They are asleep," she whispered. "I cannot believe what they have been through."

"In a way, it will be a relief to leave the cruelty of this world behind," Ashur said, but as soon as he did so, he felt Carissa's body stiffen. "But I would endure it for eternity to spend just one more lifetime with you, my love."

"Please don't," she said. "I cannot bear it any longer. The Gods have been so cruel."

"And yet, I realize now that Apollo has never really abandoned me."

"How can you say that?"

Ashur sighed and the sound was one of wheezing. "He brought us together, and together we have stayed. He allowed me what I wanted in this last part of life. I was allowed my choice." Ashur smiled and in his heart he thanked Apollo. "A father may push his child out of the home, release him from his protective embrace, but there is always a link between them, a sort of love... I see that now."

"Is it love to have you suffer so? Is it love to have Lucius, your own brother by Apollo, so tormented?"

"In a way, allowing us our choices is love."

"Lucius is not the man he once was," Carissa warned. "I could see it when he told me what Rome has done to their family. "You must speak with him before it is too late."

"One final task from father to son," Ashur said, his eyes finally growing heavy. "It is so, my love," he whispered softly as they fell asleep in the starlight upon that couch.

Morning had barely dawned over Antioch, and the streets of the Kerateion, shaded by the rocky face of Silpius, were still dark and quiet as the populace prayed in the safety of their homes.

Lucius and Caecilius were sound asleep upon the floor, their exhaustion finally having caught up with them, and Carissa slumbered upon the couch beside Ashur.

She had given everything to that mysterious man blessed and cursed by the Gods, and had enjoyed the happiest days of her life with him. Every night, as she lay herself down to try and sleep, she thought about how the pain she was feeling was worth it for the love she had lived, but then she remembered that every morning when she awoke, she might find that he was gone, and so through the long nights, she clung to him, praying to the Gods for some aid.

During those long nights, Ashur often lay awake, racked with the pain of his age, but given courage by the love Carissa held for him. He would imagine that they were young again and that the world lay before them, perhaps with a family by their side. In the darkness, he would smile at the fiction he created, his smile only visible to the Gods and the moonlight.

In the early hours of that dark morning, however, he did not imagine a life with Carissa that would never be, but rather, felt something he had not felt in many years. His spine and senses tingled like an alarm, and there was a faint music at the back of his mind. A breeze came in at the window to whirl about his face and neck, not cold or discomfiting, but rousing like spring water on a hot day. *I haven't felt such a thing since-* But Ashur's thought died upon his mute lips as he stared up at the face of his father.

The Far-Shooter stood in the cold light of the moon and stars, looking down on the son he had abandoned to pain and loneliness so many years before. The stars blazed in his timeless eyes and his demeanour was one of distance and disappointment with the sight of his one-time servant and the woman he had chosen over loyalty.

Father? Ashur said weakly. *Why have you come now, after all these years?* Tears fell from the wrinkled edges of Ashur's eyes as he spoke, for he had hoped to see the Far-Shooter one last time before he boarded the dread barge for the crossing.

Apollo stepped forward, his blue cloak wavering around his body like wind and cloud over the sea in winter. *You betrayed me, Ashur Mehrdad,* he accused.

Ashur swallowed and took a deep, shuddering breath, the pain acute as he did so. But he replied, shaking his head. *My intention was not to betray you, Lord. I was but true to myself.*

After so long, so many sunrises and sunsets, so many ages upon the earth... Apollo said.

Why have you come? Is it to heal me, Lord?

Apollo looked down and shook his head. He could not admit such to a mortal, but it did pain him to see one of his sons so tormented. Even so... *I cannot,* Apollo said. *The Laws forbid it. Just as I could not escape my exile for murder and victory, so you cannot escape the death that awaits you because of the choices you made.*

I would make those choices again, Lord...for Love...

Apollo nodded, neither angry nor happy. He had become accustomed to the ways of the world he oversaw. He looked upon the lithe artisan at Ashur's side, the one who had given up her art for him, and he knew the truth of what Ashur said. *There is something in that, at least,* he thought. *Stand with me, Ashur.*

Ashur could not easily stand, but with Apollo there at last, he tried, slipping from Carissa's side and swinging his legs over the edge of the couch. With his eyes on his father by the window, Ashur Mehrdad pushed himself up upon his shaking limbs and stood to slowly walk toward Apollo.

The god did not put out his arm to steady him, but stood close, his light giving strength to Ashur as the sun does to the world.

Why have you come? Ashur said again.

For Lucius.

Ashur nodded. *He is set upon a final path.* He looked out at the sky where the moon hung in the darkness of the heavens.

You must try to dissuade him, Apollo said. *He loves you. He will listen to you.*

And his choice?

Even you can see what it will lead to.

Ashur nodded, but said nothing.

In the great architecture of the Cosmos, there are times when the difference between gods and men is lessened. All feel the opposite pulls of order and chaos, peace and violence, love... here he looked directly at Ashur, *...and hate. All are leaves upon the winds of eternity, stars in the heavens.*

And what of a man pulled between the mortal and immortal worlds, Father? What fate befalls him? Ashur opened his arms as if to display himself, swaying upon his feet. *Would you prefer to see this state of weakness, or a strong man whose heart and will has been destroyed because he has been robbed of choice?*

All choices are a beginning, and an end. No one is fully robbed of choice.

I care no longer for riddles, Ashur said defiantly, standing as straight as he could manage, no matter how much it hurt. *I care for Carissa,* he looked to her sleeping form, *and for my brother.*

Then help him, Apollo said, his voice as close to pleading as ever it had been. *For if he pursues the path he has chosen, he will truly lose everything. He will not survive.*

Ashur leaned upon the window sill, too weak to stand any longer without aid. He looked up at the moon again, as he had so many times over the ages, and remembered when Lucius had first come to his aid in the desert. He had felt pain then, but he had healed. Apollo had commanded him to endure that pain to help Lucius. And now, in the middle of his pain, he was being asked to do so one last time. *I will speak with him,* Ashur said, *but not because you ask it of me. I will do it because I choose to, out of love for Lucius.*

Apollo nodded and tried to meet Ashur's eyes, but his son would not look upon him.

Farewell, Father, Ashur said without turning to the Far-Shooter.

Apollo nodded. *Farewell...Ashur Mehrdad...* And he was gone.

Ashur crumpled to the floor then as the first rays of sunlight peeked over the eastern edge of the world, but he hung onto the window sill, determined to hold himself up a little longer, to gaze out at the street and sky on his own.

"Ashur?" Carissa turned in their bed to see him clinging to the window sill, nearly collapsed upon the floor. She jumped out of bed and went to his side. "Why are you here?" she asked as she helped him up, kissing his sweaty brow.

"I'm fine, my love. I wanted to see the sky clearly is all. For a few minutes, I felt stronger again." She set him upon the bed and he slumped back, his breathing heavy.

"Why do you smile?" Carissa asked, confused and a little angry with him.

"Because, my love... In some ways, I am still strong...still myself."

Lucius and Caecilius awoke to Carissa making food. The apartment above The Golden Bough was filled with sunlight, and the streets of the Kerateion were alive and bustling.

Lucius rolled over and rubbed his face. He had not slept so solidly in a long time, but he felt heavy, as if weighed down with unseen burdens.

"Good morning," Carissa said as she turned to look down at them.

Caecilius stirred beside Lucius, and together they sat up.

"I'm sorry, Carissa," Lucius said. "We did not mean to sleep so long into the morning."

"You needed it," she said. "I slept soundly too, for some reason." She wiped her hands on a ragged cloth and turned to them. "I found Ashur on the floor this morning. He had been gazing out at the moon."

Lucius stood slowly and stretched. "Is he hurt?"

"No."

Lucius made to go into the other room to see Ashur, but Carissa put up her hands. "Please don't. He is resting again. You may see him later. For now, I have prepared food for you both."

They sat at the table and ate of the steaming porridge Carissa had prepared for them. It was silent as they ate, and when they were finished, Lucius stood.

"We should go to the agora to see if we can find out any more information."

"I agree," Caecilius said, the first words he had spoken that morning. He was still haunted by a dream he had had of Clarinda weeping, alone in Delphi.

"You go," Carissa said. "But stay away from the walls about the palaces on the island. "There are guards there at all times."

"Where should we go for news?" Caecilius asked.

"Try the agora again, but not among the Christian stalls. You'll learn more at the others. Then try the forum beside the temple of Artemis. If you follow the road north out of the Kerateion, you will find it."

Lucius turned to her. "Can we get you anything?"

She shook her head. "I will go later, after I finish my work. I need those small outings into the world."

Lucius nodded. "I understand." He began to gather his things with Caecilius but turned back to her. "I hope that we are not causing you trouble, being here that is."

"On the contrary," she said. "He is revived."

When Lucius and Caecilius were gone, Carissa sat down alone at the table and wept, for she could not shake the image of Ashur upon the floor. She did not want to share his final days with anyone. *But I cannot complain,* she thought, *for I have had a life with him that none can take away.*

. . .

Lucius and Caecilius spent the better part of the day roaming the aisles of the agora in the hopes of hearing some news about the emperor's movements, but it was not as easy as they would have thought. People's lips were tight, and the talk most often was of commerce and local gossip in the agora, who had made what deals and when the next caravan was expected out of the East.

It seemed the Antiochenes were accustomed to war upon their doorstep, and so there was actually very little talk of it among those who had no hope of affecting the outcome.

Among the wafting scents of roasting meats and baking bread, the blood-soaked cobbles of the butchers' street, and the hammering chorus of the smiths' quarter, Lucius and Caecilius lingered in various places, straining their ears for anything that might be helpful.

"It's hopeless," Caecilius said. "No one here cares for the emperor or his war."

"Shh," Lucius hissed. "Keep your voice down. The Praetorians always have spies around, especially when the emperor is near, and the battlefield is not far off."

"How about we visit one of the baths?" Caecilius said.

"It's too dangerous. We don't know who might be there." Lucius knew it was paranoid, but he had a bad a feeling about visiting a public bath.

"I heard one of the Christian merchants talking about a bath that beggars are permitted to visit near the theatre south of the agora."

"You want to bathe in that water?" Lucius said, almost laughing.

"Lucius…look at us. We look like beggars. If we're going to mingle in the agora next, we might do well to clean up a little, no?"

Lucius thought about it and knew his brother was right. He too felt disgusting, and realized what it must have been like for them to enter Carissa and Ashur's home. Finally, he acquiesced. "All right. But we need to take turns watching our things. It doesn't sound like the sort of place where we can leave our valuables with the attendant slaves."

They picked their way through the crowds until they reached the colonnaded cardo maximus, crossed, and entered the neighbourhood near the theatre, just below the steep slopes of Silpius. As they walked, they could see crowds milling about the theatre, and litters and troops moving down the road that led to the palace island where, Lucius presumed from the people he saw, there were games in the circus. Even with war upon their doorstep, the Antiochenes loved their games.

The baths were not difficult to find, for a line of men, women and children, who had all seen better days, ran out of the door of the building as they awaited their turn. They were free to enter as the local governor wanted to ensure that there were no outbreaks of plague in the city. War always brought a risk of sickness - they knew that from the Parthian campaign of Marcus Aurelius and Lucius Verus - and cleanliness was important in keeping the plague at bay.

"You go first," Lucius said. "I'll wait here and see if I can overhear anything." He sat down in a niche at the back of the theatre where he could see the baths from across a small square. "The line is moving, go."

Caecilius turned and walked across the paving slabs to join the queue.

Lucius watched his brother standing there, rubbing his thick beard and looking about at the people in line with him. No one payed him any mind. In fact, they all seemed to be so upended in their misery that they had little sight for the world around them. Men struggled to stay upright because of wounds or injuries incurred in fights for survival in the dead of night, and women struggled to hold their wailing children, for all their weakness and despair. Such days were held once a week at that particular bathhouse, and that made it the highlight of their lives.

That is, until the Christians arrived from the Kerateion to the south.

After Caecilius entered the baths, Lucius watched as a group of Christians dressed in plain, brown homespun tunicae arrived with baskets full of bread which they began to distribute to those standing in line for the baths.

The atmosphere changed immediately from one of downtrodden despair to one of hope and even joy. Children's crying ceased as they were handed chunks of bread from fresh loaves, and men and women smiled at their saviours from hunger, their tears wetting the food as they ate what was, for some of them, the only food they would have that day.

Lucius recognized Peter, the carpenter from the agora on their first day. He was handing out bread from a large basket and when he was finished, his bread supply fully depleted, he stood to speak with some of the people there. At one point, the man turned to see Lucius sitting in the niche of the theatre and waved.

Lucius nodded back, but that was all, for he did not want to draw attention to himself.

After the line moved on and most of the people entered the baths, Peter came over to Lucius.

"Did you find your friend?"

"I did," Lucius said. "Thank you for your directions."

"Antioch is not so large a place as others, but its streets can be confusing, especially in the Kerateion."

Lucius pointed to the line of poor waiting for the baths. "They are fortunate to have your help," he said.

"No. It is we who are fortunate to be able to help them," Peter replied. "There is always help in the world, as well as opportunities to do so."

Lucius did not say anything, but could see Peter glimpsing his weapons.

"Tell me my friend, what are you afraid of?"

"What do you mean?" Lucius answered.

"You carry all of your possessions with you, and you are always armed. I see the way you look around, like a lion who has been ejected from the pride, waiting for an attack that may never come."

"I am no lion," Lucius said. "I but wait for my brother who is in the baths."

"No one will steal your things in there," Peter replied. "They go in with gratitude and filled hearts, having received charity. They will come out rejuvenated and able to face their next trials, which are many." He held out his hands to Lucius. "Let me help you, my friend. When your brother returns, and you have visited the baths yourself, come with us to our small church. Hear what the Lord and his apostles said of charity, and love, and forgiveness. Some of the sacred texts were written right here in a humble house in the Kerateion."

Lucius shook his head. "I have known Christians. I know what you say about love and forgiving one's enemies. That is something I cannot do."

"It might surprise you to know that I too once thought as you do. My family was murdered and I had sworn vengeance. I was filled with hate for all the world."

"I'm sorry," Lucius looked away from the man's bright eyes for a moment to see his brother coming up behind. "Did you forgive the men who did it?" Lucius asked, almost sarcastically, feeling bad even as he had spoken the words.

But Peter only smiled. "No. I found all three of them and killed them with my own hands."

"What happened after that?"

"I felt worse. I felt so empty that I wanted to take my own life." Peter looked up at the sky and his eyes closed, even though he could hear Caecilius come up beside him. "I nearly drowned in my despair and self-loathing. That is, until I heard our Lord's call. One of his followers found me and spoke to me of His word, and I knew that I was hearing it for a reason. I confessed what I had done, and he told me that the Lord would forgive me my actions if I could only help others to heal and feel again." He turned to the people coming out of the baths and pointed. "You see? They are not the same people who went in, are they?"

Caecilius looked back at the people and smiled to himself. "They're certainly cleaner!" he laughed. "Good thing the baths are fed by the aqueduct." He turned to Lucius. "They're actually quite nice inside."

Peter stopped talking and stared at Lucius. "Think on what I have said." Then, he inclined his head to Caecilius and went to go back to the Kerateion with his brothers and sisters.

"Was he giving you trouble?" Caecilius asked.

Lucius shook his head "No. He's just misguided, is all. He doesn't know." He looked up at his brother and realized what was different. "You shaved your beard off?"

Caecilius rubbed his face. "Yes. I was tired of it, and besides, it's hotter here than in Delphi."

Lucius realized that Caecilius now looked more like he remembered him, younger, more innocent. He was his younger brother again, not the mountain hunter who skinned and gutted animals with his eyes closed.

"Your turn," Caecilius said. "There's no talk in there of the emperor though. Just talk of the Christus and of bread. But it is less busy now, so you should have some space."

Lucius handed Caecilius his gladius and pugio, set down his cloak and walked across the square to go in. As he did so, Caecilius leaned against the wall of the theatre and titled his head to listen to the poet speaking within. He recognized lines from the *Metamorphosis* which Alene used to read aloud for them in the peristylium of their home in Rome.

The poet's voice was beautiful in its caedence and intonation but, even so, the words made Caecilius angry for all that they had lost over the years. As he sat there, watching the crowds of people passing by, as he listened to the poet speak of gods and of love, he felt his head begin to pound and his vision shudder and blur with intense pain.

"Not now," he mumbled, rubbing his temples and closing his eyes to the bright light of day.

Inside the baths, Lucius found a quiet corner of the apodyterium in which to undress and leave his clothes. He began to regret his decision to bathe the moment he removed his tunica, for the other bathers and attendant slaves stared at his fire-scarred body. When they spotted the dragon branded upon his chest, they turned away from him immediately. The smiles which they had been given by Peter and his charity all but disappeared.

But Lucius needed to bathe desperately, and so he accepted the clean towel, strigil and phial of oil from one of the slaves who had dared to approach him. The young man stared at Lucius' chest and the image imprinted into his flesh.

"Do you have a problem?" Lucius said, his voice hoarse and gravelly.

"No," the slave shook his head and backed away, but as Lucius turned to go into the tepidarium, the slave looked up again, staring after the man he had just seen, trying to remember who had told him about a dragon. One heard and saw a lot of things in Antioch, and people paid little attention to bath slaves. What one learned in the baths could sometimes be highly profitable. Then, it dawned on him, and he turned to help the next person who came in.

Lucius had to admit that he enjoyed the experience. The hypocausts were nice and hot and the water and steam went to work on his body and mind, helping him to scrape away the weeks of dirt and grime, and even though it pained his damaged skin to feel the hot water, the discomfort was soothed by a splash in the frigidarium. He had run out of the salves for his skin long ago, and so he accepted another phial of oil - also freely given - which he spread over his skin before dressing once more.

Sometime later, Lucius emerged from the baths to find his brother cringing with the pain of his headache along the theatre wall.

"What's wrong? Is it your old injury?"

Caecilius nodded.

"Come. Let's get back to The Golden Bough. You can rest." Lucius began gathering their things.

"No," Caecilius said, taking his satchel back from Lucius. "We didn't come all this way to have me lie in bed because of a headache. Let's get to the forum before all the people go home. I'm tired of Ovid back there." He nodded toward the theatre.

With both of them looking cleaner and more respectable, despite Lucius' injuries, they made their way to the great square of the forum of Antioch which was overlooked by the temple of Artemis and the temple of Jupiter high up on the slopes of Silpius.

As they stepped into the forum square, Lucius felt as if they were not alone, as if the Gods were watching them, waiting for something.

They found a place beside a fountain that spouted fresh water from the mountains, brought into the city via the aqueduct, and stood there pretending to talk. They listened to passersby, some of whom were civil servants in the city administration by the look of their plain togas and the piles of scrolls and wax tablets they carried. Many of these men looked tired after a long day in the law courts and administrative offices of Antioch, hearing complaints from every rank of society from Christian and Jewish beggars to men of senatorial rank who were visiting.

Lucius began to lose hope of learning anything useful. He was about to call it a day when he heard two men approach.

"But the merchants were the worst of all," one man said to his colleague as they set down their wax tablets and splashed their faces in the water of the fountain beside where Lucius and Caecilius stood. "Constant complaints about the war and disruption of trade. So many caravans have gone astray or been raided by the Parthians that there's going to be a riot soon."

"Do they expect you to end the war so trade could go on?" the other man said sarcastically. "They don't understand."

"I know! I told this man that he had to deal with the war the same as the rest of us. Look at all the work it's created for us!"

"Gods! It's a nightmare!" his colleague agreed.

"I told him," the first man turned to the other and mock pointed his finger into his chest, "I told him that if he had a problem with the war and all this friction with the Parthians, that he could petition the emperor directly."

Lucius looked at Caecilius, and then turned quickly to the two men at the fountain.

"Excuse me," Lucius said.

As soon as the men turned to him, they recoiled at the sight of his skin. They only remained because of Lucius' Latin.

"I don't mean to disturb you. I can hear you've had a nightmare of a day."

"What do you want, beggar?"

"I'm no beggar," Lucius said, flashing his gladius beneath his cloak. "I'm a veteran of the Parthica legions. I want to join up again."

"Good luck with that!" the second man said as his eyes raked over Lucius' injuries.

Lucius bit his tongue and pressed on. "I would like to petition the emperor myself for a return to service. Do you know his exact whereabouts?"

"The legions are fighting on many fronts right now," the man said, his voice more full of business now. "If you want to find the emperor, you'll need to search the roads somewhere between Zeugma, Carrhae and Edessa. The last Praetorians who left the city today said they were heading in that direction to meet up with the rest of their force. If the emperor is anywhere, he'll be with them."

"My thanks," Lucius said.

"Now," the man said, "I'd like to stop answering people's questions and get to a tavern and my favourite lupa! Do you mind if I have a life?" he yelled at Lucius and Caecilius.

The two brothers gathered their things and turned to leave without looking back at the red-faced civil servant who bent over to splash more water upon his face.

"We've got what we need," Lucius said to Caecilius as they walked back toward the Kerateion and The Golden Bough.

Lucius found Ashur sitting on the rooftop of The Golden Bough, looking out over the city walls and the river valley to the distant sea and sky. The sun warmed his face where he sat against a squat stone wall with his eyes closed, wrapped in a white cloak.

"I rarely come up here," Ashur said without opening his eyes as Lucius approached.

Lucius sat down beside Ashur and looked at the distant and bright sphere in the blue sky. "Carissa said you were up here."

"Where is Caecilius?"

"One of his headaches has arisen. It's been a long time since the last one, but when they do come, he is in great pain."

"He carries a great burden, just as you do."

Lucius looked askance at Ashur who finally opened his eyes to look back, their grey colouring lit like a small, clear spring bathed in sunlight.

"How can so many years have passed, Lucius?"

"I don't know," Lucius sighed and looked back at the sun. "How can I not have known for so long that we were brothers?"

"I am sorry. Time and truth are indeed precious," Ashur said. "But if I had told you that we shared an immortal as a father when we met, would you have believed me?"

Lucius smiled to himself. "No. But I've seen much since that time, Ashur. I've been to the Otherworld, I have lived, and I have died, and lived again. I've built a world only to see it burned around me, and all for the anger and jealousy of one man."

"Caracalla is set on burning his own world, Lucius, and you happened to be a part of it."

"Careful, Ashur Mehrdad!" Lucius growled. "My family was nearly slaughtered, and hundreds of my friends were murdered because of Caracalla. Do not tell me all this happened because I was in the wrong place!"

"That is not what-" Ashur coughed then, unable to hold back, and the cloth he put to his mouth had blood upon it. "Forgive me, Lucius," he said when he caught his breath. "That is not what I was saying."

"I didn't mean to upset you. I'm sorry." Lucius knelt before him. "Shall I go and get Carissa?"

Ashur shook his head, the sweat upon his brown lost in the wrinkles of his forehead and about his eyes. "There is nothing she can do. It has been getting worse. It always does toward the end."

Lucius was silent and sat back down beside Ashur as they watched the sun descend. He remembered what Carissa had asked of him then. "Ashur?"

"Yes?" he said weakly.

"I must say something to you."

"What?" His voice was barely audible.

"Alene's death was not your fault. I'm so sorry if I accused you of that all those years ago."

"Thank you, Lucius, but…I had my part to play in your beloved sister's death. It is one of my great regrets in this long, tiresome life."

"If that is what you think, then know that I forgive you with all my heart."

Ashur's eyes opened and there Lucius saw a questioning look. "And will you forgive yourself, *Anguis*?"

Lucius stood and walked to the edge of the far wall of the rooftop to look out over the city. He shook his head. "Once I complete my task and my family is safe. Only then will I allow myself peace."

"Do you think our father knew peace after slaying Python?" Ashur said, and Lucius turned to face him. "Do you think anyone who follows a path of vengeance really does know peace in his heart?"

"Perhaps I should follow the Christians you live among?" Lucius snapped. "Shall I turn my cheek and forgive all the horrors that have been visited upon my family and my friends? Shall I wait for the next atrocity and let it happen?" He drew his gladius and held it out. "Peace rests on the point of this! This is what I trust now! And as for my heart, it is dead, Ashur. For I have left everything behind! All I have left is vengeance, and I will see it through." Lucius headed for the small stone staircase that led down to the apartments. "I'll send Carissa up to get you."

When Lucius was gone, Ashur sighed. He knew that Lucius would not be swayed. He had been through too much pain and suffering to forget. He heard footsteps rushing up to him and a moment later, Carissa was at his side, helping him up.

"What's happened? Did you argue with Lucius?" she asked.

"It's to be expected. I tried to dissuade him from his current path."

"You know better than that," she said. "Do you want me to ask them to leave?"

"No. I want Lucius here with me at the end."

"Don't talk like that, my love," she answered, her tears welling again in her eyes. "I am here."

"And you have always been, in my arms and in my heart. I would not have it any other way." They reached the bottom of the stairs, Carissa straining to help Ashur stay up.

"No more talking, my heart. You must rest." Carissa helped Ashur through the kitchen to his bed on the other side of the curtain. Caecilius slept beneath the darkness of a blanket upon the floor, his head pounding, but Lucius was nowhere to be seen. She laid Ashur upon his bed and placed the blankets over him. "I'll get you some food and water. Rest now. He'll be back."

It was not until later that night, after everyone else was asleep, that Lucius returned to the apartment. When he entered, he found food and water waiting for him on the table beside a burning clay lamp.

He checked on Caecilius whose eyes opened thinly to look up at him. "You're back? Where did you go?" Caecilius asked.

"For a walk. I'm fine," Lucius whispered. "Sleep now. Rest your head."

Caecilius disappeared beneath the blankets again and slept while Lucius went to the dividing curtain and poked his head through to see Ashur and Carissa sleeping side-by-side upon the couch.

He felt badly for how things had gone. He knew that Ashur only wished to help him, that he did not understand what Lucius needed to do. He had not seen what Lucius had seen, felt the pain that Lucius had felt. He let the curtain fall back into place and sat at the table to eat the food that Carissa had set out for him. When he was finished, he lay down to sleep.

When he had gone out to walk alone, he had hoped to find out more specific information about Caracalla's whereabouts, but he was only disappointed. The streets were filled with drunken revellers and theatre goers, and the poor of the Kerateion who slept in doorways and beneath walls where they ate the charity presented to them by Peter and his brethren.

It upset Lucius to see people so weak and downtrodden, and unwilling to do anything about it. He would not be a lamb for slaughter, devoured by wolves in the dark of night.

I am a dragon, Lucius thought as he remembered watching the palace walls from across the river, wondering who was within. *I visit vengeance upon others, those who do evil. I will make this world a better place, even if I don't live to see it.* As he closed his eyes to sleep, he wondered what it would be like to die a second time. Would he see anyone he knew? Would he forget all the terrors of his mortal life? Would he be able to feel? He knew, one way or another, that death was inevitable.

Lucius went out early the next morning to seek a medicus for something for the pain in his brother's head, and returned with a pot of Bactrian powder which he was told to mix with water and give in small doses.

He knew he needed to speak with Ashur again, that his time was short. He did not want to leave things as they were.

After a short time, Caecilius sat up on the floor where he had been lying down and felt his temples. "That Bactrian powder worked!" he said quickly, incredulous at how good he felt. "I hope you bought enough."

Lucius came to his side and knelt. "I did. But don't get up too quickly. Take it easy and rest. Tomorrow, you'll be able to go out into the city."

"Did you find out anything new when you were out?"

"Only that the war is not going well for Rome."

Caecilius nodded, a bout of dizziness hitting him. Lucius helped him down again before standing and turning to Carissa.

"I'm sorry for last night," he said to her as he carried dirty dishes from the table to the kitchen bench.

"He forgives you," she said without looking at Lucius. "But I would ask that you don't upset him anymore, Lucius." Suddenly, she could not help but weep, her hands shaking as they scrubbed a plate.

"I'm sorry. I did do as you asked and forgave him. I told him my sister's death was not his fault."

"And yet he does not feel peace, no matter how hard I try. He relies on you for that, Lucius." She looked at Caecilius sleeping upon the floor and lowered her voice. "I know who you are, who you both are and I won't say that it doesn't frighten me somewhat. But I also know that you need to listen to what he has to say before it is too late."

"Too late?"

"You think I don't see all the blood he coughs up? How he grows weaker and weaker by the day? You've seen it over two days. I've been witness to the deterioration of that great man - my *love*! - for years now. I was not so selfish as to leave his side for my own interests."

"What do you mean, Carissa?"

She wiped her cheek and shook her head. "Just go to him and listen. It is what he wants right now. He is awake."

Lucius could see that she did not want to be around him anymore, that his very presence upset her, and so he backed away quietly and went to peer through the curtain to see Ashur sitting up and looking out the window at the falling sun again. He cleared his throat and approached.

"I'm sorry for yesterday, Ashur. I...I don't know what to say. I didn't want to upset you or make you ill."

"I am ill for other reasons, Lucius. Not because of you. Please," he coughed, "sit beside me."

Lucius took the chair and sat to face his friend.

"I have realized how important Truth is, Lucius. Having lived in the shadows with secrets, it has come to be as important to me as Love. That is why I need you to understand something..."

"What is it?"

Ashur blinked very slowly, as if gathering his thoughts and energy for what he wanted to say. "When you were in Delphi...in the temple... did you see the maxims carved upon the pronaos and interior of the temple?"

"Yes."

"There is wisdom in all of them, but the primary maxim...the one that most men focus on, but which befuddles them most, is-"

"'Know thyself'," Lucius finished.

Ashur paused to catch his breath and nodded. "Yes. Such simple words, and yet so great in their purpose, so insurmountable. After so long a life as mine, it is only near the end that I could say that I truly do know myself."

"Ashur, maybe we should have this philosophical discussion another time." Lucius made to get up from the chair, but Ashur grabbed his wrist with surprising strength and shook his head.

"No! Please. Sit down. Listen... To *truly* know oneself is to be able to meet every trial upon the road of this life. It is to know your true purpose, to be with the people who truly enrich your being and whose lives you enrich. It is true honour, true happiness to know oneself. Philotimo is truly possible when you know yourself intimately, for your purposes in everything you do are clear."

"I know my purpose, Ashur." Lucius was angry now, for Ashur's words had led him to the still pool where he could see himself, that pool he did not wish to gaze into. "When I leave here, I'm going on the hunt. One way or another, I'm going to find Caracalla and let him know that his actions have all led to his death. And I will be the one to take his life. I will stare into his eyes as I do so, just as he and his men took the lives of my friends and family, and as they burned my entire world."

"And yet, Lucius, my friend, you are the one who still carries that destructive flame…"

Lucius sat up, exasperated, but he found he could not leave Ashur's side then, for the streams of tears that ran down his cheeks were real, as was the love and pity in his eyes. "Why are you doing this?"

"Because…we *are* brothers, Lucius Metellus Anguis. And you need help."

"The world needs help, Ashur. And I'll will give it - I will make this world a better place - by doing what I intend to do."

"By dying?"

"If need be." Lucius sighed deeply. It was a sound of long-held pain and grief. "I am tired of uncertainty, Ashur. So tired…"

"Life is a crucible, Lucius. It either breaks us, or makes us stronger." He grasped Lucius' tunic sleeve and pulled him closer so that he could hear. "It doesn't matter if there is uncertainty. It is always there, and we have to live with it as part of our lives! We need to remember that, in the end, it is Love and Light and Truth that win. Not anger and hatred." He now took hold of Lucius' head with both his hands and gently kissed his brother's forehead. "Don't get stuck in the fight. Open your heart to love and compassion, Lucius, for those are what will defeat the demons you face." Ashur's eyes met Lucius more intensely then. "Lucius…" Ashur cried out in pain and coughed again, his blood spattering the blanket and Lucius' arm.

"Ashur, rest now," Lucius reached for a cloth and covered Ashur's mouth. Then he gave him a cup of water.

Ashur shook his head and pushed the cup away. "Lucius… Only by letting go can you be truly free."

"That's enough!" Carissa said from behind Lucius where she had emerged with a steaming cup of broth. "Ashur, please! You need to rest!"

Ashur released his grasp on Lucius and fell back upon his pillows, exhausted and coughing. "Gods and mortals... We're all leaves in the wind..."

Carissa pulled Lucius up off the chair and Lucius backed away to allow her the room to care for Ashur.

In watching, Lucius remembered how Adara, Phoebus and Calliope had cared for him in Ynis Wytrin, how Etain and the other priestesses had tended him out of care and gratitude.

He suddenly felt very alone. The bitterness of hatred and anger, the memory of pain had a choke hold upon his psyche that he could not break away from. Nostalgia could be a poison, and as Lucius thought back to the warmth and laughter of their hall upon the hillfort, his wife's swollen belly full of life, their family and friends and the fires that consumed it all, he drank of that poison fully, sating his anger and hatred.

Lucius was no longer able to look at Ashur, so weak upon the couch, being tended by the woman who loved him more than anything. He turned away to go into the other part of the apartment where Caecilius slept fitfully beneath a blanket, having suffered from an injury inflicted upon him by another wicked man.

I know myself. I am a dragon, Lucius thought. *It is my duty to rid the world of wicked men!*

He took his cloak and a pouch of coin, and headed down to the tavern below to be alone with his thoughts and a cup of wine.

It was early morning when Lucius emerged from The Golden Bough tavern into the street outside. He breathed deeply of the cool morning air and looked up at the sky where the stars still twinkled in the firmament. The sound of someone walking down the street startled him, and he drew his gladius quickly, turning around to face nothing.

The tavern sign swayed gently in the breeze upon its iron hinges as he looked up at it. The image of the golden tree flickered in the firelight of the torches outside the door.

Lucius watched it for a few moments, mesmerized by the gentle swaying, but then he stumbled and rushed to the side of the road to vomit. His throat burned when he had finished, and he craved a cool cup of water. The trickle of one of the roadside fountains caught his ear and, sheathing his gladius, he walked the few feet until he reached it, plunging his hands in and cupping water to his face.

"That's better," he groaned, but made a fist which he pounded into the fountain. "Ashur!" He felt guilty for the way he had treated his long-time friend - *my brother!* - for he was dying, and Lucius had met him with anger. "I never thought to see him again," he mumbled and turned to walk back to The Golden Bough to make his way up to the apartment.

The stair creaked loudly as he went, and he hoped it would not wake Caecilius, for he needed his rest to get better again before they set out.

When Lucius opened the door, Caecilius was sitting alone at the table, a worried look upon his face that was lit up by the flame of the lamp.

"I'm sorry I woke you," Lucius whispered, but there was something in his brother's eyes that stopped him short. "What?"

"Lucius, where were you?"

"Drinking downstairs. Why?" Lucius turned to hang his cloak up on the peg.

Caecilius stood and walked over to him. "It's Ashur…"

Lucius looked to the curtain and stepped quickly through to the other side.

Carissa was bent over Ashur where he lay upon the couch, and her weeping was one not of mere worry, but of deep deep sorrow, the sort of keening that heralded an end.

"Carissa?" Lucius said, his voice shaking.

She turned, and her once bright eyes were red with grief.

"He's gone," she said. The words were so short, so simple, and yet they had the power to crack the cosmos.

"No," Lucius said, his fists balled. "No! Ashur, wake up!" He rushed around the other side of the bed and fell to his knees.

Ashur's body was absolutely still, his eyes closed.

"Did he say anything?" Lucius asked through the tears that fell from his stinging eyes.

Carissa looked across the body of her true love, at the man who had burst into their home and lives at the end of Ashur's days. She did not want to share with Lucius the last words that Ashur had spoken to her, for they were for her alone, of love and happiness and a life without any regrets. Those words would be her comfort in the dark nights of the rest of her life. *Those are not for Lucius Metellus Anguis.*

She looked across Ashur's folded hands and still body, straight into Lucius' eyes .

"He said that he loves you as a brother, and that he will always believe in you."

The cries of loss that rang out would have shaken the walls of Antioch, but to Lucius then, they became part of the chorus of grief that followed him through the world.

XIX

DOLORIS TEMPESTAS

'A Storm of Grief'

A .D. 217

It would have been easy to blame the Gods for Ashur's death, just as they were reunited, for the cruel irony of it all felt like a dagger buried deep in Lucius' chest, blocking air and blood and feeling from moving freely. He would have blamed Apollo, their father, and the rest of the Gods, for abandoning Ashur Mehrdad to old age and death. To do so would have been easier.

But death was never easy, Lucius knew. And he could not blame the Gods for the sense of loss he felt, for the tears that poured from Carissa's heart.

Ashur's words had struck Lucius hard, and he rebelled against the pain they caused him. Perhaps more upsetting to Lucius was how calm and accepting Ashur had been with his impending death and all that the Gods had done to him.

He would have buried himself in his anger then but for the thought of Carissa, whom Ashur loved more than anything or anyone. She now sat alone, preparing the body of the man she had loved, facing a life of solitude she had not been prepared for. Or had she?

When Lucius entered the room where Carissa had just finished dressing Ashur in his desert robes, he found her sitting calmly, staring at him. "I can't believe he is gone," she said without turning to look at Lucius.

"I'm so sorry, Carissa."

"He knew his end was near. I just wasn't ready to accept it. We had so little time together." She bent over, her face in her hands as she met another wave of grief.

Lucius stood by her side, silent as he too looked upon Ashur's peaceful face.

After a few moments, Carissa raised her head and leaned forward to touch Ashur's body. "Our Christian neighbours would have him buried in their necropolis outside the city walls. They liked Ashur, and he respected their ways...but that is not what he wanted."

"What did he want?" Lucius asked.

"To be burned and then have his ashes left to the wind upon the slopes of Silpius. He said... He said that that way, he could follow me wherever I went in the world."

And Carissa actually smiled at the thought, and Lucius knew that there was comfort in the certainty that she had been truly loved, and that love would follow her always.

"How can I help?" Lucius asked.

She turned at last to look up at him. "If you can hire a cart to take him to the ustrinum, I would be grateful. I don't have the will for it now. He did not care to wait for the full nine days. He wanted it done immediately."

Lucius nodded and knelt before her. "Of course." He took her hands and she fell against him, her shuddering sobs wrenching his heart. "I'll take care of it."

"What will Carissa do now?" Caecilius asked as he and Lucius drove the mule cart back to The Golden Bough the next morning.

"I don't know," Lucius said. "They lived for each other. Now she's alone."

"Lucius... Maybe we should look after her?"

"We can't bring her with us."

"That's not what I mean. I heard what Ashur said to you before the end. Maybe he was right? Maybe we should let go and live our lives. We could travel back with Carissa."

Lucius yanked on the mule's reins and the animal baulked. "I came here to finish things," he growled at his younger brother. "If you don't have the stomach for it anymore, you can accompany her."

Caecilius hesitated. He had not seen Lucius like that before, and wondered if he never really knew him the way he thought he did. He knew that war and loss could change a man - that was not difficult to decipher - but he had lost too. *Could I abandon Lucius now?* he asked himself. "It was just a thought," he said to Lucius. "I'm with you. Of course I am."

"Good," Lucius snapped, but then his face softened a little. "I'm sorry. I just can't fall down that well of grief. It saps my strength for the fight to come."

I don't think his fight has ever stopped, Caecilius thought, but he did not dare say it aloud.

Lucius and Caecilius stood to either side of Carissa in the ustrinum of Antioch, just outside the city walls to the southeast, below the rocky crags of Mount Silpius. It would have been a beautiful, warm afternoon with the sun shining brightly in a sky of purest blue. But the purpose for their being there cast a long shadow.

Lucius looked up at the sun as Ashur's body was laid upon the pyre of cedar logs and the oil was spread. He could feel Carissa shaking beside him, staring silently through her tears. From beneath the black cowl of his cloak, Lucius too stared in silent disbelief at what was before him. He and Ashur had only just been reunited, and yet the meeting had been so brief, he had barely had time to come to terms with all that was said.

Apollo...if you can hear me... Grant my brother...your son...peace in the Afterlife. He may have left you, but he was loyal to the end...to us... to love.

As he watched Carissa lay a large bunch of lilies upon Ashur's chest, Lucius felt the wind pick up and swirl about them, as if the Gods had answered and come to gather up Ashur's spirit to take him away before the flames took his remains.

Lucius blinked as, for a moment, he thought he could spy Ashur rise up from his body to hug Carissa one more time before going with the tall form of a god.

The shade paused to look back at Lucius, turned and left, leaving only dry leaves and dust skittering in its wake and about the pyre.

When Carissa had said her farewells, Lucius stepped forward to take the torch from the ustrinum slave who had been waiting nearby.

"Farewell, my friend," Lucius said softly to the white-robed figure of Ashur. "I'm sorry we didn't have more time."

As the tears began to burn his eyes, and as Carissa's weeping reached a crescendo, Lucius lit the pyre and the flames jumped to life to carry out their sad duty beneath that blue sky now streaked with smoke.

It took a few hours for the body to be consumed by the fire. During that time, Carissa, Lucius and Caecilius had stood by, silently watching the surreal transfiguration of Ashur Mehrdad from a man to a pile of ash.

Neither Lucius nor Caecilius bothered Carissa during that time, for she had stood a few paces closer to the pyre, watching intently as her love was consumed.

Apollo… Please care for him at long last, Carissa had prayed. *If you do, I shall create works of beauty the rest of my days… Ashur, my love… wait for me…*

By the end, her face was blackened with smoke and streaked with the silent tears she had wept as she watched, holding only the urn in which she would place all that was left of Ashur. She held it up and turned it around to look upon it.

It was the last vase she had painted for the merchant, a work she decided to keep. Upon the surface, pressed between meanders, was an image of the warrior Ajax carrying the dead body of the hero Achilles from the battlefield. It was one of the more popular scenes she had been asked to reproduce in Antioch during their time there, but that particular specimen was different, for in the face of Achilles, Carissa had unwittingly painted Ashur's still expression.

You were my own hero, Ashur, she thought as she later stepped toward the warm pile of dust and ash. *I am no Ajax, but I will carry you with me wherever I go.*

And with that, she knelt down, refusing the slave's help, and began to fill the urn with the ashes.

Lucius watched her undertake the task in stoic silence and, though he would have helped her to place his friend's remains in the urn, he knew that she wanted to do it alone, that she wished to say farewell to Ashur as they had lived - alone.

When it was done, Carissa stood up stiffly and looked up at the slopes of Silpius. "Will you come with me?" she said without turning.

Lucius stepped closer with Caecilius following. "Of course," he said, placing his hand upon her shoulder. "We're with you."

She turned then, and the sight of her face tore at Lucius' heart. *Is this what I have done to Adara?* he wondered, his hand shaking.

"Come," Carissa said. "There is a path not far from here that will lead us to a lookout. It is there that he wanted to be released."

The sun was already making its descent. They began the trek along the goat path that led up from the city walls, through the trees and over rock and scrub, until it grew steeper and they began to stumble on loose pebbles along the way.

Carissa clung to the urn as she went, keeping it from harm as she followed the path that Ashur had taken her up a few times before to watch the sunset and listen for any whisper the Gods might offer.

The Gods had been silent whenever they had gone, but now, at the end, it was Ashur who was silent, and Carissa who had been left alone to forgive the Gods for what they had done to her love.

At last, the path levelled out and led to a flat promontory that jut out over the canyon and city of Antioch below. It was about a quarter of the way up the mountainside, and when they arrived, they stopped to look out.

Carissa pictured her path now, unable to see the end of the road ahead. She could feel the tears coming again, the shuddering pain in her stomach where an invisible grief twisted and turned. She had considered ending her life, but knew that Ashur would not have wanted that for her.

I will live for the both of us now, my love, she said, looking down at the urn in her hands and the face of the hero she had painted, known and loved.

Carissa bent down to place the urn upon the rocky ground, and then stood with her arms open to the setting sun which lit their faces like the flames of the pyre itself.

"Oh goddess Venus... Thank you for blessing us and giving us a glimpse of paradise. May he remember my love in the Afterlife until I join him." She knelt then, unwilling to be so far from the urn. "Apollo, Lord of Light and Prophecy, and of Art... Ashur forgave you in the end, for your silence and disregard, and I forgive you now. I ask you, oh Far-Shooter, to guide your son to those lands where the dead are at peace, free of pain and earthly troubles. Give him peace at last..."

Carissa stopped to wipe her eyes which were filled with the sun's radiant western fire. Then, she turned to Lucius.

Lucius stepped forward, unsure of what to say, for after so long apart, with little thought for the trials of his friend and brother, he felt like an intruder.

Carissa, however, stepped aside for him to approach the urn.

"Farewell, my brother," he whispered so that Caecilius could not hear him from where he stood several paces behind them. "Forgive me for not being there for you. I will always be grateful that our father crossed our paths in the desert all those years ago..." Lucius looked up and stared straight into the sun. "Father..." he said, and in that moment, he thought he saw Apollo's visage in the sky above. "Guide your son to safety, across the river and down the dark road to peace and plenty. Give him peace at last."

There was no answer on the wind or in the light that filled Lucius' eyes as he stared out over the world, across the land to the sea beyond. He turned back to Carissa and she approached to pick up the urn.

"Farewell, my love," she said through her grief as she tipped the urn and allowed the ashes to fall out like sand from a glass.

Ashur Mehrdad's remains fell out of the urn to be picked up by the wind and pulled out over the cliff's edge as if the Gods themselves had taken the end of a thread and pulled it until it had run its course and length.

The three of them watched the sun for a time, each left with their thoughts of the departed, and then slowly picked their way down the path to the city as the sun gave way to darkness.

That evening, in the apartment above The Golden Bough, over a simple meal of boiled beans and bread, Carissa, Lucius and Caecilius tipped wine out to Ashur and the Gods with whom he now travelled. They ate in silence, and when the meal neared its end, Lucius cleared his throat and spoke.

"What will you do now?" he asked Carissa. "Will you stay here?"

She shook her head. "No. There is nothing left for me here." She looked up from her bowl at Lucius and Caecilius. "Do you think... Would... Would Emrys mind if I joined him in Delphi?"

Caecilius smiled warmly at her, for many times, Emrys had spoken of Carissa as if she were his own, long-lost daughter. He imagined the joy, he would feel and answered her without hesitation. "I think it's what he wishes for most," Caecilius told her. "There was never a day when you did not cross his mind. He misses you, Carissa."

She nodded and smiled, though tears formed in her eyes once more. "I will go to him, if he is still there." She wiped her eyes and looked at Lucius. "Do you think he is still there, in Delphi?"

Lucius sighed. "I don't know. His heart has been broken for so long, and more so since our mother died. Grief can do strange things to a man. He also spoke of returning to Dumnonia."

At the mention of her homeland, Carissa seemed wistful. She had not been back in many years. Nor had Emrys. *Will we finally meet again, where our journey began?* she wondered. Then, she decided. "I will find him. He is the only family I have left."

"He'll be so happy," Caecilius said. "But what about all your things here?"

"They are of another life. I don't need them," Carissa said. "The Christians here have been good and charitable to us. I will return the favour. They have more need of these possessions than I do."

As Lucius listened to her, he was amazed at the depths of strength Carissa was able to plumb. She had sacrificed much for her love of Ashur, as he had. And even though the Gods had turned on him, she had remained at his side. She surprised Lucius when she reached out to clasp his hand and look him in the eye.

"Lucius. Come back to Dumnonia with me."

He wanted to pull his hand away, but found he could not. It was as if both Carissa and Ashur spoke to him as one.

"I can't, Carissa. We can't."

She released his hand and sat back. "Ashur told me what you are setting out to do. Please, Lucius. It is madness. Think of your wife and children...your family. You have something few are blessed with. Do not throw it away in anger."

"I do this for them," Lucius answered, trying to dull the sharp edge in his voice. "I don't expect you to understand. For so long, we have been hunted and tormented. Everything was taken from us."

"Not everything," she countered.

"That is why I have to end it now. Before there is nothing...or no one...left."

Carissa looked to Caecilius, hoping for a different answer, but he seemed just as set, willing to follow Lucius into the darkness he was so set on. "Caecilius?"

"I go where Lucius goes. They burned my home too. They ordered the slaying of my family, and desecrated my mother's funeral rites." He began to weep again at the thought, and he was as a little boy again, sitting at the table, contemplating the pain of all that had happened. "We're going to see this through," he said, looking across the table and nodding to Lucius.

Carissa had no words. She was finished with them. Words would not dissuade Lucius and Caecilius from the death they sought, nor would they bring Ashur back. "Then we will part ways tomorrow," she said. "May the Gods guide you on the road ahead."

"May they guide us all," Lucius added.

It was early morning, and the travellers were, all three of them, awake and ready to set out. In truth, none had slept very well at all, Lucius and Caecilius for the continuance of their journey, and Carissa for the lack of Ashur beside her.

Carissa knew that if she closed her eyes to sleep, she would descend into dreams of love and loss that would tear out her heart. *I need my strength for the journey.* However, she could feel Ashur with her already, at her side, and hoped that the long days ahead would not be so lonely. The worries that also kept her awake in the dark of night were for Lucius and his brother.

What Lucius wished to do terrified her. Was there not enough death in the world without adding to the toll needlessly? The death of peasants and soldiers was one thing, affecting the lives of those who knew them, but the death of a ruler could have far-reaching repercussions like a great boulder dropped by the Gods into the smallest of ponds. She would have stayed Lucius and Caecilius' hands, but the look in their eyes told her they would not be swayed. They had already made their decision, and loss was a terrible captain of emotion and deed.

Carissa now stood in the middle of the street before The Golden Bough, all of her possessions in the satchel over her shoulder. She carried some coin that she and Ashur had saved, her best paint brushes, some food and clothing, and a small dagger that had belonged to Ashur -

they had sold his sword long ago. She had also packed the urn that had briefly held her true love's remains, and which she would offer to Apollo upon her safe arrival in Delphi.

Her Christian neighbours wept to see her go, and offered to take her in, to help her. But Carissa kindly refused, instead giving them most of hers and Ashur's remaining possessions to distribute to those in need. They thanked her and blessed her in their way and left her to say her farewells to the two Romans in their midst as they waited in front of the tavern.

Carissa turned to Lucius and Caecilius. "Come with me," she said again, reaching out to touch Lucius' shoulder, but even as she did so one last time, she could not glimpse the kind and honourable man beneath the bitter, hate-filled man of vengeance.

"I won't," Lucius said calmly, the cracked skin around his eyes and neck seemingly worse. "But please travel safely, Carissa. The road to the sea is treacherous."

"I will. There is a caravan leaving soon for the port. I will join it at the Daphne gate."

"Good. Whenever you arrive in a port, ask after a ship called the Europa. It is captained by a man named Creticus. He will take you where you need to go, Delphi or Britannia. Tell him that you're a friend of Lucius Pen Dragon."

"Pen Dragon," she repeated.

"Lucius Metellus Anguis is no more."

I know, she thought. "I will remember." They stared at each other for a few moments, unable to further express any emotion or sentiment. The end of their time together had come, and Ashur was gone. Carissa stepped in and hugged Lucius tightly. "Take care, Lucius Pen Dragon."

Lucius held back the tears that threatened to unravel him, but he could not help but ask one last thing of her. "If you...if you see Adara and my children..."

"Yes?" she asked.

"Tell them I will love them forever."

Carissa looked down and nodded. "I will." She then turned to Caecilius and hugged him as well, for standing there, he appeared uncertain of everything, the same as the little boy she had met long ago in a domus in Rome. Now, that boy was armed and ready to kill, even though his eyes were not the eyes of a killer. "May the Gods protect you both, Caecilius."

"And you, lady. Thank you for allowing us to stay with you."

Carissa smiled sadly and looked up at the window where Ashur used to look for her coming down the street, or watch the great chariot set in the West. "Farewell," she said suddenly, and began to walk down the street without looking at them again.

Lucius and Caecilius watched her disappear into the growing crowd and through the arches of the aqueduct above until she was gone. Then, the two brothers turned away from The Golden Bough and cut into the crowd toward the eastern gate. It was time to leave Antioch.

The sky was now spread out before Lucius and Caecilius. Beneath a cover of grey cloud pierced occasionally with pale blue, the brothers had set out from Antioch upon the backs of their mules to follow the road ahead toward Zeugma on the Euphrates.

With a little coin back at the stables, they had been able to press the stable master for information, though they could not be certain of its validity. Still, what he said seemed likely, and they could find out more farther down the road. What Lucius did know was that Nisibis was the base of operations for the Parthian campaign, and the emperor would most certainly be headed there at some point. The settlements of Zeugma, Edessa, and fateful Carrhae, still haunted by the shades of Rome's soldiers, were along the road.

"You sure we can trust that stable master?" Caecilius said after they were a couple of miles out of the city.

"We'll see. We just have to wait," Lucius said as he reined in his mule and turned off of the road so that they rode up a slight rise to where a few rows of thin olive trees grew.

"What are we waiting for?" Caecilius pressed Lucius as they dismounted. He watched Lucius settle upon the ground in a position so that he could see the road. Caecilius roughly tied up his own mule and sat down in the dust, adjusting his sword and daggers. "Are you going to tell me? We're wasting time!"

But Lucius did not feel like speaking, for more than ever he felt that the destiny he sought was awaiting his grasp, that the hunt was on.

"Trust me, Brother," Lucius finally said. "We won't wait long, but if the stable master was right, it'll be worth it. Now, hide your weapons and look like you're taking a nap."

"I don't want to nap!" he snapped.

They waited there in the slight shade of those young olives for close to an hour, Lucius watching the road from Antioch keenly from beneath the cowl of his cloak.

Caecilius actually did doze a little before being startled awake by a deep thrumming in the ground. "What is that?" he said, looking around wildly.

"Shh! Stay down!" Lucius hissed. "There they are." He pointed down the road to where a big dust cloud was rising up in the direction of Antioch, and it was getting closer.

"Who is it?" Caecilius asked, but this time Lucius only watched, his eyes trying to thread their way through the dust. "Sounds like about thirty horses."

"Yes. It's them," Lucius said. "He didn't lie!"

"Just answer me who?"

"Speculatores Augusti."

"What's that?"

"Praetorian cavalrymen."

"Praetorians! Are you mad? If they find you, we're surely dead!"

"They won't find us," Lucius said, his voice almost a whisper as he watched the brawny cavalrymen canter along the road, their leather harness and pteruges slapping in the breeze, their shields and spears cutting through the dust. "We're going to follow them. Quickly, get down!"

Down by the side of the road, the centurion of the group reined in his horse to watch his men ride past, his vexillarius beside him holding up the Praetorian banner with a scorpion upon it. The centurion seemed older, but he was a big man, and strong, the sort men would listen to without question, especially with the thick, polished vinerod he clutched in his strong hands. Then, he turned to look up at them.

Caecilius pretended to be sleeping again while Lucius bowed over his lap, covered in his black cloak, his weapons invisible to the centurion.

For a few moments, the centurion peered at them, even turning his horse the better to see, but as he did so, his file of troops passed, and so he turned and rode off, followed by his vexillarius.

Caecilius could feel his heart pounding in his chest and, truthfully, so could Lucius. They had been too close to the road, and if they had been found, it could all have been over. If lowly construction workers in Delphi had been aware of the bounty upon his head, so too would be the men of the Praetorian guard.

When they were gone, both Lucius and Caecilius raised their heads and breathed.

"Are you sure this is the way you want to go, what you want to do, Lucius?"

"Absolutely," he answered as he stood and brushed the dust from his clothes. "Those Praetorians will lead us straight to the emperor. We'll track them from a distance."

"I've tracked a stag for two weeks before I was able to take it down," Caecilius said. "But I never had to take one down that was protected by a thousand others. This is madness, Brother! And I don't mean are you sure you want to follow those troops. I mean, are you sure about this hunt? Maybe Carissa was right? Maybe we should just go home?"

Lucius turned on him. "What home? They're all gone! If you want to leave…if you don't have the stomach for this hunt, then I give you permission to go, Caecilius. For myself, I'm going to follow those troops and end this once and for all!"

Caecilius was silent. He could not see the brother he had grown up with and admired. He had always hoped for a kind word from Lucius in his youth, but Lucius had rarely been there, and when he was, he had been too far distant in his thoughts to pay him much attention. He could not see him in that moment, behind the angry eyes and burned visage, but he knew he was there, and that he needed his help. "I'm with you, Lucius. Don't you dare question me! I've lost too. If you think we can do this, then I trust you."

"Good." Lucius pat Caecilius roughly on the shoulder sending dust into the air. "Now, let's get moving before they pull too far ahead of us. We'll follow the dust cloud."

They mounted their mules and kneed them back down to the road where they set off at a trot after the Praetorians. The hunt was on.

It was the strangest hunt either of them had ever been on.

For days, they tracked the Praetorians, following at a distance and camping beneath a canopy of fiery stars in the night sky. The road passed between mountains and along rocky riverbeds that flowed swiftly with spring runoff. There was little sign of the war which was, according to members of one caravan, raging south of Nisibis around Hatra and Dura Europos.

The lands between the Tigris and Euphrates were torn by war between Rome and Parthia once again, and as they travelled, Lucius thought of the waste of the war already waged successfully by Severus. Back then, he had fought his way through the crucible of battle several times over.

Now, however, Lucius had no interest in the war or the dead and dying men who, just like him, had joined the legions with a false sense of loyalty to an emperor and empire that cared little for them, who would turn on them if it suited. Lucius saw only his quarry now, the feeling of sated vengeance that he dreamed about nightly as he slept beside their campfire in the desert, his half-brother beside him.

In the dark nights beneath rockfaces and at the mouths of desert caves, the world morphed and shrugged in strange ways, like a great beast moving in its sleep. On the third night, a plunging star seemed to slowly tear a hole in the firmament, its long tail leaving a trace that made wild dogs howl, and sleeping birds fall dead out of the trees of nearby groves.

One morning, between sleep and awake, as Lucius lay beside the cold remains of their night fire, he opened his eyes to see a three-headed dog staring at them while they slept. He drew his sword quickly, the sound rousing Caecilius with a start, but the strange beast was gone as quickly as it had appeared.

He did not say so to his brother, but Lucius felt a lingering cold that day at the sight of that beast.

He also felt a chill upon his chest, for the dragon brand that he carried with him constantly, that normally burned him day and night, had grown icy cold. His heart raced when he thought of it, and he struggled to fight the rising fear. A part of him felt that he was slipping away, that his reality was shifting, but he forced himself to remember that fear did such things to a man before battle.

And this was a battle he had never fought before.

On their sixth day upon the road, with the Praetorians still in their sights, Lucius and Caecilius camped upon a small, rocky rise in the land which gave them a good vantage point of the troops' campfires. They settled in for another long night, their weapons by their sides.

"Do you ever think about our father?" Caecilius asked that night as he chewed the last of the dried goat meat that they had purchased in Antioch.

Lucius looked up at him. *Your father,* he thought, but did not say so. There was no need to disillusion Caecilius further. Then, he remembered seeing Quintus Metellus' hateful face in Annwn, and knew that, yes, he did think of him. "From time to time, yes. I do," he answered. "Do you?"

"All the time. I feel cheated by the Gods whenever I think of him. I actually used to look up to the man." Caecilius stared into the fire. "I've always been such a fool." He shook his head.

"You're anything but that." Lucius leaned forward. "You're one of the bravest men I've known. With all you went through as a child...how you stood up to defend our mother... And now you're here with me."

"I miss mother, Lucius. We didn't have enough time with her, especially you. I always felt like there was more she wanted to tell me. But it wasn't meant to be. Maybe Diodorus' teachings have helped you to see this world more clearly, the reasons for everything that has happened. But for me, this life feels like a great betrayal. I remember praying for help from the Gods of our ancestors in the mountain tomb back in Etruria, even though I was terrified. They didn't hear me. I always longed for a different life, Lucius. A new life! Is this all there is? Surviving day to day...losing loved ones...watching the wicked people of the world win out? A part of me thinks that maybe the Christians do have it right. If they forgive all the horrors they've experienced because of others, then they can live a bit more easily. I wonder how Christians sleep at night? Better, I suppose."

Lucius sighed as he looked to his brother seated beside him in the dirt. "I don't know much about the Christians, but it seems to me they would have just as much trouble sleeping in this world as the rest of us. They're mortal too, and that alone is a burden."

"Do you think the Gods carry a weight as well?"

"Absolutely," Lucius said, and his thoughts immediately went to his father and his battle with Python, the worry he knew Apollo had for him throughout his life, though Lucius had often ignored it. "We always wonder about the lives of others. We imagine that those lives are probably better than the ones we lead. What Diodorus told me was that it is up to us to better the lives the Gods have given us, not long for what is not destined to be ours."

"Easy to say that," Caecilius said. "When I was little, hiding from father's rage, or even now when my head is exploding with pain, I'm wishing very much for another life, just to make it all stop." He tossed a dried stick into the flames. "But I don't want to turn into our father. He was so jealous of you, so angry with the world around him. He hated everyone for being happy or successful or liked."

"You could never be him, Caecilius. Remember that. You're everything he was not. I'm sorry for not being there for you."

"It made me strong." He looked at Lucius wistfully. "You know, I don't have any memories of us playing as children? Isn't that strange? Brothers who never played."

"I was older, I suppose."

"Yes, but I used to pretend to play soldier with you, even when you weren't home," he smiled.

"You did?"

"When father was at the senate, I would take one of the wooden rudii and play in the atrium or garden, pretending that we were standing side-by-side in the shield wall. I had a pretty good thrust!"

They both laughed at that, but the image did wring Lucius' heart and make him think of all the other emotions those around him experienced when he was busy living his own life. *I'm sorry Adara...but I have to do this...*

"You all right?" Caecilius asked, seeing the look in his brother's eyes.

"Yes. It *is* easy to get caught up in what could be. When this is all done, Caecilius, you can come with us. Perhaps Britannia will agree with you?"

"I wouldn't want to leave Clarinda alone. She needs me."

Lucius was silent and knew, at that point, that he just wanted to finish his mission and get back to the people who mattered most to him. *And if I don't get back, at least they'll be safe.*

"We should get some sleep," Caecilius said. "You take first watch."

Lucius nodded. "All right." He tossed another stick into the fire and sparks rose up into the darkness. He looked at his brother lying there, and marvelled at the man he had become, even without all of the opportunities Lucius himself had been given. "I don't know if I've ever said it to you, Brother, but I love you very much."

Caecilius looked up at Lucius from where he lay on the ground and, though he smiled, his eyes glistened in the firelight. "I love you too."

Lucius watched Caecilius fall asleep, perhaps more soundly than he had seen since they were reunited. Then, sitting alone, his gladius across his lap, Lucius watched the fires of the Praetorian camp in the distance and wondered where they would lead them, and how soon he could get to Caracalla and finish things, so that he and his brother could return home, wherever that might be.

The night was dark and deep in that land of battles, that place where the Gods either watched with keen interest, or turned their backs without a care for what happened on the dancing floor of war. Empires would always rise and fall, men would fight and kill and be killed, and blood spilled would be swallowed by sand and river to be forgotten, while the sky and stars passed and ignited overhead. It was the way of things. It always would be.

But in the dark of that night, not all the Gods turned their backs. Nor did they interfere, for that would have been against the laws of the universe. Sometimes, all a god could do was be, and watch as their children experienced pain and torment of their choosing.

That night, Apollo watched as the beasts of night circled, and he could do nothing...

It was a loud howling in the darkness beyond their fire that woke Lucius from his unintentional slumber. He had but one moment to open his eyes and see the black beasts closing in on him, one fleeting second to see his brother's eyes open quickly. Then, pain crushed his skull and all went black, as if the Gods had blown out their fire like a lamp.

No!

It was still dark when Lucius opened his eyes and felt the cold steel of a blade against his neck, blood trickling from where it had cut him. *Caecilius!*

He looked across the fire to where two men held his brother by ropes around his neck. "Let him go!" Lucius shouted, but he was met only with laughter.

They were surrounded by several men in brown cloaks whose faces were obscured by their hoods, each of them armed, each of them crouched and ready to kill.

One of the men stepped forward into the firelight. He had a bad limp in his leg, and he looked up at the distant crescent of a moon and howled loudly.

The other men around him howled too in a grisly, blood-curdling chorus.

The man then looked down at Lucius and pushed back his hood to reveal his shaved head with the tattoo of a dog on the side of his skull. "Seems that jackals can eat dragons after all...Lucius Metellus Anguis!"

Caecilius' eyes went wide as he looked across at Lucius.

Lucius was stunned, and he felt the fear running up and down his body, willing him to freeze. He fought it in that moment, but the sight of his brother held captive made him hesitate.

"Do you remember us, Dragon?" the man said, smiling with black and brown teeth. "I told you, it's death to cross the Jackals!"

Lucius tried to muster as much confidence as he could, as he scanned the area for a way out, but the Jackals had them well-covered, their weapons confiscated. "Let us go. You have no idea what you're doing!"

The Jackals laughed. "Oh, we know exactly what we're doing," the leader said. "We've been following you for days. We knew where you were in Antioch. We were so close, we could hear your conversations. And when I heard the name 'Lucius Metellus Anguis' uttered, I knew I recognized it. We don't forget bounties as large as that!" He turned to look around the circle of his men. "We don't care if it is from Romans, Parthians, or Egyptians! Three talents of gold, is three talents of gold!"

The bandits all cheered.

The man turned back to Lucius. "All I have to do is take you down to those Praetorians over there and turn you in."

Lucius struggled at that, but the men behind him held him fast and pressed their blades to his neck.

The leader came closer to Lucius and looked back at Caecilius. "The bounty was for you and your wife and children, Dragon, but not for anyone else. Who is this man with you?"

Lucius could see Caecilius' eyes looking side to side for a weapon he could grab, anything he could use.

"He's no one. Just a man I met on the road."

"Please. You forget we've been following you. You must show the Jackals respect!" he shouted before punching Lucius across the face. "He's your brother!"

"That's right you piece of dung!" Caecilius shouted, and in a quick second he slammed his head into the face of the man on his right, the one rope about his neck slackening. But the other man yanked hard upon the other rope and Caecilius fell off of his feet.

Lucius jumped up, only just spinning away from the blades, and kicked one man behind him down the rocky slope.

But they were swarmed by the Jackals, punches and kicks raining down on them in flashes and a chorus of howls as if the bandits enjoyed every second of the brawl.

The ropes about Lucius' hands loosened and he managed to pound another in the face, breaking his nose upward, but even as he turned to run to his brother, he saw the leader holding a dagger to Caecilius' chest as if waiting for Lucius to see, and when he did see, the Jackal leader plunged the dagger into Caecilius' chest three times in quick succession.

"NOOOO!" Lucius yelled, leaping over the fire to his brother's aid.

But even as Lucius' feet touched the ground, he was knocked to the side by a club.

"NOOOO!" he yelled again, but his vision was blocked out by the Jackals closing in on him with bloody grins and razor-sharp steel.

"I think I'll kill this dragon!" the leader said. "We're rich enough!" He raised the blade that still had Caecilius' blood upon it and made to drive it into Lucius' face.

He did not see the spear soaring through the air to bury itself in the side of his head, nor did the other jackals pay much heed to the pounding of hobnailed feet upon the rocky ground as a storm of Roman steel closed in around them, cutting them down like slaughtered pigs.

There were cries in the night as the Jackals were eliminated, and then shouted orders in Latin, but all Lucius had eyes and ears for was Caecilius who lay bleeding upon the ground a few feet away.

Lucius, his head spinning, dragged himself over to his brother. "Caecilius no! Stay with me, Brother, please!"

"Luc...Lu..." Caecilius tried to speak, but he choked on the blood that erupted from his throat to pour over his pale, stubbly face.

"I'm so sorry," Lucius said through his tears of rage. "Stay with me. It'll be all right!" His hands fumbled upon his brother's chest where blood pulsed from the wounds.

Caecilius shook his head, his body convulsing violently for a moment and then, with a final shudder, he was absolutely still.

"Caecilius?" Lucius said, his hands shaking, vomit rising in his throat as his heart pounded and the world spun. "Brother?" he began to weep, but then the anger filled him. "GODS, DAMN YOU!!!" he yelled to the night as he bent over his dead brother. "AHHHH!"

"That's enough of that!" said the deep voice of a centurion who bent over Lucius and slammed his fist into his face.

Gods! Lucius begged as he was once more swallowed by darkness.

The strong scent of frankincense is what roused Lucius' senses. It tickled his nose and made him want to cough, but he fought back the urge. His head ached and spun as he did a mental check of his body to see if anything was broken. He did not know where they were, or how long they had travelled, and he was about to open his eyes to look for his brother when the harsh reality stabbed at his consciousness like so many daggers.

He grew still then and felt sick as tears burned his shut eyes. *Caecilius...no...* He breathed to calm himself, focussed on listening. He could feel that he was tied with his back to a post upon sandy ground. He was inside a tent, the musty scent and gentle flapping all too familiar a setting.

After several minutes, he could not wait any longer and very slowly opened his eyes slightly to assess his surroundings.

He was tied to the central post of a command tent. In the tent were several trunks, some open with scrolls protruding. There were racks with weapons and armour on the far side. A few bronze lamps hung from the ceiling beams, mostly around a large table where an older man sat directly in front of Lucius, making notes. He wore a plain red tunic and cloak. There was a torc about his neck and armillae about his wrists. A thick vinerod lay across the top of the table.

But it was the men behind him, the guards, that gave Lucius pause.

They stood stalk still behind their centurion, white tunicae beneath their armour, and white crests upon their helmets. The hilts of their gladii glinted, even in the dim light, and upon their scuta were the images of scorpions, eagles' wings and lightning bolts.

Praetorians, Lucius thought, feeling the dread in his gut.

Then, one of the guards behind the centurion stepped forward to whisper something to his superior.

The centurion set down his stylus and looked up.

Lucius noticed the man was older, obviously a veteran, for his hair was short and grey, and about his eyes there were leathery lines from years in the elements. He was big and strong, but there was no sign of malice in his eyes, no hatred. He was just a soldier, doing his duty.

"You're awake," the centurion said, standing slowly and walking around the table to lean on it and look down at Lucius' battered face and blood-stained countenance.

"Where am I?" Lucius asked, his voice hoarse and barely audible through his dry throat.

The centurion turned to his table, poured some water from a pitcher into a small cup, and stepped forward to press the rim to Lucius' cracked lips.

The water trickled down Lucius' throat, making him cough the first time. The second time, he was able to drink a little and felt relief. "Where am I?" he repeated.

The centurion leaned back against the table. "You're in the Praetorian camp outside of Zeugma."

"Why?"

The centurion looked back in surprise at the two guards behind him, then back down at Lucius. "We saved you from that band of marauding jackals, that's why. But I should be asking the questions. Why were you following us?"

"Where is my brother?" Lucius asked, his voice shaky.

But the centurion would not be pushed. "Why were you following us?"

Lucius' mind raced, searching for a reason to give. "We wanted to join up, to get in the fight. We didn't know where the legions were gathered, so we followed you out of Antioch. I thought that since I fought for Severus, the emperor would look favourably on my petition."

"Hmm." The centurion scratched his chin and his eyes hardened.

"There are legions all over Mesopotamia right now, mainly at Nisibis. Why would you want to join up?"

"I too am a veteran. I fought in the Parthian campaign of Emperor Severus."

"As did I, soldier," the centurion said. "What legion?"

"III Parthica."

The centurion nodded. "Good outfit. They were green at the time, but accounted for themselves well in the fighting." He looked Lucius over. "You look like you've seen better days, soldier."

Lucius stared at the man. "Please tell me... Where is my brother? He had come to join with me."

"You remember don't you?"

"What?"

"That...that your brother is dead. He was slain by the Jackals."

Lucius looked down at the blood staining his chest and legs, and nodded. "Yes. I want to know where his body is so that I can perform the rites properly."

The centurion breathed slowly. "That's not possible."

"Why? Please," Lucius said. "Let me go so that I can go back to the spot and find him, burn him properly."

"We already did, soldier. I'm sorry. We burned his body beside the bodies of all the Jackals."

"No!" Lucius pulled at his bonds, straining painfully.

"Calm down!" the centurion ordered. "The desert is littered with unburied and unburned Roman and Parthian bodies that have been left for the carrion vultures. Your brother was lucky to have received the fire. We knew that he was Roman from hearing you two speak your last. We said the prayers for him, but nothing for the Jackals.

"You're lying!" Lucius shouted.

The centurion stood up above Lucius. "Calm yourself, or I'll have to put you back to sleep." He knelt in front of Lucius and looked him in the eyes. "I swear by the Gods, by Mars and Mithras, that we gave your brother the proper rites. He was young. He deserved better than to die like that in the desert."

Lucius' breathing was rapid, his heart pounding wildly.

"Be calm, and tell me your name soldier," the centurion asked Lucius.

"My name...my name is Lucius Pen Dragon."

"'Pen Dragon'? That sounds like a barbarian name."

"It's my name."

"My name is Julius Martialis. Evocatus assigned to the Praetorian guard. I want to help you, Lucius Pen Dragon. One veteran to another. And the-" The centurion's words stuck in his throat as he noticed something strange beneath Lucius' torn tunic. "What is this?" He reached out to spread the torn and bloody tunic apart to reveal the branded dragon upon the prisoner's chest. "How did that happen? Why do you have this mark?"

But Lucius thought only of his brother's bloody face and final choked words in that moment, and he began to scream. "LET ME GO!!! AHHH!!!"

Julius Martialis brought back his fist and landed it on the side of Lucius' head yet again, making the latter slump forward, silent. "So loud!" he barked, then turned to his guards. "I order you not to say anything about this man to anyone outside the century until I have a chance to speak with the prefect."

"Yes, sir!" the men answered.

"Do you believe his story, sir?" one of them asked.

The centurion turned back to look at Lucius. "I don't know. I do think he was a soldier. That much seems true, but as for the rest? I'm not sure. I'll find out." He stood and turned to them. "Almost time for your shift change. Order the slave to bring water from the river so that this one can be cleaned up." He nodded toward Lucius. "Bring me an extra tunica, cloak, caligae and cingulum too. We can't have him meeting the prefect like this."

"Yes, Centurion!" they said, saluted, and went out into the bright sunlight.

When the guards were gone, Julius Martialis turned back to Lucius. He parted the prisoner's tunic again to see the dragon brand. "Gods. It can't be." He remembered the dream he had had a week ago, of being lost in the desert until he found such a beast, a beast that led him home. "The Gods work in mysterious ways," he said to himself and the unconscious man before him. "Maybe he can be useful?" He looked toward the tent entrance to see if anyone was coming, and when he was sure they were not, he nudged Lucius to wake him. "Wake up, soldier."

After a few moments, Lucius groaned and slowly opened his eyes. The centurion's face hovered in a blur before him.

"You need to stay calm, soldier. I want to help you, but you need to help me."

Lucius' mind spun out of control, and he struggled to regain his equilibrium of thought. *Caecilius is gone, Lucius,* he told himself. *Think now. You need to finish this!* "I know Parthia...the cities...I know how they fight. I can help."

"Many of us do, soldier. You'll need to think of something better. For now, you need to refrain from outbursts and drawing attention to yourself. I'm going to cut you loose, and get you cleaned up, but you have to promise not to do anything rash. Will you trust me?"

Lucius looked up at the man's face and eyes and slowly nodded, his head still lolling to the side from the force of his beating.

"Good man. You stay calm, we might just get you what you want - a commission as an evocatus."

"What?" Lucius found the strength to raise his head.

"That's right. We'll check the records for your name, of course, but when we confirm you were with III Parthica, it won't be a problem. I was with IV Scythica. Now, I'm a Praetorian with more pay and more respect. We can get you the same."

Lucius nodded.

"I am sorry about your brother, Pen Dragon. Truly."

"Thank you for giving him the rites," Lucius said. *But it should have been me! It's all my fault!* And he began to weep silently, tears in the dried blood upon his cheeks.

"There now. He fought at the end. He didn't go quietly. The Gods will bless him for it." The centurion took the cup of water and pressed it to Lucius' lips again. "You need your strength. Soon, I'll introduce you to the Praetorian prefect. He's a good man who appreciates veterans. He'll help, I'm sure."

Lucius nodded as he drank more thirstily.

I'm coming for you, Caracalla!

XX

EXTRA UMBRAM

'Out of the Shadows'

"Gods of our ancestors… Apollo… Mercury who leads the Dead along the paths of the Afterlife… Please guide my brother, Caecilius Metellus, to Elysium. May he be forever at peace, calm and joyous on the other side of the dark river. May he know that I loved him like a true brother, and that he will not go unremembered…"

The tears Lucius wept in the early morning sunlight on the sandy bank of the Euphrates burned and blinded him, but it was the only place he could be alone outside the rich polis of Zeugma and the Praetorian and legionary camps that were erected there.

The centurion, Julius Martialis, had ordered two men to watch him. However, they stood at a respectful distance to allow Lucius the space and time to perform rites for his brother. They observed quietly, chewing on their morning ration of dried meat and oat cakes at the base of a tall palm.

Centurion Martialis had offered to cut Lucius free, but only on his oath that he would not run. He had handed Lucius the white tunica and bracae of a Praetorian and told him to wash himself. "You can then go and make offerings to your fallen brother if you like." He also allowed Lucius to purchase a black goat with part of the remainder of his coin; the rest, Martialis held as surety, along with Lucius' weapons. The mules were confiscated for the war effort.

Lucius was grateful, and he had no plans to run.

As he knelt on the silty shore of the Euphrates, praying, he held a sacrificial knife in one hand, and a rope tied to the goat in the other.

When he finished praying, Lucius pulled the goat closer, so that its hooves danced nervously in the water before him. He looked out at the

604 THE BLOOD ROAD

blue river, the way the sunlight sparkled upon the surface, and he thought of Caecilius as he held the knife at the ready.

"I'm sorry I couldn't help you, Brother..." Lucius wept, his eyes closing only to see Caecilius' face. "Forgive me for bringing you into this..." He opened his eyes again and looked up at the intensifying sun in that clear, blue sky. "Gods...accept this offering and watch over my brother. Grant me vengeance at last, and an end to all of this..."

Without hesitating, Lucius yanked the goat's head back and slit its throat. It shuddered and bucked briefly before going limp, its lifeblood flowing across the sodden silt to be carried away on the river. Lucius then released the body by pushing it out and allowing it too to be taken away to be consumed by whichever god had heard his prayer.

He made to stand from the water and paused, shielding his eyes from the angling morning light. There, on the other side of the broad river, he thought he spied Apollo and Venus, still and watchful.

Come with us, Lucius... they seemed to say. *It is not too late...*

But Lucius shook his head and turned away from the river.

"Pen Dragon? Are you finished?" one of the Praetorians called from beneath the palm.

"I'm coming!" Lucius answered before looking back to the river and seeing the far bank deserted.

Centurion Julius Martialis had a soft-spot for the lone veteran that he and his men had found in the desert. It was not just because he had lost the younger man he claimed was his brother. There was something else about him. It was strange, but when he had been encamped that night in the desert with his men, Julius could swear he had heard the voice of Mars speaking to him in the night, telling him to gather some men and search the perimeter. That was when he had found the fire of the men following them, and the group of jackals that had been attacking caravans bound for Antioch.

Julius Martialis knew from experience that the desert could either drive a man mad, or help him to see more clearly the faces of the Gods. He decided that he would take men out to search the perimeter, and Mars had not disappointed.

The travellers should both have been dead, he thought, for the Jackals took no quarter. But perhaps they too had noticed something about the man with the branded dragon upon his chest. *The prefect will want to meet him,* Martialis thought, relieved when he saw the man returning with the two guards he had set to watch him.

As soon as they entered the tent, the two guards left Lucius and stood outside the entrance.

"Thank you for allowing me to sacrifice to my brother, Centurion," Lucius said to Martialis when they were alone.

Julius Martialis looked up at him, and set his stylus down. He then turned to pick up the black pugio and gladius that belonged to Lucius. "I can see you're a good man, Pen Dragon. We can always use good men. And I want to help a fellow veteran. No soldier should be without his weapons." He held out the cingulum with the sheathed gladius and pugio to Lucius. "Don't make me regret giving you these back."

Surprised, Lucius nodded and reached out to take them. "I thank you, Centurion. I won't betray your confidence."

"That's good." Martialis turned to pour some watered wine in two cups, and handed one to Lucius. "To your brother."

Lucius nodded, poured some on the ground, and then drank the rest along with Martialis. *My brother...*

"Of course," Martialis continued, setting his cup down, "I can't speak for the prefect. He's a busy man. Spends most of his time with the emperor now that they are together again."

Lucius noticed a change in tone when Martialis spoke of Caracalla, a hardness that was not there before, a bitterness. *Seems he doesn't like Caracalla either... Good.*

"But," Martialis continued, "the prefect is no nobleman. He's one of us. Worked hard, and worked his way up. He respects veterans, unlike... unlike others. If you don't cause trouble...if you prove useful in some way..." Martialis nodded, "he'll take you in and give you a second life." He looked Lucius in the eye. "You understand me?"

"Yes, Centurion. I certainly do." Lucius strapped on the cingulum with his pugio and gladius, both polished. "I'm not going anywhere."

"Good." He slapped Lucius on the shoulder. "We'll show them what real men are capable of in this fight."

"Yes. We will," Lucius agreed.

They spent the rest of the day in Martialis' tent where Lucius, because he could read and write, and was used to the army administration, helped the centurion prepare to move out. There had been whispers that day that the emperor would want to leave the perfumed palaces and triclinia of well-coined Zeugma for the front and fighting. Caracalla had not yet bloodied his sword, and the Parthians were, apparently, moving on Nisibis.

Martialis worried for his family in the region, and so he wanted to be ready to leave when the time came. He could do his part, at least.

Lucius felt stranded, sitting in that increasingly hot tent in the Praetorian camp, just waiting. He felt like he was now groping for the end of a thread in the darkness, and there was nothing he could do about it.

Martialis obviously liked him, but he still kept the guards close at hand. Armed or not, they would be on top of Lucius in a second if he should try to escape.

Besides, Lucius thought, *he's a good man.*

"Where have you seen action besides Parthia, Pen Dragon?" Martialis asked as he was sifting through another stack of requisition requests for his century.

Lucius stood from the stool he was sitting on and stretched, his damaged skin feeling dry and taut. "I've been around."

"Come now, soldier," Martialis said. "I know some men don't like to talk about it, but you seem tough as nails. Tell me."

Lucius sighed and sat back down. "I served in Numidia after the Parthian campaign, and then went to Britannia and Caledonia."

"You were in Caledonia with Severus?" the centurion asked, his voice almost envious. "Was the fighting good?"

"It was brutal. Nothing like fighting the Parthians out in the open. There were no pitched battles. Guerrilla fighting all the way." Lucius was quiet.

"You lost a lot of men," Martialis said, his head nodding.

"You could say that," Lucius replied. *All of them...*

"Not easy, is it?"

Lucius could not answer that time, for the dead paraded before his eyes, each of them urging him to finish the mission for all their sakes. They had all experienced betrayal and pain and suffering, and were Lucius a god, they would have heaped offerings to him upon the altars of the afterlife that he would finish the fight once and for all.

"I'm sorry, Pen Dragon," Martialis said after watching Lucius' face contort where he sat in silence. "Chin up! You'll feel better once you get back in the fight."

Lucius looked at him suddenly, and nodded. "Quite true."

They went back to their work, while Martialis continued talking. "Were you there when Severus died?"

"I...I was nearby, yes."

"Great man, he was," the centurion said.

"He was." Lucius could still feel the heat of the pyre, could see it reaching to the sky as if the flames wanted to stretch to Olympus itself as the wood crackled and the garlands about the pyre twisted and burned. He also remembered Caracalla's hateful face during the entire funeral, especially when Lucius was given a firebrand to light the emperor's pyre.

"Before Parthia, I was with him in Pannonia," Martialis said. "He was one of the good ones, Severus was. Now..." The centurion stopped himself.

"Now?" Lucius prodded.

"Well...nothing..." Martialis knew he should not speak thus, that the Praetorians had always been the emperor's personal guard. But then he remembered how Caracalla had humiliated him in Nisibis. "It's just not the same anymore, is it?"

"No, it isn't," Lucius agreed. "Times have changed."

"Only a man who has served with Severus would understand. Soldiers are afforded a different perspective by the Gods, aren't they, Pen Dragon?"

"Yes. They are." Lucius picked up a stack of wax tablets and set them in one of the many trunks along the tent wall. When he sat back down, he drank and cleared his throat. "What is the Praetorian prefect like? Is he a soldier too?"

"Marcus Opellius Macrinus is the Praetorian prefect now. He's a good man. Knows how to respect a veteran. He's not a nobleman either. Worked his way up from poor beginnings in Mauretania. From what I've heard, he was a gladiator, a venator, and then a postal courier, before becoming administrator of the via Flaminia. He knows hard work, he does. And he's a good prefect."

"Will I meet him?"

Martialis looked up from the table at Lucius. "I expect so. He does his rounds without fail to let the men see him, to check on them. If he can get away from the emperor's side, he should eventually pass this way."

"Then we should finish this work before he arrives," Lucius added.

Martialis smiled. "I knew I liked you, Pen Dragon."

That evening, as a large, red sun began to fall in the western sky, a cornu sounded in the tent rows of the Praetorian camp.

Lucius looked up from the bowl of bean soup that Martialis had given him.

"The prefect is here for his rounds," the centurion said as he stood up quickly and put on his cloak and helmet. "When Prefect Macrinus comes in here, remain quiet until I have a chance to introduce you. You aren't officially an evocatus yet, but once he knows who you are, and where you've served, I'm sure he'll take you into service."

Lucius began to feel his nerves fraying beneath his calm exterior, for all that he hoped to accomplish hung on this one interaction. If he was recognized, he would be dragged before Caracalla and killed. If he was deemed too infirm because of his injuries, he would be forced out of camp. However, if he could be given a commission as a Praetorian evocatus like Martialis, then it was only a matter of time before his opportunity came.

"He's coming!" Martialis said, as loud voices could be heard outside the tent, speaking with the guards on duty. There was laughter, a little back and forth, and then the tent flaps parted.

Lucius stood behind and to the right of Centurion Martialis who saluted sharply as the Praetorian prefect entered, flanked by two officers.

"Praefectus, welcome!" Martialis said.

"At ease, Centurion," the Praetorian prefect said, saluting back and stepping forward to take Martialis' hand. "Have you wine? There is much to discuss."

"Yes, sir! I do!" Martialis turned to his ever-silent slave in the corner and the man immediately set about gathering cups upon a tray and filling them with watered wine.

Lucius stood still behind the table from where he could observe the prefect.

Macrinus was older, but cut an imposing figure. He was certainly not a soft man. Only in the lines of his long, bearded face could his age really be discerned. His eyes were close together, but focussed intently on whatever he looked at, as if he were constantly planning. "To the

Gods!" Macrinus said, tipping some wine onto the ground and raising his cup to the others.

"To the Gods!" they repeated.

"Martialis, you know my two tribunes already, the Aurelii, Nemesianus and Apollinaris?"

"Yes, Praefectus," Martialis said politely, nodding to the two young tribunes who flanked the prefect.

"And how are things here, Martialis?" the prefect asked, his eyes taking their first close look at Lucius, as he adjusted the cloak that covered his Praetorian regalia.

"We're almost ready to leave."

"At least you are, Centurion," Tribune Nemesianus said. "Most of the other centuries aren't even close yet."

"I just find it good to be ready to leave at a moment's notice, sir," Martialis said. "Do we know when the emperor wishes to set out for Nisibis?"

Macrinus' face darkened. He looked at Apollinaris to his left and leaned forward to speak candidly with Martialis. "The emperor is hesitant. He is, naturally, wary of wading into a pitched battle with the Parthians."

Not surprising! Lucius thought as he remembered Caracalla's cowardice in Caledonia. *He only kills old men, women and children.*

"Also…" Macrinus sighed and rubbed his temples. He was about to speak again, but his eyes strayed to Lucius once more. "Who is this man? Can he be trusted?"

"Yes, sir," Martialis said, standing and allowing Lucius to step forward. "This is Lucius Pen Dragon. He's a veteran of Severus' Parthian campaign like me. He's travelled far to join up as an evocatus."

"Did you receive a summons?" Tribune Nemesianus asked as he played with the white skirt of his pteruges.

"No, sir."

"How far did you travel?" Macrinus asked. "'Pen Dragon' is not a Roman name."

"I came from Britannia, Praefectus," Lucius replied. "I fought in Caledonia as well."

Macrinus was quiet, his eyes raking Lucius over. "I see. A tough campaign by all accounts."

"It was indeed, Praefectus."

"And you received your injuries in the war?" He looked over Lucius again, and the feeling it gave was extremely discomfiting.

"Yes, sir."

"Those barbarian bastards even branded him with a dragon!" Martialis blurted, as if he were angry for Lucius. "I saw it when we took him in, sir. He was travelling with his brother to get to us here so that they could both join up."

"This was when you and your men slew the Jackals?" Apollinaris asked, flicking his red cloak back.

"Yes, Tribune," Martialis answered.

"Where is your brother now, Pen Dragon?" the tribune asked again.

"He is dead," Lucius answered, his head bowed.

"I'm sorry to hear that," Macrinus said. "Death is everywhere in this accursed land."

"Sir?" Nemesianus interrupted. "Perhaps this soldier could show us the injury the barbarians inflicted on him? I for one, am curious."

"I don't think that's necessary, Tribune," Martialis said, but the look he got from the tribunes told him to hold his tongue.

"Why not?" Macrinus said. "You don't mind, do you, soldier?"

Lucius looked at the three men standing before him, took a breath and nodded. "Not at all." He began to unbuckle his cingulum and set it upon the table in front of him. Then, he lifted his tunica up over his head to reveal his scaly skin and the hard edges of the dragon brand upon his chest. He felt like a slave for sale in the market.

"My Gods," Macrinus said as the three of them peered at Lucius. He observed the dragon quite closely, and then looked from it to Lucius' eyes and back again. While the two tribunes behind him made their own observations about the horrifying injuries, the prefect continued to take it in silently. "What are those strange shadings upon your forearms?"

"Markings from the fires they burned me with, Prefect," Lucius replied, hoping the faint outline of the dragons that were once tattooed upon him were no longer discernible.

"You may replace your tunic, soldier," Macrinus offered.

Lucius began to so do, and then strapped on his cingulum and weapons.

"They truly are barbarians in the North," Macrinus said. "Such suffering. And yet," he stood and walked over to Lucius, "you've come back to the fight when you could have retired. Have you any family?"

"I used to, sir," Lucius answered slowly.

Macrinus nodded. "I see." He then turned to Tribune Apollinaris. "Tribune, write up a commission for this man as a Praetorian evocatus. He can be an optio with Martialis here."

"Yes, Praefectus," the tribune said. "I'll see it done."

The prefect sat back down. "The Praetorian Guard needs all the good, experienced men it can get. We are the elite fighting force, and we're needed more than ever."

"What do you mean, Praefectus?" Martialis asked. "Have there been some developments?"

Macrinus was silent. He looked to his left and right at the two tribunes, and then to the tent entrance to make sure the guards were far away enough. His voice was low when he spoke. "Our emperor wishes to emulate Megas Alexandros even more now. He wishes to institute the phalanx formation for his 'Lion' guard, and then in the legions themselves."

"But that's absurd!" Martialis blurted. "Sorry, Praefectus!" he said quickly. "It's just a shock. Rome defeated the phalanx ages ago. Cohorts and centuries are much more manoeuvrable."

"You're quite right, Centurion," Macrinus said.

"What are the 'Lions', if I may ask?" Lucius said, unable to hold back his curiosity.

The four men looked at him, and for a moment he feared he had gone too far. However, the prefect nodded.

"Therein lies another problem of our emperor's fascination-"

"A kind word," Nemesianus blurted.

Macrinus carried on. "His *interest* in emulating the great Alexander. Pen Dragon is right to be curious." He looked directly at Lucius. "The 'Lions' are a bodyguard of Scythian and German slaves which the emperor captured and then manumitted after the previous campaign. They all receive the same pay and privileges as centurions and they never leave the emperor's side."

"That is a job for Praetorians!" Apollinaris said through gritted teeth. "It's not right that barbarian slaves should replace Romans!"

"Keep your voice down," Macrinus growled at the tribune, his countenance changing very suddenly.

"Yes, Praefectus."

"It is no secret that the favour shown to these 'Lions' is causing unrest among the troops, especially among the Praetorian ranks." He looked at Martialis. "That is what I wanted to tell you. I want the men to keep their disaffection to themselves. We can't afford to have the Praetorians' loyalty questioned at a time like this. Any openly treasonous words against the emperor must be punished severely, Martialis. Do you understand?"

"Yes, Praefectus!"

"Good man." Macrinus sighed. "In the meantime, the more pressing issue for me and the legionary legates is to convince the emperor that retraining and fighting in phalanx formation is-"

"Madness," Nemesianus inserted.

Macrinus turned to him and scowled. "Not in Rome's best interest."

There was an awkward silence in the tent then, and as he watched, Lucius could detect much that was unspoken among those four men.

I need to find out what's going on here, he told himself and, as if he had heard his thoughts, Macrinus' eyes focussed on Lucius in that moment.

The Praetorian prefect stood up. "Martialis, I must finish my rounds. We'll talk soon."

"Yes, Praefectus!" Martialis said.

Macrinus turned to Lucius, his white pteruges and cloak swaying as he stood. He stepped closer to Lucius, smelling of oiled leather and incense. "Lucius...Pen Dragon... Welcome to the Praetorian Guard. We will speak again."

And with that, the prefect turned and went out of the tent followed by the two tribunes.

Martialis watched them leave and then sat down heavily in his chair behind the table. "Such times," he muttered.

They went back to their work of sorting the scrolls and wax tablets, and when they had finished, Martialis poured them more watered wine.

"Don't you have to do rounds, Centurion?" Lucius asked.

Martialis shook his head. "That's the nice thing about being an evocatus. Tasks like that can be left to others."

"I can give the watchword if you like?" Lucius thought he would try, for he needed to get out and discover more about Caracalla's habits. He would not learn much by staying inside the tent all the time.

"You're not an official evocatus yet, Pen Dragon. Besides, we should rest while we can. Soon, we'll be marching out, and then who knows what will happen?"

Lucius accepted the cup of wine from Martialis and sat opposite him.

"A phalanx?" the centurion mused. "Gods help us!"

"How has the emperor been received by the legions?" Lucius asked, seeing an opportunity.

Martialis scratched his grey head and stared into his cup. "My experience with the emperor has been limited apart from a short interaction when I arrived in Nisibis." *When he humiliated me!* Martialis' jaw flexed and the muscles pulsed on either side of his head. "They're soldiers. And soldiers follow whom they must. You know that."

"I do," Lucius said, sympathetic to the veteran's obvious dislike of Caracalla. *Men who have served for a long time see leaders come and go. Some of those leaders inspire, but others can a make a man question his loyalty and actions.*

"You tell me, Pen Dragon," Martialis said. "I mean, you served in Caledonia. The emperor led that campaign because of Severus' illness, no?"

How many images flooded Lucius' mind in that moment, of the green, mud and blood-churned land, trees draped with death, the charge of his cavalry, the sight of Caracalla and Claudius Picus. *Alerio. My Sarmatians...* Lucius had not thought of it all for some time, so focussed on the task ahead had he been. "So much happened..."

"I'm sorry, Pen Dragon." Martialis said. He came around the table and leaned over Lucius. "You're among friends now. We all walk with ghosts. Dry your eyes and throw yourself into the fight. It's the only way."

Lucius looked up at the centurion. *You have no idea,* he thought. "Apologies, Centurion," Lucius said. "A momentary weakness."

"Don't worry yourself. One battle is enough to scar a man for life, and you've seen more action than I have from the sound of it."

Lucius did not reply.

"Between you and me, Pen Dragon... How was our current emperor received by the troops in Caledonia and Britannia? How did he fight?"

Lucius felt his anger pulsing through his veins again...and he welcomed it. He sat straighter, forgetting the pain and anguish of his previous remembrances, and he was brought back to task by the centurion's questions. "May I speak to you in confidence, Centurion?"

Martialis glanced at the tent entrance and then back at Lucius. "What is said will remain between us alone."

"Caesar did fight...against old men, women and children. That, while my men and I fought a bloody war against the barbarians. And when Caesar did enter a real battle, he took the credit for other men's work. He is no Alexander, of that I am certain."

Martialis stared at Lucius. "Your men?"

Lucius had slipped. He was supposed to have been a regular legionary. He knew Martialis was not stupid, and he could not go back now. "Yes, sir."

"You said you were a legionary."

"I was."

"Legionaries don't lead men. How high did you climb, Pen Dragon?" Martialis' hand slowly went to the pugio at his belt.

Lucius saw it, and breathed slowly, his hand already on his own. He did not want to hurt the man before him, for there was kindness there, honour and honesty. *I'll be honest with him, and the Gods can decide what happens next.*

"Centurion, I haven't been fully honest with you."

Martialis pulled the dagger out and pointed it at Lucius. "Then do so now, Pen Dragon."

"I was a legionary. During the Parthian campaign, I did climb through the ranks. Emperor Severus was making drastic changes to the army then, and he smiled on me. As did others, such as General Laetus-"

"You knew Laetus?" Martialis said, his pugio lowering immediately. "He was a good man."

"One of the best I knew early in my career," Lucius agreed. "He...he gave me some good advice once, before he was-"

"Executed." Martialis was silent. "Perhaps the worst thing Severus did."

"I agree."

"What advice did he give you?"

Lucius smiled sadly. "He told me that no matter how many victories we carry, or how lauded we are by our troops or in the fora of the empire, no matter how blessed we are by the Gods, the closer we stand to power, the more the risk of getting burned."

Martialis looked at Lucius' face and arms then, and the latter realized the irony of what he was saying.

Lucius continued. "He said - and I remember this clearly now that I am back in this land - 'Your life is yours to honour, but it is dust to others.'"

"Such a great man," Martialis said. "And good advice. I wept when they executed him."

"Many did," Lucius said. "He also told me that it is a dangerous world for *good* men."

They were both silent, but after a time, Lucius decided to be honest with the man before him, another good man in a dangerous world.

"After General Laetus' death, I rose up through the ranks quickly. Emperor Severus had, as I said, taken an interest in me."

"What posts, Pen Dragon? I have to say, I'm much more curious about you now than before!" The centurion smiled, and there was a sense of camaraderie there that was not felt before.

"I was a tribune...and in Britannia, a prefect."

Martialis' eyes went wide, and Lucius could not decide whether he was angry or surprised, or whether the man wanted to laugh, but when he did speak, his question was simple.

"And why come here now to fight as a soldier?"

"Are we not all soldiers in the Gods' eyes?"

"True, but by the Gods, Pen Dragon, you should outrank me!"

Lucius smiled and shook his head. "One good man does not outrank another. It is a man's deeds that matter."

"True enough, but-"

"Please, Centurion," Lucius said. "I would serve as your optio. And I would rather not anyone know about my previous ranks. I tell you in confidence."

"I hear that, but I really should at least tell Macrinus. He took me in and, besides, he would be happy to have a man such as you in the ranks. You'd make a better tribune than those two brothers who follow him everywhere."

"I've no wish to be burned so close to power again. Just as Laetus said."

Martialis nodded, then held up his cup. "To Laetus." They drank together, and then the centurion cleared his throat. "Your secret is safe with me, Pen Dragon. We'll fight this war as we were meant to."

Lucius smiled and drank.

"By the way," Martialis said, almost as an aside as he drained his cup. "I agree with you about Caracalla. He's not his father. Laughed in my face when I told him I was happy to serve again."

"It's no wonder the men don't like him," Lucius chanced to say.

"Shhh!" Martialis hissed. "Keep your voice down, Pen Dragon. What you say is true, of course, but there are spies everywhere. This stays between us, you hear me?"

"Of course, Centurion."

"Good. Now, we should get some sleep."

"My thanks again, Centurion."

"We need to stick together, Pen Dragon. Thank the Gods men like the prefect appreciate us." He blew out the lamps and lay himself down on his own double cot in the dark corner at the back of the tent. "Good night."

"Good night, Centurion," Lucius said from his own dark corner beside the tent entrance.

Lucius laid himself down with his gladius on his chest, ready should he need it. He was suddenly quite exhausted by all that had happened. There were so many things in motion that he was not quite sure how to make a start of carrying out his plan. The image of his brother haunted him as soon as he closed his eyes, and the voices of his wife and children echoed in his mind as if they were calling out to him in that moment, wishing for him to come back to them.

Not yet, Lucius thought, but he realized that he would likely never see them again. All he could do was carry out his mission to ensure that they would remain safe, even if he was not there.

There was one thought that gave him peace as he lay there in the darkness of the Praetorian camp, and that was the thought of his blade plunging into Caracalla's body and face, over and over and over again. *He's finally going to pay for all that he's done to my family!*

The next day, a still Spring morning began along the banks of the Euphrates where warblers, falcons and bulbuls skirted the surface of the water and sang among the reeds. Lucius and Martialis were already awake, making the rounds of their century.

The centurion walked around as if he had never retired, as if he had always been a centurion. He fit the role well and it seemed that the men deferred to and respected him.

It was not what Lucius would have expected in the ranks of the Prae-torians. Of course, Alerio had been a Praetorian, but so had Argus and Claudius Picus. Lucius had expected rank upon rank of arrogant and hateful men, but it was much the same as any legion, perhaps more disci-plined. What was more of a shock for Lucius was to find himself wearing a lorica again after so many years. He felt awkward walking beside Martialis, wearing that armour, the helmet with a white crest and feathers that marked him as an optio, and carrying the hastile, the long staff with a brass ball on the end. A part of him wanted to disappear, to dive back into the shadows to await his moment, to continue the hunt.

But it was too late for that. Lucius was in among Rome's eagles, in plain sight. Men looked at him directly now, curious about his appear-ance, his injuries, and his strange name. There was no hiding anymore. No running. It was a matter of time and opportunity, when it finally came.

"Well, Pen Dragon," Martialis said to Lucius as they walked back to the centurion's tent. "Everything is ready, and every man is prepared to move out when the order is given. Now, we just have to wait."

"Are we waiting for the emperor to leave?" Lucius asked. "We haven't seen him at all. I remember Severus living in the Praetorian camp when we were on campaign."

"Tosh!" Martialis barked. "Not anymore. The emperor is living it up in the palaces of Zeugma. Did you ever go into the city?"

"No."

"Me neither. It's a different world, the lives those rich merchants lead. And I'm sure they've made the emperor quite comfortable while we just wait here in the dust for when he is good and ready."

Lucius looked around and leaned in to Martialis. "Should you be speaking aloud like that, Centurion?"

Martialis stopped and turned to Lucius in the middle of the via Decumana. "Look around you, Optio. Listen. Have you heard the conversations we've interrupted on our rounds? These men are not happy, but I can't bring myself to punish them. They're in a war that, really, need not have happened, and yet they're not allowed to fight. Other Romans are dying out in the desert, while they sit here. And they're not even really the emperor's guard anymore. That job has been handed to the slaves called the 'Lions'. The prefect is the only one keeping these men in line."

"Men need a leader."

"Aye. They do, Optio. And if it weren't for Macrinus...well...who knows what would happen."

"So what now?" Lucius asked as they continued walking down one of the smaller roads of the camp to the tent.

"We wait for orders."

As they walked the rest of the way, Lucius thought back on some of the things he had overheard the men saying as they walked. There were definite grumblings. In fact, the discontent and growing anger was thick in the air of the Praetorian camp everywhere they went. Men spoke of Caracalla and his cowardice in barely hushed tones and only quietened when Martialis or some other centurion eyed them. In the past, Caracalla had shared hardships and fooled the troops into thinking he was just one of them, but that was no longer the case.

He's betrayed them all, Lucius thought, and he wondered what would be happening if Severus were still alive. *What would be happening had my men and I actually succeeded?* The thought was fruitless, and served only to remind Lucius of how he had failed his men, those Sarmatian warriors who had followed him without question into danger, who had loved him, had honoured his own family. Most were dead, and the rest were living in hiding. *My sleeping dragons.* Lucius hoped that, after he was dead and gone, they would at last find the peace they deserved and could not have while he led them.

Lucius swallowed his emotions hard as they walked, for he longed more than ever to be back with his men, among trusted friends, with his wife and children. *Had I succeeded in Eburacum, the world would have been such a different place!*

He had, however, failed. And men had died. Too many men.

Lucius remembered the Praetorian arrows that took down his men in the ambush outside the walls of Eburacum. He remembered Barta's cries as he was tortured before him. He remembered fire, and the cries of his family.

With Lucius' every thought, he forcefully cut open his old wounds to fill them with anger and blood. He cursed himself for getting caught, and hated himself to see his own Praetorian reflection in the polished surface of Martialis' helmet beside him.

As they approached the tent at last, his spiralling thoughts were quickly halted.

"Not these two," Martialis grumbled as they spotted the two tribunes, Nemesianus and Apollinaris waiting for them to return. "Salvete, Tribunes!" Martialis saluted as he and Lucius walked up.

"Centurion," Nemesianus said, eyeing Martialis and Lucius.

"Do we have the order to set out?" Martialis asked.

"No. We're here to get Optio Pen Dragon."

Lucius' hand went to his gladius' handle beneath his cloak.

"Oh?" Martialis said.

"Yes," Apollinaris added. "The prefect would like to speak with him in private."

Martialis looked at the tribunes and then at Lucius. "Of course. Optio, you're dismissed for now."

"Good. This way, Optio," Nemesianus said before he and his brother strode down the street, not waiting for Lucius to follow.

"Watch those two," Martialis whispered as Lucius left.

Lucius felt his skin itching beneath his tunica and armour as he followed the tribunes' red cloaks along the tent rows and onto the via Principalis. They then turned right, and passed the guards into the courtyard of the Praetorian principia.

The perimeter was well-guarded with burly Praetorian guardsmen who stood silently between hanging purple and white banners with eagles and scorpions upon them. At the centre of the courtyard, a large tripod burned with fragrant cedar wood and incense.

Apollinaris and Nemesianus stopped beside the tripod and turned to Lucius.

"The prefect is waiting for you, Optio," Apollinaris said, pointing to the broad, ornate tent at the back of the courtyard.

Lucius saluted and continued on to the tent where two guards stood to either side of the entrance. He could feel the tribunes staring at his back as he went, and prepared himself for whatever might happen inside. *Gods...guide and protect me...*

It took his eyes a moment to adjust to the dim light of the tent, but when they did, he released his grip on his gladius. The tent was quiet, but for a slave who was setting down a tray of fruit on the large table where Marcus Opellius Macrinus sat alone among stacks of wax tablets and papyri.

The slave glanced in Lucius' direction as he stepped forward, but said nothing.

Lucius snapped a salute and spoke. "Praefectus. You asked to see me, sir?" The words he spoke, the place he stood, and the act of saluting the Praetorian prefect all felt foreign and clumsy to him, but Lucius knew he had to play his part now, for all his dead brothers-in-arms, his friends, his family, and for Caecilius who should have been standing there with him.

Macrinus looked up after he finished writing. "Leave us," he said to his slave before turning his eyes on Lucius who stood at attention before him. "Ah, yes. Lucius...Pen Dragon. Such a strange name. I did ask the Aurelii tribunes to bring you here." He leaned back in his wood and ivory chair, but did not invite Lucius to sit. "I've been thinking about you since we met. Yours is quite a story, what with what the barbarians did to you and all. And for you to travel so far to join the army again - in retirement no less! - Is, well...quite honourable."

"Thank you, Praefectus."

"It is also unbelievable."

Lucius felt his heart skip a beat, and found his mind doing a mental check of his weapons, the space around him, and the distance to the entrance where the guards stood. "I don't understand, Praefectus."

"Oh. I think you do." He smiled, and the sight was disturbing, for Macrinus seemed relaxed and completely confident in every word he uttered. "Most of the men in the legions, including the Praetorian Guard, don't want to be here. They think this war is futile, created as a salve for the ego of a man whose proposal of marriage was rejected."

Lucius' eyes widened. "He is our emperor, Praefectus. And the Parthians are the aggressors. They are attacking Hatra and Nisibis once more."

"And what are Hatra and Nisibis?" Macrinus asked. "Dusty outposts at the edge of the empire where a few veterans have made their homes. Are they worth the Roman blood that will inevitably be spilled? And we're all Romans now, aren't we?" There was sarcasm in his voice, but Lucius could not tell if it was feigned or sincere. "You fought in Severus' Parthian campaign, did you not?"

"I did, sir, yes."

"Tell me... Is this land worth it?"

"Rome is worth it. The purpose is to secure and better the empire, is it not? We cannot do so without dealing with an aggressor like the Parthians first."

Macrinus smiled again. "There is much that could be done to *better the empire*, I agree." He stood and turned his back to Lucius so that he looked at a shelf of papyri that was flanked by busts of Severus and Caracalla. Lucius could not see the dark look upon his face then, but it was there, and the thoughts to match it whirled in Macrinus' mind in a few uncomfortable moments of silence. "What do you know of me, Optio?" He turned back to Lucius. "I'm sure Martialis has briefed you."

"I wouldn't presume, Praefectus-"

"Please. I'm not the emperor. Just tell me. I'm quite open about my origins. Tell me what you know."

Lucius cleared his throat. "Ah...well... You are from Mauretania Caesariensis, and grew up in poverty. You were a gladiator, a venator and a postal courier. I believe you held some sort of administrative position under Emperor Severus."

"All true. And I am proud of my background. Nothing was given to me. I worked hard to get where I am today, and in doing so, I had to do some things I was not proud of, things that were necessary." He stared at Lucius again. "The lessons I learned in the amphitheater have stayed with me, helped me through. You see, in the arena, tough and quick decisions are required in order to survive. But they must be the right decisions, for if you slip up, you die. It's that simple. I won every fight I was in. There was no thought of losing. There can't be." Macrinus relaxed a little. "What else do you know about me?"

Lucius shrugged. "I'm afraid that is all I know, Praefectus."

"Did you know that I was also a jurist and legal advisor for Gaius Fulvius Plautianus?"

Lucius' eyes hardened upon hearing the name of the man who had turned Argus against his family, who was responsible for the death of his sister, Alene. When a man hears the name of another he has killed, there is a change in his countenance, in his eyes. It was a look that Macrinus spotted very clearly in Lucius' eyes then.

"You remember, Plautianus, I assume?"

"I had heard of him, yes."

"He was a disgrace to the post of Praetorian prefect. And I had to deal closely with him." Macrinus' voice was bitter. He turned away and picked up a small folding wooden frame with a painted picture upon in. "I'm also a father, Pen Dragon." He held up the picture of a boy on the frame. "Diadumenian…my son. Do you have children, Pen Dragon?"

Lucius felt the guilt eating away at him, wanting to burst out, to make him scream, but he forced it down. "I did."

"Something happened then, I see."

"Ye…yes, sir. It did. Much." Lucius swallowed.

"And what would you have not done to keep them safe from harm?"

"Anything."

"I see you understand me, Optio. I had no one to shield me when I scraped my way out of poverty. I don't want my son to be so vulnerable."

Why is he telling me all this? Lucius thought. "Praefectus…with respect. I'm not quite sure why you asked me here."

"I asked you here because your story intrigues me. I wanted to speak to you alone. A good leader should know the men in his ranks, especially those with as much experience as you."

Lucius froze. "Sir?"

"You see, Lucius Pen Dragon, just as you know a little about me, I too know something about you. I would be a poor Praetorian prefect if I did not."

Lucius looked for Macrinus' weapons - a pugio upon the table, and another hanging from his belt. The man had been a gladiator, so he would know how to fight in close quarters. *He's wearing armour,* Lucius thought. *So I would have to get him in the throat to keep him quiet and kill him quickly.* His mind raced, and his fingers twitched as they slowly went to his pugio beneath his cloak.

But Macrinus smiled at Lucius, no sign of aggression or care. "Listen to me," he said evenly. "Let me tell you what *I* know…Lucius Metellus Anguis."

Lucius could feel his ears ringing, but kept as calm as he could on the exterior. "I am Lucius Pen Dragon," Lucius said, the veil of deference falling away.

"Come now," Macrinus answered, his face full of disappointment. "Let us leave pretence and lies by the wayside. I have been Praetorian prefect since Caracalla murdered his brother."

Lucius pulled back his cloak so that his weapons were fully visible now. *No more pretence.*

"Who do you think issued all those bounties for you and your family?"

"Caracalla."

"Yes. And I was the one he ordered to do it. It was not simply a matter of putting the mention of coin out there, and you were not the only one he wanted hunted down and killed." Macrinus then poured some water into two cups and gave one to Lucius.

Lucius did not touch it.

Macrinus drank and sat down, this time indicating the chair in front of his desk for Lucius to sit as well. "You have left quite a trail of blood behind you. It's most impressive. You see, my network of spies all have contacts with various bounty hunters and cutthroats, and they must check in regularly. Needless to say, many did not, and that brought about suspicion, especially in Etruria. Those were two of my best men. They helped to bring down many on Caracalla's proscription lists."

Lucius quickly drew his gladius and pointed it directly at Macrinus who parried it skilfully.

The guards rushed in at the single clang of steel but Macrinus held up his hand quickly. "Stop!"

The blades pointed at Lucius' back stopped in their transit.

"We are playing a game," Macrinus said. "Leave us."

The guards lowered their blades, saluted, and went out.

"Hear me out before you make any rash decisions, Metellus."

"I am Lucius Pen Dragon."

"I suppose we should keep that pretence up." Macrinus put his pugio down. "I spoke of having to do things one does not like in order to make the world better. I did not want to issue those orders to kill you and your family if you were alive, or the others who were on those lists. But it was a necessity for survival. I am only glad that the assassins did not succeed. Where is your family now?"

Lucius said nothing, his gladius still out, but now across his lap.

"Very well. Just know that I mean what I am saying. I know you must hate Caracalla for all that he has done to you."

"The Praetorians have done much to my family as well."

"Those were different times. Marcus Claudius Picus was an animal. I am not him. Like you in Eburacum, I want to make this empire great again. I want this to be a safe world for my son to grow up in." Macrinus sighed. "I can only guess at what you've been through. It's etched upon your very person. I can see it in your eyes. You have had to do terrible things to survive, as have I. But I think we want the same thing, Pen Dragon."

"You don't know me."

"Oh, but I do. We both know what is needed to make this world better. You've survived the amphitheatre of the world several times over, as have I, and it is time for another tough decision."

"What is that?"

"If you help me, *Pen Dragon*, I will give you what you most desire."

"Help you with what?"

"I want you to help me kill Caracalla."

Lucius was silent, his fists and mottled forearms clenching and unclenching. His heart raced again and he felt warnings throughout his entire person. *Don't trust him! He's lying!* "Why don't you just kill me and get it over with. Claim the bounty for yourself."

"I assure you, I don't need the coin. And I don't need Caracalla's praise. He's a monster, and he needs to be killed."

Lucius looked around in shock. He was in the middle of the Praetorian camp, and the prefect himself was speaking openly about killing the emperor.

"Every man near me is loyal to me alone. None of them want to be here, and they hate that Caracalla has replaced them with his 'Lions'. He has betrayed Rome and the Praetorians."

Lucius stood and leaned on the table.

Macrinus stood too, and whispered. "Help me with this. Take vengeance for your family and all that Caracalla has done to you." He raised his dark eyebrows. "That is why you came all this way, isn't it? I will make it easy for you to achieve the end you've sought all along."

As vengeance lay within his grasp, through his lense of anger and hate, Lucius could see the blood and fire that had consumed his world, his friends, his family and homes. He looked down at his burned arms where his knuckles leaned on the table. He knew that if he accepted the offer, and carried out the deed, he would not be allowed to live. *They can't let me live!* But he also knew that he may never get such a chance, that they would kill him anyway, and much sooner. *I've come too far to turn back.*

"And what happens when we succeed in killing Caracalla?" Lucius asked. "What happens to us, to me?"

"The troops will accept me as their emperor. And you...you, Lucius Metellus Anguis - Lucius *Pen Dragon* - you will go free to wherever your family is, never followed, never hunted, to make a home wherever you wish. Rome will not look for you."

Gods, Lucius thought, *I give myself over to the Fates now. Caracalla's blood will be my final offering.* "When would we do this? How would we get past Caracalla's Lions?"

"The opportunity will present itself," Macrinus smiled. "I received word from the emperor today that we are setting out for Edessa tomorrow. From there, Caracalla wishes to strike out for Carrhae to visit the temple of Luna." Macrinus' voice was low and deep then, and his eyes seemed to dilate in his face. "Before he reaches Carrhae, you must do the deed."

"But how?"

"An opportunity will present itself. Trust me."

Never, Lucius thought, but he found himself nodding and smiling. "I will do it. Whenever and however, I can. I will kill him. Then, I want to be free of Rome forever." *For my family...*

"By the Gods, I promise it shall be so," Macrinus said. "And you will not be alone in this deed. Martialis has no love of the emperor either. He will be there with you when the time comes."

Then he will be dead as well, Lucius thought of the Evocatus' family. *Such are the choices we must make.* "But *why* would he help me?"

"Trust me. He will. But do not speak of our plan to him yet. Leave that to me. And do not speak of your true identity to him. That is between us alone." Macrinus flashed a smile, stood up and extended his hand to Lucius. "To vengeance and a new world."

Lucius took the hand that was extended to him, and he felt cold, as if he were grasping Death's own. "To vengeance."

"Go now, Optio, and wait for word from my tribunes. The time will come, and when it does, you must strike quickly and without mercy, for Caracalla has never shown any."

Lucius turned without another word and stepped out into the sunlight of the principia courtyard to go back to his tent.

Macrinus watched him go and sat down, smiling to himself. "This is going to be much easier than I had hoped."

Just then, the tent wall to his far left parted and the Praetorian tribunes Apollinaris and Nemesianus emerged.

"What a fool! He actually believed you." Nemesianus chuckled. "Should we begin addressing you as 'emperor' now?"

Macrinus stood and turned on him. "For now, you keep your mouth shut, Tribune," he growled. "Any whisper of this gets out and we're all dead."

The tribune's smirk faded, and his brother stepped closer to the two of them.

"To think, he travelled all this way from Britannia. Are you really just going to let him go after Caracalla is dead?"

"Of course not," Macrinus said. "The rest of the Praetorians and the Lions will need someone to blame for this. Pen Dragon and Martialis are to be slain as soon as Caracalla is dead, and you will see to it."

XXI

DRACO INTER VIPERAE

'A Dragon among Vipers'

The emperor and his Lions, along with the Praetorian Guard, set out at a leisurely pace from Zeugma to Edessa a day later. The green banks and blue water of the Euphrates dwindled in the bright light and dust behind them as they marched.

The word among the ranks was that the fighting for them would start at Nisibis, which the Parthians were already closing in on. There were grumbles among the troops about the requirement to stop at Edessa at all, but they were reminded that their duty was to protect the emperor, and wherever he went, they followed. It was a three day journey across the Mesopotamian desert to get to Edessa. Trade traffic was thinning as the drums of war grew louder and the legions marched. There was a constant flow, however, of couriers from the imperial column to the front, mostly with reports of Parthian movements and word of the emperor's progress.

The battle was coming, and the men of the legions were preparing for the fight ahead while the emperor marched and had his Lions practice a phalanx formation along the way to demonstrate his strategy to the Praetorians who looked on, baffled.

For Lucius, it was a time of uncertainty in which he struggled to stay focussed on his mission. Ever since Macrinus had revealed that he knew his true identity, he had been waiting for daggers in the dark, or the tramp of a Praetorian contubernium come to put him in chains. He rarely slept for very long, and when he did sleep, it was with his gladius unsheathed and his pugio beneath his folded cloak, which he used as a pillow. In the dark of night, as the watch word was called out in the rows of Praetorian tents, Lucius prayed to the Gods for guidance, for some sign that he would be permitted to complete the task he had set himself, a task that began to seem more impossible by the day.

But the Gods were silent.

Lucius could see their faces, their brilliant star-whirling eyes, and yet they did not speak to him. He was on his own.

I cannot back out now, he told himself. *Caecilius is dead, I've left my family, and my world is burned.* Whenever Lucius wavered in his intent, he forced himself to think on all the pain he had seen and experienced from Britannia to that point in time, the loss, the death, all for the vanity and hate of the man who now led his men across the desert to fight an enemy they had already defeated.

The sooner I can kill him, the better, Lucius thought. *And if I die in the process, so be it.* He shut his eyes in the dark of the tent. *I'm so tired of this life.*

Then there was Centurion Martialis.

Lucius was with the centurion constantly. He worried about how much Martialis knew, and whether Macrinus or the tribunes had revealed anything to him since Lucius' meeting with the prefect.

Martialis did not seem like a man bent on assassination. In fact, he did not seem like an assassin at all.

Men would have said the same about me, in another life, Lucius told himself. *But that man is dead! Death is the only true catharsis left to me.*

In moments he took as weakness, as he rode alongside Martialis at the head of their century, the spring sun beating down, Lucius' spinning thoughts of vengeance were interrupted occasionally by Diodorus' voice, in particular a conversation they had had shortly before his old tutor had passed from the world.

"You cannot worry so about what you cannot control in the world, Lucius," Diodorus had said. They had been standing on the edge of the Capitoline hill, overlooking the Forum Romanum and the via Sacra. Diodorus had been feeling off at the time, and Lucius had noticed. The old man had also noticed the intense silence Lucius was losing himself in. He could tell that his pupil stood upon a precipice.

Lucius remembered looking at Diodorus and seeing the concern and care in the old man's eyes.

"Life is full of beauty and full of horrors. There never is one without the other. It is the way of things. You are a man of goodness, Lucius. You seek kindness and beauty in the world, but you should know that it will not always be so. In such instances, you cannot always change or control things. Life needs to happen. Even the Gods understand this. Some things should be left alone and allowed to evolve naturally. Men who try to force their will on everything eventually break. Like the Gods, sometimes men need to also step back and let things happen."

"Even if they are terrible?" Lucius had asked. "Even if people will get hurt or suffer?"

"Sometimes. It is a tragedy of life. The task for a man such as you is to know yourself and your abilities, and then decide where you can effect real change, and where it is futile to attempt to do so."

"But I can't just stand back and let evil men do whatever they want, can I?" Lucius had asked, and Diodorus had smiled at his idealistic naivety.

"Even Titans and Gods cannot forever carry the weight of the world's worries, Lucius." He had hugged Lucius tightly then, and the young man had thought he spied a tear at the corner of the older man's eyes. "Listen to me, Lucius. You are an exceptional young man, and you will become a great man. I have no doubt of that. But do not fall into the fatal trap of believing, as so many young men do, that you are a god. Fate and the Furies are not kind to such men, for their hubris can destroy lives."

As Lucius rode in the Praetorian column, Diodorus' words haunted him. It was as if the old man rode beside him. He had always sought to inspire his student with his words, but that conversation had struck a more fearful and ominous tone, and for that reason, it had stuck with Lucius. He had not thought of it for years, however. *Perhaps I didn't want to?* Lucius thought, but he gritted his teeth. "This is a change I can effect, Diodorus. You'll see."

"What's that you're saying, Optio?" Martialis was looking aside at Lucius, peering at him through the dust churned up by the marching troops ahead of them.

"Sir?"

"You said something just now."

"Oh. Sorry, sir," Lucius said, shaking his head. "Must have been thinking out loud."

"The desert does that to a man," Martialis said, looking out at the vast expanse of rock and dust. "Who is Diodorus?"

"My old tutor," Lucius answered without smiling.

"Tutor?" Martialis said, taking a swig of water from the skin that hung from his saddle horn. "Must be nice."

"I was fortunate."

They rode in silence again for some time, and several hours later, Martialis pointed ahead to where they could see walls and the green of scattered trees. "There it is... Edessa." The centurion shielded his eyes to look ahead. "I remember fighting here in the previous campaign. Do you?"

"Yes," Lucius replied, though the memories of that other life were quickly fading to nothing. "I remember it was the second city we freed. King Abgar had sided with the Parthians."

"More fool him," Martialis laughed darkly. "Never does to oppose Rome."

"Is he still alive?"

"King Abgar? Not a chance. The city has been heavily garrisoned since Rome took it back."

"How long will we stay here?" Lucius asked as they rode down toward the river crossing and the city on the other side.

"Who knows?" Martialis said. "As long as the emperor wishes."

Lucius observed the worried look on the centurion's face. He had carried it for most of that day, and Lucius wondered what dreams he had had the previous night that harassed him the whole of the day. But he said nothing as they rode.

After camp had been erected on the south side of Edessa, outside of the city walls, when Lucius and Martialis had returned from their rounds of the century, they sat together in the centurion's tent completing the lists of supplies that they needed before leaving Edessa.

When they were finished, Martialis poured them both some heavily watered wine.

"So, Pen Dragon? How does it feel to be on the march again?"

Lucius looked at the older man and observed how tired he truly was, how worried. "Honestly, Centurion, it feels strange. It's not the same as any other time."

Martialis was quiet, but he nodded in agreement. "I feel like things will never be the same again. In the previous campaign, there was an energy on the march, an excitement you could almost taste or touch. Severus rallied all those legions and almost charged to the front to get stuck into the fighting."

"I remember," Lucius agreed.

"Now…" Martialis looked around as if to see if anyone was listening. He whispered, "…now it feels like we're dragging our feet. The men around us don't have the stomach for the fight, or the will to fight. The emperor seems more concerned with emulating Alexander and training his new phalanx than reaching the legions." He downed his wine and poured some more. "I heard earlier that the fighting has intensified. Certainly at Hatra."

"Hatra was never easy."

"A death trap in the desert," Martialis agreed. "I just worry that-" He stopped himself.

"What is it, Centurion?" Lucius asked.

"Nothing. I don't want to tempt dark fate by uttering things aloud. I'm sure we'll move out soon. And if not, I'll see about petitioning the emperor. Maybe now I'm an evocatus centurion, he'll listen to me."

The emperor lingered for a few days in Edessa, and his Praetorian troops had no word of how long they would be there, how long they would wait. The men grew restless, eager to show the men of the legions how Praetorians could fight, how they were better. But that would not happen so long as they waited outside the walls of Edessa while the emperor dined with merchants and practiced phalanx manoeuvres with his Lions. Word came of more Parthian incursions on Roman-controlled settlements, swift and deadly cavalry charges usually accompanied by a hailstorm of Parthian fire arrows.

Macrinus and his commanders doubled the guard around the Praetorian camp and had three cavalry alae ready to go at any one moment.

Still, the Parthians did not approach Edessa. Still, the emperor did not move.

On the fifth day outside the walls of Edessa, Lucius was up early. He had woken to find his dry and damaged skin bleeding through his white tunic, and sweat beading on his forehead. He had dreamed that he stood before the Gods, that he could see each of them clearly, but could not speak to them or hear them speak to him, though their lips moved. He had seen Mars standing in a freshly-tilled field where the ruts in the mud had filled with blood. He had seen Epona upon a green field in the North as well. She had tried to reach out to him, but was unable to touch him as the tears streamed down her cheeks, Lucius' fallen men standing in the blood-stained field behind her, confused and forgotten. Worst of all, Lucius had seen Venus standing among the members of his family, and as they all wept without end, his wife's and children's tears turned to blood upon their pale skin. The goddess stared silently at Lucius, frozen, disappointed, and cold as death.

Apollo, what have you shown me? I beg you, Father. Guide me. Help me to finish this. I offer myself up for whatever punishment you see fit, if you will only grant me what I seek.

But in the pre-dawn quiet, Lucius was met with silence. The Gods were nowhere near him. All he could do was lay there, and grasp his black-handled weapons, and wait.

The cornu sounded some time later in the Praetorian camp, and Martialis grunted as he rose from his cot and armed himself for the day ahead.

"You all right, Centurion?" Lucius asked from his dark corner of the tent.

"The Gods tortured me this night with dreams of home." The old veteran splashed his face with water from a bowl set upon a tripod. "It weakens the resolve before a battle, and yet there is no battle."

"Do you think we'll march today?"

"I don't know anymore, Optio. I just don't know."

Lucius stood and put on his lorica.

Martialis saw him struggling with the ties, and went to help him. Then, he spotted the dried blood on his arms. "Are you ill, Pen Dragon? Why do you have blood all over yourself?"

"It's my old injuries, sir. I ran out of the ointment to treat them long ago. The desert air is too dry." Lucius shook his head. "Makes no matter."

"It does, Optio. You need to stay in fighting form. Today, I want you to stretch and exercise. Maybe the medicus has some rosemary and oil so you can treat your skin. I don't want you getting an infection."

"I'll be fine, sir."

"It's not a request, Optio. You remember orders, don't you?"

"Yes, sir. Sorry, sir. I would be grateful for the oil."

"Good. I need to speak to the camp prefect anyway about some supplies and-"

There were some voices at the tent entrance as the guards acknowl-edged visitors.

"Someone's here." Martialis said, going to the tent entrance just as one of the guards came in.

"Centurion," the man said. "Tribune Nemesianus is here for you. Something urgent."

Martialis walked past the trooper and stepped out into the dim, morning light. "Tribune." He saluted, and Lucius did the same as he joined them, also saluting. "What can I do for you, sir? Do we have orders to leave?"

Tribune Nemesianus did not seem in a hurry, but there was no mistaking the forlorn look upon his face.

"What is it, sir?" Martialis asked again.

"I'm to bring you to the prefect immediately, Centurion. There is news he wishes to give you." The tribune looked at Lucius fleetingly, and then back to the centurion.

"Of course, sir."

"Follow me," Nemesianus said. "Optio, you stay here." He shot Lucius a look, and then turned and led Martialis away to the principia.

Lucius stood in the tent entrance watching the two red cloaks disap-pear down the tent row.

"What's that all about, Optio?" one of the guards asked, Lucius.

"I have no idea," Lucius answered, though he wondered if the time had come for Macrinus to finally approach Martialis about the task. "Back to your post," Lucius said, absently, and the guards obeyed, opting not to say anything about the blood on his arms.

Julius Martialis marched along the tent rows with determined purpose, trying to compose himself for what may lie in wait for him. Though the Praetorian prefect was always civil toward him - much more than the emperor had been - he rarely had a personal audience with him. Martialis usually reported to the tribunes, but lately, he had seen the prefect more than he would have expected.

That's why he's a better leader than the emperor, Martialis told himself. *He actually cares about his men!*

When they arrived at the principia of the Praetorian camp, however, it was to find the courtyard filled with the rest of the tribunes and centurions, but also with several Scythians of the emperor's Lion guard who stood across from the Praetorians as enemies across a battlefield. They were mostly taller than the Praetorians, and variously armed with spears, clubs, longswords, and even small bows. Their chain and scale armour glinted in the sun. They were quite at odds with the purple, red, white and black ornamentation of the Praetorian camp, the flowing banners of lightning, scorpions, and eagles. There was a definite tension in the air, and there were raised voices within the command tent at the back.

"Follow me, Martialis," Nemesianus said over his shoulder as he strode through the crowd directly for the entrance.

Inside, they saw the emperor standing on the opposite side of the large table, facing the Praetorian prefect.

Nemesianus went to stand beside his brother, Apollinaris, and Martialis stood beside them.

The Scythians flanking Caracalla turned to look at the newcomers and then went back to standing guard beside their emperor.

"Sire," Macrinus was saying. "With all due respect, we should march now and join the fight. The legions need to see you in the field with all haste. The Parthians have almost overrun Nisibis!"

"What?" Martialis blurted to Nemesianus beside him, immediately bowing his head.

Caracalla turned to look at the old centurion, fire in his eyes, his brow knitted tightly together in a gorgon scowl. He said nothing, but looked back at his prefect. "We march when I say we march, Praefectus! When we engage them, we will blow the Parthians away like leaves in the wind. As soon as they see all our legions assembled, they will tremble and recall what happened when a Severan marched over these lands."

Macrinus pressed on. "The reports brought by the speculatores Augusti all point to bold new leadership in the Parthian army. Artabanus has used his rejection of your marriage proposal to his daughter as a weapon among his people to humiliate you. They are not afraid, and their bold actions confirm this. We need to march now."

Caracalla was fuming, and all those silent bystanders in the tent knew it.

As he watched, Martialis felt panic rising in his soldier's gut. *If the Parthians were already marching on Nisibis, then the lands east of there, all the way to the Tigris, could have fallen. Safira!* He thought of his wife, sons and his young daughter.

At that moment, Macrinus received a nod from Nemesianus who indicated Martialis standing beside him, his head down in thought.

"My emperor," Macrinus said, bowing his head in deference to Caracalla. "I have served you for years now. I have never led you astray. My spy network has been here since before the legions, gathering intelligence. We've enlisted the best evocati to bolster our ranks. If the Parthians take Nisibis back, we risk losing control of all the lands that the legions fought for twenty years ago under your father, may the Gods bless him." Macrinus came around the table to speak closer to Caracalla, ignoring the bulky Scythian who stood close by. "I've just received word this night that all the lands east of Nisibis have been razed to the ground. All Roman citizens have been massacred, including the families of some of our own evocati!"

Noooo! Martialis' mind reeled, and he felt like vomiting as he stood there among the officers and guards surrounding the emperor and prefect.

"How dare you raise your voice to me, Praefectus! I made you what you are! I can destroy you if I like!"

"Sire, I am loyal to you. I always have been. If we march now, directly for Nisibis, we might salvage this eastern portion of your empire."

"No one tells me when and where to march, Praefectus. That's enough!" Caracalla was shouting now, his hand upon his gladius as if he would have executed anyone who gainsaid him then and there. "What do I care for a few farmers, or has-been legionaries married to whores who birthed their bastards?"

"But they are all Roman citizens now. By your decree, sire," Macrinus said calmly. "We are duty-bound to go to their aid."

"Citizens?" Caracalla scoffed. "We all know that was to win some good will at a delicate time. "Like Alexander, when I show myself to the people along the march, to low and high-born, they will see me as their saviour and liberator from Parthian oppression. As Alexander defeated the great Persian empire, so too will I end the Parthians once and for all. But only when I decide the time is right!"

"I understand, sire," Macrinus said.

"You'd better. Or else my Lions will tear you apart!"

The two Scythians smiled at that, as if they could already smell their prey, taste his blood.

But Macrinus did not flinch. He bowed obediently to Caracalla. "Your Praetorians will be ready when you call, sire." Macrinus went back around to stand behind his desk and pour the emperor more wine.

Caracalla did not drink.

"Sire, what route do you propose to march on Nisibis?" Macrinus unrolled a large map upon the table top and the emperor stood to look at it, followed by other officers of the Praetorian and Lion guards.

Macrinus pointed at the mountain range south of them. "We cannot cross these mountains easily, so I propose a march to Batnae to the southwest of Edessa, and then, from there we can march eastward along the main road to Nisibis."

"Agreed," Caracalla said. "But we will stop at Carrhae for several days."

There was silence. The name of Carrhae was one of dread for many a Roman, for Rome's armies had experienced some of their worst defeats on that bloody plain.

"Sire, why Carrhae, if I may ask?"

"I wish to stop at the temple of Luna there and make sacrifices for Lemuria. Our Roman dead need to be appeased and honoured."

"Sire, Lemuria is over a month away. We will lose valuable time."

Caracalla reached out and grabbed Macrinus' neck kerchief, pulling him over the table to look closely at the map. "Are you questioning my orders again?" he shouted.

A couple of the officers stepped closer, but the Scythians turned, their daggers already out and pointed at them as they towered over the Romans.

"No, sire! I understand," Macrinus said, not bothering to struggle. *Yes. Put on a good show! Your time is coming!*

"Good. Now, the next person to question my authority will receive fifty lashes and no more pay for the duration of the campaign. Is that understood?"

"Yes, Imperator," Macrinus said, released now and holding his throat, his face red.

"Good!" Caracalla barked. "I'll inform Rome of our plans, and you can tell the legions at Nisibis that they need to hold that position on pain of death!"

Caracalla did not meet the eyes of the men in that tent, for if he had, he would have seen disappointment in their faces, and perhaps some hatred. But there was also acceptance, for the emperor knew what he wanted to do. His mind had been set on sacrificing at the temple of Luna at Carrhae for some time, and he would see it done. *The sun has always been my ally. Now, we shall win over the moon as well.*

"We march in three days!" Caracalla said as he turned and went out of the tent into the courtyard.

As the emperor passed with his two Scythians, Julius Martialis came out of his shock, the words he had heard still ringing violently in his ears. *No…no…no! We must go now! They may still be alive!*

"My emperor!" Martialis shouted, finding himself in the courtyard with the sun beating down on him.

All eyes turned to him, including Caracalla's.

"Gods! What is it?"

Martialis saluted. "Evocatus Centurion Julius Martialis, sire! May I speak?"

"What is it?" Caracalla said, looking annoyed as he flung back his purple cloak.

"Sire, I have a wife and three children. My family lives on the banks of the Tigris to the east of Nisibis on lands given to me in recompense for excellent service and blood that I shed willingly for your father, Emperor Severus." Martialis paused, taken aback by the eyes of so many on him, the looks from his fellow officers that told him to shut up. But he could not. He had to speak. "Sire, we cannot abandon our veterans and their families to torment at the hands of our enemies. They are all Romans! Can we not march now, and return to make sacrifices for our victories at Carrhae after we have won, after we have helped them?"

There were gasps as Caracalla looked around the gathering and began to laugh. He walked slowly toward Julius Martialis. "You want me to forego my oath to sacrifice at the temple of the Moon in order to comb through the burned rubble along the Tigris to look for the bones of your family?"

"Sire, I beg you. They may yet live, and if they do, we can help them and others. I have bled for years for this empire, and I will bleed again."

Caracalla got into Martialis' face then, his breath heavy with wine and garlic, spittle flying as he yelled. "I don't care about your whore wife and bastards, Centurion! Who do you think you are giving orders to an emperor?" He turned to Macrinus who had come out of the tent to listen. "Have all the Praetorians grown insubordinate, Praefectus? Have they? Perhaps I should replace you all with my Lions, so you can see what a real bodyguard behaves like?" Caracalla spun around, eyeing every Praetorian there fearlessly, backed by his barbarian guardsmen. He then turned on Martialis again. "We will not march to their rescue, Centurion. Nor shall you be permitted to go there yourself. You will be stationed in Nisibis when we arrive there, and the lands that you received from my father will be taken back. You are nothing, old man," he growled. He then turned to the Scythian over his right shoulder. "Fifty lashes for this one. Right now!"

"Sire, I must protest!" Macrinus said, but the Lions turned on the Praetorian officers then, leaving Martialis alone in their midst. "Stand down!" he ordered those Praetorians whose blades were out. "We are on the same side!"

"Quickly!" Caracalla barked, and four Scythians closed in around Julius Martialis to pull his weapons, cloak and armour off and throw them into the dust at their feet.

The evocatus stood there alone in his tunic. He did not struggle or protest, but looked the Lions in the eyes as they closed in and turned him forcibly, his back to the emperor so that Caracalla could see the damage to be done.

Julius Martialis waited for a moment before the lashes began to lacerate his skin. He made not a sound, but in his mind he cried out for the family that he would never see again as he felt the rivulets of blood running down his skin and soaking his tunic.

Men stood around the courtyard, amazed that the old centurion took his punishment so stoically, and when it was finished, the emperor and his Lions left without a word. Men approached Julius to touch his shoulder and pay him honour, but he was silent, numb to the world around him.

It was only when the Praetorian prefect approached him that he looked up.

"You're a true soldier, Martialis," he said, picking up the centurion's items from the dirt and handing them to him. "Come into my tent for some wine. There is something I need to speak to you about."

. . .

The entirety of that day had been lost to a rising panic in Lucius' gut, for it was dusk and he had still had no word of Martialis. One of the guards on duty told Lucius he had heard there was an argument between the emperor and the prefect, but the man had heard nothing else. Rumour was spreading, but there was no solid information.

As the sun began to fall, Lucius decided enough was enough and strapped on his weapons and packed a satchel. He would get a horse from the stables and disappear. *I won't wait around to be butchered in my sleep!*

He was about to leave the tent when he heard the tramp of hobnails coming and looked to see Centurion Martialis being escorted by a contubernium of the first cohort. Lucius could see that he was weak and that he walked stiffly, but he was not shackled. In fact, the guards took good care of him.

"Centurion," Lucius said, saluting Martialis and then stepping aside so that the men could lead him inside the tent. "What happened?" Up close now, he could see the bandages and blood staining through a new tunic.

"Optio…" Martialis grimaced. "I need to rest."

Two Praetorians led Martialis to the cot he pointed to and helped him down, while a third man set his armour and weapons upon the wooden dummy behind the table. The latter turned to Lucius. "Take care of him, Optio. He's been through a lot, and without a complaint."

Lucius nodded, and removed the helmet he had placed upon his head to set it down.

"Let us know if you need anything, Centurion," one of the guards said. "We'll be right outside."

"My thanks, soldier," Martialis said through gritted teeth.

Lucius poured some wine and sat beside his cot, but Martialis would not look him in the eye. "What happened to you?"

"I had a disagreement with the emperor and his Lions."

"What?"

The centurion's red and tired eyes turned on Lucius then. "All the lands east of Nisibis have fallen to the Parthians, and the emperor refuses to march."

"Martialis," Lucius said, not bothering with the title. "Your family?"

Martialis was silent as he stared at his old, thick and gnarled hands. *Helpless hands!* "None were left alive, the scouts say."

"No!"

Martialis shook his head. "Caracalla doesn't care, and he wouldn't let me go myself to see if they are, by some miracle of the Gods, alive."

"But why were you gone all day?"

"I challenged the emperor, and all he could do was mock and dismiss my concerns. My wife and children…they're nothing more than animals to him." The centurion hesitated, his voice quavering as if he wanted to weep for the loss of his loved ones, but he would not allow it. He shut his eyes and swallowed as his breathing evened out. "I received fifty lashes."

"Fifty?" Lucius said incredulously. "You shouldn't be standing."

"Praefectus Macrinus has a skilled medicus. He had him take good care of my wounds. That's where I was most of the day."

"Did no one try to stop it?" Lucius asked. *I would have slain Caracalla on the spot!*

"The principia was crawling with the emperor's Scythian Lions. It would have been a bloodbath. It was one of those big bastards who lashed me. Smiled as he did so!" He grimaced in pain and downed his wine. "More." He handed his cup to Lucius who refilled it. Once he had drunk more, he grew silent and turned to Lucius. "I also had a long conversation with the prefect…about you."

Lucius stared at him, and Martialis looked right back at him, taking in the dry, cracked and bleeding skin, staring at Lucius' chest where he knew the dragon brand lay beneath.

"And?" was all Lucius said.

"I know who you are, Lucius Metellus Anguis."

"That man is dead," Lucius said. "He died in fire, long ago. I am Lucius Pen Dragon now."

"And you are one of Rome's greatest warriors." Martialis reached out slowly to grasp Lucius' arm. "Even at the far eastern edge of the empire, I had heard of the 'Roman Dragon' who was defeating Rome's enemies in Caledonia…a man blessed by the Gods. Why didn't you tell me?"

Macrinus betrayed me! Lucius thought, but then he saw that there was no animosity in the centurion's eyes. There was only a great, shared sadness and exhaustion.

"I did not know you, Martialis. And, as you can see…" Lucius pulled up his sleeve to show his scars again, "…I am not blessed by the Gods.

They have turned their backs on me and grown silent. I've lost everything."

"Macrinus also told me what Caracalla has done to you and your family." Martialis shook his head in wonder. "You've been through so much."

Lucius was silent for a moment, his jaw tight as he pushed away the emotions that arose inside. He tried to tamp down the burning of the dragon brand beneath his armour. "And so have you, Julius Martialis." Lucius grasped his hand. "I'm sorry about your family. Truly sorry."

"We've all been suffering at the whims of an unfit ruler. I'm so tired of this world now," Martialis sighed and it was the closest sound to weeping he would make before Lucius.

"Me too," Lucius agreed. Then, a thought occurred to him. "Did the prefect say anything else to you?"

Martialis turned his head and nodded, his eyes darting to the entrance where the fire in the brazier without cast light into the tent, just short of where they sat in the near darkness. "He did." Martialis' voice was a whisper now. "He asked me to join you in a task."

"Yes?" Lucius wanted him to say it. He wanted confirmation that Macrinus had kept his word.

"I have never really hated a man before," Martialis said, "but I do hate Caracalla. Because of him, my wife and children lie dead upon the sand, eaten by jackals and carrion birds..." His voice shook, but he rallied himself. "And your world has been burned around you, your family hunted and your men slaughtered. There is only one thing to do, Lucius Pen Dragon."

Lucius nodded and grasped the centurion's hand.

"I will help you rid the world of this false emperor," Martialis whispered, his voice like a viper's.

Pain and loss changes us all, Lucius thought, recognizing the change in the soldier before him. "For Rome...and for our families," Lucius said.

"To the end," Martialis agreed, grasping Lucius' hand as tightly as he could. "And if we end up in Tartarus for it, at least we'll take that bastard with us."

XXII

APOTHEOSIS

'To the Gods'

J ulius Martialis did weep for the loss of his dead family.

Lucius could hear him in the darkness of the night as the watch-words were called out in the Praetorian camp, but he left him to it, said nothing of it. Lucius knew full well that he had his own share of torment and tears, for far too long. Martialis deserved his own journey through grief before he tasted vengeance.

A man's grief, his mourning, is a private affair, for him alone, and for the Gods who watch over him.

Lucius wondered what the Gods were thinking then as they watched him travelling southwest to Batnae, with Rome's Praetorians, a force of men that had given him no peace during his life. However, he knew now, having met many of them up close, that all that had happened over the years was not due to the uniform they wore, but to the men who led them, the men who gave them orders. That man was Caracalla.

It was a three day march from Edessa to Carrhae, and Lucius and Julius Martialis, who ignored the pain of his wrecked back, could feel the time approaching. They were constantly alert, armed, ready for any signal from Macrinus or the tribunes Nemesianus and Apollinaris. They kept a watch for the emperor, for any opportunity that arose, that would give them the opportunity they sought.

But no such opportunity came.

Caracalla travelled with his Lions alone, and at night, he was guarded in the centre of his own, private camp, by Scythian and Germanic steel.

On their second night, just before crossing one of the tributaries of the Euphrates, with Carrhae and the temple of Luna only another half day's march, the Praetorians encamped alongside the smaller force of Lions and the emperor.

The sky was vast, as if the Gods had stretched it out to its greatest extent to reflect the boundless Mesopotamian plain.

As evocati, Lucius and Martialis had more freedom to move about than most, and Macrinus had given orders for them to be excused from duties until the centurion had healed. Everyone knew, by then, of Martialis' courage and strength under the lash, and men saluted him as he passed with his optio.

Lucius and Martialis reached the eastern edge of camp and passed between the guards to go out and gaze upon the world.

It was strangely quiet as dusk settled and the sky began to dim enough to reveal the flickering of stars.

"It really can be a beautiful land under the right circumstances," Lucius said as he let his eyes sweep the distance toward Carrhae.

In summer the land was arid and choked with dust, especially when an army marched. But in spring, as he now saw it, Mesopotamia was covered with fragrant wildflowers, and clusters of scented pine, cypress and lemon groves. In places, grape vines had begun to sprout out of the rich red soil fed by the blood of armies, and along the rivers, barley crops whispered in the breezes off of the clear water.

"Spring was always best," Martialis said after a few minutes. "Now though…it's all poison. I wish I had never come here. The loss…it's too-" The centurion stopped talking. *Enough weeping!* he cursed himself and wiped his face roughly.

"It will be over soon," Lucius said to him.

"Good. I welcome death now, so long as I get a chance to finish the job." He walked a bit farther and bent to pick a flower that had risen out of the ground, its head turned toward the west where the sun was breathing its last for the day. "My wife used to wear these in her hair… I just can't believe this is how things have ended up. Look at this place. It's beautiful, a field for the Gods, and yet I hate everything about it. Nothing *is* beautiful to me anymore. Nothing tastes good or smells right. I want to destroy it all."

"Loss is acute," Lucius said, "and vengeance is the only way to erase it."

Martialis turned on him, doubtful. "Are you sure about that, Pen Dragon? What if they don't kill us after this deed? What then? I don't want to live anymore. There is nothing. My family is gone, and yours is lost to you."

Mine will be safe at last, away from me... Lucius thought, but he did not speak of his family much to the centurion, for he knew it would only distract and upset him.

"Macrinus promised me a great pension and honours once this is done, but what good is any of it without my family? I don't want anything but to plug my dagger into that arrogant shit and spit in his face as he dies. It's difficult when you can finally see the end of the road, but it *is* simpler."

"If it helps, Centurion, I've seen enough of palace politics to know that they will never let us live."

"Good." Julius Martialis turned and gazed out at the vast, darkening plane before them, leading up to cursed Carrhae. He held out his hand to Lucius. "To Death, then."

Lucius took his hand in his, and felt the cold closing in. "To vengeance."

In his tent at the centre of the Lion camp, Emperor Caracalla sat behind his table, spinning a golden dagger, watching the tip bore a hole into the polished cedarwood top.

The wind had picked up and the white walls of the tent, with their gold-painted acanthus borders fluttered and snapped. The burning braziers at each corner cast shadows upon the walls that made Caracalla look up each time only to see the still forms of his heavily armed Scythians standing like sentry statues, awaiting his bidding.

Suddenly, the spears of the two at the entrance dropped to block someone's approach, and Caracalla stood up, dagger in hand.

"I wish to speak with the emperor!" Macrinus said out loud, more for Caracalla's benefit than the barbarian guards.

"Let him in!" Caracalla barked before sitting back down and turning to the map he had spread out but not yet bothered to look at. "Macrinus. Come. Sit with me."

The Praetorian prefect sat down before the table, opposite the emperor. "I see that you received the wine that your mother sent you. It came to the Praetorian camp by mistake."

Caracalla looked at the open amphora that sat at the end of the table. "Yes," he said, looking to his cup. "Would you like some? It's Chian wine. One of the best." Caracalla refilled his cup from a silver pitcher and drank without waiting.

"No thank you, sire."

"Your loss then," Caracalla said. He creased his brow and rubbed his face harshly, the leather of his ornate cuirass creaking as he moved, and his golden intaglio rings clanging on the silver cup as he picked it up again. "My mother is in Antioch now," he said. "She says she will come to me once we retake Nisibis. Says she has intelligence that is only for my ears, only to be given in person." Caracalla's eyes turned on Macrinus. "You wouldn't know anything about that, would you?"

"I'm afraid I don't, sire. But I wish I did. As your head spy master, it is my duty to know all that is going on, to be aware of every threat. I swore I would keep you safe at all costs, and to that I remain true."

"I'm glad to hear it, but my mother's words were troubling. More readings from her astrologer, messages in the heavens."

"May I see the letter, sire?" Macrinus asked.

"I burned it." Caracalla turned to the bust of Alexander which he brought with him everywhere he went. "She troubles me like Olympias troubled the great Alexander. She just won't leave me alone."

"She cares for you, sire, like any mother. That is all."

"She cared more for Geta." Caracalla grew silent, but there was no sign of anger. "I wish I'd-" he stopped himself.

"Yes, sire?" Macrinus leaned forward.

Caracalla shook his head and drank again. "Alexander had his companions, and I have my Lions, and you. You are my Parmenion."

"Sire," Macrinus bowed his head, but he did not like the comparison to Alexander's old, traitorous general. He knew what Alexander had done to Parmenion. "Except that, unlike Parmenion, I am loyal to my emperor."

Caracalla looked up and his beady eyes squinted at the Praetorian prefect. Then, suddenly, he nodded. "I know. And I'm glad for it. You are no Plautianus either, that's for certain."

Macrinus felt his heart begin to pound beneath his cuirass, but he maintained his outward calm. "Sire, if I may speak."

"Yes."

"Alexander's companions…some of them betrayed him in the end. Are you sure about these Lions of yours? I do wish you would bring the Praetorians back into the fold. They feel jilted."

"I trust my Lions without question." Caracalla sat straight. "Why should my Praetorians be unhappy? They are more highly paid than any other force in Rome's history."

"True. But they would serve you more."

"Are there grumblings? Is that evocatus causing more trouble? If he is, I want him executed."

"Martialis has learned his lesson. In fact, the evocati among the Praetorians are your most loyal. They are also your most useful, for they have intelligence of the Parthians that none of the younger troops do. We can learn from them."

Caracalla looked thoughtful. "I'm too tired today, but perhaps after my offerings to Luna tomorrow, I can speak with my evocati and learn from them. Alexander was wont to learn from men with experience. So should I be, to quicken the victory."

"Yes, sire."

"I need victories now. For myself. For the men. We all need victories," Caracalla said, almost sadly. "Even Alexander's men mutinied." He turned to the bust of his misunderstood hero again. "You may go," he said, waving his hand suddenly.

Macrinus stood and bowed. "Imperator."

"One more thing!" Caracalla stood quickly, hitting the table so hard it spilled the wine on the map of Mesopotamia. "My Lions have said they've seen a burned and bleeding man walking around the Praetorian camp. He seemed strange to them. Do you know him?"

"Ah, yes. He is one of our most valuable and experienced evocati. He sustained horrific injuries in the previous Parthian campaign and has never recovered. He is one of the men I mentioned who knows much of the Parthians."

"I look forward to meeting him then. Dismissed, Praefectus."

"Sire," Macrinus said, bowing again as he turned and went out past the Lion guards. *Drink up, sire,* he thought as he smiled to himself.

Caracalla sat back down and refilled his fallen cup, drawing a path to Carrhae in the spilled wine with his finger. "Don't worry, Geta. I'll make an offering to the Moon on your behalf tomorrow, so that Luna can light your way in the darkness."

The wind gusted again, and Caracalla picked up his dagger once more, his hand shaking as he did so.

. . .

The winds persisted all night long. It had been a restless night for the Praetorians, the Lions, and for the emperor. The land of life and springtime that had lain spread out to either side of the road to Carrhae the previous day was now blurred with dust and dirt that turned the rising sun to a struggling orange blur in the eastern sky.

Lucius and Martialis had not slept. How could they when they stood on the precipice, that cliff of vengeance from which they would hurl themselves? They knew it would be the following day, for it had to be before they reached Carrhae.

The previous evening, the tribunes Nemesianus and Apollinaris had come to them to reiterate the plan and ascertain the two men's will to carry out the task. When they found Lucius and Martialis sitting together, sharpening their weapons, their question was immediately answered.

"You will both ride with Macrinus and us tomorrow, at the front of the column," Apollinaris had said to them.

"Whenever the time comes," Nemesianus whispered, "the window will be a short one. My brother and I will distract the Lions who are nearest to give you a chance."

Lucius looked up at the two tribunes and then back to Martialis. "We have a plan then."

"We do," Apollinaris said. "We'll leave you to it now. Rest up, men."

"Good night, tribunes," Martialis said, his voice as sharp as the steel blade in his hands.

The tribunes turned and left without another word. They had tolerated the two evocati long enough and looked forward to killing them when the time came.

"We'll be able to call ourselves the slayers of the 'Dragon' after it is done!" Nemesianus said to his brother as they walked back to the principia.

"Our names will be on everyone's lips. We'll be the toast of Rome!"

The march was slow, the howling wind and dust worse after the emperor's marching column crossed the river and followed the road that led to Carrhae. Conversation among the ranks of marching men and horses was difficult, and so each man journeyed in silence, following the man in front, accompanied by his own thoughts. There were no marching songs either, for the Parthians could have been near enough to launch an assault of arrows out of the dust that swirled around them.

At the front of the marching column, Caracalla rode surrounded by his mounted Lions. They were followed immediately by the aquila of the Praetorian legion, the imagines, vexilla and other banners. Following these, Macrinus rode with the tribunes Nemesianus and Apollinaris, and the two evocati, Julius Martialis and Lucius Pen Dragon.

Lucius and Martialis had been given horses to ride, but they did so in complete silence amidst the tribunes and the Praetorian prefect.

Occasionally, Lucius turned around to see the tribunes behind him and the rest of the long file of Praetorians who disappeared in clouds of dust. It was a time to think for Lucius, and he wished it was not. But the desert and the march had always pulled him in, played with his mind.

Was he ready to end things? Was he ready to die?

The questions plagued him and, though he told himself he was ready, that he was tired of the life he had been leading, tired of letting those close to him down, there was a seed of doubt which he fought to crush with his built-up anger and hate with every step his horse took. He focussed on Caracalla's outline just ahead of the Praetorian banners, his purple cloak snapping in the wind, his newly-made lion helmet dull in the dusty light. *You've caused me too much pain. I won't let you harm my family ever again!*

But being in that land, Lucius' mind continued to wander, to ponder, to go back to the people he had met in his travels, and as he looked at the stretching plains to either side of the road, he thought he could see them standing there, staring at him from within the clouds of sand, twitching flowers, and windswept trees.

General Laetus, the hero of Nisibis stood there, saluting... *It is a dangerous world, for good men,* he said.

Aelius Galenus, in Alexandria, appeared to stand among the rows of scrolls of the library to remind Lucius... *I know there is strong philotimo in you. Do not let the ways of the world burn it from your soul.*

I've already burned, Lucius argued in his mind, looking down at his arm which was bleeding again through the cracks in his skin, like water seeping through a caked desert plain. *What good has philotimo done me or my family?* He thought of all the dead, all the pain caused by the man riding a short distance ahead, but the word 'philotimo' choked Lucius where he sat. *It's almost finished, Lucius! You're almost there!*

Then, walking out of a cloud of dust to sit beneath a lone tree by the roadside, Diodorus appeared, his beard and tunic as white as ever, his smile sad and thoughtful. He seemed to look up at Lucius. *Gods and men must all deal with the consequences of the battles they choose, the choices they make... You must choose, Lucius...*

I have chosen! Lucius wanted to scream, but he knew he must remain silent, though he craned his neck to watch Diodorus pass by.

"Stay calm," Martialis whispered as he leaned in to Lucius. "What's wrong with you? You keep looking around!"

Lucius looked at the man and, for a moment, wondered if he was another apparition. "Just looking for Parthians."

"Trust me. If they hit us, we won't have time to think," Martialis said.

"That reminds me," Macrinus said casually, turning in his saddle to speak to the two evocati. "We'll be stopping soon. The emperor wishes for you both to give him what intelligence you have about the Parthians. I told him you knew much that could help him in his strategy." The Praetorian prefect eyed them sharply, but gave no other indication of anything. It was all in his eyes, as it was in the tribunes' when Lucius turned to look at them.

"We'll be happy to share what we can with our emperor, Praefectus," Martialis said.

"Good," Macrinus answered, and then looked forward again.

Lucius felt his heart begin to pound faster. He thought of his brothers, Caecilius and Ashur, both worlds apart, both dead in the end. *I'll join you soon, my brothers,* Lucius thought as he fingered the handles of his black gladius and pugio.

Lucius...only by letting go can you be truly free... Ashur's voice echoed in his mind.

I will free us all, Ashur - my family, the empire, everyone. This will be my final act! He thought of Adara, Phoebus and Calliope, their faces hovering in his mind, their voices reaching out to him. *I will keep you safe! I love you all...*

Lucius rubbed his eyes of the dust that had gathered there, but quickly removed his hands when he heard raised voices and the sound of the cornu.

"HALT!" Macrinus ordered as he observed the signal from Caracalla. "The emperor wishes to stop!"

"Halt!" Tribune Nemesianus shouted to the first cohort behind him, and the order was echoed down the line.

Lucius reined in with Martialis and the tribunes behind them while Macrinus rode ahead to confer with the emperor.

A few moments later, Macrinus rode back. "We'll stop here for a time!" he shouted, then said to Nemesianus and Apollinaris. "He needs to empty his bowels. Something about the wine he drank last night." He winked at the tribunes, then turned to Lucius and Martialis. "I just asked Caesar if he wished to hear your intelligence on the Parthians now."

"Now, Praefectus?" Martialis asked.

"Yes. Now. We cannot waste the emperor's time." He turned to Nemesianus and Apollinaris. "Tribunes, take our evocati to the emperor."

"Yes, Praefectus," the brothers said in unison, saluting Macrinus sharply and nudging their horses forward, followed by Lucius and Martialis.

"Farewell...evocati," Macrinus muttered, then turned in his saddle to ensure his men were all close. When the time came, they would have to slay many Lions and stain the plains around Carrhae with more blood.

Caracalla had ridden a little ways off of the side of the road to a private spot behind a large rock that jut out of the plain, surrounded by cypress trees. He would have preferred a cool oasis to relieve himself and wash before his offerings to Luna, but there were no oases nearby.

"Wait here for me!" the emperor commanded the two Lions who had accompanied him, tossing his reins to the one, and his lion helmet to the other before disappearing around the corner of rock.

The guards nodded and turned to scan the area where the other Lions milled about, stretching their saddle-sore legs and backs and checking the distance for any approaching forces.

A short time after the emperor had disappeared around the rock, the tribunes Nemesianus and Apollinaris approached the two guards with two evocati.

The one Lion stepped in front of them to block their way.

Martialis recognized him as the one who had lashed him, and the big Scythian smiled as he recognized him in turn.

"The emperor has asked for these two men to come to him immediately. They have valuable intelligence about the Parthians," Nemesianus said to the guard.

"None see the emperor!" the Scythian said in broken Latin.

"Listen...Lion," Nemesianus said, getting into the Scythian's face. "Your emperor commanded it!"

"What's going on?" Caracalla's voice shouted from around the corner.

"Praetorians say they have Parthian information, Emperor!" the guard answered.

"Let them through!" Caracalla responded with a grunt.

The Scythian eyed the tribunes, and then looked at Lucius and Martialis. "No weapons," he said, gripping the shaft of his spear tightly. There was no negotiation to be had.

Nemesianus turned to Lucius and Martialis. "You heard him. Give me your weapons."

Lucius and Martialis looked at each other briefly and then each withdrew their gladius and pugio and handed them to the tribunes.

"Go!" the Scythian said. "Tell the emperor what you have to tell."

Lucius and Martialis walked toward the trees and the large rock formation, the voices of the tribunes talking to the Scythians about horses fading into the background.

Lucius went first, his heart in his throat, a ringing in his ears that turned to soft music.

Love's voice emerged from that rushing wind around him, even as he stepped closer to his long-sought prey.

You came back to this life of pain for Love...not vengeance.

Please stop, Lucius pleaded. *Let me do this!*

He then caught sight of Mars, standing in the dust-choked air a short distance away. The god's arms were crossed, his eyes staring at Lucius, neither approving or disapproving. *You must choose,* Mars said. *Destruction or Creation...*

"How do we do it without our weapons?" Martialis suddenly hissed in his ear now that they were out of sight of the Scythians.

Lucius put up his hands and made fists, even as he remembered the sight of his family weeping and full of pain.

Martialis nodded. There was panic in his eyes, but also grim determination as he too saw the faces of the people he had lost, as the hate he felt for the man squatting in a crack in the rocks now spilled out.

"Si...sire?" Lucius said, coming to a stop as he saw Caracalla.

"Tell me what you know, soldier!" the emperor said, glancing up at the two evocati and frowning at the one he had ordered lashed.

"Sire, the Parthians are nearby," Lucius said.

"They...they use the dust storms to cover their movements. We should dig in when we get to Carrhae," Martialis fidgeted, eyed the gilded gladius and pugio that hung from the emperor's shoulder and cingulum.

The air about Caracalla stank, but he did not seem bothered by his audience. They were all slaves to him. He finished, rubbed sand between his hands, and stood up. "Is that all?" he asked. "Macrinus said you had important information." He scowled and seemed about to call for his guards when Lucius stepped closer.

"Sire, listen carefully. The Parthians are not what they seem. There is an enemy far more dangerous than them who is closer."

"What enemy?" Caracalla said, eyeing the blood seeping from the skin on Lucius' arms, staining his white tunic.

"Death."

"Death? What are you talking about?" Caracalla said, looking directly at Lucius then.

"Death is here for you, sire," Martialis blurted.

Caracalla's eyes went wide and he was about to scream for his guards when Lucius' fist snapped out and pounded his face three times, knocking him back into the rock wall.

Lucius and Martialis closed in quickly. Martialis grabbed Caracalla's weapons, but stumbled backward over a dried log.

Caracalla made to run again, but Lucius pounded him with all his strength and then brought his knee into the emperor's gut, winding him.

Lucius could feel the full force of his rage releasing. "Don't you recognize me? You took everything from me! You hunted my family! You burned my world and killed my friends! You burned me!"

Lucius could not help himself. His fist pounded in and out, over and over. He did not feel the bones breaking in his fists, or Caracalla's flailing retaliation into his own face, the nails scratching wildly at his already bleeding arms.

"Do it now, Pen Dragon!" Martialis hissed, standing again with the gladius poised to strike.

"Pen Dragon?" Caracalla was confused as he stared through his already swelling eyes at Lucius. "Metellus?" He began to shake his head. You're supposed to be…to be dead!"

Lucius struck again to head off his call for help.

"I am dead. I am death! You won't harm any of us again! You're no Severus and you're certainly no Alexander." His knee struck again and Caracalla bent over, but Lucius gave him no time to catch his breath and pulled him up again. "You're a murderer, Caracalla. Nothing more. And I'm going to finish this!"

Lucius grabbed the gladius from Martialis and pushed Caracalla against the rock wall with the point at his throat, his hand shaking.

Others suddenly appeared at his side, and the faces he saw there horrified him as they smiled at him and urged him to strike, to bring death.

As the blood pounded in Lucius' ears, and as his left fist struck Caracalla again and again while his right waited for the moment to strike, he could see the faces of his former enemies, of Brutus and Plautianus smiling. Then, closing in, his father and Argus nodding their assent, urging him to do it. The arrogant and smiling face of Claudius Picus was there too. *Kill him, Metellussss….* he hissed.

Everything grew still then, as if time were frozen and in amongst the pulsing of blood and the cries of Martialis to finish the job, a note of music cut through the surrounding chaos, and the voice of Apollo spoke in Lucius' mind, his heart, his soul…

Sometimes, the enemies we seek to slay…whom we need to slay…are not the ones we see before us. Let go…and be free.

Lucius stopped striking Caracalla then and held him at arm's length. His sword arm shook violently, and even as Caracalla struck out at him, he held him fast, and looked closely at him.

He no longer saw an enemy, an emperor, or a murderer. All Lucius saw when he looked upon Caracalla's bleeding and swollen face was a young man who had gone astray, a wretched son and brother.

"I'm finished with you, Caracalla," Lucius said, his grip loosening. "You can't hurt us anymore." He let the gladius fall to the ground with a clang. Pity filled Lucius now. "Go, Caesar. Your fate awaits you…and I will have no part in it."

Lucius backed away and Caracalla slumped over, exhausted by his beating.

"Gua... Guards!" Caracalla suddenly screamed. "HELP!"

But Lucius did not look back as Martialis rushed in with the pugio and plunged it into the emperor's side. He did not see the old centurion run, or the two Scythians pursue him across the plain to impale him on their spears. He did not see the two tribunes rush to Caesar's side and plunge their own blades into his gut, his side and his face over and over until Caracalla lay dead in a heap near the plain of Carrhae.

Lucius did not care anymore. It was not his fight. He had let go.

"Where did Pen Dragon go?" Nemesianus called out as he watched the Scythians finish off Martialis. "Where is he?"

Lucius walked calmly through the chaos, spears and arrows flying in every direction, the clang of battle between the Lions and Praetorians muted and far away. He had no urge to look back. He was only happy to breathe again.

He had no concept of how far he walked, but eventually the dust cleared and the air was bright and crisp and fragrant. The smell of death, and feelings of hatred and anger were utterly forgotten. He no longer walked among ghosts, but across a brilliant spring-flowered field, a firmament upon the earth, toward the sound of music. The farther he walked, the calmer he felt.

The sun rose and fell, he knew not how many times, but all was beauty, every ounce of life around him filled him once more with hope.

Then, standing beneath a tall palm in the middle of that plain exploding with colour, he looked up to see his father waiting for him.

This time, Apollo strode to him, his arms open, tears streaming from his own godly, star-whirling eyes like comets in the heavens.

As Lucius fell forward, Apollo caught him and held him tightly.

"Lucius...my son..." The Far-Shooter's voice quavered as he held Lucius and looked him in the eyes. "I never thought I could feel such pride."

Lucius looked confused. "Am I dead?"

Apollo smiled and shook his head. "No. Far, far from it. You can now live."

"But..."

"You did well, Lucius. So well… Now, you are ready…"

"I know myself," Lucius said, standing straighter, feeling for the first time the complete absence of pain, of anger, of torment and jealousy and bitter resentment. And as the realization came to him, he saw the golden light coming off of his limbs, the pulsing life. He could feel the transformation as his skin healed, as his hair grew, as his mind and body became calm and strong and the poison of evil and vengeance faded into memory.

Lucius wept then, as Apollo held him. "Thank you, Father."

"You have yourself to thank, Lucius." Apollo held him out and Lucius stood tall and strong of his own accord.

"What now?" Lucius asked.

Apollo smiled. "Everything."

And together they walked across the plain, leaving the chaos of the world of men behind them.

EPILOGUS

Antioch, A.D. 217

The imperial residence in Antioch was silent as dusk's red light filled the marble corridors. The evening sea breeze rustled the flames in braziers and the silk hangings that shivered over balconies and windows.

Julia Domna sat alone now. She had dismissed her servants and handmaids, and sent away her Syrian cousin who had just brought her the news from Carrhae.

"The emperor has been slain, my lady," he had said. "Macrinus has been acclaimed emperor by the troops."

How was it that so few words could devastate a life, a world, a soul?

I am alone now, she had thought. *This must be what Olympias thought when they brought her word of Alexander's death.*

"Leave me," she had told her cousin, and the man had slipped out as quietly as he had appeared. "Oh, my son…" she said to herself when she was alone, "…I've failed you."

She stood, the silk of her orange stola rustling like the flames in the braziers. She set down the scroll that she had been reading, the one of Philostratus' *Heroicus*. The words she had found so poetic and inspiring before, now fell to the ground, dull and grey, like ash floating through the air from a fire.

The wave of sadness began to build in her soul then, and she cursed herself for not going with Caracalla, for not riding to meet up with him to warn him of what her spies had heard - that Lucius Metellus Anguis lived, and that her son was in danger.

She had failed the Metelli as well, but an empress had to use people to achieve certain ends. How could she have known that the stars and the Gods themselves would turn their backs on her and on her son?

My son… The thought occurred to her as she searched for a reason that, perhaps, in some dark corner of her heart, she wanted her son to die. She had never quite forgotten his face as he had slain Geta in her arms. *Now, you are both gone, and I am quite alone.*

In the past, she would have pressed on, mourned her losses, and held her head high and proud as she had been taught to, as she had been forced to.

But now, Julia Domna felt that she had nothing to live for.

She took a golden dagger from her table - the one she normally used to cut the bindings on new scrolls and texts that were sent to her - and, standing beside the great marble bath that her servants had drawn for her before her cousin's tidings, she slit the stola down its length so that it fell in a pool about her feet. She stood there, naked in the chilling breeze and, for a moment, watched the smoke in the bowl of a tripod spin and whirl into the air. Before stepping into the steaming water beside her, she slit the ribbons that bound the waves of her hair so tightly to her head, and let her tresses fall about her bare shoulders.

The water was warm as she lowered herself in, but she felt nothing but a creeping cold running up her body to strangle her neck.

She knew that her sister, Julia Maesa, would not weep for her. She had waited long enough for her chance at power, and she would take it. *Oh, she will take it! My sister will tear at the empire like a fury, and Macrinus won't last long.*

A part of Julia Domna felt good not to care about what should happen tomorrow of thereafter. I want to join my husband and sons in whatever realm of the dead they may reside. *I am too tired now,* she thought before taking three deep, soothing breaths.

Then, Julia Domna took her gilded dagger, pressed it to her left wrist and cut deeply up the length of her arm. Her tears began to roll down her olive cheeks then to disappear in the steaming water, now clouding with her blood. She then put the dagger to her right wrist and cut again, though less effectively.

Her world began to blur, and she wanted to sleep.

"I'm coming, Septimius...my shining Star...Geta, my beautiful Moon. And Caracalla...Antoninus...my brilliant Sun... I'm coming..."

Britannia, A.D. 218

How does one return to the world after so many trials, so much death, anger and loss? How does one find the peace within that is required to let go of such things? How does one, be he man or god, muster the strength needed to go on after living through experiences that few could ever hope to understand?

After such trials as his, Lucius Pen Dragon found himself walking a different road than the one he had set himself upon - the road home. However, he was not as he once was - a good man fighting hard against the cruelty of the world, or against himself. Nor was he a man of vengeance. He was something else.

As he travelled from the far eastern edge of Rome's empire, Lucius found that the world was a completely different place. He saw everything in a new light, and the world about him was flooded with beauty once more.

The perspective of the Gods changes a man into something else... something more.

And yet, he was still outside of the world he sought to return to. He always would be. All he sought was the family he had been reconciled to never seeing again, the family whom he had abandoned so that he might walk a road of blood on the way to the shores of the black river.

Lucius travelled long, his thoughts constantly focussed on his wife and children, and the Gods walked with him. But when he came to sacred Delphi, he found that his family was gone, all of them. He stood in the middle of the humble domus on the slopes of Parnassus, sat beneath the lone olive tree, and turned over the shame and regret that he felt, before letting them go on the wind like wheat chaff from the hand.

"They've all gone, Lucius Pen Dragon." Theia, his father's Pythia, entered the courtyard and walked up to him. Upon seeing Lucius, she bowed her head, for she could see the transformation in the one-time man before her. She would have shielded her eyes but for the bright embers of sadness evident upon his face. *Even Gods can feel despair.*

"Where have they gone?" Lucius asked, though he knew the answer in his heart. He stood easily and as he stepped into the sunlight.

She could see that he had been renewed. With awe in her eyes, Theia reached out and took his hands. "They've gone back to Britannia."

"When?"

"Shortly after you left Delphi." Theia stared into his eyes and there she could see what many could not - the spinning stars in the heavens, beyond the peaks of Olympus itself. "Will you go?"

"Yes," Lucius answered, staring up at the sky and closing his eyes. "I must."

Theia nodded, but before she had a chance to speak again, to invite him to stay with her until he departed, he was already walking away.

As Lucius passed her, he touched her shoulder, and she felt a well spring of joy within, a burden lifted. She turned to follow him to the outer wall of the compound and watched him disappear through the slanted grove of olive trees. "Farewell, son of Apollo."

It was late summer when Lucius stood on the marshy shores of the sacred lake, the morning mist swirling around him, the sound of birdsong among the reeds and golden light growing louder and more melodic.

He stood still and thoughtful now, for the road had been long and lonely. But his hesitancy was not borne of blood and death, but rather of his own neglect of those he had always thought he fought for. He had abandoned his wife and children, his family, and in turn, they had departed without him, reconciled themselves to life without him.

How can I walk back into their lives? Lucius wondered.

"Just as each season walks into the other, Lucius Pen Dragon." The voice was soft, familiar and full of a kind of sad joy.

Lucius turned to see the thee white hounds with red-tipped ears running toward him and fussing about his legs. He bent to pet them and then looked up to see their mistress leading her glowing stallion by the reins toward him.

"You've come back," Epona said, letting the reins fall and taking Lucius' hands. "I had always hoped that-"

Her animals grew still as the goddess wept.

"I could not see you in the darkness."

"I couldn't see myself, lady." They embraced tightly, the light filling that lakeside space of green beauty. Lucius released the goddess and looked into her eyes, framed by her flaming hair. "How is my family?"

She was silent a moment as she turned to gaze across the lake. "They believed you abandoned them forever. That you chose blood over love."

Lucius felt the beauty of the world fading as he pondered his return, what his children would think, what his truest love might say or feel. "All along my travels - after the Light - I've thought of them, of returning to them and holding them close… But now that I am here on the shores of the Isle of the Blessed, I don't know if I can go on." He turned back to her. "Have they moved on? Have they forgotten me? I can see much now, but that is the one thing I have not been able to decipher when I look to the heavens."

Epona smiled sadly. "You still cling to a mortal fear when you should have moved past it. No one can ever move beyond thought of you, Lucius Pen Dragon. You touch lives in myriad ways. Go to them. Let them decide for themselves how they will meet you." Without looking away from him, Epona said, "The boat is here."

Lucius looked out to the water to see the smooth lines of a small boat floating toward him. It came unbidden, unmanned, through the spinning mist, to settle in the reeds before them. He turned to Epona and grasped her hands.

"I will see you soon," the goddess said.

Lucius smiled and stepped into the boat, but before he sat, he turned back to her. "My men? My dragons? How are they?"

"They thrive."

He looked down.

"And they remember you, their brother…their Pen Dragon."

"Thank you," Lucius said, as he sat in the boat and moved slowly into the mist.

Epona watched him for a time, lingering in the feelings of his changed presence. "He is not the same," she said.

"He never will be," came the answer as Apollo and Venus emerged from the forest behind to stand with her at the water's edge.

"He has survived his apotheosis," Love said.

"But will he survive the loneliness that comes with it?" Epona asked, feeling the tears in her divine sight. "He can never truly be one of them again."

Apollo stepped into the water to watch his son reach the far shore, the shore he had been seeking for so long. "The manner of Lucius' survival will be of his own choosing…but he will never be truly alone."

The boat reached the far shore of Ynis Wytrin to emerge into the golden light of day that suffused that blessed isle. In the distance, the faint sound of the Christian bell sounded in concert with the cawing of ravens, and late summer flames flickered upon the altars of the Gods.

Lucius' eyes, however, were drawn to the mass of the Tor itself as it came into view, its broad green ridges and soaring height giving him a sense of peace. But all of that faded away when he saw the tall, lanky form of a girl walking along the shore toward the dock at the base of Wearyall hill.

Lucius felt his throat catch as he watched her, his limbs begin to shake, and his heart shudder. "Calliope?" he said, and the girl stopped in her tracks to gaze across the swaying reeds at him.

"Baba?" her voice quavered. "Baba!" She was running now, her long legs carrying her like Diana over a forest floor.

Lucius could see the glistening tears upon her cheeks as she charged toward him, her white tunic and cloak flapping wildly like clouds in a gale, until she collided with him in an embrace that was as full of love and gratitude as was possible in the world.

"My girl," Lucius said as he held his daughter tightly upon the jetty. "I'm so sorry." *I never thought to see her again,* he realized.

Calliope looked up at him, shaking her head in disbelief. "I told them you were coming! But no one believed me. They were afraid to! But I saw you. I dreamed you were healed, that you were returning!" She reached out to touch his smooth face, and the soft lengths of his dark hair. She gazed upon his arms to make sure her sight had been true, and it had. "Oh, Baba! I missed you so much." And she wept then, for several minutes. Her tears streamed as offerings of thanks upon the Gods' altars.

When Lucius stood, his hand tightly clasping Calliope's, they turned to see Phoebus standing at the end of the jetty watching, weeping silently into the morning. *I will never doubt my sister again,* he thought as he ran toward his father.

Lucius received a second onslaught from his grown son, and held him tightly, willing every ounce of strength and calm into him, and the three stood huddled together, lingering in the return, for some time.

"I thought you were dead, Baba. I thought I would never see you again." Phoebus had many questions, but somehow, they faded upon his tongue. He would have liked to know of blood spilled and anger released, but those were thoughts for another day, another time. In that moment, he was grateful for the gift the Gods had sent them. "Your injuries?" Phoebus said, even more shocked by the sight than his sister.

"I am better now," Lucius answered. "But tell me…where is the rest of the family? Are they all here?"

Phoebus shook his head. "Grandmother and grandfather are living in Lindinis. They could not stay here."

"And Emrys and Carissa are with Einion and Briana at Din Tagell," Calliope added.

"Carissa found him?" Lucius asked, grateful that she had made her way home.

"Yes. She did. Captain Creticus brought her."

"And my sister? Clarinda?" He knew she would not be happy to see him, for he brought news that would shake her to her core.

Calliope nodded. "Etain has made her a priestess here. She said Aunt Clarinda was skilled and that a priestess of Apollo was welcome in Ynis Wytrin." Calliope realized who was missing then, and looked up at her father. "And our uncle?"

The look in Lucius' eyes told all, and the children hugged him tightly.

Lucius had so many questions, about everyone, their stories, their thoughts. They whirled like a storm in his psyche, each clearly heard unlike ever before. But there was one question that he could not hold off any longer.

"Where is your mama?"

The children grew silent, their heads downcast.

"Adara is here, Lucius."

Lucius looked up to see Etain, Weylyn and Father Gilmore waiting with Rachel and Aaron. He walked toward them with his children.

"Welcome back, Lucius Pen Dragon," Weylyn said. The old druid smiled at Lucius.

"You have travelled a long road," Etain said, reaching out her hands to Lucius. "You are well again."

"I am."

"What road did you take, Baba?" Phoebus asked.

Lucius paused and looked at his children. "The road that leads back to you." He sighed. "Where is she?" he asked Etain.

"She sits beneath the great oak everyday," Weylyn said and stepped closer to him. "Lucius. Adara is not the same. She has been lost."

Lucius felt his heart sink, his mind reel back to despair. Somehow he could feel what Adara was feeling in that moment. It felt impossible to explain, but he had been dreaming of, and dreading, seeing her again.

"Baba," Calliope said beside him. "When you left...Mama...she-" Calliope could not say the words, but turned to her brother.

"Mama lost the baby when you left, Baba. She's not been the same since."

"As soon as she got your family here safely," Etain added solemnly, "she turned inward on herself."

Lucius was silent, the world about him still. He could feel Adara's despair, the unfathomable depths of sadness in which she was drowning because of the loss of her husband and child.

"Are your hands clean of blood-guilt, Lucius Pen Dragon?" Father Gilmore asked him suddenly.

Lucius turned to the priest. "Yes. They are."

"Then go to your wife and help her to heal," Father Gilmore said. "She needs you."

Lucius looked at the faces about him, those of his children and friends, people who cared for his family, people who had become his family. They all looked at him differently, for the ravaged and pained man who had left Ynis Wytrin so long ago was gone. Now, a true dragon stood in their midst.

Without another word, Lucius left the jetty and lapping water to go to his wife.

Adara sat, as she always did, beneath the broad limbs of the ancient oak, gazing at the lake, sending her thoughts out into the world, hoping that the Gods would hear her prayers. But she knew in her heart that she had given up hope long ago, when her love had abandoned her, and when their child had died inside of her.

She was tired of the world, of her ponos, the individual struggle she was burdened with. It never ended. For a while, upon her return to Britannia, she had been happy among friends in Din Tagell, with Einion and Briana and Dagon, but after a time, they had only served to remind her of her loss, of Lucius.

True, it was peaceful in Ynis Wytrin, but it was also lonely. For many months, she had wallowed, bathed in despair, comforted only by the fact that her two children were safe, alive. The sight of them living back in Ynis Wytrin kept her alive, though she had no idea what sort of life the Gods had in store for them. Wherever she sat, there too Dread sat beside her.

That morning, Calliope had been mumbling in her sleep about her father's return yet again, but Adara had ceased to believe her after so long, wondering if her daughter had gone mad with grief after her father's departure. Phoebus too had changed, spending much time alone by the shore, swinging his gladius at reeds, practicing against unseen enemies.

Thank the Gods for Rachel and Aaron, Adara thought, for the two Christian youths had, inexplicably, helped her own children by their very presence and friendship.

That day had been much the same as any other day. Adara had risen late, made her offerings to the Gods, and sat to stare out at the wind upon the water as the sun tried to burn its way though the mist that surrounded them.

It was that very day that she had made a decision to live life on her own, not as a widow, and no longer as a doting mother. She remembered the feel of a sword in her hand, and the strength of her training in her body, her limbs. She wanted to feel that strength again, regain that clarity.

And so she had set aside her dark mourning robes for the boots, breeches and tunic of a warrior. It was the only way she could meet more days, more sunrises and sunsets. She did not know if she would stay or go, but she would not wallow any longer.

And if Death finds me at last, I will welcome it, she thought as her nails dug into the thick bark of the trunk upon which she sat.

Over the last months, she had wondered how different her life would have been if she had not come to Rome with her parents all those years ago, if she had not met Lucius. Would the Gods have found a way to bring them together anyway? Or would her choices have led her down a very different path? She knew that if she had not met Lucius, she would not have known love, had children, seen the terrible beauty of the world, and become a warrior in her own right. Rather, she would have been some other's lady, locked in a loveless marriage, nodding politely at gatherings where women and men lived separate lives, their greatest concerns being the next business venture, or the latest fashion trend.

That is not me, she knew. The life she had led was full of love and fury, inspiration and tragedy, and yet…it was hers, and hers alone.

That had been a day like any other until, looking out to the water and swirling mist, she felt a cool breeze upon the back of her neck, and the racing of her heart. Something, someone, had come into Ynis Wytrin, and as Adara turned her neck, she saw Lucius standing there before her, watching her with eyes as bright as the stars in the heavens.

"Adara?" He spoke her name as he looked upon her, but he did not yet approach.

She stood, the braids in among the strands of her hair swinging in the wind. She wanted to speak, but she found herself mute. She felt relief and love, but also a great anger and resentment. Finally after a few moments, she walked slowly to face him. She could see Phoebus and Calliope beyond his shoulder, waiting and watching.

Adara wanted to strike him for all the pain and anguish he had caused her, but she found she could not. Her children were there, their hopes fulfilled at last, and there was something in his eyes that told of unfathomable struggle, of loss and life shared.

"You came back to us," she said, her green eyes alight with emotion, but no more tears. "I thought you were dead, Lucius."

Adara's voice tore at Lucius' heart, and he knew then that the woman who had loved and trusted him was gone. She had been the true casualty of his war with himself, and a tidal wave of regret began to build far out in the seas of his mind.

"I'm sorry, my love," he said, stepping close to hold her.

She returned the embrace, her fervour and relief in the strength of her limbs as she held him, but the light that poured from him could not penetrate the cloak of resentment she had draped about herself. After a moment, she stood back, her eyes glistening.

"You broke my heart, Lucius. You left us."

"I did what I believed I had to do…for you…for our children."

She shook her head. "You robbed me of my own choices. You chose blood and revenge over love…over us."

There was a world of hurt in her voice, pain in those eyes that had once looked upon him with purest love. She reached up to touch his skin, his hair, and knew that he was healed, but that he was not the man she had known.

They had both changed.

The wounds of the body might mend, but the wounds of the heart and soul, of lacerated love, and loss and vengeance and betrayal, those were not so easily fixed.

"I was wrong, Adara. But there is hope." He turned from her to see their children. "They're alive and well. You're alive." He turned back to her.

They stared into each other's eyes, their hands clasped as if they struggled to hang onto each other from one world to the next. They had both changed.

They both knew they still loved each other, for a love such as theirs was not so easily erased by fate. But it was a different love now, a war-torn love. And they would have to live with that.

They turned to Phoebus and Calliope and waved them over.

They ran to their parents and together, the four of them huddled for a time, in love and gratitude, ignoring the demons that hungered in the shadows. For now, they stood safe in the bright light of day, rejuvenated but utterly changed.

"I love you all," Lucius whispered as he held his family close about him, and he felt the emotion more than he had ever thought possible, knew that no one could ever rob them of it, that no flame could ever burn it away.

Lucius would have stayed there the entire day and night in the embrace of his family, but there was one other person he needed to see.

He had returned alone to Britannia and Ynis Wytrin, but he had left Delphi with Caecilius. The sight of his bother dying in his arms in that faraway desert still haunted Lucius from a distance, but he relived it in detail now as he approached the well of the chalice where, Etain had told him, he would find his sister.

Lucius walked through the thick arches of ivy and fern, past the ancient yews, to find Clarinda sitting in quiet meditation beside the red-running waters of the well. She sat beside the pool where he had returned from the world beyond the living, where he had felt pain explode in his senses.

Now that I am healed, I must bring her pain, he thought as he emerged from the foliage to stand before her.

Slowly, the cowled head and dark-circled eyes looked up to see him.

"Lucius!" she cried, jumping up from her seat and rushing toward him. "I can't...I..." The tears burst forth, choking her words, and Lucius would have used his new-found strength to shield her from the pain he would bring, but it was not possible. "I prayed to Apollo that he would bring you both back safely some day," Clarinda said excitedly. Then, she began to look around. "Where is Caecilius?"

Lucius was silent as he looked upon his younger sister, upon her tightly closed and wet eyes, her quivering lips. She shook her head and buried it in his shoulder, and as she slumped to the ground, her cries burst forth to shake the leaves of that blessed isle.

It felt strange for Lucius to walk the green grass of Ynis Wytrin again, to see the sunrise from atop the Tor or witness the tree of Joseph shiver in the cool breeze on Wearyall Hill. The sight of priests and priestesses working in the angling light, the gentle sound of birdsong, and the trickle of sacred water were at odds with the growing turmoil Lucius felt within. He could not remember a greater sense of peace, or a greater sense of unease than he did in the weeks after his return.

Peace only lasts if we find comfort in the middle of the storm, he realized. *We've weathered many storms,* he thought as he watched his family go about life on the isle.

Lucius thought about travelling to Din Tagell to visit Dagon, Briana and Einion, but every time he came close to leaving, he felt he could not do so, for he had, for too long, brought them all grief.

"May I sit with you?" Father Gilmore said to Lucius one day.

"Of course." Lucius sighed.

The priest sat down beside Lucius upon the fallen trunk of a tree and together they watched Lucius' family working alongside the others at the harvest. "I must apologize to you, Lucius."

"For what?"

"For being so harsh on you before you left here."

Lucius smiled at the priest, saw a greater understanding in the older man's eyes, an understanding he had learned from his youthful charges. "It was deserved."

"Still... I hope you bear us no ill will."

"I am finished with ill will, Gilmore." Lucius smiled but it quickly faded as he looked back to his family and the distance of grass between them.

Father Gilmore had observed what was happening to Lucius and his family, and he and Etain and Weylyn had discussed it. The family had done much to help Ynis Wytrin, blind to beliefs, and they deserved what help could be offered, be it companionship as the children shared, or a kind word from one to another.

Gilmore cleared his throat and breathed deeply of the cool air. "I don't know of all that you have been through in your life, Lucius Pen Dragon. But I do know this... It is lonely to be a leader of men. Great leaders always suffer for the good...for the safety... of others. Our Christus did as much for us..."

"Yes?" Lucius said, wondering what Gilmore was getting at. They had not always got along, the two of them, but there was something different in the way the priest now spoke to Lucius. There was kindness in his voice, respect and understanding. "What do you mean?"

Gilmore sighed, and looked about embarrassed, hesitant. "I can see that you have suffered greatly...and that this sacred place...your friends...and your family are all safe as a result of your suffering."

"And many have died..." Lucius said, his voice wrung with that emerging grief that came out of quiet.

"And such is man's lot when God looks upon him...when he is picked for a purpose. There is birth, and there is death. There is good, and there is evil."

"Not much hope then," Lucius added, but Gilmore continued.

"But the more men who hold good in their hearts and deeds, the better a place the world will be. There is *always* hope."

"And we are never alone," Lucius finished.

"Never."

Lucius smiled at Gilmore. "Thank you."

Gilmore did not reach out to touch Lucius, but he smiled as warmly as he ever had in Lucius' presence. He would have said more, but he decided not to, for in saying more, he might learn more of the half-mortal man before him. And that was not a prospect he wished to explore. Some things were better left unexplored.

.　.　.

You are never alone, Apollo had often told Lucius in his most desperate hours, in the dark of night when the moon was full upon the desert sand, or shedding its silver light into the grove of a northern wood.

Lucius knew his divine father was right, but he also knew that as he sat behind the foggy veil of Ynis Wytrin, he never felt more alone. It was as if he were melding with the world, seeing everything, and yet not being seen.

Adara, Phoebus, and Calliope carried on living their lives, comforted by his return, and yet no longer orbiting his fatherly sun. They had their own roads to explore and travel, their own choices to make. Clarinda too had pulled away, lost in her grief and, despite her attempts not to do so, blaming Lucius for her brother's death.

It was the eve of Samhain once more, and Lucius watched Adara helping with baskets of apples, newly-picked from the orchards. They had been through so much together and, though they were reunited now, their individual struggles and his own choices had inexorably pulled them apart.

"I have so often been blessed and cursed by the Gods," Lucius said to himself. "I need to let go, so that they can be free."

He saw a change, not only in how his family perceived him, but also in the way everyone else spoke with him, watched him, and even avoided him. Dragons were creatures to be treated with respect, awe, and also with fear.

He looked to the October sky where clouds sped across the indigo canvas of the heavens, and dried leaves spun on the wind. He could see the stars beyond, the planets, the shivering constellations, and he knew that no one else there could see what he saw.

Back in the small guest house a while later, Lucius sat alone by the fire, his eyes stinging for the words he wanted to say, but for which he could not find earthly expression. As he stared at the radiant image of the dragon in his hands, the image that he now carried with him always upon his flesh, he could feel the winds picking up, pulling at him as the bonfires were prepared for the long, dark night. He could also feel and see clearly now, the faces of all the dragons who had gone before him. They stared at him through the thin veil of that October night.

Finally, with a deep breath, Lucius set the wrapped image of the dragon back inside the strong box, stood, put on his long black cloak, and went outside to find the path that led to the top of the Tor. As he went, he turned to look back at Phoebus and Calliope where they were sitting around a fire, smiling and talking with Rachel and Aaron and some of the other young priests and priestesses. Nearby, Adara stood solemnly with Clarinda, Etain, Weylyn and Gilmore.

I love you, Adara, Lucius said in his heart, and at that moment, she turned from the gathering and waved to him. As if they too had heard, Phoebus and Calliope turned to wave also.

"I'm so proud of you," Lucius said to himself of his children.

He then turned to begin the long climb to the top of the Tor, and as he went, all colour and light and sound was a thousand times more alive than it had ever been. When Lucius reached the top, he turned to see Ynis Wytrin and the lands beyond the veil where the Samhain fires burned brightly.

Lucius sat there for some time, thinking of many things - of loved ones, friends and enemies long gone, of victories and defeats, of the terrible beauty that had been his life in the world.

And now he was a part of a new world, a world others did not understand, could not understand.

"I hoped I would find you here, Dragon."

Lucius heard the voice, and it was louder and clearer than he had ever heard it before. It came on the rushing wind at his back, emerged from the brilliant, growing light that opened up in the dark upon the Tor.

Lucius stood slowly, and turned to see the Boar of the Selgovae standing before him once more. He stepped out of the light, and some of that light lingered in his person, but he stopped short of Lucius, his eyes wide.

"You've changed, Lucius Pen Dragon."

"How did you know?"

The Boar looked back at the gateway behind him and smiled. "There is a whole world of knowing beyond the veil...and the Dragon's name is whispered everywhere." The Boar stepped closer now. "You vanquished your enemies?"

"I vanquished myself," Lucius answered. "Now there is nothing."

"Your family is safe, Dragon. That is not nothing."

Lucius smiled at the thought, the relief that brought, but his sadness welled up even then as the fires blazed across the land, and the light shone upon him from the Otherworld as well as from the heights of Olympus itself.

"This world is not a place for Dragons," the Boar said, and he understood Lucius in a way that few others did anymore. His eyes locked onto Lucius. "In Annwn, anything is possible. You are borne of two worlds, Dragon. You have lived in one. Come back with me. Live in the other too, and see your family safe for all time."

Lucius peered past the shining warrior to the world beyond, and there he saw a vast green land of rolling hills, of forests filled with game, and mountains from the tops of which one could gaze out over the world. It was a place where gods and heroes dwelled, a place where a dragon could live freely.

"Come. I will show you a new beginning, a new life. Heroes are not meant to hide, Dragon, and every world needs a hero."

Lucius looked down the steep slope of the Tor to see his family sitting around the fire, and he found he could see them clearly, their smiles, their tears, the lines of grief and joy upon their faces. He could also feel what they felt, the love, the pain, the great sadness and confusion.

"I need to let go...for them, for my love of them..."

"It is no easy thing, I know," the Boar said. "I knew, when I rode off to battle against you, that I would not see my family again. But it was what was needed."

"And I need to let them live," Lucius said, his voice shaking before he caught his breath and felt calm fill him.

"Yes," the Boar said. "But you will be with them always. You may feel alone at times, but they will never be alone."

Lucius shook his head, but hesitated.

"The decision is yours," the Boar said. "Know only that you are welcome in Annwn...that there is a place for you, should you wish it." The Boar turned and made his way slowly back to the light. "The Gods love you, Lucius Pen Dragon. They wait for you."

Lucius watched him disappear, turned away from the light to watch his family, and to stare out into the dark of night across that land. He knew that he was no longer needed.

If the Gods could feel sadness, what Lucius felt then was a maelstrom of love and loss.

"I'm tired of the world," he whispered to himself and the Gods who were with him always. "I love you with all of my being," he said to his family down the hill. "You are never alone."

Lucius Pen Dragon then turned and walked slowly into the brilliance of that otherworldly light, and a new song began in his heart, in time, as the fires burned in the mortal world, and Annwn welcomed him.

"Farewell…"

THE END

Thank you for reading!

Did you enjoy *The Blood Road*? Here is what you can do next.

If you enjoyed this Eagles and Dragons adventure, and if you have a minute to spare, please post a short review on the web page where you purchased the book.

Reviews are a wonderful way for new readers to find this series of books and your help in spreading the word is greatly appreciated.

More Eagles and Dragons novels will be coming out in the future, so be sure to sign-up for e-mail updates at:

https://eaglesanddragonspublishing.com/newsletter-join-the-legions/

Newsletter subscribers get a FREE BOOK, and first access to new releases, special offers, and much more!

To read more about the history, people and places featured in this book, check out *The World of The Blood Road* blog series on the Eagles and Dragons Publishing website.

Become a Patron of Eagles and Dragons Publishing!

If you enjoy the books that Eagles and Dragons Publishing puts out, our blogs about history, mythology, and archaeology, our video tours of historic sites and more, then you should consider becoming an official patron.

We love our regular visitors to the website, and of course our wonderful newsletter subscribers, but we want to offer more to our 'super fans', those readers and history-lovers who enjoy everything we do and create.

You can become a patron for as little as $1 per month. For your support, you can also get fantastic rewards as tokens of our appreciation.

If you are interested, just visit the website below to watch the introductory video and check out the patronage levels and exciting rewards.

https://www.patreon.com/EaglesandDragonsPublishing

Join us for an exciting future as we bring the past to life!

AUTHOR'S NOTE

Writing *The Blood Road* has been a journey unlike any other, and there were times when I did not think that this book would be finished. It has haunted me more than any other story which I've set out to tell.

Are we our own, greatest enemies? Is the world truly dangerous for good men? Is all the torment in life a direct consequence our own actions? Am I truly good? Can one really protect loved ones from the world? Who am I? Can one only truly be free when one lets go of the struggle?

In order to tell the story, I needed to ask these same questions of myself, the better to understand the questions that tormented our hero, Lucius.

Storytelling, they say, can be a cathartic process, but I almost did not live to finish this story, for in my own struggle with the human experience, I went to some very dark places, this year of pandemic notwithstanding. I felt quite alone, and hopeless, but for the light of my loved ones. We are never alone, it is true, but that is not to say that we don't feel like it at times. Writing a story such as this is, by the very nature of the process, a supremely lonely endeavour. We all have our struggles, and we all need help to get through those struggles. As we've seen in this series, and in most stories, pride gets one nowhere, and the hero's journey is painful and real.

Lucius Metellus Anguis (Lucius Pen Dragon) made very human mistakes through his choices on his own journey, but in the end, he saved his family. In a way, he also saved me.

Some readers may not like how this story ended, but not all stories end happily, especially after such a struggle and so much suffering. Lucius' main struggle throughout the series has been to keep his family safe, even at the expense of his own happiness. As I neared the end of this tale, the ending seemed more obvious to me, more unavoidable. For those readers who would have preferred it to end differently, I know that you may not like it, but I hope that you understand it.

A lot of research went into *The Blood Road*, as is the case with all of my novels. However, it is true that there is a decided change in direction from pure history to a style more interwoven with fantasy. That said, this more mystical view of the world is also historically accurate, for our ancient ancestors believed that the Gods walked among them and actively participated in their lives. Some also believed that they were descended from the Gods themselves.

The Blood Road is not all fantasy, however, and there are certain historical facts and events that are a big part of this book. As always, my main source for this period has been Cassius Dio's *Roman History*, with some added detail taken from Herodian's *History of the Roman Empire*. These two ancient writers really are the only extent sources for the period, and though their accounts are often called into question by modern historians, they are a true gift for an author of historical fiction.

I have always tended to trust Dio's account more, since he was closer to the imperial family and likely knew them personally. His seems like more of a historical account, whereas Herodian, though rich in detail, reads more like a gossip column, full of outrageous slander about Caracalla especially.

The omen with the wolves at the beginning of the book is from Dio, and I felt that that would be an interesting way to open and lead the way with one of the most traumatic events in the Severan dynasty's history - the brutal murder of Geta. Both Dio and Herodian agree here that Geta was murdered by his brother, Caracalla (Antoninus) in the arms of his mother, Julia Domna, and that her clothes were soaked with her son's blood. There are small differences in detail during this time, with Herodian talking about Julia Domna's desperate attempts to reconcile her sons prior to this horrific event, but to no avail, and Dio goes into detail about the number of Geta's followers Caracalla executes after he murders his younger brother. According to Dio, Caracalla executed twenty-thousand men, women, and children who may have had any relation or interaction with Geta. Rome was bathed in blood once more.

Both Dio and Herodian talk of Caracalla's German campaign and how he adopted Germans and Scythians to form a special guard. They speak of the various ways in which Caracalla's mental health degrades and his acts continue in horrifying manner with the execution of Vestal Virgins, and a subsequent massacre at Alexandria. I did not include all the deeds of Caracalla in this novel simply for the fact that, as darkly entertaining as they are, they would have taken up too much space, and this is not a story about him, but rather about Lucius.

Still, details such as his obsession with Alexander the Great and the introduction of the Greek phalanx formation were just too enticing to leave out, as was his anger with the Parthians for rejecting his offer of marriage to their princess. To Caracalla, it probably seemed that the world was mocking him, and if the events in the sources are to be believed, this only enflamed his insecurity and madness which, according to Dio, caused him to have visions and dreams of his father and brother.

Other details from the sources are also interesting. The rise of Marcus Opellius Macrinus does seem very strange indeed. It is true that he rose from having nothing in Mauretania, to making a living as a gladiator, a hunter, a postal courier, an administrator of the via Flaminia, and a legal advisor for the dreaded Praetorian prefect, Plautianus. Whatever the reasons Caracalla had for appointing Macrinus to the position of Praetorian prefect, it is clear that Macrinus was a man of ambition.

According to Dio, Caracalla would mock Macrinus publicly, and so the stage was set for a murder. It gets interesting when we learn from Dio that an African oracle warned of Macrinus' future treachery and this information was sent to Julia Domna who sent a letter to her son to warn him. Another letter was sent to Macrinus that he was in danger from Caracalla. It seems that Julia Domna's warning to her son never reached him, and so his fate was sealed.

Perhaps one of the most helpful pieces of information which Cassius Dio's account contributed to this book are the names of the men whom Macrinus enlisted to murder Caracalla on the road to Carrhae. Julius Martialis is indeed mentioned as a retired legionary who was serving as a centurion evocatus. The tribune brothers, Aurelius Nemesianus and Aurelius Apollinaris are also mentioned. According to Dio, Martialis was the first to plunge his blade into Caracalla when he stopped to relieve himself on the road, and when he failed to finish the job and ran - only to be slain by the emperor's bodyguards - Nemesianus and Apollinaris swept in to finish the job.

Julius Martialis, according to Dio, hated the emperor for humiliating him and for not giving him the post of centurion which, in our story, Macrinus does. Feeling that this was not enough motive to attempt to slay an emperor, I created the backstory of Martialis' family and their death at the hands of the Parthians.

The meeting of Caracalla's three would-be assassins felt like the perfect opportunity to grant Lucius entry into that inner circle, so that he could carry out his mission of revenge.

In a way, Caracalla and Lucius mirror each other in this book in that they are both victims of their own choices along a road drenched with blood. In the end, however, Lucius is saved by his decision to let go, whereas Caracalla's decisions culminate in his humiliating death by the roadside.

Herodian tells us that, stricken by grief at the death of Geta first, and then of Caracalla, Julia Domna died in Antioch, either by her own hand, or by order of Macrinus. After so many years at the head of this dynasty, the revered 'Philosopher', Augusta Julia Domna, must have been tired of life, and so it seemed a logical end to her life. Surely, she would have seen what was coming, and would not have given Macrinus the satisfaction of executing her.

Chaos was to reign in the empire once more. Macrinus was acclaimed emperor by the Praetorians and he soon made his son, Diadumenian, Caesar. But the upstart emperor would only rule for about a year before Julia Maesa made her move and set her grandson, Elagabalus, upon the imperial throne after the battle of Antioch in A.D. 218.

It certainly seems that every road, in Roman history, is a blood road, and the Severan dynasty was no exception.

For more information about the history, people and places in this novel, be sure to check out *The World of The Blood Road* blog series on the Eagles and Dragons Publishing website.

After reading this book, some readers may be wondering if this is the end of the Eagles and Dragons series.

Let me assure you, it is not.

The series is far from finished, but like anything else in this world, it will change and evolve. Characters will come and go, but their deeds will be remembered. These books are a big part of my life, and it has been inspiring to me to receive e-mails from readers who have told me that the story and characters are a big part of their own lives, that they have helped them to get through their own adversity. It is the dream of every novelist to be blessed with such readers, to be able to help and inspire, and I am excited to continue the journey with you.

Will we see Lucius Pen Dragon again in the world of men? Only the

Gods know. But as we have seen in the world of Eagles and Dragons, anything is possible.

Thank you for reading.

Adam Alexander Haviaras
Stratford, Ontario
February, 2021

GLOSSARY

adyton – the innermost sanctuary or shrine in the cella of a Greek or Roman temple

aedes – a temple; sometimes a room

aedituus – a keeper of a temple

aestivus – relating to summer; a summer camp or pasture

agora – Greek word for the central gathering place of a city or settlement

ala – an auxiliary cavalry unit

amita – an aunt

amphitheatre – an oval or round arena where people enjoyed gladiatorial combat and other spectacles

anguis – a dragon, serpent or hydra; also used to refer to the 'Draco' constellation

angusticlavius – 'narrow stripe' on a tunic; Lucius Metellus Anguis is a *tribunus angusticlavius*

apodyterium – the changing room of a bath house

aquila – a legion's eagle standard which was made of gold during the Empire

aquilifer – senior standard bearer in a Roman legion who carried the legion's eagle

ara – an altar

armilla – an arm band that served as a military decoration

augur – a priest who observes natural occurrences to determine if omens are good or bad; a soothsayer

aureus – a Roman gold coin; worth twenty-five silver *denarii*

auriga – a charioteer

avia – grandmother

avus – grandfather

ballista – an ancient missile-firing weapon that fired either heavy 'bolts' or rocks

bireme – a galley with two banks of oars on either side

bracae – knee or full-length breeches originally worn by barbarians but adopted by the Romans caldarium – the 'hot' room of a bath house; from the Latin *calidus*

caligae – military shoes or boots with or without hobnail soles

cardo – a hinge-point or central, north-south thoroughfare in a fort or settlement, the *cardo maximus*

castrum – a Roman fort

cataphract – a heavy cavalryman; both horse and rider were armoured

cella – the inner chamber of a Greek or Roman temple

cena– the principal, afternoon meal of the Romans

cetus – (plur. ceti) a whale

chiton – a long woollen tunic of Greek fashion

chryselephantine – ancient Greek sculptural medium using gold and ivory; used for cult statues

civica – relating to 'civic'; the civic crown was awarded to one who saved a Roman citizen in war

civitas – a settlement or commonwealth; an administrative centre in tribal areas of the empire

clepsydra – a water clock

cognomen – the surname of a Roman which distinguished the branch of a gens

collegia – an association or guild; e.g. *collegium pontificum* means 'college of priests'

colonia – a colony; also used for a farm or estate

consul – an honorary position in the Empire; during the Republic they presided over the Senate

contubernium – a military unit of ten men within a century who shared a tent

contus – a long cavalry spear

corbita – a large, Roman merchant ship capable of carrying very large cargoes

cornicen – the horn blower in a legion

cornu – a curved military horn

cornucopia – the horn of plenty

corona – a crown; often used as a military decoration

cubiculum – a bedchamber

curule – refers to the chair upon which Roman magistrates would sit (e.g. *curule aedile*) decumanus – refers to the tenth; the *decumanus maximus* ran east to west in a Roman fort or city

dediticii – a class of persons who were neither slaves, Latin allies, or Roman citizens

denarius – A Roman silver coin; worth one hundred brass *sestertii*

dignitas – a Roman's worth, honour and reputation

domus – a home or house

draco – a military standard in the shape of a dragon's head first used by Sarmatians and adopted by Rome

draconarius – a military standard bearer who held the draco

eques – a horseman or rider

equites – cavalry; of the order of knights in ancient Rome

fabrica – a workshop

fabula – an untrue or mythical story; a play or drama

falcata – curved, single-edged blade capable of delivering extremely heavy blows

familia – a Roman's household, including slaves

flammeum – a flame-coloured bridal veil

forum – an open square or marketplace; also a place of public business (e.g. the *Forum Romanum*)

fossa – a ditch or trench; a part of defensive earthworks

frigidarium – the 'cold room' of a bath house; a cold plunge pool

funeraticia – from *funereus* for funeral; the *collegia funeraticia* assured all received decent burial

garum – a fish sauce that was very popular in the Roman world

gladius – a Roman short sword

gorgon – a terrifying visage of a woman with snakes for hair; also known as Medusa

greaves – armoured shin and knee guards worn by high-ranking officers

groma – a surveying instrument; used for accurately marking out towns, marching camps and forts etc.

hasta – a spear or javelin

horreum – a granary

hydraulis – a water organ

hypocaust – area beneath a floor in a home or bath house that is heated by a furnace

imperator – a commander or leader; commander-in-chief

    insula – a block of flats leased to the poor

    intervallum – the space between two palisades

    itinere – a road or itinerary; the journey

lanista – a gladiator trainer

    lemure – a ghost

    libellus – a little book or diary

    lituus – the curved staff or wand of an augur; also a cavalry trumpet

    lorica – body armour; can be made of mail, scales or metal strips; can also refer to a cuirass

    lustratio – a ritual purification, usually involving a sacrifice

manica – handcuffs; also refers to the long sleeves of a tunic

    marita - wife

    maritus - husband

    matertera – a maternal aunt

    maximus – meaning great or 'of greatness'

    missum – used as a call for mercy by the crowd for a gladiator who had fought bravely

    mortarium – wide Roman kitchen vessel used for grounding, mixing and pounding food

    murmillo – a heavily armed gladiator with a helmet, shield and sword

nomen – the gens of a family (as opposed to *cognomen* which was the specific branch of a wider gens)

    nones – the fifth day of every month in the Roman calendar

    novendialis – refers to the ninth day

    nutrix – a wet-nurse or foster mother

    nymphaeum – a pool, fountain or other monument dedicated to the nymphs

officium – an official employment; also a sense of duty or respect onager – a powerful catapult used by the Romans; named after a wild ass because of its kick

optio – the officer beneath a centurion; second-in-command within a century

palaestra – the open space of a gymnasium where wrestling, boxing and other such events were practiced

palliatus – indicating someone clad in a pallium

pancration – a no-holds-barred sport that combined wrestling and boxing

parentalis – of parents or ancestors; (e.g. *Parentalia* was a festival in honour of the dead)

parma – a small, round shield often used by light-armed troops; also referred to as *parmula*

pater – a father

pax – peace; a state of peace as opposed to war

peregrinus – a strange or foreign person or thing

peristylum – a peristyle; a colonnade around a building; can be inside or outside of a building or home

phalerae – decorative medals or discs worn by centurions or other officers on the chest

pilum – a heavy javelin used by Roman legionaries

plebeius – of the plebeian class or the people

pompa funebris – a funeral procession

pontifex – a Roman high priest

popa – a junior priest or temple servant

primus pilus – the senior centurion of a legion who commanded the first cohort

promanteia – the right to be first to see the oracle ahead of others, granted to individuals or groups such as cities

pronaos – the porch or entrance to a building such as a temple

protome – an adornment on a work of art, usually a frontal view of an animal

pteruges – protective leather straps used on armour; often a leather skirt for officers

pugio – a dagger

quadriga – a four-horse chariot

quinqueremis – a ship with five banks of oars

retiarius – a gladiator who fights with a net and trident
rosemarinus – the herb rosemary
rusticus – of the country; e.g. a *villa rustica* was a country villa

sacrum – sacred or holy; e.g. the *via sacra* or 'sacred way'
schola – a place of learning and learned discussion
scutum – the large, rectangular, curved shield of a legionary
secutor – a gladiator armed with a sword and shield; often pitted against a *retiarius*
sestertius – a Roman silver coin worth a quarter *denarius*
sica – a type of dagger
signum – a military standard or banner
signifer – a military standard bearer
skene – the theatrical backdrop of an ancient theatre
spatha – an auxiliary trooper's long sword; normally used by cavalry because of its longer reach
spina – the ornamented, central median in stadiums such as the Circus Maximus in Rome
stadium – a measure of length approximately 607 feet; also refers to a race course
stibium – *antimony*, which was used for dyeing eyebrows by women in the ancient world
stoa – a columned, public walkway or portico for public use; often used by merchants to sell their wares
stola – a long outer garment worn by Roman women
strigilis – a curved scraper used at the baths to remove oil and grime from the skin

taberna – an inn or tavern
tabula – a Roman board game similar to backgammon; also a writing-tablet for keeping records
tepidarium – the 'warm room' of a bath house
tessera – a piece of mosaic paving; a die for playing; also a small wooden plaque
testudo – a tortoise formation created by troops' interlocking shields
thraex – a gladiator in Thracian armour

titulus – a title of honour or honourable designation

tor – Celtic word for a hill or rocky peak

torques – also 'torc'; a neck band worn by Celtic peoples and adopted by Rome as a military decoration

trepidatio – trepidation, anxiety or alarm

tribunus – a senior officer in an imperial legion; there were six per legion, each commanding a cohort

triclinium – a dining room

tunica – a sleeved garment worn by both men and women

ustrinum – the site of a funeral pyre

vallum – an earthen wall or rampart with a palisade

venator – a hunter

veterinarius – a veterinary surgeon in the Roman army

vexillarius – a Roman standard bearer who carried the *vexillum* for each unit

vexillum – a standard carried in each unit of the Roman army

vicus – a settlement of civilians living outside a Roman fort

vigiles – Roman firemen; literally 'watchmen'

vitis – the twisted 'vinerod' of a Roman centurion; a centurion's emblem of office

vittae – a ribbon or band

ACKNOWLEDGMENTS

This books is dedicated to Calliope, the Muse of epic song. That may seem strange to some, but there is a reason for it. The act of creating something, the journey of writing a book or series of books, is not an easy one. It's a long and arduous road. So what is it that motivates one to keep going through all the hardship, the self-doubt, the doubt of others who ask what it is you actually do in life? What is it that urged a fifteen-year-old boy who skateboarded and listened to punk music, who never really read much, to suddenly and completely dedicate all of his time and mental energy to studying history and expressing his deep love of history through fiction?

Now, I'm not really a religious man, but in the last thirty years I have certainly become a man of faith in the act and importance of creation. I've come to believe that when writing stories like the Eagles and Dragons series, I am not alone. In those early morning moments of writing, when no one else is awake, when the words come pouring out, I know that I have had help. Some might call it being in 'the Zone', but I feel that it is more like hearing the Muse whisper to me, urging me to dip my hand past that magical veil of creativity to pick up pieces of the story along the way. She has been with me from the very beginning, urging me to write, inspiring me with a font of ideas, sights and sounds that I only hope I live long enough to put into words. When I later read the words I have written, I am often surprised that I could do such a thing. For that reason, I offer my gratitude to timeless Calliope for blessing my songs.

As ever, there are also myriad mortals who have helped me along this journey whom I would like to thank.

First and foremost is my wife, Angelina. She was there for the genesis of the Eagles and Dragons series, and she was the only one who encouraged me to keep going. She always had faith in my writing, and gave me the time to do so. When others expressed doubt that I could actually write, or said that I was wasting time, she never wavered in her support. She has always been my shield wall against doubt, and her love my constant inspiration. To her, my undying love and gratitude.

I also want to thank my daughters, Alexandra and Athena, for their constant support and enthusiasm, and for always allowing me the time to write. I know it's strange to see one's father sitting there, deep in thought, lost in another world, but they tolerate it and are always keen to celebrate each victory with me. I couldn't ask for better allies. To them, my deepest love and appreciation, always.

To Kostis Diassitis of Athens, I am grateful for his help with my humble Latin translations. His help has always elevated my work and I am extremely grateful for his efforts. Of course, any errors in Latin are my own.

A heartfelt thank you to my godfather, Dennis Tini, of Detroit, Michigan. As an artist himself, he has always been a big fan and supporter of the Eagles and Dragons series and of myself in my own artistic endeavours.

My thanks also to my dear friends Jean-Francois and Heather Lamontagne for their continued enthusiasm and support of the Eagles and Dragons series. It means a great deal to know that they truly enjoy the books when others have not given them a second glance.

The creation of this book owes a lot to Catherine Comuzzi, not only for her important help in getting me through a very dark period in my life, but also for helping me, through our discussions, to explore the brutal truth of revenge and the importance of knowing when to let go of the struggle in order to be free. That, in essence, is the main theme of *The Blood Road*, and without Catherine's wisdom and insight, this story could not have reached its full potential.

As always, there is a team behind the creation of a book, and this one is no exception. A big thank you to Laura at LLPix Designs for her excellent cover design and for being so amazing to work with. I also owe an enormous debt to my editor, Angelina, at Beautiful Ink Editing. She always manages to make my books better and cleaner, and to take them to a level of professionalism that other editors have not in the past. For that, I am extremely grateful.

To the patrons of Eagles and Dragons Publishing, I offer my sincerest gratitude for their financial support and faith in what Eagles and Dragons Publishing is trying to do, to create. It really is amazing to have such a dedicated group of supporters behind us. A titanic thank you to our patrons at the time of publication: A. Diassiti, Bonnie Miller, Dig it With Raven, Edwin K. Gwaltney, Greg Hancock, Heather Parsons, J.M. Dagger, Jonas Ortega, Kathleen Larson and Michael Powell.

Lastly, I want to thank the fans of the Eagles and Dragons series. You have all helped to keep me going, and to keep writing, and to make this series a success with several 'best seller' accolades. Your support, kind words, e-mails, and all our virtual interactions mean more than you could know and are, to me, greater than any Roman general's triumph. To all of you, thank you for reading.

Adam Alexander Haviaras
Stratford, Ontario
February, 2021

ABOUT THE AUTHOR

Adam Alexander Haviaras is a writer and historian who has studied ancient and medieval history and archaeology in Canada and the United Kingdom. He currently resides in Stratford, Ontario with his wife and children where he is continuing his research and writing other works of historical fantasy.

Historical Fiction/Fantasy Titles
The Eagles and Dragons Series

The Dragon: Genesis (Prequel)
A Dragon among the Eagles (Prequel)
Children of Apollo (Book I)
Killing the Hydra (Book II)
Warriors of Epona (Book III)
Isle of the Blessed (Book IV)
The Stolen Throne (Book V)
The Blood Road (Book VI)
The Eagles and Dragons Legionary Box Set (Books 0-I-II)
The Eagles and Dragons Tribune Box Set (Books III-IV-V)

The Carpathian Interlude Series

The Carpathian Interlude - Complete Trilogy Box Set
Immortui (Part I)
Lykoi (Part II)
Thanatos (Part III)

The Mythologia Series

Chariot of the Son
Wheels of Fate

A Song for the Underworld

Heart of Fire: A Novel of the Ancient Olympics

Saturnalia: A Tale of Wickedness and Redemption in Ancient Rome

Short Stories

The Sea Released
Theoi
Nex (or, The Warrior Named for Death)

Titles in the Historia Non-fiction Series

Historia I: Celtic Literary Archetypes in *The Mabinogion*: A Study of the Ancient Tale of *Pwyll, Lord of Dyved*

Historia II: Arthurian Romance and the Knightly Ideal: A study of Medieval Romantic Literature and its Effect upon Warrior Culture in Europe

Historia III: *Y Gododdin*: The Last Stand of Three Hundred Britons - Understanding People and Events during Britain's Heroic Age

Historia IV: Camelot: The Historical, Archaeological and Toponymic Considerations for South Cadbury Castle as King Arthur's Capital

Eagles and Dragons Publishing Guides

Writing the Past: The Eagles and Dragons Publishing Guide to Researching, Writing, Publishing and Marketing Historical Fiction and Historical Fantasy

Stay Connected

To connect with Adam and learn more about the ancient world visit www.eaglesanddragonspublishing.com

Sign up for the Eagles and Dragons Publishing Newsletter at www.eagle-sanddragonspublishing.com/newsletter-join-the-legions/ to receive a FREE BOOK, first access to new releases and posts on ancient history, special offers, and much more!

Readers can also connect with Adam on Twitter @AdamHaviaras and Instagram @ adam_haviaras.

On Facebook you can 'Like' the Eagles and Dragons page to get regular updates on new historical fiction and non-fiction from Eagles and Dragons Publishing. You can also find us on Instagram at 'eaglesdragons'

Printed in Great Britain
by Amazon

11901423R00400